Strange Stories

from a Chinese Studio

Translated and annotated by

HERBERT A. GILES

Dover Publications, Inc., New York

This Dover edition, first published in 1969, is an
unabridged and unaltered republication of the third
revised edition, published by Kelly & Walsh, Limited,
in Shanghai in 1916.

Standard Book Number: 486-22395-7
Library of Congress Catalog Card Number: 73-94319

Manufactured in the United States of America
Dover Publications, Inc.
180 Varick Street
New York, N.Y. 10014

TO

MY GRANDCHILDREN

PENELOPE ESBELL LAURENCE

MARGARET VALÉRIE ST. GILES

SYLVIA SARAH GILES

ROSAMOND ST. GILES

AUSTIN LOUDON VALENTINE ST. GILES

JOHN ALLEN LAURENCE

AUDREY LAURENCE

CONTENTS

STORIES

INTRODUCTION

THE barest skeleton of a biography is all that can be formed from the very scanty materials which remain to mark the career of a writer whose work has been for the best part of two centuries as familiar throughout the length and breadth of China as are the tales of the " Arabian Nights " in all English-speaking communities. The author of " Strange Stories " was a native of Tzŭ-ch'uan, in the province of Shan-tung. His family name was P'u ; his particular name was Sung-ling ; and the designation or literary epithet by which, in accordance with Chinese usage, he was commonly known among his friends, was Liu-hsien, or " Last of the Immortals." A further fancy name, given to him probably by some enthusiastic admirer, was Liu-ch'üan, or " Willow Spring ; " but he is now familiarly spoken of simply as P'u Sung-ling. We are unacquainted with the years of his birth or death ; however, by the aid of a meagre entry in the *History of Tzŭ-ch'uan* it is possible to make a pretty good guess at the date of the former event. For we are there told that P'u Sung-ling successfully competed for the lowest or bachelor's degree before he had reached the age of twenty ; and that in 1651 he was in the position of a graduate of ten years' standing, having failed in the interim to take the second, or master's, degree. To this failure, due, as we are informed in the history above quoted, to his neglect of the beaten track of academic study, we owe the existence of his great work ; not, indeed, his only production, though the one by which, as Confucius said of his own " Spring and Autumn,"[1] men will know him. All else that we have on record of P'u Sung-ling, besides the fact that he lived in close companionship with several eminent scholars of the day, is gathered from his own words, written when, in 1679, he laid down his pen upon the completion of a task which was to raise him within a short period to a foremost rank in the Chinese world of letters. Of that record I here append a close translation, accompanied by such notes as are absolutely necessary to make it intelligible to non-students of Chinese.

AUTHOR'S OWN RECORD

" Clad in wistaria, girdled with ivy ; "[2] thus sang Ch'ü-P'ing[3] in his *Falling into Trouble.*[4] Of ox-headed devils and serpent Gods,[5] he of the long-nails[6] never wearied to tell. Each interprets in his own way the music of heaven ;[7] and whether it be discord or not, depends upon antecedent

[1] Annals of the Lu State.

[2] Said of the bogies of the hills, in allusion to their *clothes*. Here quoted with reference to the official classes, in ridicule of the title under which they hold posts which, from a literary point of view, they are totally unfit to occupy.

[3] A celebrated statesman (B.C. 332–295) who, having lost his master's favour by the intrigues of a rival, finally drowned himself in despair. The annual Dragon Festival is said by some to be a " search " for his body. The term *San Lü* used here was the name of an office held by Ch'ü-P'ing.

[4] A poem addressed by Ch'ü-P'ing to his Prince, after his disgrace. Its non-success was the immediate cause of his death.

[5] That is, of the supernatural generally.

[6] A poet of the T'ang dynasty whose eyebrows met, whose nails were very long, and who could write very fast.

[7] " You know the music of earth," said Chuang Tzū ; " but you have not heard the music of heaven."

causes.[8] As for me, I cannot, with my poor autumn fire-fly's light, match myself against the hobgoblins of the age.[9] I am but the dust in the sunbeam, a fit laughing-stock for devils.[10] For my talents are not those of Kan Pao,[11] elegant explorer of the records of the Gods; I am rather animated by the spirit of Su Tung-p'o,[12] who loved to hear men speak of the supernatural. I get people to commit what they tell me to writing and subsequently I dress it up in the form of a story; and thus in the lapse of time my friends from all quarters have supplied me with quantities of material, which, from my habit of collecting, has grown into a vast pile.[13]

Human beings, I would point out, are not beyond the pale of fixed laws, and yet there are more remarkable phenomena in their midst than in the country of those who crop their hair;[14] antiquity is unrolled before us, and many tales are to be found therein stranger than that of the nation of Flying Heads.[15] "Irrepressible bursts, and luxurious

[8] That is, to the operation of some influence surviving from a previous existence.

[9] This is another hit at the ruling classes. Hsi K'ang, a celebrated musician and alchemist (A.D. 223–262), was sitting one night alone, playing upon his lute, when suddenly a man with a tiny face walked in, and began to stare hard at him, the stranger's face enlarging all the time. "I'm not going to match myself against a devil!" cried the musician, after a few moments, and instantly blew out the light.

[10] When Liu Chüan, Governor of Wu-ling, determined to relieve his poverty by trade, he saw a devil standing by his side, laughing and rubbing its hands for glee. "Poverty and wealth are matters of destiny," said Liu Chüan; "but to be laughed at by a devil——," and accordingly he desisted from his intention.

[11] A writer who flourished in the early part of the fourth century, and composed a work in thirty books entitled *Supernatural Researches*.

[12] The famous poet, statesman, and essayist, who flourished A.D. 1036–1101.

[13] "And his friends had the habit of jotting down for his unfailing delight anything quaint or comic that they came across."—*The World* on Charles Dickens, July 24, 1878.

[14] It is related in the *Historical Record* that when T'ai Po and Yü Chung fled to the southern savages they saw men with tattooed bodies and short hair.

[15] A fabulous community, so called because the heads of the men are in the habit of leaving their bodies, and flying down to marshy places to feed on worms and crabs. A red ring is seen the night before the flight encircling the neck of the man whose head is about to fly; at daylight the head returns. Some say that the ears are used as wings; others that the hands also leave the body and fly away.

ease," [16]—such was always his enthusiastic strain. "For ever indulging in liberal thought," [17]—thus he spoke openly without restraint. Were men like these to open my book, I should be a laughing-stock to them indeed. At the cross-road [18] men will not listen to me, and yet I have some knowledge of the three states of existence [19] spoken of beneath the cliff ; [20] neither should the words I utter be set aside because of him that utters them. [21] When the bow [22] was hung at my father's door, he dreamed that a sickly-looking Buddhist priest, but half covered by his stole, entered the chamber. On one of his breasts was a round piece of plaster like a *cash* ; [23] and my father, waking from sleep, found that I, just born, had a similar black patch on my body. As a child, I was thin and constantly ailing, and unable to hold my own in the battle of life. Our own home was chill and desolate as a monastery ; and working there for my livelihood with my pen, [24] I was as poor as a priest with his alms-bowl. [25] Often and often I put my hand to my head [26] and exclaimed, "Surely he who sat with his

[16] A quotation from the admired works of Wang Po, a brilliant scholar and poet, who was drowned at the early age of twenty-eight, A.D. 676.

[17] I have hitherto failed in all attempts to identify the particular writer here intended. The phrase is used by the poet Li T'ai-po and others.

[18] The cross-road of the "Five Fathers" is here mentioned, which the commentator tells us is merely the name of the place.

[19] The past, present, and future life of the Buddhist system of metempsychosis.

[20] A certain man, who was staying at a temple, dreamt that an old priest appeared to him beneath a jade-stone cliff, and, pointing to a stick of burning incense, said to him, "That incense represents a vow to be fulfilled ; but I say unto you, that ere its smoke shall have curled away, your three states of existence will have been already accomplished." The meaning is that time on earth is as nothing to the Gods.

[21] This remark occurs in the fifteenth chapter of the Analects or Confucian Gospels.

[22] The birth of a boy was formerly signalled by hanging a bow at the door ; that of a girl, by displaying a small towel—indicative of the parts that each would hereafter play in the drama of life.

[23] See Note 2 to No. II.

[24] Literally, "ploughing with my pen."

[25] The *patra* or bowl, used by Buddhist mendicants, in imitation of the celebrated alms-dish of Shâkyamuni Buddha.

[26] Literally, "scratched my head," as is often done by the Chinese in perplexity or doubt.

face to the wall [27] was myself in a previous state of existence ; " and thus I referred my non-success in this life to the
influence of a destiny surviving from the last. I have been
tossed hither and thither in the direction of the ruling wind,
like a flower falling in filthy places ; but the six paths [28] of
transmigration are inscrutable indeed, and I have no right
to complain. As it is, midnight finds me with an expiring
lamp, while the wind whistles mournfully without ; and
over my cheerless table I piece together my tales,[29] vainly
hoping to produce a sequel to the *Infernal Regions*.[30] With
a bumper I stimulate my pen, yet I only succeed thereby
in "venting my excited feelings,"[31] and as I thus commit
my thoughts to writing, truly I am an object worthy of
commiseration. Alas! I am but the bird, that dreading the
winter frost, finds no shelter in the tree ; the autumn insect
that chirps to the moon, and hugs the door for warmth.
For where are they who know me ? [32] They are " in the
bosky grove, and at the frontier pass " [33]—wrapped in an
impenetrable gloom !

From the above curious document the reader will

[27] Alluding to Bôdhidharma, who came from India to China, and
tried to convert the Emperor Wu Ti of the Liang dynasty ; but,
failing in his attempt, because he insisted that real merit lay not in
works but in purity and wisdom combined, he retired full of mortification to a temple at Sung-shan, where he sat for nine years before
a rock, until his own image was imprinted thereon.

[28] The six *gâti* or conditions of existence, namely :—angels, men,
dèmons, hungry devils, brute beasts, and tortured sinners.

[29] Literally, " putting together the pieces under the forelegs (of
foxes) to make robes." This part of the fox-skin is the most valuable
for making fur clothes.

[30] The work of a well-known writer, named Lin I-ch'ing, who
flourished during the Sung Dynasty.

[31] Alluding to an essay by Han Fei, a philosopher of the third
century B.C., in which he laments the iniquity of the age in general,
and the corruption of officials in particular. He finally committed
suicide in prison, where he had been cast by the intrigues of a rival
minister.

[32] Confucius (*Anal*. xiv.) said, " Alas ! there is no one who knows
me (to be what I am)."

[33] The great poet Tu Fu (A.D. 712–770) dreamt that his greater
predecessor, Li T'ai-po (A.D. 705–762) appeared to him, " coming
when the maple-grove was in darkness, and returning while the
frontier-pass was still obscured ; "—that is, at night, when no one
could see him ; the meaning being that he never came at all, and
that those " who know me (P'u Sung-ling) " are equally non-existent.

gain some insight into the abstruse, but at the same time marvellously beautiful, style of this gifted writer. The whole essay—for such it is, and among the most perfect of its kind—is intended chiefly as a satire upon the scholarship of the age ; scholarship which had turned the author back to the disappointment of a private life, himself conscious all the time of the inward fire that had been lent him by heaven. It is the keynote of his own subsequent career, spent in the retirement of home, in the society of books and friends ; as also to the numerous uncomplimentary allusions which occur in all his stories relating to official life. Whether or not the world at large has been a gainer by this instance of the fallibility of competitive examinations has been already decided in the affirmative by the millions of P'u Sung-ling's own countrymen, who for the past two hundred years have more than made up to him by a posthumous and enduring reverence for the loss of those earthly and ephemeral honours which he seems to have coveted so much.

Strange Stories from a Chinese Studio, known to the Chinese as the *Liao Chai Chih I*, or more familiarly, the *Liao Chai*, has hardly been mentioned by a single foreigner without some inaccuracy on the part of the writer concerned. For instance, the late Mr. Mayers states in his *Chinese Reader's Manual*, p. 176, that this work was composed " circa A.D. 1710," the fact being that the collection was actually completed in 1679, as we know by the date attached to the "Author's Own Record " given above. I should mention, however, that the *Liao Chai* was originally, and for many years, circulated in manuscript only. P'u Sung-ling, as we are told in a colophon by his grandson to the first edition, was too poor to meet the heavy expense of block-cutting ; and it was not until so late as 1740, when the author must have been already for some time a denizen of the dark land he so much loved to describe, that his aforesaid grandson printed and published the collection now universally famous. Since then many editions have been laid before the Chinese public, the best of which is that by Tan Ming-lun, a Salt Commissioner, who flourished during the reign of Tao Kuang, and who in 1842 produced, at his own expense, an excellent edition in sixteen small octavo volumes of about 160 pages each. And as various editions will occasionally be found to contain various readings, I would here warn students of Chinese who wish to compare my rendering with the text, that it is from the edition of Tan Ming-lun, collated with that of Yü Chi, published in 1766, that this translation has been made. Many have been the commentaries and disquisitions upon the meaning of obscure passages and the general scope of this work ; to say nothing of the prefaces with which the several editions have been ushered into the world. Of the latter, I have selected one specimen, from which the reader will be able to form a tolerably accurate opinion as to the true nature of these always singular and usually difficult compositions. Here it is :—

T'ANG MÊNG-LAI'S PREFACE

The common saying, " He regards a camel as a horse with a swelled back," trivial of itself, may be used in illustration of greater matters. Men are wont to attribute an existence only to such things as they daily see with their own eyes, and they marvel at whatsoever, appearing before them at one instant, vanishes at the next. And yet it is not at the sprouting and falling of foliage, nor at the metamorphosis of insects that they marvel, but only at the manifestations of the supernatural world ; though of a truth, the whistling of the wind and the movement of streams, with nothing to set the one in motion or give sound to the other, might well be ranked among extraordinary phenomena. We are accustomed to these, and therefore do not note them. We marvel at devils and foxes : we do not marvel at man. But who is it that causes a man to move and to speak ?—to which question comes the ready answer of each individual so questioned, " *I* do." This " I do," however, is merely a personal consciousness of the facts under discussion. For a man can see with his eyes, but he cannot see what it is that makes him see ; he can hear with his ears, but he cannot hear what it is that makes him hear ; how, then, is it possible for him to understand the rationale of things he can neither see nor hear ? Whatever has come within the bounds of their own ocular or auricular experience men regard as proved to be actually existing ; and only such things.[34] But this term " experience " may be understood in various senses. For instance, people speak of something which has certain attributes as *form*, and of something else which has certain other attributes as *substance* ; ignorant as they are that form and substance are to be found existing without those particular attributes. Things which are thus constituted are inappreciable, indeed, by our ears and eyes ; but we cannot argue that therefore they do not exist. Some persons can see a mosquito's eye, while to others even a mountain is invisible ; some can hear the sound of ants battling together, while others, again, fail to catch the roar of a thunder-peal. Powers of seeing and hearing vary ; there should be no

---

[34] " Thus, since countless things exist that the senses *can* take account of, it is evident that nothing exists that the senses can *not* take account of."—The " Professor " in W. H. Mallock's *New Paul and Virginia*.

This passage recalls another curious classification by the great Chinese philosopher Han Wên-kung. " There are some things which possess form but are devoid of sound, as, for instance, jade and stones ; others have sound, but are without form, such as wind and thunder ; others, again, have both form and sound, such as men and animals ; and lastly, there is a class devoid of both, namely, *devils and spirits*."

reckless imputations of blindness. According to the
schoolmen, man at his death is dispersed like wind or fire,
the origin and end of his vitality being alike unknown ; and
as those who have seen strange phenomena are few, the
number of those who marvel at them is proportionately
great, and the " horse with a swelled back " parallel is
very widely applicable. And ever quoting the fact that
Confucius would have nothing to say on these topics, these
schoolmen half discredit such works as the *Ch'i chieh chih
kuai* and the *Yü ch'u-chii*,[35] ignorant that the Sage's
unwillingness to speak had reference only to persons of an
inferior mental calibre ; for his own *Spring and Autumn*
can hardly be said to be devoid of all allusions of the kind.
Now P'u Liu-hsien devoted himself in his youth to the
marvellous, and as he grew older was specially remarkable
for his comprehension thereof ; and being moreover a most
elegant writer, he occupied his leisure in recording whatever
came to his knowledge of a particularly marvellous nature.
A volume of these compositions of his formerly fell into
my hands, and was constantly borrowed by friends ; now,
I have another volume, and of what I read only about
three-tenths was known to me before. What there is,
should be sufficient to open the eyes of those schoolmen,
though I much fear it will be like talking of ice to a butterfly. Personally, I disbelieve in the irregularity of natural
phenomena, and regard as evil spirits only those who
injure their neighbours. For eclipses, falling stars, the
flight of herons, the nest of a mainah, talking stones, and
the combats of dragons, can hardly be classed as irregular ;
while the phenomena of nature occurring out of season, wars,
rebellions, and so forth, may certainly be relegated to the
category of evil. In my opinion the morality of P'u Liu-
hsien's work is of a very high standard, its object being
distinctly to glorify virtue and to censure vice ; and as
a book calculated to elevate mankind, it may be safely
placed side by side with the philosophical treatises of Yang
Hsiung [36] which Huan Tan [37] declared to be so worthy of
a wide circulation.

[35] I have never seen any of these works, but I believe they treat,
as implied by their titles, chiefly of the supernatural world.
[36] B.C. 53–A.D. 18.   [37] B.C. 13–A.D. 56.

With regard to the meaning of the Chinese words
Liao Chai Chih I, this title has received indifferent
treatment at the hands of different writers. Dr.
Williams chose to render it by " Pastimes of the
Study," and Mr. Mayers by " The Record of Marvels,
or Tales of the Genii ; " neither of which is sufficiently
near to be regarded in the light of a translation. Taken
literally and in order, these words stand for " Liao—
library — record — strange," " Liao " being simply
a fanciful name given by our author to his private
library or studio. An apocryphal anecdote traces the
origin of this selection to a remark once made by
himself with reference to his failure for the second
degree. " Alas ! " he is reported to have said, " I
shall now have no resource (*Liao*) for my old age ; "
and accordingly he so named his study, meaning that
in his pen he would seek that resource which fate had
denied to him as an official. For this untranslatable
" Liao " I have ventured to substitute " Chinese," as
indicating more clearly the nature of what is to follow.
No such title as " Tales of the Genii " fully expresses
the scope of this work, which embraces alike weird
stories of Taoist devilry and magic, marvellous accounts
of impossible countries beyond the sea, simple scenes
of Chinese everyday life, and notices of extraordinary
natural phenomena. Indeed, the author once had it
in contemplation to publish only the more imaginative
of the tales in the present collection under the title of
" Devil and Fox Stories ; " but from this scheme he
was ultimately dissuaded by his friends, the result
being the heterogeneous mass which is more aptly
described by the title I have given to this volume. In
a similar manner, I too had originally determined to
publish a full and complete translation of the whole of

these sixteen volumes ; but on a closer acquaintance many of the stories turned out to be quite unsuitable for the age in which we live, forcibly recalling the coarseness of our own writers of fiction in the eighteenth century.   Others, again, were utterly pointless, or mere repetitions in a slightly altered form.   From the whole, I therefore selected one hundred and sixty-four of the best and most characteristic stories, of which eight had previously been published by Mr. Allen in the *China Review,* one by Mr. Mayers in *Notes and Queries on China and Japan,* two by myself in the columns of the *Celestial Empire,* and four by Dr. Williams in a now forgotten handbook of Chinese.   The remaining one hundred and forty-nine have never before, to my knowledge, been translated into English.   To those, however, who can enjoy the *Liao Chai* in the original text, the distinctions between the various stories in felicity of plot, originality, and so on, are far less sharply defined, so impressed as each competent reader must be by the incomparable *style* in which even the meanest is arrayed.   For in this respect, as important now in Chinese eyes as it was with ourselves in days not long gone by, the author of the *Liao Chai* and the rejected candidate succeeded in founding a school of his own, in which he has since been followed by hosts of servile imitators with more or less success.   Terseness is pushed to extreme limits ; each particle that can be safely dispensed with is scrupulously eliminated ; and every here and there some new and original combination invests perhaps a single word with a force it could never have possessed except under the hands of a perfect master of his art.   Add to the above, copious allusions and adaptations from a course of reading which would seem to have been co-extensive with the whole range of Chinese literature, a wealth of metaphor and an artistic use of figures generally to which only the writings of Carlyle form an adequate parallel ; and the result is a work which for purity and beauty of style is now universally accepted in China as the best and most perfect model. Sometimes the story runs along plainly and smoothly enough ; but the next moment we may be plunged into pages of abstruse text, the meaning of which is so involved in quotations from and allusions to the poetry or history of the past three thousand years as to be recoverable only after diligent perusal of the commentary and much searching in other works of reference. In illustration of the popularity of this book, Mr. Mayers once stated that " the porter at his gate, the boatman at his midday rest, the chair-coolie at his stand, no less than the man of letters among his books, may be seen poring with delight over the elegantly-narrated marvels of the *Liao Chai ;* " but he would doubtless have withdrawn this statement in later years, with the work lying open before him. During many years in China, I made a point of never, when feasible, passing by a reading Chinaman without asking permission to glance at the volume in his hand ; and at my various stations in China I always kept up a borrowing acquaintance with the libraries of my private or official servants ; but I can safely affirm that I never once detected the *Liao Chai* in the hands of an ill-educated man. In the same connection, Mr. Mayers observed that " fairy-tales told in the style of the *Anatomy of Melancholy* would scarcely be a popular book in Great Britain ; " but except in some particular points of contact, the styles of these two works could scarcely claim even the most distant of relationships.

Such, then, is the setting of this collection of *Strange Stories from a Chinese Studio,* many of which contain, in addition to the advantages of style and plot, a very excellent moral. The intention of most of them is, in the actual words of T'ang Mêng-lai, " to glorify virtue and to censure vice,"—always, it must be borne in mind, according to the Chinese and not to a European interpretation of these terms. As an addition to our knowledge of the folk-lore of China, and as a guide to the manners, customs, and social life of that vast Empire, my translation of the *Liao Chai* may not be wholly devoid of interest. It has now been carefully revised, all inaccuracies of the first edition having been, so far as possible, corrected.

HERBERT A. GILES.

CAMBRIDGE, *July* 1908.

STRANGE STORIES FROM A CHINESE STUDIO

I. EXAMINATION FOR THE POST OF GUARDIAN ANGEL[1]

My eldest sister's husband's grandfather, named Sung Tao, was a graduate.[2] One day, while lying down from indisposition, an official messenger arrived, bringing the usual notification in his hand and leading a horse with a white forehead to summon him to the examination for his master's degree. Mr. Sung here remarked that the Grand Examiner had not yet come, and asked why there should be this hurry. The messenger did not reply to this, but pressed so earnestly that at length Mr. Sung roused himself, and getting upon the horse rode with him. The way seemed strange, and by-and-by they reached a city which resembled the capital of a prince. They then entered the Prefect's yamen,[3] the apartments of which were beautifully decorated ; and there they found some ten officials sitting at the upper end, all strangers to Mr. Sung, with the exception of one whom he recognised to be the God of War.[4] In the verandah were two tables and two stools, and at the end of one of the former a candidate was already seated,

---

[1] The tutelar deity of every Chinese city.
[2] That is, he had taken the first or bachelor's degree. I shall not hesitate to use strictly English equivalents for all kinds of Chinese terms. The three degrees are literally, (1) Cultivated Talent, (2) Raised Man, and (3) Promoted Scholar.
[3] The official residence of a mandarin above a certain rank.
[4] The Chinese Mars. A celebrated warrior, named Kuan Yü, who lived about the beginning of the third century of our era. He was raised after death to the rank of a God, and now plays a leading part in the Chinese Pantheon.

so Mr. Sung sat down alongside of him. On the table were writing materials for each, and suddenly down flew a piece of paper with a theme on it, consisting of the following eight words :—" One man, two men ; by intention, without intention." When Mr. Sung had finished his essay, he took it into the hall. It contained the following passage : " Those who are virtuous by intention, though virtuous, shall not be rewarded. Those who are wicked without intention, though wicked, shall receive no punishment." The presiding deities praised this sentiment very much, and calling Mr. Sung to come forward, said to him, " A Guardian Angel is wanted in Honan. Go you and take up the appointment." Mr. Sung no sooner heard this than he bowed his head and wept, saying, " Unworthy though I am of the honour you have conferred upon me, I should not venture to decline it but that my aged mother has reached her seventh decade, and there is no one now to take care of her. I pray you let me wait until she has fulfilled her destiny, when I will hold myself at your disposal." Thereupon one of the deities, who seemed to be the chief, gave instructions to search out his mother's term of life, and a long-bearded attendant forthwith brought in the Book of Fate. On turning it over, he declared that she still had nine years to live ; and then a consultation was held among the deities, in the middle of which the God of War said, " Very well. Let Mr. graduate Chang take the post, and be relieved in nine years' time." Then, turning to Mr. Sung, he continued, " You ought to proceed without delay to your post ; but as a reward for your filial piety, you are granted a furlough of nine years. At the expiration of that time you will receive another summons." He next addressed a few kind words to Mr. Chang ; and the two candidates, having made their *kotow*, went away together. Grasping Mr. Sung's hand, his companion, who gave " Chang Ch'i of Ch'ang-shan " as his name and address, accompanied him beyond the city walls and gave him a stanza of poetry at parting. I cannot recollect it all, but in it occurred this couplet :—

With wine and flowers we chase the hours,
  In one eternal spring :
No moon, no light, to cheer the night,
  Thyself that ray must bring.

Mr. Sung here left him and rode on, and before very long reached his own home ; here he awaked as if from a dream, and found that he had been dead three days,[5] when his mother, hearing a groan in the coffin, ran to it and helped him out. It was some time before he could speak, and then he at once inquired about Ch'ang-shan, where, as it turned out, a graduate named Chang had died that very day.

Nine years afterwards, Mr. Sung's mother, in accordance with fate, passed from this life ; and when the funeral obsequies were over, her son, having first purified himself, entered into his chamber and died also. Now his wife's family lived within the city, near the western gate ; and all of a sudden they beheld Mr. Sung, accompanied by numerous chariots and horses with carved trappings and red-tasselled bits, enter into the hall, make an obeisance, and depart. They were very much disconcerted at this, not knowing that he had become a spirit, and rushed out into the village to make inquiries, when they heard he was already dead. Mr. Sung had an account of his adventure written by himself ; but unfortunately after the insurrection it was not to be found. This is only an outline of the story.

II. THE TALKING PUPILS

AT Ch'ang-ngan there lived a scholar, named Fang Tung, who though by no means destitute of ability was a very unprincipled rake, and in the habit of following and speaking to any woman he might chance to meet. The day before the spring festival of Clear Weather,[1] he was strolling about outside the city when he saw a small carriage with red curtains and an embroidered awning, followed by a crowd of waiting-maids on horseback, one of whom was exceedingly pretty, and riding on a small palfrey. Going closer to get a better view, Mr. Fang noticed that the carriage curtain was partly open, and inside he beheld a

---

[5] Catalepsy, which is the explanation of many a story in this collection, would appear to be of very common occurrence among the Chinese. Such, however, is not the case.

[1] One of the twenty-four solar terms. It falls on or about the 5th of April, and is the special time for worshipping at the family tombs.

beautifully dressed girl of about sixteen, lovely beyond anything he had ever seen. Dazzled by the sight, he could not take his eyes off her; and, now before, now behind, he followed the carriage for many a mile. By-and-by he heard the young lady call out to her maid, and, when the latter came alongside, say to her, "Let down the screen· for me. Who is this rude fellow that keeps on staring so?" The maid accordingly let down the screen, and looking angrily at Mr. Fang said to him, "This is the bride of the Seventh Prince in the City of Immortals going home to see her parents, and no village girl that you should stare at her thus." Then taking a handful of dust, she threw it at him and blinded him. He rubbed his eyes and looked round, but the carriage and horses were gone. This frightened him, and he went off home, feeling very uncomfortable about the eyes. He sent for a doctor to examine his eyes, and on the pupils was found a small film, which had increased by next morning, the eyes watering incessantly all the time. The film went on growing, and in a few days was as thick as a cash.[2] On the right pupil there came a kind of spiral, and as no medicine was of any avail, the sufferer gave himself up to grief and wished for death. He then bethought himself of repenting of his misdeeds, and hearing that the *Kuang-ming* sutra could relieve misery, he got a copy and hired a man to teach it to him. At first it was very tedious work, but by degrees he became more composed, and spent the whole day in a posture of devotion, telling his beads. At the end of a year he had arrived at a state of perfect calm, when one day he heard a small voice, about as loud as a fly's, calling out from his left eye: "It's horridly dark in here." To this he heard a reply from the right eye, saying, "Let us go out for a stroll, and cheer ourselves up a bit." Then he felt a wriggling in his nose which. made it itch, just as if something was going out of each of the nostrils; and after a while he felt it again as if going the other way. Afterwards he heard a voice from one eye say, "I hadn't seen the garden for a long time: the epiden-

---

[2] The common European name for the only Chinese coin, about twenty of which go to a penny. Each has a square hole in the middle, for the convenience of stringing them together; hence the expression "strings of cash."

drums are all withered and dead." Now Mr. Fang was very fond of these epidendrums, of which he had planted a great number, and had been accustomed to water them himself; but since the loss of his sight he had never even alluded to them. Hearing, however, these words, he at once asked his wife why she had let the epidendrums die. She inquired how he knew they were dead, and when he told her she went out to see, and found them actually withered away. They were both very much astonished at this, and his wife proceeded to conceal herself in the room. She then observed two tiny people, no bigger than a bean, come down from her husband's nose and run out of the door, where she lost sight of them. In a little while they came back and flew up to his face, like bees or beetles seeking their nests. This went on for some days, until Mr. Fang heard from the left eye, "This roundabout road is not at all convenient. It would be as well for us to make a door." To this the right eye answered, " My wall is too thick: it wouldn't be at all an easy job." " I'll try and open mine," said the left eye, " and then it will do for both of us." Whereupon Mr. Fang felt a pain in his left eye as if something was being split, and in a moment he found he could see the tables and chairs in the room. He was delighted at this and told his wife, who examined his eye and discovered an opening in the film, through which she could see the black pupil shining out beneath, the eyeball itself looking like a cracked pepper-corn. By next morning the film had disappeared, and when his eye was closely examined it was observed to contain two pupils. The spiral on the right eye remained as before ; and then they knew that the two pupils had taken up their abode in one eye. Further, although Mr. Fang was still blind of one eye, the sight of the other was better than that of the two together. From this time he was more careful of his behaviour, and acquired in his part of the country the reputation of a virtuous man.[3]

[3] The belief that the human eye contains a tiny being of the human shape is universal in China. It originated, of course, from the reflection of oneself that is seen on looking into the pupil of anybody's eye or even, with the aid of a mirror, into one's own.

III. THE PAINTED WALL

A KIANG-SI gentleman, named Mêng Lung-t'an, was
lodging at the capital with a Mr. Chu, M.A., when one day
chance led them to a certain monastery, within which they
found no spacious halls or meditation chambers, but
only an old priest in *déshabillé*. On observing the visitors,
he arranged his dress and went forward to meet them,
leading them round and showing whatever there was to
be seen. In the chapel they saw an image of Chih Kung,
and the walls on either side were beautifully painted with
life-like representations of men and animals. On the
east side were pictured a number of fairies, among whom
was a young girl whose maiden tresses were not yet confined by the matron's knot. She was picking flowers
and gently smiling, while her cherry lips seemed about to
move, and the moisture of her eyes to overflow. Mr.
Chu gazed at her for a long time without taking his eyes
off, until at last he became unconscious of anything but
the thoughts that were engrossing him. Then, suddenly
he felt himself floating in the air, as if riding on a cloud,
and found himself passing through the wall,[1] where halls
and pavilions stretched away one after another, unlike
the abodes of mortals. Here an old priest was preaching
the Law of Buddha, surrounded by a large crowd of
listeners. Mr. Chu mingled with the throng, and after a
few moments perceived a gentle tug at his sleeve. Turning
round, he saw the young girl above-mentioned, who
walked laughing away. Mr. Chu at once followed her,
and passing a winding balustrade arrived at a small apartment beyond which he dared not venture farther. But
the young lady, looking back, waved the flowers she had
in her hand as though beckoning him to come on. He
accordingly entered and found nobody else within. Then
they fell on their knees and worshipped heaven and earth
tôgether,[2] and rose up as man and wife, after which the
bride went away, bidding Mr. Chu keep quiet until she
came back. This went on for a couple of days, when the

[1] Which will doubtless remind the reader of "Alice through the
Looking-glass, and what she saw there."
[2] The all-important item of a Chinese marriage ceremony ;
amounting, in fact, to calling God to witness the contract.

l, straining his neck to see what was going on,
tting all about his business. At the departure
est he turned round and discovered that every
is pears was gone. He then knew that those
llow had been giving away so freely were really
pears. Looking more closely at the barrow, he
d that one of the handles was missing, evidently
en newly cut off. Boiling with rage, he set out
t of the priest, and just as he turned the corner
e lost barrow-handle lying under the wall, being in
ery pear-tree the priest had cut down. But there
traces of the priest—much to the amusement of
d in the market-place.

THE TAOIST PRIEST OF LAO-SHAN

ved in our village a **Mr. Wang**, the seventh son in
amily. This gentleman had a *penchant* for the
ligion; and hearing that at Lao-shan there were
f Immortals,[1] shouldered his knapsack and went
tour thither. Ascending a peak of the mountain
ed a secluded monastery, where he found a priest
n a rush mat, with long hair flowing over his
d a pleasant expression on his face. Making a
, Wang addressed him thus: "Mysterious indeed
octrine: I pray you, Sir, instruct me therein."
ely nurtured and wanting in energy as you are,"
the priest, "I fear you could not support the
" "Try me," said Wang. So when the disciples,
re very many in number, collected together at
Vang joined them in making obeisance to the
nd remained with them in the monastery. Very
xt morning the priest summoned Wang, and giving
atchet sent him out with the others to cut firewood.
espectfully obeyed, continuing to work for over a
ntil his hands and feet were so swollen and blistered

"angels" of Taoism—immortality in a happy land being
d held out for a life on earth in accordance with the doctrines

priests are believed by some to possess an elixir of immor-
the form of a precious liquor; others again hold that the
asists solely in a virtuous conduct of life.

young lady's companions began to smell a rat and discovered Mr. Chu's hiding-place. Thereupon they all
laughed and said, "My dear, you are now a married
woman, and should leave off that maidenly *coiffure*."
So they gave her the proper hair-pins and head ornaments,
and bade her go bind her hair, at which she blushed very
much but said nothing. Then one of them cried out,
"My sisters, let us be off. Two's company, more's none."
At this they all giggled again and went away.

Mr. Chu found his wife very much improved by the
alteration in the style of her hair. The high top-knot and
the coronet of pendants were very becoming to her. But
suddenly they heard a sound like the tramping of heavy-
soled boots, accompanied by the clanking of chains and
the noise of angry discussion. The bride jumped up
in a fright, and she and Mr. Chu peeped out. They saw
a man clad in golden armour, with a face as black as jet,
carrying in his hands chains and whips, and surrounded
by all the girls. He asked, "Are you all here?" "All,"
they replied. "If," said he, "any mortal is here concealed amongst you, denounce him at once, and lay not
up sorrow for yourselves." Here they all answered as
before that there was no one. The man then made a
movement as if he would search the place, upon which
the bride was dreadfully alarmed, and her face turned
the colour of ashes. In her terror she said to Mr. Chu,
"Hide yourself under the bed," and opening a small
lattice in the wall, disappeared herself. Mr. Chu in his
concealment hardly dared to draw his breath; and in a
little while he heard the boots tramp into the room and
out again, the sound of the voices getting gradually fainter
and fainter in the distance. This reassured him, but he
still heard the voices of people going backwards and forwards outside; and having been a long time in a cramped
position, his ears began to sing as if there was a locust in
them, and his eyes to burn like fire. It was almost unbearable; however, he remained quietly awaiting the
return of the young lady without giving a thought to the
why and wherefore of his present position.

Meanwhile, Mêng Lung-t'an had noticed the sudden
disappearance of his friend, and thinking something was
wrong, asked the priest where he was. "He has gone to

hear the preaching of the Law," replied the priest. "Where?" said Mr. Mêng. "Oh, not very far," was the answer. Then with his finger the old priest tapped the wall and called out, "Friend Chu! what makes you stay away so long?" At this, the likeness of Mr. Chu was figured upon the wall, with his ear inclined in the attitude of one listening. The priest added, "Your friend here has been waiting for you some time;" and immediately Mr. Chu descended from the wall, standing transfixed like a block of wood, with starting eye-balls and trembling legs. Mr. Mêng was much terrified, and asked him quietly what was the matter. Now the matter was that while concealed under the bed he had heard a noise resembling thunder and had rushed out to see what it was.

Here they all noticed that the young lady on the wall with the maiden's tresses had changed the style of her *coiffure* to that of a married woman. Mr. Chu was greatly astonished at this and asked the old priest the reason.

He replied, "Visions have their origin in those who see them: what explanation can I give?" This answer was very unsatisfactory to Mr. Chu; neither did his friend, who was rather frightened, know what to make of it all; so they descended the temple steps and went away.

IV. PLANTING A PEAR-TREE

A COUNTRYMAN was one day selling his pears in the market. They were unusually sweet and fine flavoured, and the price he asked was high. A Taoist[1] priest in rags and

[1] That is, of the religion of *Tao*, a system of philosophy founded some six centuries before the Christian era by a man named Lao-tzŭ, "Old boy," who was said to have been born with white hair and a beard. It is now but a shadow of its former self, and is corrupted by the grossest forms of superstition borrowed from Buddhism, which has in its turn adopted many of the forms and beliefs of Taoism, so that the two religions are hardly distinguishable one from the other.

"What seemed to me the most singular circumstance connected with the matter, was the presence of half a dozen Taoist priests, who joined in all the ceremonies, doing everything that the Buddhist priests did, and presenting a very odd appearance, with their top-knots and cues, among their closely shaven Buddhist brethren. It seemed strange that the worship of Sakyamuni by celibate Buddhist priests, with shaved heads, into which holes were duly burned at their initiation, should be participated in by married Taoist priests,

tatters stopped at the
The countryman told hi
do so he began to curse a
"You have several hund
for a single one, the loss
Why then get angry?"
man to give him an infer
he obstinately refused
of the place, finding the
a pear and handed it to
it with a bow and turnin
have left our homes and
are at a loss to understa
others. Now I have som
do myself the honour to
body asked, "Since you
you eat those?" "Beca
wanted one of these pips t
he munched up the pear;
a pip in his hand, unstrap
proceeded to make a hole
deep, wherein he deposited
before. He then asked th
water to water it with, and
a joke fetched him some boil
shop. The priest poured t
had made the hole, and ev
when sprouts were seen shoo
ing larger and larger. By-a
branches sparsely covered wi
last of all fine, large, sweet-sm
profusion. These the priest
to the assembled crowd until
his pick and hacked away f
finally cutting it down. Thi
all, and sauntered quietly a
beginning, our friend the cou

whose heads are not wholly shaven,
Initiation of Buddhist Priests at Ko

Taoist priests are credited with a
black art in general.

[2] A celibate priesthood belongs
not a doctrine of the Taoist church.

the crow
and forg
of the p
one of
the old
his own
also fou
having
in pursu
he saw
fact the
were no
the crow

V

THERE
an old
Taoist
plenty
off for
he read
sitting
neck,
low bo
is the
"Delic
replied
fatigue
who
dusk,
priest
early
him a
Wang
montl

[1] T
the rev
of Ta
Tac
tality
elixir

that he secretly meditated returning home. One evening when he came back he found two strangers sitting drinking with his master. It being already dark, and no lamp or candles having been brought in, the old priest took some scissors and cut out a circular piece of paper like a mirror, which he proceeded to stick against the wall. Immediately it became a dazzling moon, by the light of which you could have seen a hair or a beard of corn. The disciples all came crowding round to wait upon them, but one of the strangers said, " On a festive occasion like this we ought all to enjoy ourselves together." Accordingly he took a kettle of wine from the table and presented it to the disciples, bidding them drink each his fill ; whereupon our friend Wang began to wonder how seven or eight of them could all be served out of a single kettle. The disciples, too, rushed about in search of cups, each struggling to get the first drink for fear the wine should be exhausted. Nevertheless, all the candidates failed to empty the kettle, at which they were very much astonished, when suddenly one of the strangers said, " You have given us a fine bright moon ; but it's dull work drinking by ourselves. Why not call Ch'ang-ngo [2] to join us ? " He then seized a chop-stick and threw it into the moon, whereupon a lovely girl stepped forth from its beams. At first she was only a foot high, but on reaching the ground lengthened to the ordinary size of woman. She had a slender waist and a beautiful neck, and went most gracefully through the Red Garment figure.[3] When this was finished she sang the following words :—

Ye fairies ! ye fairies ! I'm coming back soon,
Too lonely and cold is my home in the moon.

Her voice was clear and well sustained, ringing like the notes of a flageolet, and when she had concluded her song she pirouetted round and jumped up on the table, where, with every eye fixed in astonishment upon her, she once more became a chop-stick. The three friends laughed

[2] The beautiful wife of a legendary chieftain named Hou I, who flourished about 2500 B.C. She is said to have stolen from her husband the elixir of immortality, and to have fled with it to the moon.

[3] The name of a celebrated *pas seul* of antiquity.

loudly, and one of them said, " We are very jolly to-night, but I have hardly room for any more wine. Will you drink a parting glass with me in the palace of the moon ? " They then took up the table and walked into the moon, where they could be seen drinking so plainly that their eyebrows and beards appeared like reflections in a looking-glass. By-and-by the moon became obscured ; and when the disciples brought a lighted candle they found the priest sitting in the dark alone. The viands, however, were still upon the table and the mirror-like piece of paper on the wall. " Have you all had enough to drink ? " asked the priest ; to which they answered that they had. " In that case," said he, "you had better get to bed, so as not to be behind-hand with your wood-cutting in the morning." So they all went off, and among them Wang, who was delighted at what he had seen, and thought no more of returning home. But after a time he could not stand it any longer ; and as the priest taught him no magical arts he determined not to wait, but went to him and said, " Sir, I have travelled many long miles for the benefit of your instruction. If you will not teach me the secret of Immortality, let me at any rate learn some trifling trick, and thus soothe my cravings for a knowledge of your art. I have now been here two or three months, doing nothing but chop firewood, out in the morning and back at night, work to which I was never accustomed in my own home." " Did I not tell you," replied the priest, " that you would never support the fatigue ? To-morrow I will start you on your way home." " Sir," said Wang, " I have worked for you a long time. Teach me some small art, that my coming here may not have been wholly in vain." " What art ? " asked the priest. " Well," answered Wang, " I have noticed that whenever you walk about anywhere, walls and so on are no obstacle to you. Teach me this, and I'll be satisfied." The priest laughingly assented, and taught Wang a formula which he bade him recite. When he had done so he told him to walk through the wall ; but Wang, seeing the wall in front of him, didn't like to walk at it. As, however, the priest bade him try, he walked quietly up to it and was there stopped. The priest here called out, " Don't go so slowly. Put your head down and rush at it." So Wang stepped back

a few paces and went at it full speed ; and the wall yielding
to him as he passed, in a moment he found himself outside.
Delighted at this, he went in to thank the priest, who told
him to be careful in the use of his power, or otherwise there
would be no response, handing him at the same time some
money for his expenses on the way. When Wang got
home, he went about bragging of his Taoist friends and
his contempt for walls in general ; but as his wife dis-
believed his story, he set about going through the performance as before. Stepping back from the wall, he
rushed at it full speed with his head down ; but coming
in contact with the hard bricks, finished up in a heap on
the floor. His wife picked him up and found he had a
bump on his forehead as big as a large egg, at which she
roared with laughter ; but Wang was overwhelmed with
rage and shame, and cursed the old priest for his base
ingratitude.

VI. THE BUDDHIST PRIEST OF CH'ANG-CH'ING

AT Ch'ang-ch'ing there lived a Buddhist priest of exceptional virtue and purity of conduct, who, though over
eighty years of age, was still hale and hearty. One day
he fell down and could not move ; and when the other
priests rushed to help him up, they found he was already
gone. The old priest was himself unconscious of death,
and his soul flew away to the borders of the province of
Honan. Now it chanced that the scion of an old family
residing in Honan had gone out that very day with some
ten or a dozen followers to hunt the hare with falcons ; [1]

---

[1] This form of sport may still be seen in the north of China. A
hare being started, two Chinese greyhounds (which are very slow) are
slipped from their leash in pursuit. But, as the hare would easily run
straight away from them, a falcon is released almost simultaneously.
The latter soars to a considerable height, and then swoops down on
the hare, striking it a violent blow with the "pounce," or claw.
This partially stuns the hare, and allows the dogs to regain lost
ground, by which time the hare is ready once more, and off they go
again. The chase is ended by the hare getting to earth in a fox's
burrow, or being ultimately overtaken by the dogs. In the latter
case the heart and liver are cut out on the spot, and given to the
falcon ; otherwise he would hunt no more that day. Two falcons
are often released, one shortly after the other. They wear hoods,

but his horse having run away with him he fell off and was killed. 'Just at that moment the soul of the priest came by and entered into the body, which thereupon gradually recovered consciousness. The servants crowded round to ask him how he felt, when opening his eyes wide, he cried out, "How did I get here?" They assisted him to rise, and led him into the house, where all his ladies came to see him and inquire how he did. In great amazement he said, "I am a Buddhist priest. How came I hither?" His servants thought he was wandering, and tried to recall him by pulling his ears. As for himself, he could make nothing of it, and closing his eyes refrained from saying anything further. For food he would only eat rice, refusing all wine and meat; and avoided the society of his wives.² After some days he felt inclined for a stroll, at which all his family were delighted; but no sooner had he got outside and stopped for a little rest than he was besieged by servants begging him to take their accounts as usual. However, he pleaded illness and want of strength, and no more was said. He then took occasion to ask if they knew the district of Ch'ang-ch'ing, and on being answered in the affirmative expressed his intention of going thither for a trip, as he felt anxious about those he had left to their own resources, at the same time bidding the servants look after his affairs at home. They tried to dissuade him from this on the ground of his having but recently risen from a sick bed; but he paid no heed to their remonstrances, and on the very next day set out. Arriving in the Ch'ang-ch'ing district, he found everything unchanged; and without being put to the

which are removed at the moment of flying, and are attached by a slip-string from one leg to the falconer's wrist. During the night previous to a day's hunting they are not allowed to sleep. Each falconer lies down with one falcon on his left wrist, and keeps up an incessant tapping with the other hand on the bird's head. This is done to make them fierce. Should the quarry escape, a hare's skin is thrown down, by which means the falcons are secured, and made ready for a further flight. Occasionally, but rarely, the falcon misses its blow at the hare, with the result of a broken or injured "arm."

² Abstinence from wine and meat, and celibacy, are among the most important rules of the Buddhist church, as specially applied to its priesthood. At the door of every Buddhist monastery may be seen a notice that "No wine or meat may enter here!" Even the laity are not supposed to drink wine.

necessity of asking the road, made his way straight to the monastery. His former disciples received him with every token of respect as an honoured visitor; and in reply to his question as to where the old priest was, they informed him that their worthy teacher had been dead for some time. On asking to be shown his grave, they led him to a spot where there was a solitary mound some three feet high, over which the grass was not yet green. Not one of them knew his motives for visiting this place ; and by-and-by he ordered his horse, saying to the disciples, "Your master was a virtuous priest. Carefully preserve whatever relics of him you may have, and keep them from injury." They all promised to do this, and he then set off on his way home. When he arrived there, he fell into a listless state and took no interest in his family affairs. So much so, that after a few months he ran away and went straight to his former home at the monastery, telling the disciples that he was their old master. This they refused to believe, and laughed among themselves at his pretensions ; but he told them the whole story, and recalled many incidents of his previous life among them, until at last they were convinced. He then occupied his old bed and went through the same daily routine as before, paying no attention to the repeated entreaties of his family, who came with carriages and horses to beg him to return.

About a year subsequently, his wife sent one of the servants with splendid presents of gold and silk, all of which he refused with the exception of a single linen robe. And whenever any of his old friends passed this monastery, they always went to pay him their respects, finding him quiet, dignified, and pure. He was then barely thirty, though he had been a priest for more than eighty years.[3]

[3] Having renewed his youth by assuming the body of the young man into which his soul had entered.

VII. THE MARRIAGE OF THE FOX'S DAUGHTER

A PRESIDENT of the Board of Civil Office,[1] named Yin,
and a native of Li-ch'êng, when a young man, was very
badly off, but was endowed with considerable physical
courage. Now in this part of the country there was a
large establishment, covering several acres, with an unbroken succession of pavilions and verandahs, and belonging to one of the old county families ; but because ghosts
and apparitions were frequently seen there, the place had
for a long time remained untenanted, and was overgrown
with grass and weeds, no one venturing to enter in even
in broad daylight. One evening when Yin was carousing
with some fellow-students, one of them jokingly said, " If
anybody will pass a night in the haunted house, the rest of
us will stand him a dinner." Mr. Yin jumped up at this,
and cried out, "What is there difficult in that ? " So,
taking with him a sleeping-mat, he proceeded thither,
escorted by all his companions as far as the door, where
they laughed and said, " We will wait here a little while.
In case you see anything, shout out to us at once." " If
there are any goblins or foxes," replied Yin, " I'll catch
them for you." He then went in, and found the paths
obliterated by long grass, which had sprung up, mingled
with weeds of various kinds. It was just the time of the
new moon, and by its feeble light he was able to make
out the door of the house. Feeling his way, he walked
on until he reached the back pavilion, and then went
up on to the Moon Terrace, which was such a pleasant spot
that he determined to stop there. Gazing westwards, he
sat for a long time looking at the moon—a single thread of
light embracing in its horns the peak of a hill [2]—without
hearing anything at all unusual ; so, laughing to himself
at the nonsense people talked, he spread his mat upon the
floor, put a stone under his head for a pillow, and lay down
to sleep. He had watched the Cow-herd and the Lady [3]

---

[1] One of the " Six Boards " (now Seven) at the capital, equivalent
to our own War Office, Board of Works, &c.

[2] Which, of course, is impossible.

[3] The Chinese names for certain stars : βγ Aquilae and α Lyrae.

until they were just disappearing, and was on the point of dropping off, when suddenly he heard footsteps down below coming up the stairs. Pretending to be asleep, he saw a servant enter, carrying in his hand a lotus-shaped lantern,[4] who, on observing Mr. Yin, rushed back in a fright, and said to some one behind, " There is a stranger here ! " The person spoken to asked who it was, but the servant did not know ; and then up came an old gentleman, who, after examining Mr. Yin closely, said, " It's the future President : he's as drunk as can be. We needn't mind him ; besides, he's a good fellow, and won't give us any trouble." So they walked in and opened all the doors ; and by-and-by there were a great many other people moving about, and quantities of lamps were lighted, till the place was as light as day. About this time Mr. Yin slightly changed his position, and sneezed ; upon which the old man, perceiving that he was awake, came forward and fell down on his knees, saying, " Sir, I have a daughter who is to be married this very night. It was not anticipated that Your Honour would be here. I pray, therefore, that we may be excused." Mr. Yin got up and raised the old man, regretting that, in his ignorance of the festive occasion, he had brought with him no present.[5] " Ah, Sir," replied the old man, " your very presence here will ward off all noxious influences ; and that is quite enough for us." He then begged Mr. Yin to assist in doing the honours, and thus double the obligation already conferred. Mr. Yin readily assented, and went inside to look at the gorgeous arrangements they had made. He was here met by a lady, apparently about forty years of age, whom the old gentleman introduced as his wife ; and he had hardly made his bow when he heard the sound of flageolets,[6] and some one came hurrying in, saying, " He has come ! " The old gentleman flew out to meet this personage, and Mr. Yin also stood up, awaiting his arrival. In no long time, a bevy of people with gauze lanterns ushered in the bridegroom himself, who seemed to be about seventeen or eighteen years old, and of a most refined and prepossessing appearance. The old gentleman

---

[4] Lanterns very prettily made to resemble all kinds of flowers are to be seen at the Chinese New Year.

[5] This is, as with us, obligatory on all friends invited to a marriage.

[6] The accompaniment of all weddings and funerals in China.

bade him pay his respects first to their worthy guest; and
upon his looking towards Mr. Yin, that gentleman came
forward to welcome him on behalf of the host. Then
followed ceremonies between the old man and his son-
in-law ; and when these were over, they all sat down
to supper. Hosts of waiting-maids brought in profuse
quantities of wine and meats, with bowls and cups of
jade or gold, till the table glittered again. And when the
wine had gone round several times, the old gentleman told
one of the maids to summon the bride. This she did, but
some time passed and no bride came. So the old man
rose and drew aside the curtain, pressing the young lady
to come forth ; whereupon a number of women escorted
out the bride, whose ornaments went *tinkle tinkle* as she
walked along, sweet perfumes being all the time diffused
around. Her father told her to make the proper salutation, after which she went and sat by her mother. Mr.
Yin took a glance at her, and saw that she wore on her
head beautiful ornaments made of kingfisher's feathers,
her beauty quite surpassing anything he had ever seen.
All this time they had been drinking their wine out of
golden goblets big enough to hold several pints, when it
flashed across him that one of these goblets would be a
capital thing to carry back to his companions in evidence
of what he had seen. So he secreted it in his sleeve, and
pretending to be tipsy,[7] leaned forward with his head upon
the table as if going off to sleep. "The gentleman is
drunk," said the guests ; and by-and-by Mr. Yin heard
the bridegroom take his leave, and there was a general
trooping downstairs to the tune of a wedding march.
When they were all gone the old gentleman collected the
goblets, one of which was missing, though they hunted
high and low to find it. Some one mentioned the sleeping
guest ; but the old gentleman stopped him at once for
fear Mr. Yin should hear, and before long silence reigned

[7] The soberest people in the world, amongst whom anything like
sottishness is comparatively unknown, think it no disgrace, but
rather complimentary, to get pleasantly tipsy on all festive occasions;
and people who are physically unable to do so frequently go so far
as to hire substitutes to drink for them. Mandarins specially
suffer very much from the custom of being obliged to take " wine "
with a large number of guests. For further on this subject, see
No. LIV., note 1.

throughout. Mr. Yin then arose. It was dark, and he had no light ; but he could detect the lingering smell of the food, and the place was filled with the fumes of wine. Faint streaks of light now appearing in the east, he began quietly to make a move, having first satisfied himself that the goblet was still in his sleeve. Arriving at the door, he found his friends already there ; for they had been afraid he might come out after they left, and go in again early in the morning. When he produced the goblet they were all lost in astonishment ; and on hearing his story, they were fain to believe it, well knowing that a poor student like Yin was not likely to have such a valuable piece of plate in his possession.

Later on Mr. Yin took his doctor's degree, and was appointed magistrate over the district of Fei-ch'iu, where there was an old-established family of the name of Chu. The head of the family asked him to a banquet in honour of his arrival, and ordered the servants to bring in the large goblets. After some delay a slave-girl came and whispered something to her master which seemed to make him very angry. Then the goblets were brought in, and Mr. Yin was invited to drink. He now found that these goblets were of precisely the same shape and pattern as the one he had at home, and at once begged his host to tell him where he had had these made. " Well," said Mr. Chu, " there should be eight of them. An ancestor of mine had them made, when he was a minister at the capital, by an experienced artificer. They have been handed down in our family from generation to generation, and have now been carefully laid by for some time ; but I thought we would have them out to-day as a compliment to your Honour. However, there are only seven to be found. None of the servants can have touched them, for the old seals of ten years ago are still upon the box, unbroken. I don't know what to make of it." Mr. Yin laughed, and said, " It must have flown away ! Still, it is a pity to lose an heirloom of that kind ; and as I have a very similar one at home, I shall take upon myself to send it to you." When the banquet was over, Mr. Yin went home, and taking out his own goblet, sent it off to Mr. Chu. The latter was somewhat surprised to find that it was identical with his own, and hurried away to thank

the magistrate for his gift, asking him at the same time
how it had come into his possession. Mr. Yin told him the
whole story, which proves conclusively that although a fox
may obtain possession of a thing, even at a distance of many
hundred miles, he will not venture to keep it altogether.[8]

VIII. MISS CHIAO-NO

K'UNG HSÜEH-LI was a descendant of Confucius.[1] He was
a man of considerable ability, and an excellent poet.[2] A
fellow-student, to whom he was much attached, became
magistrate at T'ien-t'ai, and sent for K'ung to join him.
Unfortunately, just before K'ung arrived his friend died,
and he found himself without the means of returning
home ; so he took up his abode in a Buddhist monastery,
where he was employed in transcribing for the priests.
Several hundred paces to the west of this monastery there
was a house belonging to a Mr. Shan, a gentleman who
had known better days, but who had spent all his money
in a heavy law-suit ; and then, as his family was a small
one, had gone away to live in the country and left his
house vacant. One day there was a heavy fall of snow
which kept visitors away from the monastery ; and K'ung,
finding it dull, went out. As he was passing by the door
of the house above-mentioned, a young man of very elegant
appearance came forth, who, the moment he saw K'ung,
ran up to him, and with a bow, entered into conversation,
asking him to be pleased to walk in. K'ung was much
taken with the young man, and followed him inside. The

[8] The wedding-party was, of course, composed entirely of foxes,
this animal being believed by the Chinese to be capable of appearing
at will under the human form, and of doing either good or evil to its
friends or foes. These facts will be prominently brought out in
several of the stories to follow.

[1] Lineal descendants of Confucius are to be found at this day
living together as a clan, near their founder's mausoleum in Shantung. The head of the family is an hereditary *kung* or " duke," and
each member enjoys a share of the revenues with which the family
has been endowed, in well-merited recognition of the undying
influence of China's greatest sage.

[2] More or less proficiency in the art of poetry is an absolutely
essential qualification for all who present themselves at the great
competitive tests by which successful candidates are admitted to
Chinese official life.

rooms were not particularly large, but adorned throughout
with embroidered curtains, and from the walls hung scrolls
and drawings by celebrated masters. On the table lay a
book, the title of which was " Jottings from Paradise " ;
and turning over its leaves, K'ung found therein many
strange things. He did not ask the young man his name,
presuming that as he lived in the Shan family mansion,
he was necessarily the owner of the place. The young
man, however, inquired what he was doing in that part
of the country, and expressed great sympathy with his
misfortunes, recommending him to set about taking pupils.
" Alas ! " said K'ung, " who will play the Mæcenas to
a distressed wayfarer like myself ? " " If," replied the
young man, " you would condescend so far, I for my part
would gladly seek instruction at your hands." K'ung
was much gratified at this, but said he dared not arrogate
to himself the position of teacher, and begged merely to
be considered as the young man's friend. He then asked
him why the house had been shut up for so long ; to which
the young man replied, " This is the Shan family mansion.
It has been closed all this time because of the owner's
removal into the country. My surname is Huang-fu, and
my home is in Shen-si ; but as our house has been burnt
down in a great fire, we have put up here for a while."
Thus Mr. K'ung found out that his name was not Shan.
That evening they spent in laughing and talking together,
and K'ung remained there for the night. In the morning
a lad came in to light the fire ; and the young man, rising
first, went into the private part of the house. Mr. K'ung
was sitting up with the bed-clothes still huddled round
him, when the lad looked in and said, " Master's coming ! "
So he jumped up with a start, and in came an old man
with a silvery beard, who began to thank him, saying,
" I am very much obliged to you for your condescension
in becoming my son's tutor. At present he writes a
villainous hand ; and I can only hope you will not allow
the ties of friendship to interfere with discipline." Thereupon, he presented Mr. K'ung with an embroidered suit
of clothes, a sable hat, and a set of shoes and stockings ;
and when the latter had washed and dressed himself he
called for wine and food. K'ung could not make out what
the valances of the chairs and tables were made of ; they

were so very bright-coloured and dazzling. By-and-by, when the wine had circulated several times, the old gentleman picked up his walking-stick and took his leave. After breakfast the young man handed in his theme, which turned out to be written in an archaic style, and not at all after the modern fashion of essay-writing. K'ung asked him why he had done this, to which the young man replied that he did not contemplate competing at the public examinations. In the evening they had another drinking-bout, but it was agreed that there should be no more of it after that night. The young man then called the boy and told him to see if his father was asleep or not ; adding that if he was, he might quietly summon Miss Perfume. The boy went off, first taking a guitar out of a very pretty case ; and in a few minutes in came a very nice-looking young girl. The young man bade her play the *Death of Shun* ; [3] and seizing an ivory plectrum she swept the chords, pouring forth a vocal melody of exquisite sweetness and pathos. He then gave her a goblet of wine to drink, and it was midnight before they parted. Next morning they got up early and settled down to work. The young man proved an apt scholar : he could remember what he had once read, and at the end of two or three months had made astonishing progress. Then they agreed that every five days they would indulge in a symposium, and that Miss Perfume should always be of the party. One night when the wine had gone into K'ung's head, he seemed to be lost in a reverie ; whereupon his young friend, who knew what was the matter with him, said. " This girl was brought up by my father. I know you find it lonely, and I have long been looking out for a nice wife for you." " Let her only resemble Miss Perfume," said K'ung, " and she will do." " Your experience," said the young man, laughing, " is but limited, and, consequently, anything is a surprise to you. If Miss Perfume is your *beau ideal*, why, it will not be difficult to satisfy you."

[3] One of the two celebrated but legendary rulers of China in the golden ages of antiquity. Yao—who abdicated 2357 B.C.—nominated as his successor a young and virtuous husbandman named Shun, giving him both his daughters in marriage. At the death of Shun, these ladies are said to have wept so much that their tears literally drenched the bamboos which grew beside their husband's grave ; and the speckled bamboo is now commonly known as the bamboo of Shun's wives.

Some six months had passed away, when one day Mr. K'ung took it into his head that he would like to go out for a stroll in the country. The entrance, however, was carefully closed; and on asking the reason, the young man told him that his father wished to receive no guests for fear of causing interruption to his studies. So K'ung thought no more about it; and by-and-by, when the heat of summer came on, they moved their study to a pavilion in the garden. At this time Mr. K'ung had a swelling on the chest about as big as a peach, which, in a single night, increased to the size of a bowl. There he lay groaning with the pain, while his pupil waited upon him day and night. He slept badly and took hardly any food; and in a few days the place got so much worse that he could neither eat nor drink. The old gentleman also came in, and he and his son lamented over him together. Then the young man said, "I was thinking last night that my sister, Chiao-no, would be able to cure Mr. K'ung, and accordingly I sent over to my grandmother's asking her to come. She ought to be here by now." At that moment a servant entered and announced Miss Chiao-no, who had come with her cousin, having been at her aunt's house. Her father and brother ran out to meet her, and then brought her in to see Mr. K'ung. She was between thirteen and fourteen years old, and had beautiful eyes with a very intelligent expression in them, and a most graceful figure besides. No sooner had Mr. K'ung beheld this lovely creature than he quite forgot to groan, and began to brighten up. Meanwhile the young man was saying, "This respected friend of mine is the same to me as a brother. Try, sister, to cure him." Miss Chiao-no immediately dismissed her blushes, and rolling up her long sleeves approached the bed to feel his pulse.[4] As she was grasping his wrist, K'ung became conscious of a perfume more delicate than that of the epidendrum; and then she laughed, saying, "This illness was to be expected; for the heart is touched. Though it is severe, a cure can be effected; but, as there is already a swelling, not without using the knife." Then

[4] Volumes have been written by Chinese doctors on the subject of the pulse. They profess to distinguish as many as twenty-four different kinds, among which is one well known to our own practitioners—namely, the "thready" pulse; they, moreover, make a point of feeling the pulses of *both* wrists.

she drew from her arm a gold bracelet which she pressed down upon the suffering spot, until by degrees the swelling rose within the bracelet and overtopped it by an inch and more, the outlying parts that were inflamed also passing under, and thus very considerably reducing the extent of the tumour: With one hand she opened her robe and took out a knife with an edge as keen as paper, and pressing the bracelet down all the time with the other, proceeded to cut lightly round near the root of the swelling. The dark blood gushed forth, and stained the bed and the mat; but Mr. K'ung was delighted to be near such a beauty,— not only felt no pain, but would willingly have continued the operation that she might sit by him a little longer. In a few moments the whole thing was removed, and looked like a growth which had been cut off a tree. Here Miss Chiao-no called for water to wash the wound, and from between her lips she took a red pill as big as a bullet, which she laid upon the flesh, and, after drawing the skin together, passed round and round the place. The first turn felt like the searing of a hot iron; the second like a gentle itching; and at the third he experienced a sensation of lightness and coolness which penetrated into his very bones and marrow. The young lady then returned the pill to her mouth, and said, " He is cured," hurrying away as fast as she could. Mr. K'ung jumped up to thank her, and found that his complaint had quite disappeared. Her beauty, however, had made such an impression on him that his troubles were hardly at an end. From this moment he gave up his books, and took no interest in anything. This state of things was soon noticed by the young man, who said to him, " My brother, I have found a fine match for you." " Who is it to be ? " asked K'ung. " Oh, one of the family," replied his friend. Thereupon Mr. K'ung remained some time lost in thought, and at length said, " Please don't ! " Then turning his face to the wall, he repeated these lines :—

> Speak not of lakes and streams to him who once has seen the sea ;
> The clouds that circle Wu's peak are the only clouds for me.[5]

The young man guessed to whom he was alluding, and replied, " My father has a very high opinion of your talents

[5] By a famous poet, named Yüan Chên, A.D. 779–831.

and would gladly receive you into the family, but that he
has only one daughter, and she is much too young. My
cousin, Ah-sung, however, is seventeen years old, and not at
all a bad-looking girl. If you doubt my word, you can
wait in the verandah until she takes her daily walk in the
garden, and thus judge for yourself." This Mr. K'ung
acceded to, and accordingly saw Miss Chiao-no come out
with a lovely girl—her black eyebrows beautifully arched,
and her tiny feet encased in phœnix-shaped shoes—as like
one another as they well could be. He was of course
delighted, and begged the young man to arrange all preliminaries ; and the very next day his friend came to tell
him that the affair was finally settled. A portion of the
house was given up to the bride and bridegroom, and the
marriage was celebrated with plenty of music and hosts
of guests, more like a fairy wedding than anything else.
Mr. K'ung was very happy, and began to think that the
position of Paradise had been wrongly laid down, until one
day the young man came to him and said, " For the trouble
you have been at in teaching me, I shall ever remain your
debtor. At the present moment, the Shan family law-
suit has been brought to a termination, and they wish to
resume possession of their house immediately. We therefore propose returning to Shen-si, and as it is unlikely that
you and I will ever meet again, I feel very sorrowful at the
prospect of parting." Mr. K'ung replied that he would go
too, but the young man advised him to return to his old
home. This, he observed, was no easy matter ; upon
which the young man said, " Don't let that trouble you :
I will see you safe there." By-and-by his father came in
with Mr. K'ung's wife, and presented Mr. K'ung with one
hundred ounces of gold ; and then the young man gave
the husband and wife each one of his hands to grasp,
bidding them shut their eyes. The next instant they
were floating away in the air, with the wind whizzing in
their ears. In a little while he said, " You have arrived,"
and opening his eyes, K'ung beheld his former home. Then
he knew that the young man was not a human being.
Joyfully he knocked at the old door, and his mother was
astonished to see him arrive with such a nice wife. They
were all rejoicing together, when he turned round and
found that his friend had disappeared. His wife attended

on her mother-in-law with great devotion, and acquired a reputation both for virtue and beauty, which was spread round far and near. Some time passed away, and then Mr. K'ung took his doctor's degree, and was appointed Governor of the Gaol in Yen-ngan. He proceeded to his post with his wife only, the journey being too long for his mother, and by-and-by a son was born. Then he got into trouble by being too honest an official, and threw up his appointment ; but had not the wherewithal to get home again. One day when out hunting he met a handsome young man riding on a nice horse, and seeing that he was staring very hard looked closely at him. It was young Huang-fu. So they drew bridle, and fell to laughing and crying by turns,—the young man then inviting K'ung to go along with him. They rode on together until they had reached a village thickly shaded with trees, so that the sun and sky were invisible overhead, and entered into a most elaborately-decorated mansion, such as might belong to an old-established family. K'ung asked after Miss Chiao-no, and heard that she was married ; also that his own mother-in-law was dead, at which tidings he was greatly moved. Next day he went back and returned again with his wife. Chiao-no also joined them, and taking up K'ung's child, played with it, saying, " Your mother played us truant." Mr. K'ung did not forget to thank her for her former kindness to him, to which she replied, " You're a great man now. Though the wound has healed, haven't you forgotten the pain yet ? " Her husband, too, came to pay his respects, returning with her on the following morning. One day the young Huang-fu seemed troubled in spirit, and said to Mr. K'ung, " A great calamity is impending. Can you help us ? " Mr. K'ung did not know what he was alluding to, but readily promised his assistance. The young man then ran out and summoned the whole family to worship in the ancestral hall, at which Mr. K'ung was alarmed, and asked what it all meant. " You know," answered the young man, " I am not a man but a fox. To-day we shall be attacked by thunder ; [6] and if only you will aid us in our trouble, we may still

---

[6] The Chinese believe that wicked people are struck by the God of Thunder, and killed in punishment for some hidden crime. They regard lightning merely as an arrangement with a mirror by which the God is enabled to see his victim.

hope to escape. If you are unwilling, take your child and go, that you may not be involved with us." Mr. K'ung protested he would live or die with them, and so the young man placed him with a sword at the door, bidding him remain quiet there in spite of all the thunder. He did as he was told, and soon saw black clouds obscuring the light until it was all as dark as pitch. Looking round, he could see that the house had disappeared, and that its place was occupied by a huge mound and a bottomless pit. In the midst of his terror, a fearful peal was heard which shook the very hills, accompanied by a violent wind and driving rain. Old trees were torn up, and Mr. K'ung became both dazed and deaf. Yet he stood firm until he saw in a dense black column of smoke a horrid thing with a sharp beak and long claws, with which it snatched some one from the hole, and was disappearing up with the smoke. In an instant K'ung knew by her clothes and shoes that the victim was no other than Chiao-no, and instantly jumping up he struck the devil violently with his sword, and cut it down. Immediately the mountains were riven, and a sharp peal of thunder laid K'ung dead upon the ground. Then the clouds cleared away, and Chiao-no gradually came round, to find K'ung dead at her feet. She burst out crying at the sight, and declared that she would not live since K'ung had died for her. K'ung's wife also came out, and they bore the body inside. Chiao-no then made Ah-sung hold her husband's head, while her brother prised open his teeth with a hair-pin, and she herself arranged his jaw. She next put a red pill into his mouth, and bending down breathed into him. The pill went along with the current of air, and presently there was a gurgle in his throat, and he came round. Seeing all the family about him, he was disturbed as if waking from a dream. However, they were all united together, and fear gave place to joy; but Mr. K'ung objected to live in that out-of-the-way place, and proposed that they should return with him to his native village. To this they were only too pleased to assent—all except Chiao-no; and when Mr. K'ung invited her husband, Mr. Wu, as well, she said she feared her father and mother-in-law would not like to lose the children. They had tried all day to persuade her, but without success, when suddenly in rushed one of the Wu family's servants, dripping with perspiration and quite out of breath. They asked what was the matter, and the servant replied that the Wu family had been visited by a calamity on the very same day, and had every one perished. Chiao-no cried very bitterly at this, and could not be comforted ; but now there was nothing to prevent them from all returning together. Mr. K'ung went into the city for a few days on business, and then they set to work packing-up night and day. On arriving at their destination, separate apartments were allotted to young Mr. Huang-fu, and these he kept carefully shut up, only opening the door to Mr. K'ung and his wife.

Mr. K'ung amused himself with the young man and his sister Chiao-no, filling up the time with chess,[7] wine, conversation, and good cheer, as if they had been one family. His little boy, Huan, grew up to be a handsome young man, but with a touch of the fox in his composition ; so that when he showed himself abroad, he was immediately recognised as the son of a fox.

IX. MAGICAL ARTS

A CERTAIN Mr. Yü was a spirited young fellow, fond of boxing and trials of strength. He was able to take two kettles and swing them round about with the speed of the wind. Now, during the reign of Ch'ung Chêng,[1] when up for the final examination at the capital, his servant became seriously ill. Much troubled at this, he applied to a necromancer in the market-place [2] who was skilful at determining

---

[7] Chinese "chess" is similar to, but not identical with, our game. The board is divided by a river, and the king is confined to a small square of moves on his own territory. The game *par excellence* in China is *wei-ch'i*, an account of which I contributed to the *Temple Bar* magazine for January 1877.

[1] The last emperor of the Ming dynasty. Began to reign A.D. 1628.

[2] The trade of fortune-teller is one of the most flourishing in China. A large majority of the candidates who are unsuccessful at the public examinations devote their energies in this direction ; and in every Chinese city there are regular establishments whither the superstitious people repair to consult the oracle on every imaginable subject ;—not to mention hosts of itinerant soothsayers, both in town and country, whose stock-in-trade consists of a trestle-table, pen, ink, and paper, and a few other mysterious implements of their art. The nature of the response, favourable or otherwise, is determined by an inspection of the year, month, day, and hour at which the applicant was born, taken in combination with other particulars referring to the question at issue.

the various leases of life allotted to men. Before he had uttered a word, the necromancer asked him, saying, " Is it not about your servant, Sir, that you would consult me ? " Mr. Yü was startled at this, and replied that it was. " The sick man," continued the necromancer, " will come to no harm ; you, Sir, are the one in danger." Mr. Yü then begged him to cast his nativity, which he proceeded to do, finally saying to Mr. Yü, " You have but three days to live ! " Dreadfully frightened, he remained some time in a state of stupefaction, when the necromancer quietly observed that he possessed the power of averting this calamity by magic, and would exert it for the sum of ten ounces of silver. But Mr. Yü reflected that Life and Death are already fixed,[3] and he didn't see how magic could save him. So he refused, and was just going away, whereupon the necromancer said, " You grudge this trifling outlay. I hope you will not repent it." Mr. Yü's friends also urged him to pay the money, advising him rather to empty his purse than not secure the necromancer's compassion. Mr. Yü, however, would not hear of it, and the three days slipped quickly away. Then he sat down calmly in his inn to see what was going to happen. Nothing did happen all day, and at night he shut his door and trimmed the lamp ; then, with a sword at his side, he awaited the approach of death.

By-and-by, the clepsydra [4] showed that two hours had already gone without bringing him any nearer to dissolution ; and he was thinking about lying down, when he

[3] A firm belief in predestination is an important characteristic of the Chinese mind. " All is destiny " is a phrase daily in the mouth of every man, woman, and child, in the empire. Confucius himself, we are told, objected to discourse to his disciples upon this topic ; but it is evident from many passages in the *Lun Yu*, or *Confucian Gospels* [Book VI. ch. 8, Book XIV. ch. 38, &c.], that he believed in a certain pre-arrangement of human affairs, against which all efforts would be unavailing.

[4] An appliance of very ancient date in China, now superseded by cheap clocks and watches. A large clepsydra, consisting of four copper jars standing on steps one above the other, is still, however, to be seen in the city of Canton, and is in excellent working order, the night-watches being determined by reference to its indicator in the lower jar. By its aid, coils of " joss-stick," or pastille, are regulated to burn so many hours, and are sold to the poor, who use them both for the purpose of guiding their extremely vague notions of time, and for lighting the oft-recurring tobacco-pipe.

heard a scratching at the window, and then saw a tiny little man creep through, carrying a spear on his shoulder, who, on reaching the ground, shot up to the ordinary height. Mr. Yü seized his sword and at once struck at it ; but only succeeded in cutting the air. His visitor instantly shrank down small again, and made an attempt to escape through the crevice of the window ; but Yü redoubled his blows and at last brought him to the ground. Lighting the lamp, he found only a paper man,[5] cut right through the middle. This made him afraid to sleep, and he sat up watching, until in a little time he saw a horrid hobgoblin creep through the same place. No sooner did it touch the ground than he assailed it lustily with his sword, at length cutting it in half. Seeing, however, that both halves kept on wriggling about, and fearing that it might get up again, he went on hacking at it. Every blow told, giving forth a hard sound, and when he came to examine his work, he found a clay image all knocked to pieces. Upon this he moved his seat near to the window, and kept his eye fixed upon the crack. After some time, he heard a noise like a bull bellowing outside the window, and something pushed against the window-frame with such force as to make the whole house tremble and seem about to fall. Mr. Yü, fearing he should be buried under the ruins, thought he could not do better than fight outside ; so he accordingly burst open the door with a crash and rushed out. There he found a huge devil, as tall as the house, and he saw by the dim light of the moon that its face was as black as coal.

[5] " Paper men " are a source of great dread to the people at large. During the year 1876 whole provinces were convulsed by the belief that some such superstitious agency was at work to deprive innocent persons of their tails ; and the so-called " Pope " of the Taoist religion even went so far as to publish a charm against the machinations of the unseen. It ran as follows :—" Ye who urge filthy devils to spy out the people !—the Master's spirits are at hand and will soon discover you. With this charm anyone may travel by sunlight, moonlight, or starlight all over the earth." At one time popular excitement ran so high that serious consequences were anticipated ; and the mandarins in the affected districts found it quite as much as they could do to prevent lynch-law being carried out on harmless strangers who were unlucky enough to give rise to the slightest suspicion.

Taoist priests are generally credited with the power of cutting out human, animal, or other figures, of infusing vitality into them on the spot, and of employing them for purposes of good or evil.

Its eyes shot forth yellow fire : it had nothing either upon its shoulders or feet ; but held a bow in its hand and had some arrows at its waist. Mr. Yü was terrified ; and the devil discharged an arrow at him which he struck to the ground with his sword. On Mr. Yü preparing to strike, the devil let off another arrow which the former avoided by jumping aside, the arrow quivering in the wall beyond with a smart crack. The devil here got very angry, and drawing his sword flourished it like a whirlwind, aiming a tremendous blow at Mr. Yü. Mr. Yü ducked, and the whole force of the blow fell upon the stone wall of the house, cutting it right in two. Mr. Yü then ran out from between the devil's legs, and began hacking at its back—whack ! whack ! The devil now became furious, and roared like thunder, turning round to get another blow at his assailant. But Mr. Yü again ran between his legs, the devil's sword merely cutting off a piece of his coat. Once more he hacked away—whack !—whack ! and at length the devil came tumbling down flat. Mr. Yü cut at him right and left, each blow resounding like the watchman's wooden gong,[6] and then, bringing a light, he found it was a wooden image about as tall as a man. The bow and arrows were still there, the latter attached to its waist. Its carved and painted features were most hideous to behold ; and wherever Mr. Yü had struck it with his sword, there was blood. Mr. Yü sat with the light in his hand till morning, when he awaked to the fact that all these devils had been sent by the necromancer in order to kill him, and so evidence his own magical power. The next day, after having told the story far and wide, he went with some others to the place where the necromancer had his stall ; but the latter, seeing them coming, vanished in the twinkling of an eye. Some one observed that the blood of a dog would reveal a person who had made himself invisible, and Mr. Yü immediately procured some and went back with it. The necromancer disappeared as before, but on the spot where he had been standing they quickly threw down the dog's blood. Thereupon they saw his head and face all smeared

[6] Watchmen in China, when on their nightly rounds, keep up an incessant beating on what, for want of a better term, we have called a wooden gong. The object is to let thieves know they are awake and on the look-out.

over with blood, his eyes glaring like a devil's ; and at once seizing him, they handed him over to the authorities, by whom he was put to death.

X. JOINING THE IMMORTALS

A MR. CHOU, of Wên-têng, had in his youth been fellow-student with a Mr. Ch'êng, and a firm friendship was the result. The latter was poor, and depended very much upon Chou, who was the elder of the two. He called Chou's wife his " sister," and had the run of the house just as if he was one of the family. Now this wife happening to die in child-bed, Chou married another named Wang ; but as she was quite a young girl, Ch'êng did not seek to be introduced.[1] One day her younger brother came to visit her, and was being entertained in the " inner " apartments [2] when Ch'êng chanced to call. The servant announced his arrival, and Chou bade him ask Mr. Ch'êng in. But Ch'êng would not enter, and took his leave. Thereupon Chou caused the entertainment to be moved into the public part of the house, and, sending after Ch'êng, succeeded in bringing him back. They had hardly sat down before some one came in to say that a former servant of the establishment had been severely beaten at the magistrate's yamên ; the facts of the case being that a cow-boy of the Huang family connected with the Board of Rites had driven his cattle across the Chou family's land, and that words had arisen between the two servants in consequence ; upon which the Huang family's servant had complained to his master, who had seized the other and had sent him in to the magistrate's, where he had been bambooed. When Mr. Chou found out what the matter was, he was exceedingly angry, and said, " How dares this pig-boy fellow behave thus ? Why, only a generation ago his master was my father's servant ! He emerges a little from his obscurity, and immediately thinks himself I don't

[1] This is a characteristic touch. Only the most intimate of friends ever see each other's wives.

[2] Where the women of the family live, and into which no stranger ever penetrates. Among other names by which a Chinese husband speaks of his wife, a very common one is " the inner [wo]man."

know what ! " Swelling with rage, he rose to go in quest
of Huang, but Ch'êng held him back, saying, "The age is
corrupt : there is no distinction between right and wrong.
Besides, the officials of the day are half of them thieves,
and you will only get yourself into hot water." Chou,
however, would not listen to him ; and it was only when
tears were added to remonstrances that he consented to
let the matter drop. But his anger did not cease, and he
lay tossing and turning all night. In the morning he said
to his family, " I can stand the insults of Mr. Huang ; but
the magistrate is an officer of the Government, and not the
servant of influential people. If there is a case of any kind,
he should hear both plaintiff and defendant, and not act
like a dog, biting anybody he is set upon. I will bring an
action against the cow-boy, and see what the magistrate
will do to him." As his family rather egged him on, he
accordingly proceeded to the magistrate's and entered a
formal plaint ; but that functionary tore up his petition,
and would have nothing to do with it. This roused Chou's
anger, and he told the magistrate plainly what he thought
of him, in return for which contempt of court he was at once
seized and bound. During the forenoon Mr. Ch'êng called
at his house, where he learnt that Chou had gone into the
city to prosecute the cow-boy, and immediately hurried
after him with a view to stop proceedings. But his friend
was already in the gaol, and all he could do was to stamp
his foot in anger. Now it happened that three pirates had
just been caught ; and the magistrate and Huang, putting
their heads together, bribed these fellows to say that Chou
was one of their gang, whereupon the higher authorities
were petitioned to deprive him of his status as a graduate,[3]
and the magistrate then had him most unmercifully bambooed.[4] Mr. Ch'êng gained admittance to the gaol, and,
after a painful interview, proposed that a petition should

[3] Until which he would be safe, by virtue of his degree, from the
degrading penalty of the bamboo.
[4] This is the instrument commonly used for flogging criminals in
China, and consists of a strip of split bamboo planed down smooth.
Strictly speaking there are two kinds, the *heavy* and the *light* :
the former is now hardly if ever used. Until the reign of K'ang Hsi
all strokes were given across the back ; but that humane Emperor
removed the *locus operandi* lower down, " for fear of injuring the
liver or the lungs."

be presented direct to the Throne. " Alas ! " said Chou,
" here am I bound and guarded, like a bird in a cage. I
have indeed a young brother, but it is as much as he can do
to provide me with food." Then Ch'êng stepped forward,
saying, " I will perform this service. Of 'what use are
friends who will not assist in the hour of trouble ? " So
away he went, and Chou's brother provided him with
money to defray his expenses. After a long journey he
arrived at the capital, where he found himself quite at a
loss as to how he should get the petition presented. However, hearing that the Emperor was about to set out on a
hunting tour, he concealed himself in the market-place,
and when His Majesty passed by, prostrated himself on the
ground with loud cries and gesticulations. The Emperor
received his petition, and sent it to the Board of Punishments,[5] desiring to be furnished with a report on the case.
It was then more than ten months since the beginning of
the affair, and Chou, who had been made to confess [6] to
this false charge, was already under sentence of death ;
so that the officers of the Board were very much alarmed
when they received the Imperial instructions, and set to
work to re-hear the case in person. Huang was also much
alarmed, and devised a plan for killing Mr. Chou by bribing
the gaolers to stop his food and drink ; so that when his
brother brought provisions he was rudely thrust back and
prevented from taking them in. Mr. Ch'êng complained
of this to the Viceroy of the province, who investigated the
matter himself, and found that Chou was in the last stage
of starvation, for which the gaolers were bambooed to
death. Terrified out of his wits, Huang, by dint of bribing
heavily, succeeded in absconding and escaping a just
punishment for his crimes. The magistrate, however,
was banished for perversion of the law, and Chou was
permitted to return home, his affection for Ch'êng being
now very much increased. But ever after the prosecution
and his friend's captivity, Mr. Ch'êng took a dismal view
of human affairs, and one day invited Chou to retire with
him from the world. The latter, who was deeply attached

[5] See No. VII., note 1.
[6] It is a principle of Chinese jurisprudence that no sentence can
be passed until the prisoner has confessed his guilt—a principle,
however, frequently set aside in practice.

to his young wife, threw cold water on the proposition, and Mr. Ch'êng pursued the subject no farther, though his own mind was fully made up. Not seeing him for some days afterwards, Mr. Chou sent to inquire about him at his house ; but there they all thought he was at Chou's, neither family, in fact, having seen anything of him. This looked suspicious, and Chou, aware of his peculiarity, sent off people to look for him, bidding them search all the temples and monasteries in the neighbourhood. He also from time to time supplied Ch'êng's son with money and other necessaries.

Eight or nine years had passed away, when suddenly Ch'êng re-appeared, clad in a yellow cap and stole, and wearing the expression of a Taoist priest. Chou was delighted, and seized his arm, saying, " Where have you been ? —letting me search for you all over the place." " The solitary cloud and the wild crane," replied Ch'êng, laughing, " have no fixed place of abode. Since we last met my equanimity has happily been restored." Chou then ordered wine, an'd they chatted together on what had taken place in the interval. He also tried to persuade Ch'êng to detach himself from the Taoist persuasion, but the latter only smiled and answered nothing. " It is absurd ! " argued Chou. " Why cast aside your wife and child as you would an old pair of shoes ? " " Not so," answered Ch'êng ; " if men wish to cast me aside, who is there who can do so now ? " Chou asked where he lived, to which he replied, " In the Great Pure Mansion on Mount Lao." They then retired to sleep on the same bed ; and by-and-by Chou dreamt that Ch'êng was lying on his chest so that he could not breathe. In a fright he asked him what he was doing, but got no answer ; and then he waked up with a start. Calling to Ch'êng and receiving no reply, he sat up and stretched out his hand to touch him. The latter, however, had vanished, he knew not whither. When he got calm, he found he was lying at Ch'êng's end of the bed, which rather startled him. " I was not tipsy last night," reflected he ; " how could I have got over here ? " He next called his servants, and when they came and struck a light, lo ! he was Ch'êng. Now Chou had had a beard, so he put up his hand to feel for it, but found only a few straggling hairs. He then seized a mirror to look at himself, and cried out in

alarm : " If this is Mr. Ch'êng, where on earth am I ? "
By this time he was wide awake, and knew that Ch'êng
had employed magic to induce him to retire from the world.
He was on the point of entering the ladies' apartments ;
but his brother, not recognising who he was, stopped him,
and would not let him go in ; and as he himself was unable to prove his own identity, he ordered his horse that
he might go in search of Ch'êng. After some days' journey
he arrived at Mount Lao ; and, as his horse went along at
a good rate, the servant could not keep up with him.
By-and-by he rested awhile under a tree, and saw a great
number of Taoist priests going backwards and forwards,
and among them was one who stared fixedly at him. So
he inquired of him where he should find Ch'êng ; whereat
the priest laughed and said, " I know the name. He is
probably in the Great Pure Mansion." When he had given
this answer he went on his way, Chou following him with
his eyes about a stone's-throw, until he saw him speak
with some one else, and, after saying a few words, proceed
onwards as before. The person whom he had spoken
with came on to where Chou was, and turned out to be
a fellow-townsman of his. He was much surprised at
meeting Chou, and said, " I haven't seen you for some
years. They told me you had gone to Mount Lao to be
a Taoist priest. How is it you are still amusing yourself
among mortals ? ' Chou told him who he really was ;
upon which the other replied, " Why, I thought the gentleman I just met was you ! He has only just left me, and
can't have got very far." " Is it possible," cried Chou,
" that I didn't know my own face ? " Just then the
servant came up, and away they went full speed, but
could not discover the object of their search. All around
them was a vast desert, and they were at a loss whether
to go on or to return. But Chou reflected that he had no
longer any home to receive him, and determined to carry
out his design to the bitter end ; but as the road was
dangerous for riding, he gave his horse to the servant,
and bade him go back. On he went cautiously by himself,
until he spied a boy sitting by the wayside alone. He
hurried up to him and asked the boy to direct him where
he could find Mr. Ch'êng. " I am one of his disciples,"
replied the lad ; and, shouldering Chou's bundle, started

off to show the way. They journeyed on together, taking their food by the light of the stars, and sleeping in the open air, until, after many miles of road, they arrived in three days at their destination. But this Great Pure locality was not like that generally spoken of in the world. Though as late as the middle of the tenth moon, there was a great profusion of flowers along the road, quite unlike the beginning of winter. The lad went in and announced the arrival of a stranger, whereupon Mr. Ch'êng came out, and Chou recognised his own features. Ch'êng grasped his hand and led him inside, where he prepared wine and food, and they began to converse together. Chou noticed many birds of strange plumage, so tame that they were not afraid of him ; and these from time to time would alight on the table and sing with voices like Pan-pipes. He was very much astonished at all this, but a love of mundane pleasures had eaten into his soul, and he had no intention of stopping. On the ground were two rush-mats, upon which Ch'êng invited his friend to sit down with him. Then about midnight a serene calm stole over him ; and while he was dozing off for a moment, he seemed to change places with Ch'êng. Suspecting what had happened, he put his hand up to his chin, and found it covered with a beard as before. At dawn he was anxious to return home, but Ch'êng pressed him to stay ; and when three days had gone by Ch'êng said to him, " I pray you take a little rest now : to-morrow I will set you on your way." Chou had barely closed his eyelids before he heard Ch'êng call out, " Everything is ready for starting ! " So he got up and followed him along a road other than that by which he had come, and in a very short time he saw his home in the distance. In spite of Chou's entreaties, Ch'êng would not accompany him so far, but made Chou go, waiting himself by the roadside. So the latter went alone, and when he reached his house, knocked at the door. Receiving no answer, he determined to get over the wall, when he found that his body was as light as a leaf, and with one spring he was over. In the same manner he passed several inner walls, until he reached the ladies' apartments, where he saw by the still burning lamp that the inmates had not yet retired for the night. Hearing people talking within, he licked a hole in the

paper window [7] and peeped through, and saw his wife
sitting drinking with a most disreputable-looking fellow.
Bursting with rage, his first impulse was to surprise them
in the act ; but seeing there were two against one, he stole
away and let himself out by the entrance-gate, hurrying
off to Ch'êng, to whom he related what he had seen, and
finally begged his assistance. Ch'êng willingly went along
with him ; and when they reached the room, Chou seized
a big stone and hammered loudly at the door. All was
then confusion inside, so Chou hammered again, upon
which the door was barricaded more strongly than before.
Here Ch'êng came forward with his sword, [8] and burst
the door open with a crash. Chou rushed in, and the man
inside rushed out ; but Ch'êng was there, and with his
sword cut his arm right off. Chou rudely seized his wife,
and asked what it all meant ; to which she replied that the
man was a friend who sometimes came to take a cup of
wine with them. Thereupon Chou borrowed Ch'êng's
sword and cut off her head, [9] hanging up the trunk on a
tree in the courtyard. He then went back with Ch'êng.
By-and-by he awaked and found himself on the bed, at
which he was somewhat disturbed, and said, " I have
had a strangely confused dream, which has given me a
fright." " My brother,' 'replied Ch'êng, smiling, " you
look upon dreams as realities : you mistake realities for
dreams." Chou asked what he meant by these words ;
and then Ch'êng showed him his sword besmeared with
blood. Chou was terrified, and sought to destroy himself ; but all at once it occurred to him that Ch'êng might
be deceiving him again. Ch'êng divined his suspicions,

[7] Wooden frames covered with a semi-transparent paper are used
all over the northern provinces of China ; in the south, oyster-
shells, cut square and planed down thin, are inserted tile-fashion in
the long narrow spaces of a wooden frame made to receive them,
and used for the same purpose. But glass is gradually finding its
way into the houses of the well-to-do, large quantities being made
at Canton and exported to various parts of the empire.

[8] Every Taoist priest has a magic sword, corresponding to our
" magician's wand."

[9] In China, a man has the right to slay his adulterous wife, but
he must slay her paramour also ; both or neither. Otherwise, he
lays himself open to a prosecution for murder. The act completed,
he is further bound to proceed at once to the magistrate of the
district and report what he has done.

and made haste at once to see him home. In a little while they arrived at the village gate, and then Ch'êng said, " Was it not here that, sword in hand, I awaited you that night ? I cannot look upon the unclean spot. I pray you go on, and let me stay here. If you do not return by the afternoon, I will depart alone." Chou then approached his house, which he found all shut up as if no one was living there ; so he went into his brother's.

The latter, when he beheld Chou, began to weep bitterly, saying, " After your departure, thieves broke into the house and killed my sister-in-law, hanging her body upon a tree. Alas ! alas ! The murderers have not yet been caught." Chou then told him the whole story of his dream, and begged him to stop further proceedings ; at all of which his brother was perfectly lost in astonishment. Chou then asked after his son, and his brother told the nurse to bring him in ; whereupon the former said, " Upon this infant are centred the hopes of our race.[10] Tend him well ; for I am going to bid adieu

[10] The importance of male offspring in Chinese social life is hardly to be expressed in words. To the son is confided the task of worshipping at the ancestral tombs, the care of the ancestral tablets, and the due performance of all rites and ceremonies connected with the departed dead. No Chinaman will die, if he can help it, without leaving a son behind him. If his wife is childless he will buy a concubine ; and we are told on page 41, vol. xiii., of the *Liao Chai*, that a good wife, " who at thirty years of age has not borne a child should forthwith pawn her jewellery and purchase a concubine for her husband ; for to be without a son is hard indeed ! " Another and a common resource is to adopt a nephew ; and sometimes a boy is bought from starving parents, or from a professional kidnapper. Should a little boy die, no matter how young, his parents do not permit even him to be without the good offices of a son. They adopt some other child on his behalf ; and when the latter grows up it becomes his duty to perform the proper ceremonies at his baby father's tomb. Girls do not enjoy the luxury of this sham posterity. They are quietly buried in a hole near the family vault, and their disembodied spirits are left to wander about in the realms below uncared for and unappeased. It must not be inferred, however, from this that the position of woman in China is low, as such is far from being the case. Every mother shares in the ancestral worship, and her name is recorded on the tombstone, side by side with that of her husband. Hence it is that Chinese tombstones are always to the memory either of a father or of a mother, or of both, with occasionally the addition of the grandfather and grandmother, and sometimes even that of the generation preceding.

to the world." He then took his leave, his brother
following him all the time with tears in his eyes to induce
him to remain. But he heeded him not ; and when they
reached the village gate his brother saw him go away with
Ch'êng. From afar he looked back and said, " Forbear,
and be happy ! " His brother would have replied ; but
here Ch'êng whisked his sleeve, and they disappeared.
The brother remained there for some time, and then went
back overwhelmed with grief. He was an unpractical man,
and before many years were over all the property was
gone and the family reduced to poverty. Chou's son, who
was growing up, was thus unable to secure the services of
a tutor, and had no one but his uncle to teach him. One
morning, on going into the school-room, the uncle found
a letter lying on his desk addressed to himself in his brother's
handwriting. There was, however, nothing in it but a
finger-nail about four inches in length. Surprised at
this, he laid the nail down on the ink-slab while he went
out to ask whence the letter had come. This no one knew ;
but when he went back he found that the ink-stone had
been changed into a piece of shining yellow gold. More
than ever astonished, he tried the nail on copper and iron
things, all of which were likewise turned to gold. He
thus became very rich, sharing his wealth with Ch'êng's
son ; and it was bruited about that the two families possessed the secret of transmutation.[11]

XI. THE FIGHTING QUAILS

WANG CH'ÊNG belonged to an old family in P'ing-yüan,
but was such an idle fellow that his property gradually
disappeared, until at length all he had left was an old
tumble-down house. His wife and he slept under a coarse
hempen coverlet, and the former was far from sparing her
reproaches. At the time of which we are speaking the
weather was unbearably hot ; and Wang went to pass the
night with many other of his fellow-villagers in a pavilion
which stood among some dilapidated buildings belonging
to a family named Chou. With the first streaks of dawn

[11] The belief that a knowledge of alchemy is obtainable by leading
the life of a pure and perfect Taoist is one of the numerous additions
in later ages to this ancient form of religion. See No. IV., note 1.

his comrades departed ; but Wang slept well on till about
nine o'clock, when he got up and proceeded leisurely home.
All at once he saw in the grass a gold hair-pin ; and taking
it up to look at it, found engraved thereon in small
characters—" The property of the Imperial family." Now
Wang's own grandfather had married into the Imperial
family,[1] and consequently he had formerly possessed many
similar articles ; but while he was thinking it over up came
an old woman in search of the hair-pin, which Wang, who
though poor was honest, at once produced and handed
to her. The old woman was delighted, and thanked Wang
for his goodness, observing that the pin was not worth
much in itself, but was a relic of her departed husband.
Wang asked what her husband had been ; to which she
replied, " His name was Wang Chien-chih, and he was
connected by marriage with the Imperial family." " My
own grandfather ! " cried Wang, in great surprise ; " how
could you have known him ? " " You, then," said the old
woman, " are his grandson. I am a fox, and many years
ago I was married to your grandfather ; but when he died
I retired from the world. Passing by here I lost my hair-
pin, which destiny conveyed into your hands." Wang had
heard of his grandfather's fox-wife, and believing therefore
the old woman's story, invited her to return with him,
which she did. Wang called his wife out to receive her ;
but when she came in rags and tatters, with unkempt hair
and dirty face, the old woman sighed, and said, " Alas !
alas ! has Wang Chien-chih's grandson come to this ? "
Then looking at the broken, smokeless stove, she added,
" How, under these circumstances, have you managed even
to support life ? " Here Wang's wife told the tale of their
poverty, with much sobbing and tears ; whereupon the old
woman gave her the hair-pin, bidding her go pawn it, and
with the proceeds buy some food, saying that in three days

[1] The direct issue of the Emperors of the present dynasty and
their descendants in the male line for ever are entitled to wear a
yellow girdle in token of their relationship to the Imperial family,
each generation becoming a degree lower in rank, but always re-
taining this distinctive badge. Members of the collateral branches
wear a red girdle, and are commonly known as *gioros*. With the
lapse of two hundred and fifty years, the wearers of these badges
have become numerous, and in many cases disreputable ; and they
are now to be found even among the lowest dregs of Chinese social
life.

she would visit them again. Wang pressed her to stay, but she said, " You can't even keep your wife alive ; what would it benefit you to have me also dependent on you ? " So she went away, and then Wang told his wife who she was, at which his wife felt very much alarmed ; but Wang was so loud in her praises, that finally his wife consented to treat her with all proper respect. In three days she returned as agreed, and, producing some money, sent out for a hundredweight of rice and a hundredweight of corn. She passed the night with them, sleeping with Mrs. Wang, who was at first rather frightened, but who soon laid aside her suspicions when she found that the old lady meant so well towards them. Next day the latter addressed Wang, saying, " My grandson, you must not be so lazy. You should try to make a little money in some way or another." Wang replied that he had no capital ; upon which the old lady said, " When your grandfather was alive, he allowed me to take what money I liked ; but not being a mortal, I had no use for it, and consequently did not draw largely upon him. I have, however, saved from my pin-money the sum of forty ounces of silver, which has long been lying idle for want of an investment. Take it, and buy summer cloth, which you may carry to the capital and re-sell at a profit." So Wang bought some fifty pieces of summer cloth ; and the old lady made him get ready, calculating that in six or seven days he would reach the capital. She also warned him, saying,

> Be neither lazy nor slow—
> For if a day too long you wait,
> Repentance comes a day too late.

Wang promised all obedience, and packed up his goods and went off. On the road he was overtaken by a rain-storm which soaked him through to the skin ; and as he was not accustomed to be out in bad weather, it was altogether too much for him. He accordingly sought shelter in an inn, but the rain went on steadily till night, running over the eaves of the house like so many ropes. Next morning the roads were in a horrible state ; and Wang, watching the passers-by slipping about in the slush, unable to see any path, dared not face it all, and remained until noon, when it began to dry up a little. Just then, however, the clouds closed over again, and down came the rain in torrents, causing him to stay another night before he could go on. When he was nearing the capital, he heard to his great joy that summer cloth was at a premium ; and on arrival proceeded at once to take up his quarters at an inn. There the landlord said it was a pity he had come so late, as communications with the south having been only recently opened, the supply of summer cloth had been small ; and there being a great demand for it among the wealthy families of the metropolis, its price had gone up to three times the usual figure. " But," he added, " two days ago several large consignments arrived, and the price went down again, so that the late comers have lost their market." Poor Wang was thus left in the lurch, and as every day more summer cloth came in, the value of it fell in a corresponding ratio. Wang would not part with his at a loss, and held on for some ten days, when his expenses for board and lodging were added to his present distress. The landlord urged him to sell even at a loss, and turn his attention to something else, which he ultimately did, losing over ten ounces of silver on his venture. Next day he rose in the morning to depart, but on looking in his purse found all his money gone. He rushed away to tell the landlord, who, however, could do nothing for him. Some one then advised him to take out a summons and make the landlord reimburse him ; but he only sighed, and said, " It is my destiny, and no fault of the landlord's." Thereupon the landlord was very grateful to him, and gave him five ounces of silver to enable him to go home. He did not care, however, to face his grandmother empty-handed, and remained in a very undecided state, until suddenly he saw a quail-catcher winning heaps of money by fighting his birds, and selling them at over 100 *cash* a-piece. He then determined to lay out his five ounces of silver in quails, and pay back the landlord out of the profits. The latter approved very highly of this plan, and not only agreed to lend him a room, but also to charge him little or nothing for his board. So Wang went off rejoicing, and bought two large baskets of quails, with which he returned to the city, to the great satisfaction of the landlord, who advised him to lose no time in disposing of them. All that night it poured in torrents, and the next morning the streets were like rivers, the rain still continuing to fall. Wang waited for it to clear up, but several days passed and still there were no signs of fine weather. He then went to look at his quails, some of which he found dead and others dying. He was much alarmed at this, but was quite at a loss what to do ; and by the next day a lot more had died, so that only a few were left, which he fed all together in one basket. The day after this he went again to look at them, and lo ! there remained but a single quail. With tears in his eyes he told the landlord what had happened, and he, too, was much affected. Wang then reflected that he had no money left to carry him home, and that he could not do better than cease to live. But the landlord spoke to him and soothed him, and they went together to look at the quail. " This is a fine bird," said the landlord, " and it strikes me that it has simply killed the others. Now, as you have got nothing to do, just set to work and train it ; and if it is good for anything, why, you'll be able to make a living out of it." Wang did as he was told ; and when the bird was trained, the landlord bade him take it into the street and gamble for something to eat. This, too, he did, and his quail won every main ; whereupon the landlord gave him some money to bet with the young fellows of the neighbourhood. Everything turned out favourably, and by the end of six months he had saved twenty ounces of silver, so that he became quite easy in his mind and looked upon the quail as a dispensation of his destiny.

Now one of the princes was passionately fond of quail-fighting, and always at the Feast of Lanterns anybody who owned quails might go and fight them in the palace against the Prince's birds. The landlord therefore said to Wang, " Here is a chance of enriching yourself by a single stroke ; only I can't say what your luck will do for you." He then explained to him what it was, and away they went together, the landlord saying, " If you lose, burst out into lamentations ; but if you are lucky enough to win, and the Prince wishes, as he will, to buy your bird, don't consent. If he presses you very much, watch for a nod from me before you agree." This settled, they proceeded to the palace, where they found crowds of quail-fighters already on the ground ; and then the Prince came forth, heralds proclaiming to the multitude that any who wished to fight their birds might come up. Some man at once stepped forward, and the

Prince gave orders for the quails to be released ; but at the first strike the stranger's quail was knocked out of time. The Prince smiled, and by-and-by won several more mains, until at last the landlord said, " Now's our time," and went up together with Wang. The Prince looked at their bird and said, " It has a fierce-looking eye and strong feathers. We must be careful what we are doing." So he commanded his servants to bring out Iron Beak to oppose Wang's bird ; but, after a couple of strikes, the Prince's quail was signally defeated. He sent for a better bird, but that shared the same fate ; and then he cried out, " Bring the Jade Bird from the palace ! " In a little time it arrived, with pure white feathers like an egret, and an unusually martial appearance. Wang was much alarmed, and falling on his knees prayed to be excused this main, saying, " Your Highness's bird is too good. I fear lest mine should be wounded, and my livelihood be taken from me." But the Prince laughed and said, " Go on. If your quail is killed I will make it up to you handsomely." Wang then released his bird, and the Prince's quail rushed at it at once ; but when the Jade Bird was close by, Wang's quail awaited its coming head down and full of rage. The former made a violent peck at its adversary, and then sprang up to swoop down on it. Thus they went on up and down, backwards and forwards, until at length they got hold of each other, and the Prince's bird was beginning to show signs of exhaustion. This enraged it all the more, and it fought more violently than ever ; but soon a perfect snowstorm of feathers began to fall, and, with drooping wings, the Jade Bird made its escape. The spectators were much moved by the result ; and the Prince himself, taking up Wang's bird, examined it closely from beak to claws, finally asking if it was for sale. " My sole dependence," replied Wang, " is upon this bird. I would rather not part with it." " But," said the Prince, " if I give you as much as the capital, say, of an ordinary tradesman, will not that tempt you ? " Wang thought some time, and then answered, " I would rather not sell my bird ; but as your Highness has taken a fancy to it I will only ask enough to find me in food and clothes." " How much do you want ? " inquired the Prince ; to which Wang replied that he would take a thousand ounces of silver. " You fool ! " cried the

Prince ; " do you think your bird is such a jewel as all that ? " " If your Highness," said Wang, " does not think the bird a jewel, I value it more than that stone which was priced at fifteen cities." " How so ? " asked the Prince. " Why," said Wang, " I take my bird every day into the market-place. It there wins for me several ounces of silver, which I exchange for rice ; my family, over ten in number, has nothing to fear from either cold or hunger. What jewel could do that ? " " You shall not lose anything," replied the Prince ; " I will give you two hundred ounces." But Wang would not consent, and then the Prince added another hundred ; whereupon Wang looked at the landlord, who, however, made no sign. Wang then offered to take nine hundred ; but the Prince ridiculed the idea of paying such a price for a quail, and Wang was preparing to take his leave with the bird, when the Prince called him back, saying, " Here ! here ! I will give you six hundred. Take it or leave it as you please." Wang here looked at the landlord, and the landlord remained motionless as before. However, Wang was satisfied himself with this offer, and being afraid of missing his chance, said to his friend, " If I get this price for it I shall be quite content. If we go on haggling and finally come to no terms, that will be a very poor end to it all." So he took the Prince's offer, and the latter, overjoyed, caused the money to be handed to him. Wang then returned with his earnings, but the landlord said to him, " What did I say to you ? You were in too much of a hurry to sell. Another minute, and you would have got eight hundred." When Wang got back he threw the money on the table and told the landlord to take what he liked ; but the latter would not, and it was only after some pressing that he would accept payment for Wang's board. Wang then packed up and went home, where he told his story and produced his silver, to the great delight of all of them. The old lady counselled the purchase of a quantity of land, the building of a house, and the purchase of implements ; and in a very short time they became a wealthy family. The old lady always got up early in the morning and made Wang attend to the farm, his wife to her spinning ; and rated them soundly at any signs of laziness. The husband and wife henceforth lived in peace, and no longer abused each other, until at the expiration of three years the old lady declared her intention of bidding them adieu. They both tried to stop her, and with the aid of tears succeeded in persuading her ; but the next day she had disappeared.[2]

XII. THE PAINTED SKIN

AT T'ai-yüan there lived a man named Wang. One morning he was out walking when he met a young lady carrying a bundle and hurrying along by herself. As she moved along with some difficulty,[1] Wang quickened his pace and caught her up, and found she was a pretty girl of about sixteen. Much smitten, he inquired whither she was going so early, and no one with her. " A traveller like you," replied the girl, " cannot alleviate my distress ; why trouble yourself to ask ? " " What distress is it ? " said Wang ; " I'm sure I'll do anything I can for you." " My parents," answered she, " loved money, and they sold me as concubine into a rich family, where the wife was very jealous, and beat and abused me morning and night. It was more than I could stand, so I have run away." Wang asked her where she was going ; to which she replied that a runaway had no fixed place of abode. " My house," said Wang, " is at no great distance ; what do you say to coming there ? " She joyfully acquiesced ; and Wang, taking up her bundle, led the way to his house. Finding no one there, she asked Wang where his family were ; to which he

[2] Quail fighting is not so common now in China as it appears to have been formerly. Cricket-fighting is, however, a very favourite form of gambling, large quantities of these insects being caught every year for this purpose, and considerable sums frequently staked on the result of a contest between two champions.

[1] Impeded, of course, by her bound feet. This practice is said to have originated about A.D. 970, with Yao Niang, the concubine of the pretender Li Yü, who wished to make her feet like the " new moon." The Manchu or Tartar ladies never adopted this custom, and therefore the Empresses of modern times have had feet of the natural size ; neither is it in force among the Hakkas or among the hill-tribes of China and Formosa and others. The practice was forbidden in 1664 by the Manchu Emperor, K'ang Hsi ; but popular feeling was so strong on the subject that four years afterwards the prohibition was withdrawn. A vigorous attempt is now being made to secure natural feet for the Chinese girl, with more chance of success.

replied that that was only the library. " And a very nice place, too," said she ; " but if you are kind enough to wish to save my life, you mustn't let it be known that I am here." Wang promised he would not divulge her secret, and so she remained there for some days without anyone knowing anything about it. He then told his wife, and she, fearing the girl might belong to some influential family, advised him to send her away. This, however, he would not consent to do ; when one day, going into the town, he met a Taoist priest, who looked at him in astonishment, and asked him what he had met. " I have met nothing," replied Wang. " Why," said the priest, " you are bewitched ; what do you mean by not having met anything ? " But Wang insisted that it was so, and the priest walked away, saying, " The fool ! Some people don't seem to know when death is at hand." This startled Wang, who at first thought of the girl ; but then he reflected that a pretty young thing as she was couldn't well be a witch, and began to suspect that the priest merely wanted to do a stroke of business. When he returned, the library door was shut, and he couldn't get in, which made him suspect that something was wrong ; and so he climbed over the wall, where he found the door of the inner room shut too. Softly creeping up, he looked through the window and saw a hideous devil, with a green face and jagged teeth like a saw, spreading a human skin upon the bed and painting it with a paint brush. The devil then threw aside the brush, and giving the skin a shake out, just as you would a coat, threw it over its shoulders, when lo ! it was the girl. Terrified at this, Wang hurried away with his head down in search of the priest, who had gone he knew not whither ; subsequently finding him in the fields, where he threw himself on his knees and begged the priest to save him. " As to driving her away," said the priest, " the creature must be in great distress to be seeking a substitute for herself ;[2] besides, I could hardly endure to

[2] The disembodied spirits of the Chinese *Inferno* are permitted, under certain conditions of time and good conduct, to appropriate to themselves the vitality of some human being, who, as it were, exchanges places with the so-called " devil." The devil does not, however, reappear as the mortal whose life it has become possessed of, but is merely born again into the world ; the idea being that the amount of life on earth is a constant quantity, and cannot be

injure a living thing."[3] However, he gave Wang a fly-brush, and bade him hang it at the door of the bedroom, agreeing to meet again at the Ch'ing-ti temple. Wang went home, but did not dare enter the library; so he hung up the brush at the bedroom door, and before long heard a sound of footsteps outside. Not daring to move, he made his wife peep out; and she saw the girl standing looking at the brush, afraid to pass it. She then ground her teeth and went away; but in a little while came back, and began cursing, saying, "You priest, you won't frighten me. Do you think I am going to give up what is already in my grasp?" Thereupon she tore the brush to pieces, and bursting open the door, walked straight up to the bed, where she ripped open Wang and tore out his heart, with which she went away. Wang's wife screamed out, and the servant came in with a light; but Wang was already dead and presented a most miserable spectacle. His wife, who was in an agony of fright, hardly dared cry for fear of making a noise; and next day she sent Wang's brother to see the priest. The latter got into a great rage, and cried out, "Was it for this that I had compassion on you, devil that you are?" proceeding at once with Wang's brother to the house, from which the girl had disappeared without anyone knowing whither she had gone. But the priest, raising his head, looked all round, and said, "Luckily she's not far off." He then asked who lived in the apartments on the south side, to which Wang's brother replied that he did; whereupon the priest declared that there she would be found. Wang's brother was horribly frightened and said he did not think so; and then the priest asked him if any stranger had been to the house. To this he answered that he had been out to the Ch'ing-ti temple and couldn't possibly say: but he went off to inquire, and in a little while came back and reported that an old woman had

increased or diminished, reminding one in a way of the great modern doctrine of the conservation of energy. This curious belief has an important bearing that will be brought out in a subsequent story.

[3] Here again is a Taoist priest quoting the Buddhist command-ment, "Thou shalt not take life." The Buddhist laity in China, who do not hesitate to take life for the purposes of food, salve their consciences from time to time by buying birds, fishes, &c., and letting them go, in the hope that such acts will be set down on the credit side of their record of good and evil.

sought service with them as a maid-of-all-work, and had been engaged by his wife. " That is she," said the priest, as Wang's brother added she was still there ; and they all set out to go to the house together. Then the priest took his wooden sword, and standing in the middle of the court-yard, shouted out, " Base-born fiend, give me back my fly-brush ! " Meanwhile the new maid-of-all-work was in a great state of alarm, and tried to get away by the door ; but the priest struck her and down she fell flat, the human skin dropped off, and she became a hideous devil. There she lay grunting like a pig, until the priest grasped his wooden sword and struck off her head. She then became a dense column of smoke curling up from the ground, when the priest took an uncorked gourd and threw it right into the midst of the smoke. A sucking noise was heard, and the whole column was drawn into the gourd ; after which the priest corked it up closely and put it in his pouch.[4] The skin, too, which was complete even to the eye-brows, eyes, hands, and feet, he also rolled up as if it had been a scroll, and was on the point of leaving with it, when Wang's wife stopped him, and with tears entreated him to bring her husband to life. The priest said he was unable to do that ; but Wang's wife flung herself at his feet, and with loud lamentations implored his assistance. For some time he remained immersed in thought, and then replied, " My power is not equal to what you ask. I myself cannot raise the dead ; but I will direct you to some one who can, and if you apply to him properly you will succeed." Wang's wife asked the priest who it was ; to which he replied, " There is a maniac in the town who passes his time grovelling in the dirt. Go, prostrate yourself before him, and beg him to help you. If he insults you, show no sign of anger." Wang's brother knew the man to whom he alluded, and accordingly bade the priest adieu, and pro-ceeded thither with his sister-in-law.

They found the destitute creature raving away by the roadside, so filthy that it was all they could do to go near him. Wang's wife approached him on her knees ; at which the maniac leered at her, and cried out, " Do you love me, my beauty ? " Wang's wife told him what she had come

---

[4] This recalls the celebrated story of the fisherman in the *Arabian Nights*.

for, but he only laughed and said, " You can get plenty of other husbands. Why raise the dead one to life ? " But Wang's wife entreated him to help her ; whereupon he observed, " It's very strange : people apply to me to raise their dead as if I was king of the infernal regions." He then gave Wang's wife a thrashing with his staff, which she bore without a murmur, and before a gradually increasing crowd of spectators. After this he produced a loathsome pill which he told her she must swallow, but here she broke down and was quite unable to do so. However, she did manage it at last, and then the maniac, crying out, " How you do love me ! " got up and went away without taking any more notice of her. They followed him into a temple with loud supplications, but he had disappeared, and every effort to find him was unsuccessful. Overcome with rage and shame, Wang's wife went home, where she mourned bitterly over her dead husband, grievously repenting the steps she had taken, and wishing only to die. She then bethought herself of preparing the corpse, near which none of the servants would venture, and set to work to close up the frightful wound of which he died.

While thus employed, interrupted from time to time by her sobs, she felt a rising lump in her throat, which by-and-by came out with a pop and fell straight into the dead man's wound. Looking closely at it, she saw it was a human heart ; and then it began as it were to throb, emitting a warm vapour like smoke. Much excited, she at once closed the flesh over it, and held the sides of the wound together with all her might. Very soon, however, she got tired, and finding the vapour escaping from the crevices, she tore up a piece of silk and bound it round, at the same time bringing back circulation by rubbing the body and covering it up with clothes. In the night she removed the coverings, and found that breath was coming from the nose ; and by next morning her husband was alive again, though disturbed in mind as if awaking from a dream, and feeling a pain in his heart. Where he had been wounded there was a cicatrix about as big as a cash, which soon after disappeared.

XIII. THE TRADER'S SON

IN the province of Hunan there dwelt a man who was engaged in trading abroad ; and his wife, who lived alone, dreamt one night that some one was in her room. Waking up, she looked about, and discovered a small creature which on examination she knew to be a fox ; but in a moment the thing had disappeared, although the door had not been opened. The next evening she asked the cook-maid to come and keep her company ; as also her own son, a boy of ten, who was accustomed to sleep elsewhere. Towards the middle of the night, when the cook and the boy were fast asleep, back came the fox ; and the cook was waked up by hearing her mistress muttering something as if she had nightmare. The former then called out, and the fox ran away ; but from that moment the trader's wife was not quite herself. When night came she dared not blow out the candle, and bade her son be sure and not sleep too soundly. Later on, her son and the old woman having taken a nap as they leant against the wall, suddenly waked up and found her gone. They waited some time, but she did not return, and the cook was too frightened to go and look after her ; so her son took a light, and at length found her fast asleep in another room. She didn't seem aware that anything particular had happened, but she became queerer and queerer every day, and wouldn't have either her son or the cook to keep her company any more. Her son, however, made a point of running at once into his mother's room if he heard any unusual sounds ; and though his mother always abused him for his pains, he paid no attention to what she said. Consequently, everyone thought him very brave, though at the same time he was always indulging in childish tricks. One day he played at being a mason, and piled up stones upon the window-sill, in spite of all that was said to him ; and if anyone took away a stone, he threw himself on the ground, and cried like a child, so that nobody dared go near him. In a few days he had got both windows blocked up and the light excluded ; and then he set to filling up the chinks with mud. He worked hard all day without minding the trouble, and when it was finished he took and sharpened the kitchen chopper.

Everyone who saw him was disgusted with such antics, and would take no notice of him. At night he darkened his lamp, and, with the knife concealed on his person, sat waiting for his mother to mutter. As soon as she began he uncovered his light, and, blocking up the doorway, shouted out at the top of his voice. Nothing, however, happened, and he moved from the door a little way, when suddenly out rushed something like a fox, which was disappearing through the door when he made a quick movement and cut off about two inches of its tail, from which the warm blood was still dripping as he brought the light to bear upon it. His mother hereupon cursed and reviled him, but he pretended not to hear her, regretting only as he went to bed that he hadn't hit the brute fair. But he consoled himself by thinking that although he hadn't killed it outright, he had done enough to prevent it coming again. On the morrow he followed the tracks of blood over the wall and into the garden of a family named Ho ; and that night, to his great joy, the fox did not reappear. His mother was meanwhile prostrate, with hardly any life in her, and in the midst of it all his father came home. The boy told him what had happened, at which he was much alarmed, and sent for a doctor to attend his wife ; but she only threw the medicine away, and cursed and swore horribly. So they secretly mixed the medicine with her tea and soup, and in a few days she began to get better, to the inexpressible delight of both her husband and son. One night, however, her husband woke up and found her gone ; and after searching for her with the aid of his son, they discovered her sleeping in another room. From that time she became more eccentric than ever, and was always being found in strange places, cursing those who tried to remove her. Her husband was at his wits' end. It was of no use keeping the door locked, for it opened of itself at her approach ; and he had called in any number of magicians to exorcise the fox, but without obtaining the slightest result. One evening her son concealed himself in the Ho family garden, and lay down in the long grass with a view to detecting the fox's retreat. As the moon rose he heard the sound of voices, and, pushing aside the grass, saw two people drinking, with a long-bearded servant pouring out their wine, dressed in an old dark-brown coat.

They were whispering together, and he could not make out what they said ; but by-and-by he heard one of them remark, " Get some white wine for to-morrow," and then they went away, leaving the long-bearded servant alone. The latter then threw off his coat, and lay down to sleep on the stones ; whereupon the trader's son eyed him carefully, and saw that he was like a man in every respect except that he had a tail. The boy would then have gone home ; but he was afraid the fox might hear him, and accordingly remained where he was till near dawn, when he saw the other two come back, one at a time, and then they all disappeared among the bushes. On reaching home his father asked him where he had been, and he replied that he had stopped the night with the Ho family. He then accompanied his father to the town, where he saw hanging up at a hat-shop a fox's tail, and finally, after much coaxing, succeeded in making his father buy it for him. While the latter was engaged in a shop, his son, who was playing about beside him, availed himself of a moment when his father was not looking and stole some money from him, and went off and bought a quantity of white wine, which he left in charge of the wine-merchant. Now an uncle of his, who was a sportsman by trade, lived in the city, and thither he next betook himself. His uncle was out, but his aunt was there, and inquired after the health of his mother. " She has been better the last few days," replied he ; " but she is now very much upset by a rat having gnawed a dress of hers, and has sent me to ask for some poison." His aunt opened the cupboard and gave him about the tenth of an ounce in a piece of paper, which he thought was very little ; so, when his aunt had gone to get him something to eat, he took the opportunity of being alone, opened the packet, and abstracted a large handful. Hiding this in his coat, he ran to tell his aunt that she needn't prepare anything for him, as his father was waiting in the market, and he couldn't stop to eat it. He then went off ; and having quietly dropped the poison into the wine he had bought, went sauntering about the town. At nightfall he returned home, and told his father that he had been at his uncle's. This he continued to do for some time, until one day he saw among the crowd his long-bearded friend. Marking him closely, he followed him, and at length entered into conversation, asking him where he lived. " I live at Pei-ts'un," said he ; " where do you live ? " " I," replied the trader's son, falsely, " live in a hole on the hillside." The long-bearded man was considerably startled at his answer, but much more so when he added, " We've lived there for generations : haven't *you* ? " The other man asked his name, to which the boy replied, " My name is Hu.[1] I saw you with two gentlemen in the Ho family garden, and haven't forgotten you." Questioning him more fully, the long-bearded man was still in a half-and-half state of belief and doubt, when the trader's son opened his coat a little bit, and showed him the end of the tail he had bought, saying, " The like of us can mix with ordinary people, but unfortunately we can never get rid of this." The long-bearded man then asked him what he was doing there, to which he answered that his father had sent him to buy wine ; thereupon the former remarked that that was exactly what he had come for, and the boy then inquired if he had bought it yet or not. " We are poor," replied the stranger, " and as a rule I prefer to steal it." " A difficult and dangerous job," observed the boy. " I have my masters' instructions to get some," said the other, " and what am I to do ? " The boy then asked him who his masters were, to which he replied that they were the two brothers the boy had seen that night. " One of them has bewitched a lady named Wang ; and the other, the wife of a trader who lives near. The son of the last-mentioned lady is a violent fellow, and cut off my master's tail, so that he was laid up for ten days. But he is putting her under spells again now." He was then going away, saying he should never get his wine ; but the boy said to him, " It's much easier to buy than steal. I have some at the wine-shop there which I will give to you. My purse isn't empty, and I can buy some more." The long-bearded man hardly knew how to thank him ; but the boy said, " We're all one family. Don't mention such a trifle. When I have time I'll come and take a drink with you." So they went off together to the wine-shop, where the boy gave him the wine, and they then separated. That night his mother

[1] *Hu* is the sound of the character for " fox " ; it is also the sound of quite a different character, which is used as a sur-name.

slept quietly and had no fits, and the boy knew that something must have happened. He then told his father, and
they went to see if there were any results ; when lo ! they
found both foxes stretched out dead in the arbour. One
of the foxes was lying on the grass, and out of its mouth
blood was still trickling. The wine-bottle was there ; and
on shaking it they heard that some was left. Then his
father asked him why he had kept it all so secret ; to which
the boy replied that foxes were very sagacious, and would
have been sure to scent the plot. Thereupon his father
was mightily pleased, and said he was a perfect Ulysses [2]
for cunning. They then carried the foxes home, and saw
on the tail of one of them the scar of a knife-wound. From
that time they were left in peace ; but the trader's wife
became very thin, and though her reason returned, she
shortly afterwards died of consumption. The other lady,
Mrs. Wang, began to get better as soon as the foxes had
been killed ; and as to the boy, he was taught riding and
archery [3] by his proud parent, and subsequently rose to high
rank in the army.

XIV. JUDGE LU

At Ling-yang there lived a man named Chu Erh-tan, whose
literary designation[1] was Hsiao-ming. He was a fine manly

[2] The name of the Chinese type was Ch'ên P'ing.
[3] Skill in archery was until quite lately *de rigueur* for all Manchus,
and for those who would rise in the Chinese army.
[1] Every Chinese man and woman inherits a family name or surname. A woman takes her husband's surname, followed in official
documents by her maiden name. Children usually have a pet name
given to them soon after birth, which is dropped after a few years.
Then there is the *ming* or name, which once given is unchangeable,
and by which the various members of a family are distinguished.
But only the Emperor, a man's father and mother, and certain
other relatives are allowed to use this. Friends call each other by
their literary designations or " book-names," which are given generally by the teacher to whom the boy's education is first entrusted.
Brothers and sisters and others have all kinds of nick-names, as
with us. Dogs and cats are called by such names as " Blacky,"
" Whitey," " Yellowy," " Jewell," " Pearly," &c., &c. Junks are
christened " Large Profits," " Abounding Wealth," " Favourite of
Fortune," &c., &c. Places are often named after some striking
geographical feature ; *e.g., Hankow*—" mouth of the Han river,'

fellow, but an egregious dunce, though he tried hard to learn. One day he was taking wine with a number of fellow-students, when one of them said to him, by way of a joke, " People credit you with plenty of pluck. Now, if you will go in the middle of the night to the Chamber of Horrors,[2] and bring back the Infernal Judge from the left-hand porch, we'll stand you a dinner." For at Ling-yang there was a representation of the Ten Courts of Purgatory, with the gods and devils carved in wood, and almost life-like in appearance ; and in the eastern vestibule there was a full-length image of the Judge with a green face, and a red beard, and a hideous expression in his features. Some-times sounds of examination under the whip were heard to issue during the night from both porches, and persons who went in found their hair standing on end from fear ; so the other young men thought it would be a capital test for Mr. Chu. Thereupon Chu smiled, and rising from his seat went straight off to the temple ; and before many minutes had elapsed they heard him shouting outside, " His Excel-lency has arrived ! " At this they all got up, and in came Chu with the image on his back, which he proceeded to deposit on the table, and then poured out a triple libation in its honour. His comrades, who were watching what he did, felt ill at ease, and did not like to resume their seats ; so they begged him to carry the Judge back again. But he first poured some wine upon the ground, invoking the image as follows : " I am only a foolhardy, illiterate fellow : I pray your Excellency excuse me. My house is close by, and whenever your Excellency feels so disposed I shall be glad to take a cup of wine with you in a friendly

i.e., its point of junction with the Yang-tsze ; or they have fancy names, such as *Fuhkien*—" happily established ; " *Tientsin*— " Heaven's ford ; " or names implying a special distinction, such as *Nanking*—" southern capital ; " *Shan-tung*—" east of the mountains," &c.

[2] The name given by foreigners in China to the imitation of the ten torture-chambers of purgatory, as seen in every *Ch'êng-huang* or municipal temple. The various figures of the devil-lictors and the tortured sinners are made either of clay or wood, and painted in very bright colours ; and in each chamber is depicted some specimen of the horrible tortures that wicked people will undergo in the world to come. I have given in the *Appendix* a translation of the *Yü-li-ch'ao*, a celebrated Taoist work on this subject, which should at any rate be glanced at by persons who would understand the drift of some of these stories.

way." He then carried the Judge back, and the next day his friends gave him the promised dinner, from which he went home half-tipsy in the evening. But not feeling that he had had enough, he brightened up his lamp, and helped himself to another cup of wine, when suddenly the bamboo curtain was drawn aside, and in walked the Judge. Mr. Chu got up and said, " Oh, dear ! Your Excellency has come to cut off my head for my rudeness the other night." The Judge parted his thick beard, and smiling, replied, " Nothing of the kind. You kindly invited me last night to visit you ; and as I have leisure this evening, here I am." Chu was delighted at this, and made his guest sit down, while he himself wiped the cups and lighted a fire.[3] " It's warm weather," said the Judge ; " let's drink the wine cold." Chu obeyed, and putting the bottle on the table, went out to tell his servants to get some supper. His wife was much alarmed when she heard who was there, and begged him not to go back ; but he only waited until the things were ready, and then returned with them. They drank out of each other's cups,[4] and by-and-by Chu asked the name of his guest. " My name is Lu," replied the Judge ; " I have no other names." They then conversed on literary subjects, one capping the other's quotation as echo responds to sound. The Judge then asked Chu if he understood composition ; to which he answered that he could just tell good from bad ; whereupon the former repeated a little infernal poetry which was not very different from that of mortals. He was a deep drinker, and took off ten goblets at a draught ; but Chu, who had been at it all day, soon got dead drunk and fell fast asleep with his head on the table. When he waked up the candle had burnt out and day was beginning to break, his guest having already departed ; and from this time the Judge was in the habit of dropping in pretty often, until a close friendship sprang up between them. Sometimes the latter would pass the night at the house, and Chu would show him his essays, all of which the Judge scored and underlined as being good for nothing. One night Chu got tipsy and went to bed first, leaving the Judge drinking by himself. In his drunken sleep he seemed to feel a pain in his stomach, and

[3] To heat the wine, which is almost invariably taken hot.
[4] In token of their mutual good feeling.

waking up he saw that the Judge, who was standing by the side of the bed, had opened him and was carefully arranging his inside. "What harm have I done you," cried Chu, "that you should thus seek to destroy me?" "Don't be afraid," replied the Judge, laughing; "I am only providing you with a more intelligent heart." [5] He then quietly put back Chu's viscera, and closed up the opening, securing it with a bandage tied tightly round his waist. There was no blood on the bed, and all Chu felt was a slight numbness in his inside. Here he observed the Judge place a piece of flesh upon the table, and asked him what it was. "Your heart," said the latter, "which wasn't at all good at composition, the proper orifice being stuffed up.[6] I have now provided you with a better one, which I procured from Hades, and I am keeping yours to put in its place."[7] He then opened the door and took his leave. In the morning Chu undid the bandage, and looked at his waist, the wound on which had quite healed up, leaving only a red seam. From that moment he became an apt scholar, and found his memory much improved; so much so, that a few days afterwards he showed an essay to the Judge for which he was very much commended. "However," said the latter, "your success will be limited to the master's degree. You won't get beyond that." "When shall I take it?" asked Chu. "This year," replied the Judge. And so it turned out. Chu passed first on the list for the bachelor's degree, and then among the first five for the master's degree. His old comrades, who had been accustomed to make a laughing-stock of him, were now astonished to find him a full-blown M.A., and when they learned how it had come about, they begged Chu to speak to the Judge on their behalf. The Judge promised to assist them, and they made all ready to receive him; but when in the evening he did come, they were so frightened at his red beard and flashing eyes that their teeth chattered in their heads, and one by one they stole away. Chu then took the Judge home with him to have

[5] The Chinese as a nation believe to this day that the heart is the seat of the intellect and the emotions.

[6] The heart itself is supposed to be pierced by a number of "eyes," which pass right through; and in physical and mental health these passages are believed to be clear.

[7] See No. XII., note 2.

a cup together, and when the wine had mounted well into his head, he said, " I am deeply grateful to your Excellency's former kindness in arranging my inside ; but there is still another favour I venture to ask which possibly may be granted." The Judge asked him what it was ; and Chu replied, " If you can change a person's inside, you surely could also change his face. Now my wife is not at all a bad figure, but she is very ugly. I pray your Excellency try the knife upon her." The Judge laughed, and said he would do so, only it would be necessary to give him a little time. Some days subsequently, the Judge knocked at Chu's door towards the middle of the night ; whereupon the latter jumped up and invited him in. Lighting a candle, it was evident that the Judge had something under his coat, and in answer to Chu's inquiries, he said, " It's what you asked me for. I have had great trouble in procuring it." He then produced the head of a nice-looking young girl, and presented it to Chu, who found the blood on the neck was still warm. " We must make haste," said the Judge, " and take care not to wake the fowls or dogs." [8] Chu was afraid his wife's door might be bolted ; but the Judge laid his hand on it and it opened at once. Chu then led him to the bed where his wife was lying asleep on her side ; and the Judge, giving Chu the head to hold, drew from his boot a steel blade shaped like the handle of a spoon. He laid this across the lady's neck, which he cut through as if it had been a melon, and the head fell over the back of the pillow. Seizing the head he had brought with him, he now fitted it on carefully and accurately, and pressing it down to make it stick, bolstered the lady up with pillows placed on either side. When all was finished, he bade Chu put his wife's old head away, and then took his leave. Soon after Mrs. Chu waked up, and perceived a curious sensation about her neck, and a scaly feeling about the jaws. Putting her hand to her face, she found flakes of dry blood ; and much frightened called a maid-servant to bring water to wash it off. The maid-servant was also greatly alarmed at the appearance of her face, and proceeded to wash off

[8] The *Hsi-yüan-lu*, a well-known work on Chinese medical jurisprudence and *an officially authorised book*, while giving an absurd antidote against a poison that never existed, gravely insists that it is to be prepared at certain dates only, " in some place quite away from women, fowls, and dogs."

the blood, which coloured a whole basin of water ; but when she saw her mistress's new face she was almost frightened to death. Mrs. Chu took a mirror to look at herself, and was staring at herself in utter astonishment, when her husband came in and explained what had taken place. On examining her more closely, Chu saw she had a well-featured pleasant face, of a high order of beauty ; and when he came to look at her neck, he found a red seam all round, with the parts above and below of a different coloured flesh. Now the daughter of an official named Wu was a very nice-looking girl, who, though nineteen years of age, had not yet been married, two gentlemen who were engaged to her having died before the day.[9] At the Feast of Lanterns,[10] this young lady happened to visit the Chamber of Horrors, whence she was followed home by a burglar, who that night broke into the house and killed her. Hearing a noise, her mother told the servant to go and see what was the matter ; and the murder being thus discovered, every member of the family got up. They placed the body in the hall, with the head alongside, and gave themselves up to weeping and wailing the live-long night. Next morning, when they removed the coverings, the corpse was there, but the head had disappeared. The waiting-maids were accordingly flogged for neglect of duty, and consequent loss of the head, and Mr. Wu brought the matter to the notice of the Prefect. This officer took very energetic measures, but for three months no clue could be obtained ; and then the story of the changed head in the Chu family gradually reached Mr. Wu's ears. Suspecting something, he sent an old woman to make inquiries ; and she at once recognised

[9] It was almost a wonder that she got a second *fiancé*, few people caring to affiance their sons in a family where such a catastrophe has once occurred. The death of an engaged girl is a matter of much less importance, but is productive of a very curious ceremony. Her betrothed goes to the house where she is lying dead and steps over the coffin containing her body, returning home with a pair of the girl's shoes. He thus severs all connection with her, and her spirit cannot haunt him as it otherwise most certainly. would do.

[10] Held annually on the 15th of the first Chinese month—*i.e.*, at the first full moon of the year, when coloured lanterns are hung at every door. It was originally a ceremonial worship in the temple of the First Cause, and dates from about the time of the Han dynasty, or nearly two thousand years ago.

her late young mistress's features, and went back and reported to her master. Thereupon Mr. Wu, unable to make out why the body should have been left, imagined that Chu had slain his daughter by magical arts, and at once proceeded to the house to find out the truth of the matter ; but Chu told him that his wife's head had been changed in her sleep, and that he knew nothing about it, adding that it was unjust to accuse him of the murder. Mr. Wu refused to believe this, and took proceedings against him ; but as all the servants told the same story, the Prefect was unable to convict him.   Chu returned home and took counsel with the Judge, who told him there would be no difficulty, it being merely necessary to make the murdered girl herself speak.   That night Mr. Wu dreamt that his daughter came and said to him, " I was killed by Yang Ta-nien, of Su-ch'i.   Mr. Chu had nothing to do with it ; but desiring a better-looking face for his wife, Judge Lu gave him mine, and thus my body is dead while my head still lives.   Bear Chu no malice."   When he awaked, he told his wife, who had dreamt the same dream ; and there-upon he communicated these facts to the officials. Subsequently, a man of that name was captured, who confessed under the bamboo that he had committed the crime ; so Mr. Wu went off to Chu's house, and asked to be allowed to see his wife, regarding Chu from that time as his son-in-law.   Mrs. Chu's old head was fitted on to the young lady's body, and the two parts were buried together.

Subsequent to these events Mr. Chu tried three times for his doctor's degree, but each time without success, and at last he gave up the idea of entering into official life.   Then when thirty years had passed away, Judge Lu appeared to him one night, and said, " My friend, you cannot live for ever.   Your hour will come in five days' time."   Chu asked the Judge if he could not save him ; to which he replied, " The decrees of Heaven cannot be altered to suit the purposes of mortals.   Besides, to an intelligent man life and death are much the same.[11]   Why necessarily regard life as a boon and death as a misfortune ? "   Chu

---

[11] It was John Stuart Mill who pointed out that the fear of death is due to " the illusion of imagination, which makes one conceive oneself as if one were alive and feeling oneself dead " (*The Utility of Religion*).

could make no reply to this, and forthwith proceeded to
order his coffin and shroud ; and then, dressing himself
in his grave-clothes,[12] yielded up the ghost. Next day, as
his wife was weeping over his bier, in he walked at the front
door, to her very great alarm. " I am now a disembodied
spirit," said Chu to her, " though not different from what
I was in life ; and I have been thinking much of the widow
and orphan I left behind." His wife, hearing this, wept
till the tears ran down her face, Chu all the time doing his
best to comfort her. " I have heard tell," said she, " of
dead bodies returning to life ; and since your vital spark is
not extinct, why does it not resume the flesh ? " " The
ordinances of Heaven," replied her husband, " may not be
disobeyed." His wife here asked him what he was doing
in the infernal regions ; and he said that Judge Lu had got
him an appointment as Registrar, with a certain rank
attached, and that he was not at all uncomfortable. Mrs.
Chu was proceeding to inquire further, when he interrupted
her, saying, " The Judge has come with me ; get some wine
ready and something to eat." He then hurried out, and
his wife did as he had told her, hearing them laughing and
drinking in the guest chamber just like old times come
back again. About midnight she peeped in, and found
that they had both disappeared ; but they came back once
in every two or three days, often spending the night, and
managing the family affairs as usual. Chu's son was
named Wei, and was about five years old ; and whenever
his father came he would take the little boy upon his knee.
When he was about eight years of age, Chu began to teach
him to read ; and the boy was so clever that by the time

---

[12] " Boards of old age " and " Clothes of old age sold here "
are common shop-signs in every Chinese city ; death and burial
being always, if possible, spoken of euphemistically in some such
terms as these. A dutiful son provides, when he can afford it,
decent coffins for his father and mother. They are generally stored
in the house, sometimes in a neighbouring temple ; and the old
people take pleasure in seeing that their funeral obsequies are
properly provided for, though the subject is never raised in conversation. Chinese coffins are beautifully made ; and when the
body has been in for a day or two, a candle is closely applied to
the seams all round to make sure it is air-tight—any crack, however fine, being easily detected by the flickering of the flame in
the escaping gas. Thus bodies may be kept unburied for a long
time, until the geomancer has selected an auspicious site for the
grave.

he was nine he could actually compose. At fifteen he took his bachelor's degree, without knowing all this time that he had no father. From that date Chu's visits became less frequent, occurring not more than once or so in a month ; until one night he told his wife that they were never to meet again. In reply to her inquiry as to whither he was going, he said he had been appointed to a far-off post, where press of business and distance would combine to prevent him from visiting them any more. The mother and son clung to him, sobbing bitterly, but he said, " Do not act thus. The boy is now a man, and can look after your affairs. The dearest friends must part some day." Then, turning to his son, he added, " Be an honourable man, and take care of the property. Ten years hence we shall meet again." With this he bade them farewell, and went away.

Later on, when Wei was twenty-five years of age, he took his doctor's degree, and was appointed to conduct the sacrifices at the Imperial tombs. On his way thither he fell in with a retinue of an official, proceeding along with all the proper insignia,[13] and, looking carefully at the individual sitting in the carriage, he was astonished to find that it was his own father. Alighting from his horse, he prostrated himself with tears at the side of the road ; whereupon his father stopped and said, " You are well spoken of. I now take leave of this world." Wei remained on the ground, not daring to rise ; and his father, urging on his carriage, hurried away without saying any more. But when he had gone a short distance, he looked back, and unloosing a sword from his waist, sent it as a present to his son, shouting out to him, " Wear this and you will succeed." Wei tried to follow him ; but, in an instant, carriage, retinue, and horses had vanished with the speed of wind. For a long time his son gave himself up to grief, and then seizing the sword began to examine it closely. It was of exquisite workmanship, and on the blade was engraved this legend : *" Be bold, but cautious ; round in disposition, square in action."* [14] Wei subsequently rose to

[13] Gongs, red umbrellas, men carrying boards on which the officer's titles are inscribed in large characters, a huge wooden fan, &c., &c.

[14] " Be like a cash " (see No. II., note 2) is a not uncommon saying among the Chinese, the explanation of which rests upon the

high honours, and had five sons named Ch'ên, Ch'ien, Wu, Hun, and Shên. One night he dreamt that his father told him to give the sword to Hun, which he accordingly did ; and Hun rose to be a Viceroy of great administrative ability.

XV. MISS YING-NING, OR THE LAUGHING GIRL

At Lo-tien, in the province of Shantung, there lived a youth named Wang Tzŭ-fu, who had been left an orphan when quite young. He was a clever boy, and took his bachelor's degree at the age of fourteen, being quite his mother's pet, and not allowed by her to stray far away from home. One young lady to whom he had been betrothed having unhappily died, he was still in search of a wife when, on the occasion of the Feast of Lanterns, his cousin Wu asked him to come along for a stroll. But they had hardly got beyond the village before one of his uncle's servants caught them up and told Wu he was wanted. The latter accordingly went back ; but Wang, seeing plenty of nice girls about and being in high spirits himself, proceeded on alone. Amongst others, he noticed a young lady with her maid. She had just picked a sprig of plum-blossom, and was the prettiest girl he had ever heard of, her smiling face being very captivating. He stared and stared at her quite regardless of appearances ; and when she had passed by, she said to her maid, " That young fellow has a wicked look in his eyes." As she was walking away, laughing and talking, the flower dropped out of her hand ; and Wang, picking it up, stood there disconsolate as if he had lost his wits. He then went home in a very melancholy mood ; and, putting the flower under his pillow, lay down to sleep. He would neither talk nor eat ; and his mother became very anxious about him, and called in the aid of the priests.[1] By degrees, he fell off in flesh and

fact that a cash is " round in shape and convenient for use," which words are pronounced identically with a corresponding number of words meaning " round in disposition, square in action." It is, in fact, a play on words.

[1] Sickness being supposed to result from evil influences, witchcraft, &c., just as often as from more natural causes.

got very thin ; and the doctor felt his pulse and gave him medicines to bring out the disease. Occasionally, he seemed bewildered in his mind, but in spite of all his mother's inquiries would give no clue as to the cause of his malady.   One day when his cousin Wu came to the house, Wang's mother told him to try and find out what was the matter ; and the former, approaching the bed, gradually and quietly led up to the point in question.   Wang, who had wept bitterly at the sight of his cousin, now repeated to him the whole story, begging him to lend some assistance in the matter.   " How foolish you are, cousin," cried Wu ; " there will be no difficulty at all, I'll make inquiries for you.   The girl herself can't belong to a very aristocratic family to be walking alone in the country.   If she's not already engaged, I have no doubt we can arrange the affair ; and even if she is unwilling, an extra outlay will easily bring her round.[2]   You make haste and get well : I'll see to it all."   Wang's features relaxed when he heard these words ; and Wu left him to tell his mother how the case stood, immediately setting on foot inquiries as to the whereabouts of the girl.   All his efforts, however, proved fruitless, to the great disappointment of Wang's mother ; for since his cousin's visit Wang's colour and appetite had returned. In a few days Wu called again, and in answer to Wang's questions falsely told him the affair was settled.   " Who do you think the young lady is ? " said he.   " Why, a cousin of ours, who is only waiting to be betrothed ; and though you two are a little near,[3] I dare say this difficulty may be overcome."   Wang was overjoyed, and asked where she lived ; so Wu had to tell another lie, and say, " On the south-west hills, about ten miles from here." Wang begged him again and again to do his best for him,

[2] The rule which guides betrothals in China is that " the doors should be opposite "—i.e., that the families of the bride and bride-groom should be of equal position in the social scale. Any un-pleasantness about the value of the marriage presents, and so on, is thereby avoided.

[3] Marriage between persons of the same surname, except in special cases, is forbidden by law, for such are held to be blood relations, descended lineally from the original couple of that name. Inasmuch, however, as the line of descent is traced through the male branches only, a man may marry his cousins on the maternal side without let or hindrance except that of sentiment, which is sufficiently strong to keep these alliances down to a minimum.

and Wu undertook to get the betrothal satisfactorily arranged. He then took leave of his cousin, who from this moment was rapidly restored to health. Wang drew the flower from underneath his pillow, and found that, though dried up, the leaves had not fallen away. He often sat playing with this flower and thinking of the young lady ; but by-and-by, as Wu did not reappear, he wrote a letter and asked him to come. Wu pleaded other engagements, being unwilling to go ; at which Wang got into a rage and quite lost his good spirits ; so that his mother, fearing a relapse, proposed to him a speedy betrothal in another quarter. Wang shook his head at this, and sat day after day waiting for Wu, until his patience was thoroughly exhausted. He then reflected that ten miles was no great distance, and that there was no particular reason for asking anybody's aid ; so, concealing the flower in his sleeve, he went off in a huff by himself without letting it be known. Having no opportunity of asking the way, he made straight for the hills ; and after about ten miles' walking, found himself right in the midst of them, enjoying their exquisite verdure, but meeting no one, and with nothing better than mountain paths to guide him. Away down in the valley below, almost buried under a densely luxuriant growth of trees and flowers, he espied a small hamlet, and began to descend the hill and make his way thither. He found very few houses, and all built of rushes, but otherwise pleasant enough to look at. Before the door of one, which stood at the northern end of the village, were a number of graceful willow trees, and inside the wall plenty of peach and apricot trees, with tufts of bamboo between them, and birds chirping on the branches. As it was a private house, he did not venture to go in, but sat down to rest himself on a huge smooth stone opposite the front door. By-and-by he heard a girl's voice from within calling out Hsiao-jung ; and noticing that it was a sweet-toned voice, set himself to listen, when a young lady passed with a bunch of apricot-flowers in her hand, which she was sticking into her bent-down head. As soon as she raised her face she saw Wang, and stopped putting in the flowers ; then, smothering a laugh, she gathered them together and ran in. Wang perceived to his intense delight that she was none other than his heroine of the Feast of Lanterns ; but recollecting

that he had no right to follow her in, was on the point of
calling after her as his cousin. There was no one, however,
in the street, and he was afraid lest he might have made
a mistake ; neither was there anybody at the door of whom
he could make inquiries. So he remained there in a very
restless state till the sun was well down in the west, and
his hopes were almost at an end, forgetting all about food
and drink. He then saw the young lady peep through the
door, apparently very much astonished to find him still
there ; and in a few minutes out came an old woman leaning
on a stick, who said to him, " Whence do you come, Sir ?
I hear you have been here ever since morning. What is it
you want ? Aren't you hungry ? " Wang got up, and
making a bow, replied that he was in search of some
relatives of his ; but the old woman was deaf and didn't
catch what he said, so he had to shout it out again at the
top of his voice. She asked him what their names were,
but he was unable to tell her ; at which she laughed and
said, " It is a funny thing to look for people when you don't
know their names. I am afraid you are an unpractical
gentleman. You had better come in and have something
to eat ; we'll give you a bed, and you can go back to-morrow
and find out the names of the people you are in quest of."
Now Wang was just beginning to get hungry, and, besides,
this would bring him nearer to the young lady ; so he readily
accepted and followed the old woman in. They walked
along a paved path banked on both sides with hibiscus, the
leaves of which were scattered about on the ground ; and
passing through another door, entered a courtyard full of
trained creepers and other flowers. The old woman
showed Wang into a small room with beautifully white
walls and a branch of a crab-apple tree coming through the
window, the furniture being also nice and clean. They
had hardly sat down when it was clear that someone was
taking a peep through the window ; whereupon the old
woman cried out, " Hsiao-jung ! make haste and get
dinner," and a maid from outside immediately answered
" Yes, ma'am." Meanwhile, Wang had been explaining
who he was ; and then the old lady said, " Was your
maternal grandfather named Wu ? " " He was," replied
Wang. " Well, I never ! " cried the old woman ; " he was
my uncle, and your mother and I are cousins. But in

consequence of our poverty, and having no sons, we have kept quite to ourselves, and you have grown to be a man without my knowing you." " I came here," said Wang, " about my cousin, but in the hurry I forgot your name." " My name is Ch'in," replied the old lady ; " I have no son : only a girl, the child of a concubine, who, after my husband's death, married again [4] and left her daughter with me. She's a clever girl, but has had very little education ; full of fun and ignorant of the sorrows of life. I'll send for her by-and-by to make your acquaintance." The maid then brought in the dinner—a well-grown fowl—and the old woman pressed him to eat. When they had finished, and the things were taken away, the old woman said, " Call Miss Ning," and the maid went off to do so. After some time there was a giggling at the door, and the old woman cried out, " Ying-ning ! your cousin is here." There was then a great tittering as the maid pushed her in, stopping her mouth all the time to try and keep from laughing. " Don't you know better than to behave like that ? " asked the old woman, " and before a stranger, too." So Yingning controlled her feelings, and Wang made her a bow, the old woman saying, " Mr. Wang is your cousin ; you have never seen him before. Isn't that funny ? " Wang asked how old his cousin was, but the old woman didn't hear him, and he had to say it again, which sent Ying-ning off into another fit of laughter. " I told you," observed the old woman, " she hadn't much education ; now you see it. She is sixteen years old, and as foolish as a baby." " One year younger than I am," remarked Wang. " Oh, you're seventeen, are you ? Then you were born in the year ——, under the sign of the horse" [5] Wang nodded assent, and then the old woman asked who his wife was, to which Wang replied that he had none. " What ! a clever,

[4] A very unjustifiable proceeding in Chinese eyes, unless driven to it by actual poverty.

[5] The Chinese years are distinguished by the names of twelve animals—namely, rat, ox, tiger, hare, dragon, serpent, horse, sheep, monkey, cock, dog, and boar. To the common question, " What is your honourable age ? " the reply is frequently, " I was born under the —— ; " and the hearer by a short mental calculation can tell at once how old the speaker is, granting, of course, the impossibility of making an error of so much as twelve years.

handsome young fellow of seventeen not yet engaged ? [6]
Ying-ning is not engaged either : you two would make
a nice pair if it wasn't for the relationship." Wang said
nothing, but looked hard at his cousin ; and just then the
maid whispered to her, " It is the fellow with the wicked
eyes ! He's at his old game." Ying-ning laughed, and
proposed to the maid that they should go and see if the
peaches were in blossom or not ; and off they went together,
the former with her sleeve stuffed into her mouth until she
got outside, where she burst into a hearty fit of laughing.
The old woman gave orders for a bed to be got ready for
Wang, saying to him, " It's not often we meet : you must
spend a few days with us now you are here, and then we'll
send you home. If you are at all dull, there's a garden
behind where you can amuse yourself, and books for you
to read." So next day Wang strolled into the garden,
which was of moderate size, with a well-kept lawn and
plenty of trees and flowers. There was also an arbour
consisting of three posts with a thatched roof, quite shut
in on all sides by the luxuriant vegetation. Pushing his
way among the flowers, Wang heard a noise from one of the
trees, and looking up saw Ying-ning, who at once burst out
laughing and nearly fell down. " Don't ! don't ! " cried
Wang, " you'll fall ! " Then Ying-ning came down,
giggling all the time, until, when she was near the ground,
she missed her hold, and tumbled down with a run. This
stopped her merriment, and Wang picked her up, gently
squeezing her hand as he did so. Ying-ning began laughing
again, and was obliged to lean against a tree for support, it
being some time before she was able to stop. Wang waited
till she had finished, and then drew the flower out of his
sleeve and handed it to her. " It's dead," said she ; " why
do you keep it ? " " You dropped it, cousin, at the Feast
of Lanterns," replied Wang, " and so I kept it." She then
asked him what was his object in keeping it, to which he
answered, " To show my love, and that I have not forgotten
you. Since that day when we met, I have been very ill
from thinking so much of you, and am quite changed from

---

[6] Parents in China like to get their sons married as early as
possible, in the hope of seeing themselves surrounded by grandsons,
and the family name in no danger of extinction. Girls are generally married at from fifteen to seventeen.

what I was. But now that it is my unexpected good fortune to meet you, I pray you have pity on me." "You needn't make such a fuss about a trifle," replied she, "and with your own relatives, too. I'll give orders to supply you with a whole basketful of flowers when you go away." Wang told her she did not understand, and when she asked what it was she didn't understand, he said, "I didn't care for the flower itself; it was the person who picked the flower." "Of course," answered she, "everybody cares for their relations; you needn't have told me that." "I wasn't talking about ordinary relations," said Wang, "but about husbands and wives." "What's the difference?" asked Ying-ning. "Why," replied Wang, "husband and wife are always together." "Just what I shouldn't like," cried she, " to be always with anybody."[7] At this juncture up came the maid, and Wang slipped quietly away. By-and-by they all met again in the house, and the old woman asked Ying-ning where they had been; whereupon she said they had been talking in the garden. "Dinner has been ready a long time. I can't think what you have had to say all this while," grumbled the old woman. "My cousin," answered Ying-ning, "has been talking to me about husbands and wives." Wang was much disconcerted, and made a sign to her to be quiet, so she smiled and said no more; and the old woman luckily did not catch her words, and asked her to repeat them. Wang immediately put her off with something else, and whispered to Ying-ning that she had done very wrong. The latter did not see that; and when Wang told her that what he had said was private, answered him that she had no secrets from her old mother. "Besides," added she, "what harm can there be in talking on such a common topic as husbands and wives?" Wang was angry with her for being so dull,

[7] This scene should for ever disabuse people of the notion that there is no "such thing as "making love" among the Chinese. That the passion is just as much a disease in China as it is with us will be abundantly evident from several subsequent stories; though by those who have lived and mixed with the Chinese people, no such confirmation will be needed. I have even heard it gravely asserted by an educated native that not a few of his countrymen had "died for love" of the beautiful Miss Lin, the charming but fictitious heroine of the so-called *Dream of the Red Chamber*.

Playgoers can here hardly fail to notice a very striking similarity to the close of the first act of Sir W. S. Gilbert's "Sweethearts."

but there was no help for it ; and by the time dinner was
over he found some of his mother's servants had come in
search of him, bringing a couple of donkeys with them.
It appeared that his mother, alarmed at his non-appear-
ance, had made strict search for him in the village ; and
when unable to discover any traces of him, had gone off to
the Wu family to consult.　There her nephew, who recollected what he had previously said to young Wang, advised
that a search should be instituted in the direction of the
hills ; and accordingly the servants had been to all the
villages on the way until they had at length recognised him
as he was coming out of the door.　Wang went in and told
the old woman, begging that he might be allowed to take
Ying-ning with him.　" I have had the idea in my head
for several days," replied the old woman, overjoyed ; " but
I am a feeble old thing myself, and couldn't travel so far.
If, however, you will take charge of my girl and introduce
her to her aunt, I shall be very pleased."　So she called
Ying-ning, who came up laughing as usual ; whereupon the
old woman rebuked her, saying, " What makes you always
laugh so ?　You would be a very good girl but for that silly
habit.　Now, here's your cousin, who wants to take you
away with him.　Make haste and pack up."　The servants
who had come for Wang were then provided with refreshment, and the old woman bade them both farewell, telling
Ying-ning that her aunt was quite well enough off to
maintain her, and that she had better not come back.　She
also advised her not to neglect her studies, and to be very
attentive to her elders, adding that she might ask her aunt
to provide her with a good husband.　Wang and Ying-ning
then took their leave ; and when they reached the brow of
the hill, they looked back and could just discern the old
woman leaning against the door and " gazing towards the
north."[8]　On arriving at Wang's home, his mother, seeing
a nice-looking young girl with him, asked in astonishment
who she might be ; and Wang at once told her the whole
story.　" But that was all an invention of your cousin
Wu's ! " cried his mother ; " I haven't got a sister, and
consequently I can't have such a niece."　Ying-ning here
observed, " I am not the daughter of the old woman ; my
father was named Ch'in and died when I was a little baby,

[8] q.d. Looking sorrowfully after them.

so that I can't remember anything." " I *had* a sister,"
said Wang's mother, " who actually did marry a Mr. Ch'in,
but she died many years ago, and can't be still living, of
course." However, on inquiring as to facial appearance
and characteristic marks, Wang's mother was obliged to
acknowledge the identity, wondering at the same time how
her sister could be alive when she had died many years
before. Just then in came Wu, and Ying-ning retired
within ; and when he heard the story, remained some time
lost in astonishment, and then said, " Is this young lady's
name Ying-ning ? " Wang replied that it was, and asked
Wu how he came to know it. " Mr. Ch'in," answered he,
" after his wife's death was bewitched by a fox, and subsequently died. The fox had a daughter named Ying-ning,
as was well known to all the family ; and when Mr. Ch'in
died, as the fox still frequented the place, the Taoist Pope[9]
was called in to exorcise it. The fox then went away,
taking Ying-ning with it, and now here she is." While
they were thus discussing, peals of laughter were heard
coming from within, and Mrs. Wang took occasion to
remark what a foolish girl she was. Wu begged to be introduced, and Mrs. Wang went in to fetch her, finding her
in an uncontrollable fit of laughter, which she subdued only
with great difficulty, and by turning her face to the wall.
By-and-by she went out ; but, after making a bow, ran
back and burst out laughing again, to the great amusement
of all the ladies. Wu then said he would go and find out
for them all about Ying-ning and her queer story, so as to
be able to arrange the marriage ; but when he reached the
spot indicated, village and houses had all vanished, and
nothing was to be seen except hill-flowers scattered about
here and there. He recollected that Mrs. Ch'in had been
buried at no great distance from that spot ; he found,

[9] The semi-divine head of the Taoist religion, wrongly called
the Master of Heaven. In his body is supposed to reside the soul
of a celebrated Taoist, an ancestor of his, who actually discovered
the elixir of life and became an immortal some eighteen hundred
years ago. At death, the precious soul above-mentioned will take
up its abode in the body of some youthful member of the family
to be hereinafter revealed. Meanwhile, the present Pope makes
a very respectable income from the sale of charms, by working
miracles, and so forth ; and only about 1877 he visited Shanghai,
where he was interviewed by several foreigners.

however, that the grave had disappeared, and he was no longer able to determine its position. Not knowing what to make of it all, he returned home, and then Mrs. Wang, who thought the girl must be a disembodied spirit, went in and told her what Wu had said. Ying-ning showed no signs of alarm at this remark; neither did she cry at all when Mrs. Wang began to condole with her on no longer having a home. She only laughed in her usual silly way, and fairly puzzled them all. Sharing Miss Wang's room, she now began to take her part in the duties of a daughter of the family; and as for needlework, they had rarely seen anything like hers for fineness. But she could not get over that trick of laughing, which, by the way, never interfered with her good looks, and consequently rather amused people than otherwise, amongst others a young married lady who lived next door. Wang's mother fixed an auspicious day for the wedding, but still feeling suspicious about Ying-ning, was always secretly watching her. Finding, however, that she had a proper shadow,[10] she had her dressed up when the day came, in all the finery of a bride; and would have made her perform the usual ceremonies, only Ying-ning laughed so much she was unable to kneel down.[11] They were accordingly obliged to excuse her, but Wang began to fear that such a foolish girl would never be able to keep the family counsel. Luckily, she was very reticent and did not indulge in gossip; and moreover, when Mrs. Wang was in trouble or out of temper, Ying-ning could always bring her round with a laugh. The maid-servants, too, if they expected a whipping for anything, would always ask her to be present when they appeared before their mistress, and thus they often escaped punishment. Ying-ning had a perfect passion for flowers. She got all she could out of her relations, and even secretly pawned her jewels to buy rare specimens; and by the end of a few months the whole place was one mass of flowers. Behind the house there was one especial tree[12] which

[10] Disembodied spirits are supposed to have no shadow, and but very little appetite. There are also certain occasions on which they cannot stand the smell of sulphur. Fiske, in his *Myths and Myth-makers* (page 230), says, " Almost universally, ghosts, however impervious to thrust of sword or shot of pistol, can eat and drink like Squire Westerns."   [11] See No. III., note 2.
[12] The *Muh-siang* or *Rosa Banksiæ*, R. Br.

belonged to the neighbours on that side ; but Ying-ning
was always climbing up and picking the flowers to stick
in her hair, for which Mrs. Wang rebuked her severely,
though without any result. One day the owner saw her,
and gazed at her some time in rapt astonishment ; however,
she didn't move, deigning only to laugh. The gentleman
was much smitten with her ; and when she smilingly
descended the wall on her own side, pointing all the time
with her finger to a spot hard by, he thought she was
making an assignation. So he presented himself at nightfall at the same place, and sure enough Ying-ning was
there. Seizing her hand, to tell his passion, he found that
he was grasping only a log of wood which stood against the
wall ; and the next thing he knew was that a scorpion had
stung him violently on the finger. There was an end of his
romance, except that he died of the wound during the
night, and his family at once commenced an action against
Wang for having a witch-wife. The magistrate happened
to be a great admirer of Wang's talent, and knew him to
be an accomplished scholar ; he therefore refused to grant
the summons, and ordered the prosecutor to be bambooed
for false accusation.[13] Wang interposed and got him off
this punishment, and returned home himself. His mother
then scolded Ying-ning well, saying, " I knew your too
playful disposition would some day bring sorrow upon you.
But for our intelligent magistrate we should have been in
a nice mess. Any ordinary hawk-like official would have
had you publicly interrogated in court ; and then how
could your husband ever have held up his head again ? "
Ying-ning looked grave and swore she would laugh no
more ; and Mrs. Wang continued, " There's no harm in
laughing as long as it is seasonable laughter ; " but from
that moment Ying-ning laughed no more, no matter what
people did to make her, though at the same time her
expression was by no means gloomy. One evening she
went in tears to her husband, who wanted to know what
was the matter. " I couldn't tell you before," said she,
sobbing ; " we had known each other such a short time.
But now that you and your mother have been so kind to
me, I will keep nothing from you, but tell you all. I am
the daughter of a fox. When my mother went away she

[13] Strictly in accordance with Chinese criminal law.

put me in the charge of the disembodied spirit of an old woman, with whom I remained for a period of over ten years. I have no brothers : only you to whom I can look. And now my foster-mother is lying on the hill-side with no one to bury her and appease her discontented shade. If not too much, I would ask you to do this, that her spirit may be at rest, and know that it was not neglected by her whom she brought up." Wang consented, but said he feared they would not be able to find her grave ; on which Ying-ning said there was no danger of that, and accordingly they set forth together. When they arrived, Ying-ning pointed out the tomb in a lonely spot amidst a thicket of brambles, and there they found the old woman's bones. Ying-ning wept bitterly, and then they proceeded to carry her remains home with them, subsequently interring them in the Ch'in family vault. That night Wang dreamt that the old woman came to thank him, and when he waked he told Ying-ning, who said that she had seen her also, and had been warned by her not to frighten Mr. Wang. Her husband asked why she had not detained the old lady ; but Ying-ning replied, " She is a disembodied spirit, and would be ill at ease for any time surrounded by so much life." [14] Wang then inquired after Hsiao-jung, and his wife said, " She was a fox too, and a very clever one. My foster-mother kept her to wait on me, and she was always getting fruit and cakes for me, so that I have a friendship for her and shall never forget her. My foster-mother told me yesterday she was married."

After this, whenever the great fast-day [15] came round, husband and wife went off without fail to worship at the Ch'in family tomb ; and by the time a year had passed she gave birth to a son, who wasn't a bit afraid of strangers, but laughed at everybody, and in fact took very much after his mother.

[14] These disembodied spirits are unable to stand for any length of time the light and life of this upper world, darkness and death being as it were necessary to their existence and comfort.

[15] The day before the annual spring festival.

XVI. THE MAGIC SWORD

NING TS'AI-CH'EN was a Chekiang man, and a good-natured, honourable fellow, fond of telling people that he had only loved once. Happening to go to Chinhua, he took shelter in a temple to the north of the city; very nice as far as ornamentation went, but overgrown with grass taller than a man's head, and evidently not much frequented. On either side were the priests' apartments, the doors of which were ajar, with the exception of a small room on the south side, where the lock had a new appearance. In the east corner he espied a group of bamboos, growing over a large pool of water-lilies in flower; and, being much pleased with the quiet of the place, determined to remain; more especially as, the Grand Examiner being in the town, all lodgings had gone up in price. So he roamed about waiting till the priests should return; and in the evening a gentleman came and opened the door on the south side. Ning quickly made up to him, and with a bow informed him of his design. "There is no one here whose permission you need ask," replied the stranger; "I am only lodging here, and if you don't object to the loneliness, I shall be very pleased to have the benefit of your society." Ning was delighted, and made himself a straw bed, and put up a board for a table, as if he intended to remain some time; and that night, by the beams of the clear bright moon, they sat together in the verandah and talked. The stranger's name was Yen Ch'ih-hsia, and Ning thought he was a student up for the provincial examination, only his dialect was not that of a Chekiang man. On being asked, he said he came from Shensi; and there was an air of straight forwardness about all his remarks. By-and-by, when their conversation was exhausted, they bade each other good night and went to bed; but Ning, being in a strange place, was quite unable to sleep; and soon he heard sounds of voices from the room on the north side. Getting up, he peeped through a window, and saw, in a small courtyard the other side of a low wall, a woman of about forty with an old maid-servant in a long faded gown, humped-backed and feeble-looking. They were chatting by the light of the moon, and the mistress said, "Why doesn't Hsiao-

ch'ien come ? " " She ought to be here by now," replied
the other. " She isn't offended with you, is she ? " asked
the lady. " Not that I know of," answered the old servant ;
" but she seems to want to give trouble." " Such people
don't deserve to be treated well," said the other ; and she
had hardly uttered these words when up came a young girl
of seventeen or eighteen, and very nice looking. The old
servant laughed, and said, " Don't talk of people behind
their backs. We were just mentioning you as you came
without our hearing you ; but fortunately we were saying
nothing bad about you. And, as far as that goes," added
she, " if I were a young fellow, why, I should certainly fall
in love with you." " If *you* don't praise me," replied the
girl, " I'm sure I don't know who will ; " and then the lady
and the girl said something together, and Mr. Ning, thinking
they were the family next door, turned round to sleep
without paying further attention to them. In a little
while no sound was to be heard ; but, as he was dropping
off to sleep, he perceived that somebody was in the room.
Jumping up in great haste, he found it was the young lady
he had just seen ; and detecting at once that she was going
to attempt to bewitch him, sternly bade her begone. She
then produced a lump of gold which he threw away, and
told her to go after it or he would call his friend. So she
had no alternative but to go, muttering something about
his heart being like iron or stone. Next day, a young
candidate for the examination came and lodged in the east
room with his servant. He, however, was killed that very
night, and his servant the night after ; the corpses of both
showing a small hole in the sole of the foot as if bored by
an awl, and from which a little blood came. No one knew
who had committed these murders, and when Mr. Yen
came home, Ning asked him what he thought about it.
Yen replied that it was the work of devils, but Ning was a
brave fellow, and that didn't frighten him much. In the
middle of the night Hsiao-ch'ien appeared to him again,
and said, " I have seen many men, but none with a steel-
cold heart like yours. You are an upright man, and I will
not attempt to deceive you. I, Hsiao-ch'ien, whose family
name is Nieh, died when only eighteen, and was buried
alongside of this temple. A devil then took possession of

me, and employed me to bewitch people by my beauty, contrary to my inclination. There is now nothing left in this temple to slay, and I fear that imps will be employed to kill you." Ning was very frightened at this, and asked her what he should do. "Sleep in the same room with Mr. Yen," replied she. "What!" asked he, "cannot the spirits trouble Yen?" "He is a strange man," she answered, "and they don't like going near him." Ning then inquired how the spirits worked. "I bewitch people," said Hsiao-ch'ien, "and then they bore a hole in the foot which renders the victim senseless, and proceed to draw off the blood, which the devils drink. Another method is to tempt people by false gold, the bones of some horrid demon; and if they receive it, their hearts and livers will be torn out. Either method is used according to circumstances." Ning thanked her, and asked when he ought to be prepared; to which she replied, "To-morrow night." At parting she wept, and said, "I am about to sink into the great sea, with no friendly shore at hand. But your sense of duty is boundless, and you can save me. If you will collect my bones and bury them in some quiet spot, I shall not again be subject to these misfortunes." Ning said he would do so, and asked where she lay buried. "At the foot of the aspen-tree on which there is a bird's nest," replied she; and passing out of the door, disappeared. The next day Ning was afraid that Yen might be going away somewhere, and went over early to invite him across. Wine and food were produced towards noon; and Ning, who took care not to lose sight of Yen, then asked him to remain there for the night. Yen declined, on the ground that he liked being by himself; but Ning wouldn't hear any excuses, and carried all Yen's things to his own room, so that he had no alternative but to consent. However, he warned Ning, saying, "I know you are a gentleman and a man of honour. If you see anything you don't quite understand, I pray you not to be too inquisitive; don't pry into my boxes, or it may be the worse for both of us." Ning promised to attend to what he said, and by-and-by they both lay down to sleep; and Yen, having placed his boxes on the window-sill, was soon snoring loudly. Ning himself could not sleep; and after some time he saw a figure moving stealthily outside, at length approaching the window to peep through. Its eyes flashed like lightning, and Ning in a terrible fright was just upon the point of calling Yen, when something flew out of one of the boxes like a strip of white silk, and dashing against the window-sill returned at once to the box, disappearing very much like lightning. Yen heard the noise and got up, Ning all the time pretending to be asleep in order to watch what happened. The former then opened the box, and took out something which he smelt and examined by the light of the moon. It was dazzlingly white like crystal, and about two inches in length by the width of an onion leaf in breadth. He then wrapped it up carefully and put it back in the broken box, saying, " A bold-faced devil that, to dare thus to break my box ; " upon which he went back to bed ; but Ning, who was lost in astonishment, arose and asked him what it all meant, telling at the same time what he himself had seen. " As you and I are good friends," replied Yen, " I won't make any secret of it. The fact is I am a Taoist priest. But for the window-sill the devil would have been killed ; as it is, he is badly wounded." Ning asked him what it was he had there wrapped up, and he told him it was his sword,[1] on which he had smelt the presence of the devil. At Ning's request he produced the weapon, a bright little miniature of a sword ; and from that time Ning held his friend in higher esteem than ever.

Next day he found traces of blood outside the window which led round to the north of the temple ; and there among a number of graves he discovered the aspen tree with the bird's nest at its summit. He then fulfilled his promise and prepared to go home, Yen giving him a farewell banquet, and presenting him with an old leather case which he said contained a sword, and would keep at a distance from him all devils and bogies. Ning then wished to learn a little of Yen's art ; but the latter replied that although he might accomplish this easily enough, being as he was an upright man, yet he was well off in life, and not in a condition where it would be of any advantage to him. Ning then pretending that he had a younger sister buried here, dug up Hsiao-ch'ien's bones, and, having wrapped

[1] See No. X., note 8.

them up in grave-clothes, hired a boat, and set off on his way home. On his arrival, as his library looked towards the open country, he made a grave hard by and buried the bones there, sacrificing, and invoking Hsiao-ch'ien as follows :—" In pity for your lonely ghost, I have placed your remains near my humble cottage, where we shall be near each other, and no devil will dare annoy you. I pray you reject not my sacrifice, poor though it be." After this, he was proceeding home when he suddenly heard himself addressed from behind, the voice asking him not to hurry ; and turning round he beheld Hsiao-ch'ien, who thanked him, saying, " Were I to die ten times for you I could not discharge my debt. Let me go home with you and wait upon your father and mother ; you will not repent it." Looking closely at her, he observed that she had a beautiful complexion, and feet as small as bamboo shoots,[2] being altogether much prettier now that he came to see her by daylight. So they went together to his home, and bidding her wait awhile, Ning ran in to tell his mother, to the very great surprise of the old lady. Now Ning's wife had been ill for a long time, and his mother advised him not to say a word about it to her for fear of frightening her ; in the middle of which in rushed Hsiao-ch'ien, and threw herself on the ground before them. " This is the young lady," said Ning ; whereupon his mother in some alarm turned her attention to Hsiao-ch'ien, who cried out, " A lonely orphan, without brother or sister, the object of your son's kindness and compassion, begs to be allowed to give her poor services as some return for favours shown." Ning's mother, seeing that she was a nice, pleasant-looking girl, began to lose fear of her, and replied, " Madam, the prefer- ence you show for my son is highly pleasing to an old body like myself ; but this is the only hope of our family, and I hardly dare agree to his taking a devil-wife." " I have but one motive in what I ask," answered Hsiao-ch'ien, " and if you have no faith in disembodied people then let me regard him as my brother, and live under your pro- tection, serving you like a daughter." Ning's mother could not resist her straightforward manner, and Hsiao- ch'ien asked to be allowed to see Ning's wife, but this was

[2] Which, well cooked, are a very good substitute for asparagus.

denied on the plea that the lady was ill. Hsiao-ch'ien then went into the kitchen and got ready the dinner, running about the place as if she had lived there all her life. Ning's mother was, however, much afraid of her, and would not let her sleep in the house ; so Hsiao-ch'ien went to the library, and was just entering when suddenly she fell back a few steps, and began walking hurriedly backwards and forwards in front of the door. Ning seeing this, called out and asked her what it meant ; to which she replied, " The presence of that sword frightens me, and that is why I could not accompany you on your way home." Ning at once understood her, and hung up the sword-case in another place ; whereupon she entered, lighted a candle, and sat down. For some time she did not speak : at length asking Ning if he studied at night or not—" For," said she, " when I was little I used to repeat the Lêngyen *sutra* ; but now I have forgotten more than half, and, therefore, I should like to borrow a copy, and when you are at leisure in the evening you might hear me." Ning said he would, and they sat silently there for some time, after which Hsiao-ch'ien went away and took up her quarters elsewhere. Morning and night she waited on Ning's mother, bringing water for her to wash in, occupying herself with household matters, and endeavouring to please her in every way. In the evening before she went to bed, she would always go in and repeat a little of the *sutra*, and leave as soon as she thought Ning was getting sleepy. Now the illness of Ning's wife had given his mother a great deal of extra trouble—more, in fact, than she was equal to ; but ever since Hsiao-ch'ien's arrival all this was changed, and Ning's mother felt kindly disposed to the girl in consequence, gradually growing to regard her almost as her own child, and forgetting quite that she was a spirit. Accordingly, she didn't make her leave the house at night ; and Hsiao-ch'ien, who being a devil had not tasted meat or drink since her arrival,[3] now began at the end of six months to take a little thin gruel. Mother and son alike became very fond of her, and henceforth never mentioned what she really was ; neither were strangers able to detect the fact. By-and-by, Ning's wife died, and his mother secretly wished him to espouse Hsiao-ch'ien, though she rather

[3] See note 10 to the last story.

dreaded any unfortunate consequences that might arise. This Hsiao-ch'ien perceived, and seizing an opportunity said to Ning's mother, " I have been with you now more than a year, and you ought to know something of my disposition. Because I was unwilling to injure travellers I followed your son hither. There was no other motive ; and, as your son has shown himself one of the best of men, I would now remain with him for three years in order that he may obtain for me some mark of Imperial approbation [4] which will do me honour in the realms below." Ning's mother knew that she meant no evil, but hesitated to put the family hopes of a posterity into jeopardy. Hsiao-ch'ien, however, reassured her by saying that Ning would have three sons, and that the line would not be interrupted by his marrying her. On the strength of this the marriage was arranged, to the great joy of Ning, a feast prepared, and friends and relatives invited ; and when in response to a call the bride herself came forth in her gay wedding-dress, the beholders took her rather for a fairy than for a devil. After this, numbers of congratulatory presents were given by the various female members of the family, who vied with one another in making her acquaintance ; and these Hsiao-ch'ien returned by gifts of paintings of flowers, done by herself, in which she was very skilful, the receivers being extremely proud of such marks of her friendship. One day she was leaning at the window in a despondent mood, when suddenly she asked where the sword-case was. "Oh," replied Ning, " as you seemed afraid of it, I moved it elsewhere." " I have now been so long under the influence of surrounding life," [5] said Hsiao-ch'ien, " that I sha'n't be afraid of it any more. Let us hang it on the bed." " Why so ? " asked Ning. " For the last three days," explained she, " I have been much agitated in mind ; and I fear that the devil at the temple, angry at my escape, may come suddenly and carry me off." So Ning brought the sword-case, and Hsiao-ch'ien, after examining it closely, remarked, " This is where the magician puts people. I wonder how many were slain before it got old and worn out as it is now.

[4] Such as are from time to time bestowed upon virtuous widows and wives, filial sons and daughters, and others. These consist of some laudatory scroll or tablet, and are much prized by the family of the recipient.

[5] See note 14 to last story.

Even now when I look at it my flesh creeps." The case
was then hung up, and next day removed to over the door.
At night they sat up and watched, Hsiao-ch'ien warning
Ning not to go to sleep ; and suddenly something fell down
flop like a bird. Hsiao-ch'ien in a fright got behind the
curtain ; but Ning looked at the thing, and found it was an
imp of darkness, with glaring eyes and a bloody mouth,
coming straight to the door. Stealthily creeping up, it
made a grab at the sword-case, and seemed about to tear
it in pieces, when bang !—the sword-case became as big as
a wardrobe, and from it a devil protruded part of his body
and dragged the imp in. Nothing more was heard,
and the sword-case resumed its original size. Ning was
greatly alarmed, but Hsiao-ch'ien came out rejoicing,
and said, " There's an end of my troubles." In the
sword-case they found only a few quarts of clear water ;
nothing else.

After these events Ning took his doctor's degree and
Hsiao-ch'ien bore him a son. He then took a concubine,
and had one more son by each, all of whom became in time
distinguished men.

XVII. THE *SHUI-MANG* PLANT

THE *shui-mang*[1] is a poisonous herb. It is a creeper, like
the bean, and has a similar red flower. Those who eat of
it die, and become *shui-mang* devils, tradition asserting
that such devils are unable to be born again unless they can
find some one else who has also eaten of this poison to take
their place.[2] These *shui-mang* devils abound in the province of Hunan, where, by the way, the phrase " same-
year man " is applied to those born in the same year, who
exchange visits and call each other brother, their children
addressing the father's " brother " as uncle. This has now
become a regular custom there.[3]

[1] Probably the *Illicium religiosum*, S. & Z., is meant.
[2] See No. XII., note 2.
[3] The common application of the term " same-year men " is to
persons who have graduated at the same time.

A young man named Chu was on his way to visit a same-year friend of his, when he was overtaken by a violent thirst. Suddenly he came upon an old woman sitting by the roadside under a shed and distributing tea gratis,[4] and immediately walked up to her to get a drink. She invited him into the shed, and presented him with a bowl of tea in a very cordial spirit ; but the smell of it did not seem like the smell of ordinary tea, and he would not drink it, rising up to go away. The old woman stopped him, and called out, " San-niang ! bring some good tea." Immediately a young girl came from behind the shed, carrying in her hands a pot of tea. She was about fourteen or fifteen years old, and of very fascinating appearance, with glittering rings and bracelets on her fingers and arms. As Chu received the cup from her his reason fled ; and drinking down the tea she gave him, the flavour of which was unlike any other kind, he proceeded to ask for more. Then, watching for a moment when the old woman's back was turned, he seized her wrist and drew a ring from her finger. The girl blushed and smiled ; and Chu, more and more inflamed, asked her where she lived. " Come again this evening," replied she, " and you'll find me here." Chu begged for a handful of her tea, which he stowed away with the ring, and took his leave. Arriving at his destination, he felt a pain in his heart, which he at once attributed to the tea, telling his friend what had occurred. " Alas ! you are undone," cried the other; " they were *shui-mang* devils. My father died in the same way, and we were unable to save him. There is no help for you." Chu was terribly frightened, and produced the handful of tea, which his friend at once pronounced to be leaves of the *shui-mang* plant. He then showed him the ring, and told him what the girl had said ; whereupon his friend, after some reflection, said, " She must be San-niang, of the K'ou family." " How could you know her name ? " asked Chu, hearing his friend use the same words as the old woman.

---

[4] This is by no means an uncommon form of charity. During the temporary distress at Canton, in the summer of 1877, large tubs of gruel were to be seen standing at convenient points, ready for any poor person who might wish to stay his hunger. It is thus, and by similar acts of benevolence, such as building bridges, repairing roads, &c., &c., that the wealthy Chinaman strives to maintain an advantageous balance in his record of good and evil.

" Oh," replied he, " there was a nice-looking girl of that name who died some years ago from eating of the same herb. She is doubtless the girl you saw." Here some one observed that if the person so entrapped by a devil only knew its name, and could procure an old pair of its shoes, he might save himself by boiling them in water and drinking the liquor as medicine. Chu's friend thereupon rushed off at once to the K'ou family, and implored them to give him an old pair of their daughter's shoes ; but they, not wishing to prevent their daughter from finding a substitute in Chu, flatly refused his request. So he went back in anger and told Chu, who ground his teeth with rage, saying, " If I die, she shall not obtain her transmigration thereby." His friend then sent him home ; and just as he reached the door he fell down dead. Chu's mother wept bitterly over his corpse, which was in due course interred ; and he left behind one little boy barely a year old. His wife did not remain a widow, but in six months married again and went away, putting Chu's son under the care of his grandmother, who was quite unequal to any toil, and did nothing but weep morning and night. One day she was carrying her grandson about in her arms, crying bitterly all the time, when suddenly in walked Chu. His mother, much alarmed, brushed away her tears, and asked him what it meant. " Mother," replied he, " down in the realms below I heard you weeping. I am therefore come to tend you. Although a departed spirit, I have a wife, who has likewise come to share your toil. Therefore do not grieve." His mother inquired who his wife was, to which he replied, " When the K'ou family sat still and left me to my fate I was greatly incensed against them ; and after death I sought for San-niang, not knowing where she was. I have recently seen my old same-year friend, and he told me where she was. She had come to life again in the person of the baby-daughter of a high official named Jen ; but I went thither and dragged her spirit back. She is now my wife, and we get on extremely well together." A very pretty and well-dressed young lady here entered, and made obeisance to Chu's mother, Chu saying, " This is San-niang, of the K'ou family ; " and although not a living being, Mrs. Chu at once took a great fancy to her. Chu sent her off to help in the work of the house, and, in spite of not being accustomed to this sort of thing, she was so obedient to her mother-in-law as to excite the compassion of all. The two then took up their quarters in Chu's old apartments, and there they continued to remain.

Meanwhile San-niang asked Chu's mother to let the K'ou family know ; and this she did, notwithstanding some objections raised by her son. Mr. and Mrs. K'ou were much astonished at the news, and, ordering their carriage, proceeded at once to Chu's house. There they found their daughter, and parents and child fell into each other's arms. San-niang entreated them to dry their tears ; but her mother, noticing the poverty of Chu's household, was unable to restrain her feelings. " We are already spirits," cried San-niang ; " what matters poverty to us ? Besides, I am very well treated here, and am altogether as happy as I can be." They then asked her who the old woman was, to which she replied, " Her name was Ni. She was mortified at being too ugly to entrap people herself, and got me to assist her. She has now been born again at a soy-shop in the city." Then, looking at her husband, she added, " Come, since you are the son-in-law, pay the proper respect to my father and mother, or what shall I think of you ? " Chu made his obeisance, and San-niang went into the kitchen to get food ready for them, at which her mother became very melancholy, and went away home, whence she sent a couple of maid-servants, a hundred ounces of silver, and rolls of cloth and silk, besides making occasional presents of food and wine, so that Chu's mother lived in comparative comfort. San-niang also went from time to time to see her parents, but would never stay very long, pleading that she was wanted at home, and such excuses ; and if the old people attempted to keep her, she simply went off by herself. Her father built a nice house for Chu with all kinds of luxuries in it ; but Chu never once entered his father-in-law's door.

Subsequently a man of the village who had eaten *shui-mang*, and had died in consequence, came back to life, to the great astonishment of everybody. However, Chu explained it, saying, " I brought him back to life. He was the victim of a man named Li Chiu ; but I drove off Li's spirit when it came to make the other take his place." Chu's mother then asked her son why he did not get a substitute for himself; to which he replied, "I do not like to do this. I am anxious to put an end to, rather than take advantage of, such a system. Besides, I am very happy waiting on you, and have no wish to be born again." From that time all persons who had poisoned themselves with *shui-mang* were in the habit of feasting Chu and obtaining his assistance in their trouble. But in ten years' time his mother died, and he and his wife gave themselves up to sorrow, and would see no one, bidding their little boy put on mourning, beat his breast, and perform the proper ceremonies. Two years after Chu had buried his mother, his son married the granddaughter of a high official named Jen. This gentleman had had a daughter by a concubine, who had died when only a few months old; and now, hearing the strange story of Chu's wife, he came to call on her and arrange the marriage. He then gave his granddaughter to Chu's son, and a free intercourse was maintained between the two families. However, one day Chu said to his son, "Because I have been of service to my generation, God has appointed me Keeper of the Dragons; and I am now about to proceed to my post." Thereupon four horses appeared in the court-yard, drawing a carriage with yellow hangings, the flanks of the horses being covered with scale-like trappings. Husband and wife came forth in full dress, and took their seats, and, while son and daughter-in-law were weeping their adieus, disappeared from view. That very day the K'ou family saw their daughter arrive, and, bidding them farewell, she told them the same story. The old people would have kept her, but she said, "My husband is already on his way," and, leaving the house, parted from them for ever. Chu's son was named Ngo, and his literary name was Li-ch'ên. He begged San-niang's bones from the K'ou family, and buried them by the side of his father's.

XVIII. LITTLE CHU

A MAN named Li Hua dwelt at Ch'ang-chou.   He was very
well off, and about fifty years of age, but he had no sons ;
only one daughter, named Hsiao-hui, a pretty child on
whom her parents doted.   When she was fourteen she had
a severe illness and died, leaving their home desolate and
depriving them of their chief pleasure in life.   Mr. Li then
bought a concubine, and she by-and-by bore him a son,
who was perfectly idolised, and called Chu, or the Pearl.
This boy grew up to be a fine manly fellow, though so
extremely stupid that when five or six years old he didn't
know pulse from corn, and could hardly talk plainly.
His father, however, loved him dearly, and did not observe
his faults.

   Now it chanced that a one-eyed priest came to collect
alms in the town, and he seemed to know so much about
everybody's private affairs that the people all looked upon
him as superhuman.   He himself declared he had control
over life, death, happiness, and misfortune ; and consequently no one dared refuse him whatever sum he chose
to ask of them.   From Li he demanded one hundred
ounces of silver, but was offered only ten, which he refused
to receive.   This sum was increased to thirty ounces,
whereupon the priest looked sternly at Li and said, " I
must have one hundred ; not a fraction less."   Li now got
angry, and went away without giving him any, the priest,
too, rising up in a rage and shouting after him, " I hope
you won't repent."   Shortly after these events little Chu
fell sick, and crawled about the bed scratching the mat, his
face being of an ashen paleness.   This frightened his father,
who hurried off with eighty ounces of silver, and begged
the priest to accept them.   " A large sum like this is no
trifling matter to earn," said the priest, smiling ; " but
what can a poor recluse like myself do for you ? "   So Li
went home, to find that little Chu was already dead ; and
this worked him into such a state that he immediately
laid a complaint before the magistrate.   The priest was
accordingly summoned and interrogated ; but the magistrate wouldn't accept his defence, and ordered him to be
bambooed.   The blows sounded as if falling on leather,

upon which the magistrate commanded his lictors to search him ; and from about his person they drew forth two wooden men, a small coffin, and five small flags. The magistrate here flew into a passion, and made certain mystic signs with his fingers, which when the priest saw he was frightened, and began to excuse himself ; but the magistrate would not listen to him, and had him bambooed to death. Li thanked him for his kindness, and, taking his leave, proceeded home. In the evening, after dusk, he was sitting alone with his wife, when suddenly in popped a little boy, who said, " Pa ! why did you hurry on so fast ? I couldn't catch you up." Looking at him more closely, they saw that he was about seven or eight years old, and Mr. Li, in some alarm, was on the point of questioning him, when he disappeared, reappearing again like smoke, and, curling round and round, got upon the bed. Li pushed him off, and he fell down without making any sound, crying out, " Pa ! why do you do this ? " and in a moment he was on the bed again. Li was frightened, and ran away with his wife, the boy calling after them, " Pa ! Ma ! boo-oo-oo." They went into the next room, bolting the door after them ; but there was the little boy at their heels again. Li asked him what he wanted, to which he replied, " I belong to Su-chou ; my name is Chan ; at six years of age I was left an orphan ; my brother and his wife couldn't bear me, so they sent me to live at my maternal grandfather's. One day, when playing outside, a wicked priest killed me by his black art underneath a mulberry-tree, and made of me an evil spirit, dooming me to everlasting devildom without hope of transmigration. Happily you exposed him ; and I would now remain with you as your son." " The paths of men and devils," replied Li, " lie in different directions. How can we remain together ? " " Give me only a tiny room," cried the boy, " a bed, a mattress, and a cup of cold gruel every day. I ask for nothing more." So Li agreed, to the great delight of the boy, who slept by himself in another part of the house, coming in the morning and walking in and out like any ordinary person. Hearing Li's concubine crying bitterly, he asked how long little Chu had been dead, and she told him seven days. " It's cold weather now," said he, " and the body can't have decomposed. Have the grave opened, and let me see it ; if not too far

gone, I can bring him to life again." Li was only too
pleased, and went off with the boy ; and when they opened
the grave they found the body in perfect preservation ;
but while Li was controlling his emotions, lo ! the boy had
vanished from his sight. Wondering very much at this,
he took little Chu's body home, and had hardly laid it on
the bed when he noticed the eyes move. Little Chu then
called for some broth, which put him into a perspiration,
and then he got up. They were all overjoyed to see him
come to life again ; and, what is more, he was much brighter
and cleverer than before. At night, however, he lay
perfectly stiff and rigid, without showing any signs of life ;
and, as he didn't move when they turned him over and
over, they were much frightened, and thought he had died
again. But towards daybreak he awaked as if from a
dream, and in reply to their questions said that when he
was with the wicked priest there was another boy named
Ko-tzŭ ;[1] and that the day before, when he had been unable
to catch up his father, it was because he had stayed behind
to bid adieu to Ko-tzŭ ; that Ko-tzŭ was now the son of an
official in Purgatory named Chiang, and very comfortably
settled ; and that he had invited him (Chan) to go and play
with him that evening, and had sent him back on a white-
nosed horse. His mother then asked him if he had seen
little Chu in Purgatory, to which he replied, " Little Chu
has already been born again. He and our father here had
not really the destiny of father and son. Little Chu was
merely a man named Yen Tzŭ-fang, from Chin-ling, who
had come to reclaim an old debt."[2] Now Mr. Li had
formerly traded to Chin-ling, and actually owed money for
goods to a Mr. Yen ; but he had died, and no one else knew
anything about it, so that he was now greatly alarmed
when he heard this story. His mother next asked (the
quasi) little Chu if he had seen his sister, Hsiao-hui ; and
he said he had not, promising to go again and inquire about
her. A few days afterwards he told his mother that Hsiao-
hui was very happy in Purgatory, being married to a son
of one of the Judges ; and that she had any quantity of

[1] It may be necessary here to remind the reader that Chan's
spirit is speaking from Chu's body.
[2] We shall come by-and-by to a story illustrative of this extraordinary belief.

jewels,[3] and crowds of attendants when she went abroad.
" Why doesn't she come home to see her parents ? " asked
his mother. " Well," replied the boy, " dead people, you
know, haven't got any flesh or bones ; however, if you can
only remind them of something that happened in their past
lives, their feelings are at once touched. So yesterday I
managed, through Mr. Chiang, to get an interview with
Hsiao-hui ; and we sat together on a cʋral couch, and
I spoke to her of her father and mother at home, all of
which she listened to as if she was asleep. I then remarked,
' Sister, when you were alive you were very fond of embroidering double-stemmed flowers ; and once you cut
your finger with the scissors, and the blood ran over the
silk, but you brought it into the picture as a crimson cloud.
Your mother has that picture still, hanging at the head of
her bed, a perpetual souvenir of you. Sister, have you
forgotten this ? ' Then she burst into tears, and promised
to ask her husband to let her come and visit you." His
mother asked when she would arrive, but he said he could
not tell. However, one day he ran in and cried out,
" Mother, Hsiao-hui has come, with a splendid equipage
and a train of servants ; we had better get plenty of wine
ready." In a few moments he came in again, saying,
" Here is my sister," at the same time asking her to take
a seat and rest. He then wept ; but none of those present
saw anything at all. By-and-by he went out and burnt
a quantity of paper money[4] and made offerings of wine
outside the door, returning shortly and saying he had sent
away her attendants for a while ; also that Hsiao-hui
asked if the green coverlet, a small portion of which had
been burnt by a candle, was still in existence. " It is,"
replied her mother, and, going to a box, she at once produced the coverlet. " Hsiao-hui would like a bed made
up for her in her old room," said her (quasi) brother ; " she

---

[3] The *summum bonum* of many a Chinese woman.

[4] Chinese silver, called sycee (from the Cantonese *sai see*, " fine
silk ; " because, if pure, it may be drawn out under the application
of heat into fine silk threads), is cast in the form of " shoes," weighing from one to one hundred ounces. Paper imitations of these
are burnt for the use of the spirits in the world below. The sharp
edges of a " shoe " of sycee are caused by the mould containing
the molten silver being gently shaken until the metal has set, with
a view to secure uniform fineness throughout the lump.

wants to rest awhile, and will talk with you again in the morning."

Now their next-door neighbour, named Chao, had a daughter who was formerly a great friend of Hsiao-hui's, and that night she dreamt that Hsiao-hui appeared with a turban on her head and a red mantle over her shoulders, and that they talked and laughed together precisely as in days gone by. "I am now a spirit," said Hsiao-hui, "and my father and mother can no more see me than if I was far separated from them. Dear sister, I would borrow your body, from which to speak to them. You need fear nothing." On the morrow, when Miss Chao met her mother, she fell on the ground before her and remained some time in a state of unconsciousness, at length saying, "Madam, it is many years since we met ; your hair has become very white." "The girl's mad," said her mother, in alarm ; and, thinking something had gone wrong, proceeded to follow her out of the door. Miss Chao went straight to Li's house, and there with tears embraced Mrs. Li, who did not know what to make of it all. "Yesterday," said Miss Chao, "when I came back, I was unhappily unable to speak with you. Unfilial wretch that I was, to die before you and leave you to mourn my loss. How can I redeem such behaviour ?" Her mother thereupon began to understand the scene, and, weeping, said to her, "I have heard that you hold an honourable position, and this is a great comfort to me ; but living as you do in the palace of a Judge, how is it you are able to get away ?" "My husband," replied she, "is very kind ; and his parents treat me with all possible consideration. I experience no harsh treatment at their hands." Here Miss Chao rested her cheek upon her hand, exactly as Hsiao-hui had been wont to do when she was alive ; and at that moment in came her brother to say that her attendants were ready to return. "I must go," said she, rising up and weeping bitterly all the time ; after which she fell down, and remained some time unconscious as before.

Shortly after these events Mr. Li became dangerously ill, and no medicines were of any avail, so that his son feared they would not be able to save his life. Two devils sat at the head of his bed, one holding an iron staff, the other a nettle-hemp rope four or five feet in length. Day and night his son implored them to go, but they would not move ; and Mrs. Li in sorrow began to prepare the funeral clothes.[5] Towards evening her son entered and cried out, " Strangers and women leave the room ! My sister's husband is coming to see his father-in-law." He then clapped his hands, and burst out laughing. " What is the matter ? " asked his mother. " I am laughing," answered he, " because when the two devils heard my sister's husband was coming, they both ran under the bed, like terrapins, drawing in their heads." By-and-by, looking at nothing, he began to talk about the weather, and ask his sister's husband how he did, and then he clapped his hands and said, " I begged the two devils to go, but they would not ; it's all right now." After this he went out to the door and returned, saying, " My sister's husband has gone. He took away the two devils tied to his horse. My father ought to get better now. Besides, Hsiao-hui's husband said he would speak to the Judge, and obtain a hundred years' lease of life both for you and my father." The whole family rejoiced exceedingly at this, and when night came Mr. Li was better, and in a few days quite well again. A tutor was engaged for the (quasi) little Chu, who showed himself an apt pupil, and at eighteen years of age took his bachelor's degree. He could also see things of the other world ; and when anyone in the village was ill, he pointed out where the devils were, and burnt them out with fire, so that everybody got well. However, before long he himself became very ill, and his flesh turned green and purple, whereupon he said, " The devils afflict me thus because I let out their secrets. Henceforth I shall never divulge them again."

XIX. MISS QUARTA HU

MR. SHANG was a native of T'ai-shan, and lived quietly with his books alone. One autumn night when the Silver River [1]

---

[5] Death is regarded as a summons from the authorities of Purgatory ; lictors are sent to arrest the doomed man armed with a written warrant similar to those issued on earth from a magistrate's yamên.

[1] The Milky Way is known to the Chinese under this name— unquestionably a more poetical one than our own.

was unusually distinct and the moon shining brightly in the sky, he was walking up and down under the shade, with his thoughts wandering somewhat at random, when lo ! a young girl leaped over the wall, and, smiling, asked him, " What are you thinking about, Sir, all so deeply ? " Shang looked at her, and seeing that she had a pretty face, asked her to walk in. She then told him her name was Hu,[2] and that she was called Tertia ; but when he wanted to know where she lived, she laughed and would not say. So he did not inquire any further ; and by degrees they struck up a friendship, and Miss Tertia used to come and chat with him every evening. He was so smitten that he could hardly take his eyes off her, and at last she said to him, " What *are* you looking at ? " " At you," cried he, " my lovely rose, my beautiful peach. I could gaze at you all night long." " If you think so much of poor me," answered she, " I don't know where your wits would be if you saw my sister Quarta." Mr. Shang said he was sorry he didn't know her, and begged that he might be introduced ; so next night Miss Tertia brought her sister, who turned out to be a young damsel of about fifteen, with a face delicately powdered and resembling the lily, or like an apricot-flower seen through mist ; and altogether as pretty a girl as he had ever seen. Mr. Shang was charmed with her, and inviting them in, began to laugh and talk with the elder, while Miss Quarta sat playing with her girdle, and keeping her eyes on the ground. By-and-by Miss Tertia got up and said she was going, whereupon her sister rose to take leave also ; but Mr. Shang asked her not to be in a hurry, and requested the elder to assist in persuading her. " You needn't hurry," said she to Miss Quarta ; and accordingly the latter remained chatting with Mr. Shang without reserve, and finally told him she was a fox. However, Mr. Shang was so occupied with her beauty that he didn't pay any heed to that ; but she added, " And my sister is very dangerous ; she has already killed three people. Anyone bewitched by her has no chance of escape. Happily, you have bestowed your affections on me, and I shall not allow you to be destroyed. You must break off your acquaintance with her at once." Mr. Shang was very frightened, and implored her to help him ; to which

[2] See No. XIII., note 1.

she replied, " Although a fox, I am skilled in the arts of the Immortals ;[3] I will write out a charm for you which you must paste on the door, and thus you will keep her away." So she wrote down the charm, and in the morning when her sister came and saw it, she fell back, crying out, " Ungrateful minx ! you've thrown me up for him, have you ? You two being destined for each other, what have I done that you should treat me thus ? " She then went away ; and a few days afterwards Miss Quarta said she too would have to be absent for a day, so Shang went out for a walk by himself, and suddenly beheld a very nice-looking young lady emerge from the shade of an old oak that was growing on the hill-side. " Why so dreadfully pensive ? " said she to him ; " those Hu girls can never bring you a single cent." She then presented Shang with some money, and bade him go on ahead and buy some good wine, adding, " I'll bring something to eat with me, and we'll have a jolly time of it." Shang took the money and went home, doing as the young lady had told him ; and by-and-by in she herself came, and threw on the table a roast chicken and a shoulder of salt pork, which she at once proceeded to cut up. They now set to work to enjoy themselves, and had hardly finished when they heard some one coming in, and the next minute in walked Miss Tertia and her sister. The strange young lady didn't know where to hide, and managed to lose her shoes ; but the other two began to revile her, saying, " Out upon you, base fox ; what are you doing here ? " They then chased her away after some trouble, and Shang began to excuse himself to them, until at last they all became friends again as before.

One day, however, a Shensi man arrived, riding on a donkey, and coming to the door said, " I have long been in search of these evil spirits : now I have got them." Shang's father thought the man's remark rather strange, and asked him whence he had come. " Across much land and sea," replied he ; " for eight or nine months out of every year I am absent from my native place. These devils killed my brother with their poison, alas ! alas ! and I have sworn to exterminate them ; but I have travelled many miles without being able to find them. They are now

[3] That is, of the Taoists. See No. IV., note 1.

in your house, and if you do not cut them off, you will die even as my brother." Now Shang and the young ladies had kept their acquaintanceship very dark ; but his father and mother had guessed that something was up, and, much alarmed, bade the Shensi man walk in and perform his exorcisms. The latter then produced two bottles which he placed upon the ground, and proceeded to mutter a number of charms and cabalistic formulæ ; whereupon four wreaths of smoke passed two by two into each bottle. " I have the whole family," cried he, in an ecstasy of delight ; as he proceeded to tie down the mouths of the bottles with pig's bladder, sealing them with the utmost care. Shang's father was likewise very pleased, and kept his guest to dinner ; but the young man himself was sadly dejected, and approaching the bottles unperceived, bent his ear to listen. " Ungrateful man," said Miss Quarta from within, " to sit there and make no effort to save me." This was more than Shang could stand, and he immediately broke the seal, but found that he couldn't untie the knot. " Not so," cried Miss Quarta ; " merely lay down the flag that now stands on the altar, and with a pin prick the bladder, and I can get out." Shang did as she bade him, and in a moment a thin streak of white smoke issued forth from the hole and disappeared in the clouds. When the Shensi man came out, and saw the flag lying on the ground, he started violently, and cried out, " Escaped ! This must be your doing, young Sir." He then shook the bottle and listened, finally exclaiming, " Luckily only one has got away. She was fated not to die, and may therefore be pardoned."[4] Thereupon he took the bottles and went his way.

Some years afterwards Shang was one day superin-tending his reapers cutting the corn, when he descried Miss Quarta at a distance, sitting under a tree. He approached, and she took his hand, saying, " Ten years have rolled away since last we met. Since then I have gained the prize of

[4] Predestination *after the event* is, luckily for China, the form of this superstition which really appeals to her all-practical children. Not a larger percentage than with ourselves allow belief in an irremediable destiny to divert their efforts one moment from the object in view ; though thousands upon thousands are ready enough to acknowledge the " will of heaven " in any national or individual calamities that may have befallen. See No. IX., note 3.

immortality ; [5] but I thought that perhaps you had not quite forgotten me, and so I came to see you once more." Shang wished her to return home with him ; to which she replied, " I am no longer what I was that I should mingle in the affairs of mortals. We shall meet again." And as she said this, she disappeared ; but twenty years later, when Shang was one day alone, Miss Quarta walked in. Shang was overjoyed, and began to address her ; but she answered him, saying, " My name is already enrolled in the register of the Immortals, and I have no right to return to earth. However, out of gratitude to you I determined to announce to you the date of your dissolution, that you might put your affairs in order. Fear nothing ; I will see you safely through to the happy land." She then departed, and on the day named Shang actually died. A relative of a friend of mine, Mr. Li Wên-yü, frequently met the above-mentioned Mr. Shang.[6]

XX. MR. CHU, THE CONSIDERATE HUSBAND

AT the village of Chu in Chi-yang, there was a man named Chu, who died at the age of fifty and odd years. His family at once proceeded to put on their mourning robes, when suddenly they heard the dead man cry out. Rushing up to the coffin, they found that he had come to life again ; and began, full of joy, to ask him all about it. But the old gentleman replied only to his wife, saying, " When I died I did not expect to come back. However, by the time I had got a few miles on my way, I thought of the poor old body I was leaving behind me, dependent for everything on others, and with no more enjoyment of life. So I made up my mind to return, and take you away with me." The bystanders thought this was only the disconnected talk of

---

[5] Any disembodied spirit whose conduct for a certain term of years is quite satisfactory is competent to obtain this reward. Thus, instead of being born again on earth, perhaps as an animal, they become angels or good spirits, and live for ever in heaven in a state of supreme beatitude.

[6] Our author occasionally ends up with a remark of this kind ; and these have undoubtedly had their weight with his too credulous countrymen.

a man who had just regained consciousness, and attached no importance to it ; but the old man repeated it, and then his wife said, " It's all very well, but you have only just come to life ; how can you go and die again directly ? " " It is extremely simple," replied her husband ; " you go and pack up everything ready." The old lady laughed and did nothing ; upon which Mr. Chu urged her again to prepare, and then she left the house. In a short time she returned, and pretended that she had done what he wanted. " Then you had better dress," said he ; but Mrs. Chu did not move until he pressed her again and again, after which she did not like to cross him, and by-and-by came out all fully equipped. The other ladies of the family were laughing on the sly, when Mr. Chu laid his head upon the pillow, and told his wife to do likewise. " It's too ridiculous," she was beginning to say, when Mr. Chu banged the bed with his hand, and cried out, " What is there to laugh at in dying ? " upon which the various members of the family, seeing the old gentleman was in a rage, begged her to gratify his whim. Mrs. Chu then lay down alongside of her husband, to the infinite amusement of the spectators ; but it was soon noticed that the old lady had ceased to smile, and by-and-by her two eyes closed. For a long time not a sound was heard, as if she was fast asleep ; and when some of those present approached to touch her, they found she was as cold as ice, and no longer breathing ; then, turning to her husband, they perceived that he also had passed away.

This story was fully related to me by a younger sister-in-law of Mr. Chu's, who, in the twenty-first year of the reign K'ang Hsi,[1] was employed in the house of a high official named Pi.

XXI. THE MAGNANIMOUS GIRL

At Chin-ling there lived a young man named Ku, who had considerable ability but was very poor ; and having an old mother, he was very loth to leave home. So he employed himself in writing or painting [1] for people, and gave his

---

[1] A.D. 1682.

[1] The usual occupation of poor scholars who are ashamed to go into trade, and who have not enterprise enough to start as doctors

mother the proceeds, going on thus till he was twenty-five years of age without taking a wife. Opposite to their house was another building, which had long been untenanted ; and one day an old woman and a young girl came to occupy it, but there being no gentleman with them young Ku did not make any inquiries as to who they were or whence they hailed. Shortly afterwards it chanced that just as Ku was entering the house he observed a young lady come out of his mother's door. She was about eighteen or nineteen, very clever and refined-looking, and altogether such a girl as one rarely sets eyes on ; and when she noticed Mr. Ku, she did not run away, but seemed quite self-possessed. " It was the young lady over the way ; she came to borrow my scissors and measure," said his mother, " and she told me that there was only her mother and herself. They don't seem to belong to the lower classes. I asked her why she didn't get married, to which she replied that her mother was old. I must go and call on her to-morrow, and find out how the land lies. If she doesn't expect too much, you could take care of her mother for her." So next day Ku's mother went, and found that the girl's mother was deaf, and that they were evidently poor, apparently not having a day's food in the house. Ku's mother asked what their employment was, and the old lady said they trusted for food to her daughter's ten fingers. She then threw out some hints about uniting the two families, to which the old lady seemed to agree ; but, on consultation with her daughter, the latter would not consent. Mrs. Ku returned home and told her son, saying, " Perhaps she thinks we are too poor. She doesn't speak or laugh, is very nice-looking, and as pure as snow ; truly no ordinary girl." There ended that ; until one day, as Ku was sitting in his study, up came a very agreeable young fellow, who said he was from a neighbouring village, and engaged Ku to draw a picture for him. The two youths soon struck up a firm friendship and met constantly, when it happened that the stranger chanced to see the young lady of over

or fortune-tellers. Besides painting pictures and fans, and illustrating books, these men write fancy scrolls in the various ornamental styles so much prized by the Chinese ; they keep accounts for people, and write or read business and private letters for the illiterate masses.

the way. " Who is that ? " said he, following her with
his eyes. Ku told him, and then he said, " She is certainly
pretty, but rather stern in her appearance." By-and-by
Ku went in, and his mother told him the girl had come
to beg a little rice, as they had had nothing to eat all day.
" She's a good daughter," said his mother, " and I'm very
sorry for her. We must try and help them a little." Ku
thereupon shouldered a peck of rice, and, knocking at
their door, presented it with his mother's compliments.
The young lady received the rice but said nothing ; and
then she got into the habit of coming over and helping
Ku's mother with her work and household affairs, almost
as if she had been her daughter-in-law, for which Ku was
very grateful to her, and whenever he had anything nice
he always sent some of it in to her mother, though the young
lady herself never once took the trouble to thank him.
So things went on until Ku's mother got an abscess on her
leg, and lay writhing in agony day and night. Then the
young lady devoted herself to the invalid, waiting on her
and giving her medicine with such care and attention
that at last the sick woman cried out, " Oh, that I could
secure such a daughter-in-law as you, to see this old body
into its grave ! " The young lady soothed her, and replied,
" Your son is a hundred times more filial than I, a poor
widow's only daughter." " But even a filial son makes
a bad nurse," answered the patient ; " besides I am now
drawing towards the evening of my life, when my body will
be exposed to the mists and the dews, and I am vexed in
spirit about our ancestral worship and the continuance of
our line." As she was speaking Ku walked in ; and his
mother, weeping, said, " I am deeply indebted to this
young lady ; do not forget to repay her goodness." Ku
made a low bow, but the young lady said, " Sir, when
you were kind to my mother, I did not thank you ; why,
then, thank me ? " Ku thereupon became more than
ever attached to her ; but could never get her to depart
in the slightest degree from her cold demeanour towards
himself. One day, however, he managed to squeeze her
hand, upon which she told him never to do so again ; and
then for some time he neither saw nor heard anything of
her. She had conceived a violent dislike to the young
stranger above-mentioned ; and one evening when he was

sitting talking with Ku, the young lady reappeared. After a while she got angry at something he said, and drew from her robe a glittering knife about a foot long. The young man, seeing her do this, ran out in a fright and she after him, only to find that he had vanished. She then threw her dagger up into the air, and whish ! a streak of light like a rainbow, and something came tumbling down with a flop. Ku got a light, and ran to see what it was ; and lo ! there lay a white fox, head in one place and body in another. "There is your *friend*," cried the girl ; "I knew he would cause me to destroy him sooner or later." Ku dragged it into the house, and said, "Let us wait till to-morrow to talk it over ; we shall then be more calm." Next day the young lady arrived, and Ku inquired about her knowledge of the black art ; but she told Ku not to trouble himself about such affairs, and to keep it secret or it might be prejudicial to his happiness. Ku then entreated her to consent to their union, to which she replied that she had already been as it were a daughter-in-law to his mother, and there was no need to push the thing further. "Is it because I am poor ? " asked Ku. "Well, I am not rich," answered she, "but the fact is I had rather not." She then took her leave, and the next evening when Ku went across to their house to try once more to persuade her, the young lady had disappeared, and was never seen again.

XXII. THE BOON-COMPANION

ONCE upon a time there was a young man named Ch'ê, who was not particularly well off, but at the same time very fond of his wine ; so much so, that without his three stoups of liquor every night, he was quite unable to sleep, and bottles were seldom absent from the head of his bed. One night he had waked up and was turning over and over, when he fancied some one was in the bed with him ; but then, thinking it was only the clothes which had slipped off, he put out his hand to feel, and, lo ! he touched something silky like a cat, only larger. Striking a light, he found it was a fox, lying in a drunken sleep like a dog ; and then looking at his wine bottle he saw that it had been emptied. "A boon-companion," said he, laughing, as he avoided startling the animal, and covering it up, lay down to sleep with his arm across it, and the candle alight so as to see what transformation it might undergo. About midnight, the fox stretched itself, and Ch'ê cried, "Well, to be sure, you've had a nice sleep!" He then drew off the clothes, and beheld an elegant young man in a scholar's dress; but the young man jumped up, and making a low obeisance, returned his host many thanks for not cutting off his head. "Oh," replied Ch'ê, "I am not averse to liquor myself; in fact they say I'm too much given to it. You shall play Pythias to my Damon; [1] and if you have no objection, we'll be a pair of bottle-and-glass chums." So they lay down and went to sleep again, Ch'ê urging the young man to visit him often, and saying that they must have faith in each other. The fox agreed to this, but when Ch'ê awoke in the morning his bedfellow had already disappeared. So he prepared a goblet of first-rate wine in expectation of his friend's arrival, and at nightfall sure enough he came. They then sat together drinking, and the fox cracked so many jokes that Ch'ê said he regretted he had not known him before. "And truly I don't know how to repay your kindness," replied the former, "in preparing all this nice wine for me." "Oh," said Ch'ê, "what's a pint or so of wine?—nothing worth speaking of." "Well," rejoined the fox, "you are only a poor scholar, and money isn't so easily to be got. I must try if I can't secure a little wine capital for you." Next evening, when he arrived, he said to Ch'ê, "Two miles down towards the south-east you will find some silver lying by the wayside. Go early in the morning and get it." So on the morrow Ch'ê set off, and actually obtained two lumps of silver, with which he bought some choice morsels to help them out with their wine that evening. The fox now told him that there was a vault in his backyard which he ought to open; and when he did so, he found therein more than a hundred strings of cash. [2] "Now then," cried Ch'ê, delighted, "I shall have no more anxiety about funds for buying wine with all this in my purse." "Ah," replied the fox, "the water in a puddle

---

[1] Kuan Chung and Pao Shu are the Chinese types of friendship. They were two statesmen of considerable ability, who flourished in the seventh century B.C.   [2] Say about £10. See No. II., note 2.

is not inexhaustible.   I must do something further for you."
Some days afterwards the fox said to Ch'ê, " Buckwheat
is very cheap in the market just now.   Something is to
be done in this line."   Accordingly, Ch'ê bought over
forty tons, and thereby incurred general ridicule ; but
by-and-by there was a bad drought and all kinds of grain
and beans were spoilt.   Only buckwheat would grow, and
Ch'ê sold off his stock at a profit of one thousand per cent.
His wealth thus began to increase ; he bought two hundred
acres of rich land, and always planted his crops, corn,
millet, or what not, upon the advice of the fox secretly
given him beforehand.   The fox looked on Ch'ê's wife as
a sister, and on Ch'ê's children as his own ; but when,
subsequently, Ch'ê died, it never came to the house again.

XXIII. MISS LIEN-HSIANG

THERE was a young man named Sang Tzŭ-ming, a native
of I-chou, who had been left an orphan when quite young.
He lived near the Saffron market, and kept himself very
much to himself, only going out twice a day for his meals
to a neighbour's close by, and sitting quietly at home all
the rest of his time.   One day the said neighbour called,
and asked him in joke if he wasn't afraid of devil-foxes, so
much alone as he was.   " Oh," replied Sang, laughing,
" what has the superior man [1] to fear from devil-foxes ?
If they come as men, I have here a sharp sword for them ;
and if as women, why, I shall open the door and ask them
to walk in."   The neighbour went away, and having
arranged with a friend of his, they got a young lady of
their acquaintance to climb over Sang's wall with the help
of a ladder, and knock at the door.   Sang peeped through,
and called out, " Who's there ? " to which the girl answered,
" A devil ! " and frightened Sang so dreadfully that his
teeth chattered in his head.   The girl then ran away, and
next morning when his neighbour came to see him, Sang
told him what had happened, and said he meant to go
back to his native place.   The neighbour then clapped
his hands, and said to Sang, " Why didn't you ask her

[1] The term constantly employed by Confucius to denote the ma
of perfect probity, learning, and refinement.   The nearest, if not a
exact, translation would be " gentleman."

in ? " Whereupon Sang perceived that he had been tricked, and went on quietly again as before.

Some six months afterwards, a young lady knocked at his door ; and Sang, thinking his friends were at their old tricks, opened it at once, and asked her to walk in. She did so ; and he beheld to his astonishment a perfect Helen for beauty.[2] Asking her whence she came, she replied that her name was Lien-hsiang, and that she lived not very far off, adding that she had long been anxious to make his acquaintance. After that she used to drop in every now and again for a chat ; but one evening when Sang was sitting alone expecting her, another young lady suddenly walked in. Thinking it was Lien-hsiang, Sang got up to meet her, but found that the new-comer was somebody else. She was about fifteen or sixteen years of age, wore very full sleeves, and dressed her hair after the fashion of unmarried girls, being otherwise very stylish-looking and refined, and apparently hesitating whether to go on or go back. Sang, in a great state of alarm, took her for a fox ; but the young lady said, " My name is Li, and I am of a respectable family. Hearing of your virtue and talent, I hope to be accorded the honour of your acquaintance." Sang laughed, and took her by the hand, which he found was as cold as ice ; and when he asked the reason, she told him that she had always been delicate, and that it was very chilly outside. She then remarked that she intended to visit him pretty frequently, and hoped it would not inconvenience him ; so he explained that no one came to see him except another young lady, and that not very often. " When she comes, I'll go," replied the young lady, " and only drop in when she's not here." She then gave him an embroidered slipper, saying that she had worn it, and that whenever he shook it she would know that he wanted to see her, cautioning him at the same time never to shake it before strangers. Taking it in his hand he beheld a very tiny little shoe almost as fine-pointed as an awl, with which he was much pleased ; and next evening, when nobody was present, he produced the shoe and shook it, whereupon the young lady im-

[2] Literally, " a young lady whose beauty would overthrow a kingdom," in allusion to an old story which it is not necessary to reproduce here.

mediately walked in. Henceforth, whenever he brought
it out, the young lady responded to his wishes and appeared
before him. This seemed so strange that at last he asked
her to give him some explanation ; but she only laughed,
and said it was mere coincidence. One evening after this
Lien-hsiang came, and said in alarm to Sang, " Whatever
has made you look so melancholy ? " Sang replied that
he did not know, and by-and-by she took her leave, saying
they would not meet again for some ten days. During
this period Miss Li visited Sang every day, and on one
occasion asked him where his other friend was. Sang told
her ; and then she laughed and said, " What is your opinion
of me as compared with Lien-hsiang ? " " You are both
of you perfection," replied he, " but you are a little *colder*
of the two." Miss Li didn't much like this, and cried out,
" *Both of us perfection* is what you say to *me*. Then she must
be a downright Cynthia,[3] and I am no match for her."
Somewhat out of temper, she reckoned that Lien-hsiang's
ten days had expired, and said she would have a peep at
her, making Sang promise to keep it all secret. The next
evening Lien-hsiang came, and while they were talking she
suddenly exclaimed, " Oh, dear ! how much worse you seem
to have become in the last ten days. You must have encountered something bad." Sang asked her why so ; to which
she answered, " First of all your appearance ; and then your
pulse is very thready.[4] You've got the devil-disease."

The following evening when Miss Li came, Sang asked
her what she thought of Lien-hsiang, " Oh," said she,
" there's no question about her beauty ; but she's a fox.
When she went away I followed her to her hole on the
hill-side." Sang, however, attributed this remark to
jealousy, and took no notice of it ; but the next evening
when Lien-hsiang came, he observed, " I don't believe it
myself, but some one has told me you are a fox." Lien-
hsiang asked who had said so, to which Sang replied that
he was only joking ; and then she begged him to explain
what difference there was between a fox and an ordinary
person. " Well," answered Sang, " foxes frighten people
to death, and, therefore, they are very much dreaded."
" Don't you believe that ! " cried Lien-hsiang ; " and
now tell me who has been saying this of me." Sang

[3] The Lady of the Moon. See No. V., note 2.   [4] See No. VIII., note 4.

declared at first that it was only a joke of his, but by-and-by yielded to her instances, and let out the whole story. "Of course I saw how changed you were," said Lien-hsiang; "she is surely not a human being to be able to cause such a rapid alteration in you. Say nothing; to-morrow I'll watch her as she watched me." The following evening Miss Li came in; and they had hardly interchanged half a dozen sentences when a cough was heard outside the window, and Miss Li ran away. Lien-hsiang then entered and said to Sang, "You are lost! She is a devil, and if you do not at once forbid her coming here, you will soon be on the road to the other world." "All jealousy," thought Sang, saying nothing, as Lien-hsiang continued, "I know that you don't like to be rude to her; but I, for my part, cannot see you sacrificed, and to-morrow I will bring you some medicine to expel the poison from your system. Happily, the disease has not yet taken firm hold of you, and in ten days you will be well again." The next evening she produced a knife and chopped up some medicine for Sang, which made him feel much better; but, although he was very grateful to her, he still persisted in disbelieving that he had the devil-disease After some days he recovered and Lien-hsiang left him, warning him to have no more to do with Miss Li. Sang pretended that he would follow her advice, and closed the door and trimmed his lamp. He then took out the slipper, and on shaking it Miss Li appeared, somewhat cross at having been kept away for several days. "She merely attended on me these few nights while I was ill," said Sang; "don't be angry." At this Miss Li brightened up a little; but by-and-by Sang told her that people said she was a devil. "It's that nasty fox," cried Miss Li, after a pause, "putting these things into your head. If you don't break with her, I won't come here again." She then began to sob and cry, and Sang had some trouble in pacifying her. Next evening Lien-hsiang came and found out that Miss Li had been there again; whereupon she was very angry with Sang, and told him he would certainly die. "Why need you be so jealous?" said Sang, laughing; at which she only got more enraged, and replied, "When you were nearly dying the other day and I saved you, if I had not been jealous, where would

you have been now?" Sang pretended he was only
joking, and said that Miss Li had told him his recent illness was entirely owing to the machinations of a fox;
to which she replied, "It's true enough what you say,
only you don't see *whose* machinations, However, if
anything happens to you, I should never clear myself
even had I a hundred mouths; we will, therefore, part.
A hundred days hence I shall see you on your bed." Sang
could not persuade her to stay, and away she went; and
from that time Miss Li became a regular visitor.

Two months passed away, and Sang began to experience
a feeling of great lassitude, which he tried at first to shake
off, but by-and-by he became very thin, and could only
take thick gruel. He then thought about going back to
his native place; however, he could not bear to leave
Miss Li, and in a few more days he was so weak that he
was unable to get up. His friend next door, seeing how
ill he was, daily sent in his boy with food and drink; and
now Sang began for the first time to suspect Miss Li. So
he said to her, "I am sorry I didn't listen to Lien-hsiang
before I got as bad as this." He then closed his eyes and
kept them shut for some time; and when he opened them
again Miss Li had disappeared. Their acquaintanceship
was thus at an end, and Sang lay all emaciated as he was
upon his bed in his solitary room longing for the return of
Lien-hsiang. One day, while he was still thinking about
her, some one drew aside the screen and walked in. It
was Lien-hsiang; and approaching the bed she said with
a smile, "Was I then talking such nonsense?" Sang
struggled a long time to speak; and, at length, confessing
he had been wrong, implored her to save him. "When
the disease has reached such a pitch as this," replied Lien-
hsiang, "there is very little to be done. I merely came
to bid you farewell, and to clear up your doubts about my
jealousy." In great tribulation, Sang asked her to take
something she would find under his pillow and destroy it;
and she accordingly drew forth the slipper, which she
proceeded to examine by the light of the lamp, turning it
over and over. All at once Miss Li walked in, but when
she saw Lien-hsiang she turned back as though she would
run away, which Lien-hsiang instantly prevented by
placing herself in the doorway. Sang then began to

reproach her, and Miss Li could make no reply ; whereupon
Lien-hsiang said, " At last we meet.   Formerly you attributed this gentleman's illness to me ; what have you to
say now ? "   Miss Li bent her head in acknowledgment
of her guilt, and Lien-hsiang continued, " How is it that
a nice girl like you can thus turn love into hate ? "   Here
Miss Li threw herself on the ground in a flood of tears and
begged for mercy ; and Lien-hsiang, raising her up, inquired of her as to her past life.   " I am a daughter of a
petty official named Li, and I died young, leaving the web
of my destiny incomplete, like the silkworm that perishes
in the spring.   To be the partner of this gentleman was
my ardent wish ; but I had never any intention of causing
his death."   " I have heard," remarked Lien-hsiang,
" that the advantage devils obtain by killing people is
that their victims are ever with them after death.   Is
this so ? "   " It is not," replied Miss Li ; " the companionship of two devils gives no pleasure to either.   Were it
otherwise, I should not have wanted for friends in the
realms below.   But tell me, how do foxes manage not to
kill people."   " You allude to such foxes as suck the
breath out of people ? " replied Lien-hsiang ; " I am not
of that class.   Some foxes are harmless ; no devils are,[5]
because of the dominance of the *yin* [6] in their compositions."
Sang now knew that these two girls were really a fox and
a devil ; however, from being long accustomed to their
society, he was not in the least alarmed.   His breathing
had dwindled to a mere thread, and at length he uttered
a cry of pain.   Lien-hsiang looked round and said, " How
shall we cure him ? " upon which Miss Li blushed deeply
and drew back ; and then Lien-hsiang added, " If he
does get well, I'm afraid you will be dreadfully jealous."
Miss Li drew herself up, and replied, " Could a physician
be found to wipe away the wrong I have done to this
gentleman, I would bury my head in the ground.   How

[5] Miss Lien-hsiang was here speaking without book, as will be
seen in a story later on.
[6] The female principle.   In a properly-constituted human being
the male and female principles are harmoniously combined.   Nothing
short of a small volume would place this subject, the basis of Chinese
metaphysics, in a clear light before the uninitiated reader.   Broadly
speaking, the *yin* and the *yang* are the two primeval forces from
the interaction of which all things have been evolved.

should I look the world in the face?" Lien-hsiang here
opened a bag and drew forth some drugs, saying, "I have
been looking forward to this day. When I left this gentleman I proceeded to gather my simples, as it would take
three months for the medicine to be got ready; but then,
should the poison have brought anyone even to death's
door, this medicine is able to call him back. The only
condition is that it be administered by the very hand
which wrought the ill." Miss Li did as she was told, and
put the pills Lien-hsiang gave her one after another into
Sang's mouth. They burnt his inside like fire; but soon
vitality began to return, and Lien-hsiang cried out, "He
is cured!" Just at this moment Miss Li heard the cock
crow and vanished,[7] Lien-hsiang remaining behind in
attendance on the invalid, who was unable to feed himself.
She bolted the outside door and pretended that Sang had
returned to his native place, so as to prevent visitors from
calling. Day and night she took care of him, and every
evening Miss Li came in to render assistance, regarding
Lien-hsiang as an elder sister, and being treated by her
with great consideration and kindness. Three months
afterwards Sang was as strong and well as ever he had
been, and then for several evenings Miss Li ceased to
visit them, only staying a few moments when she did
come, and seeming very uneasy in her mind. One evening
Sang ran after her and carried her back in his arms, finding
her no heavier than so much straw; and then, being
obliged to stay, she curled herself up and lay down, to all
appearance in a state of unconsciousness, and by-and-by
she was gone. For many days they heard nothing of her,
and Sang was so anxious that she should come back that
he often took out her slipper and shook it. "I don't wonder
at your missing her," said Lien-hsiang, "I do myself very
much indeed." "Formerly," observed Sang, "when I

---

[7] *Ber.*—It was about to speak, when the cock crew.
Hor.—And then it started like a guilty thing
    Upon a fearful summons. I have heard,
    The cock, that is the trumpet to the morn,
    Doth with his lofty and shrill-sounding throat
    Awake the God of Day; and, at his warning,
    Whether in sea or fire, in earth or air,
    The extravagant and erring spirit hies
    To his confine.   *Hamlet.*

shook the slipper she invariably came. I thought it was very
strange, but I never suspected her of being a devil. And
now, alas ! all I can do is to sit and think about her with
this slipper in my hand." He then burst into a flood of tears.

Now a young lady named Yen-êrh, belonging to the
wealthy Chang family, and about fifteen years of age, had
died suddenly, without any apparent cause, and had come
to life again in the night, when she got up and wished
to go out. They barred the door and would not hear of
her doing so ; upon which she said, " I am the spirit
daughter of a petty magistrate. A Mr. Sang has been
very kind to me, and I have left my slipper at his house.
I am really a spirit ; what is the use of keeping me in ? "
There being some reason for what she said, they asked
her why she had come there ; but she only looked up
and down without being able to give any explanation.
Some one here observed, that Mr. Sang had already gone
home, but the young lady utterly refused to believe them.
The family was much disturbed at all this ; and when
Sang's neighbour heard the story, he jumped over the wall,
and peeping through beheld Sang sitting there chatting
with a pretty-looking girl. As he went in, there was some
commotion, during which Sang's visitor had disappeared,
and when his neighbour asked the meaning of it all, Sang
replied laughing, " Why, I told you if any ladies came I
should ask them in." His friend then repeated what
Miss Yen-êrh had said ; and Sang, unbolting his door,
was about to go and have a peep at her, but unfortunately
had no means of so doing. Meanwhile Mrs. Chang, hearing
that he had not gone away, was more lost in astonishment
than ever, and sent an old woman-servant to get back the
slipper. Sang immediately gave it to her, and Miss Yen-êrh
was delighted to recover it, though when she came to try
it on it was too small for her by a good inch. In considerable alarm, she seized a mirror to look at herself ;
and suddenly became aware that she had come to life
again in some one else's body. She therefore told all
to her mother, and finally succeeded in convincing her,
crying all the time because she was so changed for the
worse as regarded personal appearance from what she
had been before. And whenever she happened to see
Lien-hsiang, she was very much disconcerted, declaring

that she had been much better off as a devil than now as a human being. She would sit and weep over the slipper, no one being able to comfort her ; and finally, covering herself up with bed-clothes, she lay all stark and stiff, positively refusing to take any nourishment. Her body swelled up, and for seven days she refused all food, but did not die ; and then the swelling began to subside, and an intense hunger to come upon her which made her once more think about eating. Then she was troubled with a severe irritation, and her skin peeled entirely away ; and when she got up in the morning, she found that her shoes had fallen off. On trying to put them on again, she discovered that they did not fit her any longer ; and then she went back to her former pair, which were now exactly of the right size and shape. In an ecstasy of joy, she grasped her mirror, and saw that her features had also changed back to what they had formerly been ; so she washed and dressed herself and went in to visit her mother. Every one who met her was much astonished ; and when Lien-hsiang heard the strange story, she tried to persuade Mr. Sang to make her an offer of marriage. But the young lady was rich and Sang was poor, and he did not see his way clearly. However, on Mrs. Chang's birthday, when she completed her cycle,[8] Sang went along with the others to wish her many happy returns of the day ; and when the old lady knew who was coming, she bade Yen-êrh take a peep at him from behind the curtain. Sang arrived last of all ; and immediately out rushed Miss Yen-êrh and seized his sleeve, and said she would go back with him. Her mother scolded her well for this, and she ran in abashed ; but Sang, who had looked at her closely, began to weep, and threw himself at the feet of Mrs. Chang, who raised him up without saying anything unkind. Sang then took his leave, and got his uncle to act as medium between them ; the result being that an auspicious day was fixed upon for the wedding. At the appointed time Sang pro-

---

[8] The Chinese cycle is sixty years, and the birthday on which any person completes his cycle is considered a very auspicious occasion. The second emperor of the present dynasty, K'ang Hsi, completed a cycle in his *reign*, with one year to spare ; and his grandson, Ch'ien Lung (or Kien Lung) fell short of this only by a single year, dying in the same cyclical period as that in which he had ascended the throne.

ceeded to the house to fetch her ; and when he returned he found that, instead of his former poor-looking furniture, beautiful carpets were laid down from the very door, and thousands of coloured lanterns were hung about in elegant designs. Lien-hsiang assisted the bride to enter, and took off her veil, finding her the same bright girl as ever. She also joined them while drinking the wedding cup,[9] and inquired of her friend as to her recent transmigration ; and Yen-êrh related as follows :—" Overwhelmed with grief, I began to shrink from myself as some unclean thing ; and, after separating from you that day, I would not return any more to my grave. So I wandered about at random, and whenever I saw a living being, I envied its happy state. By day I remained among trees and shrubs, but at night I used to roam about anywhere. And once I came to the house of the Chang family, where, seeing a young girl lying upon the bed, I took possession of her mortal coil, unknowing that she would be restored to life again." When Lien-hsiang heard this she was for some time lost in thought ; and a month or two afterwards became very ill. She refused all medical aid and gradually got worse and worse, to the great grief of Mr. Sang and his wife, who stood weeping at her bedside. Suddenly she opened her eyes, and said, " You wish to live ; I am willing to die. If fate so ordains it, we shall meet again ten years hence." As she uttered these words, her spirit passed away, and all that remained was the dead body of a fox. Sang, however, insisted on burying it with all the proper ceremonies.

Now his wife had no children ; but one day a servant came in and said, " There is an old woman outside who has got a little girl for sale." Sang's wife gave orders that she should be shown in ; and no sooner had she set eyes on the girl than she cried out, " Why, she's the image of Lien-hsiang ! " Sang then looked at her, and found to his astonishment that she was really very like his old friend. The old woman said she was fourteen years old ;

[9] Bride and bridegroom drink wine together out of two cups joined by a red string, typical of that imaginary bond which is believed to unite the destinies of husband and wife long before they have set eyes on each other. Popular tradition assigns to an old man who lives in the moon the arrangement of all matches among mortals ; hence the common Chinese expression, " Marriages are made in the moon."

and when asked what her price was, declared that her
only wish was to get the girl comfortably settled, and
enough to keep herself alive, and ensure not being thrown
out into the kennel at death. So Sang gave a good price
for her ; [10] and his wife, taking the girl's hand, led her
into a room by themselves. Then, chucking her under the
chin, she asked her, smiling, " Do you know me ? " The
girl said she did not ; after which she told Mrs. Sang that
her name was Wei, and that her father, who had been
a pickle-merchant at Hsü-ch'êng, had died three years
before. Mrs. Sang then calculated that Lien-hsiang had
been dead just fourteen years ; and, looking at the girl,
who resembled her so exactly in every trait, at length
patted her on the head, saying, " Ah, my sister, you
promised to visit us again in ten years, and you have not
played us false." The girl here seemed to wake up as if
from a dream, and, uttering an exclamation of surprise,
fixed a steady gaze upon Sang's wife. Sang himself laughed,
and said, " Just like the return of an old familiar swallow."
" Now I understand," cried the girl, in tears ; " I recollect
my mother saying that when I was born I was able to
speak ; and that, thinking it an inauspicious manifestation,
they gave me dog's blood to drink, so that I should forget
all about my previous state of existence.[11] Is it all a
dream, or are you not the Miss Li who was so ashamed
of being a devil ? " Thus they chatted of their existence
in a former life, with alternate tears and smiles ; but when

[10] The bill of sale always handed to the purchaser of a child in
China, as a proof that the child is his *bonâ fide* property and has
not been kidnapped, is by a pleasant fiction called a " deed of gift,"
the amount paid over to the seller being therein denominated
" ginger and vinegar money," or compensation for the expense of
rearing and educating up to the date of sale. This phrase originates
from the fact that a dose of ginger and vinegar is administered to
every Chinese woman immediately after the delivery of her child.
We may here add that the value of male children to those who
have no heirs, and of female children to those who want servants,
has fostered a regular kidnapping trade, which is carried on with
great activity in some parts of China, albeit the penalty on discovery is instant decapitation. Some years ago I was present in
the streets of Tientsin when a kidnapper was seized by the infuriated mob, and within two hours I heard that the man had been
summarily executed.

[11] The power of recalling events which have occurred in a previous
life.will be enlarged upon in several stories to come.

it came to the day for worshipping at the tombs, Yen-êrh explained that she and her husband were in the habit of annually visiting and mourning over her grave. The girl replied that she would accompany them ; and when they got there they found the whole place in disorder, and the coffin wood all warped. " Lien-hsiang and I," said Yen-êrh to her husband, " have been attached to each other in two states of existence. Let us not be separated, but bury my bones here with hers." Sang consented, and opening Miss Li's tomb took out the bones and buried them with those of Lien-hsiang, while friends and relatives, who had heard the strange story, gathered round the grave in gala dress to the number of many hundreds.

I learnt the above when travelling through I-chou, where I was detained at an inn by rain, and read a biography of Mr Sang written by a comrade of his named Wang Tzŭ-chang. It was lent me by a Mr. Liu Tzŭ-ching, a relative of Sang's, and was quite a long account. This is merely an outline of it.

XXIV. MISS A-PAO ; OR, PERSEVERANCE REWARDED

IN the province of Kuang-si there lived a scholar of some reputation, named Sun Tzŭ-ch'u. He was born with six fingers, and such a simple fellow was he that he readily believed any nonsense he was told. Very shy with the fair sex, the sight of a woman was enough to send him flying in the opposite direction ; and once when he was inveigled into a room where there were some young ladies, he blushed down to his neck and the perspiration dripped off him like falling pearls. His companions laughed heartily at his discomfiture, and told fine stories of what a noodle he looked, so that he got the nickname of Silly Sun.

In the town where our hero resided, there was a rich trader whose wealth equalled that of any prince or noble-man, and whose connections were all highly aristocratic.[1]

---

[1] There is nothing in China like an aristocracy of birth. Any man may raise himself from the lowest level to the highest ; and as long as he and his family keep themselves there, they may be considered aristocratic. Wealth has nothing to do with the question ; official rank and literary tastes, separate or combined, these con-

He had a daughter, A-pao, of great beauty, for whom he was seeking a husband ; and the young men of position in the neighbourhood were vieing with each other to obtain her hand, but none of them met with the father's approval. Now Silly Sun had recently lost his wife ; and some one in joke persuaded him to try his luck and send in an application. Sun, who had no idea of his own shortcomings, proceeded at once to follow this advice ; but the father, though he knew him to be an accomplished scholar, rejected his suit on the ground of poverty. As the go-between [2] was leaving the house, she chanced to meet A-pao, and related to her the object of her visit. " Tell him," cried A-pao, laughing, " that if he'll cut off his extra finger, I'll marry him." The old woman reported this to Sun, who replied, " That is not very difficult ; " and, seizing a chopper, cut the finger clean off. The wound was extremely painful, and he lost so much blood that he nearly died, it being many days before he was about again. He then sought out the go-between and bade her inform Miss A-pao, which she did ; and A-pao was taken rather aback, but she told the old woman to go once more and bid him cut off the " silly " from his reputation. Sun got much excited when he heard this, and denied that he was silly ; however, as he was unable to prove it to the young lady herself, he began to think that probably her beauty was over-stated, and that she was giving herself great airs. So he ceased to trouble himself about her until the following spring festival,[3] when it was customary for both men and women to be seen abroad, and the young rips of the place would stroll about in groups and pass their remarks on all and sundry. Sun's friends urged him to join them in their expedition, and one of them asked him with a smile if he did not wish to look out for a suitable mate. Sun knew they were chaffing him, but he thought he

stitute a man's title to the esteem of his fellows. Trade is looked upon as ignoble and debasing ; and friendly intercourse between merchants and officials, the two great social divisions, is so rare as to be almost unknown.

[2] The medium, without whose good offices no marriage can be arranged. Generally, but not always, a woman.

This system of go-betweens is not confined to matrimonial engagements. No servant ever offers himself for a place ; he invariably employs some one to introduce him. So also in mercantile transactions the broker almost invariably appears upon the scene.

[3] See No. II., note 1.

should like to see the girl that had made such a fool of
him, and was only too pleased to accompany them. They
soon perceived a young lady resting herself under a tree,
with a throng of young fellows crowding round her, and
they immediately determined that she must be A-pao,
as in fact they found she was. Possessed of peerless
beauty, the ring of her admirers gradually increased,
till at last she rose up to go. The excitement among the
young men was intense ; they criticised her face and
discussed her feet,[4] Sun only remaining silent ; and when
they had passed on to something else, there they saw
Sun rooted like an imbecile to the same spot. As he made
no answer when spoken to, they dragged him along with
them, saying, " Has your spirit run away after A-pao ? "
He made no reply to this either ; but they thought nothing
of that, knowing his usual strangeness of manner, so
by dint of pushing and pulling they managed to get him
home. There he threw himself on the bed and did not
get up again for the rest of the day, lying in a state of
unconsciousness just as if he were drunk. He did not
wake when called ; and his people, thinking that his spirit
had fled, went about in the fields calling out to it to return.[5]
However, he showed no signs of improvement ; and when
they shook him, and asked him what was the matter,
he only answered in a sleepy kind of voice, " I am at
A-pao's house ; " but to further questions he would not
make any reply, and left his family in a state of keen
suspense.

Now when Silly Sun had seen the young lady get up to
go, he could not bear to part with her, and found himself
first following and then walking along by her side without
anyone saying anything to him. Thus he went back
with her to her home, and there he remained for three days,
longing to run home and get something to eat, but unfortunately not knowing the way. By that time Sun had

[4] The so-called " golden lilies " always come in for a large share
of criticism. See No. XII., note 1. This term originated with an
emperor who reigned in the fifth century, when, in ecstasies at the
graceful dancing of a concubine upon a stage ornamented with
lilies, he cried out, " Every footstep makes a lily grow."

[5] A common custom ; e.g. in the case of a little child lying dangerously ill, its mother will go outside the door into the garden or
field, and call out its name several times, in the hope of bringing
back the wandering spirit.

hardly a breath left in him ; and his friends, fearing that he was going to die, sent to beg of the rich trader that he would allow a search to be made for Sun's spirit in his house. The trader laughed and said, " He wasn't in the habit of coming here, so he could hardly have left his spirit behind him ; " but he yielded to the entreaties of Sun's family, and permitted the search to be made. Thereupon a magician proceeded to the house, taking with him an old suit of Sun's clothes and some grass matting ; and when Miss A-pao heard the reason for which he had come, she simplified matters very much by leading the magician straight to her own room. The magician summoned the spirit in due form, and went back towards Sun's house. By the time he had reached the door, Sun groaned and recovered consciousness ; and he was then able to describe all the articles of toilette and furniture in A-pao's room without making a single mistake. A-pao was amazed when the story was repeated to her, and could not help feeling kindly towards him on account of the depth of his passion. Sun himself, when he got well enough to leave his bed, would often sit in a state of abstraction as if he had lost his wits ; and he was for ever scheming to try and have another glimpse at A-pao.

One day he heard that she intended to worship at the Shui-yüeh temple on the 8th of the fourth moon, that day being the Wash-Buddha festival ; and he set off early in the morning to wait for her at the roadside. He was nearly blind with straining his eyes, and the sun was already past noontide before the young lady arrived ; but when she saw from her carriage a gentleman standing there, she drew aside the screen and had a good stare at him. Sun followed her in a great state of excitement, upon which she bade one of her maids to go and ask his name. Sun told her who he was, his perturbation all the time increasing ; and when the carriage drove on he returned home. Again he became very ill, and lay on his bed unconscious, without taking any food, occasionally calling on A-pao by name, at the same time abusing his spirit for not having been able to follow her as before. Just at this juncture a parrot that had been long with the family died ; and a child, playing with the body, laid it upon the bed. Sun then reflected that if he was only a parrot one flap of

his wings would bring him into the presence of A-pao ;
and while occupied with these thoughts, lo ! the dead
body moved and the parrot flew away. It flew straight
to A-pao's room, at which she was delighted ; and catching
it, tied a string to its leg, and fed it upon hemp-seed. "Dear
sister," cried the bird, " do not tie me by the leg : I am
Sun Tzŭ-ch'u." In great alarm A-pao untied the string,
but the parrot did not fly away. " Alas ! " said she, " your
love has engraved itself upon my heart ; but now you are
no longer a man, how shall we ever be united together ? "
" To be near your dear self," replied the parrot, " is all I
care about." The parrot then refused to take food from
anyone else, and kept close to Miss A-pao wherever she
went, day and night alike. At the expiration of three
days, A-pao, who had grown very fond of her parrot,
secretly sent some one to ask how Mr. Sun was ; but he
had already been dead three days, though the part over
his heart had not grown cold. " Oh ! come to life again as a
man," cried the young lady, " and I swear to be yours
for ever." " You are surely not in earnest," said the
parrot, " are you ? " Miss A-pao declared she was, and
the parrot, cocking its head aside, remained some time as
if absorbed in thought. By-and-by A-pao took off her
shoes to bind her feet a little tighter ; [6] and the parrot,
making a rapid grab at one, flew off with it in its beak.
She called loudly after it to come back, but in a moment
it was out of sight ; so she next sent a servant to inquire
if there was any news of Mr. Sun, and then learnt that he
had come round again, the parrot having flown in with
an embroidered shoe and dropped down dead on the ground.
Also, that directly he regained consciousness he asked for
the shoe, of which his people knew nothing ; at which
moment her servant had arrived, and demanded to know
from him where it was. " It was given to me by Miss
A-pao as a pledge of faith," replied Sun ; " I beg you will
tell her I have not forgotten her promise." A-pao was
greatly astonished at this, and instructed her maid to
divulge the whole affair to her mother, who, when she had
made some inquiries, observed that Sun was well known

---

[6] This process must be regularly gone through night and morning,
otherwise the bandages become loose, and the gait of the walker
unsteady.

as a clever fellow, but was desperately poor, " and to get such a son-in-law after all our trouble would give our aristocratic friends the laugh against us." [7] However, A-pao pleaded that with the shoe there as a proof against her, she would not marry anybody else ; and, ultimately, her father and mother gave their consent. This was immediately announced to Mr. Sun, whose illness rapidly disappeared in consequence. A-pao's father would have had Sun come and live with them ; [8] but the young lady objected, on the score that a son-in-law should not remain long at a time with the family of his wife,[9] and that as he was poor he would lower himself still more by doing so. " I have accepted him," added she, " and I shall gladly reside in his humble cottage, and share his poor fare without complaint." The marriage was then celebrated, and bride and bridegroom met as if for the first time in their lives.[10] The dowry A-pao brought with her somewhat raised their pecuniary position, and gave them a certain amount of comfort ; but Sun himself stuck only to his books, and knew nothing about managing affairs in general. Luckily his wife was clever in that respect, and did not bother him with such things ; so much so that by the end of three years they were comparatively well off, when Sun suddenly fell ill and died. Mrs. Sun was inconsolable, and refused either to sleep or take nourishment, being deaf to all entreaties on the subject ; and before long, taking advantage of the night, she hanged herself.[11] Her maid, hearing a noise, ran in and cut her down just in time :

[7] I have explained before that any great disparity of means is considered an obstacle to a matrimonial alliance between two families.

[8] This is a not unusual arrangement in cases where there are other sons in the bridegroom's family, but none in that of the bride's, especially if the advantage of wealth is on the side of the latter.

[9] Such is the Chinese rule, adopted simply with a view to the preservation of harmony.

[10] They are supposed never to see each other before the wedding-day ; but, after careful investigation of the subject, I have come to the conclusion that certainly in seven cases out of ten, the intended bridegroom secretly procures a sight of his future wife. I am now speaking of the higher classes ; among the poor, both sexes mix almost as freely as with us.

[11] This would still be considered a creditable act on the part of a Chinese widow. It is, however, of exceedingly rare occurrence.

but she still steadily refused all food.   Three days passed away, and the friends and relatives of Sun came to attend his funeral, when suddenly they heard a sigh proceeding forth from the coffin.   The coffin was then opened and they found that Sun had come to life again.   He told them that he had been before the Great Judge, who, as a reward for his upright and honourable life, had conferred upon him an official appointment.   " At this moment," said Sun, " it was reported that my wife was close at hand,[12] but the Judge, referring to the register, observed that her time had not yet come.   They told him she had taken no food for three days ; and then the Judge, looking at me, said that as a recompense for her wifely virtues I should be permitted to return to life.   Thereupon he gave orders to his attendants to put to the horses and see me safely back."   From that hour Sun gradually improved, and the next year went up for his Master's degree.   All his old companions chaffed him exceedingly before the examination, and gave him seven themes on out-of-the-way subjects, telling him privately that they had been surreptitiously obtained from the examiners.   Sun believed them as usual, and worked at them day and night until he was perfect, his comrades all the time enjoying a good laugh against him.   However, when the day came it was found that the examiners, fearing lest the themes they had chosen in an ordinary way should have been dishonestly made public,[13] took a set of fresh ones quite out of the common run—in fact, on the very subjects Sun's companions had given to him.   Consequently, he came out at the head of the list ; and the next year, after taking his Doctor's degree, he was entered among the Han-lin Academicians.[14]   The Emperor, too, happening to hear of his curious adventures, sent for him and made him repeat his story ; subsequently summoning A-pao and making her some very costly presents.

[12] Being nearly dead from hanging.

[13] This is occasionally done, great influence or a heavy bribe being brought to bear upon the Examiners, of whom there are only two for the Master's degree, and the second of these, or Assistant-Examiner, holds but a subordinate position.   See No. LXXV., note 1.

[14] Admission to the Han-lin College is the highest literary honour obtainable by a scholar.   Its members are employed in drawing up Government documents, histories, &c.

XXV. JEN HSIU

JEN CHIEN-CHIH was a native of Yü-t'ai, and a dealer in rugs and furs. One day he set off for Shensi, taking with him every penny he could scrape together ; and on the road he met a man who told him that his name was Shên Chu-t'ing, and his native place Su-ch'ien. These two soon became firm friends, and entered into a masonic bond [1] with each other, journeying on together by the same stages until they reached their destination. By-and-by Mr. Jen fell sick, and his companion had to nurse him, which he did with the utmost attention, but for ten days he gradually got worse and worse, and at length said to Shên, " My family is very poor. Eight mouths depend upon my exertions for food ; and now, alas ! I am about to die, far from my own home. You and I are brothers. At this distance there is no one else to whom I can look. Now in my purse you will find two hundred ounces of silver. Take half, and when you have defrayed my funeral expenses, use the balance for your return journey ; and give the other half to my family, that they may be able to send for my coffin.[2] If, however, you will take my mortal

---

[1] Besides the numerous secret societies so much dreaded by the Government, membership of which is punishable by death, very intimate friends are in the habit of adopting each other as sworn brothers, bound to stand by one another in cases of danger and difficulty, to the last drop of blood. The bond is cemented by an oath, accompanied by such ceremonies as fancy may at the moment dictate. The most curious of all, however, are the so-called " Golden Orchid " societies, the members of which are young girls, who have sworn never to enter into the matrimonial state. To such an extent have these sisterhoods spread in the Kuang-tung Province, that the authorities have been compelled to prohibit them under severe penalties.

[2] A Chinaman loves to be buried alongside of his ancestors, and poor families are often put to great straits to pay this last tribute of respect and affection to the deceased. At all large cities are to be found temporary burial grounds, where the bodies of strangers are deposited until their relatives can come to carry them away. Large freights of dead bodies are annually brought back to China from California, Queensland, and other parts to which the Chinese are in the habit of emigrating, to the great profit of the steamer companies concerned. Coffins are also used as a means of smuggling, respect for the dead being so great that they are only opened under the very strongest suspicion.

remains with you home to my native place, these expenses
need not be incurred." He then, with the aid of a pillow,
wrote a letter, which he handed to Shên, and that evening
he died. Thereupon Shên purchased a cheap coffin [3]
for some five or six ounces of silver ; and, as the landlord
kept urging him to take away the body, he said he would
go out and seek for a temple where it might be temporarily
deposited. But he ran away and never went back to the
inn ; and it was more than a year before Jen's family
knew what had taken place. His son was just about
seventeen years of age, and had recently been reading
with a tutor ; but now his books were laid aside, and he
proposed to go in search of his father's body. His mother
said he was too young ; and it was only when he declared
he would rather not live than stay at home, that with the
aid of the pawn-shop [4] enough money was raised to start
him on his way. An old servant accompanied him, and
it was six months before they returned and performed the
last ceremonies over Jen's remains. The family was thus
reduced to absolute destitution ; but happily young Hsiu
was a clever fellow, and when the days of mourning [5] were
over, took his Bachelor's degree. On the other hand, he
was somewhat wild and very fond of gambling ; and
although his mother strictly prohibited such diversions,

[3] See No. XIV., note 12. The price of an elaborate Chinese
coffin goes as high as £100 or £150.
[4] The never-failing resource of an impecunious Chinaman who
has any property whatever bearing an exchange value. The pawn-
shop proper is a licensed institution, where three per cent *per month*
is charged on all loans, all pledges being redeemable within sixteen
months. It is generally a very high brick structure, towering far
above the surrounding houses, with the deposits neatly packed up in
paper and arranged on the shelves of a huge wooden skeleton-like
frame, that completely fills the interior of the building, on the top
of which are ranged buckets of water in case of fire, and a quantity
of huge stones to throw down on any thieves who may be daring
enough to attempt to scale the wall. (In Peking, houses are not
allowed to be built above a certain height, as during the long
summer months ladies are in the habit of sitting to spin or sew in
their courtyards, very lightly clad.) Pawning goods in China is
not held to be so disgraceful as with us ; in fact, most people, at
the beginning of the hot weather, pawn their furs and winter
clothes, these being so much more carefully looked after there than
they might be at home.
[5] Nominally of three years'—really of twenty-eight months'—
duration.

all her prohibitions were in vain. By-and-by the Grand Examiner arrived, and Hsiu came out in the fourth class. His mother was extremely angry, and refused to take food, which brought young Hsiu to his senses, and he promised her faithfully he would never gamble again. From that day he shut himself up, and the following year took a first-class degree, coming out among the "senior" graduates.[6] His mother now advised him to take pupils, but his reputation as a disorderly fellow stuck to him, and no one would entrust their sons to his care.

Just then an uncle of his, named Chang, was about to start with merchandise for the capital, and recommended that Hsiu should go along with him, promising himself to pay all expenses, an offer which Hsiu was only too pleased to accept. When they reached Lin-ch'ing, they anchored outside the Custom House, where they found a great number of salt-junks, in fact a perfect forest of masts; and what with the noise of the water and the people it was quite impossible to sleep. Besides, as the row was beginning to subside, the clear rattle of dice from a neighbouring boat fell upon Hsiu's ear, and before long he was itching to be back again at his old games. Listening to hear if all around him were sound asleep, he drew forth a string of cash that he had brought with him, and thought he would just go across and try his luck. So he got up quietly with his money, and was on the point of going, when he suddenly recollected his mother's injunctions, and at once tying his purse-strings laid himself down to sleep. He was far too excited, however, to close his eyes; and after a while got up again and re-opened his purse. This he did three times, until at last it was too much for him, and off he went with his money. Crossing over into the boat whence the sounds proceeded, he beheld two persons engaged in gambling for high stakes; so throwing his money on the table, he begged to be allowed to join. The others readily consented, and they began to play, Hsiu winning so rapidly that soon one of the strangers had no money left, and was obliged to get the proprietor of the boat to change a large piece of silver

---

[6] These are entitled to receive from Government a small allowance of rice, besides being permitted to exercise certain petty functions, for which a certain charge is authorised.

for him, proceeding to lay down as much as several ounces of silver for a single stake.

As the play was in full swing another man walked in, who after watching for some time at length got the proprietor to change another lump of silver for him of one hundred ounces in weight, and also asked to be allowed to join. Now Hsiu's uncle, waking up in the middle of the night, and finding his nephew gone, and hearing the sound of dice-throwing hard by, knew at once where he was, and immediately followed him to the boat with a view of bringing him back. Finding, however, that Hsiu was a heavy winner, he said nothing to him, only carrying off a portion of his winnings to their own boat and making the others of his party get up and help him to fetch the rest, even then leaving behind a large sum for Hsiu to go on with. By-and-by the three strangers had lost all their ready money, and there wasn't a farthing left in the boat : upon which one of them proposed to play for lumps of silver, but Hsiu said he never went so high as that. This made them a little quarrelsome, Hsiu's uncle all the time trying to get him away ; and the proprietor of the boat, who had only his own commission in view, managed to borrow some hundred strings of cash from another boat, and started them all again. Hsiu soon took this out of them ; and, as day was beginning to dawn and the Custom House was about to open, he went off with his winnings back to his own boat.

The proprietor of the gambling-boat now found that the lumps of silver which he had changed for his customers were nothing more than so much tinsel, and rushing off in a great state of alarm to Hsiu's boat, told him what had happened and asked him to make it good ; but when he discovered he was speaking to the son of his former travelling companion, Jen Chien-chih, he hung his head and slunk away covered with shame. For the proprietor of that boat was no other than Shên Chu-t'ing, of whom Hsiu had heard when he was in Shensi ; now, however, that with supernatural aid [7] the wrongs of his father had been avenged, he determined to pursue the man no further. So going into partnership with his uncle, they proceeded

[7] One of the strangers was the disembodied spirit of Hsiu's father, helping his son to take vengeance on the wicked Shên.

north together ; and by the end of the year their capital
had increased five-fold. Hsiu then purchased the status
of *chien-shêng*,[8] and by further careful investment of his
money ultimately became the richest man in that part of
the country.

XXVI. THE LOST BROTHER

In Honan there lived a man named Chang, who originally
belonged to Shantung. His wife had been seized and
carried off by the soldiery during the period when Ching
Nan's troops were overrunning the latter province ;[1] and
as he was frequently in Honan on business, he finally
settled there and married a Honan wife, by whom he had
a son named Na. By-and-by this wife died, and he took
another, who bore him a son named Ch'êng. The last-
mentioned lady was from the Niu family, and a very
malicious woman. So jealous was she of Na, that she
treated him like a slave or a beast of the field, giving him
only the coarsest food, and making him cut a large bundle
of wood every day, in default of which she would beat
and abuse him in a most shameful manner. On the other
hand, she secretly reserved all the tit-bits for Ch'êng, and
also sent him to school. As Ch'êng grew up, and began
to understand the meaning of filial piety and fraternal love,[2]
he could not bear to see this treatment of his elder brother,
and spoke privately to his mother about it ; but she would
pay no heed to what he said.

One day, when Na was on the hills performing his task,
a violent storm came on, and he took shelter under a cliff.
However, by the time it was over the sun had set, and
he began to feel very hungry. So, shouldering his bundle,
he wended his way home, where his stepmother, displeased
with the small quantity of wood he had brought, refused.

---

[8] An intermediate step between the first and second degrees, to
which certain privileges are attached.   [1] A.D. 1400.

[2] The first of the sixteen maxims which form the so-called Sacred
Edict, embodies these two all-important family ties. The doctrine
of primogeniture is carried so far in China as to put every younger
brother in a subordinate position to every elder brother. All
property, however, of whatever kind, is equally divided among the
sons. [The Sacred Edict was delivered by the great Emperor
K'ang Hsi, and should be publicly read and explained in every city
of the Empire on the first and fifteenth of each month.]

to give him anything to eat. Quite overcome with hunger, Na went in and lay down ; and when Ch'êng came back from school, and saw the state he was in, he asked him if he was ill. Na replied that he was only hungry, and then told his brother the whole story ; whereupon Ch'êng coloured up and went away, returning shortly with some cakes, which he offered to Na. " Where did you get them ? " asked the latter. " Oh," replied Ch'êng, " I stole some flour and got a neighbour's wife to make them for me. Eat away, and don't talk." Na ate them up ; but begged his brother not to do this again, as he might get himself into trouble. " I shan't die," added he, " if I only get one meal a day." " You are not strong," rejoined Ch'êng, " and shouldn't cut so much wood as you do."

Next day, after breakfast, Ch'êng slipped away to the hills, and arrived at the place where Na was occupied with his usual task, to the great astonishment of the latter, who inquired what he was going to do. " To help you cut wood," replied Ch'êng. " And who sent you ? " asked his brother. " No one," said he ; " I came of my own accord." " Ah," cried Na, " you can't do this work ; and even if you can you must not. Run along home again." Ch'êng, however, remained, aiding his brother with his hands and feet alone, but declaring that on the morrow he would bring an axe. Na tried to stop him, and found that he had already hurt his finger and worn his shoes into holes ; so he began to cry, and said, " If you don't go home directly, I'll kill myself with my axe." Ch'êng then went away, his brother seeing him half-way home, and going back to finish his work by himself. He also called in the evening at Ch'êng's school, and told the master his brother was a delicate boy, and should not be allowed to go on the hills, where, he said, there were fierce tigers and wolves. The master replied that he didn't know where Ch'êng had been all the morning, but that he had caned him for playing truant. Na further pointed out to Ch'êng that by not doing as he had told him, he had let himself in for a beating. Ch'êng laughed, and said he hadn't been beaten ; and the very next day off he went again, and this time with a hatchet. " I told you not to come," cried Na, much alarmed ; " why have you done so ? " Ch'êng made no reply, but set to work chopping wood with such energy that the perspiration poured down his face ; and when he had cut about a bundle he went away without saying a word. The master caned him again, and then Ch'êng told him how the matter stood, at which the former became full of admiration for his pupil's kind behaviour, and no longer prevented him from going. His brother, however, frequently urged him not to come, though without the slightest success ; and one day, when they went with a number of others to cut wood, a tiger rushed down from the hills upon them. The wood-cutters hid themselves, in the greatest consternation ; and the tiger, seizing Ch'êng, ran off with him in his mouth. Ch'êng's weight caused the tiger to move slowly ; and Na, rushing after them, hacked away at the tiger's flanks with his axe. The pain only made the tiger hurry off, and in a few minutes they were out of sight. Overwhelmed with grief, Na went back to his comrades, who tried to soothe him ; but he said, " My brother was no ordinary brother, and, besides, he died for me ; why, then, should I live ? " Here, seizing his hatchet, he made a great chop at his own neck, upon which his companions prevented him from doing himself any more mischief. The wound, however, was over an inch deep, and blood was flowing so copiously that Na became faint, and seemed at the point of death. They then tore up their clothes, and, after having bandaged his neck, proceeded to carry him home. His stepmother cried bitterly, and cursed him, saying, " You have killed my son, and now you go and cut your neck in this make-believe kind of way." " Don't be angry, mother," replied Na ; " I will not live now that my brother is dead." He then threw himself on the bed ; but the pain of his wound was so great he could not sleep, and day and night he sat leaning against the wall in tears. His father, fearing that he too would die, went every now and then and gave him a little nourishment ; but his wife cursed him so for doing it, that at length Na refused all food, and in three days he died.

Now in the village where these events took place there was a magician who was employed in certain devil-work among mortals,[3] and Na's ghost, happening to fall in

---

[3] Ordinary devils being unable to stand for any length of time the light and life of the upper world, the souls of certain persons

with him, related the story of its previous sorrows, winding
up by asking where his brother's ghost was.   The magician
said he didn't know, but turned round with Na and showed
him the way to a city where they saw an official servant
coming out of the city gates.   The magician stopped him,
and inquired if he could· tell them anything about Ch'êng ;
whereupon the man drew out a list from a pouch at his
side, and, after carefully examining it, replied that among
the male and female criminals within there was no one of
the name of Chang.[4]   The magician here suggested that the
name might be on another list ; but the man replied that
he was in charge of that road, and surely ought to know.
Na, however, was not satisfied, and persuaded the magician
to enter the city, where they met many new and old devils
walking about, among whom were some Na had formerly
known in life.   So he asked them if they could direct him
to his brother ; but none of them knew where he was ;
and suddenly there was a great commotion, the devils
on all sides crying out, " P'u-sa [5] has come ! "   Then,
looking up, Na beheld a most beautiful man descending
from above, encircled by rays of glory, which shot forth
above and below, lighting up all around him.   " You are
in luck's way, Sir," said the magician to Na ; " only once
in many thousand years does P'u-sa descend into hell
and banish all suffering.   He has come to-day."   He then
made Na kneel, and all the devils began with clasped
hands to sing songs of praise to P'u-sa for his compassion
in releasing them from their misery, shaking the very
earth with the sound.   P'u-sa himself, seizing a willow-
branch, sprinkled them all with holy water ; and when
this was done the clouds and glory melted away, and he
vanished from their sight.   Na, who had felt the holy
water fall upon his neck, now became conscious that the
axe-wound was no longer painful ; and the magician then
proceeded to lead him back, not quitting him until within
sight of the village gate.   In fact, Na had been in a trance
for two days, and when he recovered he told them all

are often temporarily employed in this work by the authorities of
Purgatory, their bodies remaining meanwhile in a trance or cata-
leptic fit.
   [4] Their family name.
   [5] The Chinese corrupted form of Bodhisatva.   Now widely
employed to designate any deity of any kind.

that he had seen, asserting positively that Ch'êng was not dead. His mother, however, looked upon the story as a make-up, and never ceased reviling him ; and, as he had no means of proving his innocence, and his neck was now quite healed, he got up from the bed and said to his father, " I am going away·to seek for my brother throughout the universe ; if I do not find him, never expect to see me again, but I pray you regard me as dead." His father drew him aside and wept bitterly. However, he would not interfere with his son's design, and Na accordingly set off. Whenever he came to a large town or populous place he used to ask for news of Ch'êng ; and by-and-by, when his money was all spent, he begged his way on foot. A year had passed away before he reached Nanking, and his clothes were all in tatters—as ragged as a quail's tail,[6] when suddenly he met some ten or a dozen horsemen, and drew away to the roadside. Among them was a gentleman of about forty, who appeared to be a mandarin, with numerous lusty attendants and fiery steeds accompanying him before and behind. One young man on a small palfrey, whom Na took to be the mandarin's son, and at whom, of course, he did not venture to stare, eyed him closely for some time, and at length stopped his steed, and, jumping off, cried out, " Are you not my brother ? " Na then raised his head, and found that Ch'êng stood before him. Grasping each other's hands, the brothers burst into tears, and at length Ch'êng said, " My brother, how is it you have strayed so far as this ? " Na told him the circumstances, at which he was much affected ; and Ch'êng's companions, jumping off their horses to see what was the matter, went off and informed the mandarin. The latter ordered one of them to give up his horse to Na, and thus they rode together back to the mandarin's house. Ch'êng then told his brother how the tiger had carried him away, and how he had been thrown down in the road, where he had passed a whole night ; also how the mandarin, Mr. Chang,[7] on his return from the capital, had seen him there, and observing that he was no common-looking youth, had set to work and brought him round again. Also

---

[6] The usual similitude for a Chinese tatterdemalion.
[7] The surnames Chang, Wang, and Li correspond in China to our Brown, Jones, and Robinson.

how he had said to Mr. Chang that his home was a great
way off, and how Mr. Chang had taken him to his own
home, and finally cured him of his wounds ; when, having
no son of his own, he had adopted him. And now, happening to be out with his father, he had caught sight of his
brother. As he was speaking Mr. Chang walked in, and
Na thanked him very heartily for all his kindness ; Ch'êng,
meanwhile, going into the inner apartments to get some
clothes for his brother. Wine and food was placed on
the table ; and while they were chatting together the
mandarin asked Na about the number of their family in
Honan. "There is only my father," replied Na, "and he
is a Shantung man who came to live in Honan." "Why,
I am a Shantung man too," rejoined Mr. Chang ; "what
is the name of your father's native place ? " " I have
heard that it was in the Tung-ch'ang district," replied Na.
"Then we are from the same place," cried the mandarin.
"Why did your father go away to Honan ? " "His first
wife," said Na, "was carried off by soldiers, and my father
lost everything he possessed ; so, being in the habit of
trading to Honan, he determined to settle down there
for good." The mandarin then asked what his father's
other name was, and when he heard, he sat some time
staring at Na, and at length hurried away within. In a
few moments out came an old lady, and when they had
all bowed to her, she asked Na if he was Chang Ping-chih's
grandson. On his replying in the affirmative, the old
lady wept, and, turning to Mr. Chang, said, "These two
are your younger brothers." And then she explained
to Na and Ch'êng as follows :—"Three years after my
marriage with your father, I was carried off to the north
and made a slave [8] in a mandarin's family. Six months

[8] Slavery, under a modified form, exists in China at the present
day. All parents, having absolute power over their children, are at
liberty to sell them as servants or slaves to their wealthier neighbours. This is not an infrequent occurrence in times of distress,
the children even going so far as to voluntarily sell themselves, and
exposing themselves in some public thoroughfare, with a notice
affixed to a kind of arrow on their backs, stating that they are for
sale, and the amount required from the purchaser. This I have
seen with my own eyes. The chief source, however, from which
the supply of slaves is kept up is kidnapping. [See No. XXIII.,
note 10.] As to the condition of the slaves themselves, it is by no

afterwards your elder brother here was born, and in another six months the mandarin died. Your elder brother being his heir, he received this appointment, which he is now resigning. I have often thought of my native place, and have not unfrequently sent people to inquire about my husband, giving them the full particulars as to name and clan ; but I could never hear anything of him. How should I know that he had gone to Honan ? " Then, addressing Mr. Chang, she continued, " That was rather a mistake of yours, adopting your own brother." " He never told me anything about Shantung," replied Mr. Chang ; " I suppose he was too young to remember the story." For, in point of age, the elder of the brothers was forty-one ; Ch'êng, the younger, being only sixteen ; and Na, twenty years of age. Mr. Chang was very glad to get two young brothers ; and when he heard the tale of their separation, proposed that they should all go back to their father. Mrs. Chang was afraid her husband would not care to receive her back again ; but her eldest son said, " We will cast our lot together ; all or none. How can there be a country where fathers are not valued ? " They then sold their house and packed up, and were soon on the way to Honan. When they arrived, Ch'êng went in first to tell his father, whose third wife had died since Na left, and who now was a desolate old widower, left alone with only his own shadow. He was overjoyed to see Ch'êng again, and, looking fondly at his son, burst into a flood of tears. Ch'êng told him his mother and brothers

means an unhappy one. Their master has nominally the power of life and death over them, but no Chinaman would ever dream of availing himself of this dangerous prerogative. They are generally well fed, and fairly well clothed, being rarely beaten, for fear they should run away, and either be lost altogether or entail much expense to secure their capture. The girls do not have their feet compressed ; hence they are infinitely more useful than small-footed women ; and, on reaching a marriageable age, their masters are bound to provide them with husbands. They live on terms of easy familiarity with the whole household ; and, ignorant of the meaning and value of liberty, seem quite contented with a lot which places them beyond the reach of hunger and cold. Slaves take the surnames of their masters, and the children of slaves are likewise slaves. Manumission is not uncommon ; and Chinese history furnishes more than one example of a quondam slave attaining to the highest offices of State.

were outside, and the old man was then perfectly transfixed with astonishment, unable either to laugh or to cry.   Mr. Chang next appeared, followed by his mother ; and the two old people wept in each other's arms, the late solitary widower hardly knowing what to make of the crowd of men and women-servants that suddenly filled his house. Here Ch'êng, not seeing his own mother, asked where she was ; and when he heard she was dead, he fainted away, and did not come round for a good half-hour.   Mr. Chang found the money for building a fine house, and engaged a tutor for his two brothers.   Horses pranced in the stables, and servants chattered in the hall—it was quite a large establishment.

XXVII. THE THREE GENII

THERE was a certain scholar who, passing through Su-ch'ien on his way to Nanking, where he was going to try for his master's degree, happened to fall in with three other gentle-men, all graduates like himself, and was so charmed with their unusual refinement that he purchased a quantity of wine, and begged them to join him in drinking it.   While thus pleasantly employed, his three friends told him their names.   One was Chieh Ch'iu-hêng ; the second, Ch'ang Fêng-lin ;   and the other, Ma Hsi-ch'ih.   They drank away and enjoyed themselves very much, until evening had crept upon them unperceived, when Chieh said, " Here we, who ought to have been playing the host, have been feasting at a stranger's expense.   This is not right. But, come, my house is close by ; I will provide you with a bed."   Ch'ang and Ma got up, and, taking our hero by the arm, bade his servant come along with them.   When they reached a hill to the north of the village, there before them was a house and grounds, with a stream of clear water in front of the door, all the apartments within being beauti-fully clean and nice.   Chieh then gave orders to light the lamps and see after his visitor's servant ; whereupon Ma observed, " Of old it was customary to set intellectual refreshments before one's friends ; let us not miss the opportunity of this lovely evening, but decide on four themes, one for each of us ; and then, when we have finished our essays, we can set to work on the wine."[1] To this the others readily agreed ; and each wrote down a theme and threw it on the table. These were next divided amongst them as they sat, and before the second watch [2] was over the essays were all completed and handed round for general inspection ; and our scholar was so struck with the elegance and vigour of those by his three friends, that he ran off a copy of them and put it in his pocket. The host then produced some excellent wine, which was drunk by them in such bumpers that soon they were all tolerably tipsy. The other two now took their leave ; but Chieh led the scholar into another room, where, so overcome was he with wine, that he went to bed in his boots and clothes.

The sun was high in the heavens when our hero awaked, and, looking round, he saw no house or grounds, only a dell on the hill-side, in which he and his servant had been sleeping. In great alarm he called out to the servant, who also got up, and then they found a hole with a rill of water trickling down before it. Much astonished at all this, he felt in his pocket, and there, sure enough, was the paper on which he had copied the three essays of his friends. On descending the hill and making inquiries, he found that he had been to the Grotto of the Three Genii—namely, Crab, Snake, and Frog, three very wonderful beings, who often came out for a stroll, and were occasionally visible to mortal eyes. Subsequently, when our hero entered the examination hall, lo! the three themes set were those of the Three Genii, and he came out at the top of the list.

[1] No Chinese wine-party is complete without more or less amusement of a literary character. Capping verses, composing impromptu odes on persons or places, giving historical and mythological allusions, are among the ordinary diversions of this kind.

[2] The Chinese night lasts from 7 P.M. to 5 A.M., and is divided into five watches of two hours each, which are subdivided into five "beats" of the watchman's wooden tom-tom.

XXVIII. THE SINGING FROGS

WANG TZU-SUN told me that when he was at the capital
he saw a man in the street who gave the following performance :—He had a wooden box, divided by partitions
into twelve holes, in each of which was a frog ; and whenever he tapped any one of these frogs on the head with a
tiny wand, the frog so touched would immediately begin
to sing.   Some one gave him a piece of silver, and then he
tapped the frogs all round, just as if he was striking a gong ;
whereupon they all sang together, with their *Do, Ré, Mi,
Fa*, in perfect time and harmony.

XXIX. THE PERFORMING MICE

MR. WANG also told me that there was a man at Ch'ang-an
who made his living by exhibiting performing mice.   He
had a pouch on his back in which he kept some ten of these
little animals ; and whenever he got among a number of
people he would fix a little frame on his back, exactly
resembling a stage.   Then beating a drum he would sing
some old theatrical melody, at the first sounds of which
the mice would issue forth from the pouch, and then, with
masks on their faces, and arrayed in various costumes,
they would climb up his back on to the stage ; where,
standing on their hind-legs, they would go through a
performance portraying the various emotions of joy and
anger, exactly like human actors of either sex.[1]

XXX. THE TIGER OF CHAO-CH'ÊNG

AT Chao-ch'êng there lived an old woman more than
seventy years of age, who had an only son.   One day he
went up to the hills and was eaten by a tiger, at which

[1] The *rôles* of women are always played in China by men, dressed
up so perfectly, small feet and all, as to be quite undistinguishable
from real women.

his mother was so overwhelmed with grief that she hardly
wished to live. With tears and lamentations she ran and
told her story to the magistrate of the place, who laughed
and asked her how she thought the law could be brought
to bear on a tiger. But the old woman would not be
comforted, and at length the magistrate lost his temper
and bade her begone. Of this, however, she took no notice ;
and then the magistrate, in compassion for her great age
and unwilling to resort to extremities, promised her
that he would have the tiger arrested. Even then she
would not go until the warrant had been actually issued ;
so the magistrate, at a loss what to do, asked his attendants
which of them would undertake the job.[1] Upon this
one of them, Li Nêng, who happened to be gloriously
drunk, stepped forward and said that he would ; whereupon the warrant was immediately issued and the old
woman went away. When our friend, Li Nêng, got sober,
he was sorry for what he had done ; but reflecting that
the whole thing was a mere trick of his master's to get rid
of the old woman's importunities, did not trouble himself
much about it, handing in the warrant as if the arrest
had been made. " Not so," cried the magistrate, " you

---

[1] All underlings (and we might add overlings) in China being
unpaid, it behoves them to make what they can out of the opportunities afforded. In most *yamêns*, the various warrants and such
documents are distributed to the runners in turn, who squeeze the
victims thus handed over to them. For a small bribe they will go
back and report " Not at home ; " for a larger one " Has absconded,"
and so on.

Gatekeepers charge a fee on every petition that passes through
their hands ; gaolers, for a consideration and with proper security,
allow their prisoners to be at large until wanted ; clerks take bribes
to use their influence, honestly or dishonestly, with the magistrate
who is to try the case ; and all the servants share equally in the
gratuities given by anyone to whom their master may send presents.
The amount, whatever it may be, is enclosed in a red envelope and
addressed to the sender of the present, with the words " Instead of
tea," in large characters ; the meaning being that the refreshments
which should have been set before the servants who brought the
gifts have been commuted by a money payment. This money is
put into a general fund and equally divided at stated periods.

All Government officers holding a post, from the highest to the
lowest, are entitled to a nominal, and what would be a quite in-
adequate, salary ; but no one ever sees this. It is customary to
refuse acceptance of it on some such grounds as want of merit, and
refund it to the Imperial Treasury.

said you could do this, and now I shall not let you off."
Li Nêng was at his wits' end, and begged that he might be
allowed to impress the hunters of the district.[2] This was
conceded ; so collecting together these men, he proceeded
to spend day and night among the hills in the hope of
catching a tiger, and thus making a show of having fulfilled
his duty.

A month passed away, during which he received several
hundred blows with the bamboo,[3] and at length, in despair,
he betook himself to the Ch'êng-huang temple in the
eastern suburb, where, falling on his knees, he prayed
and wept by turns. By-and-by a tiger walked in, and Li
Nêng, in a great fright, thought he was going to be eaten
alive. But the tiger took no notice of anything, remaining
seated in the doorway. Li Nêng then addressed the
animal as follows :—" O tiger, if thou didst slay that
old woman's son, suffer me to bind thee with this cord ; "
and, drawing a rope from his pocket, threw it over the
animal's neck. The tiger drooped its ears, and, allowing
itself to be bound, followed Li Nêng to the magistrate's
office. The latter then asked it, saying, " Did you eat
the old woman's son ? " to which the tiger replied by
nodding its head ; whereupon the magistrate rejoined,
" That murderers should suffer death has ever been the
law.[4] Besides, this old woman had but one son, and by
killing him you took from her the sole support of her
declining years. But if now you will be as a son to her,
your crime shall be pardoned." The tiger again nodded

[2] Anybody is liable to be " impressed " at any moment for the
service of the Government. Boat owners, sedan-chair and coolie
proprietors especially dread the frequent and heavy calls that are
made upon them for assistance, the remuneration they receive being
in all cases insufficient to defray mere working expenses. But inasmuch as Chinese officials may not seize any men, or boats, or carts,
holding passes to show that they are in the employ of a foreign
merchant, a lively trade in such documents has sprung up in certain
parts of China between the dishonest of the native and foreign
commercial circles.

[3] Constables, detectives, and others are liable to be bambooed
at intervals, generally of three or five days, until the mission on
which they are engaged has been successfully accomplished. In
cases of theft and non-restoration of the stolen property within a
given time, the detectives or constables employed may be required
to make it good.

[4] Extended by the Chinese to certain cases of simple manslaughter.

assent, and accordingly the magistrate gave orders that he should be released, at which the old woman was highly incensed, thinking that the tiger ought to have paid with its life for the destruction of her son.

Next morning, however, when she opened the door of her cottage, there lay a dead deer before it ; and the old woman, by selling the flesh and skin, was able to purchase food. From that day this became a common event, and sometimes the tiger would even bring her money and valuables, so that she became quite rich, and was much better cared for than she had been even by her own son. Consequently, she became very well-disposed to the tiger, which often came and slept in the verandah, remaining for a whole day at a time, and giving no cause of fear either to man or beast. In a few years the old woman died, upon which the tiger walked in and roared its lamentations in the hall. However, with all the money she had saved, she was able to have a splendid funeral ; and while her relatives were standing round the grave, out rushed a tiger, and sent them all running away in fear. But the tiger merely went up to the mound, and, after roaring like a thunder-peal, disappeared again. Then the people of that place built a shrine in honour of the Faithful Tiger, and it remains there to this day.

XXXI. A DWARF

In the reign of K'ang Hsi, there was a magician who carried about with him a wooden box, in which he had a dwarf not much more than a foot in height. When people gave him money he would open the box and bid the little creature come out. The dwarf would then sing a song and go in again. Arriving one day at Yeh, the magistrate there seized the box, and taking it into his *yamên* asked the dwarf whence he came. At first he dared not reply, but on being pressed told the magistrate everything. He said he belonged to a respectable family, and that once when returning home from school he was stupefied by the magician, who gave him some drug which made his limbs shrink, and then took him about to exhibit to people. The magistrate was very angry, and had the magician beheaded, himself taking charge of the dwarf. He was subsequently very anxious to get him cured, but unable to obtain the proper prescription.[1]

XXXII. HSIANG-JU'S MISFORTUNES

AT Kuang-p'ing there lived an old man named Fêng, who had an only son called Hsiang-ju. Both of them were graduates; and the father was very particular and strict, though the family had long been poor. Mrs. Fêng and Hsiang-ju's wife had died, one shortly after the other, so that the father and son were obliged to do their household work for themselves.

One night Hsiang-ju was sitting out in the moonlight, when suddenly a young lady from next door got on the wall to have a look at him. He saw she was very pretty, and as he approached her she began to laugh. He then beckoned to her with his hand; but she did not move either to come or to go away. At length, however, she accepted his invitation, and descended the ladder that he had placed for her. In reply to Hsiang-ju's inquiries, the young lady said her name was Hung-yü, and that she lived next door; so Hsiang-ju, who was much taken with her beauty, begged her to come over frequently and have a chat. To this she readily assented, and continued to do so for several months, until one evening old Mr. Fêng, hearing sounds of talking and laughing in his son's room, got up and looked in. Seeing Miss Hung-yü, he was exceedingly angry, and called his son out, saying, " You good-for-nothing fellow! poor as we are, why aren't you at your books, instead of wasting your time like this? A pretty thing for the neighbours to hear of !— and even if they don't hear of it, somebody else will, and

---

[1] The Cantonese believe the following to be the usual process :— " Young children are bought or stolen at a tender age and placed in a *ch'ing*, or vase with a narrow neck, and having in this case a movable bottom. In this receptacle the unfortunate little wretches are kept for years in a sitting posture, their heads outside, being all the while carefully tended and fed. . . . When the child has reached the age of twenty or over, he or she is taken away to some distant place and ' discovered ' in the woods as a wild man or woman."—*China Mail*, May 15, 1878.

shorten your life accordingly." [1] Hsiang-ju fell on his knees, and with tears implored forgiveness ; whereupon his father turned to the young lady, and said, " A girl who behaves like this disgraces others as well as herself ; and if people find this out, we shan't be the only ones to suffer." The old man then went back to bed in a rage, and Miss Hung-yü, weeping bitterly, said to Hsiang-ju, " Your father's reproaches have overwhelmed me with shame. Our friendship is now at an end." " I could say nothing," replied he, " as long as my father was here ; but if you have any consideration for me, I pray you think nothing of his remarks." Miss Hung-yü protested, however, that they could meet no more, and then Hsiang-ju also burst into tears. " Do not weep," cried she, " our friendship was an impossible one, and time must sooner or later have put an end to these visits. Meanwhile, I hear there is a very good match to be made in the neighbourhood." Hsiang-ju replied that he was poor ; but Miss Hung-yü told him to meet her again the following evening, when she would endeavour to do something for him. At the appointed time she arrived, and, producing forty ounces of silver, presented them to Hsiang-ju ; telling him that at a village some distance off there was a Miss Wei, eighteen years of age, who was not yet married because of the exorbitant demands of her parents, but that a little extra outlay would secure for him the young lady's hand. Miss Hung-yü then bade him farewell, and Hsiang-ju went off to inform his father, expressing a desire to go and make inquiries, but saying nothing about the forty ounces. His father, thinking that they were not sufficiently well off, urged him not to go ; however, by dint of argument, he finally persuaded the old man that, at any rate, there was no harm in trying. So he borrowed horses and attendants, and set off to the house of Mr. Wei, who was a man of considerable property ; and when he got there he asked Mr. Wei to come outside and accord him a few minutes' conversation. Now the latter knew that Hsiang-ju belonged to a very good family ; and when he saw all the retinue that Hsiang-ju had brought

---

[1] Meaning that it would become known to the Arbiter of life and death in the world below, who would punish him by shortening his appointed term of years. See *The Wei-ch'i Devil*, No. CXXXI.

with him, he inwardly consented to the match, though he was afraid that perhaps his would-be son-in-law might not be as liberal as he would like. Hsiang-ju soon perceived what Mr. Wei's feelings were, and emptied his purse on the table, at which Mr. Wei was delighted, and begged a neighbour to allow the marriage contract to be drawn up in his house.[2] Hsiang-ju then went in to pay his respects to Mrs. Wei, whom he found in a small, miserable room, with Miss Wei hiding behind her. Still he was pleased to see that, in spite of her homely toilette, the young lady herself was very nice-looking; and, while he was being entertained in the neighbour's house, the old lady said, " It will not be necessary for you, Sir, to come and fetch our daughter. As soon as we have made up a small trousseau for her, we will send her along to you." [3] Hsiang-ju then agreed with them upon a day for the wedding, and went home and informed his father, pretending that the Wei family only asked for respectability, and did not care about money. His father was overjoyed to hear this; and when the day came, the young lady herself arrived. She proved to be a thrifty housekeeper and an obedient wife, so that she and her husband got along capitally together. In two years she had a son, who was called Fu-êrh. And once, on the occasion of the great spring festival, she was on her way to the family tombs, with her boy in her arms, when she chanced to meet a man named Sung, who was one of the gentry of the neighbourhood. This Mr. Sung had been a Censor,[4] but had purchased his retirement, and was now

[2] One important preliminary consists in the exchange of the four pairs of characters which denote the year, month, day, and hour of the births of the contracting parties. It remains for a geomancer to determine whether these are in harmony or not; and a very simple expedient for backing out of a proposed alliance is to bribe him to declare that the nativities of the young couple could not be happily brought together.

[3] The bridegroom invariably fetches the bride from her father's house, conveying her to his home in a handsomely-gilt red sedan-chair, closed in on all sides, and accompanied by a band of music.

[4] The Censorate is a body of fifty-six officials, whose duty it is to bring matters to the notice of the Emperor which might otherwise have escaped attention; to take exception to any acts, including those of his Majesty himself, calculated to interfere with the welfare of the people; and to impeach, as occasion may require, the high provincial authorities, whose position, but for this whole-

leading a private life, characterised by many overbearing and violent acts. He was returning from his visit to the graves of his ancestors when he saw Hsiang-ju's wife, and, attracted by her beauty, found out who she was; and imagining that, as her husband was a poor scholar, he might easily be induced for a consideration to part with the lady, sent one of his servants to find out how the land lay. When Hsiang-ju heard what was wanted, he was very angry; but, reflecting on the power of his adversary, controlled his passion, and passed the thing off with a laugh. His father, however, to whom he repeated what had occurred, got into a violent rage, and, rushing out, flung his arms about, and called Mr. Sung every name he could lay his tongue to. Mr. Sung's emissary slunk off and went home; and then a number of men were sent by the enraged Sung, and these burst into the house and gave old Fêng and his son a most tremendous beating. In the middle of the hubbub Hsiang-ju's wife ran in, and, throwing her child down on the bed, tore her hair and shrieked for help. Sung's attendants immediately surrounded her and carried her off, while there lay her husband and his father, wounded on the ground, and the baby squalling on the bed. The neighbours, pitying their wretched condition, helped them up on to the couches, and by the next day Hsiang-ju could walk with a stick; however, his father's anger was not to be appeased, and, after spitting a quantity of blood, he died. Hsiang-ju wept bitterly at this, and taking his child in his arms, used every means to bring the offenders to justice, but without the slightest success. He then heard that his wife had put an end to her own existence, and with this his cup of misery was full. Unable to get his wrongs redressed, he often meditated assassinating Sung in the open street,[5] but was deterred from attempting this by the number of his retainers and the fear of leaving his son with no one to protect him. Day and night he mourned

some check, would be almost unassailable. Censors are popularly termed the " ears and eyes " of the monarch.

[5] In the *Book of Rites* (I. Pt. i. v. 10), which dates, in its present form, only from the first century B.C., occurs this passage : " With the slayer of his father, a man may not live under the same heaven ; " and in the *Family Sayings* (Bk. X. *ab init.*), a work which professes, though on quite insufficient authority, to record a number of the conversations and apophthegms of Confucius not given iu the *Lun-yü*, or Confucian Gospels, we find the following

over his lot, and his eyelids were never closed in sleep, when suddenly in walked a personage of striking appearance to condole with him on his losses. The stranger's face was covered with a huge curly beard; and Hsiang-ju, not knowing who he was, begged him to take a seat, and was about to ask whence he came, when all at once he began, "Sir! have you forgotten your father's death, your wife's disgrace?" Thereupon Hsiang-ju, suspecting him to be a spy from the Sung family, made some evasive reply, which so irritated the stranger that he roared out, "I thought you were a man; but now I know that you are a worthless, contemptible wretch." Hsiang-ju fell on his knees and implored the stranger to forgive him, saying, "I was afraid it was a trick of Sung's: I will speak frankly to you. For days I have lain, as it were, upon thorns, my mouth filled with gall, restrained only by pity for this little one and fear of breaking our ancestral line. Generous friend, will you take care of my child if I fall?" "That," replied the stranger, "is the business of women; I cannot undertake it. But what you wish others to do for you, do yourself; and that which you would do yourself, I will do for you." When Hsiang-ju heard these words he knocked his head upon the ground; but the stranger took no more notice of him, and walked out. Following him to the door, Hsiang-ju asked his name, to which he replied, "If I cannot help you I shall not wish to have your reproaches; if I do help you, I shall not wish to have your gratitude." The stranger then disappeared, and Hsiang-ju, having a presentiment that some misfortune was about to happen, fled away with his child.

course laid down for a man whose father has been murdered :—
"He must sleep upon a grass mat, with his shield for his pillow; he must decline to take office; he must not live under the same heaven (with the murderer). When he meets him in the court or in the market-place, he must not return for a weapon, but engage him there and then;" being always careful, as the commentator observes, to carry a weapon about with him. Sir John Davis and Dr. Legge agree in stigmatising this as "one of the objectionable principles of Confucius." It must, however, be admitted that (1) a patched-up work which appeared as we have it now from two to three centuries after Confucius's death, and (2) a confessedly apocryphal work such as the *Family Sayings*, are hardly sufficient grounds for affixing to the fair fame of China's great Sage the positive inculcation of a dangerous principle of blood-vengeance like that I have just quoted.

When night came, and the members of the Sung family were wrapped in sleep, some one found his way into their house and slew the ex-Censor and his two sons, besides a maid-servant and one of the ladies. Information was at once given to the authorities ; and as the Sung family had no doubt that the murderer was Hsiang-ju, the magistrate, who was greatly alarmed,[6] sent out lictors to arrest him. Hsiang-ju, however, was nowhere to be found, a fact which tended to confirm the suspicions of the Sung family ; and they, too, despatched a number of servants to aid the mandarin in effecting his capture. Towards evening the lictors and others reached a hill, and, hearing a child cry, made for the sound, and thus secured the object of their search, whom they bound and led away. As the child went on crying louder than ever, they took it from him and threw it down by the wayside, thereby nearly causing Hsiang-ju to die of grief and rage. On being brought before the magistrate he was asked why he had killed these people ; to which he replied that he was falsely accused, " For," said he, " they died in the night, whereas I had gone away in the daytime. Besides," added he, " how, with a crying baby in my arms, could I scale walls and kill people ? " " If you didn't kill people," cried the magistrate, " why did you run away ? " Hsiang had no answer to make to this, and he was accordingly ordered to prison ; whereupon he wept and said, " I can die without regret ; but what has my child done that he, too, should be punished ? " " You," replied the magistrate, " have slain the children of others ; how can you complain if your child meets the same fate ? " Hsiang-ju was then stripped of his degree [7] and subjected to all kinds of indignities, but they were unable to wring a confession from his lips ; [8] and that very night, as the magistrate lay down, he heard a sharp noise of something striking the bed, and, jumping up in a fright, found, by the light of a candle, a small, keen blade sticking in the wood at the head of his couch so tightly that it could not be drawn out. Terribly alarmed at this, the magistrate

[6] The Chinese theory being that every official is responsible for the peace and well-being of the district committed to his charge, and even liable to punishment for occurrences over which he could not possibly have had any control.

[7] See No. X., note 3.   [8] See No. X., note 6.

walked round the room with a spear over his shoulder,
but without finding anything; and then, reflecting that
nothing more was to be feared from Sung, who was dead,
as well as his two sons, he laid Hsiang-ju's case before the
higher authorities, and obtained for him an acquittal.
Hsiang-ju was released and went home. His cupboard,
however, was empty, and there was nothing except his
own shadow within the four walls of his house. Happily,
his neighbours took pity on him and supplied him with
food; and whenever he thought upon the vengeance
that had been wreaked, his countenance assumed an
expression of joy; but as often as his misfortunes and
the extinction of his family came into his mind, his tears
would begin to flow. And when he remembered the
poverty of his life and the end of his ancestral line, he
would seek out some solitary spot, and there burst into
an ungovernable fit of grief. Thus things went on for
about six months, when the search after the murderer
began to be relaxed; and then Hsiang-ju petitioned
for the recovery of his wife's bones, which he took home
with him and buried. His sorrows made him wish to die,
and he lay tossing about on the bed without any object
in life, when suddenly he heard somebody knock at the
door. Keeping quiet to listen, he distinguished the
sound of a voice outside talking with a child; and, getting
up to look, he perceived a young lady, who said to him,
" Your great wrongs are all redressed, and now, luckily,
you have nothing to ail you." The voice seemed familiar
to him, but he could not at the moment recall where he
had heard it; so he lighted a candle, and Miss Hung-yü
stood before him. She was leading a small, happy-looking
child by the hand; and after she and Hsiang-ju had
expressed their mutual satisfaction at meeting once more,
Miss Hung-yü pushed the boy forward, saying, " Have
you forgotten your father ? " The boy clung to her dress,
and looked shyly at Hsiang-ju, who, on examining him
closely, found that he was Fu-êrh. " Where did he come
from ? " asked his father, in astonishment, not unmingled
with tears. " I will tell you all," replied Miss Hung-yü.
" I was only deceiving you when I said I belonged to a
neighbouring family. I am really a fox, and, happening
to go out one evening, I heard a child crying in a ditch.

I took him home and brought him up ; and, now that your troubles are over, I return him to you, that father and son may be together." Hsiang-ju wiped away his tears and thanked her heartily ; but Fu-êrh kept close to Miss Hung-yü, whom he had come to regard as a mother, and did not seem to recognise his father again. Before daybreak Miss Hung-yü said she must go away ; but Hsiang-yü fell upon his knees and entreated her to stop, until at. last she said she was only joking, adding that, in a new establishment like theirs, it would be a case of early to rise and late to bed. She then set to work cutting fuel and sweeping up, toiling hard as if she had been a man, which made Hsiang-ju regret that he was too poor to have all this done for her. However, she bade him mind his books, and not trouble himself about the state of their affairs, as they were not likely to die of hunger. She also produced some money, and bought implements for spinning, besides renting a few acres of land and hiring labourers to till them. Day by day she would shoulder her hoe and work in the fields, or employ herself in mending the roof, so that her fame as a good wife spread abroad, and the neighbours were more than ever pleased to help them. In half-a-year's time their home was like that of a well-to-do family, with plenty of servants about ; but one day Hsiang-ju said to Miss Hung-yü, " With all that you have accomplished on my behalf, there is still one thing left undone." On her asking him what it was, he continued :—" The examination for master's degree is at hand, and I have not yet recovered the bachelor's degree of which I was stripped." " Ah," replied she, " some time back I had your name replaced upon the list ; had I waited for you to tell me, it would have been too late." Hsiang-ju marvelled very much at this, and accordingly took his master's degree. He was then thirty-six years of age, the master of broad lands and fine houses ; and Miss Hung-yü, who looked delicate enough to be blown away by the wind, and yet worked harder than an ordinary labourer's wife, keeping her hands smooth and nice in spite of winter weather, gave herself out to be thirty-eight, though no one took her to be much more than twenty.

XXXIII. CHANG'S TRANSFORMATION

CHANG YÜ-TAN, of Chao-yüan, was a wild fellow, who pursued his studies at the Hsiao temple. Now it chanced that the magistrate of the district, Mr. Tsêng of San-han, had a daughter who was very fond of hunting, and that one day young Chang met her in the fields, and was much struck with her great beauty. She was dressed in an embroidered sable jacket, and rode about on a small palfrey, for all the world like a girl in a picture. Chang went home with the young lady still in his thoughts, his heart being deeply touched; but he soon after heard, to his infinite sorrow and dismay, that Miss Tsêng had died suddenly. Their own home being at a distance,[1] her father deposited the coffin in a temple;[2] the very temple, in fact, where her lover was residing. Accordingly Chang paid to her remains the same respect he would have offered to a god; he burnt incense every morning, and poured out libations at every meal, always accompanied by the following invocation :—" I had hardly seen you when your spirit became ever present to me in my dreams. But you passed suddenly away; and now, near as we are together, we are as far apart as if separated by hills and rivers. Alas ! alas ! In life you were under the control of your parents; now, however, there is nothing to restrain you, and with your supernatural power, I should be hearing the rustle of your robe as you approach to ease the sorrow of my heart." Day and night he prayed thus, and when some six months had passed away, and he was one night trimming his lamp to read, he raised his head and saw a young lady standing, all smiles, before him. Rising up, he inquired who she was; to which his visitor replied, " Grateful to you for your love of me, I was unable to resist the temptation of coming to thank you myself." Chang then offered her a seat, and they sat together chatting for some time. From this date the young lady used to come in every evening, and on one occasion said to Chang, " I was formerly very fond of riding and archery, shooting the musk and slaying the deer; my crime is so great that I can find no repose in death. If you have any friendly feelings towards me, I pray you recite for

---

[1] No man being allowed to hold office in his own province.
[2] This is a very common custom all over China.

me the Diamond *sutra* [3] five thousand and forty-eight
times, and I will never forget your kindness." Chang
did as he was asked, getting up every night and telling
his beads before the coffin, until the occasion of a certain
festival, when he wished to go home to his parents, and
take the young lady with him. Miss Tsêng said she was
afraid her feet were too tender to walk far ; but Chang
offered to carry her, to which she laughingly assented.
It was just like carrying a child, she was so light ; [4] and
by degrees Chang got so accustomed to taking her about
with him, that when he went up for his examination she
went in too. [5] The only thing was she could not travel
except at night. Later on, Chang would have gone up
for his master's degree, but the young lady told him it
was of no use to try, for it was not destined that he should
pass ; and accordingly he desisted from his intention.
Four or five years afterwards, Miss Tsêng's father resigned
his appointment, and so poor was he that he could not
afford to pay for the removal of his daughter's coffin, but
wanted to bury it economically where it was. Unfortunately, he had no ground of his own, and then Chang
came forward and said that a friend of his had a piece of
waste land near the temple, and that he might bury it
there. Mr. Tsêng was very glad to accept, and Chang
kindly assisted him with the funeral,—for what reason
the former was quite unable to guess. One night after
this, as Miss Tsêng was sitting by Chang's side, her father
having already returned home, she burst into a flood of
tears, and said, " For five years we have been good friends ;
we must now part. I can never repay your goodness
to me." Chang was alarmed, and asked her what she
meant ; to which she replied, " Your sympathy has told
for me in the realms below. The sum of my *sutras* is complete, and to-day I am to be born again in the family of
a high official, Mr. Lu, of Ho-pei. If you do not forget
the present time, meet me there in fifteen years from now,
on the 16th of the 8th moon." " Alas ! " cried Chang,

[3] Of all the Buddhist *sutras*, this is perhaps the favourite with
the Chinese.
[4] Contrary to the German notion that the spirit of the dead
mother, coming back at night to suckle the child she has left behind, makes an impress on the bed alongside the baby.
[5] Being, of course, invisible to all except himself.

" I am already over thirty, and in fifteen years more I shall be drawing near the wood.[6] What good will our meeting do ? " " I can be your servant," replied Miss Tsêng, " and so make some return to you. But come, escort me a few miles on my way ; the road is beset with brambles, and I shall have some trouble with my dress." So Chang carried her as before, until they reached a high road, where they found a number of carriages and horses, the latter with one or two riders on the backs of each, and three or four, or even more persons, in every carriage. But there was one richly-decorated carriage, with embroidered curtains and red awnings, in which sat only one old woman, who, when she saw Miss Tsêng, called out, " Ah, there you are." " Here I am," replied Miss Tsêng ; and then she turned to Chang and said, " We must part here ; do not forget what I told you." Chang promised he would remember ; and then the old woman helped her up into the carriage, round went the wheels, off went the attendants, and they were gone. Sorrowfully Chang wended his way home, and there wrote upon the wall the date mentioned by Miss Tsêng ; after which, bethinking himself of the efficacy of prayer, he took to reciting *sutras* more energetically than ever. By-and-by he dreamed that an angel appeared to him, and said, " The bent of your mind is excellent indeed, but you must visit the Southern Sea." [7] Asking how far off the Southern Sea was, the angel informed him it was close by ; and then waking up, and understanding what was required of him, he fixed his sole thoughts on Buddha, and lived a purer life than before. In three years' time his two sons, Ming and Chêng, came out very high on the list at the examination for the second degree, in spite of which worldly successes Chang continued to lead his usual holy life. Then one night he dreamed that another angel led him among beautiful halls and palaces, where he saw a personage sitting down who resembled Buddha himself. This personage said to him, " My son, your virtue is a matter of great joy ; unhappily your term of life is short,

[6] A very ancient expression signifying "the grave," the word "wood" being used by synecdoche for "coffin."

[7] The supposed residence of Kuan-yin, the Chinese Goddess of Mercy, she who "hears prayers," and is the giver of children.

and I have, therefore, made an appeal to God [8] on your behalf." Chang prostrated himself, and knocked his head upon the ground ; upon which he was commanded to rise, and was served with tea, fragrant as the epidendrum. A boy was next instructed to take him to bathe in a pool, the water of which was so exquisitely clear that he could count the fishes swimming about therein. He found it warm as he walked in, and scented like the leaves of the lotus-flower ; and gradually the water got deeper and deeper, until he went down altogether and passed through with his head under water. He then waked up in a fright ; but from this moment he became more robust and his sight improved. As he stroked his beard the white hairs all came out, and by-and-by the black ones too ; the wrinkles on his face were smoothed away, and in a few months he had the beardless face of a boy of fifteen or sixteen. He also grew very fond of playing about like other boys, and would sometimes tumble head over heels, and be picked up by his sons. Soon afterwards his wife died of old age, and his sons begged him to marry again into some good family ; but he said he should be obliged to go to Ho-pei first ; and then, calculating his dates, found that the appointed time had arrived. So he ordered his horses and servants, and set off for Ho-pei, where he discovered that there actually was a high official named Lu. Now Mr. Lu had a daughter, who when born was able to talk,[9] and became very clever and beautiful as she grew up. She was the idol of her parents, and had been asked in marriage by many suitors, but would not accept any of them ; and when her father and mother inquired her motives for refusal, she told them the story of of her engagement in her former life. " Silly child,' said they, reckoning up the time, and laughing at her ; " that Mr. Chang would now be about fifty years of age, a changed and feeble old man. Even if he is still alive, his hair will be white and his teeth gone." But their daughter would not listen to them ; and, finding her so obstinate in her determination, they instructed the doorkeeper to admit no strangers until the appointed time should have passed,

---

[8] The great Supreme Ruler, who is supposed to have absolute sway over the various other deities of the Chinese Pantheon.

[9] Generally spoken of as an inauspicious phenomenon.

that thus her expectations might be brought to naught. Before long, Chang arrived, but the doorkeeper would not let him in, and he went back to his inn in great distress, not knowing what to do. He then took to walking about the fields, and secretly making inquiries concerning the family. Meanwhile Miss Tsêng thought that he had broken his engagement, and refused all food, giving herself up to tears alone. Her mother argued that he was probably dead, or in any case that the breach of engagement was no fault of her daughter's; to none of which, however, would Miss Tsêng listen, lying where she was the livelong day. Mr. Lu now became anxious about her, and determined to see what manner of man this Chang might be; so, on the plea of taking a walk, he went out to meet him in the fields, and to his astonishment found quite a young man. They sat down together on some leaves, and after chatting awhile Mr. Lu was so charmed with his young friend's bearing that he invited him to his house. No sooner had they arrived, than Mr. Lu begged Chang to excuse him a moment, and ran in first to tell his daughter, who exerted herself to get up and take a peep at the stranger. Finding, however, that he was not the Chang she had formerly known, she burst into tears and crept back to bed, upbraiding her parents for trying to deceive her thus. Her father declared he was no other than Chang, but his daughter replied only with tears; and then he went back very much upset to his guest, whom he treated with great want of courtesy. Chang asked him if he was not the Mr. Lu, of such and such a position, to which he replied in a vacant kind of way that he was, looking the other way all the time and paying no attention to Chang. The latter did not approve of this behaviour, and accordingly took his leave; and in a few days Miss Tsêng had cried herself to death. Chang then dreamed that she appeared to him, and said, " Was it you after all that I saw? You were so changed in age and appearance that when I looked upon your face I did not know you. I have already died from grief; but if you make haste to the little street shrine and summon my spirit back, I may still recover. Be not late! " Chang then waked, and immediately made inquiries at Mr. Lu's house, when he found that the young lady had been dead two days.

Telling her father his dream, they went forth to summon the spirit back ; and on opening the shroud, and throwing themselves with lamentations over the corpse, a noise was heard in the young lady's throat, and her cherry lips parted.   They moved her on to a bed, and soon she began to moan, to the great joy of Mr. Lu, who took Chang out of the room and, over a bumper of wine, asked some questions about his family.   He was glad to find that Chang was a suitable match for his daughter, and an auspicious day was fixed for the wedding.   In a fortnight the event came off, the bride being escorted to Chang's house by her father, who remained with them six months before going home again.   They were a youthful pair, and people who didn't know the story mistook Chang's son and daughter-in-law for his father and mother.   A year later Mr. Lu died ; and his son, a mere child, having been badly wounded by some scoundrels, and the family property being almost gone, Chang made him come and live with them, and be one of their own family.

XXXIV. A TAOIST PRIEST

ONCE upon a time there was a Mr. Han, who belonged to a wealthy family, and was fond of entertaining people. A man named Hsü, of the same town, frequently joined him over the bottle ; and on one occasion when they were together a Taoist priest came to the door with his alms-bowl[1] in his hand.   The servants threw him some money and food, but the priest would not accept them, neither would he go away ; and at length they would take no more notice of him.   Mr. Han heard the noise of the priest knocking his bowl[2] going on for a long time, and asked his

[1] This is the Buddhist *patra*, which modern writers have come to regard as an instrumental part of the Taoist religion. See No. IV., note 1.

[2] To call attention to his presence. Beggars in China accomplish their purpose more effectually by beating a gong in the shop where they ask for alms so loudly as to prevent the shopkeeper from hearing his customers speak ; or they vary the performance by swinging about some dead animal tied to the end of a stick.   Mendicity not being prohibited in China, there results a system of blackmail payable by every householder to a beggars' guild, and this frees them from the visits of the beggars of their own particular

servants what was the matter ; and they had hardly told
him when the priest himself walked in. Mr. Han begged
him to be seated ; whereupon the priest bowed to both
gentlemen and took his seat. On making the usual
inquiries, they found that he lived at an old tumbledown
temple to the east of the town, and Mr. Han expressed
regret at not having heard sooner of his arrival, so that he
might have shown him the proper hospitality of a resident.
The priest said that he had only recently arrived, and had
no friends in the place ; but hearing that Mr. Han was
a jovial fellow, he had been very anxious to take a glass
with him. Mr. Han then ordered wine, and the priest soon
distinguished himself as a hard drinker ; Mr. Hsü treating
him all the time with a certain amount of disrespect in
consequence of his shabby appearance, while Mr. Han made
allowances for him as being a traveller. When he had
drunk over twenty large cups of wine, the priest took his
leave, returning subsequently whenever any jollification
was going on, no matter whether it was eating or drinking.
Even Han began now to tire a little of him ; and on one
occasion Hsü said to him in raillery, " Good priest, you
seem to like being a guest ; why don't you play the host
sometimes for a change ? " " Ah," replied the priest,
" I am much the same as yourself—a mouth carried
between a couple of shoulders." [3] This put Hsü to shame,
and he had no answer to make ; so the priest continued,
" But although that is so, I have been revolving the
question with myself for some time, and when we do meet
I shall do my best to repay your kindness with a cup of my
own poor wine." When they had finished drinking, the
priest said he hoped he should have the pleasure of their
company the following day at noon ; and at the appointed
time the two friends went together, not expecting, however,
to find anything ready for them. But the priest was
waiting for them in the street ; and passing through a
handsome courtyard, they beheld long suites of elegant
apartments stretching away before them. In great aston-

district ; many, however, do not subscribe, but take their chance in
the struggle as to who will tire out the other first, the shopkeeper,
who has all to lose, being careful to stop short of anything like
manual violence, which would forthwith bring down upon him the
myrmidons of the law, and subject him to innumerable " squeezes."
    [3] *Sc.* a " sponge."

ishment, they remarked to the priest that they had not visited this temple for some time, and asked when it had been thus repaired ; to which he replied that the work had been only lately completed.   They then went inside, and there was a magnificently-decorated apartment, such as would not be found even in the houses of the wealthy. This made them begin to feel more respect for their host ; and no sooner had they sat down than wine and food were served by a number of boys, all about sixteen years of age, and dressed in embroidered coats, with red shoes.   The wine and eatables were delicious, and very nicely served ; and when the dinner was taken away, a course of rare fruits was put on the table, the names of all of which it would be impossible to mention.   They were arranged in dishes of crystal and jade, the brilliancy of which lighted up the surrounding furniture ; and the goblets in which the wine was poured were of glass,[4] and more than a foot in circumference.   The priest here cried out, " Call the Shih sisters," whereupon one of the boys went out and in a few moments two elegant young ladies walked in.   The first was tall and slim like a willow wand ; the other was short and very young, both being exceedingly pretty girls.   Being told to sing while the company were drinking, the younger beat time and sang a song, while the elder accompanied her on the flageolet.   They acquitted themselves admirably ; and, when the song was over, the priest, holding his goblet bottom upwards in the air, challenged his guests to follow his example, bidding his servants pour out more wine all round.   He then turned to the girls, and remarked that they had not danced for a long time, asking if they were still able to do so ; upon which a carpet was spread by one of the boys, and the two young ladies proceeded to dance, their long robes waving about and perfuming the air around. The dance concluded, they leant against a painted screen, while the two guests gradually became more and more confused, and were at last irrecoverably drunk.   The priest took no notice of them ; but when he had finished drinking, he got up and said, " Pray, go on with your wine ; I am going to rest awhile, and will return by-and-by."   He then went away, and lay down on a splendid couch at the other

---

[4] First manufactured in China A.D. 424.   The term here used (*pʋ-li*) occurs as early as A.D. 643, and is of foreign origin.

end of the room ; at which Hsü was very angry, and shouted
out, " Priest, you are a rude fellow," at the same time
making towards him with a view of rousing him up. The
priest then ran out, and Han and Hsü lay down to sleep,
one at each end of the room, on elaborately-carved couches
covered with beautiful mattresses. When they woke up,
they found themselves lying in the road, Mr. Hsü with his
head in a dirty drain. Hard by were a couple of rush
huts ; but everything else was gone.

XXXV. THE FIGHT WITH THE FOXES

IN the province of Chih-li, there was a wealthy family in
want of a tutor. One day a graduate presented himself at
the door, and was asked by the master of the house to walk
in ; and he conversed so pleasantly that in a short time it
was clear to both sides that they were mutually pleased
with each other. The tutor said his name was Hu ; and
when the usual present had been made to him, he was
forthwith provided with apartments, and entered very
energetically upon his duties, proving himself a scholar of
no mean order. He was, however, very fond of roaming,
and generally came back in the middle of the night, not
troubling himself to knock if the door was locked, but
suddenly appearing on the inside. It was therefore suspected that he was a fox, though as his intentions seemed
to be harmless, he was treated extremely well, and not
with any want of courtesy as if he had been something
uncanny. By-and-by he discovered that his master had
a daughter,[1] and being desirous of securing the match was
always dropping hints to that effect, which his master, on
the other hand, invariably pretended not to understand.
One day he went off for a holiday, and on the next day
a stranger called ; who, tying a black mule at the door,
accepted the invitation of the master to take a seat within.
He was about fifty years of age, very neat and clean in his
dress, and gentlemanly in his manners. When they were
seated, the stranger began by saying that he was come with

[1] The women's apartments being quite separate from the rest of
a Chinese house, male visitors consequently know nothing about
their inhabitants.

proposals of marriage on behalf of Mr. Hu ; to which his host, after some consideration, replied that he and Mr. Hu got along excellently well as friends, and there was no object in bringing about a closer connection. " Besides," added he, " my daughter is already betrothed, and I beg you, therefore, to ask Mr. Hu to excuse me." The stranger said he was quite sure the young lady was not engaged, and inquired what might be the objection to the match : but it was all of no avail, until at length he remarked, " Mr. Hu is of a good family ; I see no reason why you should have such an aversion to him." " Well, then," replied the other, " I will tell you what it is. We don't like his *species*." The stranger here got very angry, and his host also lost his temper, so that they came to high words, and were already on the way to blows, when the latter bade his servants give the stranger a beating and turn him out. The stranger then retired, leaving his mule behind him ; and when they drew near to look at it they found a huge creature with black hair, drooping ears, and a long tail. They tried to lead it away, but it would not move ; and on giving it a shove with the hand from behind, it toppled over and was discovered to be only of straw. In consequence of the angry words that had been said, the master of the house felt sure that there would be an attempt at revenge, and accordingly made all preparations ; and sure enough the next day a whole host of fox-soldiers arrived, some on horseback, some on foot, some with spears, and others with cross-bows, men and horses trampling along with an indescribable din. The family were afraid to leave the house, and the foxes shouted out to set the place on fire, at which the inmates were dreadfully alarmed ; but just then one of the bravest of them rushed forth with a number of the servants to engage the foxes. Stones and arrows flew about in all directions, and many on both sides were wounded ; at length, however, the foxes drew off, leaving their swords on the field. These glittered like frost or snow, but when picked up turned out to be only millet-stalks. " Is this all their cunning ? " cried their adversary, laughing, at the same time making still more careful preparations in case the foxes should come again. Next day they were deliberating together, when suddenly a giant descended upon them from the sky. He was over ten feet in height by several feet in breadth, and brandished a sword as broad as half a door ; but they attacked him so vigorously with arrows and stones that he was soon stretched dead upon the ground, when they saw that he was made of grass. Our friends now began to make light of their fox-foes, and as they saw nothing more of them for three days their precautions were somewhat relaxed. The foxes, however, soon reappeared, armed with bows and arrows, and succeeded in shooting the master of the house in the back, disappearing when he summoned his servants and proceeded to attack them. Then, drawing the arrow from his back, he found it was a long thorn ; and thus the foxes went on for a month or so, coming and going, and making it necessary to take precautions, though not really inflicting any serious injury. This annoyed the master of the family very much, until one day Mr. Hu [2] himself appeared with a troop of soldiers at his back, and he immediately went out to meet him. Mr. Hu withdrew among his men, but the master called to him to come forth, and then asked him what he had done that soldiers should be thus brought against his family. The foxes were now on the point of discharging their arrows ; Mr. Hu, however, stopped them ; whereupon he and his old master shook hands, and the latter invited him to walk into his old room. Wine being served, his host observed, " You, Mr. Hu, are a man of intelligence, and I trust you will make allowances for me. Friends as we were, I should naturally have been glad to form a connection with you ; your carriages, however, horses, houses, &c., are not those of ordinary mortals ; and even had my daughter consented, you must know the thing would have been impossible, she being still a great deal too young." Mr. Hu was somewhat disconcerted at this, but his host continued, " It's of no consequence ; we can still be friends as before, and if you do not despise us earthly creatures, there is my son whom you have taught ; he is fifteen years old, and I should be proud to see him connected with you if such an arrangement should be feasible." Mr. Hu was delighted, and said, " I have a daughter one year younger than your son ; she is neither ugly nor stupid. How would she do ? " His host got up and made a low

[2] See No. XIII., note 1.

bow, which Mr. Hu forthwith returned, and they then became the best of friends, forgetting all about the former unpleasantness. Wine was given to Mr. Hu's attendants, and everyone was made happy. The host now inquired where Mr. Hu lived, that the ceremony of pouring out a libation to the geese [3] might be performed; but Mr. Hu said. this would not be necessary, and remained drinking till night, when he went away again. From this time there was no more trouble ; and a year passed without any news of Mr. Hu, so that it seemed as if he wished to get out of his bargain. The family, however, went on waiting, and in six months more Mr. Hu reappeared, when, after a few general remarks, he declared that his daughter was ready, and requested that an auspicious day might be fixed for her to come to her husband's home. This being arranged, the young lady arrived with a retinue of sedan-chairs, and horses, and a beautiful trousseau that nearly filled a room.[4] She was unusually respectful to her father and mother-in-law, and the former was much pleased with the match. Her father and a younger brother of his had escorted her to the house, and conversing away in a most refined style they sat drinking till daybreak before they went away. The bride herself had the gift of foreknowing whether the harvest would be good or bad, and her advice was always taken in such matters. Mr. Hu and his brother, and also their mother, often came to visit her in her new home, and were then very frequently seen by people.

XXXVI. THE KING

A CERTAIN Governor of Hu-nan despatched a magistrate to the capital in charge of treasure to the amount of six hundred thousand ounces of silver. On the road the magistrate encountered a violent storm of rain, which so

[3] A very ancient custom in China, originating in a belief that these birds never mate a second time. The libation is made on the occasion of the bridegroom fetching his bride from her father's house.

[4] A Chinese trousseau, in addition to clothes and jewels, consists of tables and chairs, and all kinds of house furniture and ornaments.

delayed him that night came on before he was able to reach
the next station. He therefore took refuge in an old
temple ; but, when morning came, he was horrified to find
that the treasure had disappeared. Unable to fix the guilt
on anyone, he returned forthwith to the Governor and told
him the whole story. The latter, however, refused to
believe what the magistrate said, and would have had him
severely punished, but that each and all of his attendants
stoutly corroborated his statements ; and accordingly he
bade him return and endeavour to find the missing silver.
When the magistrate got back to the temple, he met an
extraordinary-looking blind man, who informed him that
he could read people's thoughts, and further went on to say
that the magistrate had come there on a matter of money.
The latter replied that it was so, and recounted the misfortune that had overtaken him ; whereupon the blind man
called for sedan-chairs, and told the magistrate to follow
and see for himself, which he accordingly did, accompanied
by all his retinue. If the blind man said east, they went
east ; or if north, north ; journeying along for five days
until far among the hills, where they beheld a large city
with a great number of inhabitants. They entered the
gates and proceeded on for a short distance, when suddenly
the blind man cried " Stop ! " and, alighting from his
chair, pointed to a lofty door facing the west, at which he
told the magistrate to knock and make what inquiries were
necessary. He then bowed and took his leave, and the
magistrate obeyed his instructions, whereupon a man came
out in reply to his summons. He was dressed in the fashion
of the Han dynasty,[1] and did not say what his name was ;
but as soon as the magistrate informed him wherefore he
had come, he replied that if the latter would wait a few
days he himself would assist him in the matter. The man
then conducted the magistrate within, and giving him
a room to himself, provided him regularly with food and
drink. One day he chanced to stroll away to the back of
the building, and there found a beautiful garden with dense
avenues of pine-trees and smooth lawns of fine grass. After
wandering about for some time among the arbours and
ornamental buildings, the magistrate came to a lofty
kiosque, and mounted the steps, when he saw hanging on

[1] Which ended some seventeen hundred years ago.

the wall before him a number of human skins, each with its eyes, nose, ears, mouth, and heart.[2] Horrified at this, he beat a hasty retreat to his quarters, convinced that he was about to leave his own skin in this out-of-the-way place, and giving himself up for lost. He reflected, however, that he should probably gain nothing by trying to escape, and made up his mind to wait ; and on the following day the same man came to fetch him, saying he could now have an audience. The magistrate replied that he was ready ; and his conductor then mounted a fiery steed, leaving the other to follow on foot. By-and-by they reached a door like that leading into a Viceroy's *yamên*, where stood on either side crowds of official servants, preserving the utmost silence and decorum. The man here dismounted and led the magistrate inside ; and after passing through another door they came into the presence of a king, who wore a cap decorated with pearls, and an embroidered sash, and sat facing the south. The magistrate rushed forward and prostrated himself on the ground ; upon which the King asked him if he was the Hu-nan official who had been charged with the conveyance of treasure. On his answering in the affirmative, the King said, " The money is all here ; it's a mere trifle, but I have no objection to receive it as a present from the Governor." The magistrate here burst into tears, and declared that his term of grace had already expired : that he would be punished if he went back thus, especially as he would have no evidence to adduce in substantiation of his story. " That is easy enough," replied the King, and put into his hands a thick letter, which he bade him give to the Governor, assuring him that this would prevent him from getting into any trouble. He also provided him with an escort ; and the magistrate, who dared not argue the point further, sorrowfully accepted the letter and took his departure. The road he travelled along was not that by which he had come ; and when the hills ended, his escort left him and went back. In a few days more he reached Ch'ang-sha, and respectfully informed the Governor of what had taken place ; but the Governor thought he was telling more lies, and in a great

[2] Corresponding with our five " senses," the heart taking the place of the brain, and being regarded by Chinese doctors as the seat not only of intelligence and the passions, but also of all sensation.

rage bade the attendants bind him hand and foot. The magistrate then drew the letter forth from his coat ; and when the Governor broke the seal and saw its contents, his face turned deadly pale. He gave orders for the magistrate to be unbound, remarking that the loss of the treasure was of no importance, and that the magistrate was free to go. Instructions were next issued that the amount was to be made up in some way or other and forwarded to the capital ; and meanwhile the Governor fell sick and died.

Now this Governor had had a wife of whom he was dotingly fond ; and one morning when they waked up, lo ! all her hair was gone. The whole establishment was in dismay, no one knowing what to make of such an occurrence. But the letter above-mentioned contained that hair, accompanied by the following words :—" Ever since you first entered into public life your career has been one of peculation and avarice. The six hundred thousand ounces of silver are safely stored in my treasury. Make good this sum from your own accumulated extortions. The officer you charged with the treasure is innocent ; he must not be wrongly punished. On a former occasion I took your wife's hair as a gentle warning. If now you disobey my injunctions, it will not be long before I have your head. Herewith I return the hair as an evidence of what I say." When the Governor was dead, his family divulged the contents of the letter ; and some of his subordinates sent men to search for the city, but they only found range upon range of inaccessible mountains, with nothing like a road or path.

XXXVII. ENGAGED TO A NUN

At I-ling, in Hupei, there lived a young man named Chên Yü, the son of a graduate. He was a good scholar and a handsome fellow, and had made a reputation for himself even before he arrived at manhood. When quite a boy, a physiognomist had predicted that he would marry a Taoist nun ; but his parents regarded it only as a joke, and made several attempts to get him a different kind of wife. Their efforts, however, had not hitherto proved successful, the difficulty being to find a suitable match.

Now his maternal grandmother lived at Huang-kang; and on one occasion, when young Chên was paying her a visit, he heard some one say that of the four Yüns at Huang-chou the youngest had no peer. This remark referred to some very nice-looking nuns who lived in a temple [1] a few miles from his grandmother's house; and accordingly Chên secretly set off to see them, and knocking at the door, was very cordially received by the four ladies, who were persons of considerable refinement. The youngest was a girl of incomparable beauty, and Chên could not keep his eyes off her, until at last she put her hand up to her face and looked the other way. Her companions now going out of the room to get tea for their visitor, Chên availed himself of the opportunity to ask the young lady's name; to which she replied that she was called Yün-ch'i, and that her surname was Ch'en. "How extraordinary!" cried Chên; "and mine is P'an." [2] This made her blush very much, and she bent her head down, and made no answer; by-and-by rising up and going away. The tea then came in, accompanied by some nice fruit, and the nuns began telling him their names. One was Pai Yün-shên, and thirty odd years of age; another was Shêng Yün-mien, just twenty; and the third was Liang Yün-tung, twenty-four or five years old, but the junior in point of religious standing. [3] Yün-ch'i did not reappear, and at length Chên grew anxious to see her again, and asked where she was. Miss Pai told him her sister was afraid of strangers, and Chên then got up and took his leave in spite of their efforts to detain him. "If you want to see Yün-ch'i you had better come again to-morrow," said Miss Pai; and Chên, who went home thinking of nothing but Yün-ch'i, did return to the temple on the following day. All the nuns

---

[1] These nunneries, of which there are plenty in China, are well worth visiting, and may be freely entered by both sexes. Sometimes there are as many as a hundred nuns living together in one temple, and to all appearances devoting their lives to religious exercises; report, however, tells many tales of broken vows, and makes sad havoc generally with the reputation of these fair vestals.

[2] In corresponding English, this would be:—The young lady said her name was Eloïsa. "How funny!" cried Chên, "and mine is Abelard."

[3] That is, she was the last to take the vows.

were there except Yün-ch'i, but he hardly liked to begin
by inquiring after her ; and then they pressed him to stay
and take dinner with them, accepting no excuses, Miss
Pai herself setting food and chop-sticks before him, and
urging him to eat.   When he asked where Yün-ch'i was,
they said she would come directly ; but evening gradually
drew on, and Chên rose to go home.   Thereupon they all
entreated him to stay, promising that if he did so they
would make Yün-ch'i come in.   Chên then agreed to remain ; the lamps were lighted, and wine was freely served
round, until at last he said he was so tipsy he couldn't
take any more.   "Three bumpers more," cried Miss Pai,
" and then we will send for Yün-ch'i."   So Chên drank off
his three cups, whereupon Miss Liang said he must also
drink three with her, which he did, turning his wine-cup
down on the table [4] and declaring that he would have no
more.   "The gentleman won't condescend to drink with
us," said Miss Pai to Miss Liang, " so you had better call
in Yün-ch'i, and tell the fair Eloïsa that her Abelard is
awaiting her."   In a few moments Miss Liang came back
and told Chên that Yün-ch'i would not appear ; upon
which he went off in a huff, without saying a word to either
of them, and for several days did not go near the place
again.   He could not, however, forget Yün-ch'i, and was
always hanging about on the watch, until one afternoon he
observed Miss Pai go out, at which he was delighted, for
he wasn't much afraid of Miss Liang, and at once ran
up to the temple and knocked at the door.   Yün-mien
answered his knock, and from her he discovered that Miss
Liang had also gone out on business.   He then asked for
Yün-ch'i, and Yün-mien led him into another courtyard,
where she called out, " Yün-ch'i ! here's a visitor."   At
this the door of the room was immediately slammed, and
Yün-mien laughed and told Chên she had locked herself in.
Chên was on the point of saying something, when Yün-mien
moved away, and a voice was heard from the other side of
the window, " They all want to make me a bait to entice
you, Sir ; and if you come here again, I cannot answer
for my safety.   I do not wish to remain a nun, and if I
could only meet with a gentleman like you, Mr. P'an, I

---

[4] The usual signal that a person does not wish to take any more
wine.

would be a handmaid to him all the days of my life." Chên
offered his hand and heart to the young lady on the spot ;
but she reminded him that her education for the priesthood
had not been accomplished without expense. "And if you
truly love me," added she, "bring twenty ounces of silver
wherewith to purchase my freedom. I will wait for you
three years with the utmost fidelity." Chên assented to
this, and was about to tell her who he really was, when
Yün-mien returned, and they all went out together, Chên
now bidding them farewell and going back to his grandmother's. After this he always had Yün-ch'i in his
thoughts, and wanted very much to get another interview
with her and be near her once again, but at this juncture
he heard that his father was dangerously ill, and promptly
set off on his way home, travelling day and night. His
father died, and his mother, who then ruled the household,
was such a severe person that he dared not tell her what was
nearest to his heart. Meanwhile he scraped together all
the money he could ; and refused all proposals of marriage
on the score of being in mourning for his father.[5] His
mother, however, insisted on his taking a wife ; and he
then told her that when he was with his grandmother at
Huang-kang, an arrangement had been made that he
was to marry a Miss Ch'ên, to which he himself was quite
ready to accede ; and that now, although his father's
death had stopped all communications on the subject, he
could hardly do better than pay a visit to his grandmother
and see how matters stood, promising that if the affair
was not actually settled he would obey his mother's commands. His mother consented to this, and off he started
with the money he had saved ; but when he reached Huang-
kang and went off to the temple, he found the place desolate
and no longer what it had been. Entering in, he saw only
one old priestess employed in cooking her food; and on
making inquiries of her, she told him that the Abbess had
died in the previous year, and that the four nuns had gone
away in different directions. According to her, Yün-
ch'i was living in the northern quarter of the city, and
thither he proceeded forthwith ; but after asking for her
at all the temples in the neighbourhood, he could get no

[5] This would carry him well on into the third of the years during
which Yün-ch'i had promised to wait for him.

news of her, and returned sorrowfully home, pretending to his mother that his uncle had said Mr. Ch'ên had gone away, and that as soon as he came back they would send a servant to let him know.

Some months after these events, Chên's mother went on a visit to her own home, and mentioned this story in conversation with her old mother, who, to her astonishment, knew nothing at all about it, but suggested that Chên and his uncle must have concocted the thing together. Luckily, however, for Chên his uncle was away at that time, and they had no means of getting at the real truth. Meanwhile, Chên's mother went away to the Lily Hill to fulfil a vow she had made, and remained all night at an inn at the foot of the hill. That evening the landlord knocked at her door and ushered in a young priestess to share the room. The girl said her name was Yün-ch'i ; and when she heard that Chên's mother lived at I-ling, she went and sat by her side, and poured out to her a long tale of tribulation, finishing up by saying that she had a cousin named P'an, at I-ling, and begging Chên's mother to·send some one to tell him where she would be found. " Every day I suffer," added she, " and each day seems like a year. Tell him to come quickly, or I may be gone." Chên's mother inquired what his other name might be, but she said she did not know ; to which the old lady replied that it was of no consequence, as, being a graduate, it would be easy to find him out. Early in the morning Chên's mother bade the girl farewell, the latter again begging her not to forget ; and when she reached home she told Chên what had occurred. Chên threw himself on his knees, and told his mother that he was the P'an to whom the young lady alluded ; and after hearing how the engagement had come about, his mother was exceedingly angry, and said, " Undutiful boy ! how will you face your relations with a nun for a wife ? " Chên hung his head and made no reply ; but shortly afterwards when he went up for his examination, he presented himself at the address given by Yün-ch'i—only, however, to find that the young lady had gone away a fortnight before. He then returned home and fell into a bad state of health, when his grandmother died and his mother set off to assist at her funeral. On her way back she missed the right road and reached the house of some people named Ching, who turned out to be cousins of hers. They invited her in, and there she saw a young girl of about eighteen sitting in the parlour, and as great a beauty as she had ever set eyes on. Now, as she was always thinking of making a good match for her son, and curing him of his settled melancholy, she asked who the young lady might be ; and they told her that her name was Wang,—that she was a connection of their own, and that her father and mother being dead, she was staying temporarily with them. Chên's mother inquired the name of Miss Wang's betrothed, but they said she was not engaged ; and then, taking her hand, she entered into conversation, and was very much charmed with her. Passing the night there, Chên's mother took her cousin into her confidence, and the latter agreed that it would be a capital match ; "but," added she, "this young lady is somewhat ambitious, or she would hardly have remained single so long. We must think about it." Meanwhile, Chên's mother and Miss Wang got on so extremely well together that they were already on the terms of mother and daughter ; and Miss Wang was invited to accompany her home. This invitation she readily accepted, and next day they went back ; Chên's mother, who wished to see her son free from his present trouble, bidding one of the servants tell him that she had brought home a nice wife for him ; Chên did not believe this ; but on peeping through the window beheld a young lady much prettier even than Yün-ch'i herself. He now began to reflect that the three years agreed upon had already expired ; that Yün-ch'i had gone no one knew whither, and had probably by this time found another husband ; so he had no difficulty in entertaining the thought of marrying this young lady, and soon regained his health. His mother then caused the young people to meet, and be introduced to one another ; saying to Miss Wang, when her son had left the room, " Did you guess why I invited you to come home with me ? " " I did," replied the young lady, " but I don't think you guessed what was *my* object in coming. Some years ago I was betrothed to a Mr. P'an, of I-ling. I have heard nothing of him for a long time. If he has found another wife I will be your daughter-in-law ; if not, I will ever regard you as my own mother, and endeavour to repay you for your kindness to me." " As there is an actual engagement," replied Chên's mother, " I will say no more ; but when I was at the Lily Hill there was a Taoist nun inquiring after this Mr. P'an, and now you again, though, as a matter of fact, there is no Mr. P'an in I-ling at all." " What ! " cried Miss Wang, " are you that lady I met ? I am the person who inquired for Mr. P'an." " If that is so," replied Chên's mother with a smile, " then your Mr. P'an is not far off." " Where is he ? " said she ; and then Chên's mother bade a maid-servant lead her out to her son and ask him. " Is your name Yün-ch'i ? " said Chên, in great astonishment ; and when the young lady asked him how he knew it, he told her the whole story of his pretending to be a Mr. P'an. But when Yün-ch'i found out to whom she was talking, she was abashed, and went back and told his mother, who inquired how she came to have two names. " My real name is Wang," replied the young lady ; " but the old Abbess, being very fond of me, made me take her own name." Chên's mother was over-joyed at all this, and an auspicious day was immediately fixed for the celebration of their marriage.

XXXVIII. THE YOUNG LADY OF THE TUNG-T'ING LAKE

THE spirits of the Tung-t'ing lake [1] are very much in the habit of borrowing boats. Sometimes the cable of an empty junk will cast itself off, and away goes the vessel over the waves to the sound of music in the air above. The boatmen crouch down in one corner and hide their faces, not daring to look up until the trip is over and they are once more at their old anchorage.

Now a certain Mr. Lin, returning home after having failed at the examination for Master's degree, was lying down very tipsy on the deck of his boat, when suddenly strains of music and singing began to be heard. The boatmen shook Mr. Lin, but failing to rouse him, ran down and hid themselves in the hold below. Then some one came and lifted him up, letting him drop again on to the deck, where he was allowed to remain in the same drunken sleep

[1] The celebrated lake in Hu-nan, round which has gathered so much of the folk-lore of China.

as before.   By-and-by the noise of the various instruments
became almost deafening, and Lin, partially waking up,
smelt a delicious odour of perfumes filling the air around
him.   Opening his eyes, he saw that the boat was crowded
with a number of beautiful girls ; and knowing that something strange was going on, he pretended to be fast asleep.
There was then a call for Chih-ch'êng, upon which a young
waiting-maid came forward and stood quite close to Mr.
Lin's head.   Her stockings were the colour of the kingfisher's wing, and her feet encased in tiny purple shoes, no
bigger than one's finger.   Much smitten with this young
lady, he took hold of her stocking with his teeth, causing
her, the next time she moved, to fall forward flat on her
face.   Some one, evidently in authority, asked what was
the matter ; and when he heard the explanation, was very
angry, and gave orders to take off Mr. Lin's head.   Soldiers
now came and bound Lin, and on getting up he beheld a
man sitting with his face to the south, and dressed in the
garments of a king.   "Sire," cried Lin, as he was being
led away, "the king of the Tung-t'ing lake was a mortal
named Lin ; your servant's name is Lin also.   His Majesty
was a disappointed candidate ; your servant is one too.
His Majesty met the Dragon Lady, and was made immortal ;
your servant has played a trick upon this girl, and he is
to die.   Why this inequality of fortunes ?"   When the
king heard this, he bade them bring him back, and asked
him, saying, "Are you, then, a disappointed candidate ?"
Lin said he was ; whereupon the king handed him writing
materials, and ordered him to compose an ode upon a
lady's head-dress.   Some time passed before Lin, who was a
scholar of some repute in his own neighbourhood, had done
more than sit thinking about what he should write ; and at
length the king upbraided him, saying, "Come, come, a
man of your reputation should not take so long."   "Sire,"
replied Lin, laying down his pen, "it took ten years to
complete the Songs of the Three Kingdoms ; whereby
it may be known that the value of compositions depends
more upon the labour given to them than the speed with
which they are written."   The king laughed, and waited
patiently from early morning till noon, when a copy of the
verses was put into his hand, with which he declared himself
very pleased.   He now commanded that Lin should be

served with wine ; and shortly after there followed a colla-
tion of all kinds of curious dishes, in the middle of which
an officer came in and reported that the register of people
to be drowned had been made up.   " How many in all ? "
asked the king.   " Two hundred and twenty-eight," was
the reply ; and then the king inquired who had been
deputed to carry it out ; whereupon he was informed that
the generals Mao and Nan had been appointed to do the
work.   Lin here rose to take leave, and the king presented
him with ten ounces of pure gold and a crystal square,[2]
telling him it would preserve him from any danger he
might encounter on the lake.   At this moment the king's
retinue and horses ranged themselves in proper order
upon the surface of the lake ; and his Majesty, stepping from the boat into his sedan-chair, disappeared from
view.

When everything had been quiet for a long time, the
boatmen emerged from the hold, and proceeded to shape
their course northwards.   The wind, however, was against
them, and they were unable to make any headway ; when
all of a sudden an iron cat appeared floating on the top of
the water.   " General Mao has come," cried the boatmen,
in great alarm ; and they and all the passengers on board
fell down on their faces.   Immediately afterwards a great
wooden beam stood up from the lake, nodding itself backwards and forwards, which the boatmen, more frightened
than ever, said was General Nan.   Before long a tremendous sea was raging, the sun was darkened in the
heavens, and every vessel in sight was capsized.   But
Mr. Lin sat in the middle of the boat, with the crystal
square in his hand, and the mighty waves broke around
without doing them any harm.   Thus were they saved, and
Lin returned home ; and whenever he told his wonderful
story, he would assert that, although unable to speak
positively as to the facial beauty of the young lady he had
seen, he dared say that she had the most exquisite pair of
feet in the world.

Subsequently, having occasion to visit the city of Wu-
ch'ang, he heard of an old woman who wished to sell her
daughter, but was unwilling to accept money, giving out

[2] The instrument used by masons is here meant.

that anyone who had the fellow of a certain crystal square in her possession should be at liberty to take the girl. Lin thought this very strange ; and taking his square with him sought out the old woman, who was delighted to see him, and told her daughter to come in. The young lady was about fifteen years of age, and possessed of surpassing beauty ; and after saying a few words of greeting, she turned round and went within again. Lin's reason had almost fled at the sight of this peerless girl, and he straightway informed the old woman that he had such an article as she required, but could not say whether it would match hers or not. So they compared their squares together, and there was not a fraction of difference between them, either in length or breadth. The old woman was overjoyed, and inquiring where Lin lived, bade him go home and get a bridal chair, leaving his square behind him as a pledge of his good faith. This he refused to do ; but the old woman laughed, and said, " You are too cautious, Sir ; do you think I should run away for a square ? " Lin was thus constrained to leave it behind him, and hurrying away for a chair, made the best of his way back. When, however, he got there, the old woman was gone. In great alarm he inquired of the people who lived near as to her whereabouts ; no one, however, knew ; and it being already late he returned disconsolately to his boat. On the way, he met a chair coming towards him, and immediately the screen was drawn aside, and a voice cried out, " Mr. Lin ! why so late ? " Looking closely, he saw that it was the old woman, who, after asking him if he hadn't suspected her of playing him false, told him that just after he left she had had the offer of a chair ; and knowing that he, being only a stranger in the place, would have some trouble in obtaining one, she had sent her daughter on to his boat. Lin then begged she would return with him, to which she would not consent ; and accordingly, not fully trusting what she said, he hurried on himself as fast as he could, and, jumping into the boat, found the young lady already there. She rose to meet him with a smile, and then he was astonished to see that her stockings were the colour of a kingfisher's wing, her shoes purple, and her appearance generally like that of the girl he had met on the Tung-t'ing lake. While he was still confused, the young lady remarked,

" You stare, Sir, as if you had never seen me before ! "
but just then Lin noticed the tear in her stocking made by
his own teeth, and cried out in amazement, " What !
are you Chih-ch'êng ? "   The young lady laughed at this ;
whereupon Lin rose, and, making her a profound bow,
said, " If you are that divine creature, I pray you tell me at
once, and set my anxiety at rest."   " Sir," replied she, " I
will tell you all.   That personage you met on the boat was
actually the king of the Tung-t'ing lake.   He was so pleased
with your talent that he wished to bestow me upon you ;
but, because I was a great favourite with her Majesty the
Queen, he went back to consult with her.   I have now
come at the Queen's own command."   Lin was highly
pleased ; and washing his hands, burnt incense, with his
face towards the lake, as if it were the Imperial Court,
and then they went home together.

Subsequently, when Lin had occasion to go to Wu-ch'ang,
his wife asked to be allowed to avail herself of the opportunity to visit her parents ; and when they reached the lake,
she drew a hair-pin from her hair, and threw it into the
water.   Immediately a boat rose from the lake, and Lin's
wife, stepping into it, vanished from sight like a bird on the
wing.   Lin remained waiting for her on the prow of his
vessel, at the spot where she had disappeared ; and by-and-
by, he beheld a houseboat approach, from the window of
which there flew a beautiful bird, which was no other than
Chih-ch'êng.   Then some one handed out from the same
window gold and silk, and precious things in great
abundance, all presents to them from the Queen.   After
this, Chih-ch'êng went home regularly twice every year,
and Lin soon became a very rich man, the things he had
being such as no one had ever before seen or heard of.

XXXIX.   THE MAN WHO WAS CHANGED
INTO A CROW

MR. YÜ JUNG was a Hu-nan man.   The person who told me
his story did not recollect from what department or district
he came.   His family was very poor ; and once, when
returning home after failure at the examination, he ran

quite out of funds. Being ashamed to beg, and feeling uncomfortably hungry, he turned to rest awhile in the Wu Wang [1] temple, where he poured out all his sorrows at the feet of the God. His prayers over, he was about to lie down in the outer porch, when suddenly a man took him and led him into the presence of Wu Wang; and then falling on his knees, said, " Your Majesty, there is a vacancy among the black-robes; the appointment might be bestowed on this man." The King assented, and Yü received a suit of black clothes; and when he had put these on he was changed into a crow, and flew away. Outside he saw a number of fellow-crows collected together, and immediately joined them, settling with them on the masts of the boats, and imitating them in catching and eating the meat or cakes which the passengers and boatmen on board threw up to them in the air.[2] In a little while he was no longer hungry, and, soaring aloft, alighted on the top of a tree, quite satisfied with his change of condition. Two or three days passed, and the King, now pitying his solitary state, provided him with a very elegant mate, whose name was Chu-ch'ing, and who took every opportunity of warning him when he exposed himself too much in search of food. However, he did not pay much attention to this, and one day a soldier shot him in the breast with a cross-bow; but luckily Chu-ch'ing got away with him in her beak, and he was not captured. This enraged the other crows very much, and with their wings they flapped the water into such big waves that all the boats were upset. Chu-ch'ing now procured food and fed her husband; but his wound was a severe one, and by the end of the day he was dead— at which moment he waked, as it were, from a dream, and found himself lying in the temple.

The people of the place had found Mr. Yü to all appearance dead; and not knowing how he had come by his death, and finding that his body was not quite cold, had set some one to watch him. They now learnt what had happened to him, and, making up a purse between them, sent him away

---

[1] The guardian angel of crows.

[2] In order to secure a favourable passage. The custom here mentioned was actually practised at more than one temple on the river Yang-tsze, and allusions to it will be found in more than one serious work.

home.   Three years afterwards he was passing by the same
spot, and went in to worship at the temple ;   also preparing
a quantity of food, and inviting the crows to come down
and eat it.   He then prayed, saying, " If Chu-ch'ing is
among you, let her remain."   When the crows had eaten
the food they all flew away ;   and by-and-by Yü returned,
having succeeded in obtaining his master's degree.   Again
he visited Wu Wang's temple, and sacrificed a sheep as a
feast for the crows ;   and again he prayed as on the previous
occasion.   That night he slept on the lake, and, just as the
candles were lighted and he had sat down, suddenly there
was a noise as of birds settling, and lo ! a beautiful young
lady about twenty years of age stood before him.   " Have
you been quite well since we parted ? " asked she ;   to
which Yü replied that he should like to know whom he had
the honour of addressing.   " Don't you remember Chu-
ch'ing ? " said the young lady ;   and then Yü was overjoyed, and inquired how she had come.   " I am now,"
replied Chu-ch'ing, " a spirit of the Han river, and seldom
go back to my old home ;   but in consequence of what
you did on two occasions, I have come to see you once
more."   They then sat talking together like husband and
wife reunited after long absence, and Yü proposed that she
should return with him on his way south.   Chu-ch'ing,
however, said she must go west again, and upon this point
they could not come to any agreement.   Next morning
when Yü waked up, he found himself in a lofty room with
two large candles burning brightly, and no longer in his
own boat.   In utter amazement he arose and asked where
he was.   " At Han-yang," replied Chu-ch'ing ;   " my home
is your home ;   why need you go south ? "   By-and-by,
when it got lighter, in came a number of serving-women
with wine, which they placed on a low table on the top of a
broad couch ;   and then husband and wife sat down to
drink together.   " Where are all my servants ? " asked Yü ;
and when he heard they were still on the boat, he said he
was afraid the boat people would not be able to wait.
" Never mind," replied Chu-ch'ing ;   " I have plenty of
money, and I'll help you to make it up to them."   Yü
therefore remained with her, feasting and enjoying himself,
and forgetting all about going home.   As for the boatmen,
when they walked up and found themselves at Han-

yang, they were greatly astonished ; and seeing that the servants could find no trace of their missing master, they wished to go about their own business. They were unable, however, to undo the cable, and so they all remained there together for more than a couple of months, by the end of which time Mr. Yü became anxious to return home, and said to Chu-ch'ing, " If I stay here, my family connections will be completely severed. Besides, as we are husband and wife, it is only right that you should pay a visit to my home." " That," replied Chu-ch'ing, " I cannot do ; and even were I able to go, you have a wife there already, and where would you put me ? It is better for me to stop where I am, and thus you will have a second family." Yü said she would be so far off that he could not always be dropping in ; whereupon Chu-ch'ing produced a black suit, and replied, " Here are your old clothes. Whenever you want to see me, put these on and come, and on your arrival I will take them off for you." She then prepared a parting feast for her husband, at which he got very tipsy ; and when he waked up he was on board his boat again, and at his old anchorage on the lake. The boatmen and his servants were all here, and they looked at one another in mutual amazement ; and when they asked Yü where he had been, he hardly knew what to say. By the side of his pillow he discovered a bundle in which were some new clothes Chu-ch'ing had given him, shoes, stockings, &c. ; and folded up with them was the suit of black. In addition to these he found an embroidered belt for tying round the waist, which was stuffed full of gold. He now started on his way south, and, when he reached the end of his journey, dismissed the boatmen with a handsome present.

After being at home for some months, his thoughts reverted to Han-yang ; and, taking out the black clothes, he put them on, when wings immediately grew from his ribs, and with a flap he was gone. In about four hours he arrived at Han-yang, and, wheeling round and round in the air, espied below him a solitary islet, on which stood a house, and there he proceeded to alight. A maid-servant had already seen him coming, and cried out, " Here's master ! " and in a few moments out came Chu-ch'ing, and bade the attendants take off Mr. Yü's feathers. They were not long in setting him free, and then, hand in hand, he and Chu-ch'ing went into the house together. " You have come at a happy moment," said his wife, as they sat down to tell each other all the news ; and in three days' time she gave birth to a boy, whom they called Han-ch'an, which means " born on the Han river." Three days after the event all the river-nymphs came to congratulate them, and brought many handsome presents. They were a charming band, not one being over thirty years of age ; and, going into the bedroom and approaching the bed, each one pressed her thumb on the baby's nose, saying, " Long life to thee, little one ! " Yü asked who they all were, and Chu-ch'ing told him they belonged to the same family of spirits as herself ; " And the two last of all," said she, " dressed in pale lilac, are the nymphs who gave away their girdles at Hankow." [3]

A few months passed away, and then Chu-ch'ing sent her husband back in a boat to his old home. No sails or oars were used, but the boat sped along of itself ; and at the end of the river journey there were men waiting with horses to convey him to his own door. After this he went backwards and forwards very frequently ; and in time Han-ch'an grew up to be a fine boy, the apple of his father's eye. Unhappily his first wife had no children, and she was extremely anxious to see Han-ch'an ; so Yü communicated this to Chu-ch'ing, who at once packed up a box and sent him back with his father, on the understanding that he was to return in three months. However, the other wife became quite as fond of him as if he had been her own child, and ten months passed without her being able to bear the thought of parting with him. But one day Han-ch'an was taken violently ill, and died ; upon which Yü's wife was overwhelmed with grief, and wished to die too. Yü then set off for Han-yang, to carry the tidings to Chu-ch'ing ; and when he arrived, lo ! there was Han-ch'an, with his shoes and socks off, lying on the bed. He was greatly rejoiced at this, and asked Chu-ch'ing what it all meant. " Why," replied she, " the term agreed upon by us had long

[3] Alluding to a legend of a young man meeting two young ladies at Hankow, each of whom wore a girdle adorned with a pearl as big as a hen's egg. The young man begged them to give him these girdles, and they did so ; but the next moment they had vanished, and the girdles too.

expired, and, as I wanted my boy, I sent for him." Yü then told her how much his other wife loved Han-ch'an, but Chu-ch'ing said she must wait until there was another child, and then she should have him. Later on Chu-ch'ing had twins, a boy and a girl, the former named Han-shêng and the latter Yü-p'ei ; whereupon Han-ch'an went back again with his father, who, finding it inconvenient to be travelling backwards and forwards three or four times in a year, removed with his family to the city of Han-yang. At twelve years of age Han-ch'an took his bachelor's degree ; and his mother, thinking there was no girl among mortals good enough for her son, sent for him to come home, that she herself might find a wife for him, which she did in the person of a Miss Chih-niang, who was the daughter of a spirit like herself. Yü's first wife then died, and the three children all went to mourn her loss, Han-ch'an remaining in Hu-nan after the funeral, but the other two returning with their father, and not leaving their mother again.

XL.   THE FLOWER NYMPHS

At the lower temple on Mount Lao the camellias are twenty feet in height, and many spans in circumference. The peonies are more than ten feet high ; and when the flowers are in bloom the effect is that of gorgeous tapestry. There was a Mr. Huang, of Chiao-chow, who built himself a house at that spot, for the purposes of study ; and one day he saw from his window a young lady dressed in white wandering about amongst the flowers. Reflecting that she could not possibly belong to the monastery,[1] he went out to meet her, but she had already disappeared. After this he frequently observed her, and once hid himself in a thick-foliaged bush, waiting for her to come. By-and-by she appeared, bringing with her another young lady dressed in red, who, as he noticed from his distant point of observation, was an exceedingly good-looking girl. When they approached nearer, the young lady in the red dress ran back, saying, " There is a man here ! " whereupon Mr. Huan jumped out upon them, and away they went in a scare, with their skirts and long sleeves fluttering in the breeze, and

[1] Women, of course, being excluded.

perfuming the air around. Huang pursued them as far as a low wall, where they suddenly vanished from his gaze. In great distress at thus losing the fair creatures, he took a pencil and wrote upon a tree the following lines:—

> The pangs of love my heart enthrall
> As I stand opposite this wall.
> I dread some hateful tyrant's power,
> With none to save you in that hour.

Returning home he was absorbed in his own thoughts, when all at once the young lady walked in, and he rose up joyfully to meet her. "I thought you were a brigand," said his visitor, smiling; "you nearly frightened me to death. I did not know you were a great scholar whose acquaintance I now hope to have the honour of making." Mr. Huang asked the young lady her name, &c., to which she replied, "My name is Hsiang-yü, and I belong to P'ing-k'ang-hsiang; but a magician has condemned me to remain on this hill much against my own inclination." "Tell me his name," cried Huang, "and I'll soon set you free." "There is no need for that," answered the young lady; "I suffer no injury from him, and the place is not an inconvenient one for making the acquaintance of such worthy gentlemen as yourself." Huang then inquired who was the young lady in red, and she told him that her name was Chiang-hsüeh, and that they were half-sisters; "and now," added she, "I will sing you a song; but please don't laugh at me." She then began as follows:—

> In pleasant company the hours fly fast,
> And through the window daybreak peeps at last.
> Ah, would that, like the swallow and his mate,
> To live together were our happy fate.

Huang here grasped her hand [2] and said, "Beauty without and intellect within—enough to make a man love

---

[2] Although the Chinese do not "shake hands" in our sense of the term, it is a sign of affection to seize the hand of a parting or returning friend. "The Book of Rites," however, lays down the rule that persons of opposite sexes should not, in passing things from one to the other, *let their hands touch*; and the question was gravely put to Mencius (Book IV.) as to whether a man might even pull his drowning sister-in-law out of the water. Mencius replied that it was indeed a general principle that a man should avoid touching a

you and forget all about death, only one day's absence being like the separation of a thousand miles. I pray you come again whenever an opportunity may present itself." From this time the young lady would frequently walk in to have a chat, but would never bring her sister with her in spite of all Mr. Huang's entreaties. Huang thought they weren't friends, but Hsiang said her sister did not care for society in the same way that she herself did, promising at the same time to try and persuade her to come at some future day. One evening Hsiang-yü arrived in a melancholy frame of mind, and told Huang that he was wanting more when he couldn't even keep what he had got ; " for to-morrow," said she, " we part." Huang asked what she meant ; and then, wiping away her tears with her sleeve, Hsiang-yü declared it was destiny, and that she couldn't well tell him. " Your former pro- phecy," continued she, " has come too true ; and now it may well be said of me—

> Fallen into the tyrant's power,
> With none to save me in that hour."

Huang again tried to question her, but she would tell him nothing ; and by-and-by she rose and took her leave. This seemed very strange ; however, next day a visitor came, who, after wandering round the garden, was much taken with a white peony,[3] which he dug up and carried away with him. Huang now awaked to the fact that Hsiang-yü was a flower nymph, and became very disconso- late in consequence of what had happened ; but when he subsequently heard that the peony only lived a few days after being taken away, he wept bitterly, and composed an elegy in fifty stanzas, besides going daily to the hole from which it had been taken, and watering the ground with his tears. One day, as he was returning thence, he espied the young lady of the red clothes also wiping away her tears alongside the hole and immediately walked back gently towards her. She did not run away, and Huang,

---

woman's hand, but that he who could not make an exception in such a case would be no better than a wolf. Neither, according to the Chinese rule, should men and women hang their clothes on the same rack, which reminds one of the French prude who would not allow male and female authors to be ranged upon the same bookshelf.   [3] The *Pæonia albiflora*, Pall.

grasping her sleeve, joined with her in her lamentations. When these were concluded he invited her to his house, and then she burst out with a sigh, saying, " Alas ! that the sister of my early years should be thus suddenly taken from me. Hearing you, Sir, mourn as you did, I have also been moved to tears. Those you shed have sunk down deep to the realms below, and may perhaps succeed in restoring her to us ; but the sympathies of the dead are destroyed for ever, and how then can she laugh and talk with us again ? " " My luck is bad," said Huang, " that I should injure those I love, neither can I have the good fortune to draw towards me another such a beauty. But tell me, when I often sent messages by Hsiang-yü to you, why did you not come ? " " I knew," replied she, " what nine young fellows out of ten are ; but I did not know what you were." She then took leave, Huang telling her how dull he felt without Hsiang-yü, and begging her to come again. For some days she did not appear ; and Huang remained in a state of great melancholy, tossing and turning on his bed and wetting the pillow with his tears, until one night he got up, put on his clothes, and trimmed the lamp ; and having called for pen and ink, he composed the following lines :—

> On my cottage roof the evening rain-drops beat ;
> I draw the blind and near the window take my seat.
> To my longing gaze no loved one appears ;
> Drip, drip, drip, drip : fast flow my tears.

This he read aloud ; and when he had finished, a voice outside said, " You want some one to cap your verses there ! " Listening attentively, he knew it was Chiang-hsüeh and opening the door he let her in. She looked at his stanza and added impromptu—

> She is no longer in the room ;
> A single lamp relieves the gloom ;
> One solitary man is there ;
> He and his shadow make a pair.

As Huang read these words his tears fell fast ; and then, turning to Chiang-hsüeh, he upbraided her for not having been to see him. " I can't come so often as Hsiang-yü did," replied she, " but only now and then when you are very dull." After this she used to drop in occasionally, and Huang said Hsiang-yü was his beloved wife, and she his dear friend, always trying to find out every time she came which flower in the garden she was, that he might bring her home with him, and save her from the fate of Hsiang-yü. "The old earth should not be disturbed," said she, "and it would not do any good to tell you. If you couldn't keep your wife always with you, how will you be sure of keeping a friend?" Huang, however, paid no heed to this, and seizing her arm, led her out into the garden, where he stopped at every peony and asked if this was the one; to which Chiang-hsüeh made no reply, but only put her hand to her mouth and laughed.

At New Year's time Huang went home, and a couple of months afterwards he dreamt that Chiang-hsüeh came to tell him she was in great trouble, begging him to hurry off as soon as possible to her rescue. When he woke up, he thought his dream a very strange one; and ordering his servant and horses to be ready, started at once for the hills. There he found that the priests were about to build a new room; and finding a camellia in the way, the contractor had given orders that it should be cut down. Huang now understood his dream, and immediately took steps to prevent the destruction of the flower. That night Chiang-hsüeh came to thank him, and Huang laughed and said, "It serves you right for not telling me which you were. Now I know you, and if you don't come and see me, I'll get a firebrand and make it hot for you." "That's just why I didn't tell you before," replied she. "The presence of my dear friend," said Huang, after a pause, "makes me think more of my lost wife. It is long since I have mourned for her. Shall we go and bemoan her loss together?" So they went off and shed many a tear on the spot where formerly Hsiang-yü had stood, until at last Chiang-hsüeh wiped her eyes and said it was time to go. A few evenings later Huang was sitting alone, when suddenly Chiang-hsüeh entered, her face radiant with smiles. "Good news!" cried she, "the Flower-God,[4] moved by

[4] The various subdivisions of the animal and vegetable kingdoms are each believed by the Chinese to be under the sway of a ruler holding his commission from and responsible to the one Supreme Power or God, fully in accordance with the general scheme of supernatural government accepted in other and less civilised communities.

your tears, has granted Hsiang-yü a return to life. Huang
was overjoyed, and asked when she would come ; to which
Chiang-hsüeh replied, that she could not say for certain,
but that it would not be long. "I came here on your
account," said Huang ; "don't let me be duller than you
can help." "All right," answered she, and then went
away, not returning for the next two evenings. Huang
then went into the garden and threw his arms around her
plant, entreating her to come and see him, though without
eliciting any response. He accordingly went back, and
began twisting up a torch, when all at once in she came,
and snatching the torch out of his hand, threw it away,
saying, "You're a bad fellow, and I don't like you, and
I sha'n't have any more to do with you." However,
Huang soon succeeded in pacifying her, and by-and-by in
walked Hsiang-yü herself. Huang now wept tears of joy
as he seized her hand, and drawing Chiang-hsüeh towards
them, the three friends mingled their tears together. They
then sat down and talked over the miseries of separation,
Huang meanwhile noticing that Hsiang-yü seemed to be
unsubstantial, and that when he grasped her hand his
fingers seemed to close only on themselves, and not as in
the days gone by. This Hsiang-yü explained, saying,
"When I was a flower-nymph I had a body ; but now I am
only the disembodied spirit of that flower. Do not regard
me as a reality, but rather as an apparition seen in a dream."
"You have come at the nick of time," cried Chiang-hsüeh ;
"your husband there was just getting troublesome."
Hsiang-yü now instructed Huang to take a little powdered
white-berry and mixing it with some sulphur, to pour out a
libation to her, adding, "This day next year I will return
your kindness." The young ladies then went away, and
next day Huang observed the shoots of a young peony
growing up where Hsiang-yü had once stood. So he made
the libation as she had told him, and had the plant very
carefully tended, even building a fence all round to protect
it. Hsiang-yü came to thank him for this, and he proposed
that the plant should be removed to his own home ; but
to this she would not agree, "for," said she, "I am not very
strong, and could not stand being transplanted. Besides,
all things have their appointed place ; and as I was not
originally intended for your home, it might shorten my life

to be sent there. We can love each other very well here."
Huang then asked why Chiang-hsüeh did not come ; to
which Hsiang-yü replied that they must make her, and
proceeded with him into the garden, where, after picking a
blade of grass, she measured upwards from the roots of
Chiang-hsüeh's plant to a distance of four feet six inches,
at which point she stopped and Huang began to scratch a
mark on the place with his nails. At that moment Chiang-
hsüeh came from behind the plant, and in mock anger cried
out, " You hussy you ! what do you aid that wretch for ? "
" Don't be angry, my dear," said Hsiang-yü ; " help me
to amuse him for a year only, and then you sha'n't be
bothered any more." So they went on, Huang watching
the plant thrive, until by the spring it was over two feet
in height. He then went home, giving the priests a handsome present, and bidding them take great care of it. Next
year, in the fourth moon, he returned and found upon the
plant a bud just ready to break ; and as he was walking
round, the stem shook violently as if it would snap, and
suddenly the bud opened into a flower as large as a plate,
disclosing a beautiful maiden within, sitting upon one of the
pistils, and only a few inches in height. In the twinkling
of an eye she had jumped out, and lo ! it was Hsiang-yü.
" Through the wind and the rain I have waited for you,"
cried she ; " why have you come so late ? " They then
went into the house, where they found Chiang-hsüeh
already arrived, and sat down to enjoy themselves as they
had done in former times. Shortly afterwards Huang's
wife died, and he took up his abode at Mount Lao for good
and all. The peonies were at that time as large round as
one's arm ; and whenever Huang went to look at them, he
always said, " Some day my spirit will be there by your
sides ; " to which the two girls used to reply with a laugh,
and say, " Mind you don't forget." Ten years after these
events, Huang became dangerously ill, and his son, who
had come to see him, was very much distressed about him.
" I am about to be born," cried his father ; " I am not going
to die. Why do you weep ? " He also told the priests
that if later on they should see a red shoot, with five leaves,
thrusting itself forth alongside of the peony, that would be
himself. This was all he said, and his son proceeded to
convey him home, where he died immediately on arrival.

Next year a shoot did come up exactly as he had mentioned ; and the priests, struck by the coincidence, watered it and supplied it with earth. In three years it was a tall plant, and a good span in circumference, but without flowers. When the old priest died, the others took no care of it ; and as it did not flower they cut it down. The white peony then faded and died ; and before long the camellia was dead too.

XLI. TA-NAN IN SEARCH OF HIS FATHER

HSI CH'ÊNG-LIEH was a Ch'êng-tu man. He had a wife and a concubine, the latter named Ho Chao-jung. His wife dying, he took a second by name Shên, who bullied the concubine dreadfully, and by her constant wrangling made his life perfectly unbearable, so that one day in a fit of anger he ran away and left them. Shortly afterwards Ho gave birth to a son, and called him Ta-nan ; but as Hsi did not return, the wife Shên turned them out of the house, making them a daily allowance of food. By degrees Ta-nan became a big boy ; and his mother, not daring to ask for an increase of victuals, was obliged to earn a little money by spinning. Meanwhile, Ta-nan, seeing all his companions go to school and learn to read, told his mother he should like to go too ; and accordingly, as he was still very young, she sent him for a few days' probation. He turned out to be so clever that he soon beat the other boys ; at which the master of the school was much pleased, and offered to teach him for nothing.[1] His mother, therefore, sent him regularly, making what trifling presents she could to the master ; and by the end of two or three years he had a first-rate knowledge of the Sacred Books.[2] One day he came home and asked his mother, saying, " All the fellows at our school get money from their fathers to buy cakes.

[1] This is by no means uncommon. The debt of gratitude between pupil and teacher is second only to that existing between child and parent ; and a successful student soon has it in his power to more than repay any such act of kindness as that here mentioned.

[2] Which form the unvarying curriculum of a Chinese education. These are (1) the *Four Books*, consisting of the teachings of Confucius and Mencius ; and (2) the *Five Canons* (in the ecclesiastical sense of the word) or the Canons of Changes, History, Poetry, the Record of Rites, and Spring and Autumn.

Why don't I ? " " Wait till you are grown up," replied
his mother, " and I will explain it to you." " Why, mother,"
cried he, " I'm only seven or eight years old. What a
time it will be before I'm grown up." " Whenever you pass
the temple of the God of War on your way to school,"
said his mother, " you should go in and pray awhile ;
that would make you grow faster." Ta-nan believed she
was serious ; and every day, going and coming, he went
in and worshipped at that temple. When his mother found
this out, she asked him how soon he was praying to be grown
up ; to which he replied that he only prayed that by the
following year he might be as big as if he were fifteen or
sixteen years old. His mother laughed ; but Ta-nan went
on, increasing in wisdom and stature alike, until by the
time he was ten he looked quite thirteen or fourteen, and
his master was no longer able to correct his essays. Then he
said to his mother, ' You promised me that when I grew
up you would tell me where my father is. Tell me now."
" By-and-by, by-and-by," replied his mother ; so he waited
another year, and then pressed her so eagerly to tell him
that she could no longer refuse, and related to him the whole
story. He heard her recital with tears and lamentations, and
expressed a wish to go in search of his father ; but his
mother objected that he was too young, and also that no
one knew where his father was. Ta-nan said nothing ;
however, in the middle of the day he did not come home
as usual, and his mother at once sent off to the school, where
she found he had not shown himself since breakfast. In great
alarm, and thinking that he had been playing truant, she
paid some people to go and hunt for him everywhere, but
was unable to obtain the slightest clue to his whereabouts.
As to Ta-nan himself, when he left the house he followed
the road without knowing whither he was going, until at
length he met a man who was on his way to K'uei-chou,
and said his name was Ch'ien. Ta-nan begged of him
something to eat, and went along with him ; Mr. Ch'ien
even procuring an animal for him to ride because he walked
too slowly. The expenses of the journey were all defrayed
by Ch'ien ; and when they arrived at K'uei-chou they
dined together, Ch'ien secretly putting some drug in Ta-
nan's food which soon reduced him to a state of unconsciousness. Ch'ien then carried him off to a temple, and, pre-

tending that Ta-nan was his son, offered him to the priests [3] on the plea that he had no money to continue his journey. The priests, seeing what a nice-looking boy he was, were only too ready to buy him ; and when Ch'ien had got his money he went away. They then gave Ta-nan a draught which brought him round ; but as soon as the abbot heard of the affair and saw Ta-nan himself, he would not allow them to keep him, sending him away with a purse of money in his pocket. Ta-nan next met a gentleman named Chiang, from Lu-chou, who was returning home after having failed at the examination ; and this Mr. Chiang was so pleased with the story of his filial piety that he took him to his own home at Lu-chou. There he remained for a month and more, asking everybody he saw for news of his father, until one day he was told that there was a man named Hsi among the Fokien traders. So he bade goodbye to Mr. Chiang, and set off for Fokien, his patron providing him with clothes and shoes, and the people of the place making up a subscription for him. On the road he met two traders in cotton cloth who were going to Fu-ch'ing, and he joined their party ; but they had not travelled many stages before these men found out that he had money, and taking him to a lonely spot, bound him hand and foot and made off with all he had. Before long a Mr. Ch'ên, of Yung-fu, happened to pass by, and at once unbound him, and giving him a seat in one of his own vehicles, carried him off home. This Mr. Ch'ên was a wealthy man, and in his house Ta-nan had opportunities of meeting with traders from all quarters. He therefore begged them to aid him by making inquiries about his father, himself remaining as a fellow student with Mr. Ch'ên's sons, and roaming the country no more, neither hearing any news of his former and now distant home.

Meanwhile, his mother, Ho, had lived alone for three or four years, until the wife, Shên, wishing to reduce the expenses, tried to persuade her to find another husband. As Ho was now supporting herself, she steadfastly refused to do this ; and then Shên sold her to a Chung-ch'ing trader, who took her away with him. However, she so frightened this man by hacking herself about with a knife, that when the wounds were healed he was only too happy to get rid

[3] See No. XXIII., note 10.

of her to a trader from Yen-t'ing, who in his turn, after Ho had nearly disembowelled herself, readily listened to her repeated cries that she wished to become a nun. However, he persuaded her to hire herself out as housekeeper to a friend of his, as a means of reimbursing himself for his outlay in purchasing her ; but no sooner had she set eyes on the gentleman in question than she found it was her own husband. For Hsi had given up the career of a scholar, and gone into business ; and as he had no wife, he was consequently in want of a housekeeper. They were very glad to see each other again ; and on relating their several adventures, Hsi knew for the first time that he had a son who had gone forth in search of his father. Hsi then asked all the traders and commercial travellers to keep a look-out for Ta-nan, at the same time raising Ho from the status of concubine to that of wife. In consequence, however, of the many hardships Ho had gone through, her health was anything but good, and she was unable to do the work of the house ; so she advised her husband to buy a concubine. This he was most unwilling to do, remembering too well the former squabbling he had to endure ; but ultimately he yielded, asked a friend to buy for him an oldish woman— at any rate more than thirty years of age. A few months afterwards his friend arrived, bringing with him a person of about that age ; and, on looking closely at her, Hsi saw that she was no other than his own wife Shên !

Now this lady had lived by herself for a year and more when her brother Pao advised her to marry again, which she accordingly agreed to do. She was prevented, however, by the younger branches of the family from selling the landed property ; but she disposed of everything else, and the proceeds passed into her brother's hands. About that time a Pao-ning trader, hearing that she had plenty of money, bribed her brother to marry her to himself ; and afterwards, finding that she was a disagreeable woman, took possession of everything she had, and advertised her for sale. No one caring to buy a woman of her age, and her master being on the eve of starting for K'uei-chou, took her with him, finally getting rid of her to Hsi, who was in the same line of business as himself. When she stood before her former husband, she was overwhelmed with shame and fear, and had not a word to say ; but Hsi gathered an outline of what had happened from the trader, and then said to her, " Your second marriage with this Pao-ning gentleman was doubtless contracted after you had given up all hope of seeing me again. It doesn't matter in the least, as now I am not in search of a wife but only of a concubine. So you had better begin by paying your respects to your mistress here, my wife Ho Chao-jung." Shên was ashamed to do this : but Hsi reminded her of the time when she had been in the wife's place, and in spite of all Ho's intercession insisted that she should do so, stimulating her to obedience by the smart application of a stick. Shên was therefore compelled to yield, but at the same time she never tried to gain Ho's favour, and kept away from her as much as possible. Ho, on the other hand, treated her with great consideration, and never took her to task on the performance of her duties ; whilst Hsi himself, whenever he had a dinner-party, made her wait at table, though Ho often entreated him to hire a maid.

Now the magistrate at Yen-t'ing was named Ch'ên Tsung-ssŭ, and once when Hsi had some trifling difficulty with one of the neighbours he was further accused to this official of having forced his wife to assume the position of concubine. The magistrate, however, refused to take up the case, to the great satisfaction of Hsi and his wife, who lauded him to the skies as a virtuous mandarin. A few nights after, at rather a late hour, the servant knocked at their door, and called out, " The magistrate has come ! " Hsi jumped up in a hurry, and began looking for his clothes and shoes ; but the magistrate was already in their bedroom without either of them understanding what it all meant : when suddenly Ho, examining him closely, cried out, " It is my son ! " She then burst into tears, and the magistrate, throwing himself on the ground, wept with his mother. It seemed he had taken the name of the gentleman with whom he had lived, and had since entered upon an official career. That on his way to the capital [4] he had made a *détour* and visited his old home, where he heard to his infinite sorrow that both his mothers had married again ; and that his relatives, finding him already a man of position, had restored to him the family property, of which he had left some one in charge in the hope that his father might return. That

---

[4] To be presented to the Emperor before taking up his post.

then he had been appointèd to Yen-t'ing, but had wished
to throw up the post and travel in search of his father, from
which design he had been dissuaded by Mr. Ch'ên.   Also
that he had met a fortune-teller from whom he obtained
the following response to his inquiries : " The lesser is the
greater ; the younger is the elder.   Seeking the cock, you
find the hen ; seeking one, you get two.   Your official life
will be successful."   Ch'ên then took up his appointment,
but not finding his father he confined himself entirely to
a vegetable diet, and gave up the use of wine.[5] The above-
mentioned case had subsequently come under his notice, and
seeing the name Hsi, he quietly sent his private servant to
find out, and thus discovered that this Hsi was his father.
At nightfall he set off himself, and when he saw his mother
he knew that the fortune-teller had told him true.   Bidding
them all say nothing to anybody about what had occurred,
he provided money for the journey, and sent them back
home.   On arriving there, they found the place newly
painted, and with their increased retinue of servants and
horses, they were quite a wealthy family.   As to Shên,
when she found what a great man Ta-nan had become, she
put still more restraint upon herself ; but her brother Pao
brought an action for the purpose of reinstating her as wife.
The presiding official happened to be a man of probity,
and delivered the following judgment :—" Greedy of gain,
you urged your sister to remarry.   After she had driven
Hsi away, she took two fresh husbands.   How have you
the face to talk about reinstating her as wife ? "   He
thereupon ordered Pao to be severely bambooed, and from
this time there was no longer any doubt about Shên's
status.   She was the lesser and Ho the greater ; and yet in
the matter of clothes and food Ho showed herself by no
means grasping.   Shên was at first afraid that Ho would
pay her out, and was consequently more than ever repentant ;
and Hsi himself, letting bygones be bygones, gave orders
that Shên should be called *madam* by all alike, though of
course she was excluded from any titles that might be
gained for them by Ta-nan.[6]

[5] Hoping thus to interest Buddha in his behalf.
[6] In accordance with Chinese usage, by which titles of nobility
are often conferred upon the *dead* parents of a distinguished son.

XLII. THE WONDERFUL STONE

IN the prefecture of Shun-t'ien [1] there lived a man named
Hsing Yün-fei, who was an amateur mineralogist and
would pay any price for a good specimen. One day as he
was fishing in the river, something caught his net, and
diving down he brought up a stone about a foot in diameter,
beautifully carved on all sides to resemble clustering hills
and peaks. He was quite as pleased with this as if he had
found some precious stone ; and having had an elegant
sandal-wood stand made for it, he set his prize upon the
table. Whenever it was about to rain, clouds, which from
a distance looked like new cotton-wool, would come forth
from each of the holes or grottoes on the stone, and appear
to close them up. By-and-by an influential personage
called at the house and begged to see the stone, immediately
seizing it and handing it over to a lusty servant, at the same
time whipping his horse and riding away. Hsing was in
despair ; but all he could do was to mourn the loss of his
stone, and indulge his anger against the thief. Meanwhile,
the servant, who had carried off the stone on his back,
stopped to rest at a bridge ; when all of a sudden his hand
slipped and the stone fell into the water. His master was
extremely put out at this, and gave him a sound beating ;
subsequently hiring several divers, who tried every means
in their power to recover the stone, but were quite unable
to find it. He then went away, having first published a
notice of reward, and by these means many were tempted
to seek for the stone. Soon after, Hsing himself came to
the spot, and as he mournfully approached the bank, lo !
the water became clear, and he could see the stone lying at
the bottom. Taking off his clothes, he quickly jumped
in and brought it out, together with the sandal-wood
stand, which was still with it. He carried it off home,
but being no longer desirous of showing it to people, he
had an inner room cleaned and put it in there. Some time
afterwards an old man knocked at the door and asked to
be allowed to see the stone ; whereupon Hsing replied
that he had lost it a long time ago. " Isn't that it in the

---

[1] In which Peking is situated.

inner room ? " said the old man smiling. " Oh, walk in
and see for yourself if you don't believe me," answered
Hsing ; and the old man did walk in, and there was the
stone on the table. This took Hsing very much aback ;
and the old man then laid his hand upon the stone and
said, " This is an old family relic of mine : I lost it many
months since. How does it come to be here ?   I pray you
now restore it to me." Hsing didn't know what to say,
but declared he was the owner of the stone ; upon which
the old man remarked, " If it is really yours, what evidence
can you bring to prove it ? " Hsing made no reply ;
and the old man continued, " To show you that I know
this stone, I may mention that it has altogether ninety-
two grottoes, and that in the largest of these are five words :

A stone from Heaven above."

Hsing looked and found that there were actually some small
characters, no larger than grains of rice, which by straining
his eyes a little he managed to read ; also, that the number
of grottoes was as the old man had said. However, he
would not give him the stone ; and the old man laughed,
and asked, " Pray, what right have you to keep other
people's things ? " He then bowed and went away, Hsing
escorting him as far as the door ; but when he returned to
the room, the stone had disappeared. In a great fright,
he ran after the old man, who had walked slowly and was
not far off, and seizing his sleeve entreated him to give
back the stone. "Do you think," said the latter, " that I
could conceal a stone a foot in diameter in my sleeve ? "
But Hsing knew that he must be superhuman, and led
him back to the house, where he threw himself on his knees
and begged that he might have the stone. " Is it yours or
mine ? " asked the old man. " Of course it is yours,"
replied Hsing, " though I hope you will consent to deny
yourself the pleasure of keeping it." " In that case,"
said the old man, " it is back again ; " and going into
the inner room, they found the stone in its old place. " The
jewels of this world," observed Hsing's visitor, " should
be given to those who know how to take care of them.
This stone can choose its own master, and I am very pleased
that it should remain with you ; at the same time I must
inform you that it was in too great a hurry to come into

the world of mortals, and has not yet been freed from all contingent calamities. I had better take it away with me, and three years hence you shall have it again. If, however, you insist on keeping it, then your span of life will be shortened by three years, that your terms of existence may harmonise together. Are you willing ? " Hsing said he was ; whereupon the old man with his fingers closed up three of the stone's grottoes, which yielded to his touch like mud. When this was done, he turned to Hsing and told him that the grottoes on that stone represented the years of his life ; and then he took his leave, firmly refusing to remain any longer, and not disclosing his name.

More than a year after this, Hsing had occasion to go away on business, and in the night a thief broke in and carried off the stone, taking nothing else at all. When Hsing came home, he was dreadfully grieved, as if his whole object in life was gone ; and made all possible inquiries and efforts to get it back, but without the slightest result. Some time passed away, when one day going into a temple Hsing noticed a man selling stones, and amongst the rest he saw his old friend. Of course he immediately wanted to regain possession of it ; but as the stone-seller would not consent, he shouldered the stone and went off to the nearest mandarin. The stone-seller was then asked what proof he could give that the stone was his ; and he replied that the number of grottoes was eighty-nine. Hsing inquired if that was all he had to say, and when the other acknowledged that it was, he himself told the magistrate what were the characters inscribed within, also calling attention to the finger marks at the closed-up grottoes. He therefore gained his case, and the mandarin would have bambooed the stone-seller, had he not declared that he bought it in the market for twenty ounces of silver,— whereupon he was dismissed.

A high official next offered Hsing one hundred ounces of silver for it ; but he refused to sell it even for ten thousand, which so enraged the would-be purchaser that he worked up a case against Hsing,[2] and got him put in prison. Hsing was thereby compelled to pawn a great deal of his property ;

[2] A common form of revenge in China, and one which is easily carried through when the prosecutor is a man of wealth and influence.

and then the official sent some one to try if the affair could not be managed through his son, to which Hsing, on hearing of the attempt, steadily refused to consent, saying that he and the stone could not be parted even in death. His wife, however, and his son, laid their heads together, and sent the stone to the high official, and Hsing only heard of it when he arrived home from the prison. He cursed his wife and beat his son, and frequently tried to make away with himself, though luckily his servants always managed to prevent him from succeeding.[3] At night he dreamt that a noble-looking personage appeared to him, and said, "My name is Shih Ch'ing-hsü—(Stone from Heaven). Do not grieve. I purposely quitted you for a year and more ; but next year on the 20th of the eighth moon, at dawn, come to the Hai-tai Gate and buy me back for two strings of cash." Hsing was overjoyed at this dream, and carefully took down the day mentioned. Meanwhile the stone was at the official's private house ; but as the cloud manifestations ceased, the stone was less and less prized ; and the following year when the official was disgraced for maladministration and subsequently died, Hsing met some of his servants at the Hai-tai Gate going off to sell the stone, and purchased it back from them for two strings of cash.

Hsing lived till he was eighty-nine ; and then having prepared the necessaries for his interment, bade his son bury the stone with him,[4] which was accordingly done. Six months later robbers broke into the vault [5] and made off with the stone, and his son tried in vain to secure their capture ; however, a few days afterwards, he was travelling with his servants, when suddenly two men rushed forth dripping with perspiration, and looking up into the air,

[3] Another favourite method of revenging oneself upon an enemy, who is in many cases held responsible for the death thus occasioned. The late Sir C. Alabaster told me an amusing story of a Chinese woman who deliberately walked into a pond until the water reached her knees, and remained there alternately putting her lips below the surface and threatening in a loud voice to drown herself on the spot, as life had been made unbearable by the presence of foreign barbarians. This was during the T'ai'ping rebellion.

[4] Valuables of some kind or other are often placed in the coffins of wealthy Chinese ; and women are almost always provided with a certain quantity of jewels with which to adorn themselves in the realms below.

[5] One of the most heinous offences in the Chinese Penal Code.

acknowledged their crime, saying, " Mr. Hsing, please don't torment us thus ! We took the stone, and sold it for only four ounces of silver." Hsing's son and his servants then seized these men, and took them before the magistrate, where they at once acknowledged their guilt. Asking what had become of the stone, they said they had sold it to a member of the magistrate's family ; and when it was produced, that official took such a fancy to it that he gave it to one of his servants and bade him place it in the treasury. Thereupon the stone slipped out of the servant's hand and broke into a hundred pieces, to the great astonishment of all present. The magistrate now had the thieves bambooed and sent them away ; but Hsing's son picked up the broken pieces of the stone, and buried them in his father's grave.

XLIII. THE QUARRELSOME BROTHERS

At K'un-yang there lived a wealthy man named Tsêng. When he died, and before he was put in the coffin, tears were seen to gush forth from both eyes of the corpse, to the infinite amazement of his six sons. His second son, T'i, otherwise called Yu-yü, who had gained for himself the reputation of being a scholar, said it was a bad omen, and warned his brothers to be careful and not give cause for sorrow to the dead,—at which the others only laughed at him as an idiot.

Tsêng's first wife and eldest son having been carried off by the rebels when the latter was only seven or eight years old, he married a second wife, by whom he had three sons, Hsiao, Chung, and Hsin ; besides three other sons by a concubine—namely, the above-mentioned T'i, or Yu-yü, Jen, and Yi. Now the three by the second wife banded themselves together against the three by the concubine, saying that the latter were a base-born lot ; and whenever a guest was present and either of them happened to be in the room, Hsiao and his two brothers would not take the slightest notice of them. This enraged Jen and Yi very much, and they went to consult with Yu-yü as to how they should avenge themselves for such slights. Yu-yü, however, tried every means in his power to pacify them, and would not take part in any plot ; and, as they were much younger than he, they took his advice,[1] and did nothing.

Hsiao had a daughter, who died shortly after her marriage to a Mr. Chou ; and her father begged Yu-yü and his other brothers to go with him and give his late daughter's mother-in-law a sound beating.[2] Yu-yü would not hear of it for a moment ; so Hsiao in a rage got his brothers Chung and Hsin, with a lot of rowdies from the neighbourhood, and went off and did it themselves, scattering the goods and chattels of the family about, and smashing everything they could lay their hands on. An action was immediately brought by the Chou family, and Hsiao and his two brothers were thrown into prison by the angry mandarin, who purposed sending the case before a higher tribunal. Yu-yü, however, whose high character was well known to that official, interceded for them, and himself went to the Chou family and tendered the most humble apologies for what had occurred. The Chou family, out of respect for Yu-yü, suffered the case to drop, and Hsiao regained his liberty, though he did not evince the slightest gratitude for his brother's exertions. Shortly after, Yu-yü's mother died ; but Hsiao and the other two refused to put on mourning for her, going on with their usual feasting and drinking as if nothing had happened. Jen and Yi were furious at this ; but Yu-yü only observed, "What they do is their own indecorous behaviour ; it does not injure us." Then, again, when the funeral was about to take place, Hsiao, Chung, and Hsin stood before the door of the vault, and would not allow the others to bury their mother there. So Yu-yü buried her alongside the principal grave. Before long Hsiao's wife died, and Yu-yü told Jen and Yi to accompany him to the house

---

[1] Deference to elder brothers is held by the Chinese to be second only in importance to filial piety.

[2] In a volume of *Chinese Sketches*, published by me in 1876, occur (p. 129) the following words :—" Occasionally a young wife is driven to commit suicide by the harshness of her mother-in-law, but this is of rare occurrence, as the consequences are terrible to the family of the guilty woman. The blood-relatives of the deceased repair to the chamber of death, and in the injured victim's hand they place a broom. They then support the corpse round the room, making its dead arm move the broom from side to side, and thus sweep away wealth, happiness, and longevity from the accursed place for ever."

and condole with the widower; to which they both
objected, saying, "He would not wear mourning for our
mother; shall we do so for his wife?" [3] Ultimately
Yu-yü had to go alone; and while he was pouring forth
his lamentations beside the bier, he heard Jen and Yi
playing drums and trumpets outside the door. Hsiao
flew into a tremendous passion, and went after them with
his own two brothers to give them a good thrashing. Yu-
yü, too, seized a big stick and accompanied them to the
house where Jen and Yi were; whereupon Jen made his
escape; but as Yi was clambering over the wall, Yu-yü
hit him from behind and knocked him down. Hsiao and
the others then set upon him with their fists and sticks,
and would never have stopped but that Yu-yü interposed
his body between them and made them desist. Hsiao
was very angry at this, and began to abuse Yu-yü, who
said, "The punishment was for want of decorum, for
which death would be too severe. I can neither connive
at their bad behaviour, nor at your cruelty. If your anger
is not appeased, strike me." Hsiao now turned his fury
against Yu-yü, and being well seconded by his two brothers,
they beat Yu-yü until the neighbours separated them and
put an end to the row. Yu-yü at once proceeded to Hsiao's
house to apologise for what had occurred; but Hsiao
drove him away, and would not let him take part in the
funeral ceremonies. Meanwhile, as Yi's wounds were very
severe, and he could neither eat nor drink, his brother
Jen went on his behalf to the magistrate, stating in the
petition that the accused had not worn mourning for their
father's concubine. The magistrate issued a warrant;
and, besides causing the arrest of Hsiao, Chung, and Hsin,
he ordered Yu-yü to prosecute them as well. Yu-yü,
however, was so much cut about the head and face that
he could not appear in court, but he wrote out a petition,
in which he begged that the case might be quashed; and
this the magistrate consented to do. Yi soon got better,
the feeling of hatred and resentment increasing in the
family day by day; while Jen and Yi, who were younger
than the others, complained to Yu-yü of their recent
punishment, saying, "The relationship of elder and younger

[3] A wife being an infinitely less important personage than a
mother in the Chinese social scale.

brothers exists for others, why not for us ? " "Ah," replied Yu-yü, "that is what I might well say ; not you." Yu-yü then tried to persuade them to forget the past ; but, not succeeding in his attempt, he shut up his house, and went off with his wife to live somewhere else, about twenty miles away. Now, although when Yu-yü was among them he did not help the two younger ones, yet his presence acted as some restraint upon Hsiao and the other two ; but now that he was gone their conduct was beyond all. bounds. They sought out Jen and Yi in their own houses, and not only reviled them, but abused the memory of their dead mother, against which Jen and Yi could only retaliate by keeping the door shut against them. However, they determined to do them some injury, and carried knives about with them wherever they went for that purpose.

One day the eldest brother, Ch'êng, who had been carried off by the rebels, returned with his wife ; and, after three days' deliberation, Hsiao and the other two determined that, as he had been so long separated from the family, he had no further claims upon them for houseroom, &c. Jen and Yi were secretly delighted at this result, and at once inviting Ch'êng to stay with them, sent news of his arrival to Yu-yü, who came back directly, and agreed with the others to hand over a share of the property to their elder brother. Hsiao and his clique were much enraged at this purchase of Ch'êng's goodwill, and, hurrying to their brothers' houses, assailed them with every possible kind of abuse. Ch'êng, who had long been accustomed to scenes of violence among the rebels, now got into a great passion, and cried out, " When I came home none of you would give me a place to live in. Only these younger ones recognised the ties of blood,[4] and you would punish them for so doing. Do you think to drive me away ? " Thereupon he threw a stone at Hsiao and knocked him down ; and Jen and Yi rushed out with clubs and gave the three of them a severe thrashing. Ch'êng did not wait for them to lay a plaint, but set off to the magistrate on the spot, and preferred a charge against his three brothers. The magistrate, as before,

[4] Literally, of hand and foot, to the mutual dependence of which that of brothers is frequently likened by the Chinese.

sent for Yu-yü to ask his opinion, and Yu-yü had no
alternative but to go, entering the *yamên* with downcast
head, his tears flowing in silence all the while. The
magistrate inquired of him how the matter stood; to
which he replied only by begging His Honour to hear the
case; which the magistrate accordingly did, deciding
that the whole of the property was to be divided equally
among the seven brothers. Thenceforth Jen and Yi became
more and more attached to Ch'êng; and one day, in
conversation, they happened to tell him the story of their
mother's funeral. Ch'êng was exceedingly angry, and
declared that such behaviour was that of brute beasts,
proposing at the same time that the vault should be opened
and that she should be re-buried in the proper place. Jen
and Yi went off and told this to Yu-yü, who immediately
came and begged Ch'êng to desist from his scheme; to
which, however, he paid no attention, and fixed a day
for her interment in the family vault. He then built a
hut near by, and, with a knife lopping the branches off
the trees, informed the brothers that any of them who
did not appear at the funeral in the usual mourning would
be treated by him in a manner similar to the trees. So
they were all obliged to go, and the obsequies were conducted in a fitting manner. The brothers were now at
peace together, Ch'êng keeping them in first-rate order,
and always treating Hsiao, Chung, and Hsin with much
more severity than the others. To Yu-yü he showed a
marked deference, and, whenever he was in a rage, would
always be appeased by a word from him. Hsiao, too,
was always going to Yu-yü to complain of the treatment
he received at Ch'êng's hands when he did anything that
Ch'êng disapproved of; and then, if Yu-yü quietly reproved
him, he would be dissatisfied, so that at last Yu-yü could
stand it no longer, and again went away and took a house
at a considerable distance, where he remained almost
entirely cut off from the others. By the time two years
had passed away Ch'êng had completely succeeded in
establishing harmony amongst them, and quarrels were
of rare occurrence. Hsiao was then forty-six years old,
and had five sons; Chi-yeh and Chi-tê, the first and third,
by his wife; Chi-kung and Chi-chi, the second and fourth,
by a concubine; and Chi-tsu, by a slave. They were

all grown up, and exactly imitated their father's former behaviour, banding themselves together one against the other, and so on, without their father being able to make them behave better. Chi-tsu had no brothers of his own, and, being the youngest, the others bullied him dreadfully; until at length, being on a visit to his wife's family, who lived not far from Yu-yü's house, he went slightly out of his way to call and see his uncle. There he found his three cousins living peaceably together and pursuing their studies, and was so pleased that he remained with them some time, and said not a word as to returning home. His uncle urged him to go back, but he entreated to be allowed to stay; and then his uncle told him it was not that he grudged his daily food: it was because his father and mother did not know where he was. Chi-tsu accordingly went home, and a few months afterwards, when he and his wife were on the point of starting to congratulate his wife's mother on the anniversary of her birthday, he explained to his father that he should not come home again. When his father asked him why not, he partly divulged his reasons for going; whereupon his father said he was afraid his uncle would bear malice for what happened in the past, and that he would not be able to remain there long. "Father," replied Chi-tsu, "uncle Yu-yü is a good and virtuous man." He set out with his wife, and when they arrived Yu-yü gave them separate quarters, and made Chi-tsu rank as one of his own sons, making him join the eldest, Chi-san, in his studies. Chi-tsu was a clever fellow, and now enrolled himself as a resident of the place where his uncle lived.[5]

Meanwhile, his brothers went on quarrelling among themselves as usual; and one day Chi-kung, enraged at an insult offered to his mother, killed Chi-yeh. He was immediately thrown into prison, where he was severely bambooed, and in a few days he died. Chi-yeh's wife, whose maiden name was Fêng, now spent the days of mourning in cursing her husband's murderer; and when Chi-kung's wife heard this, she flew into a towering passion, and said to her, "If your husband is dead, mine isn't

[5] Any permanent change of residence must be notified to the District Magistrate, who keeps a running census of all persons within his jurisdiction.

alive." She then drew a knife and killed her, completing the tragedy by herself committing suicide in a well.

Mr. Fêng, the father of the murdered woman, was very much distressed at his daughter's untimely end; and, taking with him several members of the family with arms concealed under their clothes, they proceeded to Hsiao's house, and there gave his wife a most terrific beating. It was now Ch'êng's turn to be angry. "The members of my family are dying like sheep," cried he; "what do you mean by this, Mr. Fêng?" He then rushed out upon them with a roar, accompanied by all his own brothers and their sons; and the Fêng family was utterly routed. Seizing old Fêng himself, Ch'êng cut off both his ears; and when his son tried to rescue him, Chi-chi ran up and broke both his legs with an iron crowbar. Every one of the Fêng family was badly wounded, and thus dispersed, leaving old Fêng's son lying in the middle of the road. The others not knowing what to do with him, Ch'êng took him under his arm, and having thrown him down in the Fêng village, returned home, giving orders to Chi-Chi to go immediately to the authorities and enter their plaint the first.[6]

The Fêng family had, however, anticipated them, and all the Tsêngs were accordingly thrown into prison, except Chung, who managed to escape. He ran away to the place where Yu-yü lived, and was pacing backwards and forwards before the door, afraid lest his brother should not have forgiven past offences, when suddenly Yu-yü, with his son and nephew, arrived on their return from the examination. "What do you want, my brother?" asked Yu-yü; whereupon Chung prostrated himself at the roadside, and then Yu-yü, seizing his hand, led him within to make further inquiries. "Alas! alas!" cried Yu-yü, when he had heard the story, "I knew that some dreadful calamity would be the result of all this wicked behaviour. But why have you come hither? I have been absent so long that I am no more acquainted with the local authorities; and if I now went to ask a favour of them, I should probably only be insulted for my pains. However, if none of the Fêng family die of their wounds, and

[6] To be thus beforehand with one's adversary is regarded as *prima facie* evidence of being in the right.

if we three may chance to be successful in our examination, something may perhaps be done to mitigate this
calamity." [7] Yu-yü then kept Chung to dinner, and at
night he shared their room, which kind treatment made
him at once grateful and repentant. By the end of ten
days he was so struck with the behaviour of the father,
sons, uncle, nephew, and cousins, one towards the other,
that he burst into tears, and said, " Now I know how badly
I behaved in days gone by." His brother was overjoyed
at his repentance, and sympathised with his feelings, when
suddenly it was announced that Yu-yü and his son had
both passed the examination for master's degree, and
that Chi-tsu was *proxime accessit*. This delighted them
all very much. They did not, however, attend the Fu-t'ai's
congratulatory feast,[8] but went off first to worship at the
tombs of their ancestors.

Now, at the time of the Ming dynasty a man who had
taken his master's degree was a very considerable personage,[9] and the Fêngs accordingly began to draw in their
horns. Yu-yü, too, met them half-way. He got a friend
to convey to them presents of food and money to help
them in recovering from their injuries, and thus the prosecution was withdrawn. Then all his brothers implored
him with tears in their eyes to return home, and, after
burning incense with them,[10] and making them enter into
a bond with him that bygones should be bygones, he
acceded to their request. Chi-tsu, however, would not
leave his uncle ; and Hsiao himself said to Yu-yü, " I
don't deserve such a son as that. Keep him, and teach
him as you have done hitherto, and let him be as one of
your own children ; but if at some future time he succeeds

[7] By means of the *status* which a graduate of the second degree
would necessarily have.

[8] A sham entertainment given by the Fu-t'ai, or governor, to all
the successful candidates. I say *sham*, because the whole thing is
merely nominal ; a certain amount of food is contracted for, but
there is never anything fit to eat, most of the money being embezzled
by the underlings to whose management the banquet is entrusted.

[9] Much more so than at present.

[10] Thereby invoking the Gods as witnesses. A common method
of making up a quarrel in China is to send the aggrieved party an
olive and a piece of red paper in token that peace is restored.
Why the *olive* should be specially employed I have in vain tried to
ascertain.

in his examination, then I will beg you to return him to me." Yu-yü consented to this; and three years afterwards Chi-tsu did take his master's degree, upon which he sent him back to his own family.

Both husband and wife were very loth to leave their uncle's house, and they had hardly been at home three days before one of their children, only three years old, ran away and went back, returning to his great-uncle's as often as he was recaptured. This induced Hsiao to remove to the next house to Yu-yü's, and, by opening a door between the two, they made one establishment of the whole. Ch'êng was now getting old, and the family affairs devolved entirely upon Yu-yü, who managed things so well that their reputation for filial piety and fraternal love was soon spread far and wide.

XLIV. THE YOUNG GENTLEMAN WHO COULDN'T SPELL [1]

AT Chia-p'ing there lived a certain young gentleman of considerable talent and very prepossessing appearance. When seventeen years of age he went up for his bachelor's degree; and as he was passing the door of a house, he saw within a pretty-looking girl, who not only riveted his gaze, but also smiled and nodded her head at him. Quite pleased at this, he approached the young lady and began to talk, she, meanwhile, inquiring of him where he lived, and if alone or otherwise. He assured her he was quite by himself; and then she said, " Well, I will come and see you, but you mustn't let any one know." The young gentleman agreed, and when he got home he sent all the servants to another part of the house, and by-and-by the young lady arrived. She said her name was Wên-chi, and that her admiration for her host's noble bearing had made her visit him, unknown to her mistress. " And gladly," added she, " would I be your handmaid for life." Our hero was delighted, and proposed to purchase her from the mistress she mentioned; and from this time she was in the habit of coming in every other day or so.

[1] Of course there is no such thing as spelling, in our sense of the term, in Chinese. But characters are frequently written with too many or too few strokes, and may thus be said to be incorrectly spelt.

On one occasion it was raining hard, and, after hanging up her wet cloak upon a peg, she took off her shoes, and bade the young gentleman clean them for her. He noticed that they were newly embroidered with all the colours of the rainbow, but utterly spoilt by the soaking rain; and was just saying what a pity it was, when the young lady cried out, " I should never have asked you to do such menial work except to show my love for you." All this time the rain was falling fast outside, and Wên-chi now repeated the following line :—

A nipping wind and chilly rain fill the river and the city.

"There," said she, " cap that." The young gentle-man replied that he could not, as he did not even understand what it meant. " Oh, really," retorted the young lady, " if you're not more of a scholar than that, I shall begin to think very little of you." She then told him he had better practise making verses, and he promised he would do so.

By degrees Miss Wên-chi's frequent visits attracted the notice of the servants, as also of a brother-in-law named Sung, who was likewise a gentleman of position; and the latter begged our hero to be allowed to have a peep at her. He was told in reply that the young lady had strictly forbidden that any one should see her; however, he concealed himself in the servants' quarters, and when she arrived he looked at her through the window. Almost beside himself, he now opened the door; whereupon Wên-chi, jumping up, vaulted over the wall and disappeared. Sung was really smitten with her, and went off to her mistress to try and arrange for her purchase; but when he mentioned Wên-chi's name, he was informed that they had once had such a girl, who had died several years previously. In great amazement Sung went back and told his brother-in-law, and he now knew that his beloved Wên-chi was a disembodied spirit. So when she came again he asked her if it was so; to which she replied, " It is; but as you wanted a nice wife and I a handsome husband, I thought we should be a suitable pair. What matters it that one is a mortal and the other a spirit ? " The young gentleman thoroughly coincided in her view of the case; and when his examination was over, and he was homeward bound, Wên-chi accompanied him, invisible to others and visible to him alone. Arriving at his parents' house, he installed her in the library; and the day she went to pay the customary bride's visit to her father and mother,[2] he told his own mother the whole story. She and his father were greatly alarmed, and ordered him to have no more to do with her; but he would not listen to this, and then his parents tried by all kinds of devices to get rid of the girl, none of which met with any success.

One day our hero had left upon the table some written instructions for one of the servants, wherein he had made a number of mistakes in spelling, such as *paper* for *pepper*, *jinjer* for *ginger*, and so on; and when Wên-chi saw this, she wrote at the foot :—

> Paper for pepper do I see ?
> Jinjer for ginger—can it be ?
> Of such a husband I'm afraid ;
> I'd rather be a servant-maid.

She then said to the young gentleman, " Imagining you to be a man of culture, I hid my blushes and sought you out the first.[3] Alas, your qualifications are on the outside ; should I not thus be a laughing-stock to all ? " She then disappeared, at which the young gentleman was much hurt ; but not knowing to what she alluded, he gave the instructions to his servant, and so made himself the butt of all who heard the story.

XLV. THE TIGER GUEST

A YOUNG man named Kung, a native of Min-chou, on his way to the examination at Hsi-ngan, rested awhile in an inn, and ordered some wine to drink. Just then a very tall and noble-looking stranger walked in, and, seating himself by the side of Kung, entered into conversation with him. Kung offered him a cup of wine, which the stranger did not refuse ; saying, at the same time, that his name was Miao. But he was a rough, coarse fellow ; and Kung, therefore, when the wine was finished, did not call for any more. Miao then rose, and observing that Kung did not appreciate a man of his capacity, went out

---

[2] A ceremonial visit made on the third day after marriage.
[3] Contrary to all Chinese notions of modesty and etiquette.

into the market to buy some, returning shortly with a huge bowl full. Kung declined the proffered wine ; but Miao, seizing his arm to persuade him, gripped it so painfully that Kung was forced to drink a few more cups, Miao himself swilling away as hard as he could go out of a soupplate. " I am not good at entertaining people," cried Miao, at length ; " pray go on or stop just as you please." Kung accordingly put together his things and went off ; but he had not gone more than a few miles when his horse was taken ill, and lay down in the road. While he was waiting there with all his heavy baggage, revolving in his mind what he should do, up came Mr. Miao ; who, when he heard what was the matter, took off his coat and handed it to the servant, and lifting up the horse, carried it off on his back to the nearest inn, which was about six or seven miles distant. Arriving there he put the animal in the stable, and before long Kung and his servant arrived too. Kung was much astonished at Mr. Miao's feat ; and, believing him to be superhuman, began to treat him with the utmost deference, ordering both wine and food to be procured for their refreshment. " My appetite," remarked Miao, " is one that you could not easily satisfy. Let us stick to wine." So they finished another stoup together, and then Miao got up and took his leave, saying, " It will be some time before your horse is well ; I cannot wait for you." He then went away.

After the examination several friends of Kung's invited him to join them in a picnic to the Flowery Hill ; and just as they were all feasting and laughing together, lo ! Mr. Miao walked up. In one hand he held a large flagon, and in the other a ham, both of which he laid down on the ground before them. " Hearing," said he, " that you gentlemen were coming here, I have tacked myself on to you, like a fly to a horse's tail." [1] Kung and his friends then rose and received him with the usual ceremonies, after which they all sat down promiscuously.[2] By-and-by,

[1] Alluding to a well-known expression which occurs in the *Historical Record*, and is often used in the sense of deriving advantage from connection with some influential person.

[2] Without any regard to precedence, which plays quite as important a part at a Chinese as at a Western dinner-party. In China, however, the most honoured guest sits at (what may be called) the head of the table, the host at the foot. I say " what

when the wine had gone round pretty freely, some one proposed capping verses ; whereupon Miao cried out, " Oh, we're very jolly drinking like this ; what's the use of making oneself uncomfortable ? " The others, however, would not listen to him, and agreed that as a forfeit a huge goblet of wine should be drunk by any defaulter. " Let us rather make death the penalty," said Miao ; to which they replied, laughing, that such a punishment was a trifle too severe ; and then Miao retorted that if it was not to be death, even a rough fellow like himself might be able to join. A Mr. Chin, who was sitting at the top of the line, then began :—

From the hill-top high, wide extends the gaze—

upon which Miao immediately carried on with

Redly gleams the sword o'er the shattered vase.[3]

The next gentleman thought for a long time, during which Miao was helping himself to wine ; and by-and-by they had all capped the verse, but so wretchedly that Miao called out, " Oh, come ! if we aren't to be fined for these,[4] we had better abstain from making any more." As none of them would agree to this, Miao could stand it no longer, and roared like a dragon till the hills and valleys echoed again. He then went down on his hands and knees,

may be called," as Chinese dining tables are almost invariably square, and position alone determines which is the head and which the foot. They are usually made to accommodate eight persons ; hence the fancy name " eight-angel table," in allusion to the eight famous angels, or Immortals, of the Taoist religion. (See No. V., note 1.) Occasionally, round tables are used ; especially in cases where the party consists of some such number as ten.

[3] It is almost impossible to give in translation the true spirit of a Chinese antithetical couplet. There are so many points to be brought out, each word of the second line being in opposition both in tone and sense to a corresponding word in the first, that anything beyond a rough rendering of the idea conveyed would be superfluous in a work like this. Suffice it to say that Miao has here successfully capped the verse given ; and the more so because he has introduced, through the medium of " sword " and " shattered vase," an allusion to a classical story in which a certain Wang Tun, when drunk with wine, beat time on a vase with his sword, and smashed the lip.

[4] This is the *vel ego vel Cluvienus* style of sarcasm, his own verse having been particularly good.

and jumped about like a lion, which utterly confused the
poets, and put an end to their lucubrations. The wine
had now been round a good many times, and being half
tipsy each began to repeat to the other the verses he had
handed in at the recent examination,[5] all at the same time
indulging in any amount of mutual flattery. This so
disgusted Miao that he drew Kung aside to have a game
at " guess-fingers ; "[6] but as they went on droning away
all the same, he at length cried out, " Do stop your rubbish,
fit only for your own wives,[7] and not for general company."
The others were much abashed at this, and so angry were
they at Miao's rudeness that they went on repeating all
the louder. Miao then threw himself on the ground in a
passion, and with a roar changed into a tiger, immediately
springing upon the company, and killing them all except
Kung and Mr. Chin. He then ran off roaring loudly.
Now this Mr. Chin succeeded in taking his master's degree ;
and three years afterwards, happening to revisit the
Flowery Hill, he beheld a Mr. Chi, one of those very gentlemen who had previously been killed by the tiger. In
great alarm he was making off, when Chi seized his bridle
and would not let him proceed. So he got down from his
horse, and inquired what was the matter ; to which Chi
replied, " I am now the slave of Miao, and have to endure
bitter toil for him. He must kill some one else before I
can be set free.[8] Three days hence a man, arrayed in the

[5] Many candidates, successful or otherwise, have their verses
and essays printed, and circulate them among an admiring circle of
friends.

[6] Accurately described in Tylor's *Primitive Culture*, Vol. I.,
p. 75 :—" Each player throws out a hand, and the sum of all the
fingers shown has to be called, the successful caller scoring a point;
practically each calls the total before he sees his adversary's hand."
The insertion of the word " simultaneously " after " called " would
improve this description. This game is so noisy that the Hong-
kong authorities have forbidden it, except within certain authorised
limits, between the hours of 11 p.m. and 6 a.m.—Ordinance No. 2
of 1872.

[7] This delicate stroke is of itself sufficient to prove the truth of
the oft-quoted Chinese saying, that all between the Four Seas are
brothers.

[8] The " substitution " theory, by which disembodied spirits are
enabled to find their way back to the world of mortals. A very
interesting and important example of this belief occurs in a later
story (No. CVI.), for which place I reserve further comments.

robes and cap of a scholar, should be eaten by the tiger at the foot of the Ts'ang-lung Hill. Do you on that day take some gentleman thither, and thus help your old friend." Chin was too frightened to say much, but promising that he would do so, rode away home. He then began to consider the matter over with himself, and, regarding it as a plot, he determined to break his engagement, and let his friend remain the tiger's devil. He chanced, however, to repeat the story to a Mr. Chiang who was a relative of his, and one of the local scholars ; and as this gentleman had a grudge against another scholar, named Yu, who had come out equal with him at the examination, he made up his mind to destroy him. So he invited Yu to accompany him on that day to the place in question, mentioning that he himself should appear in undress only. Yu could not make out the reason for this ; but when he reached the spot there he found all kinds of wine and food ready for his entertainment. Now that very day the Prefect had come to the hill ; and being a friend of the Chiang family, and hearing that Chiang was below, sent for him to come up. Chiang did not dare to appear before him in undress, and borrowed Yu's clothes and hat ; but he had no sooner got them on than out rushed the tiger and carried him away in its mouth.

XLVI. THE SISTERS

HIS EXCELLENCY the Grand Secretary Mao came from an obscure family in the district of Yeh, his father being only a poor cow-herd. At the same place there resided a wealthy gentleman, named Chang, who owned a burial-ground in the neighbourhood ; and some one informed him that while passing by he had heard sounds of wrangling from within the grave, and voices saying, " Make haste and go away ; do not disturb His Excellency's home." Chang did not much believe this ; but subsequently he had several dreams in which he was told that the burial-ground in question really belonged to the Mao family, and that he had no right whatever to it. From this moment the affairs of his house began to go wrong ;[1] and at length he listened to the remonstrances of friends and removed his dead elsewhere.

One day Mao's father, the cow-herd, was out near this burial-ground, when, a storm of rain coming on, he took refuge in the now empty grave, while the rain came down harder than ever, and by-and-by flooded the whole place and drowned the old man. The Grand Secretary was then a mere boy, and his mother went off to Chang to beg a piece of ground wherein to bury her dead husband. When Chang heard her name he was greatly astonished ; and on going to look at the spot where the old man was drowned, found that it was exactly at the proper place for the coffin. More than ever amazed, he gave orders that the body should be buried there in the old grave, and also bade Mao's mother bring her son to see him. When the funeral was over, she went with Mao to Mr. Chang's house, to thank him for his kindness ; and so pleased was he with the boy that he kept him to be educated, ranking him as one of his own sons. He also said he would give him his eldest daughter as a wife, an offer which Mao's mother hardly dared accept ; but Mrs. Chang said that the thing was settled and couldn't be altered, so then she was obliged to consent. The young lady, however, had a great contempt for Mao, and made no effort to disguise her feelings ; and if any one spoke to her of him, she would put her fingers in her ears, declaring she would die sooner than marry the cow-boy. On the day appointed for the wedding, the bridegroom arrived, and was feasted within, while outside the door a handsome chair was in waiting to convey away the bride, who all this time was standing crying in a corner, wiping her eyes with her sleeve, and absolutely refusing to dress. Just then the bridegroom sent in to say he was going,[2] and the drums and trumpets struck up the wedding march, at

[1] Such is the dominant belief regarding the due selection of an auspicious site, whether for a house or grave ; and with this superstition deeply ingrained in the minds of the people, it is easy to understand the hold on the public mind possessed by the pseudo-scientific professors of Fêng-Shui, or the geomantic art.

[2] The bridegroom leads off the procession, and the bride follows shortly afterwards in an elaborately-gilt sedan-chair, closed in on all sides so that the occupant cannot be seen.

which the bride's tears only fell the faster as her hair
hung dishevelled down her back. Her father managed
to detain Mao awhile, and went in to urge his daughter
to make haste, she weeping bitterly as if she did not hear
what he was saying. He now got into a rage, which only
made her cry the louder; and in the middle of it all a
servant came to say the bridegroom wished to take his
leave. The father ran out and said his daughter wasn't
quite ready, begging Mao to wait a little longer; and then
hurried back again to the bride. Thus they went on for
some time, backwards and forwards, until at last things
began to look serious, for the young lady obstinately
refused to yield; and Mr. Chang was ready to commit
suicide for want of anything better. Just then his second
daughter was standing by upbraiding her elder sister
for her disobedience, when suddenly the latter turned
round in a rage, and cried out, "So you are imitating
the rest of them, you little minx; why don't you go and
marry him yourself?" "My father did not betroth me
to Mr. Mao," answered she, "but if he had I should not
require you to persuade me to accept him." Her father
was delighted with this reply, and at once went off and
consulted with his wife as to whether they could venture
to substitute the second for the elder; and then her
mother came and said to her, "That bad girl there won't
obey her parents' commands; we wish, therefore, to put
you in her place: will you consent to this arrangement?"
The younger sister readily agreed, saying that had they
told her to marry a beggar she would not have dared to
refuse, and that she had not such a low opinion of Mr.
Mao as all that. Her father and mother rejoiced exceedingly at receiving this reply; and dressing her up
in her sister's clothes, put her in the bridal chair and sent
her off. She proved an excellent wife, and lived in harmony
with her husband; but she was troubled with a disease
of the hair, which caused Mr. Mao some annoyance. Later
on, she told him how she had changed places with her
sister, and this made him think more highly of her than
before. Soon after Mao took his bachelor's degree, and
then set off to present himself as a candidate for the
master's degree. On the way he passed by an inn, the
landlord of which had dreamt the night before that a

spirit appeared to him and said, " To-morrow Mr. Mao, first on the list, will come. Some day he will extricate you from a difficulty." Accordingly the landlord got up early, and took especial note of all guests who came from the eastward, until at last Mao himself arrived. The landlord was very glad to see him, and provided him with the best of everything, refusing to take any payment for it all, but telling what he had dreamt the night before. Mao now began to give himself airs ; and, reflecting that his wife's want of hair would make him look ridiculous, he determined that so soon as he attained to rank and power he would find another spouse. But alas ! when the list of successful candidates was published, Mao's name was not among them ; and he retraced his steps with a heavy heart, and by another road, so as to avoid meeting the innkeeper. Three years afterwards he went up again, and the landlord received him with precisely the same attentions as on the previous occasion ; upon which Mao said to him, " Your former words did not come true ; I am now ashamed to put you to so much trouble." " Ah," replied the landlord, " you meant to get rid of your wife, and the Ruler of the world below struck out your name.[3] My dream couldn't have been false." In great astonishment, Mao asked what he meant by these words ; and then he learnt that after his departure the landlord had had a second dream informing him of the above facts. Mao was much alarmed at what he heard, and remained as motionless as a wooden image, until the landlord said to him, ' You, Sir, as a scholar, should have more self-respect, and you will certainly take the highest place." By-and-by when the list came out, Mao was the first of all ; and almost simultaneously his wife's hair began to grow quite thick, making her much better-looking than she had hitherto been.

Now her elder sister had married a rich young fellow of good family, who lived in the neighbourhood, which made the young lady more contemptuous than ever ; but he was so extravagant and so idle that their property was soon gone, and they were positively in want of food.

---

[3] Here again we have the common Chinese belief that fate is fate only within certain limits, and is always liable to be altered at the will of heaven.

Hearing, too, of Mr. Mao's success at the examination, she was overwhelmed with shame and vexation, and avoided even meeting her sister in the street. Just then her husband died and left her destitute; and about the same time Mao took his doctor's degree, which so aggravated her feelings that, in a passion, she became a nun. Subsequently, when Mao rose to be a high officer of state, she sent a novice to his *yamên* to try and get a subscription out of him for the temple; and Mao's wife, who gave several pieces of silk and other things, secretly inserted a sum of money among them. The novice, not knowing this, reported what she had received to the elder sister, who cried out in a passion, "I wanted money to buy food with; of what use are these things to me?" So she bade the novice take them back; and when Mao and his wife saw her return, they suspected what had happened, and opening the parcel found the money still there. They now understood why the presents had been refused; and taking the money, Mao said to the novice, "If one hundred ounces of silver is too much luck for your mistress to secure, of course she could never have secured a high official, such as I am now, for her husband." He then took fifty ounces, and giving them to the novice, sent her away, adding, "Hand this to your mistress; I'm afraid more would be too much for her."[4] The novice returned and repeated all that had been said; and then the elder sister sighed to think what a failure her life had been, and how she had rejected the worthy to accept the worthless. After this, the innkeeper got into trouble about a case of murder, and was imprisoned; but Mao exerted his influence, and obtained the man's pardon.

XLVII. FOREIGN [1] PRIESTS

THE Buddhist priest, T'i-k'ung, relates that when he was at Ch'ing-chou he saw two foreign priests of very extraordinary appearance. They wore rings in their ears,

[4] This is another curious phase of Chinese superstition, namely, that each individual is so constituted by nature as to be able to absorb only a given quantity of good fortune and no more, any superfluity of luck doing actual harm to the person on whom it falls.
[1] The word here used is *fan*, generally translated "barbarian."

were dressed in yellow cloth, and had curly hair and beards. They said they had come from the countries of the west ; and hearing that the Governor of the district was a devóted follower of Buddha, they went to visit him. The Governor sent a couple of servants to escort them to the monastery of the place, where the abbot, Ling-p'ei, did not 'receive them very cordially ; but the secular manager, seeing that they were not ordinary individuals, entertained them and kept them there for the night. Some one asked if there were many strange men in the west, and what magical arts were practised by the Lohans ; [2] whereupon one of them laughed, and putting forth his hand from his sleeve, showed a small pagoda, fully a foot in height, and beautifully carved, standing upon the palm. Now very high up in the wall there was a niche ; and the priest threw the pagoda up to it, when lo! it stood there firm and straight. After a few moments the pagoda began to incline to one side, and a glory, as from a relic of some saint, was diffused throughout the room. The other priest then bared his arms and stretched out his left until it was five or six feet in length, at the same time shortening his right arm until it dwindled to nothing. He then stretched out the latter until it was as long as his left arm.

XLVIII. THE SELF-PUNISHED MURDERER

MR. LI was a *chü-jen* of Yung-nien.[1] On the 28th of the 9th moon of the 4th year of K'ang Hsi,[2] he killed his wife. The neighbours reported the murder to the officials, and the high authorities instructed the district magistrate to investigate the case. At this juncture Mr. Li was standing at the door of his residence ; and snatching a butcher's knife from a stall hard by, he rushed into the Ch'êng-huang [3] temple, where, mounting the theatrical stage,[4] he threw himself on his knees, and spoke as follows :—

[2] The disciples of Shakyamuni Buddha. Same as *Arhans*.
[1] In the province of Chihli. " Chü-jen " = second or master's degree.
[2] In 1665, that is between fourteen and fifteen years previous to the completion of the *Liao Chai*.
[3] See No. I., note 1.
[4] Religion and the drama work hand in hand in China.

" The spirit here will punish me. I am not to be prosecuted by evil men who, from party motives, confuse right and wrong. The spirit moves me to cut off an ear." There- upon he cut off his left ear and threw it down from the stage. He then said the spirit was going to fine him a hand for cheating people out of their money; and he forthwith chopped off his left hand. Lastly, he cried out that he was to be punished severely for all his many crimes ; and immediately cut his own throat. The Viceroy sub- sequently received the Imperial permission to deprive him of his rank [5] and bring him to trial ; but he was then being punished by a higher power in the realms of darkness below. See the *Peking Gazette.*[6]

XLIX. THE MASTER THIEF

BEFORE his rebellion,[1] Prince Wu frequently told his soldiers that if any one of them could catch a tiger unaided he would give him a handsome pension and the title of the Tiger Daunter. In his camp there was a man named Pao-chu, as strong and agile as a monkey ; and once when a new tower was being built, the wooden framework having only just been set up, Pao-chu walked along the eaves, and finally got up on the very tip-top beam, where he ran backwards and forwards several times. He then jumped down, alighting safely on his feet.

Now Prince Wu had a favourite concubine, who was a skilful player on the guitar ; and the nuts of the instru- ment she used were of warm jade,[2] so that when played upon there was a general feeling of warmth throughout the room. The young lady was extremely careful of this treasure, and never produced it for any one to see unless on receipt of the Prince's written order. One night, in

[5] Always the first step in the prosecution of a graduate. In this case, the accused was also an official.

[6] Of what date, our author does not say, or it would be curious to try and hunt up the official record of this case as it appeared in the Government organ of the day. The unfortunate man was in all probability insane.

[1] A.D. 1675. His full name was Wu San-kuei.

[2] Such is the literal translation of a term which I presume to be the name of some particular kind of jade, which is ordinarily dis- tinguished from the imitation article by its comparative *coldness.*

the middle of a banquet, a guest begged to be allowed to
see this wonderful guitar; but the Prince, being in a lazy
mood, said it should be exhibited to him on the following
day. Pao-chu, who was standing by, then observed that
he could get it without troubling the Prince to write an
order. Some one was therefore sent off beforehand to
instruct all the officials to be on the watch, and then the
Prince told Pao-chu he might go; and after scaling
numerous walls the latter found himself near the lady's
room. Lamps were burning brightly within; the doors
were bolted and barred, and it was impossible to effect an
entrance. Under the verandah, however, was a cockatoo
fast asleep on its perch; and Pao-chu, first mewing several
times like a cat, followed it up by imitating the voice of
the bird, and cried out as though in distress, "The cat!
the cat!" He then heard the concubine call to one of
the slave girls, and bid her go rescue the cockatoo, which
was being killed; and, hiding himself in a dark corner,
he saw a girl come forth with a light in her hand. She
had barely got outside the door when he rushed in, and
there he saw the lady sitting with the guitar on a table
before her. Seizing the instrument he turned and fled;
upon which the concubine shrieked out "Thieves!
thieves!" And the guard, seeing a man making off with
the guitar, at once started in pursuit. Arrows fell round
Pao-chu like drops of rain, but he climbed up one of a
number of huge ash trees growing there, and from its top
leaped on to the top of the next, and so on, until he had
reached the furthermost tree, when he jumped on to the
roof of a house, and from that to another, more as if he
were flying than anything else. In a few minutes he had
disappeared, and before long presented himself suddenly
at the banquet-table with the guitar in his hand, the
entrance-gate having been securely barred all the time,
and not a dog or a cock aroused.

L. A FLOOD

IN the twenty-first year of K'ang Hsi [1] there was a severe
drought, not a green blade appearing in the parched ground
all through the spring and well into the summer.   On
the 13th of the 6th moon a little rain fell, and people began
to plant their rice.   On the 18th there was a heavy fall,
and beans were sown.

Now at a certain village there was an old man, who,
noticing two bullocks fighting on the hills, told the villagers
that a great flood was at hand, and forthwith removed
with his family to another part of the country.   The
villagers all laughed at him ; but before very long rain
began to fall in torrents, lasting all through the night,
until the water was several feet deep, and carrying away
the houses.   Among the others was a man, who, neglecting
to save his two children, with his wife assisted his aged
mother to reach a place of safety, from which they looked
down at their old home, now only an expanse of water,
without hope of ever seeing the children again.   When the
flood had subsided, they went back, to find the whole place
a complete ruin ; but in their own house they discovered
the two boys playing and laughing on the bed as if nothing
had happened.   Some one remarked that this was a reward
for the filial piety of the parents.   It happened on the
20th of the 6th moon.[2]

LI. DEATH BY LAUGHING

A MR. SUN CHING-HSIA, a Director of Studies, told me that
in his village there was a certain man who had been killed
by the rebels when they passed through the place.   The

---

[1] A.D. 1682 ; that is, three years after the date of our author's
preface. See *Introduction*.

[2] A curious note here follows in the original :—" In 1696 a severe
earthquake occurred at P'ing-yang, and seven or eight out of every
ten of the inhabitants were killed, the city and suburbs were utterly
destroyed, only one house remaining uninjured—a house inhabited
by a filial son. And thus, when in the crash of a collapsing universe,
filial piety is specially marked out for protection, who shall say that
God Almighty does not know black from white ? "

man's head was left hanging down on his chest; and as soon as the rebels had gone, his servants secured the body and were about to bury it. Hearing, however, a sound of breathing, they looked more closely, and found that the windpipe was not wholly severed; and, setting his head in its proper place, they carried him back home. In twenty-four hours he began to moan; and by dint of carefully feeding him with a spoon, within six months he had quite recovered.

Some ten years afterwards he was chatting with a few friends, when one of them made a joke which called forth loud applause from the others. Our hero, too, clapped his hands; but, as he was bending backwards and forwards with laughter, the seam on his neck split open, and down fell his head with a gush of blood. His friends now found that he was quite dead, and his father immediately commenced an action against the joker; [1] but a sum of money was subscribed by those present and given to the father, who buried his son and stopped further proceedings.

LII. PLAYING AT HANGING

A NUMBER of wild young fellows were one day out walking when they saw a young lady approach, riding on a pony.[1] One of them said to the others, " I'll back myself to make that girl laugh," and a supper was at once staked by both sides on the result. Our hero then ran out in front of the pony, and kept on shouting " I'm going to die! I'm going to die!" at the same time pulling out from over the top of a wall a stalk of millet, to which he attached his own waistband, and, tying the latter round his neck,

---

[1] The Chinese distinguish five degrees of homicide, of which accidental homicide is one (see *Penal Code*, Book VI.). Thus, if a gun goes off of itself in a man's hand and kills a bystander, the holder of the gun is guilty of homicide; but were the same gun lying on a table, it would be regarded as the will of Heaven. Similarly, a man is held responsible for any death caused by an animal belonging to him; though in such cases the affair can usually be hushed up by a money payment, no notice being taken of crimes in general unless at the instigation of a prosecutor, at whose will the case may be subsequently withdrawn. Where the circumstances are purely accidental, the law admits of a money compensation.

[1] Women in China ride astride.

made a pretence of hanging himself. The young lady did laugh as she passed by, to the great amusement of the assembled company ; but as when she was already some distance off their friend did not move, the others laughed louder than ever. However, on going up to him they saw that his tongue protruded, and that his eyes were glazed ; he was, in fact, quite dead. Was it not strange that a man should be able to hang himself on a millet stalk ? [2] It is a good warning against practical joking.

LIII. THE RAT WIFE

Hsi Shan was a native of Kao-mi, and a trader by occupation. He used constantly to travel between Mêng-yin and I-shui (in Shantung). One day he was delayed on the road by rain, and when he arrived at his usual quarters it was already late in the night. He knocked at all the doors, but no one answered ; and he was walking backwards and forwards in the piazza when suddenly a door flew open and an old man came out. He invited the traveller to enter, an invitation to which Hsi Shan gladly responded ; and, tying up his mule, he went in. The place was totally unfurnished ; and the old man began by saying that it was only out of compassion that he had asked him in, as his house was not an inn. " There are only three or four of us," added he ; " and my wife and daughter are fast asleep. We have some of yesterday's food, which I will get ready for you ; you must not object to its being cold." He then went within, and shortly afterwards returned with a low couch, which he placed on the ground, begging his guest to be seated, at the same time hurrying back for a low table, and soon for a number of other things, until at last Hsi Shan was quite uncomfortable, and entreated his host to rest himself awhile. By-and-by a young lady came out, bringing some wine ; upon which the old man said, " Oh, our A-ch'ien has got up." She was about sixteen or seventeen, a slender and pretty-looking girl ; and as Hsi Shan had an unmarried brother, he began to think directly that she would do for him. So he inquired of the old man his name and address, to which

[2] Which, although tolerably stout and strong, is hardly capable of sustaining a man's weight.

the latter replied that his name was Ku, and that his
children had all died save this one daughter. "I didn't
like to wake her just now, but I suppose my wife told her
to get up." Hsi Shan then asked the name of his son-in-
law, and was informed that the young lady was not yet
engaged,—at which he was secretly very much pleased.
A tray of food was now brought in, evidently the remains
from the day before ; and when he had finished eating,
Hsi Shan began respectfully to address the old man as
follows :—"I am only a poor wayfarer, but I shall never
forget the kindness with which you have treated me. Let
me presume upon it, and submit to your consideration
a plan I have in my head. My younger brother, San-
lang, is seventeen years old. He is a student, and by no
means unsteady or dull. May I hope that you will unite
our families together, and not think it presumption on my
part ? " "I, too, am but a temporary sojourner," replied
the old man, rejoicing; "and if you will only let me have
a part of your house, I shall be very glad to come and live
with you." Hsi Shan consented to this, and got up and
thanked him for the promise of his daughter ; upon which
the old man set to work to make him comfortable for the
night, and then went away. At cock-crow he was outside,
calling his guest to come and have a wash ; and when
Hsi Shan had packed up ready to go, he offered to pay for
his night's entertainment. This, however, the old man
refused, saying, "I could hardly charge a stranger anything for a single meal ; how much less could I take money
from one who is to be a connection by marriage ? " They
then separated, and in about a month Hsi Shan returned ;
but when he was a short distance from the village he met
an old woman with a young lady, both dressed in deep
mourning. As they approached he began to suspect it
was A-ch'ien ; and the young lady, after turning round
to look at him, pulled the old woman's sleeve, and whispered
something in her ear, which Hsi Shan himself did not hear.
The old woman stopped immediately, and asked if she
was addressing Mr. Hsi ; and when informed that she was,
she said mournfully, " Alas ! my husband has been killed
by the falling of a wall. We are going to bury him to-day.
There is no one at home ; but please wait here, and we
will be back by-and-by." They then disappeared among

the trees ; and, returning after a short absence, they walked along together in the dusk of the evening. The old woman complained bitterly of their lonely and helpless state, and Hsi Shan himself was moved to compassion by the sight of her tears. She told him that the people of the neighbourhood were a bad lot, and that if A-ch'ien was to marry into his family, no time should be lost. Hsi Shan said he was willing ; and when they reached the house the old woman, after lighting the lamp and setting food before him, proceeded to speak as follows :—" Knowing, Sir, that you would shortly arrive, we sold all our grain except about twenty piculs. We cannot take this with us so far ; but a mile or so to the north of the village, at the first house you come to, there lives a man named T'an Erh-ch'üan, who often buys grain from me. Don't think it too much trouble to oblige me by taking a sack with you on your mule and proceeding thither at once. Tell Mr. T'an that the old lady of the southern village has several piculs of grain which she wishes to sell in order to get money for a journey, and beg him to send some animals to carry it." The old woman then gave him a sack of grain ; and Hsi Shan, whipping up his mule, was soon at the place ; and, knocking at the door, a great fat fellow came out, to whom he told his errand. Emptying the sack he had brought, he went back himself first ; and before long a couple of men arrived leading five mules. The old woman took them into the granary, which was a cellar below ground, and Hsi Shan, going down himself, held the measure and grasped the smoothing-bar, while the mother poured the grain into the measure and the daughter received it in the sack. In a little while the men had got a load, with which they went off, returning altogether four times before all the grain was exhausted. They then paid the old woman, who kept one man and two mules, and, packing up her things, set off towards the east. After travelling some seven miles day began to break ; and by-and-by they reached a market-town, where the old woman hired animals and sent back T'an's servant. When they arrived at Hsi Shan's home he related the whole story to his parents, who were very pleased at what had happened, and provided separate apartments for the old lady ; and after choosing a lucky day, A-ch'ien was married to San-lang. The old woman prepared a handsome trousseau; and as for A-ch'ien herself, she spoke but little, seldom losing her temper, and if anyone addressed her she would only reply with a smile. She employed all her time in spinning, and thus became a general favourite with all alike. "Tell your brother," said she to San-lang, "that when he happens to pass our old residence he will do well not to make any mention of my mother and myself."

In three or four years' time the Hsi family had made plenty of money, and San-lang had taken his bachelor's degree, when one day Hsi Shan happened to pass a night with the people who lived next door to the house where he had met A-ch'ien. After telling them the story of his having had nowhere to sleep, and taking refuge with the old man and woman, his host said to him, "You must make a mistake, Sir; the house you allude to belongs to my uncle, but was abandoned three years ago in consequence of its being haunted. It has now been uninhabited for a long time. What old man and woman can have entertained you there?" Hsi Shan was very much astonished at this, but did not put much faith in what he heard; meanwhile his host continued, "For ten years no one dared enter the house; however, one day the back wall fell down, and my uncle, going to look at it, found, half-buried underneath the ruins, a large rat, almost as big as a cat. It was still moving, and my uncle went off to call for assistance, but when he got back the rat had disappeared. Every one suspected some supernatural agency to be at work, though on returning to the spot ten days afterwards nothing was to be either heard or seen; and about a year subsequently the place was inhabited once more." Hsi Shan was more than ever amazed at what he now heard, and on reaching home told the family what had occurred; for he feared that his brother's wife was not a human being, and became rather anxious about him. San-lang himself continued to be much attached to A-ch'ien; but by-and-by the other members of the family let A-ch'ien perceive that they had suspicions about her. So one night she complained to San-lang, saying, "I have been a good wife to you for some years, but now I am no longer regarded as a human being. I pray you

give me my divorce,[1] and seek for yourself some worthier
mate." She then burst into a flood of tears ; whereupon
San-lang said, " You should know my feelings by this
time. Ever since you entered the house the family has
prospered ; and that prosperity is entirely due to you.
Who can say it is not so ? " " I know full well," replied
A-ch'ien, " what you feel ; still there are the others, and
I do not wish to share the fate of an autumn fan." [2] At
length San-lang succeeded in pacifying her ; but Hsi Shan
could not dismiss the subject from his thoughts, and gave
out that he was going to get a first-rate mouser, with a
view to testing A-ch'ien. She did not seem very frightened
at this, though evidently ill at ease ; and one night she
told San-lang that her mother was not very well, and that
he needn't come to bid her good-night as usual. In the
morning mother and daughter had disappeared ; at which
San-lang was greatly alarmed, and sent out to look for
them in every direction. No traces of the fugitives could
be discovered, and San-lang was overwhelmed with grief,
unable either to eat or to sleep. His father and brother
thought it was a lucky thing for him, and advised him to

[1] The Chinese acknowledge seven just causes for putting away a
wife. (1) Bad behaviour towards the husband's father and mother.
(2) Adultery. (3) Jealousy. (4) Garrulity. (5) Theft. (6) Disease.
(7) Barrenness. The right of divorce may not, however, be enforced
if the husband's father and mother have died since the marriage, as
thus it would be inferred that the wife had served them well up to
the time of their death ; or if the husband has recently risen to
wealth and power (hence the saying, " The wife of my porridge
days shall not go down from my hall ") ; or, thirdly, if the wife's
parents and brothers are dead, and she has no home in which she
can seek shelter.
[2] This simile is taken from a song ascribed to Pan Chieh-yü,
a favourite of the Emperor Ch'êng Ti of the Han dynasty, written
when her influence with the Son of Heaven began to wane. I
venture to reproduce it here.

> " O fair white silk, fresh from the weaver's loom ;
> Clear as the frost, bright as the winter's snow !
> See ! friendship fashions out of thee a fan,
> Round as the round moon shines in heaven above.
> At home, abroad, a close companion thou,
> Stirring at every move the grateful gale.
> And yet I fear, ah, me ! that autumn chills,
> Cooling the dying Summer's torrid rage,
> Will see thee laid neglected on the shelf,
> All thought of bygone days, like them, bygone."

console himself with another wife. This, however, he refused to do ; until, about a year afterwards, nothing more having been heard of A-ch'ien, he could not resist their importunities any longer, and bought himself a concubine. But he never ceased to think of A-ch'ien ; and some years later, when the prosperity of the family was on the wane, they all began to regret her loss.

Now San-lang had a step-brother, named Lan, who, when travelling to Chiao-chou on business, passed a night at the house of a relative named Lu. He noticed that during the night sounds of weeping and lamentation proceeded from their next-door neighbours, but he did not inquire the reason of it ; however, on his way back he heard the same sounds, and then asked what was the cause of such demonstrations. Mr. Lu told him that a few years ago an old widow and her daughter had come there to live, and that the mother had died about a month previously, leaving her child quite alone in the world. Lan inquired what her name was, and Mr. Lu said it was Ku ; "But," added he, "the door is closely barred, and as they never had any communication with the village, I know nothing of their antecedents." "It's my sister-in-law," cried Lan, in amazement, and at once proceeded to knock at the door of the house. Some one came to the front door, and said, in a voice that betokened recent weeping, "Who's there ? There are no men in this house."[3] Lan looked through a crack, and saw that the young lady really was his sister-in-law ; so he called out, "Sister, open the door. I am your step-brother A-sui." A-ch'ien immediately opened the door and asked him in, and recounted to him the whole story of her troubles. "Your husband," said Lan, "is always thinking of you. For a trifling difference you need hardly have run away so far from him." He then proposed to hire a vehicle and take her home ; but A-ch'ien replied, "I came hither with my mother to hide because I was not regarded as a human being, and should make myself ridiculous by now returning thus. If I am to go back, my elder brother Hsi Shan must no longer live with us ; otherwise, I will immediately poison myself." Lan then went home and told San-lang, who set off and travelled all night until he

---

[3] Signifying that it would be impossible for him to enter.

reached the place where A-ch'ien was. Husband and wife were overjoyed to meet again, and the following day San-lang notified the landlord of the house where A-ch'ien had been living. Now this landlord had long desired to secure A-ch'ien as a concubine for himself; and, after making no claim for rent for several years, he began to hint as much to her mother. The old lady, however, refused flatly; but shortly afterwards she died, and then the landlord thought that he might be able to succeed. At this juncture San-lang arrived, and the landlord sought to hamper him by putting in his claim for rent; and, as San-lang was anything but well off at the moment, it really did annoy him very much. A-ch'ien here came to the rescue, showing San-lang a large quantity of grain she had in the house, and bidding him use it to settle accounts with the landlord. The latter declared he could not accept grain, but must be paid in silver; whereupon A-ch'ien sighed and said it was all her unfortunate self that had brought this upon them, at the same time telling San-lang of the landlord's former proposition. San-lang was very angry, and was about to take out a summons against him, when Mr. Lu interposed, and, by selling the grain in the neighbourhood, managed to collect sufficient money to pay off the rent. San-lang and his wife then returned home; and the former, having explained the circumstances to his parents, separated his household from that of his brother. A-ch'ien now proceeded to build, with her own money, a granary, which was a matter of some astonishment to the family, there not being a hundred-weight of grain in the place. But in about a year the granary was full,[4] and before very long San-lang was a rich man, Hsi Shan remaining as poor as before. Accordingly, A-ch'ien persuaded her husband's parents to come and live with them, and made frequent presents of money to the elder brother; so that her husband said, "Well, at any rate, you bear no malice." "Your brother's behaviour," replied she, "was from his regard for you. Had it not been for him, you and I would never have met." After this there were no more supernatural manifestations.

---

[4] The result of A-ch'ien's depredations as a rat.

LIV. THE MAN WHO WAS THROWN
DOWN A WELL

MR. TAI, of An-ch'ing, was a wild fellow when young. One day as he was returning home tipsy,[1] he met by the way a dead cousin of his named Chi; and having, in his drunken state, quite forgotten that his cousin was dead, he asked him where he was going. " I am already a disembodied spirit," replied Chi; " don't you remember ? " Tai was a little disturbed at this; but, being under the influence of liquor, he was not frightened, and inquired of his cousin what he was doing in the realms below. " I am employed as scribe," said Chi, " in the court of the Great King." " Then you must know all about our happiness and misfortunes to come," cried Tai. " It is my business," answered his cousin, " so of course I know. But I see such an enormous mass that, unless of special reference to myself or family, I take no notice of any of it. Three days ago, by the way, I saw your name in the register." Tai immediately asked what there was about himself, and his cousin replied, " I will not deceive you; your name was put down for a dark and dismal hell." Tai was dreadfully alarmed, and at the same time sobered, and entreated his cousin to assist him in some way. " You may try," said Chi, " what merit will do for you as a means of mitigating your punishment; but the register of your sins is as thick as my finger, and nothing short of the most deserving acts will be of any avail. What can a poor fellow like myself do for you ? Were you to

---

[1] I have already discussed the subject of drunkenness in China (*Chinese Sketches*, pp. 113, 114), and shall not return to it here, further than to quote a single sentence, to which I adhere as firmly now as when the book in question was published :—" Who ever sees in China a tipsy man reeling about a crowded thoroughfare, or lying with his head in a ditch by the side of some country road ? "
It is not, however, generally known that the Chinese, with their usual quaintness, distinguish between five kinds of drunkenness, different people being differently affected, according to the physical constitution of each. Wine may fly (1) to the heart, and produce maudlin emotions; or (2) to the liver, and incite to pugnacity; or (3) to the stomach, and cause drowsiness, accompanied by a flushing of the face; or (4) to the lungs, and induce hilarity; or (5) to the kidneys, and excite desire.

perform one good act every day, you would not complete the necessary total under a year and more, and it is now too late for that. But henceforth amend your ways, and there may still be a chance of escape for you." When Tai heard these words he prostrated himself on the ground, imploring his cousin to help him ; but, on raising his head, Chi had disappeared ; he therefore returned sorrowfully home, and set to work to cleanse his heart and order his behaviour.

Now Tai's next-door neighbour had long suspected him of paying too much attention to his wife ; and one day meeting Tai in the fields shortly after the events narrated above, he inveigled him into inspecting a dry well, and then pushed him down. The well was many feet deep, and the man felt certain that Tai was killed ; however, in the middle of the night he came round, and sitting up at the bottom, he began to shout for assistance, but could not make any one hear him. On the following day, the neighbour, fearing that Tai might possibly have recovered consciousness, went to listen at the mouth of the well ; and hearing him cry out for help, began to throw down a quantity of stones. Tai took refuge in a cave at the side, and did not dare utter another sound ; but his enemy knew he was not dead, and forthwith filled the well almost up to the top with earth. In the cave it was as dark as pitch, exactly like the Infernal Regions ; and not being able to get anything to eat or drink, Tai gave up all hopes of life. He crawled on his hands and knees further into the cave, but was prevented by water from going further than a few paces, and returned to take up his position at the old spot. At first he felt hungry ; by-and-by, however, this sensation passed away ; and then reflecting that there, at the bottom of a well, he could hardly perform any good action, he passed his time in calling loudly on the name of Buddha. Before long he saw a number of Will-o'-the-Wisps flitting over the water and illuminating the gloom of the cave ; and immediately prayed to them, saying, " O Will-o'-the-Wisps, I have heard that ye are the shades of wronged and injured people. I have not long to live, and am without hope of escape ; still I would gladly relieve the monotony of my situation by exchanging a few words with you." Thereupon, all the Wills came

flitting across the water to him ; and in each of them was
a man of about half the ordinary size. Tai asked them
whence they came ; to which one of them replied, " This
is an old coal-mine. The proprietor, in working the coal,
disturbed the position of some graves ; [2] and Mr. Lung-fei
flooded the mine and drowned forty-three workmen. We
are the shades of those men." He further said he did not
know who Mr. Lung-fei was, except that he was secretary
to the City God, and that in compassion for the misfortunes
of the innocent workmen, he was in the habit of sending
them a quantity of gruel every three or four days. " But
the cold water," added he, " soaks into our bones, and
there is but small chance of ever getting them removed.
If, Sir, you some day return to the world above, I pray
you fish up our decaying bones and bury them in some
public burying-ground. You will thus earn for yourself
boundless gratitude in the realms below." Tai promised
that if he had the luck to escape he would do as they
wished ; " but how," cried he, " situated as I am, can I
ever hope to look again upon the light of day ? " He then
began to teach the Wills to say their prayers, making for
them beads [3] out of bits of mud, in order to keep record
of the number of invocations uttered. He could not tell
night from morning ; he slept when he felt tired, and
when he waked he sat up. Suddenly, he perceived in
the distance the light of lamps, at which the shades all
rejoiced, and said, " It is Mr. Lung-fei with our food."
They then invited Tai to go with them ; and when he
said he couldn't because of the water, they bore him along
over it so that he hardly seemed to walk. After twisting
and turning about for nearly a quarter of a mile, he reached
a place at which the Wills bade him walk by himself ; and
then he appeared to mount a flight of steps, at the top of
which he found himself in an apartment lighted by a
candle as thick round as one's arm. Not having seen the
light of fire for some time, he was overjoyed and walked

[2] A religious and social offence of the deepest dye, sure to entail
punishment in the world to come, even if the perpetrator escapes
detection in this life.

[3] The Buddhist rosary consists of 108 beads, which number is the
same as that of the compartments in the *Phrabat*, or sacred foot-
print of Buddha.

in ; but observing an old man in a scholar's dress and cap
seated in the post of honour, he stopped, not liking to
advance further. But the old man had already caught
sight of him, and asked him how he, a living man, had
come there. Tai threw himself on the ground at his feet,
and told him all ; whereupon the old man cried out, " My
great-grandson ! " He then bade him get up ; and
offering him a seat, explained that his own name was
Tai Ch'ien, and that he was otherwise known as Lung-fei.
He said, moreover, that in days gone by a worthless grandson of his named T'ang had associated himself with a lot
of scoundrels and sunk a well near his grave, disturbing
the peace of his everlasting night ; and that therefore he
had flooded the place with salt water and drowned them.
He then inquired as to the general condition of the family
at that time.

   Now Tai was a descendant of one of five brothers,
from the eldest of whom T'ang himself was also descended ;
and an influential man of the place had bribed T'ang to
open a mine [4] alongside the family grave. His brothers
were afraid to interfere ; and by-and-by the water rose
and drowned all the workmen ; whereupon actions for
damages were commenced by the relatives of the deceased,[5]
and T'ang and his friend were reduced to poverty, and
T'ang's descendants to absolute destitution. Tai was a
son of one of T'ang's brothers, and having heard this
story from his seniors, now repeated it to the old man.
" How could they be otherwise than unfortunate," cried
the latter, " with such an unfilial progenitor ? But since
you have come hither, you must on no account neglect
your studies." The old man then provided him with
food and wine, and spreading a volume of essays according
to the old style before him, bade him study it most carefully. He also gave him themes for composition, and
corrected his essays as if he had been his tutor. The
candle remained always burning in the room, never needing
to be snuffed and never decreasing. When he was tired

---

   [4] It here occurred to me that the word hitherto translated " well "
should have been " shaft ; " but the commentator refers expressly
to the *Tso Chuan*, where the phrase for " a dry well," as first used,
is so explained. We must accordingly fall back on the supposition
that our author has committed a trifling slip.
   [5] See No. LI., note 1.

he went to sleep, but he never knew day from night. The old man occasionally went out, leaving a boy to attend to his great-grandson's wants. It seemed that several years passed away thus, but Tai had no troubles of any kind to annoy him. He had no other book except the volume of essays, one hundred in all, which he read through more than four thousand times. One day the old man said to him, " Your term of expiation is nearly completed, and you will be able to return to the world above. My grave is near the coal-mine, and the grosser breeze plays upon my bones. Remember to remove them to the eastern plain." [6] Tai promised he would see to this ; and then the old man summoned all the shades together and instructed them to escort Tai back to the place where they had found him. The shades now bowed one after the other, and begged Tai to think of them as well, while Tai himself was quite at a loss to guess how he was going to get out.

Meanwhile, Tai's family had searched for him everywhere, and his mother had brought his case to the notice of the officials, thereby implicating a large number of persons, but without getting any trace of the missing man. Three or four years passed away, and there was a change of magistrate ; in consequence of which the search was relaxed, and Tai's wife, not being happy where she was, married another husband. Just then an inhabitant of the place set about repairing the old well, and found Tai's body in the cave at the bottom. Touching it, he found it was not dead, and at once gave information to the family. Tai was promptly conveyed home, and within a day he could tell his own story.

Since he had been down the well, the neighbour who pushed him in had beaten his own wife to death ; and his father-in-law having brought an action against him, he had been in confinement for more than a year while the case was being investigated.[7] When released he was a mere bag of bones ; [8] and then hearing that Tai had come

[6] In order to profit by the vivifying influence of the east, the quarter associated with spring.

[7] That is, as to whether or not there were extenuating circumstances, in which case no punishment would be inflicted.   ſ

[8] Such is the invariable result of confinement in a Chinese prison, unless the prisoner has the wherewithal to purchase food.

back to life, he was terribly alarmed and fled away. The family tried to persuade Tai to take proceedings against him, but this he would not do, alleging that what had befallen him was a proper punishment for his own bad behaviour, and had nothing to do with the neighbour. Upon this, the said neighbour ventured to return ; and when the water in the well had dried up, Tai hired men to go down and collect the bones, which he put in coffins and buried all together in one place. He next hunted up Mr. Lung-fei's name in the family tables of genealogy, and proceeded to sacrifice all kinds of nice things at his tomb. By-and-by the Literary Chancellor [9] heard this strange story, and was also very pleased with Tai's compositions ; accordingly, Tai passed successfully through his examinations, and, having taken his master's degree, returned home and reburied Mr. Lung-fei on the eastern plain, repairing thither regularly every spring without fail.[10]

LV. THE VIRTUOUS DAUGHTER-IN-LAW

AN TA-CH'ÊNG was a Chung-ch'ing man. His father, who had gained the master's degree, died early ; and his brother Êrh-ch'êng was a mere boy. He himself had married a wife from the Ch'ên family, whose name was Shan-hu ; and this young lady had much to put up with from the violent and malicious disposition of her husband's mother.[1] However, she never complained ; and every morning dressed herself up smart, and went in to pay her respects to the old lady. Once when Ta-ch'êng was ill, his mother abused Shan-hu for dressing so nicely ; whereupon Shan-hu went back and changed her clothes ; but even then Mrs. An was not satisfied, and began to tear her own hair with rage. Ta-ch'êng, who was a very filial son, at once gave his wife a beating, and this put an end to the scene. From that moment his mother hated her more than ever, and although she was everything that a daughter-in-law could be, would never exchange a word with her. Ta-ch'êng then treated her in much the same

---

[9] The provincial examiner for the degree of bachelor.
[10] To worship at his tomb.   [1] See No. XLIII., note 2.

way, that his mother might see he would have nothing to do with her; still the old lady wasn't pleased, and was always blaming Shan-hu for every trifle that occurred. "A wife," cried Ta-ch'êng, "is taken to wait upon her mother-in-law. This state of things hardly looks like the wife doing her duty." So he bade Shan-hu begone,[2] and sent an old maid-servant to see her home : but when Shan-hu got outside the village-gate, she burst into tears, and said, "How can a girl who has failed in her duties as a wife ever dare to look her parents in the face ? I had better die." Thereupon she drew a pair of scissors and stabbed herself in the throat, covering herself immediately with blood. The servant prevented any further mischief, and supported her to the house of her husband's aunt, who was a widow living by herself, and who made Shan-hu stay with her. The servant went back and told Ta-ch'êng, and he bade her say nothing to any one, for fear his mother should hear of it. In a few days Shan-hu's wound was healed, and Ta-ch'êng went off to ask his aunt to send her away. His aunt invited him in, but he declined, demanding loudly that Shan-hu should be turned out; and in a few moments Shan-hu herself came forth, and inquired what she had done. Ta-ch'êng said she had failed in her duty towards his mother ; where-upon Shan-hu hung her head and made no answer, while tears of blood[3] trickled from her eyes and stained her dress all over. Ta-ch'êng was much touched by this spectacle, and went away without saying any more ; but before long his mother heard all about it, and, hurrying off to the aunt's, began abusing her roundly. This the aunt would not stand, and said it was all the fault of her own bad temper, adding, "The girl has already left you, and do you still claim to decide with whom she is to live ? Miss Ch'ên is staying with me, not your daughter-in-law ; so you had better mind your own business." This made Mrs. An furious ; but she was at a loss for an answer, and, seeing that the aunt was firm, she went off home abashed and in tears.

[2] See No. LIII., note I.
[3] Such is the Chinese idiom for what we should call "bitter" tears. This phrase is constantly employed in the notices of the death of a parent sent round to friends and relatives.

Shan-hu herself was very much upset, and determined to seek shelter elsewhere, finally taking up her abode with Mrs. An's elder sister, a lady of sixty odd years of age, whose son had died, leaving his wife and child to his mother's care. This Mrs. Yü was extremely fond of Shan-hu ; and when she heard the facts of the case, said it was all her sister's horrid disposition, and proposed to send Shan-hu back. The latter, however, would not hear of this, and they continued to live together like mother and daughter ; neither would Shan-hu accept the invitation of her two brothers to return home and marry some one else, but remained there with Mrs. Yü, earning enough to live upon by spinning and such work.

Ever since Shan-hu had been sent away, Ta-ch'êng's mother had been endeavouring to get him another wife ; but the fame of her temper had spread far and wide, and no one would entertain her proposals. In three or four years Erh-ch'êng had grown up, and he had to be married first. His wife was a young lady named Tsang-ku, whose temper turned out to be something fearful, and far more ungovernable even than her mother-in-law's. When the latter only looked angry, Tsang-ku was already at the shrieking stage ; and Erh-ch'êng, being of a very meek disposition, dared not side with either. Thus it came about that Mrs. An began to be in mortal fear of Tsang-ku ; and whenever her daughter-in-law was in a rage she would try and turn off her anger with a smile. She seemed never to be able to please Tsang-ku, who in her turn worked her mother-in-law like a slave, Ta-ch'êng himself not venturing to interfere, but only assisting his mother in washing the dishes and sweeping the floor. Mother and son would often go to some secluded spot, and there in secret tell their griefs to one another ; but before long Mrs. An was stretched upon a sick-bed with nobody to attend to her except Ta-ch'êng. He watched her day and night without sleeping, until both eyes were red and inflamed ; and then when he went to summon the younger son to take his place, Tsang-ku told him to leave the house. Ta-ch'êng now went off to inform Mrs. Yü, hoping that she would come and assist ; and he had hardly finished his tale of woe before Shan-hu walked in. In great confusion at seeing her, he would have left immediately had

not Shan held out her arms across the door ; whereupon
he bolted underneath them and escaped. He did not
dare to tell his mother, and shortly afterwards Mrs. Yü
arrived, to the great joy of Ta-ch'êng's mother, who made
her stay in the house. Every day something nice was
sent for Mrs. Yü, and even when she told the servants
that there was no occasion for it, she having all she wanted
at her sister's, the things still came as usual. However,
she kept none of them for herself, but gave what came to
the invalid, who gradually began to improve. Mrs. Yü's
grandson also used to come by his mother's orders, and
inquire after the sick lady's health, besides bringing a
packet of cakes and so on for her. " Ah, me ! " cried
Mrs. An, " what a good daughter-in-law you have got,
to be sure. What have you done to her ? " " What
sort of a person was the one you sent away ? " asked her
sister in reply. " She wasn't as bad as some one I know
of," said Mrs. An, " though not so good as yours."
" When she was here you had but little to do," replied
Mrs. Yü ; " and when you were angry she took no notice
of it. How was she not as good ? " Mrs. An then burst
into tears, and saying how sorry she was, asked if Shan-hu
had married again ; to which Mrs. Yü replied that she
did not know, but would make inquiries. In a few more
days the patient was quite well, and Mrs. Yü proposed to
return ; her sister, however, begged her to stay, and declared she should die if she didn't. Mrs. Yü then advised
that Erh-ch'êng and his wife should live in a separate
house, and Erh-ch'êng spoke about it to his wife ; but
she would not agree, and abused both Ta-ch'êng and Mrs.
Yü alike. It ended by Ta-ch'êng giving up a large share
of the property, and ultimately Tsang-ku consented, and
a deed of separation was drawn up. Mrs. Yü then went
away, returning next day with a sedan-chair to carry her
sister back ; and no sooner had the latter put her foot
inside Mrs. Yü's door, than she asked to see the daughter-
in-law, whom she immediately began to praise very highly.
" Ah," said Mrs. Yü, " she's a good girl, with her little
faults like the rest of us ; but even if your daughter-in-
law were as good as mine, you would not be able to
appreciate her." " Alas ! " replied her sister, " I must
have been as senseless as a statue not to have seen what

she was." "I wonder what Shan-hu, whom you turned out of doors, says of you?" rejoined Mrs. Yü. "Why, swears at me, of course," answered Mrs. An. "If you examine yourself honestly and find nothing which should make people swear at you, is it at all likely you would be sworn at?" asked Mrs. Yü. "Well, all people are fallible," replied the other, "and as I know she is not perfect, I conclude she would naturally swear at me." "If a person has just cause for resentment, and yet does not indulge that resentment, it is obvious how he will repay kindness; or if any one has just cause for leaving another and yet does not do so, it is obvious how he will act under good treatment. Now, all the things that were sent when you were ill, and all the various little attentions, did not come from my daughter-in-law, but from yours." Mrs. An was amazed at hearing this, and asked for some explanation; whereupon Mrs. Yü continued, "Shan-hu has been living here for a long time. Everything she sent to you was bought with money earned by her spinning, and that, too, continued late into the night." Mrs. An here burst into tears, and begged to be allowed to see Shan-hu, who came in at Mrs. Yü's summons, and threw herself on the ground at her mother-in-law's feet. Mrs. An was much abashed, and beat her head with shame; but Mrs. Yü made it all up between them, and they became mother and daughter as at first. In about ten days they went home, and, as their property was not enough to support them, Ta-ch'êng had to work with his pen while his wife did the same with her needle. Erh-ch'êng was quite well off, but his brother would not apply to him, neither did he himself offer to help them. Tsang-ku, too, would have nothing to do with her sister-in-law, because she had been divorced; and Shan-hu in her turn, knowing what Tsang-ku's temper was, made no great efforts to be friendly. So the two brothers lived apart; [4] and when Tsang-ku was in one of her outrageous moods, all the others would stop their ears, till at length there was only her husband and the servants upon whom to vent her spleen. One day a maid-servant of hers committed suicide, and the father of the girl brought an action against Tsang-ku

---

[4] A disgraceful state of things, in the eyes of the Chinese. See the paraphrase of the *Sacred Edict*, Maxim 1.

for having caused her death. Erh-ch'êng went off to the
mandarin's to take her place as defendant, but only got
a good beating for his pains, as the magistrate insisted
that Tsang-ku herself should appear and answer to the
charge, in spite of all her friends could do. The consequence was she had her fingers squeezed [5] until the flesh
was entirely taken off ; and the magistrate, being a grasping
man, a very severe fine was inflicted as well. Erh-ch'êng
had now to mortgage his property before he could raise
enough money to get Tsang-ku released ; but before long
the mortgagee threatened to foreclose, and he was obliged
to enter into negotiations for the sale of it to an old gentleman of the village named Jen. Now Mr. Jen knowing
that half the property had belonged to Ta-ch'êng, said
the deed of sale must be signed by the elder brother as
well ; however, when Ta-ch'êng reached his house, the
old man cried out, " I am Mr. An, M.A. ; who is this
Jen that he should buy my property ? " Then, looking
at Ta-ch'êng, he added, " The filial piety of you and your
wife has obtained for me in the realms below this interview ; " upon which Ta-ch'êng said, " O father, since
you have this power, help my younger brother." " The
unfilial son and the vixenish daughter-in-law," said the
old man, " deserve no pity. Go home and quickly buy
back our ancestral property." " We have barely enough
to live upon," replied Ta-ch'êng ; " where, then, shall we
find the necessary money ? " " Beneath the crape myrtle-
tree," [6] answered his father, " you will find a store of
silver, which you may take and use for this purpose."
Ta-ch'êng would have questioned him further, but the
old gentleman said no more, recovering consciousness
shortly afterwards [7] without knowing a word of what

[5] An illegal form of punishment, under the present dynasty,
which authorises only *bambooing* of two kinds, each of five degrees
of severity ; *banishment*, of three degrees of duration ; *transporta-
tion* for life, of three degrees of distance ; and *death*, of two kinds,
namely, by strangulation and decapitation. That torture is occasionally resorted to by Chinese officials is an indisputable fact ;
that it is commonly employed by the whole body of mandarins
could only be averred by those who have not had the opportunities
or the desire to discover the actual truth.

[6] *Lagerstræmia indica*, L.

[7] That is, old Mr. Jen's body had been possessed by the disembodied spirit of Ta-ch'êng's father.

had happened. Ta-ch'êng went back and told his brother, who did not altogether believe the story; Tsang-ku, however, hurried off with a number of men, and had soon dug a hole four or five feet deep, at the bottom of which they found a quantity of bricks and stones, but no gold. She then gave up the idea and returned home, Ta-ch'êng having meanwhile warned his mother and wife not to go near the place while she was digging. When Tsang-ku left, Mrs. An went herself to have a look, and seeing only bricks and earth mingled together, she too, retraced her steps. Shan-hu was the next to go, and she found the hole full of silver bullion; and then Ta-ch'êng repaired to the spot and saw that there was no mistake about it. Not thinking it right to apply this heirloom to his own private use, he now summoned Erh-ch'êng to share it; and having obtained twice as much as was necessary to redeem the estate, the brothers returned to their homes. Erh-ch'êng and Tsang-ku opened their half together, when lo! the bag was full of tiles and rubbish. They at once suspected Ta-ch'êng of deceiving them, and Erh-ch'êng ran off to see how things were going at his brother's. He arrived just as Ta-ch'êng was spreading the silver on the table, and with his mother and wife rejoicing over their acquisition; and when he had told them what had occurred, Ta-ch'êng expressed much sympathy for him, and at once presented him with his own half of the treasure. Erh-ch'êng was delighted, and paid off the mortgage on the land, feeling very grateful to his brother for such kindness. Tsang-ku, however, declared it was a proof that Ta-ch'êng had been cheating him; "for how otherwise," argued she, "can you understand a man sharing anything with another, and then resigning his own half?"

Erh-ch'êng himself did not know what to think of it; but next day the mortgagee sent to say that the money paid in was all imitation silver, and that he was about to lay the case before the authorities. Husband and wife were greatly alarmed at this, and Tsang-ku exclaimed, "Well, I never thought your brother was as bad as this. He's simply trying to take your life." Erh-ch'êng himself was in a terrible fright, and hurried off to the mortgagee to entreat for mercy; but as the latter was extremely angry and would hear of no compromise, Erh-ch'êng was obliged to make over the property to him to dispose of himself. The money was then returned, and when he got home he found that two lumps had been cut through, showing merely an outside layer of silver, about as thick as an onion-leaf, covering nothing but copper within. Tsang-ku and Erh-ch'êng then agreed to keep the broken pieces themselves, but send the rest back to Ta-ch'êng, with a message, saying that they were deeply indebted to him for all his kindness, and that they had ventured to retain two of the lumps of silver out of compliment to the giver ; also that the property which remained to them was still equal to Ta-ch'êng's, that they had no use for much land, and accordingly had abandoned it, and that Ta-ch'êng could redeem it or not as he pleased. Ta-ch'êng, who did not perceive the intention in all this, refused to accept the land ; however, Erh-ch'êng entreated him to do so, and at last he consented. When he came to weigh the money, he found it was five ounces short, and therefore bade Shan-hu pawn something from her jewel-box to make up the amount, with which he proceeded to pay off the mortgage. The mortgagee, suspecting it was the same money that had been offered him by Erh-ch'êng, cut the pieces in halves, and saw that it was all silver of the purest quality. Accordingly he accepted it in liquidation of his claim, and handed the mortgage back to Ta-ch'êng. Meanwhile, Erh-ch'êng had been expecting some catastrophe ; but when he found that the mortgaged land had been redeemed, he did not know what to make of it. Tsang-ku thought that at the time of the digging Ta-ch'êng had concealed the genuine silver, and immediately rushed off to his house, and began to revile them all round. Ta-ch'êng now understood why they had sent him back the money ; and Shan-hu laughed and said, "The property is safe ; why, then, this anger ? " Thereupon she made Ta-ch'êng hand over the deeds to Tsang-ku.

One night after this Erh-ch'êng's father appeared to him in a dream, and reproached him, saying, "Unfilial son, unfraternal brother, your hour is at hand. Wherefore usurp rights that do not belong to you ? " In the morning Erh-ch'êng told Tsang-ku of his dream, and proposed to return the property to his brother ; but she only laughed at him for a fool. Just then the eldest of his two sons, a boy of seven, died of small-pox, and this frightened Tsang-ku so that she agreed to restore the deeds. Ta-ch'êng would not accept them ; and now the second child, a boy of three, died also ; whereupon Tsang-ku seized the deeds, and threw them into her brother-in-law's house. Spring was over, but the land was in a terribly neglected state ; so Ta-ch'êng set to work and put it in order again. From this moment Tsang-ku was a changed woman towards her mother- and sister-in-law ; and when, six months later, Mrs. An died, she was so grieved that she refused to take any nourishment. "Alas!" cried she, "that my mother-in-law has died thus early, and prevented me from waiting upon her. Heaven will not allow me to retrieve my past errors." Tsang-ku had thirteen children,[8] but as none of them lived, they were obliged to adopt one of Ta-ch'êng's,[9] who, with his wife, lived to a good old age, and had three sons, two of whom took their doctor's degree. People said this was a reward for filial piety and brotherly love.

LVI. DR. TSÊNG'S DREAM

THERE was a Fuhkien gentleman named Tsêng, who had just taken his doctor's degree. One day he was out walking with several other recently elected doctors, when they heard that at a temple hard by there lived an astrologer, and accordingly the party proceeded thither to get their fortunes told. They went in and sat down, and the astrologer made some very complimentary remarks to Tsêng, at which he fanned himself and smiled, saying, "Have I any chance of ever wearing the dragon robes and the jade girdle?"[1] The astrologer[2] immediately put on a serious face, and replied that he would be a Secretary of State during twenty years of national tranquillity. Thereupon Tsêng was much pleased, and began to give himself greater airs than ever. A slight rain coming on, they sought shelter in the priest's quarters,

[8] Five is considered a large number for an ordinary Chinese woman.

[9] In order to leave some one behind to look after their graves and perform the duties of ancestral worship. No one can well refuse to give a son to be adopted by a childless brother.

[1] That is, of rising to the highest offices of State.

[2] The Chinese term used throughout is "star-man."

where they found an old bonze, with sunken eyes and a
big nose, sitting upon a mat. He took no notice of the
strangers, who, after having bowed to him, stretched
themselves upon the couches to chat, not forgetting to
congratulate Tsêng upon the destiny which had been
foretold him. Tsêng, too, seemed to think the thing was
a matter of certainty, and mentioned the names of several
friends he intended to advance, amongst others the old
family butler. Roars of laughter greeted this announce-
ment, mingled with the patter-patter of the increasing
rain outside. Tsêng then curled himself up for a nap,
when suddenly in walked two officials bearing a commission under the Great Seal appointing Tsêng to the
Grand Secretariat. As soon as Tsêng understood their
errand, he rushed off at once to pay his respects to the
Emperor, who graciously detained him some time in conversation, and then issued instructions that the promotion
and dismissal of all officers below the third grade [3] should
be vested in Tsêng alone. He was next presented with
the dragon robes, the jade girdle, and a horse from the
imperial stables, after which he performed the *k'o-t'ou* [4]
before His Majesty and took his leave. He then went
home, but it was no longer the old home of his youth.
Painted beams, carved pillars, and a general profusion of
luxury and elegance, made him wonder where on earth
he was ; until, nervously stroking his beard, he ventured
to call out in a low tone. Immediately the responses of
numberless attendants echoed through the place like
thunder. Presents of costly food were sent to him by all
the grandees, and his gate was absolutely blocked up
by the crowds of retainers who were constantly coming
and going. When Privy Councillors came to see him, he
would rush out in haste to receive them ; when Under-
Secretaries of State visited him, he made them a polite
bow ; but to all below these he would hardly vouchsafe
a word. The Governor of Shansi sent him twelve singing-
girls, two of whom, Ni-ni and Fairy, he made his favourites.
All day long he had nothing to do but find amusement as
best he could, until he bethought himself that formerly

---

[3] Chinese official life is divided into nine grades.
[4] Prostrating himself three times, and knocking his head on the
ground thrice at each prostration.

a man named Wang had often assisted him with money.
Thereupon he memorialised the Throne and obtained
official employment for him. Then he recollected that
there was another man to whom he owed a long-standing
grudge. He at once caused this man, who was in the
Government service, to be impeached and stripped of
his rank and dignities. Thus he squared accounts with
both. One day when out in his chair a drunken man
bumped against one of his tablet-bearers.[5] Tsêng had
him seized and sent in to the mayor's *yamên*, where he
died under the bamboo. Owners of land adjoining his
would make him a present of the richest portions, fearing
the consequences if they did not do so ; and thus he became
very wealthy, almost on a par with the State itself. By-
and-by, Ni-ni and Fairy died, and Tsêng was overwhelmed
with grief. Suddenly he remembered that in former years
he had seen a beautiful girl whom he wished to purchase
as a concubine, but want of money had then prevented
him from carrying out his intention. Now there was no
longer that difficulty ; and accordingly he sent off two
trusty servants to get the girl by force. In a short time
she arrived, when he found that she had grown more
beautiful than ever ; and so his cup of happiness was
full. But years rolled on, and gradually his fellow-officials
became estranged, Tsêng taking no notice of their behaviour, until at last one of them impeached him to
the Throne in a long and bitter memorial. Happily,
however, the Emperor still regarded him with favour, and
for some time kept the memorial by him unanswered.
Then followed a joint memorial from the whole of the
Privy Council, including those who had once thronged
his doors, and had falsely called him their dear father.

[5] The *retinue* of a high mandarin is composed as follows :—
First, gong-bearers, then banner-men, tablet-bearers (on which
tablets are inscribed the titles of the official), a large red umbrella,
mounted attendants, a box containing a change of clothes, bearers
of regalia, a second gong, a small umbrella or sunshade, a large
wooden fan, executioners, lictors from hell, who wear tall hats ;
a mace (called a " golden melon "), bamboos for " bambooing,"
incense-bearers, more attendants, and now the great man himself,
followed by a body-guard of soldiers and a few personal attendants,
amounting in all to nearly one hundred persons, many of whom are
mere street-rowdies or beggars, hired at a trifling outlay when
required to join what might otherwise be an imposing procession.

The Imperial rescript to this document was " Banishment to Yünnan," [6] his son, who was Governor of P'ing-yang, being also implicated in his guilt. When Tsêng heard the news, he was overcome with fear ; but an armed guard was already at his gate, and the lictors were forcing their way into his innermost apartments. They tore off his robe and official hat, and bound him and his wife with cords. Then they collected together in the hall his gold, his silver, and bank-notes,[7] to the value of many hundred thousands of taels. His pearls, and jade, and precious stones filled many bushel baskets. His curtains, and screens, and beds, and other articles of furniture were brought out by thousands ; while the swaddling-clothes of his infant boy and the shoes of his little girl were lying littered about the steps. It was a sad sight for Tsêng ; but a worse blow was that of his concubine carried off almost lifeless before his eyes, himself not daring to utter a word. Then all the apartments, store-rooms, and treasuries were sealed up ; and, with a volley of curses, the soldiers bade Tsêng begone, and proceeded to leave the place, dragging him with them. The husband and wife prayed that they might be allowed some old cart, but this favour was denied them. After about ten *li*, Tsêng's wife could barely walk, her feet being swollen and sore. Tsêng helped her along as best he could, but another ten *li* reduced him to a state of abject fatigue. By-and-by they saw before them a great mountain, the summit of which was lost in the clouds ; and, fearing they should be made to ascend it, Tsêng and his wife stood still and began to weep. The lictors, however, clamoured round them, and would permit of no rest. The sun was rapidly sinking, and there was no place at hand where they could obtain shelter for the night. So they continued on their weary way until about half-way up the hill, when his wife's strength was quite exhausted, and she sat down by the roadside. Tsêng, too, halted to rest in spite of the soldiers and their abuse ; but they had hardly stopped a moment before down came a band of robbers upon them,

[6] A land journey of about three months, ending in a region which the Chinese have always regarded as semi-barbarous.

[7] From A.D. 1154 the use of paper money became quite common in China.

each with a sharp knife in his hand. The soldiers immediately took to their heels, and Tsêng fell on his knees
before the robbers, saying, "I am a poor criminal going
into banishment, and have nothing to give you. I pray
you spare my life." But the robbers sternly replied,
"We are all the victims of your crimes, and now we want
your wicked head." Then Tsêng began to revile them,
saying, "Dogs! though I am under sentence of banishment, I am still an officer of the State." But the robbers
cursed him again, flourishing a sword over his neck, and
the next thing he heard was the noise of his own head as
it fell with a thud to the ground. At the same instant
two devils stepped forward and seized him each by one
hand, compelling him to go with them. After a little
while they arrived at a great city where there was a
hideously ugly king sitting upon a throne judging between
good and evil. Tsêng crawled before him on his hands
and knees to receive sentence, and the king, after turning
over a few pages of his register, thundered out, "The
punishment of a traitor who has brought misfortune on
his country : the cauldron of boiling oil!" To this ten
thousand devils responded with a cry like a clap of thunder,
and one huge monster led Tsêng down alongside the
cauldron, which was seven feet in height, and surrounded
on all sides by blazing fuel, so that it was of a glowing
red heat. Tsêng shrieked for mercy, but it was all up
with him, for the devil seized him by the hair and the
small of his back and pitched him headlong in. Down he
fell with a splash, and rose and sank with the bubbling of
the oil, which ate through his flesh into his very vitals.
He longed to die, but death would not come to him. After
about half-an-hour's boiling, a devil took him out on a
pitchfork and threw him down before the Infernal King,
who again consulted his note-book, and said, "You relied
on your position to treat others with contumely and
injustice, for which you must suffer on the Sword-Hill."
Again he was led away by devils to a large hill thickly
studded with sharp swords, their points upwards like
the shoots of bamboo, with here and there the remains
of many miserable wretches who had suffered before
him. Tsêng again cried for mercy and crouched upon
the ground ; but a devil bored into him with a poisoned

awl until he screamed with pain. He was then seized and flung up high into the air, falling down right on the sword-points, to his most frightful agony. This was repeated several times until he was almost hacked to pieces. He was then brought once more before the king, who asked what was the amount of his peculations while on earth. Immediately an accountant came forward with an abacus, and said that the whole sum was 3,210,000 taels, whereupon the king replied, " Let him drink that amount." Forthwith the devils piled up a great heap of gold and silver, and, when they had melted it in a huge crucible, began pouring it into Tsêng's mouth. The pain was excruciating as the molten metal ran down his throat into his vitals ; but since in life he had never been able to get enough of the dross, it was determined he should feel no lack of it then. He was half-a-day drinking it, and then the king ordered him away to be born again as a woman [8] in Kan-chou. A few steps brought them to a huge frame, where on an iron axle revolved a mighty wheel many hundred *yojanas* [9] in circumference, and shining with a brilliant light. The devils flogged Tsêng on to the wheel, and he shut his eyes as he stepped up. Then whiz—and away he went, feet foremost, round with the wheel, until he felt himself tumble off and a cold thrill ran through him, when he opened his eyes and found he was changed into a girl. He saw his father and mother in rags and tatters, and in one corner a beggar's bowl and a staff,[10] and understood the calamity that had befallen him. Day after day he begged about the streets, and his inside rumbled for want of food ; he had no clothes to his back. At fourteen years of age he was sold to a gentleman as concubine ; and then, though food and clothes were not wanting, he had to put up with the scoldings and floggings of the wife, who one day burnt him with a hot iron.[11] Luckily the gentleman took a

[8] This contingency is much dreaded by the Chinese.

[9] A *yojana* has been variously estimated at from five to nine English miles.

[10] The *patra* and *khakkharam* of the *bikshu* or Buddhist mendicant.

[11] It is not considered quite correct to take a concubine unless the wife is childless, in which case it is held that the proposition to do so, and thus secure the much-desired posterity, should emanate from the wife herself. On page 41 of Vol. XIII. of this author, we read, " and if at thirty years of age you have no children, then sell your hair-pins and other ornaments, and buy a concubine for

fancy to him and treated him well, which kindness Tsêng repaid by an irreproachable fidelity. It happened, however, that on one occasion when they were chatting together, burglars broke into the house and killed the gentleman, Tsêng having escaped by hiding himself under the bed. Thereupon he was immediately charged by the wife with murder, and on being taken before the authorities was sentenced to die the " lingering death." [12] This sentence was at once carried out with tortures more horrible than any in all the Courts of Purgatory, in the middle of which Tsêng heard one of his companions call out " Hello, there ! you've got nightmare." Tsêng got up and rubbed his eyes, and his friends said, " It's quite late in the day, and we're all very hungry." But the old priest smiled, and asked him if the prophecy as to his future rank was true or not. Tsêng bowed and begged him to explain ; whereupon the old priest said, " For those who cultivate virtue, a lily will grow up even in the fiery pit." [13] Tsêng had gone thither full of pride and vain-glory ; he went home an altered man. From that day he thought no more of becoming a Secretary of State, but retired into the hills, and I know not what became of him after that.

LVII. THE COUNTRY OF THE CANNIBALS [1]

At Chiao-chou [2] there lived a man named Hsü, who gained his living by trading across the sea. On one occasion he was carried far out of his course by a violent tempest, and

your husband. For the childless state is a hard one to bear ; " or, as Victor Hugo puts it in his *Légende des Siècles*, there is nothing so sad as " la maison sans enfants."

[12] This is the celebrated form of death, reserved for parricide and similar awful crimes, about which so much has been written. Strictly speaking, the malefactor should be literally chopped to pieces in order to prolong his agonies ; but the sentence is now rarely, if ever, carried out in its extreme sense. A few gashes are made upon the wretched victim's body, and he is soon put out of his misery by decapitation.

[13] Alluding to a well-known Buddhist miracle, in which a *bikshu* was to be thrown into a cauldron of boiling water in a fiery pit, when suddenly a lotus-flower came forth, the fire was extinguished, and the water became cold.

[1] The Chinese term—here translated " cannibals "—is a meaningless imitation by two Chinese characters of the Sanscrit *yakcha,* or certain demons who feed upon human flesh.

[2] Hué, the capital of Cochin-China.

reached a country of high hills and dense jungle,[3] where, after making fast his boat and taking provisions with him, he landed, hoping to meet with some of the inhabitants. He then saw that the rocks were covered with large holes, like the cells of bees ; and, hearing the sound of voices from within, he stopped in front of one of them and peeped in. To his infinite horror he beheld two hideous beings, with thick rows of horrid fangs, and eyes that glared like lamps, engaged in tearing to pieces and devouring some raw deer's flesh ; and, turning round, he would have fled instantly from the spot, had not the cannibals already espied him ; and, leaving their food, they seized him and dragged him in. Thereupon ensued a chattering between them, resembling the noise of birds or beasts,[4] and they proceeded to pull off Hsü's clothes as if about to eat him ; but Hsü, who was frightened almost to death, offered them the food he had in his wallet, which they ate up with great relish, and looked inside for more. Hsü waved his hand to show it was all finished, and then they angrily seized him again ; at which he cried out, " I have a saucepan in my boat, and can cook you some." The cannibals did not understand what he said ; but, by dint of gesticulating freely, they at length seemed to have an idea of what he meant ; and, having taken him down to the shore to fetch the saucepan, they returned with him to the cave, where he lighted a fire and cooked the remainder of the deer, with the flavour of which they appeared to be mightily pleased. At night they rolled a big stone to the mouth of the cave,[5] fearing lest he should try to escape ; and Hsü himself lay down at a distance from them in doubt as to whether his life would be spared. At daybreak the cannibals went out, leaving the entrance blocked, and by-and-by came back with a deer, which they gave to Hsü to cook. Hsü flayed the carcase, and from a remote

[3] The island of Hainan, inhabited as it was in earlier times by a race of savages, is the most likely source of the following marvellous adventures.

[4] To which sounds the languages of the West have been more than once likened by the Chinese. It is only fair, however, to the lettered classes to state that they have a similar contempt for their own local dialects ; regarding *Mandarin*, or the Court dialect, as the only form of speech worthy to be employed by men.

[5] The occasional analogies to the story of the Cyclops must be evident to all readers.

corner of the cave took some water and prepared a large quantity, which was no sooner ready than several other cannibals arrived to join in the feast. When they had finished all there was, they made signs that Hsü's saucepan was too small ; and three or four days afterwards they brought him a large one, of the same shape as those in common use amongst men, subsequently furnishing him with constant supplies of wolf and deer,[6] of which they always invited him to partake. By degrees they began to treat him kindly, and not to shut him up when they went out ; and Hsü, too, gradually learnt to understand, and even to speak, a little of their language, which pleased them so much that they finally gave him a cannibal woman for his wife. Hsü was horribly afraid of her ; but, as she treated him with great consideration, always reserving tit-bits of food for him, they lived very happily together. One day all the cannibals got up early in the morning, and, having adorned themselves with strings of fine pearls, they went forth as if to meet some honoured guest, giving orders to Hsü to cook an extra quantity of meat that day. " It is the birthday of our King," said Hsü's wife to him ; and then, running out, she informed the other cannibals that her husband had no pearls. So each gave five from his own string, and Hsü's wife added ten to these, making in all fifty, which she threaded on a hempen fibre and hung around his neck, each pearl being worth over a hundred ounces of silver. Then they went away, and as soon as Hsü had finished his cooking his wife appeared and invited him to come and receive the King. So off they went to a huge cavern, covering about a mow [7] of ground, in which was a huge stone, smoothed away at the top like a table, with stone seats at the four sides. At the upper end was a dais, over which was spread a leopard's skin, the other seats having only deer-skins ; and within the cavern some twenty or thirty cannibals ranged themselves on the seats. After a short

---

[6] The animal here mentioned is the plain brown deer, or *Rusa Swinhoii*, of Formosa, in which island I should prefer to believe, but for the great distance from Hué, that the scenes here narrated took place.

[7] About one-sixth of an acre. On old title-deeds of landed property in China may still be seen measurements calculated according to the amount of grain that could be sown thereon.

interval a great wind began to stir up the dust, and they all rushed out to a creature very much resembling themselves, which hurried into the cave, and, squatting down cross-legged, cocked its head and looked about like a cormorant. The other cannibals then filed in and took up their positions right and left of the dais, where they stood gazing up at the King with their arms folded before them in the form of a cross. The King counted them one by one, and asked if they were all present ; and when they replied in the affirmative, he looked at Hsü and inquired who he was. Thereupon Hsü's wife stepped forward and said he was her husband, and the others all loudly extolled his skill in cookery, two of them running out and bringing back some cooked meat, which they set before the King. His Majesty swallowed it by handfuls, and found it so nice that he gave orders to be supplied regularly ; and then, turning to Hsü he asked him why his string of beads [8] was so short. " He has but recently arrived among us," replied the cannibals, " and hasn't got a complete set ; " upon which the King drew ten pearls from the string round his own neck and bestowed them upon Hsü. Each was as big as the top of one's finger and as round as a bullet ; and Hsü's wife threaded them for him and hung them round his neck. Hsü himself crossed his arms and thanked the King in the language of the country, after which His Majesty went off in a gust of wind as rapidly as a bird can fly, and the cannibals sat down and finished what was left of the banquet. Four years afterwards Hsü's wife gave birth to a triplet of two boys and one girl, all of whom were ordinary human beings, and not at all like the mother ; at which the other cannibals were delighted, and would often play with them and caress them.[9] Three years passed away, and the children could walk about, after which their father taught them to speak his own tongue ; and in their early babblings their human origin was manifested. The boys, as mere

[8] The king here uses the words " ku-t'u-tzu," which are probably intended by the author to be an imitation of a term in the savage tongue.

[9] Fondness for children is specially a trait of Chinese character ; and a single baby would do far more to ensure the safety of a foreign traveller in China than all the usual paraphernalia of pocket-pistols and revolvers.

children, could climb about on the mountains as easily
as though walking upon a level road ; and between them
and their father there grew up a mutual feeling of attach-
ment. One day the mother had gone out with the girl
and one of the boys, and was absent for a long time. A
strong north wind was blowing, and Hsü, filled with
thoughts of his old home, led his other son down with him
to the beach, where lay the boat in which he had formerly
reached this country. He then proposed to the boy that
they should go away together ; and, having explained to
him that they could not inform his mother, father and
son stepped on board, and after a voyage of only twenty-
four hours, arrived safely at Chiao-chou. On reaching
home Hsü found that his wife had married again ; so he
sold two of his pearls for an enormous sum of money,[10]
and set up a splendid establishment. His son was called
Piao, and at fourteen or fifteen years of age the boy could
lift a weight of three thousand catties [11] (4000 lb.). He was
extremely fond of athletics of all kinds, and thus attracted
the notice of the Commander-in-Chief, who gave him a
commission as sub-lieutenant. Just at that time there
happened to be some trouble on the frontier, and young
Piao, having covered himself with glory, was made a
colonel at the age of eighteen.

About that time another merchant was driven by stress
of weather to the country of the cannibals, and had hardly
stepped ashore before he observed a young man whom he
knew at once to be of Chinese origin. The young man
asked him whence he came, and finally took him into a
cave hid away in a dark valley and concealed by the dense
jungle. There he bade him remain, and in a little while he
returned with some deer's flesh, which he gave the merchant
to eat, saying at the same time that his own father was a
Chiao-chou man. The merchant now knew that the young
man was Hsü's son, he himself being acquainted with Hsü
as a trader in the same line of business. " Why, he's an
old friend of mine," cried the latter ; " his other son is now
a colonel." The young man did not know what was meant

---

[10] Literally, " a million of taels."
[11] Here again we have 100 *chün*, one *chün* being equal to about
40 *lb*. Chinese weights, measures, distances, numbers, &c., are often
very loosely employed ; and it is probable that not more than 100
atties, say 133 *lb.*, is here meant.

by a *colonel,* so the merchant told him it was the title of a Chinese mandarin. " And what is a *mandarin* ? " asked the youth. " A mandarin," replied the merchant, " is one who goes out with a chair and horses ; who at home sits upon a dais in the hall ; whose summons is answered by a hundred voices ; who is looked at only with sidelong eyes, and in whose presence all people stand aslant ;— this is to be a mandarin." The young man was deeply touched at this recital, and at length the merchant said to him, " Since your honoured father is at Chiao-chou, why do you remain here ? " " Indeed," replied the youth, " I have often indulged the same feeling ; but my mother is not a Chinese woman, and, apart from the difference of her language and appearance, I fear that if the other cannibals found it out they would do us some mischief." He then took his leave, being in rather a disturbed state of mind, and bade the merchant wait until the wind should prove favourable,[12] when he promised to come and see him off, and charge him with a letter to his father and brother. Six months the merchant remained in that cave, occasionally taking a peep at the cannibals passing backwards and forwards, but not daring to leave his retreat. As soon as the monsoon set in the young man arrived and urged him to hurry away, begging him, also, not to forget the letter to his father. So the merchant sailed away and soon reached Chiao-chou, where he visited the colonel and told him the whole story. Piao was much affected, and wished to go in search of those members of the family ; but his father feared the dangers he would encounter, and advised him not to think of such a thing. However, Piao was not to be deterred ; and having imparted his scheme to the Commander-in-Chief, he took with him two soldiers and set off. Adverse winds prevailed at that time, and they beat about for half a moon, until they were out of sight of all land, could not see a foot before them, and had completely lost their reckoning. Just then a mighty sea arose and capsized their boat, tossing Piao into the water, where he floated about for some time at the will of the waves, until suddenly somebody dragged him out and carried him into a house. Then he saw that his rescuer was to all appearances a cannibal, and accordingly he addressed him

[12] That is, until the change of the monsoon from S.W. to N.E.

in the language of the country, and told him whither he
himself was bound. " It is my native place," replied the
cannibal, in astonishment ; " but you will excuse my
saying that you are now 8000 *li* out of your course. This
is the way to the country of the Poisonous Dragons, and
not your route at all." He then went off to find a boat
for Piao, and, himself swimming in the water behind,
pushed it along like an arrow from a bow, so quickly that by
the next day they had traversed the whole distance. On
the shore Piao observed a young man walking up and down
and evidently watching him ; and, knowing that no human
beings dwelt there, he guessed at once that he was his
brother. Approaching more closely, he saw that he was
right ; and, seizing the young man's hand, he asked after
his mother and sister. On hearing that they were well,
he would have gone directly to see them ; but the younger
one begged him not to do so, and ran away himself to fetch
them. Meanwhile, Piao turned to thank the cannibal who
had brought him there, but he, too, had disappeared. In
a few minutes his mother and sister arrived, and, on seeing Piao, they could not restrain their tears. Piao then
laid his scheme before them, and when they said they
feared people would ill-treat them, he replied, " In China
I hold a high position, and people will not dare to show
you disrespect." Thus they determined to go. The wind,
however, was against them, and mother and son were at a
loss what to do, when suddenly the sail bellied out towards
the south, and a rustling sound was heard. " Heaven
helps us, my mother ! " cried Piao, full of joy ; and, hurrying on board at once, in three days they had reached their
destination. As they landed the people fled right and left
in fear, Piao having divided his own clothes amongst the
party ; and when they arrived at the house, and his mother
saw Hsü, she began to rate him soundly for running away
without her. Hsü hastened to acknowledge his error,
and then all the family and servants were introduced to
her, each one being in mortal dread of such a singular
personage. Piao now bade his mother learn to talk Chinese,
and gave her any quantity of fine clothes and rich meats,
to the infinite delight of the old lady. She and her daughter
both dressed in man's clothes, and by the end of a few
months were able to understand what was said to them.

The brother, named Pao (Leopard), and the sister, Yeh (Night), were both clever enough, and immensely strong into the bargain. Piao was ashamed that Pao could not read, and set to work to teach him ; and the youngster was so quick that he learnt the Sacred Books [13] and histories by merely reading them once over. However, he would not enter upon a literary career, loving better to draw a strong bow or ride a spirited horse, and finally taking the highest military degree. He married the daughter of a post-captain ; but his sister had some trouble in getting a husband, because of her being the child of a cannibal woman. At length a serjeant, named Yüan, who was under her brother's command, and had become a widower, consented to take her as his wife. She could draw a hundred-catty bow, and shoot birds at a hundred paces without ever missing. Whenever Yüan went on a campaign she went with him ; and his subsequent rise to high rank was chiefly due to her. At thirty-four years of age Pao got a command ; and in his great battles his mother, clad in armour and grasping a spear, would fight by his side, to the terror of all their adversaries ; and when he himself received the dignity of an hereditary title, he memorialised the Throne to grant his mother the title of " lady."

LVIII.   FOOT-BALL ON THE TUNG-T'ING LAKE

Wang Shih-hsiu was a native of Lu-chou, and such a lusty fellow that he could pick up a stone mortar.[1] Father and son were both good foot-ball players ; but when the former was about forty years of age he was drowned while crossing the Money Pool.[2] Some eight or nine years later our hero happened to be on his way to Hunan ; and anchoring in the Tung-t'ing lake, watched the moon rising in the east and illuminating the water into a bright sheet of light. While he was thus engaged, lo ! from out of the lake emerged five men, bringing with them a large mat, which they spread on the surface of the water so as to cover about six yards square. Wine and food were then arranged upon it, and Wang heard the sound of the dishes knocking together, but it was a dull, soft sound, not at all like that of ordinary

---

[13] See No. XLI., note 2.   [1] Used for pounding rice.
[2] A fancy name for the Tung-t'ing lake. See No. XXXVIII., note 1.

crockery. Three of the men sat down on the mat and the
other two waited upon them. One of the former was
dressed in yellow, the other two in white, and each wore a
black turban. Their demeanour as they sat there side by
side was grave and dignified ; in appearance they resembled
three of the ancients, but by the fitful beams of the moon
Wang was unable to see very clearly what they were like.
The attendants wore black serge dresses, and one of them
seemed to be a boy, while the other was many years older.
Wang now heard the man in the yellow dress say, " This is
truly a fine moonlight night for a drinking bout ; " to
which one of his companions replied, " It quite reminds
me of the night when Prince Kuang-li feasted at Pear-
blossom Island." [3] The three then pledged each other
in bumping goblets, talking all the time in such a low
tone that Wang could not hear what they were saying.
The boatmen kept themselves concealed, crouching down
at the bottom of the boat ; but Wang looked hard at the
attendants, the elder of whom bore a striking resemblance
to his father, though he spoke in quite a different tone of
voice. When it was drawing towards midnight, one of
them proposed a game at ball ; and in a moment the boy
disappeared in the water, to return immediately with a
huge ball—quite an armful in fact—apparently full of
quicksilver, and lustrous within and without. All now
rose up, and the man in the yellow dress bade the old
attendant join them in the game. The ball was kicked
up some ten or fifteen feet in the air, and was quite dazzling
in its brilliancy ; but once, when it had gone up with a
whish-h-h-h, it fell at some distance off, right in the very
middle of Wang's boat. The occasion was irresistible,
and Wang, exerting all his strength, kicked the ball with
all his might. It seemed unusually light and soft to the
touch, and his foot broke right through. Away went
the ball to a good height, pouring forth a stream of light
like a rainbow from the hole Wang had made, and making
as it fell a curve like that of a comet rushing across the
sky. Down it glided into the water, where it fizzed a
moment and then went out. " Ho, there ! " cried out
the players in anger, " what living creature is that who
dares thus to interrupt our sport ? " " Well kicked—

[3] The commentator declares himself unable to trace this allusion.

indeed!" said the old man, "that's a favourite drop-
kick of my own." At this, one of the two in white clothes
began to abuse him, saying, "What! you old baggage,
when we are all so annoyed in this manner, are you to
come forward and make a joke of it? Go at once with
the boy and bring back to us this practical joker, or your
own back will have a taste of the stick." Wang was of
course unable to flee ; however, he was not a bit afraid,
and grasping a sword stood there in the middle of the boat.
In a moment, the old man and boy arrived, also armed,
and then Wang knew that the former was really his father,
and called out to him at once, " Father, I am your son."
The old man was greatly alarmed, but father and son
forgot their troubles in the joy of meeting once again.
Meanwhile, the boy went back, and Wang's father bade
him hide, or they would all be lost. The words were
hardly out of his mouth when the three men jumped on
board the boat. Their faces were black as pitch, their
eyes as big as pomegranates, and they at once proceeded
to seize the old man. Wang struggled hard with them,
and managing to get the boat free from her moorings, he
seized his sword and cut off one of his adversaries' arms.
The arm dropped down and the man in the yellow dress
ran away ; whereupon one of those in white rushed at
Wang, who immediately cut off his head, and he fell into
the water with a splash, at which the third disappeared.
Wang and his father were now anxious to get away, when
suddenly a great mouth arose from the lake, as big and
as deep as a well, and against which they could hear the
noise of the water when it struck. This mouth blew forth
a violent gust of wind, and in a moment the waves were
mountains high and all the boats on the lake were tossing
about. The boatmen were terrified, but Wang seized
one of two huge stones there were on board for use as
anchors,[4] about 130 lb. in weight, and threw it into the
water, which immediately began to subside ; and then
he threw in the other one, upon which the wind dropped,
and the lake became calm again. Wang thought his
father was a disembodied spirit, but the old man said,
" I never died. There were nineteen of us drowned in

[4] These are bound in between several sharp-pointed stakes, and
serve their purpose very well in the inland waters of China.

the river, all of whom were eaten by the fish-goblins except myself : I was saved because I could play foot-ball. Those you saw got into trouble with the Dragon King, and were sent here. They were all marine creatures, and the ball they were playing with was a fish-bladder." Father and son were overjoyed at meeting again, and at once proceeded on their way. In the morning they found in the boat a huge fin—the arm that Wang had cut off the night before.

LIX. THE THUNDER GOD

YO YÜN-HAO and Hsia P'ing-tzŭ lived as boys in the same village, and when they grew up read with the same tutor, becoming the firmest of friends. Hsia was a clever fellow, and had acquired some reputation even at the early age of ten. Yo was not a bit envious, but rather looked up to him, and Hsia in return helped his friend very much with his studies, so that he, too, made considerable progress. This increased Hsia's fame, though try as he would he could never succeed at the public examinations, and by-and-by he sickened and died. His family was so poor they could not find money for his burial, whereupon Yo came foward and paid all expenses, besides taking care of his widow and children.

Every peck or bushel he would share with them, the widow trusting entirely to his support ; and thus he acquired a good name in the village, though not being a rich man himself he soon ran through all his own property. " Alas ! " cried he, " where talents like Hsia's failed, can I expect to succeed ? Wealth and rank are matters of destiny, and my present career will only end by my dying like a dog in a ditch. I must try something else." So he gave up book-learning and went into trade, and in six months he had a trifle of money in hand.

One day when he was resting at an inn in Nanking, he saw a great big fellow walk in and seat himself at no great distance in a very melancholy mood. Yo asked him if he was hungry, and on receiving no answer, pushed some food over towards him. The stranger immediately set to feeding himself by handfuls, and in no time the whole had disappeared. Yo ordered another supply, but that was quickly disposed of in like manner ; and then he told the landlord to bring a shoulder of pork and a quantity of boiled dumplings. Thus, after eating enough for half a dozen, his appetite was appeased and he turned to thank his benefactor, saying, " For three years I haven't had such a meal." " And why should a fine fellow like you be in such a state of destitution ? " inquired Yo ; to which the other only replied, " The judgments of heaven may not be discussed." Being asked where he lived, the stranger replied, " On land I have no home, on the water no boat ; at dawn in the village, at night in the city." Yo then prepared to depart ; but his friend would not leave him, declaring that he was in imminent danger, and that he could not forget the late kindness Yo had shown him. So they went along together, and on the way Yo invited the other to eat with him ; but this he refused, saying that he only took food occasionally. Yo marvelled more than ever at this ; and next day when they were on the river a great storm arose and capsized all their boats, Yo himself being thrown into the water with the others. Suddenly the gale abated and the stranger bore Yo on his back to another boat, plunging at once into the water and bringing back the lost vessel, upon which he placed Yo and bade him remain quietly there. He then returned once more, this time carrying in his arms a part of the cargo, which he replaced in the vessel, and so he went on until it was all restored. Yo thanked him, saying, " It was enough to save my life ; but you have added to this the restoration of my goods." Nothing, in fact, had been lost, and now Yo began to regard the stranger as something more than human. The latter here wished to take his leave, but Yo pressed him so much to stay that at last he consented to remain. Then Yo remarked that after all he had lost a gold pin, and immediately the stranger plunged into the water again, rising at length to the surface with the missing article in his mouth, and presenting it to Yo with the remark that he was delighted to be able to fulfil his commands. The people on the river were all much astonished at what they saw ; meanwhile Yo went home with his friend, and there they lived together, the big man only eating once in ten or twelve days, but then displaying an enormous appetite. One day he spoke of going away, to which Yo

would by no means consent ; and as it was just then about
to rain and thunder, he asked him to tell him what the
clouds were like, and what thunder was, also how he
could get up to the sky and have a look, so as to set his
mind at rest on the subject. " Would you like to have
a ramble among the clouds ? " asked the stranger, as
Yo was lying down to take a nap ; on awaking from which
he felt himself spinning along through the air, and not at
all as if he was lying on a bed. Opening his eyes he saw
he was among the clouds, and around him was a fleecy
atmosphere. Jumping up in great alarm, he felt giddy
as if he had been at sea, and underneath his feet he found
a soft, yielding substance unlike the earth. Above him
were the stars, and this made him think he was dreaming ;
but looking up he saw that they were set in the sky like
seeds in the cup of a lily, varying from the size of the
biggest bowl to that of a small basin. On raising his
hand he discovered that the large stars were all tightly
fixed ; but he managed to pick a small one, which he
concealed in his sleeve ; and then, parting the clouds
beneath him, he looked through and saw the sea glittering
like silver below. Large cities appeared no bigger than
beans—just at this moment, however, he bethought himself that if his foot were to slip, what a tremendous fall
he would have. He now beheld two dragons writhing
their way along, and drawing a cart with a huge vat in
it, each movement of their tails sounding like the crack
of a bullock-driver's whip. The vat was full of water,
and numbers of men were employed in ladling it out and
sprinkling it on the clouds. These men were astonished
at seeing Yo ; however, a big fellow among them called
out, " All right, he's my friend," and then they gave him
a ladle to help them throw the water out. Now it happened
to be a very dry season, and when Yo got hold of the ladle
he took good care to throw the water so that it should all
fall on and around his own home. The stranger then told
him that he was an assistant to the God of Thunder,[1] and

[1] This deity is believed to be constantly on the look-out for
wicked people, aided by the Goddess of Lightning, who flashes a
mirror on to whomsoever the God wishes to strike. " *The thief
eats thunderbolts*," means that he will bring down vengeance from
Heaven on himself. Tylor's *Primitive Culture*, Vol. I., p. 88.

that he had just returned from a three years' punishment inflicted on him in consequence of some neglect of his in the matter of rain. He added that they must now part; and taking the long rope which had been used as reins for the cart, bade Yo grip it tightly, that he might be let down to earth. Yo was afraid of this, but on being told there was no danger he did so, and in a moment whish-h-h-h-h— away he went and found himself safe and sound on *terra firma*. He discovered that he had descended outside his native village, and then the rope was drawn up into the clouds and he saw it no more. The drought had been excessive; for three or four miles round very little rain had fallen, though in Yo's own village the water-courses were all full. On reaching home he took the star out of his sleeve, and put it on the table. It was dull-looking like an ordinary stone; but at night it became very brilliant and lighted up the whole house. This made him value it highly, and he stored it carefully away, bringing it out only when he had guests, to light them at their wine. It was always thus dazzling bright, until one evening when his wife was sitting with him doing her hair, the star began to diminish in brilliancy, and to flit about like a fire-fly. Mrs. Yo sat gaping with astonishment, when all of a sudden it flitted into her mouth and ran down her throat. She tried to cough it up, but couldn't, to the very great amazement of her husband. That night Yo dreamt that his old friend Hsia appeared before him and said, "I am the Shao-wei star. Your friendship is still cherished by me, and now you have brought me back from the sky. Truly our destinies are knitted together, and I will repay your kindness by becoming your son." Now Yo was thirty years of age, but without sons; however, after this dream his wife bore him a male child, and they called his name Star. He was extraordinarily clever, and at sixteen years of age took his master's degree.

LX. THE GAMBLER'S TALISMAN

A TAOIST priest, called Han, lived at the T'ien-ch'i temple, in our district city. His knowledge of the black art was very extensive, and the neighbours all regarded him as an Immortal.[1] My late father was on intimate terms with him, and whenever he went into the city invariably paid him a visit. One day, on such an occasion, he was proceeding thither in company with my late uncle, when suddenly they met Han on the road. Handing them the key of the door, he begged them to go on and wait awhile for him, promising to be there shortly himself. Following out these instructions, they repaired to the temple, but on unlocking the door there was Han sitting inside—a feat which he subsequently performed several times.

Now a relative of mine, who was terribly given to gambling, also knew this priest, having been introduced to him by my father. And once this relative, meeting with a Buddhist priest from the T'ien-fo temple, addicted like himself to the vice of gambling, played with him until he had lost everything, even going so far as to pledge the whole of his property, which he lost in a single night. Happening to call in upon Han as he was going back, the latter noticed his exceedingly dejected appearance, and the rambling answers he gave, and asked him what was the matter. On hearing the story of his losses, Han only laughed, and said, " That's what always overtakes the gambler, sooner or later ; if, however, you will break yourself of the habit, I will get your money back for you." " Ah," cried the other, " if I can only win back my money, you may break the dice with an iron pestle when you catch me gambling again." So Han gave him a talismanic formula, written out on a piece of paper, to put in his girdle, bidding him only win back what he had lost, and not attempt to get a fraction more. He also handed him 1000 *cash*, on condition that this sum should be repaid from his winnings, and off went my relative delighted. The Buddhist, however, turned up his nose at the smallness of his means, and said it wasn't worth his while to stake so little ; but at last he was persuaded into having

[1] See No. V., note 1.

one throw for the whole lot. They then began, the priest leading off with a fair throw, to which his opponent replied by a better ; whereupon the priest doubled his stake, and my relative won again, going on and on until the latter's good luck had brought him back all that he had previously lost. He thought, however, that he couldn't do better than just win a few more strings of cash, and accordingly went on ; but gradually his luck turned, and on looking into his girdle he found that the talisman was gone.   In a great fright he jumped up, and went off with his winnings to the temple, where he reckoned up that after deducting Han's loan, and adding what he had lost towards the end, he had exactly the amount originally his.   With shame in his face he turned to thank Han, mentioning at the same time the loss of the talisman ; at which Han only laughed, and said, "That has got back before you.   I told you not to be over-greedy, and as you didn't heed me, I took the talisman away." [2]

LXI. THE HUSBAND PUNISHED

CHING HSING, of Wên-têng, was a young fellow of some literary reputation, who lived next door to a Mr. Ch'ên, their studios being separated only by a low wall.   One evening Ch'ên was crossing a piece of waste ground when he heard a young girl crying among some pine-trees hard by.   He approached, and saw a girdle hanging from one of the branches, as if its owner was just on the point of hanging herself.   Ch'ên asked her what was the matter, and then she brushed away her tears, and said, "My mother has gone away and left me in charge of my brother-in-law ; but he's a scamp, and won't continue to take care of me ; and now there is nothing left for me but to die." Hereupon the girl began crying again, and Ch'ên untied the girdle and bade her go and find herself a husband ;

[2] Gambling is the great Chinese vice, far exceeding in its ill effects all that opium has ever done to demoralise the country. Public gaming-houses are strictly forbidden by law, but their exist-ence is winked at by a too venal executive. *Fantan* is the favourite game. It consists in staking on the remainder of an unknown number of cash, after the heap has been divided by four, namely, whether it will be three, two, one or nothing ; with other variations of a more complicated nature.

to which she said there was very little chance of that;
and then Ch'ên offered to take her to his own home—an
offer which she very gladly accepted. Soon after they
arrived, his neighbour Ching thought he heard a noise,
and jumped over the wall to have a peep, when lo and
behold! at the door of Ch'ên's house stood this young
lady, who immediately ran away into the garden on seeing
Ching. The two young men pursued her, but without
success, and were obliged to return each to his own room,
Ching being greatly astonished to find the same girl now
standing at his door. On addressing the young lady, she
told him that his neighbour's destiny was too poor a one
for her,[1] and that she came from Shantung, and that her
name was Ch'i A-hsia. She finally agreed to take up her
residence with Ching; but after a few days, finding that
a great number of his friends were constantly calling, she
declared it was too noisy a place for her, and that she
would only visit him in the evening. This she continued
to do for a few days, telling him in reply to his inquiries
that her home was not very far off. One evening, however, she remarked that their present *liaison* was not very
creditable to either; that her father was a mandarin on
the western frontier, and that she was about to set out
with her mother to join him; begging him meanwhile
to make a formal request for the celebration of their
nuptials, in order to prevent them from being thus
separated. She further said that they started in ten days
or so, and then Ching began to reflect that if he married
her she would have to take her place in the family, and
that would make his first wife jealous; so he determined
to get rid of the latter, and when she came in he began
to abuse her right and left. His wife bore it as long as
she could, but at length cried out it were better she should
die; upon which Ching advised her not to bring trouble
on them all like that, but to go back to her own home.
He then drove her away, his wife asking all the time
what she had done to be sent away like this after ten
years of blameless life with him.[2] Ching, however, paid
no heed to her entreaties, and when he had got rid of her
he set to work at once to get the house whitewashed and
made generally clean, himself being on the tip-toe of

---

[1] See No. XLVI., note 4.   [2] See No. LIII., note 1.

expectation for the arrival of Miss A-hsia. But he waited and waited, and no A-hsia came ; she seemed gone like a stone dropped into the sea. Meanwhile emissaries came from his late wife's family begging him to take her back ; and when he flatly refused, she married a gentleman of position named Hsia, whose property adjoined Ching's, and who had long been at feud with him in consequence, as is usual in such cases. This made Ching furious, but he still hoped that A-hsia would come, and tried to console himself in this way. Yet more than a year passed away, and still no signs of her, until one day, at the festival of the Sea Spirits, he saw among the crowds of girls passing in and out one who very much resembled A-hsia. Ching moved towards her, following her as she threaded her way through the crowd as far as the temple gate, where he lost sight of her altogether, to his great mortification and regret. Another six months passed away, when one day he met a young lady dressed in red, accompanied by an old man-servant, and riding on a black mule. It was A-hsia. So he asked the old man the name of his young mistress, and learnt from him that she was the second wife of a gentleman named Chêng, having been married to him about a fortnight previously. Ching now thought she could not be A-hsia, but just then the young lady, hearing them talking, turned her head, and Ching saw that he was right. And now, finding that she had actually married another man, he was overwhelmed with rage, and cried out in a loud voice, "A-hsia ! A-hsia ! why did you break faith ? " The servant here objected to his mistress being thus addressed by a stranger, and was squaring up to Ching, when A-hsia bade him desist ; and, raising her veil, replied, "And you, faithless one, how do you dare meet my gaze ? " "You are the faithless one," said Ching, "not I." "To be faithless to your wife is worse than being faithless to me," rejoined A-hsia ; "if you behaved like that to her, how should I have been treated at your hands ? Because of the fair fame of your ancestors, and the honours gained by them, I was willing to ally myself with you ; but now that you have discarded your wife, your thread of official advancement has been cut short in the realms below, and Mr. Ch'ên is to take the place that should have been yours at the head of the examination list. As for myself, I am now part of the Chêng family ; think no more of me." Ching hung his head and could make no reply ; and A-hsia whipped up her mule and disappeared from his sight, leaving him to return home disconsolate. At the forthcoming examination, everything turned out as she had predicted ; Mr. Ch'ên was at the top of the list, and he himself was thrown out. It was clear that his luck was gone. At forty he had no wife, and was so poor that he was glad to pick up a meal where he could. One day he called on Mr. Chêng, who treated him well and kept him there for the night ; and while there Chêng's second wife saw him, and asked her husband if his guest's name wasn't Ching. "It is," said he ; "how could you guess that ? " "Well," replied she, "before I married you, I took refuge in his house, and he was then very kind to me. Although he has now sunk low, yet his ancestors' influence on the family fortunes is not yet exhausted ; ³ besides, he is an old acquaintance of yours, and you should try and do something for him." Chêng consented, and having first given him a new suit of clothes, kept him in the house several days. At night a slave-girl came to him with twenty ounces of silver for him, and Mrs. Chêng, who was outside the window, said, "This is a trifling return for your past kindness to me. Go and get yourself a good wife. The family luck is not yet exhausted, but will descend to your sons and grandchildren. Do not behave like this again, and so shorten your term of life." Ching thanked her and went home, using ten ounces of silver to procure a concubine from a neighbouring family, who was very ugly and ill-tempered. However, she bore him a son, and he by-and-by graduated as doctor. Mr. Chêng became Vice-President of the Board of Civil Office,⁴ and at his death A-hsia attended the funeral ; but when they opened her chair on its return home, she was gone, and then people knew for the first

³ The virtuous conduct of any individual will result not only in happiness and prosperity to himself, but a certain quantity of these will descend to his posterity, unless, as in the present case, there is one among them whose personal wickedness neutralises any benefit that would otherwise accrue therefrom. Here we have an instance where the crimes of a descendant still left a balance of good fortune surviving from the accumulated virtue of generations.

⁴ One of the six departments of State administration.

time that she was not mortal flesh and blood. Alas!
for the perversity of mankind, rejecting the old and craving
for the new,[5] until at length the nest is overthrown and
the birds fly away. Thus does heaven punish such people.

LXII. THE MARRIAGE LOTTERY

A CERTAIN labourer, named Ma T'ien-jung, lost his wife
when he was only about twenty years of age, and was
too poor to take another. One day when out hoeing in
the fields, he beheld a nice-looking young lady leave the
path and come tripping across the furrows towards him.
Her face was well painted,[1] and she had altogether such
a refined look that Ma concluded she must have lost her
way, and began to make some playful remarks in consequence. "You go along home," cried the young lady,
"and I'll be with you by-and-by." Ma doubted this
rather extraordinary promise, but she vowed and declared
she would not break her word; and then Ma went off,
telling her that his front door faced the north, &c. &c.
At midnight the young lady arrived, and then Ma saw
that her hands and face were covered with fine hair, which
made him suspect at once she was a fox. She did not
deny the accusation; and accordingly Ma said to her,
"If you really are one of those wonderful creatures you
will be able to get me anything I want; and I should be
much obliged if you would begin by giving me some money
to relieve my poverty." The young lady said she would;
and next evening, when she came again, Ma asked her
where the money was. "Dear me!" replied she, "I
quite forgot it." When she was going away, Ma reminded
her of what he wanted, but on the following evening
she made precisely the same excuse, promising to bring
it another day. A few nights afterwards Ma asked her

---

[5] This seems a curious charge to bring against a people who for a
stolid and bigoted conservatism have rarely, if ever, been equalled.
Mencius, however, uttered one golden sentence which might be
brought to bear upon the occasionally foolish opposition of the
Chinese to measures of proved advantage to the commonwealth.
"Live," said the Sage, "in harmony with the age in which you
are born."

[1] Only slave-girls and women of the poorer classes, and old women,
omit this very important part of a Chinese lady's toilet.

once more for the money, and then she drew from her sleeve two pieces of silver, each weighing about five or six ounces. They were both of fine quality, with turned-up edges,[2] and Ma was very pleased and stored them away in a cupboard. Some months after this, he happened to require some money for use, and took out these pieces ; but the person to whom he showed them said they were only pewter, and easily bit off a portion of one of them with his teeth. Ma was much alarmed, and put the pieces away directly ; taking the opportunity when evening came of abusing the young lady roundly. " It's all your bad luck," retorted she ; " real gold would be too much for your inferior destiny." [3] There was an end of that ; but Ma went on to say, " I always heard that fox-girls were of surpassing beauty ; how is it you are not ? " " Oh," replied the young lady, " we always adapt our-selves to our company. Now you haven't the luck of an ounce of silver to call your own ; and what would you do, for instance, with a beautiful princess ? [4] My beauty may not be good enough for the aristocracy ; but among your big-footed, bent-backed rustics,[5] why, it may safely be called ' surpassing.' "

A few months passed away, and then one day the young lady came and gave Ma three ounces of silver, saying, " You have often asked me for money, but in consequence of your weak luck I have always refrained from giving you any. Now, however, your marriage is at hand, and I here give you the cost of a wife, which you may also regard as a parting gift from me." Ma replied that he wasn't engaged, to which the young lady answered that in a few days a go-between would visit him to arrange the affair. " And what will she be like ? " asked Ma. " Why, as your aspirations are for ' sur-passing ' beauty," replied the young lady, " of course she will be possessed of surpassing beauty." " I hardly expect that," said Ma ; " at any rate, three ounces of silver will not be enough to get a wife." " Marriages,"

---

[2] Alluding probably to the shape of the " shoe " or ingot of silver.
[3] See No. XLVI., note 4.
[4] Literally, " One who would make wild geese alight and fish dive down for shame ; " or, as the next line from the same poem has it, " a beauty which would obscure the moon and put flowers to the blush."   [5] Slave-girls do not have their feet compressed.

explained the young lady, "are made in the moon; [6] mortals have nothing to do with them." "And why must you be going away like this?" inquired Ma. "Because," answered she, "for us to meet only by night is not the proper thing. I had better get you another wife and have done with you." Then when morning came, she departed, giving Ma a pinch of yellow powder, saying, "In case you are ill after we are separated, this will cure you." Next day, sure enough, a go-between did come, and Ma at once asked what the proposed bride was like; to which the former replied that she was very passable-looking. Four or five ounces of silver was fixed as the marriage present, Ma making no difficulty on that score, but declaring he must have a peep at the young lady.[7] The go-between said she was a respectable girl, and would never allow herself to be seen; however, it was arranged that they should go to the house together, and await a good opportunity. So off they went, Ma remaining outside while the go-between went in, returning in a little while to tell him it was all right. "A relative of mine lives in the same court, and just now I saw the young lady sitting in the hall. We have only got to pretend we are going to see my relative, and you will be able to get a glimpse of her." Ma consented, and they accordingly passed through the hall, where he saw the young lady sitting down with her head bent forward while some one was scratching her back. She seemed to be all that the go-between had said; but when they came to discuss the money, it appeared the young lady only wanted one or two ounces of silver, just to buy herself

---

[6] Wherein resides an old gentleman who ties together with a red cord the feet of those destined to become man and wife. From this bond there is no escape, no matter what distance may separate the affianced pair. The first go-between, Ku Ts'ê, was originally seen on ice, arranging matches with some one below :—

> Marriage is not a trifling thing—
> The Book and the Vermilion String!
> On ice by moonlight may be seen
> The wedded couples' go-between.
> —*A Thousand Character Essays for Girls.*

Hence the common phrase "to do the ice (business)," *i.e.*, to arrange a marriage.

[7] This proceeding is highly improper, but is winked at in a large majority of Chinese betrothals.

a few clothes, &c., which Ma thought was a very small amount, and gave the go-between a present for her trouble, which just finished up the three ounces his fox-friend had provided. An auspicious day was chosen, and the young lady came over to his house; when lo! she was hump-backed and pigeon-breasted, with a short neck like a tortoise, and regular beetle-crushers, full ten inches long. The meaning of his fox-friend's remarks then flashed upon him.

LXIII. THE LO-CH'A COUNTRY AND THE SEA-MARKET [1]

ONCE upon a time there was a young man, named Ma Chün, who was also known as Lung-mei. He was the son of a trader, and a youth of surpassing beauty. His manners were courteous, and he loved nothing better than singing and playing. He used to associate with actors, and with an embroidered handkerchief round his head the effect was that of a beautiful woman. Hence he acquired the sobriquet of the Beauty. At fourteen years of age he graduated and began to make a name for himself; but his father, who was growing old and wished to retire from business, said to him, " My boy, book-learning will never fill your belly or put a coat on your back; you had much better stick to the old thing." Accordingly, Ma from that time occupied himself with scales and weights, with principal and interest, and such matters.

He made a voyage across the sea, and was carried away by a typhoon. After being tossed about for many days and nights he arrived at a country where the people were hideously ugly. When these people saw Ma they thought he was a devil, and all ran screeching away. Ma was somewhat alarmed at this, but finding that it was they who were frightened at him, he quickly turned their fear to his own advantage. If he came across people eating and drinking he would rush upon them, and when they fled away for fear, he would regale himself upon what they had left. By-and-by he went to a village among the hills, and there the people had at any rate some facial

---

[1] The term " sea-market " is generally understood in the sense of *mirage*, or some similar phenomenon.

resemblance to ordinary men. But they were all in rags and tatters like beggars. So Ma sat down to rest under a tree, and the villagers, not daring to come near him, contented themselves with looking at him from a distance. They soon found, however, that he did not want to eat them, and by degrees approached a little closer to him. Ma, smiling, began to talk; and although their language was different, yet he was able to make himself tolerably intelligible, and told them whence he had come. The villagers were much pleased, and spread the news that the stranger was not a man-eater. Nevertheless, the very ugliest of all would only take a look and be off again; they would not come near him. Those who did go up to him were not very much unlike his own countrymen, the Chinese. They brought him plenty of food and wine. Ma asked them what they were afraid of. They replied, "We had heard from our forefathers that 26,000 *li* to the west there is a country called China. We had heard that the people of that land were the most extraordinary in appearance you can possibly imagine. Hitherto it has been hearsay; we can now believe it." He then asked them how it was they were so poor. They answered, "You see, in our country everything depends, not on literary talent, but on beauty. The most beautiful are made ministers of state; the next handsomest are made judges and magistrates; and the third class in looks are employed in the palace of the king. Thus these are enabled out of their pay to provide for their wives and families. But we, from our very birth, are regarded by our parents as inauspicious, and are left to perish, some of us being occasionally preserved by more humane parents to prevent the extinction of the family." Ma asked the name of their country, and they told him it was Lo-ch'a. Also that the capital city was some 30 *li* to the north. He begged them to take him there, and next day at cock-crow he started thitherwards in their company, arriving just about dawn. The walls of the city were made of black stone, as black as ink, and the city gate-houses were about 100 feet high. Red stones were used for tiles, and picking up a broken piece Ma found that it marked his finger-nail like vermilion. They arrived just when the Court was rising, and saw all the equipages of the officials. The

village people pointed out one who they said was Prime
Minister. His ears drooped forward in flaps ; he had
three nostrils, and his eye-lashes were just like bamboo
screens hanging in front of his eyes. Then several came
out on horseback, and they said these were the privy
councillors. So they went on, telling him the rank of
all the ugly uncouth fellows he saw. The lower they
got down in the official scale the less hideous the officials
were. By-and-by Ma went back, the people in the streets
marvelling very much to see him, and tumbling helter-
skelter one over another as if they had met a goblin.
The villagers shouted out to reassure them, and then they
stood at a distance to look at him. When he got back,
there was not a man, woman, or child in the whole nation
but knew that there was a strange man at the village ;
and the gentry and officials became very desirous of
seeing him. However, if he went to any of their houses
the porter always slammed the door in his face, and the
master, mistress, and family, in general, would only peep
at, and speak to him through the cracks. Not a single one
dared receive him face to face ; but, finally, the village
people, at a loss what to do, bethought themselves of a
man who had been sent by a former king on official business
among strange nations. " He," said they, " having seen
many kinds of men, will not be afraid of you." So they
went to his house, where they were received in a very
friendly way. He seemed to be about eighty or ninety
years of age ; his eyeballs protruded, and his beard curled
up like a hedgehog. He said, " In my youth I was sent
by the king among many nations, but I never went to
China. I am now one hundred and twenty years of age,
and that I should be permitted to see a native of your
country is a fact which it will be my duty to report to the
Throne. For ten years and more I have not been to
Court, but have remained here in seclusion ; yet I will
now make an effort on your behalf." Then followed a
banquet, and when the wine had already circulated pretty
freely, some dozen singing girls came in and sang and
danced before them. The girls all wore white embroidered
turbans, and long scarlet robes which trailed on the ground.
The words they uttered were unintelligible, and the tunes
they played perfectly hideous. The host, however,

seemed to enjoy it very much, and said to Ma, " Have you
music in China ? " He replied that they had, and the
old man asked for a specimen. Ma hummed him a tune,
beating time on the table, with which he was very much
pleased, declaring that his guest had the voice of a phœnix
and the notes of a dragon, such as he had never heard before.
The next day he presented a memorial to the Throne, and
the king at once commanded Ma to appear before him.
Several of the ministers, however, represented that his
appearance was so hideous it might frighten His Majesty,
and the king accordingly desisted from his intention. The
old man returned and told Ma, being quite upset about
it. They remained together some time until they had
drunk themselves tipsy. Then Ma, seizing a sword, began
to attitudinise, smearing his face all over with coal-dust.
He acted the part of Chang Fei,[2] at which his host was so
delighted that he begged him to appear before the Prime
Minister in the character of Chang Fei. Ma replied, " I
don't mind a little amateur acting, but how can I play
the hypocrite [3] for my own personal advantage ? " On
being pressed he consented, and the old man prepared a
great feast, and asked some of the high officials to be
present, telling Ma to paint himself as before. When the
guests had arrived, Ma was brought out to see them ;
whereupon they all exclaimed, " Ai-yah ! how is it he
was so ugly before and is now so beautiful ? " By-and-by,
when they were all taking wine together, Ma began to sing
them a most bewitching song, and they got so excited over
it that next day they recommended him to the king. The
king sent a special summons for him to appear, and asked
him many questions about the government of China, to
all of which Ma replied in detail, eliciting sighs of admiration from His Majesty. He was honoured with a banquet
in the royal guest-pavilion, and when the king had made
himself tipsy he said to him, " I hear you are a very skilful
musician. Will you be good enough to let me hear you ? "
Ma then got up and began to attitudinise, singing a plaintive
air like the girls with the turbans. The king was charmed,
and at once made him a privy councillor, giving him a

[2] A famous General who played a leading part in the wars of the
Three Kingdoms. See No. XCIII., note 8.
[3] A hit at the hypocrisy of the age.

private banquet, and bestowing other marks of royal favour. As time went on his fellow officials found out the secret of his painted face,[4] and whenever he was among them they were always whispering together, besides which they avoided being near him as much as possible. Thus Ma was left to himself, and found his position anything but pleasant in consequence. So he memorialised the Throne, asking to be allowed to retire from office, but his request was refused. He then said his health was bad, and got three months' sick leave, during which he packed up his valuables and went back to the village. The villagers on his arrival went down on their knees to him, and he distributed gold and jewels amongst his old friends. They were all very glad to see him, and said, " Your kindness shall be repaid when we go to the sea-market ; we will bring you some pearls and things." Ma asked them where that was. They said it was at the bottom of the sea, where the mermaids [5] kept their treasures, and that as many as twelve nations were accustomed to go thither to trade. Also that it was frequented by spirits, and that to get there it was necessary to pass through red vapours and great waves. "Dear Sir," they said, " do not yourself risk this great danger, but let us take your money and purchase these rare pearls for you. The season is now at hand." Ma asked them how they knew this. They said, " Whenever we see red birds flying backwards and forwards over the sea, we know that within seven days the market will open." He asked when they were going to start, that he might accompany them ; but they begged him not to think of doing so. He replied, " I am a sailor : how can I be afraid of wind and waves ? " Very soon after this people came with merchandise to forward, and so Ma packed up and went on board the vessel that was going.

This vessel held some tens of people, was flat-bottomed, with a railing all round, and, rowed by ten men, it cut through the water like an arrow. After a voyage of three days they saw afar off faint outlines of towers and minarets, and crowds of trading vessels. They soon arrived at the city, the walls of which were made of bricks as long

---

[4] Showing that hypocrisy is bad policy in the long run.
[5] The tears of Chinese mermaids are said to be pearls.

as a man's body, the tops of its buildings being lost in the Milky Way.[6] Having made fast their boat, they went in, and saw laid out in the market rare pearls and wondrous precious stones of dazzling beauty, such as are quite unknown amongst men. Then they saw a young man come forth riding upon a beautiful steed. The people of the market stood back to let him pass, saying he was the third son of the king ; but when the prince saw Ma, he exclaimed, " This is no foreigner," and immediately an attendant drew near and asked his name and country. Ma made a bow, and standing at one side told his name and family. The prince smiled, and said, " For you to have honoured our country thus is no small piece of good luck." He then gave him a horse and begged him to follow. They went out of the city gate and down to the sea-shore, whereupon their horses plunged into the water. Ma was terribly frightened and screamed out ; but the sea opened dry before them and formed a wall of water on either side. In a little time they reached the king's palace, the beams of which were made of tortoise-shell and the tiles of fishes' scales. The four walls were of crystal, and dazzled the eye like mirrors. They got down off their horses and went in, and Ma was introduced to the king. The young prince said, " Sire, I have been to the market, and have got a gentleman from China." Whereupon Ma made obeisance before the king, who addressed him as follows :—" Sir, from a talented scholar like yourself I venture to ask for a few stanzas upon our sea-market. Pray do not refuse." Ma thereupon made a k'o-t'ou, and undertook the king's command. Using an ink-slab of crystal, a brush of dragon's beard, paper as white as snow, and ink scented like the larkspur,[7] Ma immediately threw off some thousand odd verses, which he laid at the feet of the king. When His Majesty saw them, he said, " Sir, your genius does honour to these marine nations of ours." Then, summoning the members of the royal family, the king gave a great feast in the Coloured Cloud pavilion ; and, when the wine had circulated freely, seizing

[6] See No. XIX., note 1.

[7] Good ink of the kind miscalled " Indian " is usually very highly scented ; and from a habit the Chinese have of sucking their writing-brushes to a fine point, the phrase " to eat ink " has become a synonym of " to study."

a great goblet in his hand, the king rose and said before
all the guests, " It is a thousand pities, Sir, that you are
not married. What say you to entering the bonds of
wedlock ? " Ma rose blushing and stammered out his
thanks ; upon which the king, looking round, spoke a
few words to the attendants, and in a few moments in
came a bevy of Court ladies supporting the king's daughter,
whose ornaments went tinkle, tinkle, as she walked along.
Immediately the nuptial drums and trumpets began to
sound forth, and bride and bridegroom worshipped Heaven
and Earth together.[8] Stealing a glance, Ma saw that the
princess was endowed with a fairy-like loveliness. When
the ceremony was over she retired, and by-and-by the
wine party broke up. Then came several beautifully
dressed waiting-maids, who with painted candles escorted
Ma within. The bridal couch was made of coral adorned
with eight kinds of precious stones, and the curtains were
thickly hung with pearls as big as acorns. Next day at
dawn a crowd of young slave-girls trooped into the room
to offer their services ; whereupon Ma got up and went
off to Court to pay his respects to the king. He was then
duly received as royal son-in-law and made an officer of
state. The fame of his poetical talents spread far and
wide, and the kings of the various seas sent officers to
congratulate him, vieing with each other in their invitations
to him. Ma dressed himself in gorgeous clothes, and went
forth riding on a superb steed, with a mounted body-guard
all splendidly armed. There were musicians on horseback
and musicians in chariots, and in three days he had visited
every one of the marine kingdoms, making his name
known in all directions. In the palace there was a jade
tree, about as big round as a man could clasp. Its roots
were as clear as glass, and up the middle ran, as it were, a
stick of pale yellow. The branches were the size of one's
arm ; the leaves like white jade, as thick as a copper
cash. The foliage was dense, and beneath its shade the
ladies of the palace were wont to sit and sing. The flowers
which covered the tree resembled grapes, and if a single
petal fell to the earth it made a ringing sound. Taking
one up, it would be found to be exactly like carved corne-

---

[8] This all-important point in a Chinese marriage ceremony is the
equivalent of our own " signing in the vestry."

lian, very bright and pretty to look at. From time to time a wonderful bird came and sang there. Its feathers were of a golden hue, and its tail as long as its body. Its notes were like the tinkling of jade, very plaintive and touching to listen to. When Ma heard this bird sing, it called up in him recollections of his old home, and accordingly he said to the princess, " I have now been away from my own country for three years, separated from my father and mother. Thinking of them my tears flow and the perspiration runs down my back. Can you return with me ? " His wife replied, " The way of immortals is not that of men. I am unable to do what you ask, but I cannot allow the feelings of husband and wife to break the tie of parent and child. Let us devise some plan." When Ma heard this he wept bitterly, and the princess sighed and said, " We cannot both stay or both go." The next day the king said to him, " I hear that you are pining after your old home. Will to-morrow suit you for taking leave ? " Ma thanked the king for his great kindness, which he declared he could never forget, and promised to return very shortly. That evening the princess and Ma talked over their wine of their approaching separation. Ma said they would soon meet again ; but his wife averred that their married life was at an end. Then he wept afresh, but the princess said, " Like a filial son you are going home to your parents. In the meetings and separations of this life, a hundred years seem but a single day ; why, then, should we give way to tears like children ? I will be true to you ; do you be faithful to me ; and then, though separated, we shall be united in spirit, a happy pair. Is it necessary to live side by side in order to grow old together ? If you break our contract your next marriage will not be a propitious one ; but if loneliness [9] overtakes you then choose a concubine. There is one point more of which I would speak, with reference to our married life. I am about to become a mother, and I pray you give me a name for your child." To this Ma replied, " If a girl I would have her called Lung-kung ; if a boy, then name him Fu-hai." [10] The princess asked for some token of remembrance, and Ma gave her a pair

---

[9] Literally, " if you have no one to cook your food."
[10] " Dragon Palace " and " Happy Sea," respectively.

of jade lilies that he had got during his stay in the marine kingdom. She added, " On the 8th of the 4th moon, three years hence, when you once more steer your course for this country, I will give you up your child." She next packed a leather bag full of jewels and handed it to Ma, saying, " Take care of this ; it will be a provision for many generations." When the day began to break a splendid farewell feast was given him by the king, and Ma bade them all adieu. The princess, in a car drawn by snow-white sheep, escorted him to the boundary of the marine kingdom, where he dismounted and stepped ashore. " Farewell ! " cried the princess, as her returning car bore her rapidly away, and the sea, closing over her, snatched her from her husband's sight. Ma returned to his home across the ocean. Some had thought him long since dead and gone ; all marvelled at his story. Happily his father and mother were yet alive, though his former wife had married another man ; and so he understood why the princess had pledged him to constancy, for she already knew that this had taken place. His father wished him to take another wife, but he would not. He only took a concubine. Then, after the three years had passed away, he started across the sea on his return journey, when lo ! he beheld, riding on the wave-crests and splashing about the water in playing, two young children. On going near, one of them seized hold of him and sprang into his arms ; upon which the elder cried until he, too, was taken up. They were a boy and girl, both very lovely, and wearing embroidered caps adorned with jade lilies. On the back of one of them was a worked case, in which Ma found the following letter :—

" I presume my father and mother-in-law are well. Three years have passed away and destiny still keeps us apart. Across the great ocean, the letter-bird would find no path.[11] I have been with you in my dreams until I am quite worn out. Does the blue sky look down upon any grief like mine ? Yet Ch'ang-ngo[12] lives solitary in the moon, and Chih Nü[13] laments that she cannot cross the

[11] Alluding to an old legend of a letter conveyed by a bird.
[12] See No. V., note 2.
[13] The " Spinning Damsel," or name of a star in Lyra, connected with which there is a celebrated legend of its annual transit across the Milky Way.

Silver River. Who am I that I should expect happiness to be mine ? Truly this thought turns my tears into joy. Two months after your departure I had twins, who can already prattle away in the language of childhood, at one moment snatching a date, at another a pear. Had they no mother they would still live. These I now send to you, with the jade lilies you gave me in their hats, in token of the sender. When you take them upon your knee, think that I am standing by your side. I know that you have kept your promise to me, and I am happy. I shall take no second husband, even unto death. All thoughts of dress and finery are gone from me ; my looking-glass sees no new fashions ; my face has long been unpowdered, my eyebrows unblacked. You are my Ulysses, I am your Penelope ; [14] though not actually leading a married life, how can it be said that we are not husband and wife ? Your father and mother will take their grandchildren upon their knees, though they have never set eyes upon the bride. Alas ! there is something wrong in this. Next year your mother will enter upon the long night. I shall be there by the side of the grave, as is becoming in her daughter-in-law. From this time forth our daughter will be well ; later on she will be able to grasp her mother's hand. Our boy, when he grows up, may possibly be able to come to and fro. Adieu, dear husband, adieu, though I am leaving much unsaid." Ma read the letter over and over again, his tears flowing all the time. His two children clung round his neck, and begged him to take them home. "Ah, my children," said he, " where is your home ? " Then they all wept bitterly, and Ma, looking at the great ocean stretching away to meet the sky, lovely and pathless, embraced his children, and proceeded sorrowfully to return. Knowing, too, that his mother could not last long, he prepared everything necessary for the ceremony of interment, and planted a hundred young pine-trees at her grave.[15] The following year the old lady did die, and her coffin was borne to its last resting-place, when lo ! there was the princess standing by the side of the grave. The lookers-on were much

---

[14] These are of course only the equivalents of the Chinese names in the text.

[15] To keep off the much-dreaded wind, which disturbs the rest of the departed.

alarmed, but in a moment there was a flash of lightning followed by a clap of thunder and a squall of rain, and she was gone. It was then noticed that many of the young pine-trees which had died were one and all brought to life. Subsequently, Fu-hai went in search of the mother for whom he pined so much, and after some days' absence returned. Lung-kung, being a girl, could not accompany him, but she mourned much in secret. One dark day her mother entered and bade her dry her eyes, saying, " My child, you must get married. Why these tears ? " She then gave her a tree of coral eight feet in height, some Baroos camphor,[16] one hundred valuable pearls, and two boxes inlaid with gold and precious stones, as her dowry. Ma having found out she was there, rushed in, and, seizing her hand, began to weep for joy, when suddenly a violent peal of thunder rent the building and the princess had vanished.[17]

LXIV. THE FIGHTING CRICKET

DURING the reign of Hsüan Tê,[1] cricket fighting was very much in vogue at court, levies of crickets being exacted from the people as a tax. On one occasion the magistrate of Hua-yin, wishing to make friends with the Governor, presented him with a cricket which, on being set to fight, displayed very remarkable powers ; so much so that the Governor commanded the magistrate to supply him regularly with these insects. The latter, in his turn, ordered the beadles of his district to provide him with crickets ; and then it became a practice for people who had nothing else to do to catch and rear them for this purpose. Thus the price of crickets rose very high; and when the beadle's[2] runners came to exact even a single one, it was enough to ruin several families.

[16] For which a very high price is obtained in China.

[17] Episodes which appear in this story and in " The Princess of the Tung-t'ing Lake " have been woven together to form the so-called Japanese " tale of Urashima, the fisher-lad who was beloved of the Sea King's daughter." See the *Fortnightly Review*, July 1906, p. 99, and Aston's *Japanese Literature*, p. 39.

[1] Of the Ming dynasty ; reigned A.D. 1426–1436.

[2] These beadles are chosen by the officials from among the respectable and substantial of the people to preside over a small

Now in the village of which we are speaking there lived a man named Ch'êng, a student who had often failed for his bachelor's degree ; and, being a stupid sort of fellow, his name was sent in for the post of beadle. He did all he could to get out of it, but without success ; and by the end of the year his small patrimony was gone. Just then came a call for crickets, and Ch'êng, not daring to make a like call upon his neighbours, was at his wits' end, and in his distress determined to commit suicide. " What's the use of that ? " cried his wife. " You'd do better to go out and try to find some." So off went Ch'êng in the early morning, with a bamboo tube and a silk net, not returning till late at night ; and he searched about in tumble-down walls, in bushes, under stones, and in holes, but without catching more than two or three, do what he would. Even those he did catch were weak creatures, and of no use at all, which made the magistrate fix a limit of time, the result of which was that in a few days Ch'êng got one hundred blows with the bamboo. This made him so sore that he was quite unable to go after the crickets any more, and, as he lay tossing and turning on the bed, he determined once again to put an end to his life.

About that time a hump-backed fortune-teller of great skill arrived at the village, and Ch'êng's wife, putting together a trifle of money, went off to seek his assistance. The door was literally blocked up—fair young girls and white-headed dames crowding in from all quarters. A room was darkened, and a bamboo screen hung at the door, an altar being arranged outside at which the fortune-seekers burnt incense in a brazier, and prostrated themselves twice, while the soothsayer stood by the side, and, looking up into vacancy, prayed for a response. His lips opened and shut, but nobody heard what he said, all

area and be responsible for the general good behaviour of its inhabitants. The post is one of honour and occasional emolument, since all petitions presented to the authorities, all mortgages, transfers of land, &c., should bear the beadle's seal or signature in evidence of their *bona-fide* character. On the other hand, the beadle is punished by fine, and sometimes bambooed, if robberies are too frequent within his jurisdiction, or if he fails to secure the person of any malefactor particularly wanted by his superior officers. And other causes may combine to make the post a dangerous one ; but no one is allowed to refuse acceptance of it point-blank.

standing there in awe waiting for the answer. In a few moments a piece of paper was thrown from behind the screen, and the soothsayer said that the petitioner's desire would be accomplished in the way he wished. Ch'êng's wife now advanced, and, placing some money on the altar, burnt her incense and prostrated herself in a similar manner. In a few moments the screen began to move, and a piece of paper was thrown down, on which there were no words, but only a picture. In the middle was a building like a temple, and behind this a small hill, at the foot of which were a number of curious stones, with the long, spiky feelers of innumerable crickets appearing from behind. Hard by was a frog, which seemed to be engaged in putting itself into various kinds of attitudes. The good woman had no idea what it all meant ; but she noticed the crickets, and accordingly went off home to tell her husband. " Ah," said he, " this is to show me where to hunt for crickets ; " and, on looking closely at the picture, he saw that the building very much resembled a temple to the east of their village. So he forced himself to get up, and, leaning on a stick, went out to seek crickets behind the temple. Rounding an old grave, he came upon a place where stones were lying scattered about as in the picture, and then he set himself to watch attentively. He might as well have been looking for a needle or a grain of mustard-seed ; and by degrees he became quite exhausted, without finding anything, when suddenly an old frog jumped out. Ch'êng was a little startled, but immediately pursued the frog, which retreated into the bushes. He then saw one of the insects he wanted sitting at the root of a bramble ; but on making a grab at it, the cricket ran into a hole, from which he was unable to move it until he poured in some water, when out the little creature came. It was a magnificent specimen, strong and handsome, with a fine tail, green neck, and golden wings; and, putting it in his basket, he returned home in high glee to receive the congratulations of his family. He would not have taken anything for this cricket. He put it into a bowl, and fed it with white crab's flesh and with the yellow kernel of the sweet chestnut, tending it most lovingly, and waiting for the time when the magistrate should call upon him for a cricket.

Meanwhile, a son of Ch'êng's, aged nine, one day took

the opportunity of his father being out to open the bowl. Instantaneously the cricket made a spring forward and was gone ; and all efforts to catch it again were unavailing. At length the boy made a grab at it with his hand, but only succeeded in seizing one of its legs, which thereupon broke, and the little creature soon afterwards died. Ch'êng's wife turned deadly pale when her son, with tears in his eyes, told her what had happened. " Oh, you young rascal ! won't you catch it when your father comes home," said she ; at which the boy ran away, crying bitterly. Soon after Ch'êng arrived, and when he heard his wife's story he felt as if he had been turned to ice, and went in search of his son, who, however, was nowhere to be found, until at length they discovered his body lying at the bottom of a well. Their anger was thus turned to grief, and death seemed as though it would be a pleasant relief to them as they sat facing each other in silence in their thatched and smokeless [3] hut. At evening they prepared to bury the boy ; but, on touching the body, lo ! he was still breathing. Overjoyed, they placed him upon the bed, and towards the middle of the night he came round ; but they found that his mind was weak, and he wanted to go to sleep. His father, how- ever, caught sight of the empty bowl in which he had kept the cricket, and ceased to think any more about his son, never once closing his eyes all night ; and as day gradually broke, there he lay stiff and stark, until suddenly he heard the chirping of a cricket outside the house door. Jumping up in a great hurry to see, there was his lost insect ; but, on trying to catch it, away it hopped directly. At last he got it under his hand, though when he came to close his fingers on it, there was nothing in them. So he went on, chasing it up and down, until finally it hopped into a corner of the wall ; and then, looking carefully about, he espied it once more, no longer the same in appearance, but small, and of a dark red colour. Ch'êng stood looking at it, without trying to catch such a worthless specimen, when all of a sudden the little creature hopped into his sleeve ; and, on examining it more nearly, he saw that it really was a hand- some insect, with well-formed head and neck, and forthwith took it indoors. He was now anxious to try its prowess ; and it so happened that a young fellow of the village, who

[3] A favourite Chinese expression, signifying the absence of food.

had a fine cricket which used to win every bout it fought, and was so valuable to him that he wanted a high price for it, called on Ch'êng that very day. He laughed heartily at Ch'êng's champion, and, producing his own, placed it side by side, to the great disadvantage of the former. Ch'êng's countenance fell, and he no longer wished to back his cricket ; however, the young fellow urged him, and he thought that there was no use in rearing a feeble insect, and that he had better sacrifice it for a laugh ; so they put them together in a bowl. The little cricket lay quite still like a piece of wood, at which the young fellow roared again, and louder than ever when it did not move even though tickled with a pig's bristle. By dint of tickling it was roused at last, and then it fell upon its adversary with such fury, that in a moment the young fellow's cricket would have been killed outright had not its master interfered and stopped the fight. The little cricket then stood up and chirped to Ch'êng as a sign of victory; and Ch'êng, over-joyed, was just talking over the battle with the young fellow when a cock caught sight of the insect, and ran up to eat it. Ch'êng was in a great state of alarm ; but the cock luckily missed its aim, and the cricket hopped away, its enemy pursuing at full speed. In another moment it would have been snapped up, when, lo! to his great astonishment, Ch'êng saw his cricket seated on the cock's head, holding firmly on to its comb. He then put it into a cage, and by-and-by sent it to the magistrate, who, seeing what a small one he had provided, was very angry indeed. Ch'êng told the story of the cock, which the magistrate refused to believe, and set it to fight with other crickets, all of which it vanquished without exception. He then tried it with a cock, and as all turned out as Ch'êng had said, he gave him a present, and sent the cricket in to the Governor. The Governor put it into a golden cage, and forwarded it to the palace, accompanied by some remarks on its performances ; and when there, it was found that of all the splendid collection of His Imperial Majesty, not one was worthy to be placed alongside of this one. It would dance in time to music, and thus became a great favourite, the Emperor in return bestowing magnificent gifts of horses and silks upon the Governor. The Governor did not forget whence he had obtained the cricket, and the magistrate also well rewarded Ch'êng by excusing him from the duties of beadle, and by instructing the Literary Chancellor to pass him for the first degree. A few months afterwards Ch'êng's son recovered his intellect, and said that he had been a cricket, and had proved himself a very skilful fighter.[4] The Governor, too, rewarded Ch'êng handsomely, and in a few years he was a rich man, with flocks, and herds, and houses, and acres, quite one of the wealthiest of mankind.

LXV. TAKING REVENGE

HSIANG KAO, otherwise called Ch'u-tan, was a T'ai-yüan man, and deeply attached to his half-brother Shêng. Shêng himself was desperately enamoured of a young lady named Po-ssŭ,[1] who was also very fond of him : but the mother wanted too much money for her daughter. Now a rich young fellow named Chuang thought he should like to get Po-ssŭ for himself, and proposed to buy her as a concubine. "No, no," said Po-ssŭ to her mother, "I prefer being Shêng's wife to becoming Chuang's concubine." So her mother consented, and informed Shêng, who had only recently buried his first wife ; at which he was delighted and made preparations to take her over to his own house. When Chuang heard this he was infuriated against Shêng for thus depriving him of Po-ssŭ ; and chancing to meet him out one day, set to and abused him roundly. Shêng answered him back, and then Chuang ordered his attendants to fall upon Shêng and beat him well, which they did, leaving him lifeless on the ground. When Hsiang heard what had taken place he ran out and found his brother lying dead upon the ground. Overcome with grief, he proceeded to the magistrate's, and accused Chuang of

---

[4] That is to say, his spirit had entered, during his period of temporary insanity, into the cricket which had allowed itself to be caught by his father, and had animated it to fight with such extraordinary vigour in order to make good the loss occasioned by his carelessness in letting the other escape.

[1] This is the term used by the Chinese for " Persia," often put by metonymy for things which come from that country, sc. " valuables." Thus, " to be poor in Persia " is to have but few jewels, gold and silver ornaments, and even clothes.

murder ; but the latter bribed so heavily that nothing came of the accusation. This worked Hsiang to frenzy, and he determined to assassinate Chuang on the high road ; with which intent he daily concealed himself, with a sharp knife about him, among the bushes on the hill-side, waiting for Chuang to pass. By degrees, this plan of his became known far and wide, and accordingly Chuang never went out except with a strong bodyguard, besides which he engaged at a high price the services of a very skilful archer, named Chiao T'ung, so that Hsiang had no means of carrying out his intention. However, he continued to lie in wait day after day, and on one occasion it began to rain heavily, and in a short time Hsiang was wet through to the skin. Then the wind got up, and a hailstorm followed, and by-and-by Hsiang was quite numbed with the cold. On the top of the hill there was a small temple wherein lived a Taoist priest, whom Hsiang knew from the latter having occasionally begged alms in the village, and to whom he had often given a meal. This priest, seeing how wet he was, gave him some other clothes, and told him to put them on ; but no sooner had he done so than he crouched down like a dog, and found that he had been changed into a tiger, and that the priest had vanished. It now occurred to him to seize this opportunity of revenging himself upon his enemy ; and away he went to his old ambush, where lo and behold ! he found his own body lying stiff and stark. Fearing lest it should become food for birds of prey, he guarded it carefully, until at length one day Chuang passed by. Out rushed the tiger and sprang upon Chaung, biting his head off, and swallowing it upon the spot, at which Chiao T'ung, the archer, turned round and shot the animal through the heart. Just at that moment Hsiang awaked as though from a dream, but it was some time before he could crawl home, where he arrived to the great delight of his family, who didn't know what had become of him. Hsiang said not a word, lying quietly on the bed until some of his people came in to congratulate him on the death of his great enemy Chuang. Hsiang then cried out, " I was that tiger," and proceeded to relate the whole story, which thus got about until it reached the ears of Chuang's son, who immediately set to work to bring his father's murderer to justice. The magistrate, however, did not consider this wild story as sufficient evidence against him, and there-upon dismissed the case.

LXVI. THE TIPSY TURTLE

AT Lin-t'iao there lived a Mr. Fêng, whose other name the person who told me this story could not remember ; he belonged to a good family, though now somewhat falling into decay. Now a certain man, who caught turtles, owed him some money which he could not pay, but whenever he captured any turtles he used to send one to Mr. Fêng. One day he took him an enormous creature, with a white spot on its forehead ; but Fêng was so struck with something in its appearance, that he let it go again. A little while afterwards he was returning home from his son-in-law's, and had reached the banks of the river,[1] when in the dusk of the evening he saw a drunken man come rolling along, attended by two or three servants. No sooner did he perceive Fêng than he called out, " Who are you ? " to which Fêng replied that he was a traveller. " And haven't you got a name ? " shouted out the drunken man in a rage, " that you must call yourself a traveller ? " To this Fêng made no reply, but tried to pass by ; whereupon he found himself seized by the sleeve and unable to move. His adversary smelt horribly of wine, and at length Fêng asked him, saying, " And pray who are you ? " " Oh, I am the late magistrate at Nan-tu," answered he ; " what do you want to know for ? " " A nice disgrace to society you are, too," cried Fêng ; " however, I am glad to hear you are only *late* magistrate, for if you had been present magistrate there would be bad times in store for travellers." This made the drunken man furious, and he was proceeding to use violence, when Fêng cried out, " My name is So-and-so, and I'm not the man to stand this sort of thing from anybody." No sooner had he uttered these words than the drunken man's rage was turned into joy, and, falling on his knees before

[1] The name here used is the *Hêng* or " ceaseless " river, which is applied by the Chinese to the Ganges. A certain number, extending to fifty-three places of figures, is called " Ganges sand," in allusion to a famous remark that " Buddha and the Bôdhisatras knew of the creation and destruction of every grain of dust in Jambudwipa (the universe) ; how much more the number of the sand-particles in the river Ganges ? "

Fêng, he said, " My benefactor ! pray excuse my rudeness."
Then getting up, he told his servants to go on ahead and
get something ready ; Fêng at first declining to go with
him, but yielding on being pressed. Taking his hand, the
drunken man led him along a short distance until they
reached a village, where there was a very nice house and
grounds, quite like the establishment of a person of position.
As his friend was now getting sober, Fêng inquired what
might be his name. " Don't be frightened when I tell
you," said the other ; " I am the Eighth Prince of the T'iao
river. I have just been out to take wine with a friend, and
somehow I got tipsy ; hence my bad behaviour to you,
which please forgive." Fêng now knew that he was not
of mortal flesh and blood ; but, seeing how kindly he himself was treated, he was not a bit afraid. A banquet
followed, with plenty of wine, of which the Eighth Prince
drank so freely that Fêng thought he would soon be worse
than ever, and accordingly said he felt tipsy himself, and
asked to be allowed to go to bed. " Never fear," answered
the Prince, who perceived Fêng's thoughts ; " many
drunkards will tell you that they cannot remember in the
morning the extravagances of the previous night, but I tell
you this is all nonsense, and that in nine cases out of ten
those extravagances are committed wittingly and with
malice prepense.[2] Now, though I am not the same order
of being as yourself, I should never venture to behave badly
in your good presence ; so pray do not leave me thus."
Fêng then sat down again and said to the Prince, " Since
you are aware of this, why not change your ways ? "
" Ah," replied the Prince, " when I was a magistrate I
drank much more than I do now ; but I got into disgrace
with the Emperor and was banished here, since which
time, ten years and more, I have tried to reform. Now,
however, I am drawing near the wood,[3] and being unable

---

[2] Drunkenness is not recognised in China as an extenuating
circumstance ; neither, indeed, is insanity,—a lunatic who takes
another man's life being equally liable with ordinary persons to the
forfeiture of his own.

[3] A favourite Chinese figure expressive of old age. It dates back
to the celebrated commentary by Tso-ch'iu Ming on Confucius'
Spring and Autumn (see No. XLI., note 2) :—" Hsi is twenty-
three and I am twenty-five ; and marrying thus we shall approach
the wood together ; " the " wood " being, of course, that of the coffin.

to move about much, the old vice has come upon me again ; I have found it impossible to stop myself, but perhaps what you say may do me some good." While they were thus talking, the sound of a distant bell broke upon their ears ; and the Prince, getting up and seizing Fêng's hand, said, " We cannot remain together any longer ; but I will give you something by which I may in part requite your kindness to me. It must not be kept for any great length of time ; when you have attained your wishes, then I will receive it back again." Thereupon he spat out of his mouth a tiny man, no more than an inch high, and scratching Fêng's arm with his nails until Fêng felt as if the skin was gone, he quickly laid the little man upon the spot. When he let go, the latter had already sunk into the skin, and nothing was to be seen but a cicatrix well healed over. Fêng now asked what it all meant, but the Prince only laughed, and said, " It's time for you to go," and forthwith escorted him to the door. The Prince here bade him adieu, and when he looked round, Prince, village, and house had all disappeared together, leaving behind a great turtle which waddled down into the water, and disappeared likewise. He could now easily account for the Prince's present to him ; and from this moment his sight became intensely keen. He could see precious stones lying in the bowels of the earth, and was able to look down as far as Hell itself ; besides which he suddenly found that he knew the names of many things of which he had never heard before. From below his own bedroom he dug up many hundred ounces of pure silver, upon which he lived very comfortably ; and once when a house was for sale, he perceived that in it lay concealed a vast quantity of gold, so he immediately bought it, and so became immensely rich in all kinds of valuables. He secured a mirror, on the back of which was a phœnix, surrounded by water and clouds, and portraits of the celebrated wives of the Emperor Shun,[4] so beautifully executed that each hair of the head and eyebrows could easily be counted. If any woman's face came upon the mirror, there it remained indelibly fixed and not to be rubbed out ; but if the same woman looked into the mirror again, dressed in a different dress, or if some other woman chanced to look in, then the former face would gradually fade away.

[4] See No. VIII., note 3.

Now the third drincess in Prince Su's family was very
beautiful ; and Fêng, who had long heard of her fame,
concealed himself on the K'ung-tung hill, when he knew
the Princess was going there.   He waited until she alighted
from her chair, and then getting the mirror full upon her,
he walked off home.   Laying it on the table, he saw
therein a lovely girl in the act of raising her handkerchief,
and with a sweet smile playing over her face ; her lips
seemed about to move, and a twinkle was discernible in her
eyes.[5]   Delighted with this picture, he put the mirror very
carefully away ; but in about a year his wife had let the
story leak out, and the Prince, hearing of it, threw Fêng
into prison, and took possession of the mirror.   Fêng was
to be beheaded ; however, he bribed one of the Prince's
ladies to tell His Highness that if he would pardon him all
the treasures of the earth might easily become his ; whereas,
on the other hand, his death could not possibly be of any
advantage to the Prince.   The Prince now thought of
confiscating all his goods and banishing him ; but the third
princess observed, that as he had already seen her, were he
to die ten times over it would not give her back her lost
face, and that she had much better marry him.   The Prince
would not hear of this, whereupon his daughter shut herself
up and refused all nourishment, at which the ladies of the
palace were dreadfully alarmed, and reported it at once
to the Prince.   Fêng was accordingly liberated, and was to
informed of the determination of the Princess, which, however, he declined to fall in with, saying that he was not
going thus to sacrifice the wife of his days of poverty,[6] and
would rather die than carry out such an order.   He added
that if His Highness would consent, he would purchase his
liberty at the price of everything he had.   The Prince was
exceedingly angry at this, and seized Fêng again ; and
meanwhile one of the concubines got Fêng's wife into the
palace, intending to poison her.   Fêng's wife, however,
brought her a beautiful present of a coral stand for a
looking-glass, and was so agreeable in her conversation,
that the concubine took a great fancy to her, and presented

5 . . . Move these eyes ?
   . . . Here are severed lips.
                    —*Merchant of Venice*, Act III., sc. 2.
6 See No. LIII., note 1.

her to the Princess, who was equally pleased, and forthwith determined that they would both be Fêng's wives.[7] When Fêng heard of this plan, he said to his wife, "With a Prince's daughter there can be no distinctions of first and second wife;" but Mrs. Fêng paid no heed to him, and immediately sent off to the Prince such an enormous quantity of valuables that it took a thousand men to carry them, and the Prince himself had never before heard of such treasures in his life. Fêng was now liberated once more, and solemnised his marriage with the Princess.

One night after this he dreamt that the Eighth Prince came to him and asked him to return his former present, saying that to keep it too long would be injurious to his chances of life. Fêng asked him to take a drink, but the Eighth Prince said that he had forsworn wine, acting under Fêng's advice, for three years. He then bit Fêng's arm, and the latter waked up with the pain, to find that the cicatrix on his arm was no longer there.

LXVII. THE MAGIC PATH

In the province of Kuangtung there lived a scholar named Kuo, who was one evening on his way home from a friend's, when he lost his way among the hills. He got into a thick jungle, where, after about an hour's wandering, he suddenly heard the sound of laughing and talking on the top of the hill. Hurrying up in the direction of the sound, he beheld some ten or a dozen persons sitting on the ground engaged in drinking. No sooner had they caught sight of Kuo than they all cried out, "Come along! just room for one more; you're in the nick of time." So Kuo sat down with the company, most of whom, he noticed, belonged to the literati,[1] and began by asking them to direct him on his

---

[7] This method of arranging a matrimonial difficulty is a common one in Chinese fiction, but I should say quite unknown in real life.

[1] This term, while really including all literary men, of no matter what rank or standing, is more usually confined to that large section of unemployed scholarship made up of (1) those who are waiting to get started in an official career, (2) those who have taken one or more degrees and are preparing for the next, (3) those who have

way home ; but one of them cried out, " A nice sort of fellow you are, to be bothering about your way home, and paying no attention to the fine moon we have got to-night." The speaker then presented him with a goblet of wine of exquisite bouquet, which Kuo drank off at a draught, and another gentleman filled up again for him at once. Now, Kuo was pretty good in that line, and being very thirsty withal from his long walk, tossed off bumper after bumper, to the great delight of his hosts, who were unanimous in voting him a jolly good fellow. He was, moreover, full of fun, and could imitate exactly the note of any kind of bird ; so all of a sudden he began on the sly to twitter like a swallow, to the great astonishment of the others, who wondered how it was a swallow could be out so late. He then changed his note to that of a cuckoo, sitting there laughing and saying nothing, while his hosts were discussing the extraordinary sounds they had just heard. After a while he imitated a parrot, and cried, " Mr. Kuo is very drunk : you'd better see him home ; " and then the sounds ceased, beginning again by-and-by, when at last the others found out who it was, and all burst out laughing. They screwed up their mouths and tried to whistle like Kuo, but none of them could do so ; and soon one of them observed, " What a pity Madam Ch'ing isn't with us : we must rendezvous here again at mid-autumn, and you, Mr. Kuo, must be sure and come." Kuo said he would, whereupon another of his hosts got up and remarked that, as he had given them such an amusing entertainment, they would try to show him a few acrobatic feats. They all arose, and one of them planting his feet firmly, a second jumped up on to his shoulders, a third on to the second's shoulders, and a fourth on to his, until it was too high for the rest to jump up, and accordingly they began to climb as though it had been a ladder. When they were all up, and the topmost head seemed to touch the clouds, the whole column bent gradually down until it lay along the ground transformed into a path. Kuo remained for some time in a state of considerable alarm, and then, setting out along this path, ultimately reached his own home. Some days

failed to distinguish themselves at the public examinations, and eke out a small patrimony by taking pupils, and (4) scholars of sufficiently high qualifications who have no taste for official life.

afterwards he revisited the spot, and saw the remains of a feast lying about on the ground, with dense bushes on all sides, but no sign of a path. At mid-autumn he thought of keeping his engagement ; however, his friends persuaded him not to go.

LXVIII. THE FAITHLESS WIDOW [1]

MR. NIU was a Kiangsi man who traded in piece goods. He married a wife from the Chêng family, by whom he had two children, a boy and a girl. When thirty-three years of age he fell ill and died, his son Chung being then only twelve and his little girl eight or nine. His wife did not remain faithful to his memory, but, selling off all the property, pocketed the proceeds and married another man, leaving her two children almost in a state of destitution with their aunt, Niu's sister-in-law, an old lady of sixty, who had lived with them previously, and had now nowhere to seek a shelter. A few years later this aunt died, and the family fortunes began to sink even lower than before ; Chung, however, was now grown up, and determined to carry on his father's trade, only he had no capital to start with. His sister marrying a rich trader named Mao, she begged her husband to lend Chung ten ounces of silver, which he did, and Chung immediately started for Nanking. On the road he fell in with some bandits, who robbed him of all he had, and consequently he was unable to return ; but one day when he was at a pawnshop he noticed that the master of the shop was wonderfully like his late father, and on going out and making inquiries he found that this pawnbroker bore precisely the same names. In great astonishment, he forthwith proceeded to

---

[1] Unless under exceptional circumstances, it is not considered creditable in China for widows to marry again. It may here be mentioned that the honorary tablets conferred from time to time by His Imperial Majesty upon virtuous widows are only given to women who, widowed before the age of thirty, have remained in that state for a period of thirty years. The meaning of this is obvious ; temptations are supposed to be fewer and less dangerous after thirty, which is the equivalent of forty with us ; and it is wholly improbable that thirty years of virtuous life, at which period the widow would be at least fifty, would be followed by any act that might cast a stain upon the tablet thus bestowed.

frequent the place with no other object than to watch this
man, who, on the other hand, took no notice of Chung ;
and by the end of three days, having satisfied himself that
he really saw his own father, and yet not daring to disclose
his own identity, he made application through one of the
assistants, on the score of being himself a Kiangsi man,
to be employed in the shop.   Accordingly, an indenture
was drawn up ;   and when the master noticed Chung's
name and place of residence he started, and asked him
whence he came.   With tears in his eyes Chung addressed
him by his father's name, and then the pawnbroker became
lost in a deep reverie, by-and-by asking Chung how his
mother was.   Now Chung did not like to allude to his
father's death, and turned the question by saying, " My
father went away on business six years ago, and never
came back ;   my mother married again and left us, and
had it not been for my aunt our corpses would long ago
have been cast out in the kennel."   Then the pawnbroker
was much moved, and cried out, " I am your father ! "
seizing his son's hand and leading him within to see his
step-mother.   This lady was about twenty-two, and,
having no children of her own, was delighted with Chung,
and prepared a banquet for him in the inner apartments.
Mr. Niu himself was, however, somewhat melancholy,
and wished to return to his old home ; but his wife, fearing
that there would be no one to manage the business, persuaded him to remain ;   so he taught his son the trade,
and in three months was able to leave it all to him.   He
then prepared for his journey, whereupon Chung informed
his step-mother that his father was really dead, to which
she replied in great consternation that she knew him only
as a trader to the place, and that six years previously he
had married her, which proved conclusively that he couldn't
be dead.   He then recounted the whole story, which was
a perfect mystery to both of them ; and twenty-four
hours afterwards in walked his father, leading a woman
whose hair was all dishevelled.   Chung looked at her, and
saw that she was his own mother ; and Niu took her by
the ear and began to revile her, saying, " Why did you
desert my children ? " to which the wretched woman made
no reply.   He then bit her across the neck, at which she
screamed to Chung for assistance, and he, not being able

to bear the sight, stepped in between them. His father
was more than ever enraged at this, when, lo! Chung's
mother had disappeared. While they were still lost in
astonishment at this strange scene, Mr. Niu's colour
changed; in another moment his empty clothes had
dropped upon the ground, and he himself became a black
vapour and also vanished from their sight. The step-
mother and son were much overcome; they took Niu's
clothes and buried them, and after that Chung continued
his father's business, and soon amassed great wealth. On
returning to his native place he found that his mother had
actually died on the very day of the above occurrence,
and that his father had been seen by the whole family.

LXIX. THE PRINCESS OF THE TUNG-T'ING LAKE

Ch'ên Pi-chiao was a Pekingese; and being a poor man
he attached himself as secretary to the suite of a high
military official named Chia. On one occasion, while
anchored on the Tung-t'ing lake, they saw a dolphin [1]
floating on the surface of the water; and General Chia
took his bow and shot at it, wounding the creature in the
back. A fish was hanging on to its tail, and would not let
go; so both were pulled out of the water together, and
attached to the mast. There they lay gasping, the dolphin
opening its mouth as if pleading for life, until at length
young Ch'ên begged the General to let them go again;
and then he himself half jokingly put a piece of plaster
upon the dolphin's wound, and had the two thrown back
into the water, where they were seen for some time afterwards diving and rising again to the surface. About a
year afterwards, Ch'ên was once more crossing the Tung-
t'ing lake on his way home, when the boat was upset in a
squall, and he himself only saved by clinging to a bamboo
crate, which finally, after floating about all night, caught

---

[1] Literally, a "pig old-woman dragon." Porpoise (Fr. *porc-poisson*) suggests itself at once; but I think fresh-water dolphin is
the best term, especially as the Tung-t'ing lake is many hundred
miles inland. The commentator explains it by *t'o*, which would be
"alligator" or "cayman," and is of course out of the question.

in the overhanging branch of a tree, and thus enabled
him to scramble on shore. By-and-by, another body
floated in, and this turned out to be his servant ; but on
dragging him out, he found life was already extinct. In
great distress, he sat himself down to rest, and saw beautiful
green hills and waving willows, but not a single human
being of whom he could ask the way. From early dawn till
the morning was far advanced he remained in that state ;
and then, thinking he saw his servant's body move, he
stretched out his hand to feel it, and before long the man
threw up several quarts of water and recovered consciousness. They now dried their clothes in the sun, and by
noon these were fit to put on ; at which period the pangs
of hunger began to assail them, and accordingly they
started over the hills in the hope of coming upon some
habitation of man. As they were walking along, an arrow
whizzed past, and the next moment two young ladies
dashed by on handsome palfreys. Each had a scarlet
band round her head, with a bunch of pheasant's feathers
stuck in her hair, and wore a purple riding-jacket with
small sleeves, confined by a green embroidered girdle
round the waist. One of them carried a cross-bow for
shooting bullets, and the other had on her arm a dark-
coloured bow-and-arrow case. Reaching the brow of the
hill, Ch'ên beheld a number of riders engaged in beating
the surrounding cover, all of whom were beautiful girls
and dressed exactly alike. Afraid to advance any further,
he inquired of a youth who appeared to be in attendance,
and the latter told him that it was a hunting party from
the palace ; and then, having supplied him with food from
his wallet, he bade him retire quickly, adding that if he
fell in with them he would assuredly be put to death,
Thereupon Ch'ên hurried away ; and descending the hill,
turned into a copse where there was a building which
he thought would in all probability be a monastery. On
getting nearer, he saw that the place was surrounded by a
wall, and between him and a half-open red door was a
brook spanned by a stone bridge leading up to it. Pulling
back the door, he beheld within a number of ornamental
buildings circling in the air like so many clouds, and for
all the world resembling the Imperial pleasure-grounds ;
and thinking it must be the park of some official personage,

he walked quietly in, enjoying the delicious fragrance of
the flowers as he pushed aside the thick vegetation which
obstructed his way. After traversing a winding path
fenced in by balustrades, Ch'ên reached a second enclosure,
wherein were a quantity of tall willow-trees which swept
the red eaves of the buildings with their branches. The
note of some bird would set the petals of the flowers fluttering in the air, and the least wind would bring the seed-
vessels down from the elm-trees above ; and the effect
upon the eye and heart of the beholder was something
quite unknown in the world of mortals. Passing through
a small kiosque, Ch'ên and his servant came upon a swing
which seemed as though suspended from the clouds,
while the ropes hung idly down in the utter stillness that
prevailed.[2] Thinking by this that they were approaching
the ladies' apartments,[3] Ch'ên would have turned back,
but at that moment he heard sounds of horses' feet at
the door, and what seemed to be the laughter of a bevy
of girls. So he and his servant hid themselves in a bush ;
and by-and-by, as the sounds came nearer, he heard one of
the young ladies say, " We've had but poor sport to-day ; "
whereupon another cried out, " If the princess hadn't
shot that wild goose, we should have taken all this trouble
for nothing." Shortly after this, a number of girls dressed
in red came in escorting a young lady, who went and
sat down under the kiosque. She wore a hunting costume
with tight [4] sleeves, and was about fourteen or fifteen
years old. Her hair looked like a cloud of mist at the
back of her head, and her waist seemed as though a breath
of wind might snap it [5]—incomparable for beauty, even

[2] Literally, in the utter absence of anybody.

[3] In passing near to the women's quarters in a friend's house, it
is etiquette to cough slightly, that inmates may be warned and
withdraw from the doors or windows in time to escape observation.
Over and over again at interviews with mandarins of all grades I
have heard the rustling of the ladies' dresses from some coign of
vantage, whence every movement of mine was being watched by
an inquisitive crowd ; and on one occasion I actually saw an eye
peering through a small hole in the partition behind me.

[4] Literally, " bald "—i.e., without the usual width and ornamentation of a Chinese lady's sleeve.

[5] Small waists are much admired in China, but any such artificial
aids as stays and tight lacing are quite unknown. A certain Prince
Wei admitted none but the possessors of small waists into his

among the celebrities of old. Just then the attendants handed her some exquisitely fragrant tea, and stood glittering round her like a bank of beautiful embroidery. In a few moments the young lady arose and descended from the kiosque ; at which one of her attendants cried out, " Is your Highness too fatigued by riding to take a turn in the swing ? " The princess replied that she was not ; and immediately some held her under the shoulders, while others seized her arms, and others, again, arranged her petticoats and supported her feet. Thus they helped her into the swing, she herself stretching out her shining arms, and putting her feet into a suitable pair of slippers ; [6] and then — away she went, light as a flying-swallow, far up into the fleecy clouds. As soon as she had had enough, the attendants helped her out, and one of them exclaimed, " Truly, your Highness is a perfect angel ! " At this the young lady laughed, and walked away, Ch'ên gazing after her in a state of semi-consciousness, until, at length, the voices died away, and he and his servant crept forth. Walking up and down near the swing, he suddenly espied a red handkerchief near the paling, which he knew had been dropped by one of the young ladies ; and, thrusting it joyfully into his sleeve, he walked up and entered the kiosque. There, upon a table, lay writing materials, and taking out the handkerchief he indited upon it the following lines :—

> What form divine was just now sporting nigh ?—
> 'Twas she, I trow, of " golden lily " fame ;
> Her charms the moon's fair denizens might shame,
> Her fairy footsteps bear her to the sky.

Humming this stanza to himself, Ch'ên walked along seeking for the path by which he had entered ; but every door was securely barred, and he knew not what to do. So he went back to the kiosque, when suddenly one of the young ladies appeared, and asked him in astonishment what he did there. " I have lost my way," replied Ch'ên ;

harem ; hence his establishment came to be called the *Palace of Small Waists.*

[6] Probably of felt or some such material, to prevent the young lady from slipping as she stood, in this case, not sat, in the swing. Chinese girls swing either standing or sitting.

" I pray you lend me your assistance." " Do you happen
to have found a red handkerchief ? " said the girl. " I
have, indeed," answered Ch'ên, " but I fear I have made it
somewhat dirty ; " and, suiting the action to the word, he
drew it forth, and handed it to her. " Wretched man ! "
cried the young lady, " you are undone. This is a handkerchief the Princess is constantly using, and you have gone
and scribbled all over it ; what will become of you now ? "
Ch'ên was in a great fright, and begged the young lady to
intercede for him ; to which she replied, " It was bad
enough that you should come here and spy about ; however, being a scholar, and a man of refinement, I would
have done my best for you ; but after this, how am I
to help you ? " Off she then ran with the handkerchief,
while Ch'ên remained behind in an agony of suspense,
and longing for the wings of a bird to bear him away from
his fate. By-and-by the young lady returned and congratulated him, saying, " There is some hope for you. The
Princess read your verses several times over, and was not at
all angry. You will probably be released ; but, meanwhile,
wait here, and don't climb the trees, or try to get through
the walls, or you may not escape after all." Evening was
now drawing on, and Ch'ên knew not, for certain, what
was about to happen ; at the same time he was very empty,
and, what with hunger and anxiety, death would have
been almost a happy release. Before long, the young
lady returned with a lamp in her hand, and followed by
a slave-girl bearing wine and food, which she forthwith
presented to Ch'ên. The latter asked if there was any
news about himself ; to which the young lady replied that
she had just mentioned his case to the Princess, who, not
knowing what to do with him at that hour of the night, had
given orders that he should at once be provided with food,
" which, at any rate," added she, " is not bad news." The
whole night long Ch'ên walked up and down, unable to
take rest ; and it was not till late in the morning that the
young lady appeared with more food for him. Imploring
her once more to intercede on his behalf, she told him that
the Princess had not instructed them either to kill or to
release him, and that it would not be fitting for such as
herself to be bothering the Princess with suggestions.
So there Ch'ên still remained until another day had almost

gone, hoping for the welcome moment; and then the
young lady rushed hurriedly in, saying, "You are lost!
Some one has told the Queen, and she, in a fit of anger,
threw the handkerchief on the ground, and made use of
very violent language. Oh dear! Oh dear! I'm sure
something dreadful will happen." Ch'ên threw himself
on his knees, his face as pale as ashes, and begged to know
what he should do; but at that moment sounds were
heard outside, and the young lady waved her hand to him,
and ran away. Immediately a crowd came pouring in
through the door, with ropes ready to secure the object
of their search; and among them was a slave-girl, who
looked fixedly at our hero, and cried out, "Why, surely you
are Mr. Ch'ên, aren't you?" at the same time stopping
the others from binding him until she should have reported
to the Queen. In a few minutes she came back, and said
the Queen requested him to walk in; and in he went,
through a number of doors, trembling all the time with
fear, until he reached a hall, the screen before which was
ornamented with green jade and silver. A beautiful girl
drew aside the bamboo curtain at the door, and announced,
"Mr. Ch'ên;" and he himself advanced, and fell down
before a lady, who was sitting upon a dais at the other
end, knocking his head upon the ground, and crying out,
"Thy servant is from a far-off country; spare, oh! spare
his life." "Sir!" replied the Queen, rising hastily from
her seat, and extending a hand to Ch'ên, "but for you, I
should not be here to-day. Pray excuse the rudeness of
my maids." Thereupon a splendid repast was served,
and wine was poured out in chased goblets, to the no
small astonishment of Ch'ên, who could not understand
why he was treated thus. "Your kindness," observed
the Queen, "in restoring me to life, I am quite unable to
repay; however, as you have made my daughter the
subject of your verse, the match is clearly ordained by fate,
and I shall send her along to be your handmaid." Ch'ên
hardly knew what to make of this extraordinary accomplishment of his wishes, but the marriage was solemnised
there and then; bands of music struck up wedding-airs,
beautiful mats were laid down for them to walk upon, and
the whole place was brilliantly lighted with a profusion
of coloured lamps. Then Ch'ên said to the Princess, "That

a stray and unknown traveller like myself, guilty of spoiling your Highness's handkerchief, should have escaped the fate he deserved, was already more than could be expected ; but now to receive you in marriage—this, indeed, far surpasses my wildest expectations." "My mother," replied the Princess, "is married to the King of this lake, and is herself a daughter of the River Prince. Last year, when on her way to visit her parents, she happened to cross the lake, and was wounded by an arrow ; but you saved her life, and gave her plaster for the wound. Our family, therefore, is grateful to you, and can never forget your good act. And do not regard me as of another species than yourself ; the Dragon King has bestowed upon me the elixir of immortality, and this I will gladly share with you." Then Ch'ên knew that his wife was a spirit, and by-and-by he asked her how the slave-girl had recognised him ; to which she replied, that the girl was the small fish which had been found hanging to the dolphin's tail. He then inquired why, as they didn't intend to kill him, he had been kept so long a prisoner. "I was charmed with your literary talent," answered the Princess, "but I did not venture to take the responsibility upon myself ; and no one saw how I tossed and turned the livelong night." "Dear friend," said Ch'ên ; "but, come, tell me who was it that brought my food." "A trusty waiting-maid of mine," replied the Princess ; "her name is A-nien." Ch'ên then asked how he could ever repay her, and the Princess told him there would be plenty of time to think of that ; and when he inquired where the King, her father, was, she said he had gone off with the God of War to fight against Ch'ih-yu,[7] and had not returned. A few days passed, and Ch'ên began to think his people at home would be anxious about him ; so he sent off his servant with a letter to tell them he was safe and sound, at which they were all overjoyed, believing him to have been lost in the wreck of the boat, of which event news had already reached them. However, they were unable to send him any reply, and were considerably distressed

---

[7] A rebel chieftain of the legendary period of China's history, who took up arms against the Emperor Huang Ti (B.C. 2698–2598), but was subsequently defeated in what was perhaps the first decisive battle of the world.

as to how he would find his way home again. Six months
afterwards Ch'ên himself appeared, dressed in fine clothes,
and riding on a splendid horse, with plenty of money, and
valuable jewels in his pocket—evidently a man of wealth.
From that time forth he kept up a magnificent establishment ; and in seven or eight years had become the father
of five children. Every day he kept open house, and if
any one asked him about his adventures, he would readily
tell them without reservation. Now a friend of his,
named Liang, whom he had known since they were boys
together, and who, after holding an appointment for
some years in Nan-fu, was crossing the Tung-t'ing lake,
on his way home, suddenly beheld an ornamental barge,
with carved woodwork and red windows, passing over
the foamy waves to the sound of music and singing from
within. Just then a beautiful young lady leant out of
one of the windows, which she had pushed open, and by her
side Liang saw a young man sitting, in a *négligé* attitude,
while two nice-looking girls stood by and shampooed [8]
him. Liang, at first, thought it must be the party of
some high official, and wondered at the scarcity of attendants ; [9] but, on looking more closely at the young man,
he saw it was no other than his old friend Ch'ên. Thereupon he began almost involuntarily to shout out to him ;
and when Ch'ên heard his own name, he stopped the rowers,
and walked out towards the figurehead,[10] beckoning
Liang to cross over into his boat, where the remains of
their feast were quickly cleared away, and fresh supplies
of wine, and tea, and all kinds of costly foods spread out
by handsome slave-girls. " It's ten years since we met,"
said Liang, " and what a rich man you have become in the
meantime." " Well," replied Ch'ên, " do you think
that so very extraordinary for a poor fellow like me ? "
Liang then asked him who was the lady with whom he

<hr/>

[8] This favourite process consists in gently thumping the person
operated upon all over the back with the soft part of the closed
fists. Compare Lane, *Arabian Nights*, Vol. I., p. 551 :—" She then
pressed me to her bosom, and laid me on the bed, and continued
gently kneading my limbs until slumber overcame me."

[9] See No. LVI., note 5. A considerable number of the attendants
there mentioned would accompany any high official, some in the
same, the rest in another barge.

[10] Generally known as the " cut-wave God."

was taking wine, and Ch'ên said she was his wife, which very much astonished Liang, who further inquired whither they were going. "Westwards," answered Ch'ên, and prevented any further questions by giving a signal for the music, which effectually put a stop to all further conversation.[11] By-and-by, Liang found the wine getting into his head, and seized the opportunity to ask Ch'ên to make him a present of one of his beautiful slave-girls. "You are drunk,[12] my friend," replied Ch'ên ; "however, I will give you the price of one as a pledge of our old friendship." And, turning to a servant, he bade him present Liang with a splendid pearl, saying, "Now you can buy a Green Pearl ;[13] you see I am not stingy ;" adding forthwith, "but I am pressed for time, and can stay no longer with my old friend." So he escorted Liang back to his boat, and, having let go the rope, proceeded on his way. Now, when Liang reached home, and called at Ch'ên's house, whom should he see but Ch'ên himself drinking with a party of friends ! "Why, I saw you only yesterday," cried Liang, "upon the Tung-t'ing. How quickly you have got back !" Ch'ên denied this, and then Liang repeated the whole story, at the conclusion of which Ch'ên laughed, and said, "You must be mistaken. Do you imagine I can be in two places at once ?" The company were all much astonished, and knew not what to make of it ; and subsequently when Ch'ên, who died at the age of eighty, was being carried to his grave, the bearers thought the coffin seemed remarkably light, and on opening it to see, found that the body had disappeared.[14]

[11] At all great banquets in China a theatrical troupe is engaged to perform while the dinner, which may last from four to six hours, drags its slow length along.
[12] See No. LIV., note 1.
[13] The name of a celebrated beauty.
[14] See No. LXIII., note 17.

LXX. THE PRINCESS LILY

AT Chiao-chou there lived a man named Tou Hsün, other-wise known as Hsiao-hui. One day he had just dropped off to sleep when he beheld a man in serge clothes standing by the bedside, and apparently anxious to communicate something to him. Tou inquired his errand; to which the man replied that he was the bearer of an invitation from his master. "And who is your master?" asked Tou. "Oh, he doesn't live far off," replied the other; so away they went together, and after some time came to a place where there were innumerable white houses rising one above the other, and shaded by dense groves of lemon-trees. They threaded their way past countless doors, not at all similar to those usually used, and saw a great many official-looking men and women passing and repassing, each of whom called out to the man in serge, "Has Mr. Tou come?" to which he always replied in the affirmative. Here a mandarin met them and escorted Tou into a palace, upon which the latter remarked, "This is really very kind of you; but I haven't the honour of knowing you, and I feel somewhat diffident about going in." "Our Prince," answered his guide, "has long heard of you as a man of good family and excellent principles, and is very anxious to make your acquaintance." "Who is your Prince?" inquired Tou. "You'll see for yourself in a moment," said the other; and just then out came two girls with banners, and guided Tou through a great number of doors until they came to a throne, upon which sat the Prince. His Highness immediately descended to meet him, and made him take the seat of honour; after which ceremony exquisite viands of all kinds were spread out before them. Looking up, Tou noticed a scroll, on which was inscribed, *The Cassia Court*, and he was just beginning to feel puzzled as to what he should say next, when the Prince addressed him as follows:—"The honour of having you for a neighbour is, as it were, a bond of affinity between us. Let us, then, give ourselves up to enjoyment, and put away suspicion and fear." Tou murmured his acquies-cence; and when the wine had gone round several times there arose from a distance the sound of pipes and singing, unaccompanied, however, by the usual drum, and very much subdued in volume. Thereupon the Prince looked about him and cried out, "We are about to set a verse for any of you gentlemen to cap ; here you are :—*Genius seeks the Cassia Court.*" While the courtiers were all engaged in thinking of some fit antithesis,[1] Tou added, "*Refinement loves the Lily flower ;*" upon which the Prince exclaimed, "How strange ! Lily is my daughter's name ; and, after such a coincidence, she must come in for you to see her." In a few moments the tinkling of her ornaments and a delicious fragrance of musk announced the arrival of the Princess, who was between sixteen and seventeen, and endowed with surpassing beauty. The Prince bade her make an obeisance to Tou, at the same time introducing her as his daughter Lily ; and as soon as the ceremony was over the young lady moved away. Tou remained in a state of stupefaction, and, when the Prince proposed that they should pledge each other in another bumper, paid not the slightest attention to what he said. Then the Prince, perceiving what had distracted his guest's attention, remarked that he was anxious to find a consort for his daughter, but that unfortunately there was the difficulty of *species*, and he didn't know what to do ; but again Tou took no notice of what the Prince was saying, until at length one of the bystanders plucked his sleeve, and asked him if he hadn't seen that the Prince wished to drink with him, and had just been addressing some remarks to him. Thereupon Tou started, and, recovering himself at once, rose from the table and apologised to the Prince for his rudeness, declaring that he had taken so much wine he didn't know what he was doing. "Besides," said he, "your Highness has doubtless business to transact ; I will therefore take my leave." "I am extremely pleased to have seen you," replied the Prince, "and only regret that you are in such a hurry to be gone. However, I won't detain you now ; but, if you don't forget all about us, I shall be very glad to invite you here again." He then gave orders that Tou should be escorted home ; and on the way one of the courtiers

---

[1] In this favourite pastime of the literati in China the important point is that each word in the second line should be a due and proper antithesis of the word in the first line to which it corresponds.

asked the latter why he had said nothing when the Prince had spoken of a consort for his daughter, as his Highness had evidently made the remark with an eye to securing Tou as his son-in-law. The latter was now sorry that he had missed his opportunity ; meanwhile they reached his house, and he himself awoke. The sun had already set, and there he sat in the gloom thinking of what had happened. In the evening he put out his candle, hoping to continue his dream ; but, alas ! the thread was broken, and all he could do was to pour forth his repentance in sighs. One night he was sleeping at a friend's house, when suddenly an officer of the Court walked in and summoned him to appear before the Prince ; so up he jumped, and hurried off at once to the palace, where he prostrated himself before the throne. The Prince raised him and made him sit down, saying that since they had last met he had become aware that Tou would be willing to marry his daughter, and hoped that he might be allowed to offer her as a handmaid. Tou rose and thanked the Prince, who thereupon gave orders for a banquet to be prepared ; and when they had finished their wine it was announced that the Princess had completed her toilet. Immediately a bevy of young ladies came in with the Princess in their midst, a red veil covering her head, gliding with tiny footsteps as they led her up to be introduced to Tou. When the ceremonies were concluded, Tou said to the Princess, "In your presence, Madam, it would be easy to forget even death itself ; but, tell me, is not this all a dream ? " "And how can it be a dream," asked the Princess, "when you and I are here together ? "

Next morning Tou amused himself by helping the Princess to paint her face,[2] and then with a girdle he began to measure the size of her waist [3] and with his fingers the length of her feet. "Are you crazy ? " cried she, laughing ; to which Tou replied, "I have been deceived so often by dreams, that I am now making a careful record. If such it turns out to be, I shall still have something as a souvenir of you." While they were thus chatting a maid rushed into the room, shrieking out, "Alas ! alas ! a great monster has got into the palace: the Prince has

[2] See No. LXII., note 1.
[3] See No. LXIX., note 5.

fled into a side chamber : destruction is surely come upon us." Tou was in a great fright when he heard this, and rushed off to see the Prince, who grasped his hand and, with tears in his eyes, begged him not to desert them. " Our relationship," cried he, " was cemented when Heaven sent this calamity upon us ; and now my kingdom will be overthrown. What shall I do ? " Tou begged to know what was the matter ; and then the Prince laid a despatch upon the table, telling Tou to open it and make himself acquainted with its contents. This despatch ran as follows :—" The Grand Secretary of State, Black Wings, to His Royal Highness, announcing the arrival of an extraordinary monster, and advising the immediate removal of the Court in order to preserve the vitality of the empire. A report has just been received from the officer in charge of the Yellow Gate stating that, ever since the 6th of the 5th moon, a huge monster, 10,000 feet in length, has been lying coiled up outside the entrance to the palace, and that it has already devourèd 13,800 and odd of your Highness's subjects, and is spreading desolation far and wide. On receipt of this information your servant proceeded to make a reconnaissance, and there beheld a venomous reptile with a head as big as a mountain and eyes like vast sheets of water. Every time it raised its head, whole buildings disappeared down its throat ; and, on stretching itself out, walls and houses were alike laid in ruins. In all antiquity there is no record of such a scourge. The fate of our temples and ancestral halls is now a mere question of hours ; we therefore pray your Royal Highness to depart at once with the Royal Family and seek somewhere else a happier abode." [4] When Tou had read this document his face turned ashy pale ; and just then a messenger rushed in, shrieking out, " Here is the monster ! " at which the whole Court burst into lamentations as if their last hour was at hand. The Prince was beside himself with fear ; all he could do was to beg Tou to look to his own safety without regarding the wife through whom he was involved in their misfortunes. The Princess, however, who

---

[4] The language in which this fanciful document is couched is precisely such as would be used by an officer of the Government in announcing some national calamity ; hence the value of these tales, —models as they are of the purest possible style.

was standing by bitterly lamenting the fate that had fallen
upon them, begged Tou not to desert her ; and, after a
moment's hesitation, he said he should be only too happy
to place his own poor home at their immediate disposal
if they would only deign to honour him. " How can we
talk of *deigning*," cried the Princess, " at such a moment
as this ? I pray you take us there as quickly as possible."
So Tou gave her his arm, and in no time they had arrived
at Tou's house, which the Princess at once pronounced
to be a charming place of residence, and better even than
their former kingdom. " But I must now ask you," said
she to Tou, " to make some arrangement for my father and
mother, that the old order of things may be continued here."
Tou at first offered objections to this ; whereupon the
Princess said that a man who would not help another in
his hour of need was not much of a man, and immediately
went off into a fit of hysterics, from which Tou was trying
his best to recall her, when all of a sudden he awoke and
found that it was all a dream. However, he still heard a
buzzing in his ears which he knew was not made by any
human being, and, on looking carefully about, he discovered two or three bees which had settled on his pillow.
He was very much astonished at this, and consulted with
his friend, who was also greatly amazed at his strange
story ; and then the latter pointed out a number of other
bees on various parts of his dress, none of which would
go away even when brushed off. His friend now advised
him to get a hive for them, which he did without delay ;
and immediately it was filled by a whole swarm of bees,
which came flying from over the wall in great numbers.
On tracing whence they had come, it was found that they
belonged to an old gentleman who lived near, and who had
kept bees for more than thirty years previously. Tou
thereupon went and told him the story ; and when the old
gentleman examined his hive he found the bees all gone.
On breaking it open he discovered a large snake inside of
about ten feet in length, which he immediately killed,
recognising in it the " huge monster " of Tou's adventure.
As for the bees, they remained with Tou, and increased
in numbers every year.

LXXI. THE DONKEY'S REVENGE

CHUNG CH'ING-YÜ was a scholar of some reputation, who lived in Manchuria. When he went up for his master's degree, he heard that there was a Taoist priest at the capital who would tell people's fortunes, and was very anxious to see him ; and at the conclusion of the second part of the examination,[1] he accidentally met him at Pao-t'u-ch'üan.[2] The priest was over sixty years of age, and had the usual white beard flowing down over his breast. Around him stood a perfect wall of people inquiring their future fortunes, and to each the old man made a brief reply : but when he saw Chung among the crowd, he was overjoyed, and, seizing him by the hand, said, " Sir, your virtuous intentions command my esteem." He then led him up behind a screen, and asked if he did not wish to know what was to come ; and when Chung replied in the affirmative, the priest informed him that his prospects were bad. " You may succeed in passing this examination," continued he, " but on returning covered with honour to your home, I fear that your mother will be no longer there." Now Chung was a very filial son ; and as soon as he heard these words, his tears began to flow, and he declared that he would go back without competing any further. The priest observed that if he let this chance slip, he could never hope for success ; to which Chung replied that, on the other hand, if his mother were to die he could never hope to have her back again, and that even the rank of Viceroy would not repay him for her loss. " Well," said the priest, " you and I were connected in a former existence, and I must do my best to help you now." So he took out a pill which he gave to Chung, and told him that if he sent it post-haste by some one to his mother, it would prolong her life for seven days, and thus he would be able to see her once again after the examination was over. Chung took the pill, and went off in very low spirits ; but he soon reflected

[1] The examination consists of three bouts of three days each, during which periods the candidates remain shut up in their examination cells day and night.
[2] The name of a place.

that the span of human life is a matter of destiny, and
that every day he could spend at home would be one more
day devoted to the service of his mother. Accordingly,
he got ready to start at once, and, hiring a donkey, actually
set out on his way back. When he had gone about half-a-
mile, the donkey turned round and ran home ; and when
he used his whip, the animal threw itself down on the
ground. Chung got into a great perspiration, and his
servant recommended him to remain where he was ; but
this he would not hear of, and hired another donkey,
which served him exactly the same trick as the other one.
The sun was now sinking behind the hills, and his servant
advised his master to stay and finish his examination
while he himself went back home before him. Chung
had no alternative but to assent, and the next day he
hurried through with his papers, starting immediately
afterwards, and not stopping at all on the way either to
eat or to sleep. All night long he went on, and arrived
to find his mother in a very critical state ; however,
when he gave her the pill she so far recovered that he was
able to go in and see her. Grasping his hand, she begged
him not to weep, telling him that she had just dreamt
she had been down to the Infernal Regions, where the
King of Hell had informed her with a gracious smile that
her record was fairly clean, and that in view of the filial
piety of her son she was to have twelve years more of life.
Chung was rejoiced at this, and his mother was soon
restored to her former health.

   Before long the news arrived that Chung had passed
his examination ; upon which he bade adieu to his mother,
and went off to the capital, where he bribed the eunuchs
of the palace to communicate with his friend the Taoist
priest. The latter was very much pleased, and came out
to see him, whereupon Chung prostrated himself at his
feet. " Ah," said the priest, " this success of yours, and
the prolongation of your good mother's life, is all a reward
for your virtuous conduct. What have I done in the
matter ? " Chung was very much astonished that the
priest should already know what had happened ; however,
he now inquired as to his own future. " You will never
rise to high rank," replied the priest, " but you will attain

the years of an octogenarian. In a former state of existence you and I were once travelling together, when you threw a stone at a dog, and accidentally killed a frog. Now that frog has reappeared in life as a donkey, and according to all principles of destiny you ought to suffer for what you did ; but your filial piety has touched the Gods, a protecting star-influence has passed into your nativity sheet, and you will come to no harm. On the other hand, there is your wife ; in her former state she was not as virtuous as she might have been, and her punishment in this life was to be widowed quite young ; you, however, have secured the prolongation of your own term of years, and therefore I fear that before long your wife will pay the penalty of death." Chung was much grieved at hearing this ; but after a while he asked the priest where his second wife to be was living. "At Chung-chou," replied the latter ; "she is now fourteen years old." The priest then bade him adieu, telling him that if any mischance should befall him he was to hurry off towards the south-east. About a year after this, Chung's wife did die ; and his mother then desiring him to go and visit his uncle, who was a magistrate in Kiangsi, on which journey he would have to pass through Chung-chou, it seemed like a fulfilment of the old priest's prophecy. As he went along, he came to a village on the banks of a river, where a large crowd of people was gathered together round a theatrical performance which was going on there. Chung would have passed quietly by, had not a stray donkey followed so close behind him that he turned round and hit it over the ears. This startled the donkey so much that it ran off full gallop, and knocked a rich gentleman's child, who was sitting with its nurse on the bank, right into the water, before any one of the servants could lend a hand to save it. Immediately there was a great outcry against Chung, who gave his mule the rein and dashed away, mindful of the priest's warning, towards the south-east. After riding about seven miles, he reached a mountain village, where he saw an old man standing at the door of a house, and, jumping off his mule, made him a low bow. The old man asked him in, and inquired his name and whence he came ; to which Chung replied by telling him the whole adventure. "Never fear,"

said the old man ; "you can stay here, while I send out
to learn the position of affairs." By the evening his
messenger had returned, and then they knew for the first
time that the child belonged to a wealthy family. The old
man looked grave and said, " Had it been anybody else's
child, I might have helped you ; as it is I can do nothing."
Chung was greatly alarmed at this ; however, the old
man told him to remain quietly there for the night, and
see what turn matters might take. Chung was overwhelmed with anxiety, and did not sleep a wink ; and next
morning he heard that the constables were after him,
and that it was death to any one who should conceal him.
The old man changed countenance at this, and went inside,
leaving Chung to his own reflections; but towards the
middle of the night he came and knocked at Chung's
door, and, sitting down, began to ask how old his wife
was. Chung replied that he was a widower ; at which
the old man seemed rather pleased, and declared that
in such case help would be forthcoming ; " for," said he,
" my sister's husband has taken the vows, and become a
priest,[3] and my sister herself has died, leaving an orphan
girl who has now no home ; and if you would only marry
her . . ." Chung was delighted, more especially as this
would be both the fulfilment of the Taoist priest's prophecy
and a means of extricating himself from his present difficulty ; at the same time, he declared he should be sorry
to implicate his future father-in-law. "Never fear about
that," replied the old man ; " my sister's husband is pretty
skilful in the black art. He has not mixed much with
the world of late ; but when you are married, you can
discuss the matter with my niece." So Chung married
the young lady, who was sixteen years of age, and very
beautiful ; but whenever he looked at her he took occasion to sigh. At last she said, " I may be ugly ; but you

[3] This interesting ceremony is performed by placing little conical
pastilles on a certain number of spots, varying from three to twelve,
on the candidate's head. These are then lighted and allowed to
burn down into the flesh, while the surrounding parts are vigorously
rubbed by attendant priests in order to lessen the pain. The whole
thing lasts about twenty minutes, and is always performed on the
eve of Shâkyamuni Buddha's birthday. The above was well described by Mr. S. L. Baldwin in the *Foochow Herald*.

needn't be in such a hurry to let me know it ; " whereupon Chung begged her pardon, and said he felt himself only too lucky to have met with such a divine creature ; adding that he sighed because he feared some misfortune was coming on them which would separate them for ever. He then told her his story, and the young lady was very angry that she should have been drawn into such a difficulty without a word of warning. Chung fell on his knees, and said he had already consulted with her uncle, who was unable himself to do anything, much as he wished it. He continued that he was aware of her power ; and then, pointing out that his alliance was not altogether beneath her, made all kinds of promises if she would only help him out of this trouble. The young lady was no longer able to refuse, but informed him that to apply to her father would entail certain disagreeable consequences, as he had retired from the world, and did not any more recognise her as his daughter. That night they did not attempt to sleep, spending the interval in padding their knees with thick felt concealed beneath their clothes ; and then they got into chairs and were carried off to the hills. After journeying some distance, they were compelled by the nature of the road to alight and walk ; and it was only by a great effort that Chung succeeded at last in getting his wife to the top. At the door of the temple they sat down to rest, the powder and paint on the young lady's face having all mixed with the perspiration trickling down ; but when Chung began to apologise for bringing her to this pass, she replied that it was a mere trifle compared with what was to come. By-and-by, they went inside ; and threading their way to the wall behind, found the young lady's father sitting in contemplation,[4] his eyes closed, and a servant-boy standing by with a chowry.[5] Everything was beautifully clean and nice, but before the dais were sharp stones scattered about as thick as the stars in the sky. The young lady did not venture to select a favourable spot ; she fell on her knees at once, and Chung did likewise behind her. Then her father opened

---

[4] There is a room in most Buddhist temples specially devoted to this purpose.

[5] The Buddhist emblem of cleanliness ; generally a yak's tail, and commonly used as a fly-brush.

his eyes, shutting them again almost instantaneously; whereupon the young lady said, " For a long time I have not paid my respects to you. I am now married, and I have brought my husband to see you." A long time passed away, and then her father opened his eyes and said, " You're giving a great deal óf trouble," immediately relapsing into silence again. There the husband and wife remained until the stones seemed to pierce into their very bones ; but after a while the father cried out, " Have you brought the donkey ? " His daughter replied that they had not ; whereupon they were told to go and fetch it at once, which they did, not knowing what the meaning of this order was. After a few more days' kneeling, they suddenly heard that the murderer of the child had been caught and beheaded, and were just congratulating each other on the success of their scheme, when a servant came in with a stick in his hand, the top of which had been chopped off. " This stick," said the servant, " died instead of you. Bury it reverently, that the wrong done to the tree may be somewhat atoned for." [6] Then Chung saw that at the place where the top of the stick had been chopped off there were traces of blood ; he therefore buried it with the usual ceremony, and immediately set off with his wife, and returned to his own home.

LXXII. THE WOLF DREAM

MR. PAI was a native of Chih-li, and his eldest son was called Chia. The latter had been some two years holding an appointment [1] as magistrate in the south ; but because of the great distance between them, his family had heard nothing of him. One day a distant connection, named Ting, called at the house ; and Mr. Pai, not having seen this gentleman for a long time, treated him with much cordiality. Now Ting was one of those persons who are occasionally employed by the Judge of the Infernal Regions

[6] Tree-worship can hardly be said to exist in China at the present day ; though at a comparatively recent epoch this phase of religious sentiment must have been widely spread. See *The Flower Nymphs* and *Mr. Willow*.

[1] Literally, " had been allotted the post of Nan-fu magistrate," such appointments being always determined by drawing lots.

to make arrests on earth ; [2] and, as they were chatting together, Mr. Pai questioned him about the realms below. Ting told him all kinds of strange things, but Pai did not believe them, answering only by a smile. Some days afterwards, he had just lain down to sleep when Ting walked in and asked him to go for a stroll ; so they went off together, and by-and-by reached the city. " There," said Ting, pointing to a door, "lives your nephew," alluding to a son of Mr. Pai's elder sister, who was a magistrate in Honan ; and when Pai expressed his doubts as to the accuracy of this statement, Ting led him in, when, lo and behold ! there was his nephew sitting in his court dressed in his official robes. Around him stood the guard, and it was impossible to get near him ; but Ting remarked that his son's residence was not far off, and asked Pai if he would not like to see him too. The latter assenting, they walked along till they came to a large building, which Ting said was the place. However, there was a fierce wolf at the entrance,[3] and Mr. Pai was afraid to go in. Ting bade him enter, and accordingly they walked in, when they found that all the employés of the place, some of whom were standing about and others lying down to sleep, were all wolves. The central pathway was piled up with whitening bones, and Mr. Pai began to feel horribly alarmed ; but Ting kept close to him all the time, and at length they got safely in. Pai's son, Chia, was just coming out ; and when he saw his father accompanied by Ting, he was overjoyed, and, asking them to sit down, bade the attendants serve some refreshments. Thereupon a great big wolf brought in in his mouth the carcase of a dead man, and set it before them, at which Mr. Pai rose up in consternation, and asked his son what this meant. " It's only a little refreshment for you, father," replied Chia ; but this did not calm Mr. Pai's agitation, who would have retired precipitately, had it not been for the crowd of

---

[2] Such is one common explanation of catalepsy (see No. I., note 5), it being further averred that the proper lictors of the Infernal Regions are unable to remain long in the *light* of the upper world.

[3] Upon a wall at the entrance to every official residence is painted a huge fabulous animal, called *Greed*, in such a position that the resident mandarin must see it every time he goes out of his front gates. It is to warn him against greed and the crimes that are sure to flow from it.

wolves which barred the path. Just as he was at a loss
what to do, there was a general stampede among the
animals, which scurried away, some under the couches
and some under the tables and chairs ; and while he was
wondering what the cause of this could be, in marched
two knights in golden armour, who looked sternly at
Chia, and, producing a black rope, proceeded to bind him
hand and foot. Chia fell down before them, and was
changed into a tiger with horrid fangs ; and then one of
the knights drew a glittering sword and would have cut
off its head, had not the other cried out, "Not yet ! not
yet ! that is for the fourth month next year. Let us now
only take out its teeth." Immediately that knight produced
a huge mallet, and, with a few blows, scattered the tiger's
teeth all over the floor, the tiger roaring so loudly with
pain as to shake the very hills, and frightening all the wits
out of Mr. Pai—who woke up with a start. He found he
had been dreaming, and at once set off to invite Ting to
come and see him ; but Ting sent back to say he must
beg to be excused. Then Mr. Pai, pondering on what he
had seen in his dream, despatched his second son with
a letter to Chia, full of warnings and good advice ;
and lo ! when his son arrived, he found that his elder
brother had lost all his front teeth, these having been
knocked out, as he averred, by a fall he had had from his
horse when tipsy ; and, on comparing dates, the day of
that fall was found to coincide with the day of his father's
dream. The younger brother was greatly amazed at
this, and took out their father's letter, which he gave to
Chia to read. The latter changed colour, but immediately
asked his brother what there was to be astonished at in
the coincidence of a dream. And just at that time he was
busily engaged in bribing his superiors to put him first
on the list for promotion, so that he soon forgot all about
the circumstance ; while the younger, observing what
harpies Chia's subordinates were, taking presents from
one man and using their influence for another, in one unbroken stream of corruption, sought out his elder brother,
and, with tears in his eyes, implored him to put some
check upon their rapacity. "My brother," replied Chia,
"your life has been passed in an obscure village ; you
know nothing of our official routine. We are promoted

or degraded at the will of our superiors, and not by the voice of the people. He, therefore, who gratifies his superiors is marked out for success ; [4] whereas he who consults the wishes of the people is unable to gratify his superiors as well." Chia's brother saw that his advice was thrown away ; he accordingly returned home and told his father all that had taken place. The old man was much affected, but there was nothing that he could do in the matter, so he devoted himself to assisting the poor, and such acts of charity, daily praying the Gods that the wicked son alone might suffer for his crimes, and not entail misery on his innocent wife and children. The next year it was reported that Chia had been recommended for a post in the Board of Civil Office,[5] and friends crowded the father's door, offering their congratulations upon the happy event. But the old man sighed and took to his bed, pretending he was too unwell to receive visitors. Before long another message came, informing them that Chia had fallen in with bandits while on his way home, and that he and all his retinue had been killed. Then his father arose and said, " Verily the Gods are good unto me, for they have visited his sins upon himself alone ; " and he immediately proceeded to burn incense and return thanks. Some of his friends would have persuaded him that the report was probably untrue ; but the old man had no doubts as to its correctness, and made haste to get ready his son's grave. But Chia was not yet dead. In the fatal fourth moon he had started on his journey and had fallen in with bandits, to whom he had offered all his money and valuables ; upon which the latter cried out, " We have come to avenge the cruel wrongs of many hundreds of victims ; do you imagine we want only *that* ? " They then cut off his head, and the head of his wicked secretary, and the heads of several of his servants who had been foremost in carrying out his shameful orders, and were now accompanying him to the capital. They then divided the booty between them, and made off with all speed. Chia's soul remained near his body for some time, until at length a high mandarin passing by asked

[4] Such, indeed, is the case at the present day in China, and elsewhere.

[5] See No. VII., note 1.

who it was that was lying there dead. One of his servants replied that he had been a magistrate at such and such a place, and that his name was Pai. "What!" said the mandarin, "the son of old Mr. Pai? It is hard that his father should live to see such sorrow as this. Put his head on again." [6] Then a man stepped forward and placed Chia's head upon his shoulders again, when the mandarin interrupted him, saying, "A crooked-minded man should not have a straight body: put his head on sideways." By-and-by Chia's soul returned to its tenement; and when his wife and children arrived to take away the corpse, they found that he was still breathing. Carrying him home, they poured some nourishment down his throat, which he was able to swallow; but there he was at an out-of-the-way place, without the means of continuing his journey. It was some six months before his father heard the real state of the case, and then he sent off the second son to bring his brother home. Chia had indeed come to life again, but he was able to see down his own back, and was regarded ever afterwards more as a monstrosity than as a man. Subsequently the nephew, whom old Mr. Pai had seen sitting in state surrounded by officials, actually became an Imperial Censor, so that every detail of the dream was thus strangely realised.

LXXIII. THE UNJUST SENTENCE

MR. CHU was a native of Yang-ku, and, as a young man, was much given to playing tricks and talking in a loose kind of way. Having lost his wife, he went off to ask a certain old woman to arrange another match for him; and on the way he chanced to fall in with a neighbour's wife who took his fancy very much. So he said in joke to the old woman, "Get me that stylish-looking, handsome lady, and I shall be quite satisfied." "I'll see what I can do," replied the old woman, also joking, "if you will manage to kill her present husband;" upon which Chu laughed and said he certainly would do so. Now about

---

[6] The great sorrow of decapitation as opposed to strangulation is that the body will appear in the realms below without a head. The family of any condemned man who may have sufficient means always bribe the executioner to sew it on again.

a month afterwards, the said husband, who had gone out to collect some money due to him, was actually killed in a lonely spot ; and the magistrate of the district immediately summoned the neighbours and beadle [1] and held the usual inquest, but was unable to find any clue to the murderer. However, the old woman told the story of her conversation with Chu, and suspicion at once fell upon him. The constables came and arrested him ; but he stoutly denied the charge ; and the magistrate now began to suspect the wife of the murdered man. Accordingly, she was severely beaten and tortured in several ways until her strength failed her, and she falsely acknowledged her guilt. [2] Chu was then examined, and he said, " This delicate woman could not bear the agony of your tortures ; what she has stated is untrue ; and, even should her wrong escape the notice of the Gods, for her to die in this

[1] See No. LXIV., note 2.

[2] Such has, doubtless, been the occasional result of torture in China ; but the singular keenness of the mandarins, as a body, in recognising the innocent and detecting the guilty,—that is, when their own avaricious interests are not involved,—makes this contingency so rare as to be almost unknown. A good instance came under my own notice at Swatow in 1876. For years a Chinese servant had been employed at the foreign Custom House to carry a certain sum of money every week to the bank, and at length his honesty was above suspicion. On the occasion to which I allude he had been sent as usual with the bag of dollars, but after a short absence he rushed back with a frightful gash on his right arm, evidently inflicted by a heavy chopper, and laying the bone bare. The money was gone. He said he had been invited into a teahouse by a couple of soldiers whom he could point out ; that they had tried to wrest the bag from him, and that at length one of them seized a chopper and inflicted so severe a wound on his arm, that in his agony he dropped the money, and the soldiers made off with it. The latter were promptly arrested and confronted with their accuser ; but, with almost indecent haste, the police magistrate dismissed the case against them, and declared that he believed the man had made away with the money and inflicted the wound on himself. And so it turned out to be, under overwhelming evidence. This servant of proved fidelity had given way to a rash hope of making a little money at the gaming-table ; had hurried into one of these hells and lost everything in three stakes ; had wounded himself on the right arm (he was a left-handed man), and had concocted the story of the soldiers, all within the space of about twenty-five minutes. When he saw that he was detected, he confessed everything, without having received a single blow of the bamboo ; but up to the moment of his confession the foreign feeling against that police-magistrate was undeniably strong.

way with a stain upon her name is more than I can endure. I will tell the whole truth. I killed the husband that I might secure the wife : she knew nothing at all about it." And when the magistrate asked for some proof, Chu said his bloody clothes would be evidence enough ; but when they sent to search his house, no bloody clothes were forthcoming. He was then beaten till he fainted ; yet when he came round he still stuck to what he had said. "It is my mother," cried he, "who will not sign the death-warrant of her son. Let me go myself and I will get the clothes." So he was escorted by a guard to his home, and there he explained to his mother that whether she gave up or withheld the clothes, it was all the same ; that in either case he would have to die, and it was better to die early than late. Thereupon his mother wept bitterly, and going into the bedroom, brought out, after a short delay, the required clothes, which were taken at once to the magistrate's. There was now no doubt as to the truth of Chu's story ; and as nothing occurred to change the magistrate's opinion, Chu was thrown into prison to await the day for his execution. Meanwhile, as the magistrate was one day inspecting his gaol, suddenly a man appeared in the hall, who glared at him fiercely and roared out, "Dull-headed fool! unfit to be the guardian of the people's interests!"—whereupon the crowd of servants standing round rushed forward to seize him, but with one sweep of his arms he laid them all flat on the ground. The magistrate was frightened out of his wits, and tried to escape, but the man cried out to him, "I am one of Kuan Ti's [3] lieutenants. If you move an inch you are lost." So the magistrate stood there, shaking from head to foot with fear, while his visitor continued, "The murderer is Kung Piao : Chu had nothing to do with it."

The lieutenant then fell down on the ground, and was to all appearance lifeless ; however, after a while he recovered, his face having quite changed, and when they asked him his name, lo! it was Kung Piao. Under the application of the bamboo he confessed his guilt. Always an unprincipled man, he had heard that the murdered man was going out to collect money, and thinking he would be sure to bring it back with him, he had killed him, but had

[3] See No. I., note 4.

found nothing. Then when he learnt that Chu acknowledged the crime as his own doing, he had rejoiced in secret at such a stroke of luck. How he had got into the magistrate's hall he was quite unable to say. The magistrate now called for some explanation of Chu's bloody clothes, which Chu himself was unable to give ; but his mother, who was at once sent for, stated that she had cut her own arm to stain them, and when they examined her they found on her left arm the scar of a recent wound. The magistrate was lost in amazement at all this ; unfortunately for him, the reversal of his sentence cost him his appointment, and he died in poverty, unable to find his way home. As for Chu, the widow of the murdered man married him [4] in the following year, out of gratitude for his noble behaviour.

LXXIV. A RIP VAN WINKLE [1]

[THE story runs that a Mr. Chia, after obtaining, with the assistance of a mysterious friend, his master's degree, became alive to the vanity of mere earthly honours, and determined to devote himself to the practice of Taoism, in the hope of obtaining the elixir of immortality.[2]]

So early one morning Chia and his friend, whose name was Lang, stole away together, without letting Chia's family know anything about it ; and by-and-by they found themselves among the hills, in a vast cave where there was another world and another sky. An old man was sitting there in great state, and Lang presented Chia to him as his future master. "Why have you come so soon ? " asked the old man ; to which Lang replied, "My friend's determination is firmly fixed : I pray you receive him amongst you." "Since you have come," said the old man, turning to Chia, "you must begin by putting away from you your earthly body." Chia murmured his assent, and was then escorted by Lang to a sleeping-chamber, where he was provided with food, after which Lang went away.

---

[4] See No. LXVIII., note 1. The circumstances which led to this marriage would certainly be considered " exceptional."

[1] This being a long and tedious story, I have given only such part of it as is remarkable for its similarity to Washington Irving's famous narrative.　　　　　[2] See No. IV., note 1.

The room was beautifully clean : [3] the doors had no panels and the windows no lattices ; and all the furniture was one table and one couch. Chia took off his shoes and lay down, with the moon shining brightly into the room ; and beginning soon to feel hungry, he tried one of the cakes on the table, which he found sweet and very satisfying. He thought Lang would be sure to come back, but there he remained hour after hour by himself, never hearing a sound. He noticed, however, that the room was fragrant with a delicious perfume ; his viscera seemed to be removed from his body, by which his intellectual faculties were much increased ; and every one of his veins and arteries could be easily counted. Then suddenly he heard a sound like that of a cat scratching itself ; and, looking out of the window, he beheld a tiger sitting under the verandah. He was horribly frightened for the moment, but immediately recalling the admonition of the old man, he collected himself and sat quietly down again. The tiger seemed to know that there was a man inside, for it entered the room directly afterwards, and walking straight up to the couch sniffed at Chia's feet. Whereupon there was a noise outside, as if a fowl were having its legs tied, and the tiger ran away. Shortly afterwards a beautiful young girl came in, suffusing an exquisite fragrance around ; and going up to the couch where Chia was, she bent over him and whispered, " Here I am." Her breath was like the sweet odour of perfumes ; but as Chia did not move, she whispered again, " Are you sleeping ? " The voice sounded to Chia remarkably like that of his wife ; however, he reflected that these were all probably nothing more than tests of his determination, so he closed his eyes firmly for a while. But by-and-by the young lady called him by his pet name, and then he opened his eyes wide to discover that she was no other than his own wife. On asking her how she had come there, she replied that Mr. Lang was afraid her husband would be lonely, and had sent an old woman to guide her to him. Just then they heard the old man outside in a towering rage, and Chia's wife, not knowing where to conceal herself, jumped over a low wall near by and disappeared. In came the old man, and gave Lang a severe beating before

[3] Borrowed from Buddhism.

Chia's face, bidding him at once to get rid of his visitor ;
so Lang led Chia away over the low wall, saying, " Because
I entertained extravagant hopes of you, I made the mistake
of too hastily introducing you ; but now I see that your
time has not yet come : hence this beating I have had.
Good-bye : we shall meet again some day." He then
showed Chia the way to his home, and waving his hand
bade him farewell. Chia looked down—for he was in
the moon—and beheld the old familiar village ; and
recollecting that his wife was not a good walker and would
not have got very far, hurried on to overtake her. Before
long he was at his own door, but he noticed that the place
was all tumble-down and in ruins, and not as it was when
he went away. As for the people he saw, old and young
alike, he did not recognise one of them ; and recollecting
the story of how Liu and Yüan came back from heaven,[4]
he was afraid to go in at the door. So he sat down and
rested outside ; and after a while an old man leaning on a
staff came out, whereupon Chia asked him which was
the house of Mr. Chia. " This is it," replied the old man ;
" you probably wish to hear the extraordinary story
connected with the family ? I know all about it. They
say that Mr. Chia ran away just after he had taken his
master's degree, when his son was only seven or eight
years old ; and that about seven years afterwards the
child's mother went into a deep sleep from which she did
not awake. As long as her son was alive he changed
his mother's clothes for her according to the seasons, but
when he died, her grandsons fell into poverty, and had
nothing but an old shanty to put the sleeping lady into.
Last month she awaked, having been asleep for over a
hundred years. People from far and near have been
coming in great numbers to hear the strange story ; of
late, however, there have been rather fewer." Chia was
amazed when he heard all this, and, turning to the old
man, said, " I am Chia Fêng-chih." This astonished the

---

[4] Alluding to a similar story, related in the *Record of the Immortals*, of how these two friends lost their way while gathering
simples on the hills, and were met and entertained by two lovely
young damsels for the space of half-a-year. When, however, they
subsequently returned home, they found that ten generations had
passed away.

old man very much, and off he went to make the announce-
ment to Chia's family. The eldest grandson was dead ;
and the second, a man of about fifty, refused to believe
that such a young-looking man was really his grandfather ;
but in a few moments out came Chia's wife, and she recognised her husband at once. They then fell upon each
other's necks and mingled their tears together.

[After which the story is drawn out to a considerable
length, but is quite devoid of interest.] [5]

LXXV. THE THREE STATES OF EXISTENCE

A CERTAIN man of the province of Hunan could recall what
had happened to him in three previous lives. In the first,
he was a magistrate ; and, on one occasion, when he had
been nominated Assistant-Examiner, a candidate, named
Hsing, was unsuccessful. Hsing went home dreadfully
mortified, and soon after died ; but his spirit appeared
before the King of Purgatory, and read aloud the rejected
essay, whereupon thousands of other shades, all of whom
had suffered in a similar way, thronged around, and
unanimously elected Hsing as their chief. The Examiner
was immediately summoned to take his trial, and when he
arrived the King asked him, saying, " As you are appointed
to examine the various essays, how is it that you throw
out the able and admit the worthless ? " " Sire," replied
he, " the ultimate decision rests with the Grand Examiner ;
I only pass them on to him." The King then issued a
warrant for the apprehension of the Grand Examiner, and
as soon as he appeared, he was told what had just now

[5] Besides the above, there is the story of a man named Wang,
who, wandering one day in the mountains, came upon some old
men playing a game of *wei-ch'i* ; and after watching them for some
time, he found that the handle of an axe he had with him had
mouldered away into dust. Seven generations of men had passed
away in the interval. Also, a similar legend of a horseman, who,
when riding over the hills, saw several old men playing a game
with rushes, and tied his horse to a tree while he himself approached
to observe them. A few minutes afterwards he turned to depart,
but found only the skeleton of his horse and the rotten remnants
of the saddle and bridle. He then sought his home, but that was
gone too ; and so he laid himself down upon the ground and died
of a broken heart.

been said against him ; to which he answered, " I am only able to make a general estimate of the merits of the candidates. Valuable essays may be kept back from me by my Associate-Examiners, in which case I am powerless."[1] But the King cried out, "It's all very well for you two thus to throw the blame on each other ; you are both guilty, and both of you must be bambooed according to law." This sentence was about to be carried into effect, when Hsing, who was not at all satisfied with its lack of severity, set up such a fearful screeching and howling, in which he was well supported by all the other hundreds and thousands of shades, that the King stopped short, and inquired what was the matter. Thereupon Hsing informed His Majesty that the sentence was too light, and that the Examiners should both have their eyes gouged out, so as not to be able to read essays any more. The King would not consent to this, explaining to the noisy rabble that the Examiners did not purposely reject good essays, but only because they themselves were naturally wanting in capacity. The shades then begged that, at any rate, their hearts might be cut out, and to this the King was obliged to yield ; so the Examiners were seized by the attendants, their garments stripped off, and their bodies ripped open with sharp knives. The blood poured out on the ground, and the victims screamed with pain ; at which all the shades rejoiced exceedingly, and said, " Here we have been pent

---

[1] If there is one institution in the Chinese Empire which is jealously guarded and honestly administered, it is the great system of competitive examinations which has obtained in China now for many centuries. And yet frauds do take place, in spite of the exceptionally heavy penalties incurred upon detection. Friends are occasionally smuggled through by the aid of marked essays ; and dishonest candidates avail themselves of " sleeve editions," as they are called, of the books in which they are to be examined. On the whole, the result is a successful one. As a rule, the best candidates pull through ; while, in exceptional cases, unquestionably good men are rejected. Of the latter class, the author of this work is a most striking instance. Excelling in literary attainments of the highest order, he failed more than once to obtain his master's degree, and finally threw up in disgust. Thenceforward he became the enemy of the mandarinate ; and how he has lashed the corruption of his age may be read in such stories as *The Wolf Dream*, and many others, while the policy that he himself would have adopted, had he been fortunate enough to succeed, must remain for ever a matter of doubt and speculation.

up, with no one to redress our wrongs ; but now Mr. Hsing
has come, our injuries are washed away." They then
dispersed with great noise and hubbub. As for our
Associate-Examiner, after his heart had been cut out, he
came to life again as the son of a poor man in Shensi ; and
when he was twenty years old he fell into the hands of the
rebels, who were at that time giving great trouble to the
country. By-and-by, a certain official was sent at the head
of some soldiers to put down the insurrection, and he succeeded in capturing a large number of the rebels, among
whom was our hero. The latter reflected that he himself
was no rebel, and he was hoping that he would be able to
obtain his release in consequence, when he noticed that the
officer in charge was also a man of his own age, and, on
looking more closely, he saw that it was his old enemy,
Hsing. "Alas ! " cried he, "such is destiny ; " and so
indeed it turned out, for all the other prisoners were forthwith released, and he alone was beheaded. Once more his
spirit stood before the King of Purgatory, this time with an
accusation against Hsing. The King, however, would not
summon Hsing at once, but said he should be allowed to
complete his term of official life on earth ; and it was not
till thirty years afterwards that Hsing appeared to answer
to the charge. Then, because he had made light of the
lives of his people, he was condemned to be born again as
a brute-beast ; and our hero, too, inasmuch as he had been
known to beat his father and mother, was sentenced to
a similar fate. The latter, fearing the future vengeance of
Hsing, persuaded the King to give him the advantage of
size ; and, accordingly, orders were issued that he was to be
born again as a big, and Hsing as a little, dog. The big
dog came to life in a shop in Shun-t'ien Fu, and was one
day lying down in the street, when a trader from the south
arrived, bringing with him a little golden-haired dog, about
the size of a wild cat, which, lo and behold ! turned out to
be Hsing. The other, thinking Hsing's size would render
him an easy prey, seized him at once ; but the little one
caught him from underneath by the throat, and hung there
firmly, like a bell. The big dog tried hard to shake him
off, and the people of the shop did their best to separate
them, but all was of no avail, and in a few moments both
dogs were dead. Upon their spirits presenting themselves,

as usual, before the King, each with its grievance against the other, the King cried out, "When will ye have done with your wrongs and your animosities ? I will now settle the matter finally for you ; " and immediately commanded that Hsing should become the other's son-in-law in the next world. The latter was then born at Ch'ing-yün, and when he was twenty-eight years of age took his master's degree. He had one daughter, a very pretty girl, whom many of his wealthy neighbours would have been glad to get for their sons ; but he would not accept any of their offers. On one occasion he happened to pass through the prefectural city, just as the examination for bachelor's degree was over; and the candidate who had come out at the top of the list, though named Li, was no other than Mr. Hsing. So he led this man away, and took him to an inn, where he treated him with the utmost cordiality, finally arranging that, as Mr. Li was still unmarried, he should marry his pretty daughter. Every one, of course, thought that this was done in admiration of Li's talents, ignorant that destiny had already decreed the union of the young couple. No sooner were they married than Li, proud of his own literary achievements, began to slight his father-in-law, and often passed many months without going near him ; all of which the father-in-law bore very patiently, and when, at length, Li had repeatedly failed to get on any farther in his career, he even went so far as to set to work, by all manner of means, to secure his success ; after which they lived happily together as father and son.

LXXVI. IN THE INFERNAL REGIONS

HSI FANG-P'ING was a native of Tung-an. His father's name was Hsi Lien—a hasty-tempered man, who had quarrelled with a neighbour named Yang. By-and-by Yang died; and some years afterwards, when Lien was on his death-bed, he cried out that Yang was bribing the devils in hell to torture him. His body then swelled up and turned red, and in a few moments he had breathed his last. His son wept bitterly and refused all food, saying, "Alas ! my poor father is now being maltreated by cruel devils ; I must go down and help to redress his wrongs." Thereupon he ceased speaking, and sat for a long time like one dazed, his soul having already quitted its tenement of clay. To himself he appeared to be outside the house, not knowing in what direction to go, so he inquired from one of the passers-by which was the way to the district city.[1] Before long he found himself there, and, directing his steps towards the prison, found his father lying outside [2] in a very shocking state. When the latter beheld his son, he burst into tears, and declared that the gaolers had been bribed to beat him, which they did both day and night, until they had reduced him to his present sorry plight. Then Fang-p'ing turned round in a great rage, and began to curse the gaolers. " Out upon you ! " cried he ; " if my father is guilty he should be punished according to law, and not at the will of a set of scoundrels like you." Thereupon he hurried away, and prepared a petition, which he took with him to present at the morning session of the City God ; but his enemy, Yang, had meanwhile set to work, and bribed so effectually, that the City God dismissed his petition for want of corroborative evidence.[3] Fang-p'ing was furious, but could do nothing ; so he started at once for the prefectural city, where he managed to get his plaint received, though it was nearly a month before it came on for hearing, and then all he got was a reference back to the district city, where he was severely tortured, and escorted back to the door of his own home, for fear he should give further trouble. However, he did not go in, but stole away and proceeded to lay his complaint before one of the ten Judges of Purgatory ; whereupon the two mandarins who had previously ill-used him, came forward and secretly offered him a thousand ounces of silver if he would withdraw the charge. This he positively refused to do ; and some days subsequently the landlord of the inn, where he was staying, told him he had been a fool for his pains, and that he would now get neither money nor justice, the Judge himself having already been tampered with.

[1] The Infernal Regions are supposed to be pretty much a counterpart of the world above, except in the matter of light.

[2] The visitor to Canton cannot fail to observe batches of prisoners with chains on them sitting in the street outside the prisons, many of them engaged in plying their particular trades.

[3] The judge in a Chinese court is necessarily very much dependent on his secretaries ; and, except in special cases, he takes his cue almost entirely from them. They take theirs from whichever party to the case knows best how to " cross the palm."

Fang-p'ing thought this was mere gossip, and would not believe it ; but, when his case was called, the Judge utterly refused to hear the charge, and ordered him twenty blows with the bamboo, which were administered in spite of all his protestations. He then cried out, " Ah ! it's all because I have no money to give you ; " which so incensed the Judge, that he told the lictors to throw Fang-p'ing on the fire-bed. This was a great iron couch, with a roaring fire underneath, which made it red-hot ; and upon that the devils cast Fang-p'ing, having first stripped off his clothes, pressing him down on it, until the fire ate into his very bones, though in spite of that he could not die. After a while the devils said he had had enough, and made him get off the iron bed, and put his clothes on again. He was just able to walk, and when he went back into court, the Judge asked him if he wanted to make any further complaints. " Alas ! " cried he, " my wrongs are still unredressed, and I should only be lying were I to say I would complain no more." The Judge then inquired what he had to complain of ; to which Fang-p'ing replied that it was of the injustice of his recent punishment. This enraged the Judge so much that he ordered his attendants to saw Fang-p'ing in two. He was then led away by devils, to a place where he was thrust in between a couple of wooden boards, the ground on all sides being wet and sticky with blood. Just at that moment he was summoned to return before the Judge, who asked him if he was still of the same mind ; and, on his replying in the affirmative, he was taken back again, and bound between the two boards. The saw was then applied, and as it went through his brain he experienced the most cruel agonies, which, however, he managed to endure without uttering a cry. " He's a tough customer," said one of the devils, as the saw made its way gradually through his chest ; to which the other replied, " Truly, this is filial piety ; and, as the poor fellow has done nothing, let us turn the saw a little out of the direct line, so as to avoid injuring his heart." Fang-p'ing then felt the saw make a curve inside him, which caused him even more pain than before ; and, in a few moments, he was cut through right down to the ground, and the two halves of his body fell apart, along with the boards to which they were tied, one on either side. The devils went back to report progress, and were then ordered to join Fang-p'ing together again, and bring him in. This they accordingly did,—the cut all down Fang-p'ing's body hurting him dreadfully, and feeling as if it would re-open every minute. But, as Fang-p'ing was unable to walk, one of the devils took out a cord and tied it round his waist, as a reward, he said, for his filial piety. The pain immediately ceased, and Fang-p'ing appeared once more before the Judge, this time promising that he would make no more complaints. The Judge now gave orders that he should be sent up to earth, and the devils, escorting him out of the north gate of the city, showed him his way home, and went away. Fang-p'ing now saw that there was even less chance of securing justice in the Infernal Regions than upon the earth above ; and, having no means of getting at the Great King to plead his case, he bethought himself of a certain upright and benevolent God, called Erh Lang, who was a relative of the Great King's, and him he determined to seek. So he turned about and took his way southwards, but was immediately seized by some devils, sent out by the Judge to watch that he really went back to his home. These devils hurried him again into the Judge's presence, where he was received, contrary to his expectation, with great affability ; the Judge himself praising his filial piety, but declaring that he need trouble no further in the matter, as his father had already been born again in a wealthy and illustrious family. "And upon you," added the Judge, " I now bestow a present of one thousand ounces of silver to take home with you, as well as the old age of a centenarian, with which I hope you will be satisfied." He then showed Fang-p'ing the stamped record of this, and sent him away in charge of the devils. The latter now began to abuse him for giving them so much trouble, but Fang-p'ing turned sharply upon them, and threatened to take them back before the Judge. They were then silent, and marched along for about half-a-day, until at length they reached a village, where the devils invited Fang-p'ing into a house, the door of which was standing half-open. Fang-p'ing was just going in, when suddenly the devils gave him a shove from behind, and . . . there he was, born again on earth as a little girl. For three days he pined and cried, without taking any food, and then he died. But his spirit did not forget Erh Lang, and set out at once in search of that God. He had not gone far when he fell in with the retinue of some high personage, and one of the attendants seized him for getting in the way, and hurried him before his master. He was taken to a chariot, where he saw a handsome young man, sitting in great state ; and thinking that now was his chance, he told the young man, who he imagined to be a high mandarin, all his sad story from beginning to end. His bonds were then loosed, and he went along with the young man until they reached a place where several officials came out to receive them ; and to one of these he confided Fang-p'ing, who now learnt that the young man was no other than God himself, the officials being the nine princes of heaven and the one to whose care he was entrusted no other than Erh Lang. This last was very tall, and had a long white beard, not at all like the popular representation of a God ; and when the other princes had gone, he took Fang-p'ing into a court-room, where he saw his father and their old enemy, Yang, besides all the lictors and others who had been mixed up in the case. By-and-by, some criminals were brought in in cages, and these turned out to be the Judge, Prefect, and Magistrate. The trial was then commenced, the three wicked officers trembling and shaking in their shoes ; and when he had heard the evidence, Erh Lang proceeded to pass sentence upon the prisoners, each of whom he sentenced, after enlarging upon the enormity of their several crimes, to be roasted, boiled, and otherwise put to most excruciating tortures. As for Fang-p'ing, he accorded him three extra decades of life, as a reward for his filial piety, and a copy of the sentence was put in his pocket. Father and son journeyed along together, and at length reached their home ; that is to say, Fang-p'ing was the first to recover consciousness, and then bade the servants open his father's coffin, which they immediately did, and the old man at once came back to life. But when Fang-p'ing looked for his copy of the sentence, lo ! it had disappeared. As for the Yang family, poverty soon overtook them, and all their lands passed into Fang-p'ing's hands ; for as sure as any one else bought them, they became sterile forthwith, and would produce nothing ; but Fang-p'ing and his father lived on happily, both reaching the age of ninety and odd years.[4]

[4] The whole story is of course simply a satire upon the venality and injustice of the ruling classes in China.

LXXVII. SINGULAR CASE OF OPHTHALMIA

A MR. KU, of Chiang-nan, was stopping in an inn at Chi-hsia, when he was attacked by a very severe inflammation of the eyes. Day and night he lay on his bed groaning, no medicines being of any avail ; and when he did get a little better, his recovery was accompanied by a singular phenomenon. Every time he closed his eyes, he beheld in front of him a number of large buildings, with all their doors wide open, and people passing and repassing in the background, none of whom he recognised by sight. One day he had just sat down to have a good look, when, all of a sudden, he felt himself passing through the open doors. He went on through three court-yards without meeting any one ; but, on looking into some rooms on either side, he saw a great number of young girls sitting, lying, and kneeling about on a red carpet, which was spread on the ground. Just then a man came out from behind the building, and, seeing Ku, said to him, " Ah, the Prince said there was a stranger at the door ; I suppose you are the person he meant." He then asked Ku to walk in, which the latter was at first unwilling to do ; however, he yielded to the man's instances, and accompanied him in, asking whose palace it was. His guide told him it belonged to the son of the Ninth Prince, and that he had arrived at the nick of time, for a number of friends and relatives had chosen this very day to come and congratulate the young gentleman on his recent recovery from a severe illness. Meanwhile another person had come out to hurry them on, and they soon reached a spot where there was a pavilion facing the north, with an ornamental terrace and red balustrades, supported by nine pillars. Ascending the steps, they found the place full of visitors, and then espied a young man seated with his face to the north,[1] whom they at once knew to be the Prince's son, and thereupon they prostrated themselves before him, the whole company rising as they did so.

[1] In Book V. of Mencius' works we read that Shun, the perfect man, stood with his face to the south, while the Emperor Yao (see No. VIII., note 3) and his nobles faced the north. This arrangement is said to have been adopted in deference to Shun's virtue ; for in modern times the Emperor always sits facing the south.

The young Prince made Ku sit down to the east of him,
and caused wine to be served ; after which some singing-
girls came in and performed the Hua-fêng-chu.[2] They
had got to about the third scene, when, all of a sudden,
Ku heard the landlord of the inn and his servant shouting
out to him that dinner was ready, and was dreadfully
afraid that the young Prince, too, had heard. No one,
however, seemed to have noticed anything, so Ku begged
to be excused a moment, as he wished to change his clothes,
and immediately ran out. He then looked up, and saw
the sun low in the west, and his servant standing by his
bedside, whereupon he knew that he had never left the
inn. He was much chagrined at this, and wished to go
back as fast as he could ; he, therefore, dismissed his
servant, and on shutting his eyes once more, he found everything just as he had left it, except that where, on the first
occasion, he had observed the young girls, there were
none now to be seen, but only some dishevelled hump-
backed creatures, who cried out at him, and asked him
what he meant by spying about there. Ku didn't dare
reply, but hurried past them as quickly as he could, and
on to the pavilion of the young Prince. There he found
him still sitting, but with a black beard over a foot in
length ; and the Prince was anxious to know where he had
been, saying that seven scenes of the play were already
over. He then seized a big goblet of wine, and made
Ku drink it as a penalty, by which time the play was
finished, and the list was handed up for a further selection.
The " Marriage of P'eng Tsu " was selected, and then the
singing-girls began to hand round the wine in cocoa-nuts
big enough to hold about five quarts, which Ku declined,
on the ground that he was suffering from weak eyes, and
was consequently afraid to drink too much. " If your
eyes are bad," cried the young Prince, " the Court physician
is at hand, and can attend to you." Thereupon, one of
the guests sitting to the east came forward, and, opening
Ku's eyes with his fingers, touched them with some white
ointment, which he applied from the end of a jade pin.
He then bade Ku close his eyes, and take a short nap ;
so the Prince had him conducted into a sleeping-room,
where he found the bed so soft, and surrounded by such

[2] Name of a celebrated play.

delicious perfume, that he soon fell into a deep slumber.
By-and-by he was awaked by what appeared to be the
clashing of cymbals, and fancied that the play was still
going on; but on opening his eyes, he saw that it was
only the inn-dog, which was licking an oilman's gong.[3]
His ophthalmia, however, was quite cured; and when he
shut his eyes again he could see nothing.

LXXVIII. CHOU K'O-CH'ANG AND
HIS GHOST

AT Huai-shang there lived a graduate named Chou T'ien-i,
who, though fifty years of age, had but one son, called
K'o-ch'ang, whom he loved very dearly. This boy, when
about thirteen or fourteen, was a handsome, well-favoured
fellow, strangely averse to study, and often playing truant
from school, sometimes for the whole day, without any
remonstrance on the part of his father. One day he
went away and did not come back in the evening; neither,
after a diligent search, could any traces of him be discovered.
His father and mother were in despair, and hardly cared
to live; but after a year and more had passed away, lo
and behold! K'o-ch'ang returned, saying that he had
been beguiled away by a Taoist priest, who, however,
had not done him any harm, and that he had seized a
moment while the priest was absent to escape and find
his way home again. His father was delighted, and asked
him no more questions, but set to work to give him an
education; and K'o-ch'ang was so much cleverer and
more intelligent than he had been before, that by the
following year he had taken his bachelor's degree and
made quite a name for himself. Immediately all the
good families of the neighbourhood wanted to secure him
as a son-in-law. Among others proposed there was an
extremely nice girl, the daughter of a gentleman named
Chao, who had taken his doctor's degree, and K'o-ch'ang's
father was very anxious that he should marry the young

---

[3] These are about as big as a cheese-plate and attached to a short
stick, from which hangs suspended a small button of metal in such
a manner as to clash against the face of the gong at every turn of
the hand. The names and descriptions of various instruments employed by costermongers in China would fill a good-sized volume.

lady. The youth himself would not hear of it, but stuck to his books and took his master's degree, quite refusing to entertain any thought of marriage ; and this so exasperated his mother that one day the good lady began to rate him soundly. K'o-ch'ang got up in a great rage and cried out, " I have long been wanting to get away, and have only remained for your sakes. I shall now say farewell, and leave Miss Chao for any one that likes to marry her." At this his mother tried to detain him, but in a moment he had fallen forwards on the ground, and there was nothing left of him but his hat and clothes. They were all dreadfully frightened, thinking that it must have been K'o-ch'ang's ghost who had been with them, and gave themselves up to weeping and lamentation ; however, the very next day K'o-ch'ang arrived, accompanied by a retinue of horses and servants, his story being that he had formerly been kidnapped [1] and sold to a wealthy trader, who, being then childless, had adopted him, but who, when he subsequently had a son born to him by his own wife, sent K'o-ch'ang back to his old home. And as soon as his father began to question him as to his studies, his utter dullness and want of knowledge soon made it clear that he was the real K'o-ch'ang of old ; but he was already known as a man who had got his master's degree (that is, the ghost of him had got it), so it was determined in the family to keep the whole affair secret. This K'o-ch'ang was only too ready to espouse Miss Chao ; and before a year had passed over their heads his wife had presented the old people with the much-longed-for grandson.

LXXIX.　THE SPIRITS OF THE PO-YANG LAKE

An official, named Chai, was appointed to a post at Jaochou, and on his way thither crossed the Po-yang lake. Happening to visit the shrine of the local spirits, he noticed a carved image of the patriotic Ting P'u-lang,[1] and another

---

[1] See No. XXIII., note 10.
[1] A famous soldier, who distinguished himself at the battle of Po-yang, A.D. 1363. Even when his head had been taken off, he still grasped his sword and remained standing in an attitude of attack.

of a namesake of his own, the latter occupying a very inferior position. "Come! come!" said Chai, "my patron saint sha'n't be put in the background like that;" so he moved the image into a more honourable place, and then went back on board his boat again. Soon after, a great wind struck the vessel, and carried away the mast and sails; at which the sailors, in great alarm, set to work to howl and cry. However, in a few moments they saw a small skiff come cutting through the waves, and before long they were all safely on board. The man who rowed it was strangely like the image in the shrine, the position of which Chai had changed; but they were hardly out of danger when the squall had passed over, and skiff and man had both vanished.

LXXX. THE STREAM OF CASH

A CERTAIN gentleman's servant was one day in his master's garden, when he beheld a stream of cash [1] flowing by, two or three feet in breadth and of about the same depth. He immediately seized two large handfuls, and then threw himself down on the top of the stream in order to try and secure the rest. However, when he got up he found that it had all flowed away from under him, none being left except what he had got in his two hands.

["Ah!" says the commentator, "money is properly a circulating medium, and is not intended for a man to lie upon and keep all to himself."] [2]

[1] See No. II., note 2.

[2] The Chinese, fond as they are of introducing water, under the form of miniature lakes, into their gardens and pleasure-grounds, do not approve of a running stream near the dwelling-house. I myself knew a case of a man, provided with a pretty little house, rent-free, alongside of which ran a mountain rill, who left the place and paid for lodgings out of his own pocket rather than live so close to a stream which he averred *carried all his good luck away*. Yet this man was a fair scholar and a graduate to boot.

LXXXI. THE INJUSTICE OF HEAVEN

MR. Hsü was a magistrate in Shantung. A certain upper chamber of his house was used as a store-room ; but some creature managed so frequently to get in and make havoc among the stores, for which the servants were always being scolded, that at length some of the latter determined to keep watch. By-and-by they saw a huge spider as big as a peck measure, and hurried off to tell their master, who thought it so strange that he gave orders to the servants to feed the insect with cakes. It thus became very tame, and would always come forth when hungry, returning as soon as it had taken enough to eat.[1] Years passed away, and one day Mr. Hsü was consulting his archives, when suddenly the spider appeared and ran under the table. Thinking it was hungry, he bade his servants give it a cake ; but the next moment he noticed two snakes, of about the thickness of a chop-stick, lying one on each side. The spider drew in its legs as if in mortal fear, and the snakes began to swell out until they were as big round as an egg ; at which Mr. Hsü was greatly alarmed, and would have hurried away, when crash ! went a peal of thunder, killing every person in the house. Mr. Hsü himself recovered consciousness after a little while, but only to see his wife and servants, seven persons in all, lying dead ; and after a month's illness he, too, departed this life. Now Mr. Hsü was an upright, honourable man, who really had the interests of the people at heart. A subscription was accordingly raised to pay his funeral expenses, and on the day of his burial the air was rent for miles round with cries of weeping and lamentation.

[Hereon the author makes the following remark :— " That dragons play with pearls [2] I have always regarded as an old woman's tale. Is it possible, then, that the story

---

[1] That Chinaman thinks his a hard lot who cannot " eat till he is full." It may be noticed here that the Chinese seem not so much to enjoy the process of eating, as the subsequent state of repletion. As a rule, they bolt their food, and get their enjoyment out of it afterwards.

[2] The disc, spoken of as a pearl, which is often figured between two dragons, is really the symbol of thunder rolling.

is a fact ? I have heard, too, that the thunder strikes
only the guilty man ; and, if so, how could a virtuous
official be visited with this dire calamity ? " Are not
the inconsistencies of God Almighty many indeed ?]

LXXXII. THE SEA-SERPENT

A TRADER named Chia was voyaging on the south seas,
when one night it suddenly became as light as day on
board his ship. Jumping up to see what was the matter,
he beheld a huge creature with its body half out of the water,
towering up like a hill. Its eyes resembled two suns, and
threw a light far and wide ; and when the trader asked
the boatmen what it was, there was not one who could say.
They all crouched down and watched it ; and by-and-by
the monster gradually disappeared in the water again,
leaving everything in darkness as before. And when they
reached port, they found all the people talking about a
strange phenomenon of a great light that had appeared
in the night, the time of which coincided exactly with the
strange scene they themselves had witnessed.[1]

LXXXIII. THE MAGIC MIRROR [1]

" . . . BUT if you would really like to have something
that has belonged to me," said she, " you shall." Whereupon she took out a mirror and gave it to him, saying,
"Whenever you want to see me, you must look for me in
your books ; otherwise I shall not be visible ; "—and in
a moment she had vanished. Liu went home very melancholy at heart ; but when he looked in the mirror, there

---

[1] The " sea-serpent " in this case was probably nothing more or
less than some meteoric phenomenon.
[1] The following is merely a single episode taken from a long and
otherwise uninteresting story. Miss Fêng-hsien was a fox ; hence
her power to bestow such a singular present as the mirror here
described, the object of which was to incite her lover to success—
the condition of their future union.

was Fêng-hsien, standing with her back to him, gazing, as it were, at some one who was going away, and about a hundred paces from her. He then bethought himself of her injunctions, and settled down to his studies, refusing to receive any visitors; and a few days subsequently, when he happened to look in the mirror, there was Fêng-hsien, with her face turned towards him, and smiling in every feature. After this, he was always taking out the mirror to look at her; however, in about a month his good resolutions began to disappear, and he once more went out to enjoy himself and waste his time as before. When he returned home and looked in the mirror, Fêng-hsien seemed to be crying bitterly; and the day after, when he looked at her again, she had her back turned towards him as on the day he received the mirror. He now knew that it was because he had neglected his studies, and forthwith set to work again with all diligence, until in a month's time she had turned round once again. Henceforward, whenever anything interrupted his progress, Fêng-hsien's countenance became sad; but whenever he was getting on well, her sadness was changed to smiles. Night and morning Liu would look at the mirror, regarding it quite in the light of a revered preceptor; and in three years' time he took his degree in triumph. "Now," cried he, "I shall be able to look Fêng-hsien in the face." And there, sure enough, she was, with her delicately-pencilled arched eyebrows, and her teeth just showing between her lips, as happy-looking as she could be, when, all of a sudden, she seemed to speak, and Liu heard her say, "A pretty pair we make, I must allow"—and the next moment Fêng-hsien stood by his side.

LXXXIV. COURAGE TESTED

MR. TUNG was a Hsü-chou man, very fond of playing broad-sword, and a light-hearted, devil-may-care fellow, who was often involving himself in trouble. One day he fell in with a traveller who was riding on a mule and going the same way as himself; whereupon they entered into conversation, and began to talk to each other about

feats of strength and so on. The traveller said his name
was T'ung,[1] and that he belonged to Liao-yang ; that he
had been twenty years away from home, and had just
returned from beyond the sea. " And I venture to say,"
cried Tung, " that in your wanderings on the Four Seas [2]
you have seen a great many people ; but have you seen
any supernaturally clever ones ? " T'ung asked him
to what he alluded ; and then Tung explained what his
own particular hobby was, adding how much he would
like to learn from them any tricks in the art of broad-sword.
" Supernaturals," replied the traveller, " are to be found
everywhere. It needs but that a man should be a loyal
subject and a filial son for him to know all that the supernaturals know." " Right you are, indeed ! " cried Tung,
as he drew a short sword from his belt, and, tapping the
blade with his fingers, began to accompany it with a song.
He then cut down a tree that was by the wayside, to show
T'ung how sharp it was ; at which T'ung smoothed his
beard and smiled, begging to be allowed to have a look
at the weapon. Tung handed it to him, and, when he
had turned it over two or three times, he said, " This is
a very inferior piece of steel ; now, though I know nothing
about broad-sword myself, I have a weapon which is really
of some use." He then drew from beneath his coat a
sword, a foot or so in length, and with it he began to pare
pieces off Tung's sword, which seemed as soft as a melon,
and which he cut quite away like a horse's hoof. Tung
was greatly astonished, and borrowed the other's sword
to examine it, returning it after carefully wiping the blade.
He then invited T'ung to his house, and made him stay
the night ; and after begging him to explain the mystery
of his sword, began to nurse his leg and sit listening respect-

---

[1] Besides the all-important aspirate, this name is pronounced in
a different *tone* from the first-mentioned " Tung ; " and is, moreover,
expressed in writing by a totally different character. To a Chinese
ear, the two words are as unlikely to be confounded as Brown and
Jones.

[2] The Four Seas are supposed by the Chinese to bound the
habitable portions of the earth, which, by the way, they further
believe to be square. In the centre of all is China, extending far
and wide in every direction,—the eye of the universe, the Middle
Kingdom. Away at a distance from her shores lie a number of
small islands, wherein dwell such barbarous nations as the English,
French, Dutch, &c,

fully without saying a word. It was already pretty late, when suddenly there was a sound of scuffling next door, where Tung's father lived ; and, on putting his ear to the wall, he heard an angry voice saying, "Tell your son to come here at once, and then I will spare you." This was followed by other sounds of beating and a continued groaning, in a voice which Tung knew to be his father's. He therefore seized a spear, and was about to rush forth, but T'ung held him back, saying, " You'll be killed for a certainty if you go. Let us think of some other plan." Tung asked what plan he could suggest ; to which the other replied, " The robbers are killing your father : there is no help for you ; but as you have no brothers, just go and tell your wife and children what your last wishes are, while I try and rouse the servants." Tung agreed to this, and ran in to tell his wife, who clung to him and implored him not to go, until at length all his courage had ebbed away, and he went upstairs with her to get his bow and arrows ready to resist the robbers' attack. At that juncture he heard the voice of his friend T'ung, outside on the eaves of the house, saying, with a laugh, " All right ; the robbers have gone ; " but on lighting a candle, he could see nothing of him. He then stole out to the front door, where he met his father with a lantern in his hand, coming in from a party at a neighbour's house; and the whole court-yard was covered with the ashes of burnt grass, whereby he knew that T'ung the traveller was himself a supernatural.[3]

LXXXV. THE DISEMBODIED FRIEND

MR. CH'ÊN, M.A., of Shun-t'ien Fu, when a boy of sixteen, went to school at a Buddhist temple.[1]   There were a great many scholars besides himself, and, among others, one named Ch'u, who said he came from Shantung.   This

---

[3] The author adds a note to this story which might be summed up in our own—

The [wo]man that deliberates is lost.

[1] Buddhist priests not unusually increase the revenue of their monastery by taking pupils ; and it is only fair to them to add that the curriculum is strictly secular, the boys learning precisely what they would at an ordinary school and nothing else.

Ch'u was a very hard-working fellow; he never seemed to be idle, and actually slept in the schoolroom, not going home at all. Ch'ên became much attached to him, and one day asked him why he never went away. "Well, you see," replied Ch'u, "my people are very poor, and can hardly afford to pay for my schooling; but, by dint of working half the night, two of my days are equal to three of anybody else's." Thereupon Ch'ên said he would bring his own bed to the school, and that they would sleep there together; to which Ch'u replied that the teaching they got wasn't worth much, and that they would do better by putting themselves under a certain old scholar named Lü. This they were easily able to do, as the arrangement at the temple was monthly, and at the end of each month any one was free to go or to come. So off they went to this Mr. Lü, a man of considerable literary attainments, who had found himself in Shun-t'ien Fu without a cash in his pocket, and was accordingly obliged to take pupils. He was delighted at getting two additions to his number; and Ch'u showing himself an apt scholar, the two soon became very great friends, sleeping in the same room and eating at the same table. At the end of the month Ch'u asked for leave of absence, and, to the astonishment of all, ten days elapsed without anything being heard of him. It then chanced that Ch'ên went to the T'ien-ning temple, and there he saw Ch'u under one of the verandahs, occupied in cutting wood for lucifer-matches.[2] The latter was much disconcerted by the arrival of Ch'ên, who asked him why he had given up his studies; so the latter took him aside, and explained that he was so poor as to be obliged to work half a month to scrape together funds enough for his next month's schooling. "You come along back with me," cried Ch'ên, on hearing this, "I

---

[2] These consist simply of thin slips of wood dipped in brimstone, and resemble those used in England as late as the first quarter of the nineteenth century. They are said to have been invented by the people of Hang-chou, the capital of Chekiang; but it is quite possible that the hint may have first reached China from the West. They were called *yin kuang*, "bring light" (*lucifer*), *fa chu*, "give forth illumination," and other names. Lucifer matches are now generally spoken of as *tzŭ lai huo*, "self-come fire," and are almost universally employed, except in remote parts where the flint and steel still hold sway.

will arrange for the payment," which Ch'u immediately
consented to do on condition that Ch'ên would keep the
whole thing a profound secret. Now Ch'ên's father was
a wealthy tradesman, and from his till Ch'ên abstracted
money wherewith to pay for Ch'u ; and by-and-by, when
his father found him out, he confessed why he had done so.
Thereupon Ch'ên's father called him a fool, and would not
let him resume his studies ; at which Ch'u was much
hurt, and would have left the school too, but that old Mr.
Lü discovered what had taken place, and gave him the
money to return to Ch'ên's father, keeping him still at
the school, and treating him quite like his own son. So
Ch'ên studied no more, but whenever he met Ch'u he always
asked him to join in some refreshment at a restaurant,
Ch'u invariably refusing, but yielding at length to his
entreaties, being himself loth to break off their old
acquaintanceship.

Thus two years passed away, when Ch'ên's father died,
and Ch'ên went back to his books under the guidance of
old Mr. Lü, who was very glad to see such determination.
Of course Ch'ên was now far behind Ch'u ; and in about
six months Lü's son arrived, having begged his way in
search of his father, so Mr. Lü gave up his school and
returned home with a purse which his pupils had made
up for him, Ch'u adding nothing thereto but his tears.
At parting, Mr. Lü advised Ch'ên to take Ch'u as his
tutor, and this he did, establishing him comfortably in
the house with him. The examination was very shortly
to commence, and Ch'ên felt convinced that he should not
get through; but Ch'u said he thought he should be able
to manage the matter for him. On the appointed day he
introduced Ch'ên to a gentleman who he said was a cousin
of his, named Liu, and asked Ch'ên to accompany this
cousin, which Ch'ên was just proceeding to do when Ch'u
pulled him back from behind,[3] and he would have fallen
down but that the cousin pulled him up again, and then,
after having scrutinised his appearance, carried him off
to his own house. There being no ladies there, Ch'ên was
put into the inner apartments ; and a few days afterwards Liu said to him, " A great many people will be at
the gardens to-day ; let us go and amuse ourselves awhile,

[3] The whole point of the story hinges on this.

and afterwards I will send you home again." He then
gave orders that a servant should proceed on ahead with
tea and wine, and by-and-by they themselves went, and
were soon in the thick of the fête. Crossing over a bridge,
they saw beneath an old willow tree a little painted skiff,
and were soon on board, engaged in freely passing round
the wine. However, finding this a little dull, Liu bade
his servant go and see if Miss Li, the famous singing-girl,
was at home ; and in a few minutes the servant returned
bringing Miss Li with him. Ch'ên had met her before,
and so they at once exchanged greeetings, while Liu
begged her to be good enough to favour them with a song.
Miss Li, who seemed labouring under a fit of melancholy,
forthwith began a funeral dirge ; at which Ch'ên was not
much pleased, and observed that such a theme was hardly
suitable to the occasion. With a forced smile, Miss Li
changed her key, and gave them a love-song ; whereupon
Ch'ên seized her hand, and said, " There's that song of the
Huan-sha river,[4] which you sang once before ; I have read
it over several times, but have quite forgotten the words."
Then Miss Li began—

Eyes overflowing with tears, she sits gazing into her mirror ;
Lifting the bamboo screen, one of her comrades approaches.
She bends her head and seems intent on her bow-like slippers,
And forces her eyebrows to arch themselves into a smile.
With her scarlet sleeve she wipes the tears from her fragrant cheek,
In fear and trembling lest they should guess the thoughts that
  overwhelm her.

Ch'ên repeated this over several times, until at length
the skiff stopped, and they passed through a long verandah,
where a great many verses had been inscribed on the
walls,[5] to which Ch'ên at once proceeded to add a stanza
of his own. Evening was now coming on, and Liu remarked
that the candidates would be just about leaving the exami-
nation-hall ;[6] so he escorted him back to his own home,

---

[4] Beside which lived Hsi Shih, the famous beauty of the fifth
century after Christ.

[5] The Chinese have precisely the same mania as our Browns,
Joneses, and Robinsons, for scribbling and carving their names and
compositions all over the available parts of any place of public
resort. The literature of inn walls alone would fill many ponderous
tomes.

[6] The examination, which lasts nine days, has been going on all
this time.

and there left him. The room was dark, and there was
no one with him ; but by-and-by the servants ushered
in some one whom at first he took to be Ch'u. However,
he soon saw that it was not Ch'u, and in another moment
the stranger had fallen against him and knocked him
down. "Master's fainted!" cried the servants, as they
ran to pick him up ; and then Ch'ên discovered that
the one who had fallen down was really no other than
himself.[7] On getting up, he saw Ch'u standing by his
side ; and when they had sent away the servants the latter
said, "Don't be alarmed : I am nothing more than a disembodied spirit. My time for reappearing on earth[8] is
long overdue, but I could not forget your great kindness
to me, and accordingly I have remained under this form
in order to assist in the accomplishment of your wishes.
The three bouts [9] are over, and your ambition will be
gratified." Ch'ên then inquired if Ch'u could assist him
in like manner for his doctor's degree ; to which the latter
replied, "Alas ! the luck descending to you from your
ancestors is not equal to that.[10] They were a niggardly
lot, and unfit for the posthumous honours you would thus
confer on them." Ch'ên next asked him whither he was
going ; and Ch'u replied that he hoped, through the
agency of his cousin, who was a clerk in Purgatory, to be
born again in old Mr. Lü's family. They then bade each
other adieu ; and, when morning came, Ch'ên set off
to call on Miss Li, the singing-girl ; but on reaching her
house he found that she had been dead some days.[11] He
walked on to the gardens, and there he saw traces of verses
that had been written on the walls, and evidently rubbed
out, so as to be hardly decipherable. In a moment it
flashed across him that the verses and their composers
belonged to the other world. Towards evening Ch'u
reappeared in high spirits, saying that he had succeeded
in his design, and had come to wish Ch'ên a long farewell.

[7] That is, his own body, into which Ch'u's spirit had temporarily
passed, his own occupying, meanwhile, the body of his friend.
[8] That is, for being born again, the sole hope and ambition of a
disembodied shade.
[9] See No. LXXI., note 1.
[10] See No. LXI., note 3.
[11] His own spirit in Ch'u's body had met her in a disembodied
state.

Holding out his open palms, he requested Ch'ên to write the word *Ch'u* on each ; and then, after refusing to take a parting cup, he went away, telling Ch'ên that the examination-list would soon be out, and that they would meet again before long. Ch'ên brushed away his tears and escorted him to the door, where a man, who had been waiting for him, laid his hand on Ch'u's head and pressed it downwards until Ch'u was perfectly flat. The man then put him in a sack and carried him off on his back. A few days afterwards the list came out, and, to his great joy, Ch'ên found his name among the successful candidates ; whereupon he immediately started off to visit his old tutor, Mr. Lü.[12] Now Mr. Lü's wife had had no children for ten years, being about fifty years of age, when suddenly she gave birth to a son, who was born with both fists doubled up so that no one could open them. On his arrival Ch'ên begged to see the child, and declared that inside its hands would be found written the word Ch'u. Old Mr. Lü laughed at this ; but no sooner had the child set eyes on Ch'ên than both its fists opened spontaneously, and there was the word as Ch'ên had said. The story was soon told, and Ch'ên went home, after making a handsome present to the family ; and later on, when Mr. Lü went up for his doctor's degree [13] and stayed at Ch'ên's house, his son was thirteen years old, and had already matriculated as a candidate for literary honours.

LXXXVI. THE CLOTH MERCHANT

A CERTAIN cloth merchant went to Ch'ing-chou, where he happened to stroll into an old temple, all tumble-down and in ruins. He was lamenting over this sad state of things, when a priest who stood by observed that a devout believer like himself could hardly do better than put the place into repair, and thus obtain favour in the eyes of Buddha. This the merchant consented to do ; whereupon the priest invited him to walk into the private quarters of the temple, and treated him with much courtesy ; but

---

[12] Such is the invariable custom. Large presents are usually made by those who can afford the outlay, and the tutor's name has ever afterwards an honourable place in the family records.

[13] See No. XLVIII., note 1.

he went on to propose that our friend the merchant should also undertake the general ornamentation of the place both inside and out.[1] The latter declared he could not afford the expense, and the priest began to get very angry, and urged him so strongly that at last the merchant, in terror, promised to give all the money he had. After this he was preparing to go away, but the priest detained him, saying, " You haven't given the money of your own free will, and consequently you'll be owing me a grudge : I can't do better than make an end of you at once." Thereupon he seized a knife, and refused to listen to all the cloth merchant's entreaties, until at length the latter asked to be allowed to hang himself, to which the priest consented ; and, showing him into a dark room, told him to make haste about it.

At this juncture, a Tartar-General[2] happened to pass by the temple ; and from a distance, through a breach in the old wall, he saw a damsel in a red dress pass into the priest's quarters. This roused his suspicions,[3] and dismounting from his horse, he entered the temple and searched high and low, but without discovering anything. The dark room above-mentioned was locked and double-barred, and the priest refused to open it, saying the place was haunted. The General in a rage burst open the door, and there beheld the cloth merchant hanging from a beam.

---

[1] The elaborate gilding and woodwork of an ordinary Chinese temple form a very serious item in the expense of restoration. Public subscriptions are usually the means employed for raising sufficient funds, the names of subscribers and amount given by each being published in some conspicuous position. Occasionally devout priests—black swans, indeed, in China—shut themselves up in boxes studded with nails, one of which they pull out every time a certain donation is given, and there they remain until every nail is withdrawn. But after all it is difficult to say whether they endure these trials so much for the faith's sake as for the funds from which they derive more of the luxuries of life, and the temporary notoriety gained by thus coming before the public. A Chinese proverb says, " The image-maker doesn't worship Buddha. He knows too much about it ; " and the application of this saying may safely be extended to the majority of Buddhist priests in China.

[2] This is the title generally applied to the Manchu commanders of Manchu garrisons, who are stationed at certain of the most important points of the Chinese Empire, and whose presence is intended as a check upon the action of the civil authorities.

[3] See No. VI., note 2.

He cut him down at once, and in a short time he was brought round and told the General the whole story. They then searched for the damsel, but she was nowhere to be found, having been nothing more than a divine manifestation. The General cut off the priest's head and restored the cloth merchant's property to him, after which the latter put the temple in thorough repair, and kept it well supplied with lights and incense ever afterwards. Mr. Chao, M.A., told me this story, with all its details.[4]

LXXXVII. A STRANGE COMPANION

HAN KUNG-FU, of Yü-ch'êng, told me that he was one day travelling along a road with a man of his village, named P'êng, when all of a sudden the latter disappeared, leaving his mule to jog along with an empty saddle. At the same moment, Mr. Han heard his voice calling for assistance, and apparently proceeding from inside one of the panniers strapped across the mule's back ; and on looking closely, there indeed he was in one of the panniers, which, however, did not seem to be at all displaced by his weight. On trying to get him out the mouth of the pannier closed itself tightly ; and it was only when he cut it open with a knife that he saw P'êng curled up in it like a dog. He then helped him out, and asked him how he managed to get in ; but this he was unable to say. It further appeared that his family was under fox influence, many strange things of this kind having happened before.

LXXXVIII. SPIRITUALISTIC SÉANCES

IT is customary in Shantung, when any one is sick, for the womenfolk to engage an old sorceress or medium, who strums on a tambourine and performs certain mysterious antics. This custom obtains even more in the capital, where young ladies of the best families frequently organise such séances among themselves. On a table in the hall

---

[4] The moral being, of course, that Buddha protects those who look after his interests on earth.

they spread out a profusion of wine and meat, and burn huge candles which make the place as light as day. Then the sorceress, shortening her skirts, stands on one leg and performs the *shang-yang*,[1] while two of the others support her, one on each side. All this time she is chattering unintelligible sentences,[2] something between a song and a prayer, the words being confused but uttered in a sort of tune ; while the hall resounds with the thunder of drums, enough to stun a person, with which her vaticinations are mixed up and lost. By-and-by her head begins to droop, and her eyes to look aslant ; and but for her two supporters she would inevitably fall to the ground. Suddenly she stretches forth her neck and bounds several feet into the air, upon which the other women regard her in terror, saying, " The spirits have come to eat ; " and immediately all the candles are blown out and everything is in total darkness. Thus they remain for about a quarter of an hour, afraid to speak a word, which in any case would not be heard through the din, until at length the sorceress calls out the personal name of the head of the family[3] and some others ; whereupon they immediately relight the candles and hurry up to ask if the reply of the spirits is favourable or otherwise. They then see that every scrap of the food and every drop of the wine has disappeared. Meanwhile, they watch the old woman's expression, whereby they can tell if the spirits are well disposed ; and each one asks her some question, to which she as promptly replies. Should there be any unbelievers among the party, the spirits are at once aware of their presence ; and the old sorceress, pointing her finger at such a one, cries out,

---

[1] It is related in the *Family Sayings*, an apocryphal work which professes to give conversations of Confucius, that a number of one-legged birds having suddenly appeared in Ch'i, the Duke of Ch'i sent off to ask the Sage what was the meaning of this strange phenomenon. Confucius replied, " The bird is the *shang-yang*, and portends beneficial rain." And formerly the boys and girls in Shantung would hop about on one leg, crying, " The *shang-yang* has come ; " after which rain would be sure to follow.

[2] Speaking in the unknown tongue, like the Irvingites and others.

[3] This is a clever hit. The " personal " name of a man may not be uttered except by the Emperor, his father or mother, grand-father, grandmother, &c. Thus, the mere use of the personal name of the *head of a family* proves conclusively that the spirit of some one of his ancestors must be present.

"Disrespectful mocker! where are your trousers?"
upon which the mocker alluded to looks down, and lo!
her trousers are gone—gone to the top of a tree in the
court-yard, where they will subsequently be found.[4]

Manchu women and girls, especially, are firm believers
in spiritualism. On the slightest provocation they consult
their medium, who comes into the room gorgeously dressed,
and riding on an imitation horse or tiger.[5] In her hand
she holds a long spear, with which she mounts the couch [6]
and postures in an extraordinary manner, the animal
she rides snorting or roaring fiercely all the time. Some
call her Kuan Ti,[7] others Chang Fei, and others, again,
Chou Kung, from her terribly martial aspect, which strikes
fear into all beholders. And should any daring fellow try
to peep in while the *séance* is going on, out of the window
darts the spear, transfixes his hat, and draws it off his head
into the room, while women and girls, young and old, hop
round one after the other like geese, on one leg, without
seeming to get the least fatigued.

LXXXIX. THE MYSTERIOUS HEAD

SEVERAL traders who were lodging at an inn in Peking
occupied a room which was divided from the adjoining
apartment by a partition of boards from which a piece

[4] The above is a curious story to be found in a Chinese work over
200 years old ; but no part of it more so than the forcible removal
of some part of the clothing, which has been so prominent a feature
in the *séances* of our own day. It may be added that in many a
court-yard in Peking will be found one or more trees, which cause
the view from the city wall to be very pleasing to the eye.

[5] The arrangement being that of the hobby-horse of bygone
days.

[6] The couches of the North of China are brick beds, heated by a
stove underneath, and covered with a mat. Upon one of these is
generally a dwarf table and a couple of pillows ; and here it is that
the Chinaman loves to recline, his wine-kettle, opium-pipe, or tea-
pot within reach, and a friend at his side, with whom he may converse far into the night.

[7] See No. LXXIII., note 3. Chang Fei was the bosom friend of
the last, and was his associate-commander in the wars of the Three
Kingdoms. Chou Kung was a younger brother of the first Emperor
of the Chou dynasty, and a pattern of wisdom and virtue. He is
said by the Chinese to have invented the compass ; but the legend
will not bear investigation.

was missing, leaving an aperture about as big as a basin. Suddenly a girl's head appeared through the opening, with very pretty features and nicely dressed hair ; and the next moment an arm, as white as polished jade. The traders were much alarmed, and, thinking it was the work of devils, tried to seize the dead, which, however, was quickly drawn in again out of their reach. This happened a second time, and then, as they could see nobody belonging to the head, one of them took a knife in his hand and crept up against the partition underneath the hole. In a little while the head reappeared, when he made a chop at it and cut it off, the blood spurting out all over the floor and wall. The traders hurried off to tell the landlord, who immediately reported the matter to the authorities, taking the head with him, and the traders were forthwith arrested and examined ; but the magistrate could make nothing of the case, and, as no one appeared for the prosecution, the accused, after about six months' incarceration, were accordingly released, and orders were given for the girl's head to be buried.

XC. THE SPIRIT OF THE HILLS

A MAN named Li, of I-tu, was once crossing the hills when he came upon a number of persons sitting on the ground engaged in drinking. As soon as they saw Li they begged him to join them, and vied with each other in filling his cup. Meanwhile, he looked about him and noticed that the various trays and dishes contained all kinds of costly food ; the wine only seemed to him a little rough on the palate. In the middle of their fun up came a stranger with a face about three feet long and a very tall hat ; whereupon the others were much alarmed, and cried out, " The hill spirit ! the hill spirit ! " running away in all directions as fast as they could go. Li hid himself in a hole in the ground ; and when by-and-by he peeped out to see what had happened, the wine and food had disappeared, and there was nothing there but a few dirty potsherds and some pieces of broken tiles with efts and lizards crawling over them.[1]

---

[1] Mr. Li had, doubtless, taken " a drop too much " before he started on his mountain walk.

XCI. INGRATITUDE PUNISHED

K'U TA-YU was a native of the Yang district, and managed to get a military appointment under the command of Tsu Shu-shun.[1] The latter treated him most kindly, and finally sent him as Major-General of some troops by which he was then trying to establish the dynasty of the usurping Chous. K'u soon perceived that the game was lost, and immediately turned his forces upon Tsu Shu-shun, whom he succeeded in capturing, after Tsu had been wounded in the hand, and whom he at once forwarded as a prisoner to headquarters. That night he dreamed that the Judge of Purgatory appeared to him, and, reproaching him with his base ingratitude, bade the devil-lictors seize him and scald his feet in a cauldron of boiling oil. K'u then woke up with a start, and found that his feet were very sore and painful; and in a short time they swelled up, and his toes dropped off. Fever set in, and in his agony he shrieked out, " Ungrateful wretch that I was indeed," and fell back and expired.

XCII. SMELLING ESSAYS [1]

Now as they wandered about the temple they came upon an old blind priest sitting under the verandah, engaged in selling medicines and prescribing for patients. " Ah ! " cried Sung, " there is an extraordinary man who is well versed in the arts of composition ; " and immediately he sent back to get the essay they had just been reading, in order to obtain the old priest's opinion as to its merits. At the same moment up came their friend from Yü-hang, and all three went along together. Wang began by addressing him as " Professor ; " whereupon the priest, who thought the stranger had come to consult him as a doctor, inquired what might be the disease from which he was suffering. Wang then explained what his mission was ; upon which the priest smiled and said, " Who's been

---

[1] Of whom I can learn nothing.

[1] The following extract from a long and otherwise tedious story tells its own tale. Wang is the modest man, and the young man from Yü-hang the braggart. Sung is merely a friend of Wang's.

telling you this nonsense ? How can a man with no eyes discuss with you the merits of your compositions ? " Wang replied by asking him to let his ears do duty for his eyes ; but the priest answered that he would hardly have patience to sit out Wang's three sections, amounting perhaps to some two thousand and more words. "However," added he, "if you like to burn it, I'll try what I can do with my nose." Wang complied, and burnt the first section there and then ; and the old priest, snuffing up the smoke, declared that it wasn't such a bad effort, and finally gave it as his opinion that Wang would probably succeed at the examination. The young scholar from Yü-hang didn't believe that the old priest could really tell anything by these means, and forthwith proceeded to burn an essay by one of the old masters ; but the priest no sooner smelt the smoke than he cried out, "Beautiful indeed ! beautiful indeed ! I do enjoy this. The light of genius and truth is evident here." The Yü-hang scholar was greatly astonished at this, and began to burn an essay of his own ; whereupon the priest said, "I had had but a taste of that one ; why change so soon to another ? " "The first paragraph," replied the young man, "was by a friend ; the rest is my own composition." No sooner had he uttered these words than the old priest began to retch violently, and begged that he might have no more, as he was sure it would make him sick. The Yü-hang scholar was much abashed at this, and went away ; but in a few days the list came out, and his name was among the successful ones, while Wang's was not. He at once hurried off to tell the old priest, who, when he heard the news, sighed and said, "I may be blind with my eyes, but I am not so with my nose, which I fear is the case with the examiners. Besides," added he, "I was talking to you about composition : I said nothing about *destiny*." [2]

---

[2] This is one of our author's favourite shafts—a sneer at examiners in general, and those who rejected him in particular.

XCIII. HIS FATHER'S GHOST

A MAN named T'ien Tzŭ-ch'êng, of Chiang-ning, was crossing the Tung-t'ing lake, when the boat was capsized, and he was drowned. His son, Liang-ssŭ, who, towards the close of the Ming dynasty, took the highest degree, was then a baby in arms; and his wife, hearing the bad news, swallowed poison forthwith,[1] and left the child to the care of his grandmother. When Liang-ssŭ grew up, he was appointed magistrate in Hu-pei, where he remained about a year. He was then transferred to Hu-nan, on military servce; but, on reaching the Tung-t'ing lake, his feelings overpowered him, and he returned to plead inability as an excuse for not taking up his post. Accordingly, he was degraded to the rank of Assistant-Magistrate, which he at first declined, but was finally compelled to accept; and thenceforward gave himself up to roaming about on the lakes and streams of the surrounding country, without paying much attention to his official duties.

One night he had anchored his boat alongside the bank of a river, when suddenly the cadence of a sweetly-played flageolet broke upon his ear; so he strolled along by the light of the moon in the direction of the music, until, after a few minutes' walking, he reached a cottage standing by itself, with a few citron-trees round it, and brilliantly lighted inside. Approaching a window, he peeped in, and saw three persons sitting at a table, engaged in drinking. In the place of honour was a graduate of about thirty years of age; an old man played the host, and at the side sat a much younger man playing on the flageolet. When he had finished, the old man clapped his hands in admiration; but the graduate turned away with a sigh, as if he had not heard a note. "Come now, Mr. Lu," cried the old man, addressing the latter, "kindly favour us with one of your songs, which, I know, must be worth hearing." The graduate then began to sing as follows :—

---

[1] This would be regarded as a very meritorious act by the Chinese.

Over the river the wind blows cold on lonely me :
Each flow'ret trampled under foot, all verdure gone.
At home a thousand *li* away, I cannot be ;
So towards the Bridge my spirit nightly wanders on.

The above was given in such melancholy tones that the
old man smiled and said, " Mr. Lu, these must be experiences
of your own," and, immediately filling a goblet, added,
" I can do nothing like that ; but if you will let me, I
will give you a song to help us on with our wine." He
then sang a verse from Li T'ai-po,[2] and put them all in
a lively humour again ; after which the young man said
he would just go outside and see how high the moon was,
which he did, and, observing Liang-ssŭ outside, clapped
his hands, and cried out to his companions, " There is a
man at the window, who has seen all we have been doing."
He then led Liang-ssŭ in ; whereupon the other two rose,
and begged him to be seated, and to join them in their
wine. The wine, however, was cold,[3] and he therefore
declined ; but the young man at once perceived his reason,
and proceeded to warm some for him. Liang-ssŭ now
ordered his servant to go and buy some more, but this
his host would not permit him to do. They next inquired
Liang-ssŭ's name, and whence he came, and then the old
man said, " Why, then, you are the father and mother [4]
of the district in which I live. My name is River : I am
an old resident here. This young man is a Mr. Tu, of
Kiang-si ; and this gentleman," added he, pointing to
the graduate, " is Mr. Rushten,[5] a fellow-provincial of
yours." Mr. Rushten looked at Liang-ssŭ in rather a
contemptuous way, and without taking much notice of
him ; whereupon Liang-ssŭ asked him whereabouts he
lived in Chiang-ning, observing that it was strange he
himself should never have heard of such an accomplished
gentleman. " Alas ! " replied Rushten, " it is many a

[2] The Byron of China.

[3] Chinese wine—or, more correctly, *spirits*—is always taken hot ;
hence the term wine-kettle, which frequently occurs in these pages.

[4] The Magistrate ; who is supposed to be towards the people
what a father is to his children.

[5] This singularly un-Chinese surname is employed to keep up a
certain play upon words which exists in the original, and which is
important to the *dénouement* of the story. " River " is the simple
translation of a name actually in use.

long day since I left my home, and I know nothing even of my own family. Alas, indeed ! " These words were uttered in so mournful a tone of voice that the old man broke in with, " Come, come, now ! talking like this, instead of drinking when we're all so jolly together ; this will never do." He then drained a bumper himself, and said, " I propose a game of forfeits. We'll throw with three dice ; and whoever throws so that the spots on one die [6] equal those on the other two shall give us a verse with a corresponding classical allusion in it." He then threw himself, and turned up an ace, a two, and a three ; whereupon he sang the following lines :—

An ace and a deuce on one side, just equal a three on the other :
For Fan a chicken was boiled, though three years had passed, by
    Chang's mother.[7]
                Thus friends love to meet !

Then the young musician threw, and turned up two twos and a four ; whereupon he exclaimed, " Don't laugh at the feeble allusion of an unlearned fellow like me :—

    Two deuces are equal to a four ;
    Four men united their valour in the old city.[8]
        Thus brothers love to meet ! "

Mr. Rushten followed with two aces and a two, and recited these lines :—

---

[6] Chinese dice are the exact counterpart of our own, except that the ace and the four are coloured red : the ace because the combination of black and white would be unlucky, and the four because this number once turned up in response to the call of an Emperor of the T'ang dynasty, who particularly wanted a four to win him the *partie*. All letters, despatches, and such documents, have invariably something *red* about them, this being the lucky colour, and to the Chinese emblematic of prosperity and joy.

[7] Alluding to an ancient story of a promise by a Mr. Fan that he would be at his friend Chang's house that day three years. When the time drew near, Chang's mother ridiculed the notion of a man keeping a three years' appointment ; but, acceding to her son's instances, she prepared a boiled chicken, which was barely ready when Fan arrived to eat of it.

[8] Alluding to the celebrated oath of confederation sworn in the peach garden between Kuan Yü, or Kuan Ti (see No. I., note 4), Chang Fei (see No. LXIII., note 2), Liu Pei, who subsequently proclaimed himself Emperor, A.D. 221, and Chu-ko Liang, his celebrated minister, to whose sage counsels most of the success of the undertaking was due.

Two aces are equal to a two :
Lu-hsiang stretched out his two arms and embraced his father.[9]
Thus father and son love to meet !

Liang then threw, and turned up the same as Mr. Rushten ; whereupon he said :—

Two aces are equal to a two :
Mao-jung regaled Lin-tsung with two baskets.[10]
Thus host and guest love to meet !

When the *partie* was over Liang-ssŭ rose to go, but Mr. Rushten said, " Dear me ! why are you in such a hurry ; we haven't had a moment to speak of the old place. Please stay : I was just going to ask you a few questions." So Liang-ssŭ sat down again, and Mr. Rushten proceeded. " I had an old friend," said he, " who was drowned in the Tung-t'ing lake. He bore the same name as yourself ; was he a relative ? " " He was my father," replied Liang-ssŭ ; " how did you know him ? " " We were friends as boys together ; and when he was drowned, I recovered and buried his body by the river-side." [11] Liang-ssŭ here burst into tears, and thanked Mr. Rushten very warmly, begging him to point out his father's grave. " Come again to-morrow," said Mr. Rushten, " and I will show it to you. You could easily find it yourself. It is close by here, and has ten stalks of water-rush growing on it." Liang-ssŭ now took his leave, and went back to his boat, but he could not sleep for thinking of what Mr. Rushten had told him ; and at length, without waiting for the dawn, he set out to look for the grave. To his great astonishment, the house where he had spent the previous evening had disappeared ; but hunting about in the direction indicaetd by Mr. Rushten, he found a grave with ten

[9] Alluding to the story of a young man who went in search of his missing father.

[10] Lin-tsung saw his host kill a chicken which he thought was destined for himself. However, Mao-jung served up the dainty morsel to his mother, while he and his guest regaled themselves with two baskets of common vegetables. At this instance of filial piety, Lin-tsung had the good sense to be charmed.

[11] The Chinese recognise no act more worthy a virtuous man than that of burying stray bones, covering up exposed coffins, and so forth. By such means the favour of the Gods is most surely obtained, to say nothing of the golden opinions of the living.

water-rushes growing on it, precisely as Mr. Rushten had
described. It then flashed across him that Mr. Rushten's
name had a special meaning, and that he had been holding
converse with none other than the disembodied spirit of
his own father. And, on inquiring of the people of the
place, he learnt that twenty years before, a benevolent
old gentleman, named Kao, had been in the habit of collecting the bodies of persons found drowned, and burying
them in that spot. Liang then opened the grave, and
carried off his father's remains to his own home, where
his grandmother, to whom he described Mr. Rushten's
appearance, confirmed the suspicion he himself had formed.
It also turned out that the young musician was a cousin
of his, who had been drowned when nineteen years of
age ; and then he recollected that the boy's father had
subsequently gone to Kiang-si, and that his mother had
died there, and had been buried at the Bamboo Bridge,
to which Mr. Rushten had alluded in his song. But he
did not know who the old man was.[12]

XCIV. THE BOAT-GIRL BRIDE

WANG KUEI-AN was a young man of good family. It
happened once when he was travelling southwards, and
had moored his boat to the bank, that he saw in another
boat close by a young boat-girl embroidering shoes. He
was much struck by her beauty, and continued gazing at
her for some time, though she took not the slightest notice
of him. By-and-by he began singing—

> The Lo-yang lady lives over the way :
> [Fifteen years is her age I should say].[1]

---

[12] This is merely our author's way of putting the question of the
old man's identity. He was the Spirit of the Waters—his name,
it will be recollected, was River—just, in fact, as we say Old Father
Thames.

[1] From a poem by Wang Wei, a noted poet of the T'ang dynasty;
he lived A.D. 699–759. The second line is not given in the text.

to attract her attention, and then she seemed to perceive that he was addressing himself to her; but, after just raising her head and glancing at him, she resumed her embroidery as before. Wang then threw a piece of silver towards her, which fell on her skirt; however, she merely picked it up, and flung it on to the bank, as if she had not seen what it was, so Wang put it back in his pocket again. He followed up by throwing her a gold bracelet, to which she paid no attention whatever, never taking her eyes off her work. A few minutes after her father appeared, much to the dismay of Wang, who was afraid he would see the bracelet; but the young girl quietly placed her feet over it, and concealed it from his sight. The boatman let go the painter, and away they went down stream, leaving Wang sitting there, not knowing what to do next. And, having recently lost his wife, he regretted that he had not seized this opportunity to make another match; the more so, as when he came to ask the other boat-people of the place, no one knew anything about them. So Wang got into his own boat, and started off in pursuit; but evening came on, and, as he could see nothing of them, he was obliged to turn back and proceed in the direction where business was taking him. When he had finished that, he returned, making inquiries all the way along, but without hearing anything about the object of his search. On arriving at home, he was unable either to eat or to sleep, so much did this affair occupy his mind; and about a year afterwards he went south again, bought a boat, and lived in it as his home, watching carefully every single vessel that passed either up or down, until at last there was hardly one he didn't know by sight. But all this time the boat he was looking for never reappeared.

Some six months passed away thus, and then, having exhausted all his funds, he was obliged to go home, where he remained in a state of general inaptitude for anything. One night he dreamed that he entered a village on the river-bank, and that, after passing several houses, he saw one with a door towards the south, and a palisade of bamboos inside. Thinking it was a garden, he walked in, and beheld a beautiful magnolia, covered with blossoms, which reminded him of the line—

And Judas-tree in flower before the door.[2]

A few steps farther on was a neat bamboo hedge, on the other side of which, towards the north, he found a small house, with three columns, the door of which was locked ; and another, towards the south, with its window shaded by the broad leaves of a plaintain-tree. The door was barred by a clothes-horse,[3] on which was hanging an embroidered petticoat ; and, on seeing this, Wang stepped back, knowing that he had got to the ladies' quarters ; but his presence had already been noticed inside, and, in another moment, out came his heroine of the boat. Overjoyed at seeing her, he was on the point of grasping her hand, when suddenly the girl's father arrived, and, in his consternation, Wang waked up, and found that it was all a dream. Every incident of it, however, remained clear and distinct in his mind, and he took care to say nothing about it to anybody, for fear of destroying its reality.

Another year passed away, and he went again to Chinkiang, where lived an official, named Hsü, who was an old friend of the family, and who invited Wang to come and take a cup of wine with him. On his way thither, Wang lost his way, but at length reached a village which seemed familiar to him, and which he soon found, by the door with the magnolia inside, to be identical in every particular with the village of his dream. He went in through the

[2] From a poem by P'an T'ang-shên, which runs :—

> Her rustic home stands by the Tung-t'ing lake.
> Ye who would there a pure libation pour,
> Look for mud walls, a roof of rushy make,
> And Judas-tree in flower before the door.

The Chinese believe that the Judas-tree will only bloom where fraternal love prevails.

[3] I have already observed that men and women should not let their hands touch when passing things to each other (see No. XL., note 2) ; neither is it considered proper for persons of different sexes to hang their clothes on the same clothes-horse. (See *Appendix*, note 42.)

With regard to shaking hands, I have omitted to mention how objectionable this custom is in the eyes of the Chinese, as in vogue among foreigners, without reference to sex. They believe that a bad man might easily secrete some noxious drug in the palm of his hand, and so convey it into the system of any woman, who would then be at his mercy.

doorway, and there was everything as he had seen it in his dream, even to the boat-girl herself. She jumped up on his arrival, and, shutting the door in his face, asked what his business was there. Wang inquired if she had forgotten about the bracelet, and went on to tell her how long he had been searching for her, and how, at last, she had been revealed to him in a dream. The girl then begged to know his name and family; and when she heard who he was, she asked what a gentleman like himself could want with a poor boat-girl like her, as he must have a wife of his own. " But for you," replied Wang, " I should, indeed, have been married long ago." Upon which the girl told him if that was really the case, he had better apply to her parents, " although," added she, " they have already refused a great many offers for me. The bracelet you gave me is here, but my father and mother are just now away from home; they will be back shortly. You go away now and engage a match-maker, when I dare say it will be all right if the proper formalities are observed." Wang then retired, the girl calling after him to remember that her name was Mêng Yün, and her father's Mêng Chiang-li. He proceeded at once on his way to Mr. Hsü's, and after that sought out his intended father-in-law, telling him who he was, and offering him at the same time one hundred ounces of silver, as betrothal-money for his daughter. " She is already promised," replied the old man; upon which Wang declared he had been making careful inquiries, and had heard, on all sides, that the young lady was not engaged, winding up by begging to know what objection there was to his suit. " I have just promised her," answered her father, " and I cannot possibly break my word;" so Wang went away, deeply mortified, not knowing whether to believe it or not. That night he tossed about a good deal; and next morning, braving the ridicule with which he imagined his friend would view his wished-for alliance with a boat-girl, he went off to Mr. Hsü, and told him all about it. " Why didn't you consult me before?" cried Mr. Hsü; " her father is a connection of mine." Wang then went on to give fuller particulars, which his friend interrupted by saying, " Chiang-li is indeed poor, but he has never been a boatman. Are you sure you are not making a mistake?" He then sent off his elder son to make inquiries; and to him the girl's father said, " Poor I am, but I don't *sell* my daughter.[4] Your friend imagined that I should be tempted by the sight of his money to forego the usual ceremonies, and so I won't have anything to do with him. But if your father desires this match, and everything is in proper order, I will just go in and consult with my daughter, and see if she is willing." He then retired for a few minutes, and when he came back he raised his hands in congratulation, saying, " Everything is as you wish ; " whereupon a day was fixed, and the young man went home to report to his father. Wang now sent off betrothal presents, with the usual formalities, and took up his abode with his friend, Mr. Hsü, until the marriage was solemnised, three days after which he bade adieu to his father-in-law, and started on his way northwards. In the evening, as they were sitting on the boat together, Wang said to his wife, " When I first met you near this spot, I fancied you were not of the ordinary boating-class. Where were you then going ? " " I was going to visit my uncle," she replied. " We are not a wealthy family, you know, but we don't want anything through an improper channel ; and I couldn't help smiling at the great eyes you were making at me, all the time trying to tempt me with money. But when I heard you speak, I knew at once you were a man of refinement, though I guessed you were a bit of a rake ; and so I hid your bracelet, and saved you from the wrath of my father." " And yet," replied Wang, " you have fallen into my snare after all ; " adding, after a little pressure, " for I can't conceal from you much longer the fact that I have already a wife, belonging to a high official family." This she did not believe, until he began to affirm it seriously ; and then she jumped up and ran out of the cabin. Wang followed at once, but, before he could reach her, she was already in the river ; whereupon he shouted out to boats to come to their assistance, causing quite a commotion all round about ; but nothing was to be seen in the river, save only the reflection of the stars shining brightly on the water. All night long Wang went sorrowfully up and down, and offered a

---

[4] Alluding to Wang's breach of etiquette in visiting the father himself, instead of sending a go-between, who would have offered the same sum in due form as the usual dowry or present to the bride's family.

high reward for the body, which, however, was not forthcoming. So he went home in despair, and then, fearing
lest his father-in-law should come to visit his daughter,
he started on a visit to a connection of his, who had an
appointment in Honan. In the course of a year or two,
when on his homeward journey, he chanced to be detained by
bad weather at a roadside inn of rather cleaner appearance
than usual. Within he saw an old woman playing with
a child, which, as soon as he entered, held out its arms to
him to be taken. Wang took the child on his knee, and
there it remained, refusing to go back to its nurse ; and,
when the rain had stopped, and Wang was getting ready
to go, the child cried out, " Pa-pa gone ! " The nurse
told it to hold its tongue, and, at the same moment, out
from behind the screen came Wang's long-lost wife. " You
bad fellow," said she, " what am I to do with this ? "
pointing to the child ; and then Wang knew that the boy
was his own son. He was much affected, and swore by
the sun [5] that the words he had uttered had been uttered
in jest, and by-and-by his wife's anger was soothed. She
then explained how she had been picked up by a passing
boat, the occupant of which was the owner of the house
they were in, a man of sixty years of age, who had no
children of his own, and who kindly adopted her.[6] She
also told him how she had had several offers of marriage,

[5] Witnesses in a Chinese court of justice take no oath, in our
sense of the term. Their written depositions, however, are always
ended with the words " the above evidence is the truth ! " In
ordinary life people call heaven and earth to witness, or, as in this
case, the sun ; or they declare themselves willing to forfeit their
lives ; and so on, if their statements are not true. " Saucer-break-
ing " is one of those pleasant inductions from probably a single
instance, which may have been the fancy of a moment ; at any rate,
it is quite unknown in China as a national custom. " Cock-killing "
usually has reference to the ceremonies of initiation performed by
the members of the numerous secret societies which exist over the
length and breadth of the Empire, in spite of Government prohibitions, and the penalty of death incurred upon detection.

[6] Adoption is common all over China, and is regulated by law.
For instance, an adopted son excludes all the daughters of the
family. A man is not allowed to marry a girl whom he has adopted
until he shall have given her away to be adopted in a family of a
different surname from his own ; after which fictitious ceremony, his
marriage with her becomes legal (see No. XV., note 3) ; for the
child adopted takes the same surname as that of the family into
which he is adopted, and is so far cut off from his own relations,

all of which she had refused, and how her child was born, and that she had called him Chi-shêng, and that he was then a year old. Wang now unpacked his baggage again, and went in to see the old gentleman and his wife, whom he treated as if they had actually been his wife's parents. A few days afterwards they set off together towards Wang's home, where they found his wife's real father awaiting them. He had been there more than two months, and had been considerably disconcerted by the mysterious remarks of Wang's servants ; but the arrival of his daughter and her husband made things all smooth again, and when they told him what had happened, he understood the demeanour of the servants which had seemed so strange to him at first.

XCV. THE TWO BRIDES [1]

Now Chi-shêng, or Wang Sun, was one of the cleverest young fellows in the district ; and his father and mother, who had foreseen his ability from the time when, as a baby in long clothes, he distinguished them from other people, loved him very dearly. He grew up into a handsome lad ; at eight or nine he could compose elegantly, and by fourteen he had already entered his name as a candidate for the first degree, after which his marriage became a question for consideration. Now his father's younger sister, Erh-niang, had married a gentleman named Chêng Tzŭ-ch'iao, and they had a daughter called Kuei-hsiu, who was extremely pretty, and with whom Chi-shêng fell deeply in love, being soon unable either to eat or to sleep. His parents became extremely uneasy about him, and inquired what it was that ailed him ; and when he told them, they

that he would not venture even to put on mourning for his real parents without first obtaining the consent of those who had adopted him. A son or daughter may be sold, but an adopted child may not ; neither may the adopted child be given away in adoption to any one else without the specific consent of his real parents. The general object in adopting children is to leave some one behind at death to look after the duties of ancestral worship. For this boys are preferred ; but the *Fortunate Union* gives an instance in which these rites were very creditably performed by the heroine of the tale.

[1] This story is a sequel to the last.

at once sent off a match-maker to Mr. Chêng. The latter, however, was rather a stickler for the proprieties, and replied that the near relationship precluded him from accepting the offer.[2] Thereupon Chi-shêng became dangerously ill, and his mother, not knowing what to do, secretly tried to persuade Erh-niang to let her daughter come over to their house; but Mr. Chêng heard of it, and was so angry that Chi-shêng's father and mother gave up all hope of arranging the match.

At that time there was a gentleman named Chang living near by, who had five daughters, all very pretty, but the youngest, called Wu-k'o, was singularly beautiful, far surpassing her four sisters. She was not betrothed to any one, when one day, as she was on her way to worship at the family tombs, she chanced to see Chi-shêng, and at her return home spoke about him to her mother. Her mother guessed what her meaning was, and arranged with a match-maker, named Mrs. Yü, to call upon Chi-shêng's parents. This she did precisely at the time when Chi-shêng was so ill, and forthwith told his mother that her son's complaint was one she, Mrs. Yü, was quite competent to cure; going on to tell her about Miss Wu-k'o and the proposed marriage, at which the good lady was delighted, and sent her in to talk about it to Chi-shêng herself. "Alas!" cried he, when he had heard Mrs. Yü's story, "you are bringing me the wrong medicine for my complaint." "All depends upon the efficacy of the medicine," replied Mrs. Yü; "if the medicine is good, it matters not what is the name of the doctor who administers the draught; while to set your heart on a particular person, and to lie there and die because that person doesn't come, is surely foolish in the extreme." "Ah," rejoined Chi-shêng, "there's no medicine under heaven that will do me any good." Mrs. Yü told him his experience was limited, and proceeded to expatiate by speaking and gesticulating on the beauty and liveliness of Wu-k'o. But all Chi-shêng said was that she was not what he wanted, and, turning round his face to the wall, would listen to no more about her. So Mrs. Yü was obliged to go away, and Chi-shêng became worse and worse every day, until

[2] The surnames would in this case be different, and no obstacle could be offered on that score. See No. XV., note 3.

suddenly one of the maids came in and informed him that
the young lady herself was at the door. Immediately he
jumped up and ran out, and lo ! there before him stood
a beautiful girl, whom, however, he soon discovered not
to be Kuei-hsiu. She wore a light yellow robe with a fine
silk jacket and an embroidered petticoat, from beneath
which her two little feet peeped out ; and altogether she
more resembled a fairy than anything else. Chi-shêng
inquired her name ; to which she replied that it was Wu-k'o,
adding that she couldn't understand his devoted attach-
ment to Kuei-hsiu, as if there was nobody else in the world.
Chi-shêng apologised, saying that he had never before
seen any one so beautiful as Kuei-hsiu, but that he was now
aware of his mistake. He then swore everlasting fidelity
to her, and was just grasping her hand when he awoke
and found his mother rubbing him. It was a dream, but
so accurately defined in all its details that he began to
think if Wu-k'o was really such as he had seen her, there
would be no further need to try for his impracticable cousin.
So he communicated his dream to his mother ; and she,
only too delighted to notice this change of feeling, offered
to go to Wu-k'o's house herself ; but Chi-shêng would not
hear of this, and arranged with an old woman who knew
the family to find some pretext for going there, and to
report to him what Wu-k'o was like. When she arrived
Wu-k'o was ill in bed, and lay with her head propped up
by pillows, looking very pretty indeed. The old woman
approached the couch and asked what was the matter ;
to which Wu-k'o made no reply, her fingers fidgetting all
the time with her waistband. " She's been behaving
badly to her father and mother," cried the latter, who was
in the room ; " there's many a one has offered to marry her,
but she says she'll have none but Chi-shêng : and then
when I scold her a bit, she takes on and won't touch her
food for days." " Madam," said the old woman, " if
you could get that young man for your daughter they
would make a truly pretty pair ; and as for him, if he
could only see Miss Wu-k'o, I'm afraid it would be too much
for him. What do you think of my going there and getting
them to make proposals ? " " No, thank you," replied
Wu-k'o ; " I would rather not risk his refusal ; " upon
which the old woman declared she would succeed, and

hurried off to tell Chi-shêng, who was delighted to find from her report that Wu-k'o was exactly as he had seen her in his dream, though he didn't trust implicitly in all the old woman said. By-and-by, when he began to get a little better, he consulted with the old woman as to how he could see Wu-k'o with his own eyes ; and, after some little difficulty, it was arranged that Chi-shêng should hide himself in a room from which he would be able to see her as she crossed the yard supported by a maid, which she did every day at a certain hour. This Chi-shêng proceeded to do, and in a little while out she came, accompanied by the old woman as well, who instantly drew her attention either to the clouds or the trees, in order that she should walk more leisurely. Thus Chi-shêng had a good look at her, and saw that she was truly the young lady of his dream. He could hardly contain himself for joy; and when the old woman arrived and asked if she would do instead of Kuei-hsiu, he thanked her very warmly and returned to his own home. There he told his father and mother, who sent off a match-maker to arrange the preliminaries ; but the latter came back and told them that Wu-k'o was already betrothed. This was a terrible blow for Chi-shêng, who was soon as ill as ever, and offered no reply to his father and mother when they charged him with having made a mistake. For several months he ate nothing but a bowl of rice-gruel a day, and he became as emaciated as a fowl, when all of a sudden the old woman walked in and asked him what was the matter. "Foolish boy," said she, when he had told her all; "before you wouldn't have her, and do you imagine she is bound to have you now ? But I'll see if I can help you ; for were she the Emperor's own daughter, I should still find some way of getting her." Chi-shêng asked what he should do, and she then told him to send a servant with a letter next day to Wu-k'o's house, to which his father at first objected for fear of another repulse ; but the old woman assured him that Wu-k'o's parents had since repented, besides which no written contract had as yet been made ; "and you know the proverb," added she, "that those who are first at the fire will get their dinner first." So Chi-shêng's father agreed, and two servants were accordingly sent, their mission proving a complete success. Chi-shêng

now rapidly recovered his health, and thought no more
of Kuei-hsiu, who, when she heard of the intended match,
became in her turn very seriously ill, to the great anger of
her father, who said she might die for all he cared, but
to the great sorrow of her mother, who was extremely
fond of her daughter. The latter even went so far as
to propose to Mr. Chêng that Kuei-hsiu should go as second
wife, at which he was so enraged that he declared he would
wash his hands of the girl altogether. The mother then
found out when Chi-shêng's wedding was to take place ;
and, borrowing a chair and attendants from her brother
under pretence of going to visit him, put Kuei-hsiu inside
and sent her off to her uncle's house. As she arrived at
the door, the servants spread a carpet for her to walk on,
and the band struck up the wedding march. Chi-shêng
went out to see what it was all about, and there met a
young lady in a bridal veil, from whom he would have
escaped had not her servants surrounded them, and, before
he knew what he was doing, he was making her the usual
salutation of a bridegroom. They then went in together,
and, to his further astonishment, he found that the young
lady was Kuei-hsiu ; and, being now unable to go and
meet Wu-k'o, a message was sent to her father, telling
him what had occurred. He, too, got into a great rage,
and vowed he would break off the match ; but Wu-k'o
herself said she would go all the same, her rival having
only got the start of her in point of time. And go she did ;
and the two wives, instead of quarrelling, as was expected,
lived very happily together like sisters, and wore each
other's clothes and shoes without distinction, Kuei-hsiu
taking the place of an elder sister as being somewhat older
than Wu-k'o.[3] One day, after these events, Chi-shêng
asked Wu-k'o why she had refused his offer ; to which
she replied that it was merely to pay him out for having
previously refused her father's proposal. " Before you
had seen me, your head was full of Kuei-hsiu ; but after
you had seen me, your thoughts were somewhat divided ;
and I wanted to know how I compared with her, and whether

[3] The *dénouement* of the *Yü chiao li*, a small novel which was
translated into French by Rémusat, and again by Julien under the
title of *Les Deux Cousines*, is effected by the hero of the tale marrying
both the heroines.

you would fall ill on my account as you had on hers, that we mightn't quarrel about our looks." "It was a cruel revenge," said Chi-shêng; "but how should I ever have got a sight of you had it not been for the old woman?" "What had she to do with it?" replied Wu-k'o; "I knew you were behind the door all the time. When I was ill I dreamt that I went to your house and saw you, but I looked upon it only as a dream until I heard that you had dreamt that I had actually been there, and then I knew that my spirit must have been with you." Chi-shêng now related to her the particulars of his vision, which coincided exactly with her own; and thus, strangely enough, had the matrimonial alliances of both father and son been brought about by dreams.

XCVI. A SUPERNATURAL WIFE

A CERTAIN Mr. Chao, of Ch'ang-shan, lodged in a family of the name of T'ai. He was very badly off, and, falling sick, was brought almost to death's door. One day they moved him into the verandah, that it might be cooler for him; and, when he awoke from a nap, lo! a beautiful girl was standing by his side. "I am come to be your wife," said the girl, in answer to his question as to who she was; to which he replied that a poor fellow like himself did not look for such luck as that; adding that, being then on his death-bed, he would not have much occasion for the services of a wife. The girl said she could cure him; but he told her he very much doubted that; "And even," continued he, "should you have any good prescription, I have not the means of getting it made up." "I don't want medicine to cure you with," rejoined the girl, proceeding at once to rub his back and sides with her hand, which seemed to him like a ball of fire. He soon began to feel much better, and asked the young lady what her name was, in order, as he said, that he might remember her in his prayers. "I am a spirit," replied she; "and you, when alive under the Han dynasty as Ch'u Sui-lang, were a benefactor of my family. Your kindness being engraven on my heart, I have at length succeeded in my search for you, and am able in some measure to requite you." Chao was dreadfully ashamed of his poverty-stricken state, and

afraid that his dirty room would spoil the young lady's
dress ; but she made him show her in, and accordingly
he took her into his apartment, where there were neither
chairs to sit upon, nor signs of anything to eat, saying, " You
might, indeed, be able to put up with all this ; but you
see my larder is empty, and I have absolutely no means
of supporting a wife." " Don't be alarmed about that,"
cried she ; and in another moment he saw a couch covered
with costly robes, the walls papered with a silver-flecked
paper, and chairs and tables appear, the latter laden with
all kinds of wine and exquisite viands. They then began
to enjoy themselves, and lived together as husband and
wife, many people coming to witness these strange things,
and being all cordially received by the young lady, who
in her turn always accompanied Mr. Chao when he went
out to dinner anywhere.[1] One day there was an unprincipled young graduate among the company, which she
seemed immediately to become aware of ; and, after
calling him several bad names, she struck him on the
side of the head, causing his head to fly out of the window
while his body remained inside; and there he was, stuck
fast, unable to move either way, until the others interceded for him and he was released. After some time
visitors became too numerous, and if she refused to see
them they turned their anger against her husband. At
length, as they were sitting together drinking with some
friends at the Tuan-yang festival,[2] a white rabbit ran in,
whereupon the girl jumped up and said, " The doctor [3] has
come for me ; " then, turning to the rabbit, she added,

---

[1] The sexes do not dine together. On the occasion of a dinner-
party, private or official, the ladies give a separate entertainment to
the wives of the various guests in the " inner " or women's apartments, as an adjunct to which a theatrical troupe is often engaged,
precisely as in the case of the opposite sex. Singing-girls are, however, present at and share in the banquets of the *roués* of China.

[2] This occurs on the 5th of the 5th moon, and is commonly
known as the Dragon-Boat Festival, from a practice of racing on
that day in long, narrow boats. It is said to have been instituted
in memory of a patriotic statesman named Ch'ü Yüan, who drowned
himself (B.C. 295) because his counsels were unheeded.

[3] A hare or rabbit is believed to sit at the foot of the cassia-tree
in the moon, pounding the drugs out of which is concocted the
elixir of immortality. The first allusion to this occurs in the poems
of Ch'ü Yüan (see preceding note).

" You go on : I'll follow you." So the rabbit went away, and then she ordered them to get a ladder and place it against a high tree in the back yard, the top of the ladder overtopping the tree. The young lady went up first and Chao close behind her ; after which she called out to anybody who wished to join them to make haste up. None ventured to do so with the exception of a serving-boy belonging to the house, who followed after Chao ; and thus they went up, up, up, up, until they disappeared in the clouds and were seen no more. However, when the bystanders came to look at the ladder, they found it was only an old door-frame with the panels knocked out ; and when they went into Mr. Chao's room, it was the same old, dirty, unfurnished room as before. So they determined to find out all about it from the serving-boy when he came back ; but this he never did.

XCVII. BRIBERY AND CORRUPTION

At Pao-ting Fu there lived a young man, who having purchased the lowest [1] degree was about to proceed to Peking, in the hope of obtaining, by the aid of a little bribery, an appointment as District Magistrate. His boxes were all ready packed, when he was taken suddenly ill and was confined to his bed for more than a month. One day the servant entered and announced a visitor ; whereupon our sick man jumped up and ran to the door as if there was nothing the matter with him. The visitor was elegantly dressed like a man of some position in society ; and, after bowing thrice, he walked into the house, explaining that he was Kung-sun Hsia, [2] tutor to the Eleventh Prince, and that he had heard our Mr. So-and-so wished to arrange for the purchase of a magistracy. " If that is really so," added he, " would you not do better to buy a prefecture ? " So-and-so thanked him warmly, but said his funds would not be sufficient ; upon which Mr. Kung-sun declared he should be delighted to assist him with half

---

[1] By which he would become eligible for Government employ. The sale of degrees has been extensively carried on under the present dynasty, as a means of replenishing an empty Treasury.

[2] Kung-sun is an example of a Chinese double surname.

the purchase-money, which he could repay after taking up the post.[3] He went on to say that being on intimate terms with the various provincial Governors the thing could be easily managed for about five thousand taels ; and also that at that very moment Chên-ting Fu being vacant, it would be as well to make an early effort to get the appointment. So-and-so pointed out that this place was in his native province ;[4] but Kung-sun only laughed at his objection, and reminded him that money [5] could obliterate all distinctions of that kind. This did not seem quite satisfactory ; however, Kung-sun told him not to be alarmed, as the post of which he was speaking was below in the infernal regions. " The fact is," said he, " that your term of life has expired, and that your name is already on the death list ; by these means you will take your place in the world below as a man of official position. Farewell ! In three days we shall meet again." He then went to the door and mounted his horse and rode away. So-and-so now opened his eyes and spoke a few parting words to his wife and children, bidding them take money from his strong room [6] and go buy large quantities of paper ingots,[7]

[3] Such is the common system of repaying the loan, by means of which an indigent nominee is enabled to defray the expenses of his journey to the post to which he has been appointed, and other calls upon his purse. These loans are generally provided by some "western " merchant, which term is an ellipsis for a " Shansi " banker, Shansi being literally " west of the mountains." Some one accompanies the newly-made official to his post, and holds his commission in pawn until the amount is repaid ; which settlement is easily effected by the issue of some well-understood proclamation, calling, for instance, upon the people to close all gambling-houses within a given period. Immediately the owners of these hells forward presents of money to the incoming official, the Shansi banker gets his principal with interest, perhaps at the rate of 2 per cent. *per month*, the gambling-houses carry on as usual, and everybody is perfectly satisfied.

[4] Which fact would disqualify him from taking the post.

[5] Literally, " square hole." A common name for the Chinese cash. See No. II., note 2.

[6] In the case of wealthy families these strong rooms often contain, in addition to bullion, jewels to a very great amount belonging to the ladies of the house ; and, as a rule, the door may not be opened unless in the presence of a certain number of the male representatives of the house.

[7] Pieces of silver and gold paper made up to represent the ordinary Chinese " shoes " of bullion (see No. XVIII., note 4), and burnt

which they immediately did, quite exhausting all the shops. This was piled in the court-yard with paper images of men, devils, horses, &c., and burning went on day and night until the ashes formed quite a hill. In three days Kung-sun returned, bringing with him the money; upon which So-and-so hurried off to the Board of Civil Office,[8] where he had an interview with the high officials, who, after asking his name, warned him to be a pure and upright officer, and then calling him up to the table handed him his letter of appointment. So-and-so bowed and took his leave; but recollecting at once that his purchased degree would not carry much weight with it in the eyes of his subordinates,[9] he sent off to buy elaborate chairs and a number of horses for his retinue, at the same time despatching several devil lictors to fetch his favourite wife in a beautifully adorned sedan-chair. All arrangements were just completed when some of the Chên-ting staff came to meet the new Prefect,[10] others awaiting him all along the line of road, about half a mile in length. He was immensely gratified at this reception, when all of a sudden the gongs before him ceased to sound, and the banners were lowered to the ground. He had hardly time to ask what was the matter before he saw those of his servants who were on horseback jump hastily to the ground and dwindle down to about a foot in height, while their horses shrank to the size of foxes or racoons. One of the attendants near his chariot cried out in alarm, "Here's Kuan Ti!"[11] and then he, too, jumped out in a fright, and saw in the distance Kuan Ti himself slowly approaching them, followed by four or five retainers on horseback. His great beard covered the lower half of his face, quite unlike ordinary mortals; his aspect was terrible to behold, and his eyes reached nearly to his ears. "Who is this?" roared he to his servants; and they immediately informed him that it was the new Prefect of Chên-ting. "What!" cried he; "a petty fellow like that to have a retinue like

for the use of the dead. Generally known to foreigners in China as "joss-paper."

[8] See No. VII., note I. In this case the reference is to a similar Board in the Infernal Regions.

[9] These would be sure to sneer at him behind his back.

[10] A compliment usually paid to an incoming official.

[11] See No. I., note 4.

this ? " [12] Whereupon So-and-so's flesh began to creep with fear, and in a few moments he found that he too had shrunk to the size of a little boy of six or seven. Kuan Ti bade his attendants bring the new Prefect with them, and went into a building at the roadside, where he took up his seat facing the south [13] and calling for writing materials told So-and-so to write down his name and address. When this was handed to him he flew into a towering passion, and said, "The scribbly scrawl of a placeman, indeed! [14] Can such a one be entrusted with the welfare of the people ? Look me up the record of his good works." A man then advanced, and whispered something in a low tone ; upon which Kuan Ti exclaimed in a loud voice, " The crime of the briber is comparatively trifling ; the heavy guilt lies with those who sell official posts for money." So-and-so was now seized by angels in golden armour, and two of them tore off his cap and robes, and administered to him fifty blows with the bamboo, until hardly any flesh remained on his bones. He was then thrust outside the door, and lo! his carriages and horses had disappeared, and he himself was lying, unable to walk for pain, at no great distance from his own house. However, his body seemed as light as a leaf, and in a day and a night he managed to crawl home. When he arrived, he awoke as it were from a dream, and found himself groaning upon the bed; and to the inquiries of his family he only replied that he felt dreadfully sore. Now he really had been dead for seven days ; and when he came round thus, he immediately asked for A-lien, which was the name of his favourite wife. But the very day before, while chatting with the other members of the family, A-lien had suddenly cried out that her husband was made Prefect of Chên-ting, and that his lictors had come to escort her thither. Accordingly she retired to dress herself in her best clothes, and, when ready to start, she fell back and expired. Hearing this sad story, So-and-so began to mourn and beat his

---

[12] The retinue of a Mandarin should be in accordance with his rank. I have given elsewhere (see No. LVI., note 5) what would be that of an official of the highest rank.

[13] See No. LXXVII., note 1.

[14] Good writing holds a much higher place in the estimation of the Chinese than among Western nations. The very nature of their characters raises calligraphy almost to the rank of an art.

breast, and he would not allow her to be buried at once, in the hope that she might yet come round ; but this she never did. Meanwhile So-and-so got slowly better, and by the end of six months was able to walk again. He would often exclaim, "The ruin of my career and the punishment I received—all this I could have endured ; but the loss of my dear A-lien is more than I can bear." [15]

XCVIII. A CHINESE JONAH

A MAN named Sun Pi-chên was crossing the river [1] when a great thunder-squall broke upon the vessel and caused her to toss about fearfully, to the great terror of all the passengers. Just then, an angel in golden armour appeared standing upon the clouds above them, holding in his hand a scroll inscribed with certain characters, also written in gold, which the people on the vessel easily made out to be three in number, namely *Sun Pi-chên*. So, turning at once to their fellow-traveller, they said to him, "You have evidently incurred the displeasure of Heaven ; get into a boat by yourself, and do not involve us in your punishment." And without giving him time to reply whether he would do so or not, they hurried him over the side into a small boat and set him adrift ; but when Sun Pi-chên looked back, lo ! the vessel itself had capsized. [2]

[15] The author here adds a somewhat similar case, which actually occurred in the reign of K'ang Hsi, of a Viceroy, who was modestly attended, falling in with the gorgeous retinue of a Magistrate, and being somewhat rudely treated by the servants of the latter. On arriving at his destination, the Viceroy sent for that Magistrate, and sternly bade him retire from office, remarking that no simple magistrate could afford to keep such a retinue of attendants unless by illegal exactions from the suffering people committed to his charge.

[1] The Yang-tze : sometimes spoken of as the Long River.

[2] The full point of this story can hardly be conveyed in translation. The man's surname was Sun, and his prænomen, Pi-chên (which in Chinese *follows* the nomen), might be rendered "Must-be-saved." However, there is another word meaning "struck," precisely similar in sound and tone, though written differently, to the above *chên* ; and, so far as the ear alone is concerned, our hero's name might have been either *Sun Must-be-saved* or *Sun Must-be-struck*. That the merchants mistook the character *chên*, "saved," for *chên* "struck," is evident from the catastrophe which overtook their vessel, while Mr. Sun's little boat rode safely through the storm.

XCIX. CHANG PU-LIANG

A CERTAIN trader who was travelling in the province of Chih-li, being overtaken by a storm of rain and hail, took shelter among some standing crops by the wayside. There he heard a voice from heaven, saying, "These are Chang Pu-liang's fields ; do not injure his crops." The trader began to wonder who this Chang Pu-liang could be, and how, if he was *pu liang* (not virtuous), he came to be under divine protection ; so when the storm was over and he had reached the neighbouring village, he made inquiries on the subject, and told the people there what he had heard. The villagers then informed him that Chang Pu-liang was a very wealthy farmer, who was accustomed every spring to make loans of grain to the poor of the district, and who was not too particular about getting back the exact amount he had lent,—taking, in fact, whatever they brought him without discussion ; hence the sobriquet of *pu liang*, "no measure" (*i.e.*, the man who doesn't measure the repayments of his loans).[1] After that, they all proceeded in a body to the fields, where it was discovered that vast damage had been done to the crops generally, with the exception of Chang Pu-liang's, which had escaped uninjured.

C. THE DUTCH CARPET

FORMERLY, when the Red Heads [1] were permitted to trade with China, the officer in command of the coast defences would not allow them, on account of their great numbers, to come ashore. The Dutch begged very hard for the

[1] Here again we have a play upon words similar to that in the last story.

[1] We read in the *History of Amoy* :—" In the year 1622 the red-haired barbarians seized the Pescadores and attacked Amoy." From the Pescadores they finally retired, on a promise that trade would be permitted, to Formosa, whence they were expelled by the famous Koxinga in 1662. " Red-haired barbarians," a term now commonly applied to all foreigners, was first used in the records of the Ming dynasty to designate the Dutch.

grant of a piece of land such as a carpet would cover; and the officer above-mentioned, thinking that this could not be very large, acceded to their request. A carpet was accordingly laid down, big enough for about two people to stand on ; but by dint of stretching, it was soon enough for four or five ; and so they went on, stretching and stretching, until at last it covered about an acre, and by-and-by, with the help of their knives, they had filched a piece of ground several miles in extent.[2]

CI. CARRYING A CORPSE

A WOODSMAN who had been to market was returning home with his pole across his shoulder,[1] when suddenly he felt it become very heavy at the end behind him, and looking round he saw attached to it the headless trunk of a man. In great alarm, he got his pole quit of the burden and struck about him right and left, whereupon the body disappeared. He then hurried on to the next village, and when he arrived there in the dusk of the evening, he found several men holding lights to the ground as if looking for something. On asking what was the matter, they told him that while sitting together a man's head had fallen from the sky into their midst ; that they had noticed the hair and beard were all draggled, but in a moment the head had vanished. The woodsman then related what had happened to himself ; and thus one whole man was accounted for, though no one could tell whence he came. Subsequently, another man was carrying a basket when some one saw a man's head in it, and called out to him ; whereupon he dropped the basket in a fright, and the head rolled away and disappeared.

[2] Our author would here seem to have heard of the famous bull's hide which is mentioned in the first book of the *Æneid*. In any case, the substitution of " stretching " is no improvement on the cele-brated device by which the bull's hide was made to enclose so large a space.

[1] The common method of porterage in China is by a bamboo pole over the shoulder with well-balanced burdens hanging from each end. I have often seen children carried thus, sitting in wicker baskets ; sometimes for long journeys.

CII. A TAOIST DEVOTEE

CHÜ YAO-JU was a Ch'ing-chou man, who, when his wife died, left his home and became a priest.[1] Some years afterwards he returned, dressed in the Taoist garb, and carrying his praying-mat [2] over his shoulder ; and after staying one night he wanted to go away again. His friends, however, would not give him back his cassock and staff ; so at length he pretended to take a stroll outside the village, and when there, his clothes and other belongings came flying out of the house after him, and he got safely away.

CIII. JUSTICE FOR REBELS

DURING the reign of Shun Chih,[1] of the people of T'êng-i, seven in ten were opposed to the Manchu dynasty. The officials dared not touch them ; and subsequently, when the country became more settled, the magistrates used to distinguish them from the others by always deciding any cases in their favour : for they feared lest these men should revert to their old opposition. And thus it came about that one litigant would begin by declaring himself to have been a "rebel," while his adversary would follow up by showing such statement to be false ; so that before any case could be heard on its actual merits, it was necessary to determine the status both of plaintiff and defendant, whereby infinite labour was entailed upon the Registrars.

Now it chanced that the yamên of one of the officials was haunted by a fox, and the official's daughter was bewitched by it. Her father, therefore, engaged the services of a magician, who succeeded in capturing the animal and putting it into a bottle ; but just as he was going to commit

---

[1] It would be more usual to " renew the guitar string," as the Chinese idiom runs. In the paraphrase of the first maxim of the *Sacred Edict* we are told that " The closest of all ties is that of husband and wife ; but suppose your wife dies, why, you can marry another. But if your brother were to die," &c. &c.

[2] This, as well as the staff mentioned below, belongs to Buddhism. See No. IV., note 1.

[1] The first Manchu ruler of the Empire of China. He came to the throne in A.D. 1644.

it to the flames, the fox cried out from inside the bottle, " I'm a rebel ! " at which the bystanders were unable to suppress their laughter.

CIV. THEFT OF THE PEACH

WHEN I was a little boy I went one day to the prefectural city.[1] It was the time of the Spring festival,[2] and the custom was that on the day before, all the merchants of the place should proceed with banners and drums to the judge's yamên : this was called " bringing in the Spring." I went with a friend to see the fun ; the crowd was immense, and there sat the officials in crimson robes arranged right and left in the hall ; but I was small and didn't know who they were, my attention being attracted chiefly by the hum of voices and the noise of the drums.   In the middle of it all, a man leading a boy with his hair unplaited and hanging down his back, walked up to the dais.   He carried a pole on his shoulder, and appeared to be saying something which I couldn't hear for the noise ; I only saw the officials smile, and immediately afterwards an attendant came down, and in a loud voice ordered the man to give a performance. ' What shall it be ? " asked the man in reply ; whereupon, after some consultation between the officials on the dais, the attendant inquired what he could do best.   The man said he could invert the order of nature ; and then, after another pause, he was instructed to produce some peaches ; to this he assented ; and taking off his coat, laid it on his box, at the same time observing that they had set him a hard task, the winter frost not having broken up, and adding that he was afraid the gentlemen would be angry with him, &c., &c.   His son here reminded him that he had agreed to the task and couldn't well get out of it ; so, after fretting and grumbling awhile, he cried out, " I have it ! with snow on the ground we shall never get peaches here ; but I guess there are some up in heaven in the Royal Mother's garden,[3] and there we must try."

---

[1] It is worth noting that the author professes actually to have witnessed the following extraordinary scene.

[2] The vernal equinox, which would fall on or about the 20th of March.

[3] A fabulous lady said to reside at the summit of the K'un-lun

" How are we to get up, father ? " asked the boy ; where-upon the man said, " I have the means," and immediately proceeded to take from his box a cord some tens of feet in length. This he carefully arranged, and then threw one end of it high up into the air, where it remained as if caught by something. He now paid out the rope, which kept going up higher and higher until the end he had thrown up disappeared in the clouds and only a short piece was left in his hands. Calling his son, he then explained that he himself was too heavy, and, handing him the end of the rope, bade him go up at once. The boy, however, made some difficulty, objecting that the rope was too thin to bear his weight up to such a height, and that he would surely fall down and be killed ; upon which his father said that his promise had been given and that repentance was now too late, adding that if the peaches were obtained they would surely be rewarded with a hundred ounces of silver, which should be set aside to get the boy a pretty wife. So his son seized the rope and swarmed up, like a spider running up a thread of its web ; and in a few moments he was out of sight in the clouds. By-and-by down fell a peach as large as a basin, which the delighted father handed up to his patrons on the dais, who were some time coming to a conclusion whether it was real or imitation. But just then down came the rope with a run, and the affrighted father shrieked out, " Alas ! alas ! some one has cut the rope : what will my boy do now ? " and in another minute down fell something else, which was found on examination to be his son's head. " Ah me ! " said he, weeping bitterly and showing the head ; " the gardener has caught him, and my boy is no more." After that, his arms, and legs, and body, all came down in like manner ; and the father, gathering them up, put them in the box and said, " This was my only son, who accompanied me everywhere ; and now what a cruel fate is his. I must away and bury him." He then approached the dais and said, " Your peach, gentlemen, was obtained at the cost of my boy's life ; help me now to pay his funeral expenses,

mountain, where, on the border of the Gem Lake, grows the peach-tree of the Gods, the fruit of which confers immortality on him who eats it. For her identification with Juno, see *Adversaria Sinica*, No. 1, 1905.

and I will be ever grateful to you." The officials, who had been watching the scene in horror and amazement, forthwith collected a good purse for him ; and when he had received the money, he rapped on his box and said, " Pa-pa'rh ! why don't you come out and thank the gentlemen ? " Thereupon, there was a thump on the box from the inside, and up came the boy himself, who jumped out and bowed to the assembled company. I have never forgotten this strange trick, which I subsequently heard could be done by the White Lily sect,[4] who probably got it from this source.[5]

CV. KILLING A SERPENT

AT Ku-chi island in the eastern sea, there were camellias of all colours which bloomed throughout the year. No one, however, lived there, and very few people ever visited the spot. One day, a young man of Têng-chou, named Chang, who was fond of hunting and adventure, hearing of the beauties of the place, put together some wine and food, and rowed himself across in a small open boat. The flowers were just then even finer than usual, and their perfume was diffused for a mile or so around ; while many of the

[4] One of the most celebrated of the numerous secret societies of China, the origin of which dates back to about A.D. 1350. Its members have always been credited with a knowledge of the black art.

[5] Of Chinese jugglers, Ibn Batuta writes as follows :—" They produced a chain fifty cubits in length, and in my presence threw one end of it towards the sky, where it remained, as if fastened to something in the air. A dog was then brought forward, and, being placed at the lower end of the chain, immediately ran up, and reaching the other end immediately disappeared in the air. In the same manner a hog, a panther, a lion, and a tiger were alternately sent up the chain, and all equally disappeared at the upper end of it. At last they took down the chain, and put it into a bag, no one ever discerning in what way the different animals were made to vanish into the air in the mysterious manner above described. This, I may venture to affirm, was beyond measure strange and surprising."

A propos of which passage, Mr. Maskelyne, the prince of all black-artists, ancient or modern, says :—" These apparent effects were, doubtless, due to the aid of concave mirrors, the use of which was known to the ancients, especially in the East, but they could not have been produced in the open air."

trees he saw were several armfuls in circumference. So he
roamed about and gave himself up to enjoyment of the
scene ; and by-and-by he opened a flask of wine, regretting
very much that he had no companion to share it with him,
when all of a sudden a most beautiful young girl, with
extremely bright eyes, and dressed in red, stepped down
from one of the camellias before him.[1] "Dear me!"
said she, on seeing Mr. Chang ; "I expected to be alone
here, and was not aware that the place was already
occupied." Chang was somewhat alarmed by this apparition, and asked the young lady whence she came ; to which
she replied that her name was Chiao-ch'ang, and that she
had accompanied thither a Mr. Hai, who had gone off for
a stroll and had left her to await his return. Thereupon
Chang begged her to join him in a cup of wine, which she
very willingly did, and they were just beginning to enjoy
themselves when a sound of rushing wind was heard, and
the trees and plants bent beneath it. "Here's Mr. Hai!"
cried the young lady ; and jumping quickly up, disappeared
in a moment. The horrified Chang now beheld a huge
serpent coming out of the bushes near by, and immediately
ran behind a large tree for shelter, hoping the reptile
would not see him. But the serpent advanced and en-
veloped both Chang and the tree in its great folds, binding
Chang's arms down to his sides so as to prevent him from
moving them ; and then raising its head, darted out its
tongue and bit the poor man's nose, causing the blood to
flow freely out. This blood it was quietly sucking up,
when Chang, who thought that his last hour had come,
remembered that he had in his pocket some fox poison ;
and managing to insert a couple of fingers, he drew out
the packet, broke the paper, and let the powder lie in the
palm of his hand. He next leaned his hand over the
serpent's coils in such a way that the blood from his nose
dripped into his hand, and when it was nearly full the
serpent actually did begin to drink it. And in a few
moments the grip was relaxed ; the serpent struck the
ground heavily with its tail, and dashed away up against
another tree, which was broken in half, and then stretched
itself out and died. Chang was a long time unable to
rise, but at length he got up and carried the serpent off

[1] See No. LXXI., note 6.

with him. He was very ill for more than a month afterwards, and even suspected the young lady of being a serpent, too, in disguise.

CVI. THE RESUSCITATED CORPSE

A CERTAIN old man lived at Ts'ai-tien, in the Yang-hsin district. The village was some miles from the district city, and he and his son kept a roadside inn where travellers could pass the night. One day, as it was getting dusk, four strangers presented themselves and asked for a night's lodging ; to which the landlord replied that every bed was already occupied. The four men declared it was impossible for them to go back, and urged him to take them in somehow ; and at length the landlord said he could give them a place to sleep in if they were not too particular,—which the strangers immediately assured him they were not. The fact was that the old man's daughter-in-law had just died, and that her body was lying in the women's quarters, waiting for the coffin, which his son had gone away to buy. So the landlord led them round thither, and walking in, placed a lamp on the table. At the further end of the room lay the corpse, decked out with paper robes, &c., in the usual way ; and in the foremost section were sleeping couches for four people. The travellers were tired, and throwing themselves on the beds, were soon snoring loudly, with the exception of one of them, who was not quite off when suddenly he heard a creaking of the trestles on which the dead body was laid out, and opening his eyes, he saw by the light of the lamp in front of the corpse that the girl was raising the coverings from her and preparing to get down. In another moment she was on the floor and advancing towards the sleepers. Her face was of a light yellow hue, and she had a silk kerchief round her head ; and when she reached the beds, she blew on the other three travellers, whereupon the fourth, in a great fright, stealthily drew up the bed-clothes over his face, and held his breath to listen. He heard her breathe on him as she had done on the others, and then heard her go back again and get under the paper robes, which rustled distinctly as she did so. He now put out his head to take a peep, and saw that she was lying down as before; whereupon, not daring to make any noise, he stretched forth his foot and kicked his companions, who, however, showed no signs of moving. He now determined to put on his clothes and make a bolt for it; but he had hardly begun to do so before he heard the creaking sound again, which sent him back under the bed-clothes as fast as he could go. Again the girl came to him, and, breathing several times on him, went away to lie down as before, as he could tell by the noise of the trestles. He then put his hand very gently out of bed, and, seizing his trousers, got quickly into them, jumped up with a bound, and rushed out of the place as fast as his legs would carry him. The corpse, too, jumped up; but by this time the traveller had already drawn the bolt, and was outside the door, running along and shrieking at the top of his voice, with the corpse following close behind. No one seemed to hear him, and he was afraid to knock at the door of the inn for fear they should not let him in in time; so he made for the highway to the city, and after awhile he saw a monastery by the roadside, and, hearing the " wooden fish," [1] he ran up and thumped with all his might at the gate. The priest, however, did not know what to make of it, and would not open to him; and as the corpse was only a few yards off, he could do nothing but run behind a tree which stood close by, and there shelter himself, dodging to the right as the corpse dodged to the left, and so on. This infuriated the dead girl to madness; and at length, as tired and panting they stood watching each other on opposite sides of the tree, the corpse made a rush forward with one arm on each side in the hope of thus grabbing its victim. The traveller, however, fell backwards and escaped, while the corpse remained rigidly embracing the tree. By-and-by the priest, who had been listening from the inside, hearing no sounds for some time, came out and found the traveller lying senseless on the ground; whereupon he had him carried into the monastery, and by morning they had got him round

[1] This instrument, used by Buddhist priests in the musical accompaniment to their liturgies, is said to be so called because a fish never closes its eyes, and is therefore a fit model of vigilance to him who would walk in the paths of holiness and virtue.

again. After giving him a little broth to drink, he related the whole story ; and then in the early dawn they went out to examine the tree, to which they found the girl tightly fixed. The news being sent to the magistrate, that functionary attended at once in person,[2] and gave orders to remove the body ; but this they were at first unable to do, the girl's fingers having penetrated into the bark so far that her nails were not to be seen. At length they got her away, and then a messenger was despatched to the inn, already in a state of great commotion over the three travellers, who had been found dead in their beds. The old man accordingly sent to fetch his daughter-in-law ; and the surviving traveller petitioned the magistrate, saying, " Four of us left home, but only one will go back. Give me something that I may show to my fellow-townsmen." So the magistrate gave him a certificate and sent him home again.[3]

CVII. THE FISHERMAN AND HIS FRIEND

IN the northern parts of Tzŭ-chou there lived a man named Hsü, a fisherman by trade. Every night when he went to fish, he would carry some wine with him, and drink and fish by turns, always taking care to pour out a libation on the ground, accompanied by the following invocation —" Drink too, ye drowned spirits of the river ! " Such was his regular custom ; and it was also noticeable that, even on occasions when the other fishermen caught nothing, he always got a full basket. One night, as he was sitting drinking by himself, a young man suddenly appeared and began walking up and down near him. Hsü offered him a cup of wine, which was readily accepted, and they remained chatting together throughout the night, Hsü meanwhile not catching a single fish. However, just as he was giving up all hope of doing anything, the young man rose and said he would go a little way down the stream and beat them up towards Hsü, which he accordingly did, returning in a few minutes and warning him to be on the

[2] The duties of Coroner belong to the office of a District Magistrate in China.

[3] Without such certificate he would be liable to be involved in trouble and annoyance at the will of any unfriendly neighbour.

look-out. Hsü now heard a noise like that of a shoal coming up the stream, and, casting his net, made a splendid haul,—all that he caught being over a foot in length. Greatly delighted, he now prepared to go home, first offering his companion a share of the fish, which the latter declined, saying that he had often received kindnesses from Mr. Hsü, and that he would be only too happy to help him regularly in the same manner if Mr. Hsü would accept his assistance. The latter replied that he did not recollect ever meeting him before, and that he should be much obliged for any aid the young man might choose to afford him, regretting, at the same time, his inability to make him any adequate return. He then asked the young man his name and surname ; and the young man said his surname was Wang, adding that Hsü might address him when they met as Wang Liu-lang, he having no other name. Thereupon they parted, and the next day Hsü sold his fish and bought some more wine, with which he repaired as usual to the river-bank. There he found his companion already awaiting him, and they spent the night together in precisely the same way as the preceding one, the young man beating up the fish for him as before. This went on for some months, until at length one evening the young man, with many expressions of his thanks and his regrets, told Hsü that they were about to part for ever. Much alarmed by the melancholy tone in which his friend had communicated this news, Hsü was on the point of asking for an explanation, when the young man stopped him, and himself proceeded as follows :—" The friendship that has grown up between us is truly surprising, and, now that we shall meet no more, there is no harm in telling you the whole truth. I am a disembodied spirit— the soul of one who was drowned in this river when tipsy. I have been here many years, and your former success in fishing was due to the fact that I used secretly to beat up the fish towards you, in return for the libations you were accustomed to pour out. To-morrow my time is up : my substitute will arrive, and I shall be born again in the world of mortals.[1] We have but this one evening left, and I therefore take advantage of it to express my feelings to you." On hearing these words, Hsü was at

[1] See No. XLV., note 8.

first very much alarmed; however, he had grown so accustomed to his friend's society, that his fears soon passed away; and, filling up a goblet, he said, with a sigh, "Liu-lang, old fellow, drink this up, and away with melancholy. It's hard to lose you; but I'm glad enough for your sake, and won't think of my own sorrow." He then inquired of Liu-lang who was to be his substitute; to which the latter replied, "Come to the river-bank to-morrow afternoon and you'll see a woman drowned: she is the one." Just then the village cocks began to crow, and, with tears in their eyes, the two friends bade each other farewell.

Next day Hsü waited on the river-bank to see if anything would happen, and lo! a woman carrying a child in her arms came along. When close to the edge of the river, she stumbled and fell into the water, managing, however, to throw the child safely on to the bank, where it lay kicking and sprawling and crying at the top of its voice. The woman herself sank and rose several times, until at last she succeeded in clutching hold of the bank and pulled herself, dripping, out; and then, after resting awhile, she picked up the child and went on her way. All this time Hsü had been in a great state of excitement, and was on the point of running to help the woman out of the water; but he remembered that she was to be the substitute of his friend, and accordingly restrained himself from doing so.[2] Then when he saw the woman get out by herself,

---

[2] We have in this story the keynote to the notorious and much-to-be-deprecated dislike of the Chinese people to assist in saving the lives of drowning strangers. Some of our readers may, perhaps, not be aware that the Government of Hong-Kong has found it necessary to insert a clause on the junk-clearances issued in that colony, by which the junkmen are bound to assist to the utmost in saving life. The apparent apathy of the Chinese in this respect comes before us, however, in quite a different light when coupled with the superstition that disembodied spirits of persons who have met a violent death may return to the world of mortals if only fortunate enough to secure a substitute. For among the crowd of shades, anxious all to revisit their "sweet sons," may perchance be some dear relative or friend of the man who stands calmly by while another is drowning; and it may be that to assist the drowning stranger would be to take the longed-for chance away from one's own kith and kin. Therefore, the superstition-ridden Chinaman turns away, often perhaps, as in the story before us, with feelings of pity and remorse. And yet this belief has not prevented the

he began to suspect that Liu-lang's words had not been fulfilled. That night he went to fish as usual, and before long the young man arrived and said, "We meet once again : there is no need now to speak of separation." Hsü asked him how it was so; to which he replied, "The woman you saw had already taken my place, but I could not bear to hear the child cry, and I saw that my one life would be purchased at the expense of their two lives, wherefore I let her go, and now I cannot say when I shall have another chance.[3] The union of our destinies may not yet be worked out." "Alas!" sighed Hsü, "this noble conduct of yours is enough to move God Almighty."

After this the two friends went on much as they had done before, until one day Liu-lang again said he had come to bid Hsü farewell. Hsü thought he had found another substitute, but Liu-lang told him that his former behaviour had so pleased Almighty Heaven, that he had been appointed guardian angel of Wu-chên, in the Chao-yüan district, and that on the following morning he would start for his new post. "And if you do not forget the days of our friendship," added he, "I pray you come and see me, in spite of the long journey." "Truly," replied Hsü, "you well deserved to be made a God ; but the paths of Gods and men lie in different directions, and even if the distance were nothing, how should I manage to meet you again ? " "Don't be afraid on that score," said Liu-lang, "but come ; " and then he went away, and Hsü returned home. The latter immediately began to prepare for the journey, which caused his wife to laugh at him and say, " Supposing you do find such a place at the end of that long journey, you won't be able to hold a conversation with a clay image." Hsü, however, paid no attention to her remarks, and

establishment, especially on the river Yang-tsze, of institutions provided with lifeboats, for the express purpose of saving life in those dangerous waters ; so true is it that when the Chinese people wish to move *en masse* in any given direction, the fragile barrier of superstition is trampled down and scattered to the winds.

[3] As there are good and bad foxes, so may devils be beneficent or malicious according to circumstances ; and Chinese apologists for the discourtesy of the term " foreign devils," as applied to Europeans and Americans alike, have gone so far as to declare that in this particular instance the allusion is to the more virtuous among the denizens of the Infernal Regions.

travelled straight to Chao-yüan, where he learned from
the inhabitants that there really was a village called Wu-
chên, whither he forthwith proceeded and took up his abode
at an inn. He then inquired of the landlord where the
village temple was ; to which the latter replied by asking
him somewhat hurriedly if he was speaking to Mr. Hsü.
Hsü informed him that his name was Hsü, asking in reply
how he came to know it ; whereupon the landlord further
inquired if his native place was not Tzŭ-chou. Hsü told
him it was, and again asked him how he knew all this ; to
which the landlord made no answer, but rushed out of the
room ; and in a few moments the place was crowded with
old and young, men, women, and children, all come to
visit Hsü. They then told him that a few nights before
they had seen their guardian deity in a vision, and he
had informed them that Mr. Hsü would shortly arrive,
and had bidden them to provide him with travelling expenses, &c. Hsü was very much astonished at this, and
went off at once to the shrine, where he invoked his friend
as follows :—" Ever since we parted I have had you daily
and nightly in my thoughts ; and now that I have fulfilled
my promise of coming to see you, I have to thank you for
the orders you have issued to the people of the place. As
for me, I have nothing to offer you but a cup of wine, which
I pray you accept as though we were drinking together
on the river-bank." He then burnt a quantity of paper
money,[4] when lo ! a wind suddenly arose, which, after
whirling round and round behind the shrine, soon dropped,
and all was still. That night Hsü dreamed that his friend
came to him, dressed in his official cap and robes, and very
different in appearance from what he used to be, and thanked
him, saying, " It is truly kind of you to visit me thus : I
only regret that my position makes me unable to meet you
face to face, and that though near we are still so far. The
people here will give you a trifle, which pray accept for
my sake ; and when you go away, I will see you a short
way on your journey." A few days afterwards Hsü prepared to start, in spite of the numerous invitations to
stay which poured in upon him from all sides ; and then
the inhabitants loaded him with presents of all kinds, and
escorted him out of the village. There a whirlwind arose
and accompanied him several miles, when he turned round

4 See No. XCVII., note 7.

and invoked his friend thus :—" Liu-lang, take care of
your valued person. Do not trouble yourself to come any
farther.[5] Your noble heart will ensure happiness to this
district, and there is no occasion for me to give a word
of advice to my old friend." By-and-by the whirlwind
ceased, and the villagers, who were much astonished,
returned to their own homes. Hsü, too, travelled home-
wards, and being now a man of some means, ceased to
work any more as a fisherman. And whenever he met a
Chao-yüan man he would ask him about that guardian
angel, being always informed in reply that he was a most
beneficent God. Some say the place was Shih-k'êng-
chuang, in Chang-ch'in : I can't say which it was myself.

CVIII. THE PRIEST'S WARNING

A MAN named Chang died suddenly, and was escorted at
once by devil-lictors [1] into the presence of the King of
Purgatory. His Majesty turned to Chang's record of
good and evil, and then, in great anger, told the lictors
they had brought the wrong man, and bade them take him
back again. As they left the judgment-hall, Chang persuaded his escort to let him have a look at Purgatory ;
and, accordingly, the devils conducted him through the
nine sections,[2] pointing out to him the Knife Hill,[3] the
Sword Tree, and other objects of interest. By-and-by,
they reached a place where there was a Buddhist priest,
hanging suspended in the air head downwards, by a rope
through a hole in his leg. He was shrieking with pain,
and longing for death ; and when Chang approached,
lo ! he saw that it was his own brother. In great distress,
he asked his guides the reason of this punishment ; and
they informed him that the priest was suffering thus for
collecting subscriptions on behalf of his order, and then

[5] A phrase constantly repeated, in other terms, by a guest to a
host who is politely escorting him to the door.
[1] The spiritual lictors who are supposed to arrest the souls of
dying persons are also believed to be armed with warrants signed
and sealed in due form as in the world above.
[2] Literally, the " nine dark places," which will remind readers of
Dante of the nine " bolgie " of the *Inferno*.
[3] This is a cliff over which sinners are hurled, to alight upon the
upright points of knives below. The branches of the Sword Tree
are sharp blades which cut and hack all who pass within reach.

privately squandering the proceeds in gambling and debauchery.[4] "Nor," added they, "will he escape this torment unless he repents him of his misdeeds." When Chang came round,[5] he thought his brother was already dead, and hurried off to the Hsing-fu monastery, to which the latter belonged. As he went in at the door, he heard a loud shrieking; and, on proceeding to his brother's room, he found him laid up with a very bad abscess in his leg, the leg itself being tied up above him to the wall, this being, as his brother informed him, the only bearable position in which he could lie. Chang now told him what he had seen in Purgatory, at which the priest was so terrified, that he at once gave up taking wine and meat,[6] and devoted himself entirely to religious exercises. In a fortnight he was well, and was known ever afterwards as a most exemplary priest.

CIX. METEMPSYCHOSIS

MR. LIN, who took his master's degree in the same year as the late Mr. Wên Pi,[1] could remember what had happened to him in his previous state of existence, and once told the whole story, as follows :—I was originally of a good family, but, after leading a very dissolute life, I died at the age of sixty-two. On being conducted into the presence of the King of Purgatory, he received me civilly, bade me be seated, and offered me a cup of tea. I noticed, however, that the tea in His Majesty's cup was clear and limpid, while that in my own was muddy, like the lees of wine. It then flashed across me that this was the potion which was given to all disembodied spirits to render them oblivious of the past :[2] and, accordingly, when the King was looking

---

[4] Crimes by no means unknown to the clergy of China.
[5] That is, when the lictors had returned his soul to its tenement.
[6] See No. VI., note 2. [1] In A.D. 1621.
[2] According to the *Yü li ch'ao* (see *Appendix*, 10th Court), this potion is administered by an old beldame, named Mother Mêng, who sits upon the Terrace of Oblivion. "Whether they swallow much or little it matters not; but sometimes there are perverse devils who altogether refuse to drink. Then beneath their feet sharp blades start up, and a copper tube is forced down their throats, by which means they are compelled to swallow some."

the other way, I seized the opportunity of pouring it under the table, pretending afterwards that I had drunk it all up. My record of good and evil was now presented for inspection, and when the King saw what it was, he flew into a great passion, and ordered the attendant devils to drag me away, and send me back to earth as a horse. I was immediately seized and bound, and the devils carried me off to a house, the door-sill of which was so high I could not step over it. While I was trying to do so, the devils behind lashed me with all their might, causing me such pain that I made a great spring, and—lo and behold! I was a horse in a stable. " The mare has got a nice colt," I then heard a man call out ; but, although I was perfectly aware of all that was passing, I could say nothing myself. Hunger now came upon me, and I was glad to be suckled by the mare ; and by the end of four or five years I had grown into a fine strong horse, dreadfully afraid of the whip, and running away at the very sight of it. When my master rode me, it was always with a saddle cloth, and at a leisurely pace, which was bearable enough ; but when the servants mounted me barebacked, and dug their heels into me, the pain struck into my vitals ; and at length I refused all food, and in three days I died. Reappearing before the King of Purgatory, His Majesty was enraged to find that I had thus tried to shirk working out my time ; and, flaying me forthwith, condemned me to go back again as a dog. And when I did not move, the devils came behind me and lashed me until I ran away from them into the open country, where, thinking I had better die right off, I jumped over a cliff, and lay at the bottom unable to move. I then saw that I was among a litter of puppies, and that an old bitch was licking and suckling me by turns ; whereby I knew that I was once more among mortals. In this hateful form I continued for some time, longing to kill myself, and yet fearing to incur the penalty of skirking. At length, I purposely bit my master in the leg, and tore him badly ; whereupon he had me destroyed, and I was taken again into the presence of the King, who was so displeased with my vicious behaviour that he condemned me to become a snake, and shut me up in a dark room, where I could see nothing. After a while I managed to climb up the wall, bore a hole in the roof, and escape; and immediately I found myself lying in the grass, a veritable snake. Then I registered a vow that I would harm no living thing, and I lived for some years, feeding upon berries and suchlike, ever remembering neither to take my own life, nor by injuring any one to incite them to take it, but longing all the while for the happy release, which did not come to me. One day, as I was sleeping in the grass, I heard the noise of a passing cart, and, on trying to get across the road out of its way, I was caught by the wheel, and cut in two. The King was astonished to see me back so soon, but I humbly told my story, and, in pity for the innocent creature that loses its life, he pardoned me, and permitted me to be born again at my appointed time as a human being.

Such was Mr. Lin's story. He could speak as soon as he came into the world; and could repeat anything he had once read. In the year 1621 he took his master's degree, and was never tired of telling people to put saddle-cloths on their horses, and recollect that the pain of being gripped by the knees is even worse than the lash itself.

CX. THE FORTY STRINGS OF CASH

MR. JUSTICE WANG had a steward, who was possessed of considerable means. One night the latter dreamt that a man rushed in and said to him, " To-day you must repay me those forty strings of cash." The steward asked who he was; to which the man made no answer, but hurried past him into the women's apartments. When the steward awoke, he found that his wife had been delivered of a son; and, knowing at once that retribution was at hand, he set aside forty strings of cash to be spent solely in food, clothes, medicines, and so on, for the baby. By the time the child was between three and four years old, the steward found that of the forty strings only about seven hundred cash remained; and when the wet-nurse, who happened to be standing by, brought the child and dandled it in her arms before him, he looked at it and said, " The forty strings are all but repaid; it is time you were off again." Thereupon the child changed colour; its head fell back, and its eyes stared fixedly, and, when they tried to revive it, lo ! respiration had already ceased. The father then took the balance of the forty strings, and with it defrayed the child's funeral expenses—truly a warning to people to be sure and pay their debts.

Formerly, an old childless man consulted a great many Buddhist priests on the subject. One of them said to him, " If you owe no one anything, and no one owes you anything, how can you expect to have children ? A good son is the repayment of a former debt ; a bad son is a dunning creditor, at whose birth there is no rejoicing, at whose death no lamentations." [1]

CXI. SAVING LIFE

A CERTAIN gentleman of Shên-yu, who had taken the highest degree, could remember himself in a previous state of existence. He said he had formerly been a scholar, and had died in middle life ; and that when he appeared before the Judge of Purgatory, there stood the cauldrons, the boiling oil, and other apparatus of torture, exactly as we read about them on earth. In the eastern corner of the hall were a number of frames from which hung the skins of sheep, dogs, oxen, horses, &c. ; and when anybody was condemned to reappear in life under any one of these forms, his skin was stripped off and a skin was taken from the proper frame and fixed on to his body. The gentleman of whom I am writing heard himself sentenced to become a sheep ; and the attendant devils had already clothed him in a sheep's skin in the manner above described, when the clerk of the record informed the Judge that the criminal before him had once saved another man's life. The Judge consulted his books, and forthwith cried out, " I pardon him ; for although his sins have been many, this one act has redeemed them all." [1] The devils then tried to take off the sheep's skin, but it was so tightly stuck on him

---

[1] And such is actually the prevalent belief in China to this day.
[1] Note 2 to No. CVII. should be read here. To save life is indeed the bounden duty of every good Buddhist, for which he will be proportionately rewarded in the world to come.

that they couldn't move it. However, after great efforts, and causing the gentleman most excruciating agony, they managed to tear it off bit by bit, though not quite so cleanly as one might have wished. In fact, a piece as big as the palm of a man's hand was left near his shoulder ; and when he was born again into the world, there was a great patch of hair on his back, which grew again as fast as it was cut off.

CXII. THE SALT SMUGGLER

WANG SHIH, of Kao-wan, a petty salt huckster, was inordinately fond of gambling. One night he was arrested by two men, whom he took for lictors of the Salt Gabelle ; and, flinging down what salt he had with him, he tried to make his escape.[1] He found, however, that his legs would not move with him, and he was forthwith seized and bound. " We are not sent by the Salt Commissioner," cried his captors, in reply to an entreaty to set him free ; " we are the devil-constables of Purgatory." Wang was horribly frightened at this, and begged the devils to let him bid farewell to his wife and children ; but this they refused to do, saying, " You aren't going to die ; you are only wanted for a little job there is down below." Wang asked what the job was ; to which the devils replied, " A new Judge has come into office, and, finding the river[2] and the eighteen hells choked up with the bodies of sinners, he

---

[1] Salt is a Government monopoly in China, and its sale is only permitted to licensed dealers. It is a contraband article of commerce, whether for import or export, to foreign nations trading with China. In an account of a journey from Swatow to Canton in March–April, 1877, I wrote :—" À propos of salt, we came across a good-sized bunker of it when stowing away our things in the space below the deck. The boatmen could not resist the temptation of doing a little smuggling on the way up. . . . At a secluded point in a bamboo-shaded bend of the river, they ran the boat alongside the bank, and were instantly met by a number of suspicious-looking gentlemen with baskets, who soon relieved them of the smuggled salt and separated in different directions." Thus do the people of China seek to lighten the grievous pressure of this tax. A curious custom exists in Canton. Certain blind old men and women are allowed to hawk salt about the streets, and earn a scanty living from the profits they are able to make.

[2] The Styx.

has determined to employ three classes of mortals to clean them out. These are thieves, unlicensed founders,[3] and unlicensed dealers in salt, and, for the dirtiest work of all, he is going to take musicians." [4]

Wang accompanied the devils until at length they reached a city, where he was brought before the Judge, who was sitting in his Judgment-hall. On turning up his record in the books, one of the devils explained that the prisoner had been arrested for unlicensed trading ; whereupon the Judge became very angry, and said, " Those who drive an illicit trade in salt, not only defraud the State of its proper revenue, but also prey upon the livelihood of the people. Those, however, whom the greedy officials and corrupt traders of to-day denounce as unlicensed traders, are among the most virtuous of mankind—needy unfortunates who struggle to save a few cash in the purchase of their pint of salt.[5] Are they your unlicensed traders ? " The Judge then bade the lictors buy four pecks of salt, and send it to Wang's house for him, together with that which had been found upon him ; and, at the same time, he gave Wang an iron scourge, and told him to superintend the works at the river. So Wang followed the devils, and

---

[3] These words require some explanation. Ordinarily they would be taken in the sense of casting *cash* of a base description ; but they might equally well signify the casting of iron articles of any kind, and thereby hang some curious details. Iron foundries in China may only be. opened under license from the local officials, and the articles there made, consisting chiefly of cooking utensils, may only be sold within a given area, each district having its own particular foundries, from which alone the supplies of the neighbourhood may be derived. Free trade in iron is much feared by the authorities, as thereby pirates and rebels would be enabled to supply themselves with arms. At the framing of the Treaty of Tientsin, with its accompanying tariff and rules, iron was not specified among other prohibited articles of commerce. Consequently, British merchants would appear to have a full right to purchase iron in the interior and convey it to any of the open ports under Transit-pass. But the Chinese officials steadily refuse to acknowledge, or permit the exercise of, this right, putting forward their own time-honoured custom with regard to iron, and enumerating the disadvantages to China were such an innovation to be brought about.

[4] The allusion is to women, of a not very respectable class.

[5] No Chinese magistrate would pass sentence upon a man who stole food under stress of hunger, even if such a criminal were ever brought before him.

found the river swarming with people like ants in an ant-hill. The water was turbid and red, the stench from it being almost unbearable, while those who were employed in cleaning it out were working there naked. Sometimes they would sink down in the horrid mass of decaying bodies : sometimes they would get lazy, and then the iron scourge was applied to their backs. The assistant-superintendents had small scented balls, which they held in their mouths. Wang himself approached the bank, and saw the licensed salt-merchant of Kao-wan [6] in the midst of it all, and thrashed him well with his scourge, until he was afraid he would never come up again. This went on for three days and three nights, by which time half the workmen were dead, and the work completed ; where-upon the same two devils escorted him home again, and then he waked up.

As a matter of fact, Wang had gone out to sell some salt, and had not come back. Next morning, when his wife opened the house door, she found two bags of salt in the court-yard ; and, as her husband did not return, she sent off some people to search for him, and they discovered him lying senseless by the wayside. He was immediately conveyed home, where, after a little time, he recovered consciousness, and related what had taken place. Strange to say, the licensed salt-merchant had fallen down in a fit on the previous evening, and had only just recovered ; and Wang, hearing that his body was covered with sores— the result of the beating with the iron scourge—went off to his house to see him ; however, directly the wretched man set eyes on Wang, he hastily covered himself up with the bed-clothes, forgetting that they were no longer at the infernal river. He did not recover from his injuries for a year, after which he retired from trade.[7]

[6] His own village.

[7] The whole story is meant as a satire upon the iniquity of the Salt Gabelle.

CXIII. COLLECTING SUBSCRIPTIONS

THE FROG-GOD frequently employs a magician to deliver its oracles to those who have faith. Should the magician declare that the God is pleased, happiness is sure to follow ; but if he says the God is angry, women and children [1] sit sorrowfully about, and neglect even their meals. Such is the customary belief, and it is probably not altogether devoid of foundation.

There was a certain wealthy merchant, named Chou, who was a very stingy man. Once, when some repairs were necessary to the temple of the God of War,[2] and rich and poor were subscribing as much as each could afford, he alone gave nothing.[3] By-and-by the works were stopped for want of funds, and the committee of management were at a loss what to do next. It happened that just then there was a festival in honour of the Frog-God, at which

[1] The chief supporters of superstition in China.
[2] See No. I., note 4.
[3] Such is one of the most common causes of hostile demonstration against Chinese Christians. The latter, acting under the orders of the missionaries, frequently refuse to subscribe to the various local celebrations and processions, the great annual festivities, and ceremonies of all kinds, on the grounds that these are idolatrous and forbidden by the Christian faith. Hence bad feeling, high words, blows, and sometimes bloodshed. I say "frequently," because many cases have come to light in which converts have quietly subscribed like other people rather than risk an *emeute*.

An amusing incident came under my own special notice not very long ago. A missionary appeared before me one day to complain that a certain convert of his had been posted in his own village, and cut off from his civic rights for two years, merely because he had agreed to let a room of his house to be used as a missionary *dépôt*. I took a copy of the placard which was handed to me in proof of this statement, and found it to run thus :—" In consequence of —— having entered into an agreement with a barbarian pastor, to lease to the said barbarian pastor a room in his house to be used as a missionary chapel, we, the elders of this village, do hereby debar —— from the privilege of worshipping in our ancestral hall for the space of two years." It is needless, of course, to mention that Ancestral Worship is (or was) prohibited by all sects of missionaries in China alike ; or that, when I pointed this out to the individual in question, who could not have understood the import of the Chinese placard, the charge was promptly withdrawn.

the magician suddenly cried out, "General Chou [4] has given orders for a further subscription. Bring forth the books." The people all shouting assent to this, the magician went on to say, "Those who have already subscribed will not be compelled to do so again ; those who have not subscribed must give according to their means." Thereupon various persons began to put down their names, and when this was finished, the magician examined the books. He then asked if Mr. Chou was present ; and the latter, who was skulking behind, in dread lest he should be detected by the God, had no alternative but to come to the front. "Put yourself down for one hundred taels," said the magician to him ; and when Chou hesitated, he cried out to him in anger, "You could give two hundred for your own bad purposes : how much more should you do so in a good cause ? " alluding to a scandalous intrigue of Chou's, the consequences of which he had averted by payment of the sum mentioned. This put our friend to the blush, and he was obliged to enter his name for one hundred taels, at which his wife was very angry, and said the magician was a rogue, and whenever he came to collect the money he was put off with some excuse.

Shortly afterwards, Chou was one day going to sleep, when he heard a noise outside his house, like the blowing of an ox, and beheld a huge frog walking leisurely through the front door, which was just big enough to let it pass. Once inside, the creature laid itself down to sleep, with its head on the threshold, to the great horror of all the inmates ; upon which Chou observed that it had probably come to collect his subscription, and, burning some incense, he vowed that he would pay down thirty taels on the spot, and send the balance later on. The frog, however, did not move, so Chou promised fifty, and then there was a slight decrease in the frog's size. Another twenty brought it down to the size of a peck measure ; and when Chou said the full amount should be paid on the spot, the frog became suddenly no larger than one's fist, and disappeared through a hole in the wall. Chou immediately sent off fifty taels,

---

[4] An historical character who was formerly among the ranks of the Yellow Turban rebels, but subsequently entered the service of Kuan Yü (see No. I., note 4), and was canonised by an Emperor of the last dynasty.

at which all the other subscribers were much astonished, not knowing what had taken place. A few days afterwards the magician said Chou still owed fifty taels, and that he had better send it in soon ; so Chou forwarded ten more, hoping now to have done with the matter. However, as he and his wife were one day sitting down to dinner, the frog reappeared, and, glaring with anger, took up a position on the bed, which creaked under it, as though unable to bear the weight. Putting its head on the pillow, the frog went off to sleep, its body gradually swelling up until it was as big as a buffalo, and nearly filled the room, causing Chou to send off the balance of his subscription without a moment's delay. There was now no diminution in the size of the frog's body ; and by-and-by crowds of small frogs came hopping in, boring through the walls, jumping on the bed, catching flies on the cooking-stove, and dying in the saucepans, until the place was quite unbearable. Three days passed thus, and then Chou sought out the magician, and asked him what was to be done. The latter said he could manage it, and began by vowing on behalf of Chou twenty more taels' subscription. At this the frog raised its head, and a further increase caused it to move one foot ; and by the time a hundred taels was reached, the frog was walking out of the door. At the door, however, it stopped, and lay down once more, which the magician explained by saying, that immediate payment was required ; so Chou handed over the amount at once, and the frog, shrinking down to its usual size, mingled with its companions, and departed with them.

The repairs to the temple were accordingly completed, but for " lighting the eyes," [5] and the attendant festivities,

[5] This curious ceremony is the final touch to a newly-built or newly-restored temple, and consists in giving expression to the eyes of the freshly-painted idols, which have been purposely left blank by the painter. Up to that time these blocks of clay or wood are not supposed to have been animated by the spiritual presence of the deity in question ; but no sooner are the eyes lighted than the gratified God smiles down upon the handsome decorations thus provided by devout and trusting suppliants.

There is a cognate custom belonging to the ceremonies of ancestral worship, of great importance in the eyes of the Chinese. On a certain day after the death of a parent, the surviving head of the family proceeds with much solemnity to dab a spot of ink upon the

some further subscriptions were wanted. Suddenly, the
magician, pointing at the managers, cried out, "There is
money short ; of fifteen men, two of you are defaulters."
At this, all declared they had given what they could afford ;
but the magician went on to say, "It is not a question
of what you can afford ; you have misappropriated the
funds [6] that should not have been touched, and misfortune
would come upon you, but that, in return for your exertions,
I shall endeavour to avert it from you. The magician
himself is not without taint.[7] Let him set you a good
example." Thereupon, the magician rushed into his
house, and brought out all the money he had, saying,
"I stole eight taels myself, which I will now refund." He
then weighed what silver he had, and finding that it only
amounted to a little over six taels, he made one of the
bystanders take a note of the difference. Then the others
came forward and paid up, each what he had misappropriated from the public fund. All this time the magician
had been in a divine ecstasy, not knowing what he was
saying ; and when he came round, and was told what
had happened, his shame knew no bounds, so he pawned
some of his clothes, and paid in the balance of his own
debt. As to the two defaulters who did not pay, one of
them was ill for a month and more ; while the other
had a bad attack of boils.

memorial tablet of the deceased. This is believed to give to the
departed spirit the power of remaining near to, and watching over
the fortunes of, those left behind.

[6] Such indeed is the fate of a percentage of all public subscriptions raised and handled by Chinese of no matter what class. An
application was once made to me for a donation to a native found-
ling hospital at Swatow, on the ground that I was known as a
"read (Chinese) book man," and that consequently other persons,
both Chinese and foreigners, might be induced to follow my example.
On my declining to subscribe, the manager of the concern informed
me that if I would only put down my name for fifty dollars, say
£10, no call should be made upon me for the money ! What a
blessing it is to live in Christian England, where peculation and
corruption are unknown !

[7] The reader must recollect that these are the words of the God,
speaking from the magician's body.

CXIV. TAOIST MIRACLES

At Chi-nan Fu there lived a certain priest : I cannot say whence he came, or what was his name. Winter and summer alike he wore but one unlined robe, and a yellow girdle about his waist, with neither shirt nor trousers. He combed his hair with a broken comb, holding the ends in his mouth, like the strings of a hat. By day he wandered about the market-place ; at night he slept in the street, and to a distance of several feet round where he lay, the ice and snow would melt. When he first arrived at Chi-nan he used to perform miracles, and the people vied with each other in making him presents. One day a disreputable young fellow gave him a quantity of wine, and begged him in return to divulge the secret of his power ; and when the priest refused, the young man watched him get into the river to bathe, and then ran off with his clothes. The priest called out to him to bring them back, promising that he would do as the young man required ; but the latter, distrusting the priest's good faith, refused to do so ; whereupon the priest's girdle was forthwith changed into a snake, several spans in circumference, which coiled itself round its new master's head, and glared and hissed terribly. The young man now fell on his knees, and humbly prayed the priest to save his life ; at which the priest put his girdle on again, and a snake that had appeared to be his girdle, wriggled away and disappeared. The priest's fame was thus firmly established, and the gentry and officials of the place were constantly inviting him to join them in their festive parties. By-and-by the priest said he was going to invite his entertainers to a return feast ;[1] and at the appointed time each one of them found on his table a formal invitation to a banquet at the Water Pavilion, but no one knew who had brought the letters. However, they all went, and were met at the door by the priest, in his usual garb ; and when they got inside, the place was all desolate and bare, with no banquet ready. " I'm afraid I shall be obliged to ask you gentlemen to let me use your attendants," said the priest to

---

[1] It is considered a serious breach of Chinese etiquette to accept invitations without returning the compliment at an early date.

his guests; "I am a poor man, and keep no servants myself." To this all readily consented; whereupon the priest drew a double door upon the wall, and rapped upon it with his knuckles. Somebody answered from within, and immediately the door was thrown open, and a splendid array of handsome chairs, and tables loaded with exquisite viands and costly wines, burst upon the gaze of the astonished guests. The priest bade the attendants receive all these things from the door, and bring them outside, cautioning them on no account to speak with the people inside; and thus a most luxurious entertainment was provided, to the great amazement of all present.

Now this Pavilion stood upon the bank of a small lake, and every year, at the proper season, it was literally covered with lilies; but, at the time of this feast, the weather was cold, and the surface of the lake was of a smoky green colour. "It's a pity," said one of the guests, "that the lilies are not out"—a sentiment in which the others very cordially agreed, when suddenly a servant came running in to say that, at that moment, the lake was a perfect mass of lilies. Every one jumped up directly, and ran to look out of the window, and, lo! it was so; and in another minute the fragrant perfume of the flowers was borne towards them by the breeze. Hardly knowing what to make of this strange sight, they sent off some servants, in a boat, to gather a few of the lilies, but they soon returned empty-handed, saying, that the flowers seemed to shift their position as fast as they rowed towards them; at which the priest laughed, and said, "These are but the lilies of your imagination, and have no real existence." And later on, when the wine was finished, the flowers began to droop and fade; and by-and-by a breeze from the north carried off every sign of them, leaving the lake as it had been before.

A certain Taot'ai,[2] at Chi-nan, was much taken with this priest, and gave him rooms at his yamên. One day he had some friends to dinner, and set before them some

---

[2] A high Chinese official, known to foreigners as Intendant of Circuit; the circuit being a circuit of Prefectures, over which he has full control, subject only to the approval of the highest provincial authorities. It is with this functionary that foreign Consuls rank.

very choice old wine that he had, and of which he only brought out a small quantity at a time, not wishing to get through it too rapidly. The guests, however, liked it so much that they asked for more ; upon which the Taot'ai said, " he was very sorry but it was all finished." The priest smiled at this, and said, " I can give the gentlemen some, if they will oblige me by accepting it ; " and immediately inserted the wine-kettle [3] in his sleeve, bringing it out again directly, and pouring out for the guests. This wine tasted exactly like the choice wine they had just been drinking, and the priest gave them all as much of it as they wanted, which made the Taot'ai suspect that something was wrong ; so, after the dinner, he went into his cellar to look at his own stock, when he found the jars closely tied down, with unbroken seals, but one and all empty. In a great rage, he caused the priest to be arrested for sorcery, and proceeded to have him bambooed ; but no sooner had the bamboo touched the priest than the Taot'ai himself felt a sting of pain, which increased at every blow ; and, in a few moments, there was the priest writhing and shrieking under every cut,[4] while the Taot'ai was sitting in a pool of blood. Accordingly, the punishment was soon stopped, and the priest was commanded to leave Chi-nan, which he did, and I know not whither he went. He was subsequently seen at Nanking, dressed precisely as of old ; but on being spoken to, he only smiled and made no reply.

[3] See No. XCIII., note 3.
[4] Of course only pretending to be hurt, the pain of the blows being transferred by his magical art to the back of the Taot'ai.

CXV. ARRIVAL OF BUDDHIST PRIESTS

Two Buddhist priests having arrived from the West,[1] one
went to the Wu-t'ai hill, while the other hung up his staff [2]
at T'ai-shan. Their clothes, complexions, language, and
features were very different from those of our country.
They further said they had crossed the Fiery Mountains,
from the peaks of which smoke was always issuing as from
the chimney of a furnace ; that they could only travel
after rain, and that excessive caution was necessary to
avoid displacing any stone and thus giving a vent to the
flames. They also stated that they had passed through
the River of Sand, in the middle of which was a crystal
hill with perpendicular sides and perfectly transparent ;
and that there was a defile just broad enough to admit
a single cart, its entrance guarded by two dragons with
crossed horns. Those who wished to pass prostrated themselves before these dragons, and on receiving permission
to enter, the horns opened and let them through. The
dragons were of a white colour, and their scales and bristles
seemed to be of crystal. Eighteen winters and summers
these priests had been on the road ; and of twelve who
started from the West together, only two reached China.[3]
These two said that in their country four of our mountains
are held in great esteem, namely, T'ai, Hua, Wu-t'ai, and
Lo-chia. The people there also think that China[4] is paved
with yellow gold, that Kuan-yin and Wên-shu[5] are still
alive, and that they have only come here to be sure of their
Buddhahood and of immortal life. Hearing these words,

---

[1] That is, missionaries from India.

[2] See No. LVI., note 10.

[3] Much of the above recalls Fa Hsien's narrative of his celebrated
journey from China to India in the early years of the fifth century
of our era, with which our author was evidently well acquainted.
That courageous traveller complained that of those who had set
out with him some had stopped on the way and others had died,
leaving him only his own shadow as a companion.

[4] This may almost be said to have been the belief of the Arabs
at the date of the composition of *The Arabian Nights*.

[5] For Kuan-yin, see No. XXXIII., note 7. Wên-shu, or Man-
jusiri, is the God of Wisdom, and is generally represented as riding
on a lion, in attendance, together with P'u-hsien, the God of Action,
who rides an elephant, upon Shâkyamuni Buddha.

it struck me that this was precisely what our own people say and think about the West ; and that if travellers from each country could only meet half-way and tell each other the true state of affairs, there would be some hearty laughter on botd sides, and a saving of much unnecessary trouble.

CXVI. THE STOLEN EYES

WHEN His Excellency Mr. T'ang, of our village, was quite a child, a relative of his took him to a temple to see the usual theatrical performances.[1] He was a clever little fellow, afraid of nothing and nobody ; and when he saw one of the clay images in the vestibule staring at him with its great glass [2] eyes, the temptation was irresistible ; and, secretly gouging them out with his finger, he carried them off with him. When they reached home, his relative was taken suddenly ill, and remained for a long time speechless ; at length, jumping up, he cried out several times in a voice of thunder, " Why did you gouge out my eyes ? " His family did not know what to make of this, until little T'ang told them what he had done ; they then immediately began to pray to the possessed man, saying, " A mere child, unconscious of the wickedness of his act, took away in his fun thy sacred eyes. They shall be reverently replaced." Thereupon the voice exclaimed, " In that case, I shall go away ; " and he had hardly spoken before T'ang's relative fell flat upon the ground and lay there in a state of insensibility for some time. When he recovered, they asked him concerning what he had said ; but he remembered nothing of it. The eyes were then forthwith restored to their original sockets.

[1] See No. XLVIII., note 4.
[2] The term here used stands for a vitreous composition that has long been prepared by the Chinese.

CXVII. THE INVISIBLE PRIEST

MR. HAN was a gentleman of good family, on very intimate terms with a skilful Taoist priest and magician named Tan, who, when sitting amongst other guests, would suddenly become invisible. Mr. Han was extremely anxious to learn this art, but Tan refused all his entreaties, " Not," as he said, " because I want to keep the secret for myself, but simply as a matter of principle. To teach the superior man [1] would be well enough ; others, however, would avail themselves of such knowledge to plunder their neighbours. There is no fear that you would do this, though even you might be tempted in certain ways." Mr. Han, finding all his efforts unavailing, flew into a great passion, and secretly arranged with his servants that they should give the magician a sound beating ; and, in order to prevent his escape through the power of making himself invisible, he had his threshing-floor [2] covered with a fine ash-dust, so that at any rate his footsteps would be seen and the servants could strike just above them.[3] He then inveigled Tan to the appointed spot, which he had no sooner reached than Han's servants began to belabour him on all sides with leathern thongs. Tan immediately became invisible, but his footprints were clearly seen as he moved about hither and thither to avoid the blows, and the servants went on striking above them until finally he succeeded in getting away. Mr. Han then went home, and subsequently Tan reappeared and told the servants that he could stay there no longer, adding that before he went he intended to give them all a feast in return for many things they had done for him. And diving into his sleeve he brought forth a quantity of delicious meats and wines, which he spread out upon

---

[1] The perfect man, according to the Confucian standard.

[2] A large, smooth area of concrete, to be seen outside all country houses of any size, and used for preparing the various kinds of grain.

[3] Compare, " The not uncommon practice of strewing ashes to show the footprints of ghosts or demons takes for granted that they are substantial bodies."—Tylor's *Primitive Culture*, Vol. I., p. 455.

the table, begging them to sit down and enjoy themselves.
The servants did so, and one and all of them got drunk
and insensible ; upon which Tan picked each of them
up and stowed them away in his sleeve. When Mr. Han
heard of this, he begged Tan to perform some other trick ;
so Tan drew upon the wall a city, and knocking at the
gate with his hand it was instantly thrown open. He
then put inside it his wallet and clothes, and stepping
through the gateway himself, waved his hand and bade
Mr. Han farewell. The city gates were now closed, and
Tan vanished from their sight. It was said that he appeared
again in Ch'ing-chou, where he taught little boys to paint
a circle on their hands, and, by dabbing this on to another
person's face or clothes, to imprint the circle on the place
thus struck without a trace of it being left behind upon the
hand.

CXVIII. THE CENSOR IN PURGATORY

JUST beyond Fêng-tu [1] there is a fathomless cave which
is reputed to be the entrance to Purgatory. All the
implements of torture employed therein are of human
manufacture ; old, worn-out gyves and fetters being occasionally found at the mouth of the cave, and as regularly
replaced by new ones, which disappear the same night,
and for which the magistrate of the district makes a formal
charge [2] in his accounts.

   Under the Ming dynasty, there was a certain Censor,[3]

[1] Fêng-tu is a district city in the province of Szechuen, and near
it are said to be fire-wells, otherwise known as the entrance to Purgatory, the capital city of which is also called Fêng-tu.
   [2] To the Imperial Treasury. From what I know of the barefaced-
ness of similar official impostures, I should say that this statement
is quite within the bounds of truth. For instance, at Amoy 1 per
cent. is collected by the local mandarins on all imports, ostensibly
for the purpose of providing the Imperial table with a delicious
kind of bird's nest said to be found in the neighbourhood ! Seven-
tenths of the sum thus collected is pocketed by the various officials
of the place, and with the remaining three-tenths a certain quantity
of the ordinary article of commerce is imported from the Straits and
forwarded to Peking.
   [3] See No. XXXII., note 4.

named Hua, whose duties brought him to this place ; and hearing the story of the cave, he said he did not believe it, but would penetrate into it and see for himself. People tried to dissuade him from such an enterprise ; however, he paid no heed to their remonstrances, and entered the cave with a lighted candle in his hand, followed by two attendants. They had proceeded about half a mile, when suddenly the candle was violently extinguished, and Mr. Hua saw before him a broad flight of steps leading up to the Ten Courts, or Judgment-halls, in each of which a judge was sitting with his robes and tablets all complete. On the eastern side there was one vacant place ; and when the judges saw Mr. Hua, they hastened down the steps to meet him, and each one cried out, " So you have come at last, have you ? I hope you have been quite well since last we met." Mr. Hua asked what the place was ; to which they replied that it was the Court of Purgatory, and then Mr. Hua in a great fright was about to take his leave, when the judges stopped him, saying, " No, no, Sir ! that is your seat there ; how can you imagine you are to go back again ? " Thereupon Mr. Hua was overwhelmed with fear, and begged and implored the judges to forgive him ; but the latter declared they could not interfere with the decrees of fate, and taking down the register of Life and Death they showed him that it had been ordained that on such a day of such a month his living body would pass into the realms of darkness. When Mr. Hua read these words he shivered and shook as if iced water was being poured down his back, and thinking of his old mother and his young children, his tears began to flow. At that juncture an angel in golden armour appeared, holding in his hand a document written on yellow silk,[4] before which the judges all performed a respectful obeisance. They then unfolded and read the document, which was nothing more or less than a general pardon from the Almighty for the suffering sinners in Purgatory, by virtue of which Mr. Hua's fate would be set aside, and he would be enabled to return once more to

---

[4] An imperial mandate is always written on yellow silk, and the ceremony of opening and perusing it is accompanied by prostrations and other acts of reverential submission.

the light of day. Thereupon the judges congratulated him
upon his release, and started him on his way home ; but
he had not got more than a few steps of the way before he
found himself plunged in total darkness. He was just
beginning to despair, when forth from the gloom came a
God with a red face and a long beard, rays of light shooting
out from his body and illuminating the darkness around.
Mr. Hua made up to him at once, and begged to know
how he could get out of the cave ; to which the God curtly
replied, " Repeat the *sutras* of Buddha ! " and vanished
instantly from his sight. Now Mr. Hua had forgotten
almost all the *sutras* he had ever known ; however, he
remembered a little of the diamond *sutra*, and, clasping
his hands in an attitude of prayer, he began to repeat it
aloud. No sooner had he done this than a faint streak of
light glimmered through the darkness, and revealed to him
the direction of the path ; but the next moment he was
at a loss how to go on, and the light forthwith disappeared.
He then set himself to think hard what the next verse was,
and as fast as he recollected and could go on repeating, so
fast did the light reappear to guide him on his way, until at
length he emerged once more from the mouth of the cave.
As to the fate of the two servants who accompanied him
it is needless to inquire.

CXIX. MR. WILLOW AND THE LOCUSTS

DURING the Ming dynasty a plague of locusts [1] visited
Ch'ing-yen, and was advancing rapidly towards the I
district, when the magistrate of that place, in great tribulation at the impending disaster, retired one day to sleep
behind the screen in his office. There he dreamt that a
young graduate, named Willow, wearing a tall hat and a
green robe, and of very commanding stature, came to see
him, and declared that he could tell the magistrate how
to get rid of the locusts. " To-morrow," said he, " on

---

[1] Innumerable pamphlets have been published in China on the
best methods of getting rid of these destructive insects, but none
to my knowledge contains much sound or practical advice.

the south-west road, you will see a woman riding [2] on a large jennet: she is the Spirit of the Locusts; ask her, and she will help you." The magistrate thought this strange advice; however, he got everything ready, and waited, as he had been told, at the roadside. By-and-by, along came a woman with her hair tied up in a knot, and a serge cape over her shoulders, riding slowly northwards on an old mule; whereupon the magistrate burned some sticks of incense, and, seizing the mule's bridle, humbly presented a goblet of wine. The woman asked him what he wanted; to which he replied, "Lady, I implore you to save my small magistracy from the dreadful ravages of your locusts." "Oho!" said the woman, "that scoundrel, Willow, has been letting the cat out of the bag, has he? He shall suffer for it: I won't touch your crops." She then drank three cups of wine, and vanished out of sight. Subsequently, when the locusts did come, they flew high in the air, and did not settle on the crops; but they stripped the leaves off every willow-tree far and wide; and then the magistrate awaked to the fact that the graduate of his dream was the Spirit of the Willows. Some said that this happy result was owing to the magistrate's care for the welfare of his people.

CXX. MR. TUNG, OR VIRTUE REWARDED

At Ch'ing-chou there lived a Mr. Tung, President of one of the Six Boards, whose domestic regulations were so strict that the men and women servants were not allowed to speak to each other.[1] One day he caught a slave-girl laughing and talking with one of his attendants, and gave them both a sound rating. That night he retired to sleep, accompanied by his *valet-de-chambre*, in his library, the door of which, as it was very hot weather, was left wide open. When the night was far advanced, the valet was awakened by a noise at his master's bed: and, opening

[2] See No. LII., note 1. The mules of the North of China are marvels of beauty and strength; and the price of a fine animal often goes as high as £100.
[1] See No. XL., note 2, and No. XCIV., note 3.

his eyes, he saw, by the light of the moon, the attendant above mentioned pass out of the door with something in his hand. Recognising the man as one of the family, he thought nothing of the occurrence, but turned round and went to sleep again. Soon after, however, he was again aroused by the noise of footsteps tramping heavily across the room, and, looking up, he beheld a huge being with a red face and a long beard, very like the God of War,[2] carrying a man's head. Horribly frightened, he crawled under the bed, and then he heard sounds above him as of clothes being shaken out, and as if some one was being shampooed.[3] In a few moments, the boots tramped once more across the room and went away; and then he gradually put out his head, and, seeing the dawn beginning to peep through the window, he stretched out his hand to reach his clothes. These he found to be soaked through and through, and, on applying his hand to his nose, he smelt the smell of blood. He now called out loudly to his master, who jumped up at once; and, by the light of a candle, they saw that the bed-clothes and pillows were alike steeped in blood. Just then some constables knocked at the door, and when Mr. Tung went out to see who it was, the constables were all astonishment; "for," said they, "a few minutes ago a man rushed wildly up to our yamên, and said he had killed his master; ànd, as he himself was covered with blood, he was arrested, and turned out to be a servant of yours. He also declared that he had buried your head alongside the temple of the God of War; and when we went to look, there, indeed, was a freshly-dug hole, but the head was gone." Mr. Tung was amazed at all this story, and, on proceeding to the magistrate's yamên, he discovered that the man in charge was the attendant whom he had scolded the day before. Thereupon, the criminal was severely bambooed and released; and then Mr. Tung, who was unwilling to make an enemy of a man of this stamp, gave him the girl to wife. However, a few nights afterwards the people who lived next door to the newly-married couple heard a terrific crash in their house, and, rushing in to see what was the matter, found that husband and wife, and the bedstead

2 See No., I., note 4.
3 See No. LXIX., note 8.

as well, had been cut clean in two as if by a sword. The ways of the God are many, indeed, but few more extra-ordinary than this.[4]

CXXI. THE DEAD PRIEST

A CERTAIN Taoist priest, overtaken in his wanderings by the shades of evening, sought refuge in a small Buddhist monastery. The monk's apartment was, however, locked ; so he threw his mat down in the vestibule of the shrine, and seated himself upon it. In the middle of the night, when all was still, he heard a sound of some one opening the door behind him ; and looking round, he saw a Buddhist priest, covered with blood from head to foot, who did not seem to notice that anybody else was present. Accordingly, he himself pretended not to be aware of what was going on ; and then he saw the other priest enter the shrine, mount the altar, and remain there some time, embracing Buddha's head and laughing by turns. When morning came, he found the monk's room still locked ; and, suspecting something was wrong, he walked to a neighbouring village, where he told the people what he had seen. Thereupon the villagers went back with him, and broke open the door, and there before them lay the priest weltering in his blood, having evidently been killed by robbers, who had stripped the place bare. Anxious now to find out what had made the disembodied spirit of the priest laugh in the way it had been seen to do, they proceeded to inspect the head of the Buddha on the altar ; and, at the back of it, they noticed a small mark, scraping through which they discovered a sum of over thirty ounces of silver. This sum was forthwith used for defraying the: funeral expenses of the murdered man.

[4] It was the God of War who replaced Mr. Tung's head after it had actually been cut off and buried.

CXXII. THE FLYING COW

A CERTAIN man, who had bought a fine cow, dreamt the same night that wings grew out of the animal's back, and that it had flown away. Regarding this as an omen of some pending misfortune, he led the cow off to market again, and sold it at a ruinous loss. Wrapping up in a cloth the silver he received, he slung it over his back, and was half-way home, when he saw a falcon eating part of a hare.[1] Approaching the bird, he found it was quite tame, and accordingly tied it by the leg to one of the corners of the cloth, in which his money was. The falcon fluttered about a good deal, trying to escape ; and, by-and-by, the man's hold being for a moment relaxed, away went the bird, cloth, money, and all. " It was destiny," said the man every time he told the story ; ignorant as he was, first, that no faith should be put in dreams ; [2] and, secondly, that people shouldn't take things they see by the wayside.[3] Quadrupeds don't usually fly.

CXXIII. THE " MIRROR AND LISTEN " TRICK

AT I-tu there lived a family of the name of Chêng. The two sons were both distinguished scholars, but the elder was early known to fame, and, consequently, the favourite with his parents, who also extended their preference to his wife. The younger brother was a trifle wild, which displeased his father and mother very much, and made them regard his wife, too, with anything but a friendly eye.

---

[1] See No. VI., note 1.

[2] The highly educated Confucianist rises above the superstition that darkens the lives of his less fortunate fellow countrymen. Had such a dream as the above received an inauspicious interpretation at the hands of some local soothsayer the owner of the animal would in nine cases out of ten have taken an early opportunity of getting rid of it.

[3] The Chinese love to refer to the " good old time " of their forefathers, when a man who dropped anything on the highway would have no cause to hurry back for fear of its being carried off by a stranger.

The latter reproached her husband for being the cause of this, and asked him why he, being a man like his brother, could not vindicate the slights that were put upon her. This piqued him ; and, setting to work in good earnest, he soon gained a fair reputation, though still not equal to his brother's. That year the two went up for the highest degree ; and, on New Year's Eve, the wife of the younger, very anxious for the success of her husband, secretly tried the " mirror and listen " trick.[1] She saw two men pushing each other in jest, and heard them say, " You go and get cool," which remark she was quite unable to interpret for good or for bad, so she thought no more about the matter. After the examination, the two brothers returned home ; and one day, when the weather was extremely hot, and their two wives were hard at work in the cook-house, preparing food for their field-labourers, a messenger rode up in hot haste [2] to announce that the elder brother had passed. Thereupon his mother went into the cook-house, and, calling to her daughter-in-law, said, " Your husband has passed ; *you go and get cool.*" Rage and grief now filled the breast of the second son's wife, who, with tears in her eyes, continued her task of cooking, when suddenly another messenger rushed in to say, that the second son had passed too. At this, his wife flung down her frying-pan, and cried out, " Now I'll *go and get cool* ; " and as in the heat of her excitement she uttered these words, the recollection of her trial of the " mirror and listen " trick flashed upon her, and she knew that the words of that evening had been fulfilled.

[1] One method is to wrap an old mirror (formerly a polished metal disc) in a handkerchief, and then, no one being present, to bow seven times towards the Spirit of the Hearth : after which the first words heard spoken by any one will give a clue to the issue under investigation. Another method is to close the eyes and take seven paces, opening them at the seventh and getting some hint from the objects first seen in a mirror held in the hand, coupled with the words first spoken within the experimenter's hearing.

[2] In former days, these messengers of good tidings to candidates whose homes were in distant parts used to earn handsome sums if first to announce the news ; but now the telegraph has taken their occupation from them.

CXXIV. THE CATTLE PLAGUE

CH'ÊN HUA-FÊNG, of Mêng-shan, overpowered by the great heat, went and lay down under a tree, when suddenly up came a man with a thick comforter round his neck, who also sat down on a stone in the shade, and began fanning himself as hard as he could, the perspiration all the time running off him like a waterfall. Ch'ên rose and said to him with a smile, " If, Sir, you were to remove that comforter, you would be cool enough without the help of a fan." " It would be easy enough," replied the stranger, " to take off my comforter ; but the difficulty would be in getting it on again." He then went on to converse generally upon other matters, in a manner which betokened considerable refinement ; and by-and-by he exclaimed, " What I should like now is just a draught of iced wine to cool the twelve joints of my œsophagus."[1] " Come along, then," cried Ch'ên, " my house is close by, and I shall be happy to give you what you want." So off they went together ; and Ch'ên set before them some capital wine, which he produced from a cave, cold enough to numb their teeth. The stranger was delighted, and ,remained there drinking until late in- the evening, when, all at once, it began to rain. Ch'ên lighted a lamp ; and he and his guest, who now took off the comforter, sat talking together in *déshabille*. Every now and again the former thought he saw a light coming from the back of the stranger's head ; and when at length he had gone off into a tipsy sleep, Ch'ên took the light to examine more closely. He found behind the ears a large cavity, partitioned by a number of membranes, and looking like a lattice, with a thin skin hanging down in front of each, the spaces being apparently empty. In great astonishment Ch'ên took a hair-pin, and inserted it into one of these places, when pff ! out flew something like a tiny cow,

---

[1] Accurate anatomical descriptions must not be looked for in Chinese literature. " Man has three hundred and sixty-five bones, corresponding to the number of days it takes the heavens to revolve." From the *Hsi yüan lu*, or *Instructions to Coroners*, Book I., ch. 12. See No. XIV., note 8.

which broke through the window,[2] and was gone. This frightened Ch'ên, and he determined to play no more tricks ; just then, however, the stranger waked up. " Alas ! " cried he, " you have been at my head, and have let out the Cattle Plague. What is to be done now ? " Ch'ên asked what he meant : upon which the stranger said, " There is no object in further concealment. I will tell you all. I am the Angel of Pestilence for the six kinds of domestic animals. That form which you have let out attacks oxen, and I fear that, for miles round, few will escape alive." Now Ch'ên himself was a cattle-farmer, and when he heard this was dreadfully alarmed, and implored the stranger to tell him what to do. " What to do ! " replied he ; " why, I shall not escape punishment myself ; how can I tell you what to do ? However, you will find powdered K'u-ts'an [3] an efficacious remedy—that is, if you don't keep it a secret for your private use." [4] The stranger then departed, first of all piling up a quantity of earth in a niche in the wall, a handful of which, he told Ch'ên, given to each animal, might prove of some avail. Before long the plague did break out ; and Ch'ên, who was desirous of making a little money by it, told the remedy to no one, with the exception of his younger brother. The latter tried it on his own beasts with great success ; while, on the other hand, those belonging to Ch'ên himself died off, to the number of fifty head,[5] leaving him only four or five old cows, which showed every sign of soon sharing the same fate. In his distress, Ch'ên suddenly bethought himself of the earth in the niche ; and, as a last resource, gave some to the sick animals. By the next morning they were quite well, and then he knew that his secrecy about the remedy had caused it to have no effect. From that moment his stock went on increasing, and in a few years he had as many as ever.

[2] See No. X., note 7.

[3] *Sophora flavescens*, Ait.

[4] As the Chinese invariably do whenever they get hold of a useful prescription or remedy. Master workmen also invariably try to withhold something of their art from the apprentices they engage to teach.

[5] The text has " of two hundred hoofs."

CXXV. THE MARRIAGE OF THE
VIRGIN GODDESS

At Kuei-chi there is a shrine to the Plum Virgin, who was
formerly a young lady named Ma, and lived at Tung-wan.
Her betrothed husband dying before the wedding, she swore
she would never marry, and at thirty years of age she
died. Her kinsfolk built a shrine to her memory, and
gave her the title of the Plum Virgin. Some years afterwards, a Mr. Chin, on his way to the examination, happened
to pass by the shrine ; and entering in, he walked up and
down thinking very much of the young lady in whose
honour it had been erected. That night he dreamt that
a servant came to summon him into the presence of the
Goddess ; and that, in obedience to her command, he
went and found her waiting for him just outside the shrine.
" I am deeply grateful to you, Sir," said the Goddess,
on his approach, " for giving me so large a share of your
thoughts ; and I intend to repay you by becoming your
humble handmaid." Mr. Chin bowed an assent ; and
then the Goddess escorted him back, saying, " When
your place is ready, I will come and fetch you." On
waking in the morning, Mr. Chin was not over-pleased with
his dream ; however, that very night every one of the
villagers dreamt that the Goddess appeared and said she
was going to marry Mr. Chin, bidding them at once prepare
an image of him. This the village elders, out of respect
for their Goddess, positively refused to do ; until at length
they all began to fall ill, and then they made a clay image
of Mr. Chin and placed it on the left of the Goddess. Mr.
Chin now told his wife that the Plum Virgin had come for
him ; and, putting on his official cap and robes, he straightway died. Thereupon his wife was very angry ; and,
going to the shrine, she first abused the Goddess, and then,
getting on the altar, slapped her face well. The Goddess
is now called Chin's virgin wife.

CXXVI. THE WINE INSECT

A MR. LIN of Ch'ang-shan was extremely fat, and so fond of wine [1] that he would often finish a pitcher by himself. However, he owned about fifty acres of land, half of which was covered with millet, and being well off, he did not consider that his drinking would bring him into trouble. One day a foreign Buddhist priest saw him, and remarked that he appeared to be suffering from some extraordinary complaint. Mr. Lin said nothing was the matter with him ; whereupon the priest asked him if he often got drunk. Lin acknowledged that he did ; and the priest told him that he was afflicted by the wine insect. " Dear me ! " cried Lin, in great alarm, " do you think you could cure me ? " The priest declared there would be no difficulty in doing so ; but when Lin asked him what drugs he intended to use, the priest said he should not use any at all. He then made Lin lie down in the sun ; and tying his hands and feet together, he placed a stoup of good wine about half a foot from his head. By-and-by, Lin felt a deadly thirst coming on ; and the flavour of the wine passing through his nostrils seemed to set his vitals on fire. Just then he experienced a tickling sensation in his throat, and something ran out of his mouth and jumped into the wine. On being released from his bonds, he saw that it was an insect about three inches in length, which wriggled about in the wine like a tadpole, and had mouth and eyes all complete. Lin was overjoyed, and offered money to the priest, who refused to take it, saying, all he wanted was the insect, which he explained to Lin was the essence of wine, and which, on being stirred up in water, would turn it into wine. Lin tried this, and found it was so ; and ever afterwards he detested the sight of wine. He subsequently became very thin, and so poor that he had hardly enough to eat and drink. [2]

[1] The ordinary " wine " of China is a spirit distilled from rice. See No. XCIII., note 3.

[2] The commentator would have us believe that Mr. Lin's fondness for wine was to him an element of health and happiness rather than a disease to be cured, and that the priest was wrong in meddling with the natural bent of his constitution.

CXXVII. THE FAITHFUL DOG

A CERTAIN man of Lu-ngan, whose father had been cast into prison, and was brought almost to death's door,[1] scraped together one hundred ounces of silver, and set out for the city to try and arrange for his parent's release. Jumping on a mule, he saw that a black dog, belonging to the family, was following him. He tried in vain to make the dog remain at home ; and when, after travelling for some miles, he got off his mule to rest awhile, he picked up a large stone and threw it at the dog, which then ran off. However, he was no sooner on the road again, than up came the dog, and tried to stop the mule by holding on to its tail. His master beat it off with the whip ; whereupon the dog ran barking loudly in front of the mule, and seemed to be using every means in its power to cause his master to stop. The latter thought this a very inauspicious omen, and turning upon the animal in a rage, drove it away out of sight. He now went on to the city ; but when, in the dusk of the evening, he arrived there, he found that about half his money was gone. In a terrible state of mind, he tossed about all night ; then all of a sudden it flashed across him that the strange behaviour of the dog might possibly have some meaning ; so getting up very early, he left the city as soon as the gates were open,[2] and though, from the number of passers-by, he never expected to find his money again, he went on until he reached the spot where he had got off his mule the day before. There he saw his dog lying dead upon the ground, its hair having apparently been wetted through with

[1] In an entry on torture (see No. LXXIII., note 2) which occurs in my *Glossary of Reference* I made the following statement :— "The real tortures of a Chinese prison are the filthy dens in which the unfortunate victims are confined, the stench in which they have to draw breath, the fetters and manacles by which they are secured, the absolute insufficiency even of the disgusting rations doled out to them, and above all the mental agony which must ensue in a country with no *Habeas corpus* to protect the lives and fortunes of its citizens."

[2] For a small bribe, the soldiers at the gates of a Chinese city will usually pass people in and out by means of a ladder placed against the wall at some convenient spot.

perspiration ;[3] and, lifting up the body by one of its
ears, he found his lost silver. Full of gratitude he bought
a coffin and buried the dead animal ; and the people
now call the place the Grave of the Faithful Dog.

CXXVIII. AN EARTHQUAKE

IN 1668 there was a very severe earthquake.[1] I myself
was staying at Chi-hsia, and happened to be that night
sitting over a kettle of wine with my cousin Li Tu. All
of a sudden we heard a noise like thunder, travelling from
the south-east in a north-westerly direction. We were
much astonished at this, and quite unable to account for
the noise ; in another moment the table began to rock,
and the wine-cups were upset ; the beams and supports
of the house snapped here and there with a crash, and we
looked at each other in fear and trembling. By-and-by
we knew that it was an earthquake ; and, rushing out,
we saw houses and other buildings, as it were, fall down
and get up again ; and, amidst the sounds of crashing
walls, we heard the shrieks of women and children, the
whole mass being like a great seething cauldron. Men
were giddy and could not stand, but rolled about on the
ground ; the river overflowed its banks ; cocks crowed, and
dogs barked from one end of the city to the other. In a
little while the quaking began to subside ; and then might
be seen men and women running half naked about the
streets, all anxious to tell their own experiences, and
forgetting that they had on little or no clothing. I subsequently heard that a well was closed up and rendered
useless by this earthquake ; that a house was turned
completely round, so as to face the opposite direction ;
that the Chi-hsia hill was riven open, and that the waters
of the I river flowed in and made a lake of an acre and
more. Truly such an earthquake as this is of rare
occurrence.

[3] I believe it is with us only a recently determined fact that dogs
perspire through the skin.
[1] The exact date is given—the 17th of the 6th moon, which
would probably fall towards the end of June.

CXXIX. MAKING ANIMALS

THE tricks for bewitching people are many. Sometimes drugs are put in their food, and when they eat they become dazed, and follow the person who has bewitched them. This is commonly called *ta hsü pa* ; in Kiang-nan it is known as *ch'e hsü*. Little children are most frequently bewitched in this way. There is also what is called " making animals," which is better known on the south side of the River.[1]

One day a man arrived at an inn in Yang-chou, leading with him five donkeys. Tying them up near the stable, he told the landlord he would be back in a few minutes, and bade him give his donkeys no water. He had not been gone long before the donkeys, which were standing out in the glare of the sun, began to kick about, and make a noise ; whereupon the landlord untied them, and was going to put them in the shade, when suddenly they espied water, and made a rush to get at it. So the landlord let them drink ; and no sooner had the water touched their lips than they rolled on the ground, and changed into women. In great astonishment the landlord asked them whence they came ; but their tongues were tied, and they could not answer, so he hid them in his private apartments, and at that moment their owner returned, bringing with him five sheep. The latter immediately asked the landlord where his donkeys were ; to which the landlord replied by offering him some wine, saying, the donkeys would be brought to him directly. He then went out and gave the sheep some water, on drinking which they were all changed into boys. Accordingly, he communicated with the authorities, and the stranger was arrested and forthwith beheaded.

[1] See No. XCVIII., note 1

CXXX. CRUELTY AVENGED

A CERTAIN magistrate caused a petty oil-vendor, who was brought before him for some trifling misdemeanour, and whose statements were very confused, to be bambooed to death. The former subsequently rose to high rank; and having amassed considerable wealth, set about building himself a fine house. On the day when the great beam was to be fixed in its place,[1] among the friends and relatives who arrived to offer their congratulations, he was horrified to see the oilman walk in. At the same instant one of the servants came rushing up to announce to him the birth of a son; whereupon, he mournfully remarked, "The house not yet finished, and its destroyer already here." The bystanders thought he was joking, for they had not seen what he had seen.[2] However, when that boy grew up, by his frivolity and extravagance he quite ruined his father. He was finally obliged himself to go into service; and spent all his earnings in oil, which he swallowed in large quantities.

CXXXI. THE WEI-CH'I DEVIL

A CERTAIN general, who had resigned his command, and had retired to his own home, was very fond of roaming about and amusing himself with wine and *wei-ch'i*.[1] One

---

[1] This corresponds to our ceremony of laying the foundation stone, except that one commemorates the beginning, the other the completion, of a new building.

[2] That is, the disembodied spirit of the oilman.

[1] A most abstruse and complicated game of skill, for which the Chinese claim an antiquity of four thousand years, and which I was the first to introduce to a European public through an article in the *Temple Bar Magazine* for January 1877. *A propos* of which, an accomplished American lady, Miss A. M. Fielde, of Swatow, wrote as follows :—" The game seems to me the peer of chess. . . . It is a game for the slow, persistent, astute, multitudinous Chinese; while chess, by the picturesque appearance of the board, the variety and prominent individuality of the men, and the erratic combination of the attack,—is for the Anglo-Saxon."

day—it was the 9th of the 9th moon, when everybody goes up high [2]—as he was playing with some friends, a stranger walked up, and watched the game intently for some time without going away. He was a miserable-looking creature, with a very ragged coat, but nevertheless possessed of a refined and courteous air. The general begged him to be seated, an offer which he accepted, being all the time extremely deferential in his manner. "I suppose you are pretty good at this," said the general, pointing to the board; "try a bout with one of my friends here." The stranger made a great many apologies in reply, but finally accepted, and played a game in which, apparently to his great disappointment, he was beaten. He played another with the same result; and now, refusing all offers of wine, he seemed to think of nothing but how to get some one to play with him. Thus he went on until the afternoon was well advanced; when suddenly, just as he was in the middle of a most exciting game, which depended on a single place, he rushed forward, and throwing himself at the feet of the general, loudly implored his protection. The general did not know what to make of this; however, he raised him up, and said, "It's only a game : why get so excited ? " To this the stranger replied by begging the general not to let his gardener seize him; and when the general asked what gardener he meant, he said the man's name was Ma-ch'êng. Now this Ma-ch'êng was often employed as a lictor by the Ruler of Purgatory, and would sometimes remain away as much as ten days, serving the warrants of death; accordingly, the general sent off to inquire about him, and found that he had been in a trance for two days.[3] His master cried out that he had better not behave rudely to his guest, but at that very moment the stranger sank down to the ground, and was gone. The general was lost in astonishment; however, he now knew that the man was a disembodied spirit, and on the next day, when Ma-ch'êng came round, he asked him for full particulars. "The gentleman was a native of Hu-

---

[2] On this day, annually dedicated to kite-flying, picnics, and good cheer, everybody tries to get up to as great an elevation as possible, in the hope, as some say, of thereby prolonging life. It was this day—4th October, 1878—which was fixed for the total extermination of foreigners in Foochow.   [3] See No. XXVI., note 3.

hsiang," replied the gardener, "who was passionately addicted to *wei-ch'i*, and had lost a great deal of money by it. His father, being much grieved at his behaviour, confined him to the house ; but he was always getting out, and indulging the fatal passion, and at last his father died of a broken heart. In consequence of this, the Ruler of Purgatory curtailed his term of life, and condemned him to become a hungry devil,[4] in which state he has already passed seven years. And now that the Phœnix Tower[5] is completed, an order has been issued for the literati to present themselves, and compose an inscription to be cut on stone, as a memorial thereof, by which means they would secure their own salvation as a reward. Many of the shades failing to arrive at the appointed time, God was very angry with the Ruler of Purgatory, and the latter sent off me, and others who are employed in the same way, to hunt up the defaulters. But as you, Sir, bade me treat the gentleman with respect, I did not venture to bind him." The general inquired what had become of the stranger ; to which the gardener replied, "He is now a mere menial in Purgatory, and can never be born again." "Alas ! " cried his master, " thus it is that men are ruined by any inordinate passion." [6]

CXXXII. THE FORTUNE-HUNTER PUNISHED

A CERTAIN man's uncle had no children and the nephew, with an eye to his uncle's property, volunteered to become his adopted son.[1] When the uncle died all the property passed accordingly to his nephew, who thereupon broke faith as to his part of the contract.[2] He did the same with

---

[4] One of the *prêtas*, or the fourth of the six paths (*gati*) of existence ; the other five being (1) angels, (2) men, (3) demons, (5) brute beasts, and (6) sinners in hell. The term is often used colloquially for a self-invited guest.

[5] An imaginary building in the Infernal Regions.

[6] Mencius reckoned " to play *wei-ch'i* for money " among the five unfilial acts.

[1] See No. LV., note 9 ; and No. XCIV., note 6.

[2] That is, in carrying out the obligations he had entered into, such as conducting the ceremonies of ancestral worship, repairing the family tombs, &c.

another uncle, and thus united three properties in his own
person, whereby he became the richest man of the neighbourhood. Suddenly he fell ill, and seemed to go out of
his mind ; for he cried out, " So you wish to live in wealth,
do you ? " and immediately seizing a sharp knife, he began
hacking away at his own body until he had strewed the
floor with pieces of flesh. He then exclaimed, " You cut
off other people's posterity and expect to have posterity
yourself, do you ? " and forthwith he ripped himself open
and died. Shortly afterwards his son, too, died, and the
property fell into the hands of strangers. Is not this a
retribution to be dreaded ?

CXXXIII. LIFE PROLONGED

A CERTAIN cloth merchant of Ch'ang-ch'ing was stopping
at T'ai-ngan, when he heard of a magician who was said
to be very skilled in casting nativities. So he went off
at once to consult him ; but the magician would not
undertake the task, saying, " Your destiny is bad : you
had better hurry home." At this the merchant was dreadfully frightened, and, packing up his wares, set off towards
Ch'ang-ch'ing. On the way he fell in with a man in short
clothes,[1] like a constable ; and the two soon struck up a
friendly intimacy, taking their meals together. By-and-by
the merchant asked the stranger what his business was ;
and the latter told him he was going to Ch'ang-ch'ing
to serve summonses, producing at the same time a document and showing it to the merchant, who, on looking
closely, saw a list of names, at the head of which was
his own. In great astonishment he inquired what he had
done that he should be arrested thus ; to which his companion replied, " I am not a living being : I am a lictor
in the employ of the infernal authorities, and I presume
your term of life has expired." The merchant burst into

---

[1] The long flowing robe is a sign of respectability which all but
the very poorest classes love to affect in public. At the port of
Haiphong, *shoes* are the criterion of social standing ; but, as a rule,
the well-to-do native merchants prefer to go barefoot rather than
give the authorities a chance of exacting heavier squeezes, on the
strength of such a palpable acknowledgment of wealth.

tears and implored the lictor to spare him, which the latter declared was impossible ; " But," added he, " there are a great many names down, and it will take me some time to get through them : you go off home and settle up your affairs, and, as a slight return for your friendship, I'll call for you last." A few minutes afterwards they reached a stream where the bridge was in ruins, and people could only cross with great difficulty; at which the lictor remarked, " You are now on the road to death, and not a single cash can you carry away with you. Repair this bridge and benefit the public ; and thus from a great outlay you may possibly yourself derive some small advantage." The merchant said he would do so ; and when he got home, he bade his wife and children prepare for his coming dissolution, and at the same time set men to work and made the bridge sound and strong again. Some time elapsed, but no lictor arrived ; and his suspicions began to be aroused, when one day the latter walked in and said, " I reported that affair of the bridge to the Municipal God,[2] who communicated it to the Ruler of Purgatory ; and for that good act your span of life has been lengthened, and your name struck out of the list. I have now come to announce this to you." The merchant was profuse in his thanks ; and the next time he went to T'ai-ngan, he burnt a quantity of paper nigots,[3] and made offerings and libations to the lictor, out of gratitude for what he had done. Suddenly the lictor himself appeared and cried out, " Do you wish to ruin me ? Happily my new master has only just taken up his post, and he has not noticed this, or where should I be ? "[4] The lictor then escorted the merchant some distance ; and, at parting, bade him never return by that road, but, if he had any business at T'ai-ngan, to go thither by a roundabout way.

[2] See No. I., note 1.
[3] See No. LVI., note 7; and No. XCVII., note 7.
[4] The lictor had no right to divulge his errand when he first met the cloth merchant, or to remove the latter's name from the top to the bottom of the list.

CXXXIV. THE CLAY IMAGE

On the river I there lived a man named Ma, who married a wife from the Wang family, with whom he was very happy in his domestic life. Ma, however, died young; and his wife's parents were unwilling that their daughter should remain a widow, but she resisted all their importunities, and declared firmly she would never marry again. "It is a noble resolve of yours, I allow," argued her mother; "but you are still a mere girl, and you have no children. Besides, I notice that people who start with such rigid determinations always end by doing something discreditable, and therefore you had better get married as soon as you can, which is no more than is done every day." The girl swore she would rather die than consent, and accordingly her mother had no alternative but to let her alone. She then ordered a clay image to be made, exactly resembling her late husband;[1] and whenever she took her own meals, she would set meat and wine before it, precisely as if her husband had been there. One night she was on the point of retiring to rest, when suddenly she saw the clay image stretch itself and step down from the table, increasing all the while in height, until it was as tall as a man, and neither more nor less than her own husband. In great alarm she called out to her mother, but the image stopped her, saying, "Don't do that! I am but showing my gratitude for your affectionate care of me, and it is chill and uncomfortable in the realms below. Such devotion as yours casts its light back on generations gone by; and now I, who was cut off in my prime because my father did evil, and was condemned to be without an heir, have been permitted, in consequence of your virtuous conduct, to visit you once again, that our ancestral line may yet remain unbroken."[2] Every morning at cock-crow her husband resumed his

[1] The clay image makers of Tientsin are wonderfully clever in taking likenesses by these means. Some of the most skilful will even manipulate the clay behind their backs, and then, adding the proper colours, will succeed in producing an exceedingly good resemblance. They find, however, more difficulty with foreign faces, to which they are less accustomed in the trade.

[2] See No. LXI., note 3.

usual form and size as the clay image ; and after a time he told her that their hour of separation had come, upon which husband and wife bade each other an eternal farewell. By-and-by the widow, to the great astonishment of her mother, bore a son, which caused no small amusement among the neighbours who heard the story ; and, as the girl herself had no proof of what she stated to be the case, a certain beadle [3] of the place, who had an old grudge against her husband, went off and informed the magistrate of what had occurred. After some investigation, the magistrate exclaimed, " I have heard that the children of disembodied spirits have no shadow ; and that those who have shadows are not genuine." Thereupon they took Ma's child into the sunshine, and lo ! there was but a very faint shadow, like a thin vapour. The magistrate then drew blood from the child, and smeared it on the clay image; upon which the blood at once soaked in and left no stain. Another clay image being produced and the same experiment tried, the blood remained on the surface so that it could be wiped away.[4] The girl's story was thus acknowledged to be true ; and when the child grew up, and in every feature was the counterpart of Ma, there was no longer any room for suspicion.

CXXXV. DISHONESTY PUNISHED

At Chiao-chou there lived a man named Liu Hsi-ch'uan, who was steward to His Excellency Mr. Fa. When already over forty a son was born to him, whom he loved very dearly, and quite spoilt by always letting him have his own way. When the boy grew up he led a dissolute, extravagant life, and ran through all his father's property. By-and-by he fell sick, and then he declared that nothing would cure him but a slice off a fat old favourite mule they had ; upon which his father had another and more worthless animal killed ; but his son found out he was being tricked, and, after abusing his father soundly, his symptoms became more and more alarming. The mule was

[3] See No. LXIV., note 2.
[4] Such is the officially authorised method of determining a doubtful relationship between a dead parent and a living child, substituting a bone for the clay image here mentioned.

accordingly killed, and some of it was served up to the
sick man ; however, he only just tasted it and sent the
rest away. From that time he got gradually worse and
worse, and finally died, to the great grief of his father,
who would gladly have died too. Three or four years
afterwards, as some of the villagers were worshipping
on Mount Tai, they saw a man riding on a mule, the very
image of Mr. Liu's dead son ; and, on approaching more
closely, they saw that it was actually he.[1] Jumping
from his mule,[2] he made them a salutation, and then they
began to chat with him on various subjects, always carefully avoiding that one of his own death. They asked
him what he was doing there ; to which he replied that
he was only roaming about, and inquired of them in his
turn at what inn they were staying ; "For," added he,
"I have an engagement just now, but I will visit you
to-morrow." So they told him the name of the inn, and
took their leave, not expecting to see him again. However,
the next day he came, and, tying his mule to a post outside, went in to see them. "Your father," observed one
of the villagers, "is always thinking about you. Why
do you not go and pay him a visit ? " The young man
asked to whom he was alluding ; and, at the mention of
his father's name, he changed colour and said, "If he is
anxious to see me, kindly tell him that on the 7th of the
4th moon I will await him here." He then went away,
and the villagers returned and told Mr. Liu all that had
taken place. At the appointed time the latter was very
desirous of going to see his son ; but his master dissuaded
him, saying that he thought from what he knew of his son
that the interview might possibly not turn out as he would
desire ; "Although," added he, "if you are bent upon
going, I should be sorry to stand in your way. Let me,
however, counsel you to conceal yourself in a cupboard,
and thus, by observing what takes place, you will know
better how to act, and avoid running into any danger."
This he accordingly did, and, when his son came, Mr.

[1] "In various savage superstitions the minute resemblance
of soul to body is forcibly stated."—*Myths and Myth-makers*, by
John Fiske, p. 228.
[2] An important point in Chinese etiquette. It is not considered
polite for a person in a sitting position to address an equal who is
standing.

Fa received him at the inn. "Where's Mr. Liu?" cried
the son. "Oh, he hasn't come," replied Mr. Fa. "The
old beast! What does he mean by that?" exclaimed his
son; whereupon Mr. Fa asked him what *he* meant by
cursing his own father. "My father!" shrieked the son;
"why, he's nothing more to me than a former rascally
partner in trade, who cheated me out of all my money,
and for which I have since avenged myself on him.[3] What
sort of a father is that, I should like to know?" He then
went out of the door; and his father crept out of the
cupboard from which, with the perspiration streaming
down him and hardly daring to breathe, he had heard all
that had passed, and sorrowfully wended his way home
again.

CXXXVI. THE MAD PRIEST

A CERTAIN mad priest, whose name I do not know, lived
in a temple on the hills. He would sing and cry by turns,
without any apparent reason; and once somebody saw
him boiling a stone for his dinner. At the autumn festival
of the 9th day of the 9th moon,[1] an official of the district
went up in that direction for the usual picnic, taking
with him his chair and his red umbrellas. After luncheon
he was passing by the temple, and had hardly reached the
door, when out rushed the priest, barefooted and ragged,
and, himself opening a yellow umbrella, cried out as the
attendants of a mandarin do when ordering the people to
stand back. He then approached the official, and made
as though he were jesting at him; at which the latter was
extremely indignant, and bade his servants drive the priest
away. The priest moved off with the servants after him,
and in another moment had thrown down his yellow
umbrella, which split into a number of pieces, each piece
changing immediately into a falcon, and flying about in all
directions. The umbrella handle became a huge serpent,
with red scales and glaring eyes; and then the party
would have turned and fled, but that one of them declared

[3] By becoming his son and behaving badly to him. See No. CX.,
note 1, and the text to which it refers.
[1] See No. CXXXI., note 2.

it was only an optical delusion, and that the creature couldn't do any hurt. The speaker accordingly seized a knife and rushed at the serpent, which forthwith opened its mouth and swallowed its assailant whole. In a terrible fright the servants crowded round their master and hurried him away, not stopping to draw breath until they were fully a mile off. By-and-by several of them stealthily returned to see what was going on ; and, on entering the temple, they found that both priest and serpent had disappeared. But from an old ash-tree hard by they heard a sound proceeding,—a sound, as it were, of a donkey panting ; and at first they were afraid to go near, though after a while they ventured to peep through a hole in the tree, which was an old hollow trunk ; and there, jammed hard and fast with his head downwards, was the rash assailant of the serpent. It being quite impossible to drag him out, they began at once to cut the tree away ; but by the time they had set him free he was already perfectly unconscious. However, he ultimately came round and was carried home ; but from this day the priest was never seen again.[2]

CXXXVII. FEASTING THE RULER OF PURGATORY

At Ching-hai there lived a young man, named Shao, whose family was very poor. On the occasion of his mother completing her cycle,[1] he arranged a quantity of meat-offerings and wine on a table in the court-yard, and proceeded to invoke the Gods in the usual manner ; but when he rose from his knees, lo and behold ! all the meat and wine had disappeared. His mother thought this was a bad omen, and that she was not destined to enjoy a long life ; however, she said nothing on the subject to her son, who was himself quite at a loss to account for what had happened. A short time afterwards the Literary Chancellor [2] arrived ; and young Shao, scraping together

---

[2] The story is intended as a satire on those puffed-up dignitaries who cannot even go to a picnic without all the retinue belonging to their particular rank. See No. LVI., note 5.

[1] See No. XXIII., note 8.

[2] The examiner for the bachelor's, or lowest, degree.

what funds he could, went off to present himself as a candidate. On the road he met with a man who gave him such a cordial invitation to his house that he willingly accepted ; and the stranger led him to a stately mansion, with towers and terraces rising one above the other as far as the eye could reach. In one of the apartments was a king, sitting upon a throne, who received Shao in a very friendly manner ; and, after regaling him with an excellent banquet, said, " I have to thank you for the food and drink you gave my servants that day we passed your house." Shao was greatly astonished at this remark, when the King proceeded, " I am the Ruler of Purgatory. Don't you recollect sacrificing on your mother's birthday ? " The King then bestowed on Shao a packet of silver, saying, " Pray accept this in return for your kindness." Shao thanked him and retired ; and in another moment the palace and its occupants had one and all vanished from his sight, leaving him alone in the midst of some tall trees. On opening his packet he found it to contain five ounces of pure gold ; and, after defraying the expenses of his examination, half was still left, which he carried home and gave to his mother.

CXXXVIII. THE PICTURE HORSE

A CERTAIN Mr. Ts'ui, of Lin-ch'ing, was too poor to keep his garden walls in repair, and used often to find a strange horse lying down on the grass inside. It was a black horse marked with white, and having a scrubby tail, which looked as if the end had been burnt off ;[1] and, though always driven away, would still return to the same spot. Now Mr. Ts'ui had a friend, who was holding an appointment in Shansi ; and though he had frequently felt desirous of paying him a visit, he had no means of travelling so far. Accordingly, he one day caught the strange horse, and, putting a saddle on its back, rode away, telling his servants that if the owner of the horse should appear, he was to inform him where the animal was to be found. The horse

---

[1] The Chinese never cut the tails of their horses or mules.

started off at a very rapid pace, and, in a short time, they were thirty or forty miles from home ; but at night it did not seem to care for its food, so the next day Mr. Ts'ui, who thought perhaps illness might be the cause, held the horse in, and would not let it gallop so fast. However, the animal did not seem to approve of this, and kicked and foamed until at length Mr. Ts'ui let it go at the same old pace ; and by midday he had reached his destination. As he rode into the town, the people were astonished to hear of the marvellous journey just accomplished, and the Prince [2] sent to say he should like to buy the horse. Mr. Ts'ui, fearing that the real owner might come forward, was compelled to refuse this offer ; but when, after six months had elapsed, no inquiries had been made, he agreed to accept eight hundred ounces of silver, and handed over the horse to the Prince. He then bought himself a good mule, and returned home. Subsequently, the Prince had occasion to use the horse for some important business at Lin-ch'ing ; and when there it took the opportunity to run away. The officer in charge pursued it right up to the house of a Mr. Tsêng, who lived next door to Mr. Ts'ui, and saw it run in and disappear. Thereupon he called upon Mr. Tsêng to restore it to him ; and, on the latter declaring he had never even seen the animal, the officer walked into his private apartments, where he found, hanging on the wall, a picture of a horse, by Ch'ên Tzŭ-ang,[3] exactly like the one he was in search of, and with part of the tail burnt away by a joss-stick. It was now clear that the Prince's horse was a supernatural creature ; but the officer, being afraid to go back without it, would have prosecuted Mr. Tsêng, had not Ts'ui, whose eight hundred ounces of silver had since increased to something like ten thousand, stepped in and paid back the original purchase-money. Mr. Tsêng was exceedingly grateful to him for this act of kindness, ignorant, as he was, of the previous sale of the horse by Ts'ui to the Prince.

[2] One of the feudal Governors of bygone days.
[3] A.D. 656–698. Better known as a poet.

CXXXIX. THE BUTTERFLY'S REVENGE

MR. WANG, of Ch'ang-shan, was in the habit, when a District Magistrate, of commuting the fines and penalties of the Penal Code, inflicted on the various prisoners, for a corresponding number of butterflies. These he would let go all at once in the court, rejoicing to see them fluttering hither and thither, like so many tinsel snippings borne about by the breeze. One night he dreamt that a young lady, dressed in gay-coloured clothes, appeared to him and said, "Your cruel practice has brought many of my sisters to an untimely end, and now you shall pay the penalty of thus gratifying your tastes." The young lady then changed into a butterfly and flew away. Next day, the magistrate was sitting alone, over a cup of wine, when it was announced to him that the censor was at the door ; and out he ran at once to receive His Excellency, with a white flower, that some of his women had put in his official hat, still sticking there. His Excellency was very angry at what he deemed a piece of disrespect to himself ; and, after severely censuring Mr. Wang, turned round and went away. Thenceforward no more penalties were commuted for butterflies.

CXL. THE DOCTOR

A CERTAIN poor man, named Chang, who lived at I, fell in one day with a Taoist priest. The latter was highly skilled in the science of physiognomy ; [1] and, after looking at Chang's features, said to him, "You would make your fortune as a doctor." "Alas ! " replied Chang, "I can barely read and write ; how then could I follow such a calling as that ? " "And where, you simple fellow," asked the priest, "is the necessity for a doctor to be a scholar ? You just try, that's all." Thereupon Chang returned home ; and, being very poor, he simply collected a few of the commonest prescriptions, and set up a small stall with a handful of fishes' teeth and some dry honey-

---

[1] Advertisements of these professors of physiognomy are to be seen in every Chinese city.

comb from a wasp's nest,[2] hoping thus to earn, by his tongue, enough to keep body and soul together, to which, however, no one paid any particular attention. Now it chanced that just then the Governor of Ch'ing-chou was suffering from a bad cough, and had given orders to his subordinates to send to him the most skilful doctors in their respective districts ; and the magistrate of I, which was an out-of-the-way mountainous district, being unable to lay his hands on any one whom he could send in, gave orders to the beadle [3] to do the best he could under the circumstances. Accordingly, Chang was nominated by the people, and the magistrate put his name down to go in to the Governor. When Chang heard of his appointment, he happened to be suffering himself from a bad attack of bronchitis, which he was quite unable to cure, and he begged, therefore, to be excused ; but the magistrate would not hear of this, and forwarded him at once in charge of some constables. While crossing the hills, he became very thirsty, and went into a village to ask for a drink of water ; but water there was worth its weight in jade, and no one would give him any. By-and-by he saw an old woman washing a quantity of vegetables in a scanty supply of water, which was consequently, very thick and muddy ; and, being unable to bear his thirst any longer, he obtained this and drank it up. Shortly afterwards he found that his cough was quite cured, and then it occurred to him that he had hit upon a capital remedy. When he reached the city, he learned that a great many doctors had already tried their hand upon the patient, but without success ; so asking for a private room in which to prepare his medicines, he obtained from the town some bunches of bishop-wort, and proceeded to wash them as the old woman had done. He then took the dirty water, and gave a dose of it to the Governor, who was immediately and permanently relieved. The patient was overjoyed ; and, besides making Chang a handsome present, gave him a certificate written in golden characters, in consequence of which his fame spread far and wide ; [4] and of the numerous cases he subsequently

---

[2] In order to make some show for the public eye.
[3] See No. LXIV., note 2.
[4] A doctor of any repute generally has large numbers of such certificates, generally engraved on wood, hanging before and about

undertook, in not a single instance did he fail to effect a cure. One day, however, a patient came to him, complaining of a violent chill; and Chang, who happened to be tipsy at the time, treated him by mistake for remittent fever. When he got sober, he became aware of what he had done; but he said nothing to anybody about it, and three days afterwards the same patient waited upon him with all kinds of presents to thank him for a rapid recovery. Such cases as this were by no means rare with him; and soon he got so rich that he would not attend when summoned to visit a sick person, unless the summons was accompanied by a heavy fee and a comfortable chair to ride in.[5]

CXLI. SNOW IN SUMMER

ON the 6th day of the 7th moon [1] of the year Ting-Hai (1647) there was a heavy fall of snow at Soochow. The people were in a great state of consternation at this, and went off to the temple of the Great Prince [2] to pray. Then the spirit moved one of them to say, " You now address me as *Your Honour*. Make it *Your Excellency*, and, though I am but a lesser deity, it may be well worth your while to do so." Thereupon the people began to use the latter term, and the snow stopped at once; from

his front door.   When I was stationed at Swatow, the Chinese writer at Her Majesty's Consulate presented one to Dr. E. J. Scott, the resident medical practitioner, who had cured him of opium-smoking.   It bore two principal characters, " Miraculous Indeed ! " accompanied by a few remarks, in a smaller-sized character, laudatory of Dr. Scott's professional skill.   Banners, with graceful inscriptions written upon them, are frequently presented by Chinese passengers to the captains of coasting steamers who may have brought them safely through bad weather.

[5] The story is intended as a satire upon Chinese doctors generally, whose ranks are recruited from the swarms of half-educated candidates who have been rejected at the great competitive examinations, medical diplomas being quite unknown in China.   Doctors' fees are, by a pleasant fiction, called " horse-money ; " and all prescriptions are made up by the local apothecary, never by the physician himself.

[1] This would be exactly at the hottest season.

[2] The *Jupiter Pluvius* of the neighbourhood.

which I infer that flattery is just as pleasant to divine as to mortal ears.[3]

CXLII. PLANCHETTE [1]

At Ch'ang-shan there lived a man, named Wang Jui-t'ing, who understood the art of planchette. He called himself

[3] A sneer at the superstitious custom of praying for good or bad weather, which obtains in China from the Son of Heaven himself down to the lowest agriculturist whose interests are involved. Droughts, floods, famines, and pestilences are alike set down to the anger of Heaven, to be appeased only by prayer and repentance.

[1] Planchette was in full swing in China at the date of the composition of these stories, more than 200 years ago, and remains so at the present day. The character *chi*, used here and elsewhere for Planchette, is defined in the *Shuo Wên*, a Chinese dictionary, published A.D. 100, " to inquire by divination on doubtful topics," no mention being made of the particular manner in which responses are obtained. For the purpose of writing from personal experience, I once attended a *séance* at a temple in Amoy, and witnessed the whole performance. After much delay, I was requested to write on a slip of paper " any question I might have to put to the God ; " and, accordingly, I took a pencil and wrote down, " A humble suppliant ventures to inquire if he will win the Manila lottery." This question was then placed upon the altar, at the feet of the God ; and shortly afterwards two respectable-looking Chinamen, not priests, approached a small table covered with sand, and each seized one arm of a forked piece of wood, at the fork of which was a stumpy end, at right angles to the plane of the arms. Immediately the attendants began burning quantities of joss-paper, while the two performers whirled the instrument round and round at a rapid rate, its vertical point being all the time pressed down upon the table of sand. All of a sudden the whirling movement stopped, and the point of the instrument rapidly traced a character in the sand, which was at once identified by several of the bystanders, and forthwith copied down by a clerk in attendance. The whirling movement was then continued until a similar pause was made and another character appeared ; and so on, until I had four lines of correctly-rhymed Chinese verse, each line consisting of seven characters. The following is an almost word-for-word translation :—

" The pulse of human nature throbs from England to Cathay,
 And gambling mortals ever love to swell their gains by play ;
 For gold in this vile world of ours is everywhere a prize—
 A thousand taels shall meet the prayer that on this altar lies."

As the question is not concealed from view, all that is necessary for such a hollow deception is a quick-witted versifier who can put

a disciple of Lü Tung-pin,[2] and some one said he was probably that worthy's crane. At his *séances* the subjects were always literary—essays, poetry, and so on. The well-known scholar, Li Chih, thought very highly of him, and availed himself of his aid on more than one occasion ; so that by degrees the literati generally also patronised him. His responses to questions of doubt or difficulty were remarkable for their reasonableness ; matters of mere good or bad fortune he did not care to enter into. In 1631, just after the examination at Chi-nan, a number of the candidates requested Mr. Wang to tell them how they would stand on the list ; and after having examined their essays, he proceeded to pass his opinion on their merits.[3] Among the rest there happened to be one who was very intimate with another candidate, not present, whose name was Li Pien ; and who, being an enthusiastic student and a deep thinker, was confidently expected to appear among the successful few. Accordingly, the friend submitted Mr. Li's essay for inspection ; and in a few minutes two characters appeared on the sand—namely, "'Number one." After a short interval this sentence followed :—" The decision given just now had reference to Mr. Li's essay simply as an essay. Mr. Li's destiny is darkly obscured, and he will suffer accordingly. It is strange, indeed, that a man's literary powers and his destiny should thus be out of harmony.[4] Surely the Examiner will judge of him by his essay ;—but stay : I will go and see how matters stand." Another pause ensued, and then these words were written down :—" I have been over to the Examiner's yamên, and have found a pretty state of things going on ; instead of reading the candidates' papers himself, he has handed them over to his clerks, some half-dozen illiterate fellows who purchased their own degrees,

together a poetical response *stans pede in uno*. But in such matters the unlettered masses of China are easily outwitted, and are a profitable source of income to the more astute of their fellow-countrymen.

[2] A recluse who flourished in the eighth century of our era, and who, for his devotion to the Taoist religion, was subsequently canonised as one of the Eight Immortals. He is generally represented as riding on a crane.

[3] That is, by means of the planchette-table.

[4] Our author was here evidently thinking of his own unlucky fate.

and who, in their previous existence, had no status whatever,—'hungry devils'[5] begging their bread in all directions ; and who, after eight hundred years passed in the murky gloom of the infernal regions, have lost all discrimination, like men long buried in a cave and suddenly transferred to the light of day. Among them may be one or two who have risen above their former selves, but the odds are against an essay falling into the hands of one of these." The young men then begged to know if there was any method by which such an evil might be counteracted ; to which the planchette replied that there was, but, as it was universally understood, there was no occasion for asking the question. Thereupon they went off and told Mr. Li, who was so much distressed at the prediction that he submitted his essay to His Excellency Sun Tzŭ-mei, one of the finest scholars of the day. This gentleman examined it, and was so pleased with its literary merit that he told Li he was quite sure to pass, and the latter thought no more about the planchette prophecy. However, when the list came out, there he was down in the fourth class ; and this so much disconcerted His Excellency Mr. Sun, that he went carefully through the essay again for fear lest any blemishes might have escaped his attention. Then he cried out, "Well, I have always thought this Examiner to be a scholar ; he can never have made such a mistake as this ; it must be the fault of some of his drunken assistants, who don't know the mere rudiments of composition." This fulfilment of the prophecy raised Mr. Wang very high in the estimation of the candidates, who forthwith went and burned incense and invoked the spirit of the planchette, which at once replied in the following terms :—"Let not Mr. Li be disheartened by temporary failure. Let him rather strive to improve himself still further, and next year he may be among the first on the list." Li carried out these injunctions ; and after a time the story reached the ears of the Examiner, who gratified Li by making a public acknowledgment that there had been some miscarriage of justice at the examination ; and the following year he was passed high up on the list.[6]

5 See No. CXXXI., note 4.
6 See No. LXXV., note 1.

CXLIII. FRIENDSHIP WITH FOXES

A CERTAIN man had an enormous stack of straw, as big
as a hill, in which his servants, taking what was daily
required for use, had made quite a hole. In this hole a
fox fixed his abode, and would often show himself to the
master of the house under the form of an old man. One
day the latter invited the master to walk into the cave,
which he at first declined, but accepted on being pressed
by the fox ; and when he got inside, lo ! he saw a long
suite of handsome apartments. They then sat down, and
exquisitely perfumed tea and wine were brought ; but the
place was so gloomy that there was no difference between
night and day. By-and-by, the entertainment being over,
the guest took his leave ; and on looking back the beautiful rooms and their contents had all disappeared. The
old man himself was in the habit of going away in the
evening and returning with the first streaks of morning ;
and as no one was able to follow him, the master of the
house asked him one day whither he went. To this he
replied that a friend invited him to take wine ; and then
the master begged to be allowed to accompany him, a
proposal to which the old man very reluctantly consented.
However, he seized the master by the arm, and away they
went as though riding on the wings of the wind ; and, in
about the time it takes to cook a pot of millet, they reached
a city, and walked into a restaurant, where there were
a number of people drinking together and making a great
noise. The old man led his companion to a gallery above,
from which they could look down on the feasters below ;
and he himself went down and brought away from the
tables all kinds of nice food and wine, without appearing
to be seen or noticed by any of the company. After awhile
a man dressed in red garments came forward and laid upon
the table some dishes of cumquats ; [1] and the master at
once requested the old man to go down and get him some of
these. " Ah," replied the latter, " that is an upright man :
I cannot approach him." Thereupon the master said to

[1] Literally, " golden oranges." These are skilfully preserved by
the Cantonese, and form a delicious sweetmeat for dessert.

himself, "By thus seeking the companionship of a fox,
I then am deflected from the true course. Henceforth
I, too, will be an upright man." No sooner had he
formed this resolution, than he suddenly lost all control
over his body, and fell from the gallery down among the
revellers below. These gentlemen were much astonished
by his unexpected descent ; and he himself, looking up,
saw there was no gallery to the house, but only a large beam
upon which he had been sitting. He now detailed the
whole of the circumstances, and those present made up
a purse for him to pay his travelling expenses ; for he
was at Yu-t'ai—one thousand *li* from home.

CXLIV. THE GREAT RAT

DURING the reign of the Emperor Wan Li,[1] the palace was
troubled by the presence of a huge rat, quite as big as a cat,
which ate up all the cats that were set to catch it. Just
then it chanced that among the tribute offerings sent by
some foreign State was a lion-cat, as white as snow. This
cat was accordingly put into the room where the rat usually
appeared ; and, the door being closely shut, a secret watch
was kept. By-and-by the rat came out of its hole and
rushed at the cat, which turned and fled, finally jumping
up on the table. The rat followed, upon which the cat
jumped down.; and thus they went on up and down for
some time. Those who were watching said the cat was
afraid and of no use ; however, in a little while the rat began
to jump less briskly, and soon after squatted down out of
breath. Then the cat rushed at it, and, seizing the rat by
the back of the neck, shook and shook while its victim
squeaked and squeaked, until life was extinct. Thus they
knew that the cat was not afraid, but merely waited for
its adversary to be fatigued, fleeing when pursued and itself
pursuing the fleeing rat. Truly, many a bad swordsman
may be compared with that rat !

[1] A.D. 1573–1620, the epoch of the most celebrated " blue china."

CXLV. WOLVES

I.—A CERTAIN village butcher, who had bought some meat at market and was returning home in the evening, suddenly came across a wolf, which followed him closely, its mouth watering at the sight of what he was carrying. The butcher drew his knife and drove the animal off ; and then reflecting that his meat was the attraction, he determined to hang it up in a tree and fetch it the next morning. This he accordingly did, and the wolf followed him no further ; but when he went at daylight to recover his property, he saw something hanging up in the tree resembling a human corpse. It turned out to be the wolf, which, in its efforts to get at the meat, had been caught on the meat-hook like a fish ; and as the skin of a wolf was just then worth ten ounces of silver, the butcher found himself possessed of quite a little capital. Here we have a laughable instance of the result of " climbing trees to catch fish." [1]

II.—A butcher, while travelling alone at night, was sore pressed by a wolf, and took refuge in an old mat shed which had been put up for the watchman of the crops. There he lay, while the wolf sniffed at him from outside, and at length thrust in one of its paws from underneath. This the butcher seized hold of at once, and held it firmly, so that the wolf couldn't stir ; and then, having no other weapon at hand, he took a small knife he had with him and slit the skin underneath the wolf's paw. He now proceeded to blow into it, as butchers blow into pork ; [2] and after vigorously blowing for some time, he found that the wolf had ceased to struggle ; upon which he went outside and saw the animal lying on the ground, swelled up to the size of a cow, and unable to bend its legs or close its open

[1] A satirical remark of Mencius (Book I.), used by the sage when combating the visionary projects of a monarch of antiquity.

[2] This disgusting process is too frequently performed by native butchers at the present day, in order to give their meat a more tempting appearance. Water is also blown in through a tube, to make it heavier ; and inexperienced housekeepers are often astonished to find how light ducks and geese become after being cooked, not knowing that the fraudulent poulterer had previously stuffed their throats as full as possible of sand.

mouth. Thereupon he threw it across his shoulders and carried it off home. However, such a feat as this could only be accomplished by a butcher.

CXLVI. SINGULAR VERDICT

A SERVANT in the employ of a Mr. Sun was sleeping alone one night, when all of a sudden he was arrested and carried before the tribunal of the Ruler of Purgatory. "This is not the right man," cried His Majesty, and immediately sent him back. However, after this the servant was afraid to sleep on that bed again, and took up his quarters elsewhere. But another servant, named Kuo Ngan, seeing the vacant place, went and occupied it. A third servant, named Li Lu, who had an old standing grudge against the first, stole up to the bed that same night with a knife in his hand, and killed Kuo Ngan [1] in mistake for his enemy. Kuo's father at once brought the case before the magistrate of the place, pleading that the murdered man was his only son on whom he depended for his living ; and the magistrate decided that Kuo was to take Li Lu in the place of his dead son, much to the discomfiture of the old man. Truly the descent of the first servant into Purgatory was not so marvellous as the magistrate's decision !

CXLVII. THE GRATEFUL DOG

A CERTAIN trader who had been doing business at Wu-hu and was returning home with the large profits he had made, saw on the river-bank a butcher tying up a dog.[1] He bought the animal for much more than its value, and carried it along with him in his boat. Now the boatman had formerly been a bandit ; and, tempted by his passenger's

[1] This was the man whose destiny it was really to die just then, and appear before the Ruler of Purgatory.

[1] The city of Canton boasts several "cat and dog" restaurants ; but the consumption of this kind of food is much less universal than is generally supposed.

wealth, ran the boat among the rushes, and, drawing a knife, prepared to slay him. The trader begged the man to leave him a whole skin;[2] so the boatman wrapped him up in a carpet and threw him into the river. The dog, on seeing what was done, whined piteously, and, jumping into the river, seized the bundle with his teeth and did his best to keep the trader above water until at length a shallow spot was reached. The animal then succeeded by continuous barking in attracting the attention of some people on the bank, and they hauled the bundle out of the river, and released the trader, who was still alive. The latter asked to be taken back to Wu-hu, where he might look out for the robber boatman; but just as he was about to start, lo! the dog was missing. The trader was much distressed at this; and after spending some days at Wu-hu without being able to find, among the forest of masts collected there, the particular boat he wanted, he was on the point of returning home with a friend, when suddenly the dog reappeared, and seemed by its barking to invite its master to follow in a certain direction. This the trader did, until at length the dog jumped on a boat and seized one of the boatmen by the leg. No beating could make the animal let go; and on looking closely at the man, the trader saw he was the identical boatman who had robbed and tried to murder him. He had changed his clothes and also his boat, so that at first he was not recognisable; he was now, however, arrested, and the whole of the money was found in his boat. To think that a dog could show gratitude like that! Truly there are not a few persons who would be put to shame by that faithful animal.[3]

[2] Not in our sense of the term. It was not death, but decapitation, or even mutilation, from which the trader begged to be spared. See No. LXXII., note 6.

[3] The Chinese dog is usually an ill-fed, barking cur, without one redeeming trait in its character. Valued as a guardian of house and property, this animal does not hold the same social position as with us; its very name is a byword of reproach; and the people of Tongking explain their filthy custom of blackening the teeth on the ground that a dog's teeth are white.

CXLVIII. THE GREAT TEST

BEFORE Mr. Yang Ta-hung [1] was known to fame, he had already acquired some reputation as a scholar in his own part of the country, and felt convinced himself that his was to be no mean destiny. When the list of successful candidates at the examination was brought to where he lived, he was in the middle of dinner, and rushed out with his mouth full to ask if his name was there or not ; and on hearing that it was not, he experienced such a revulsion of feeling that what he then swallowed stuck fast like a lump in his chest and made him very ill. His friends tried to appease him by advising him to try at the further examination of the rejected, and when he urged that he had no money, they subscribed ten ounces of silver and started him on his way.

That night he dreamt that a man appeared to him and said, " Ahead of you there is one who can cure your complaint : beseech him to aid you." The man then added—

A tune on the flute 'neath the riverside willow ;
Oh, show no regret when 'tis cast to the billow !

Next day, Mr. Yang actually met a Taoist priest sitting beneath a willow tree ; and, making him a bow, asked him to prescribe for his malady. " You have come to the wrong person," replied the priest, smiling ; " I cannot cure diseases ; but had you asked me for a tune on the flute, I could have possibly helped you." Then Mr. Yang knew that his dream was being fulfilled ; and going down on his knees offered the priest all the money he had. The priest took it, but immediately threw it into the river, at which Mr. Yang, thinking how hardly he had come by his money, was moved to express his regret. " Aha ! " cried the priest at this ; " so you are not indifferent, eh ? You'll find your money all safe on the bank." There indeed Mr. Yang found it, at which he was so much astonished that he

[1] A celebrated scholar and statesman, who flourished towards the close of the Ming dynasty, and distinguished himself by his impeachment of the powerful eunuch, Wei Chung-hsien,—a dangerous step to take in those eunuch-ridden times.

addressed the priest as though he had been an angel. " I
am no angel," said the priest, " but here comes one ; "
whereupon Mr. Yang looked behind him, and the priest
seized the opportunity to give him a slap on the back,
crying out at the same time, " You worldly-minded
fellow ! " This blow brought up the lump of food that had
stuck in his chest, and he felt better at once ; but when
he looked round the priest had disappeared.[2]

CXLIX. THE ALCHEMIST [1]

At Ch'ang-ngan there lived a scholar named Chia Tzū-lung,
who one day noticed a very refined-looking stranger ; and,
on making inquiries about him, learnt that he was a Mr.
Chên who had taken lodgings hard by. Accordingly, next
day Chia called and sent in his card, but did not see Chên,
who happened to be out at the time. The same thing
occurred thrice, and at length Chia engaged some one to
watch and let him know when Mr. Chên was at home.
However, even then the latter would not come forth to
receive his guest, and Chia had to go in and rout him out.
The two now entered into conversation, and soon became
mutually charmed with each other ; and by-and-by Chia
sent off a servant to bring wine from a neighbouring wine-
shop. Mr. Chên proved himself a pleasant boon companion,
and when the wine was nearly finished, he went to a box
and took from it some wine-cups and a large and beautiful
jade tankard, into the latter of which he poured a single
cup of wine, and lo ! it was filled to the brim. They then
proceeded to help themselves from the tankard ; but how-

[2] Mr. Yang was a man of tried virtue, and had he been able to
tolerate the loss of his money, the priest would have given him, not
merely a cure for the bodily ailment under which he was suffering,
but a knowledge of those means by which he might have obtained
the salvation of his soul, and have enrolled himself among the ranks
of the Taoist Immortals. " To those, however," remarks the
author, " who lament that Mr. Yang was too worldly-minded to
secure this great prize, I reply, ' Better one more good man on earth,
than an extra angel in heaven.' "

[1] Alchemy is first mentioned in Chinese history B.C. 133, and
was widely cultivated in China during the Han dynasty by priests
of the Taoist religion.

ever much they took out, the contents never seemed to
diminish. Chia was astonished at this, and begged Mr.
Chên to tell him how it was done. " Ah," replied Mr. Chên,
" I tried to avoid making your acquaintance solely because
of your one bad quality—avarice. The art I practise is
a secret known to the Immortals only : how can I divulge
it to you ? " " You do me wrong," rejoined Chia, 'in thus
attributing avarice to me. The avaricious, indeed, are
always poor." Mr. Chên laughed, and they separated for
that day ; but from that time they were constantly together,
and all ceremony was laid aside between them. Whenever
Chia wanted money, Mr. Chên would bring out a black
stone, and, muttering a charm, would rub it on a tile or
a brick, which was forthwith changed into a lump of silver.
This silver he would give to Chia, and it was always just as
much as he actually required, neither more nor less ; and
if ever the latter asked for more, Mr. Chên would rally him
on the subject of avarice. Finally, Chia determined to try
and get possession of this stone ; and one day, when Mr.
Chên was sleeping off the fumes of a drinking-bout, he tried
to extract it from his clothes. However, Chên detected
him at once, and declared that they could be friends no
more, and next day he left the place altogether. About
a year afterwards Chia was one day wandering by the river-
bank, when he saw a handsome-looking stone, marvellously
like that in the possession of Mr. Chên ; and he picked it up
at once and carried it home with him. A few days passed
away, and suddenly Mr. Chên presented himself at Chia's
house, and explained that the stone in question possessed
the property of changing anything into gold, and had been
bestowed upon him long before by a certain Taoist priest,
whom he had followed as a disciple. " Alas ! " added he,
" I got tipsy and lost it ; but divination told me where it
was, and if you will now restore it to me, I shall take care
to repay your kindness." " You have divined rightly,"
replied Chia ; " the stone is with me ; but recollect, if you
please, that the indigent Kuan Chung [2] shared the wealth
of his friend Pao Shu." At this hint Mr. Chên said he
would give Chia one hundred ounces of silver ; to which the
latter replied that one hundred ounces was a fair offer, but
that he would far sooner have Mr. Chên teach him the

[2] See No. XXII., note 1.

formula to utter when rubbing the stone on anything, so
as just to try the thing once himself. Mr. Chên was afraid
to do this ; whereupon Chia cried out, " You are an
Immortal yourself ; you must know well enough that I
would never deceive a friend." So Mr. Chên was prevailed
upon to teach him the formula, and then Chia would have
tried the art upon the immense stone washing-block [3] which
was lying near at hand had not Mr. Chên seized his arm and
begged him not to do anything so outrageous. Chia then
picked up half a brick and laid it on the washing-block,
saying to Mr. Chên, " This little piece is not too much,
surely ? " Accordingly, Mr. Chên relaxed his hold and let
Chia proceed ; which he did by promptly ignoring the half
brick and quickly rubbing the stone on the washing-block.
Mr. Chên turned pale when he saw him do this, and made
a dash forward to get hold of the stone ; but it was too late,
the washing-block was already a solid mass of silver, and
Chia quietly handed him back the stone. " Alas ! alas ! "
cried Mr. Chên in despair, " what is to be done now ? For
having thus irregularly conferred wealth upon a mortal,[4]
Heaven will surely punish me. Oh, if you would save me,
give away one hundred coffins [5] and one hundred suits of
wadded clothes." " My friend," replied Chia, " my object
in getting money was not to hoard it up like a miser."
Mr. Chên was delighted at this ; and during the next three
years Chia engaged in trade, taking care to be all the time
fulfilling his promise to Mr. Chên. At the expiration of
that time Mr. Chên himself reappeared, and, grasping
Chia's hand, said to him, " Trustworthy and noble friend,
when we last parted the Spirit of Happiness impeached me
before God,[6] and my name was erased from the list of
angels. But now that you have carried out my request,

---

[3] These are used, together with a heavy wooden *bâton*, by the
Chinese washerman, the effect being most disastrous to a European
wardrobe.

[4] For thus interfering with the appointments of Destiny.

[5] To provide coffins for poor people has ever been regarded as an
act of transcendent merit. The tornado at Canton in April 1878,
in which several thousand lives were lost, afforded an admirable
opportunity for the exercise of this form of charity—an opportunity
which was very largely availed of by the benevolent.

[6] For usurping its prerogative by allowing Chia to obtain un-
authorised wealth.

that sentence has accordingly been rescinded. Go on as you have begun, without ceasing." Chia asked Mr. Chên what office he filled in heaven ; to which the latter replied that he was only a fox, who, by a sinless life, had finally attained to that clear perception of the Truth which leads to immortality. Wine was then brought, and the two friends enjoyed themselves together as of old ; and even when Chia had passed the age of ninety years, that fox still used to visit him from time to time.

CL. RAISING THE DEAD

MR. T'ANG P'ING, who took the highest degree in the year 1661, was suffering from a protracted illness, when suddenly he felt, as it were, a warm glow rising from his extremities upwards. By the time it had reached his knees, his feet were perfectly numb and without sensation ; and before long his knees and the lower part of his body were similarly affected. Gradually this glow worked its way up until it attacked the heart,[1] and then some painful moments ensued. Every single incident of Mr. T'ang's life from his boyhood upwards, no matter how trivial, seemed to surge through his mind, borne along on the tide of his heart's blood. At the revival of any virtuous act of his, he experienced a delicious feeling of peace and calm ; but when any wicked deed passed before his mind, a painful disturbance took place within him, like oil boiling and fretting in a cauldron. He was quite unable to describe the pangs he suffered ; however, he mentioned that he could recollect having stolen, when only seven or eight years old, some young birds from their nest, and having killed them ; and for this alone, he said, boiling blood rushed through his heart during the space of an ordinary meal-time. Then when all the acts of his life had passed one after another in panorama before him, the warm glow proceeded up his throat, and, entering the brain, issued out at the top of his head like smoke from a chimney. By-and-by Mr. T'ang's soul escaped from his body by the same aperture, and wandered far away, forgetting all about the tenement it had

[1] See No. XIV., note 5.

left behind.   Just at that moment a huge giant came along, and, seizing the soul, thrust it into his sleeve, where it remained cramped and confined, huddled up with a crowd of others, until existence was almost unbearable.   Suddenly Mr. T‘ang reflected that Buddha alone could save him from this horrible state, and forthwith he began to call upon his holy name.[2]   At the third or fourth invocation he fell out of the giant's sleeve, whereupon the latter picked him up and put him back ; but this happened several times, and at length the giant, wearied of picking him up, let him lie where he was.   The soul lay there for some time, not knowing in which direction to proceed ; however, it soon recollected that the land of Buddha was in the west, and westwards accordingly it began to shape its course.   In a little while the soul came upon a Buddhist priest sitting by the roadside, and hastening forwards, respectfully inquired of him which was the right way.   " The record of life and death 'for scholars," replied the priest, " is in the hands of Wên-ch‘ang [3] and Confucius ; any application must receive the consent of both."   The priest then directed Mr. T‘ang on his way, and the latter journeyed along until he reached a Confucian temple, in which the Sage was sitting with his face to the south.[4]   On hearing his business, Confucius referred him on to Wên-ch‘ang ; and, proceeding onwards in the direction indicated, Mr. T‘ang by-and-by arrived at what seemed to be the palace of a king, within which sat Wên-ch‘ang precisely as we depict him on earth.   " You are an upright man," replied the God, in reply to Mr. T‘ang's prayer, " and are certainly entitled to a longer span of life ; but by this time your mortal body has become decomposed, and unless you can secure the assistance of P‘u-sa,[5] I can give you no aid."   So Mr. T‘ang set off once more, and hurried along until he came to a magnificent shrine standing in a thick grove of tall bamboos ; and, entering in, he stood in the presence of the God, on whose head was the *ushnisha*,[6] whose golden

[2] See No. LIV., note 3.
[3] The God of Literature.
[4] See No. LXXVII., note 1.
[5] See No. XXVI, note 5.
[6] A fleshy protuberance on the head, which is the distinguishing mark of a Buddha.

face was round like the full moon, and at whose side was a green willow-branch bending gracefully over the lip of a vase. Humbly Mr. T'ang prostrated himself on the ground, and repeated what Wên-ch'ang had said to him; but P'u-sa seemed to think it would be impossible to grant his request, until one of the Lohans [7] who stood by cried out, " O God, Thou canst perform this miracle : take earth and make his flesh ; take a sprig of willow and make his bones." Thereupon P'u-sa broke off a piece from the willow-branch in the vase beside him ; and, pouring a little of the water upon the ground, he made clay, and, casting the whole over Mr. T'ang's soul, bade an attendant lead the body back to the place where his coffin was. At that instant Mr. T'ang's family heard a groan proceeding from within his coffin, and, on rushing to it and helping out the lately-deceased man, they found he had quite recovered. He had then been dead seven days.

CLI. FÊNG-SHUI [1]

AT I-chou there lived a high official named Sung, whose family were all ardent supporters of Fêng-Shui ; so much so, that even the women-folk read books [2] on the subject, and understood the principles of the science. When Mr.

[7] The eighteen personal disciples of Shâkyamuni Buddha. Sixteen of these are Hindoos, which number was subsequently increased by the addition of two Chinese Buddhists.

[1] Literally, " wind and water," or that which cannot be seen and that which cannot be grasped. I have explained the term in my *Chinese Sketches*, p. 143, as " a system of geomancy, by the *science* of which it is possible to determine the desirability of sites,—whether of tombs, houses, or cities, from the configuration of such natural objects as rivers, trees, and hills, and to foretell with certainty the fortunes of any family, community, or individual according to the spot selected ; by the *art* of which it is in the power of the geomancer to counteract evil influences by good ones, to transform straight and noxious outlines into undulating and propitious curves, and rescue whole districts from the devastations of flood or pestilence."

[2] As a rule, only the daughters of wealthy families receive any education to speak of.

Sung died, his two sons set up separate establishments,[3] and each invited to his own house geomancers from far and near, who had any reputation in their art, to select a spot for the dead man's grave. By degrees, they had collected together as many as a hundred apiece, and every day they would scour the country round, each at the head of his own particular regiment. After about a month of this work, both sides had fixed upon a suitable position for the grave ; and the geomancers engaged by one brother, declared that if their spot was selected he would certainly some day be made a marquis, while the other brother was similarly informed, by his geomancers, that by adopting their choice, he would infallibly rise to the rank of Secretary of State. Thus, neither brother would give way to the other, but each set about making the grave in his own particular place,— pitching marquees, and arranging banners, and making all necessary preparations for the funeral. Then when the coffin arrived at the point where roads branched off to the two graves, the two brothers, each leading on his own little army of geomancers, bore down upon it with a view to gaining possession of the corpse. From morn till dewy eve the battle raged ; and as neither gained any advantage over the other, the mourners and friends, who had come to witness the ceremony of burial, stole away one by one ; and the coolies, who were carrying the coffin, after changing the poles from one shoulder to another until they were quite worn out, put the body down by the roadside, and went off home. It then became necessary to make some protection for the coffin against the wind and rain ; whereupon the elder brother immediately set about building a hut close by, in which he purposed leaving some of his attendants to keep guard ; but he had no sooner begun than the younger brother followed his example ; and when the elder built a second and third, the younger also built a second and third ; and as this went on for the space of three whole years, by the end of that time the place had become quite a little village. By-and-by, both brothers died, one directly after the other ; and then their two wives determined to cast to

---

[3] A reprehensible proceeding in the eyes of all respectable Chinese, both from a moral and a practical point of view ; " for when brothers fall out," says the proverb, " strangers get an advantage over them."

the winds the decision of each party of geomancers. Accordingly, they went together to the two spots in question ; and after inspecting them carefully, declared that neither was suitable. The next step was to jointly engage another set of geomancers, who submitted for their approval several different spots, and ten days had hardly passed away before the two women had agreed upon the position for their father-in-law's grave, which, as the wife of the younger brother prophesied, would surely give to the family a high military degree. So the body was buried, and within three years Mr. Sung's eldest grandson, who had entered as a military cadet, actually took the corresponding degree to a literary master of arts.

[" Fêng-Shui," adds the author, " may or may not be based upon sound principles ; at any rate, to indulge a morbid belief in it is utter folly ; and thus to join issue and fight while a coffin is relegated to the roadside, is hardly in accordance with the doctrines of filial piety or fraternal love. Can people believe that mere position will improve the fortunes of their family ? At any rate, that two women should have thus quietly settled the matter is certainly worthy of record."]

CLII. THE LINGERING DEATH

THERE was a man in our village who led an exceedingly disreputable life. One morning when he got up rather early, two men appeared, and led him away to the market-place, where he saw a butcher hanging up half a pig. As they approached, the two men shoved him with all their might against the dead animal, and lo ! his own flesh began to blend with the pork before him, while his conductors hurried off in an opposite direction. By-and-by the butcher wanted to sell a piece of his meat ; and, seizing a knife, began to cut off the quantity required. At every touch of the blade our disreputable friend experienced a severe pang, which penetrated into his very marrow ; and when, at length, an old man came and haggled over the weight given him, crying out for a little bit more fat, or an extra portion of lean,[1] then, as the butcher sliced away the pork ounce by ounce, the pain was unendurable in the extreme. By about nine o'clock the pork was all sold, and our hero went home, whereupon his family asked him what he meant by staying in bed so late.[2] He then narrated all that had taken place, and on making inquiries, they found that the pork-butcher had only just come home ; besides which our friend was able to tell him every pound of meat he had sold, and every slice he had cut off. Fancy a man being put to the lingering death[3] like this before breakfast !

CLIII. DREAMING HONOURS

WANG TZU-NGAN was a Tung-ch'ang man, and a scholar of some repute, but unfortunate at the public examinations. On one occasion, after having been up for his master's degree, his anxiety was very great ; and when the time for the publication of the list drew near, he drank himself gloriously tipsy, and went and lay down on the bed. In a few moments a man rushed in, and cried out, " Sir ! you have passed ! " whereupon Wang jumped up, and said, " Give him ten strings of cash."[1] Wang's wife, seeing he was drunk, and wishing to keep him quiet, replied, " You go on sleeping : I've given him the money." So Wang lay down again, but before long in came another man who informed Wang that his name was among the successful candidates for the highest degree. " Why, I haven't been up for it yet," said Wang ; " how can I have passed ? " "What ! you don't mean to say you have forgotten the examination ? " answered the man ; and then Wang got up once more, and gave orders to present the informant with ten strings of cash. " All right," replied his wife ;

[1] Chinese tradesmen invariably begin by giving short weight in such transactions as these, partly in order to be in a position to gratify the customer by throwing in a trifle more and thus acquire a reputation for fair dealing.
[2] It was only his soul that had left the house.
[3] See No. LVI., note 12.
[1] See No. CXXIII., note 2.

" you go on sleeping : I've given him the money." Another
short interval, and in burst a third messenger to say that
Wang had been elected a member of the National Academy,
and that two official servants had come to escort him
thither. Sure enough there were the two servants bowing
at the bedside, and accordingly Wang directed that they
should be served with wine and meat, which his wife,
smiling at his drunken nonsense, declared had been already
done. Wang now bethought him that he should go out
and receive the congratulations of the neighbours, and
roared out several times to his official servants ; but without
receiving any answer. " Go to sleep," said his wife, " and
wait till I have fetched them ; " and after awhile the servants
actually came in ; whereupon Wang stamped and swore
at them for being such idiots as to go away. " What ! you
wretched scoundrel," cried the servants, " are you cursing
us in earnest, when we are only joking with you ! " At
this Wang's rage knew no bounds, and he set upon the men,
and gave them a sound beating, knocking the hat of one off
on to the ground. In the *mêlée*, he himself tumbled over,
and his wife ran in to pick him up, saying, " Shame upon
you, for getting so drunk as this ! " " I was only punishing
the servants as they deserved," replied Wang ; " why do
you call me drunk ? " " Do you mean the old woman who
cooks our rice and boils the water for your foot-bath," asked
his wife, smiling, " that you talk of servants to wait upon
your poverty-stricken carcase ? " At this sally all the
women burst out in a roar of laughter ; and Wang, who was
just beginning to get sober, waked up as if from a dream,
and knew that there was no reality in all that had taken
place. However, he recollected the spot where the servant's
hat had fallen off, and on going thither to look for it, lo !
he beheld a tiny official hat, no larger than a wine-cup,
lying there behind the door. They were all much astonished at this, and Wang himself cried out, " Formerly
people were thus tricked by devils ; and now foxes are
playing the fool with me ! " [2]

[2] A common saying is, " Foxes in the north ; devils in the south,"
as illustrative of the folk-lore of these two great divisions of China.

CLIV. THE SHE-WOLF AND THE HERD-BOYS

Two herd-boys went up among the hills and found a wolf's lair with two little wolves in it. Seizing each of them one, they forthwith climbed two trees which stood there, at a distance of forty or fifty paces apart. Before long the old wolf came back, and, finding her cubs gone, was in a great state of distress. Just then, one of the herd-boys pinched his cub and made it squeak ; whereupon the mother ran angrily towards the tree whence the sound proceeded, and tried to climb up it. At this juncture, the boy in the other tree pinched the other cub, and thereby diverted the wolf's attention in that direction. But no sooner had she reached the foot of the second tree, than the boy who had first pinched his cub did so again, and away ran the old wolf back to the tree in which her other young one was. Thus they went on time after time, until the mother was dead tired, and lay down exhausted on the ground. Then, when after some time she showed no signs of moving, the herd-boys crept stealthily down, and found that the wolf was already stiff and cold. And truly, it is better to meet a blustering foe with his hand upon his sword-hilt, by retiring within doors, and leaving him to fret his violence away unopposed ; for such is but the behaviour of brute beasts, of which men thus take advantage.

CLV. ADULTERATION [1] PUNISHED

At Chin-ling there lived a seller of spirits, who was in the habit of adulterating his liquor with water and a certain drug, the effect of which was that even a few cups would make the strongest-headed man as drunk as a jelly-fish.[2] Thus his shop acquired a reputation for having a good article on sale, and by degrees he became a rich man. One

[1] In no country in the world is adulteration more extensively practised than in China, the only formal check upon it being a religious one—the dread of punishment in the world below.

[2] The text has here a word (literally, " mud ") explained to be the name of a boneless aquatic creature, which on being removed from the water lies motionless like a lump of mud. The common term for a jelly-fish is *shui-mu*, " water-mother."

morning, on getting up, he found a fox lying drunk along-side of the spirit vat ; and tying its legs together, he was about to fetch a knife, when suddenly the fox waked up, and began pleading for its life, promising in return to do anything the spirit-merchant might require. The latter then released the animal, which instantly changed into the form of a human being. Now, at that very time, the wife of a neighbour was suffering under fox influence, and this recently-transformed animal confessed to the spirit-merchant that it was he who had been troubling her. Thereupon the spirit-merchant, who knew the lady in question to be a celebrated beauty, begged his fox friend to secretly introduce him to her. After raising some ob-jections, the fox at length consented, and conducted the spirit-merchant to a cave, where he gave him a suit of serge clothes, which he said had belonged to his late brother, and in which he told him he could easily go. The merchant put them on, and returned home, when, to his great delight, he observed that no one could see him, but that if he changed into his ordinary clothes everybody could see him as before. Accordingly he set off with the fox for his neighbour's house ; and, when they arrived, the first thing they beheld was a charm on the wall, like a great wriggling dragon. At this the fox was greatly alarmed, and said, " That scoundrel of a priest ! I can't go any farther." He then ran off home, leaving the spirit-merchant to proceed by himself. The latter walked quietly in, to find that the dragon on the wall was a real one, and preparing to fly at him, so he too turned, and ran away as fast as his legs could carry him. The fact was that the family had' engaged a priest to drive away the fox influence ; and he, not being able to go at the moment himself, gave them this charm to stick up on the wall. The following day the priest himself came, and, arranging an altar, proceeded to exorcise the fox. All the villagers crowded round to see, and among others was the spirit-merchant, who, in the middle of the ceremony, suddenly changed colour, and hurried out of the front door, where he fell on the ground in the shape of a fox, having his clothes still hanging about his arms and legs. The bystanders would have killed him on the spot, but his wife begged them to spare him ; and the priest let her take the fox home, where in a few days it died.

CLVI. A CHINESE SOLOMON

IN our district there lived two men, named Hu Ch'êng and
Fêng Ngan, between whom there existed an old feud.
The former, however, was the stronger of the two ; and
accordingly Fêng disguised his feelings under a specious
appearance of friendship, though Hu never placed much
faith in his professions. One day they were drinking
together, and being both of them rather the worse for
liquor, they began to brag of the various exploits they had
achieved. "What care I for poverty," cried Hu, "when
I can lay a hundred ounces of silver on the table at a
moment's notice ? " Now Fêng was well aware of the
state of Hu's affairs, and did not hesitate to scout such
pretensions, until Hu further informed him in perfect
seriousness that the day before he had met a merchant
travelling with a large sum of money and had tumbled him
down a dry well by the wayside ; in confirmation of which
he produced several hundred ounces of silver, which really
belonged to a brother-in-law on whose behalf he was
managing some negotiations for the purchase of land.
When they separated, Fêng went off and gave information
to the magistrate of the place, who summoned Hu to
answer to the charge. Hu then told the actual facts of the
case, and his brother-in-law and the owner of the land
in question corroborated his statement. However, on
examining the dry well by letting a man down with a rope
round him, lo ! there was a headless corpse lying at the
bottom. Hu was horrified at this, and called Heaven to
witness that he was innocent ; whereupon the magistrate
ordered him twenty or thirty blows on the mouth for lying
in the presence of such irrefragable proof, and cast him into
the condemned cell, where he lay loaded with chains.
Orders were issued that the corpse was not to be removed,
and a notification was made to the people, calling upon the
relatives of the deceased to come forward and claim the
body. Next day a woman appeared, and said deceased
was her husband ; that his name was Ho, and that he was
proceeding on business with a large sum of money about
him when he was killed by Hu. The magistrate observed
that possibly the body in the well might not be that of her

husband, to which the woman replied that she felt sure it was; and accordingly the corpse was brought up and examined, when the woman's story was found to be correct. She herself did not go near the body, but stood at a little distance making the most doleful lamentations; until at length the magistrate said, "We have got the murderer, but the body is not complete; you go home and wait until the head has been discovered, when life shall be given for life." He then summoned Hu before him, and told him to produce the head by the next day under penalty of severe torture; but Hu only wandered about with the guard sent in charge of him, crying and lamenting his fate, but finding nothing. The instruments of torture were then produced, and preparations were made as if for torturing Hu; however, they were not applied,[1] and finally the magistrate sent him back to prison, saying, "I suppose that in your hurry you didn't notice where you dropped the head." The woman was then brought before him again; and on learning that her relatives consisted only of one uncle, the magistrate remarked, "A young woman like you, left alone in the world, will hardly be able to earn a livelihood. [Here she burst into tears and implored the magistrate's pity.] The punishment of the guilty man has been already decided upon, but until we get the head, the case cannot be closed. As soon as it is closed, the best thing you can do is to marry again. A young woman like yourself should not be in and out of a police court." The woman thanked the magistrate and retired; and the latter issued a notice to the people, calling upon them to make a search for the head. On the following day, a man named Wang, a fellow villager of the deceased, reported that he had found the missing head; and his report proving to be true, he was rewarded with 1000 *cash*. The magistrate now summoned the woman's uncle above mentioned, and told him that the case was complete, but that as it involved such an important matter as the life of a human being, there would necessarily be some delay in closing it for good and all.[2]

---

[1] See No. LXXIII., note 2.

[2] There is a widespread belief that human life in China is held at a cheap rate. This may be accounted for by the fact that death is the legal punishment for many crimes not considered capital in the West; and by the severe measures that are always taken in

" Meanwhile," added the magistrate, "your niece is a young woman and has no children ; persuade her to marry again and so keep herself out of these troubles, and never mind what people may say." [3] The uncle at first refused to do this ; upon which the magistrate was obliged to threaten him, until he was ultimately forced to consent. At this, the woman appeared before the magistrate to thank him for what he had done; whereupon the latter gave out that any person who was willing to take the woman to wife was to present himself at his yamên. Immediately afterwards an application was made—by the very man who had found the head. The magistrate then sent for the woman and asked her if she could say who was the real murderer ; to which she replied that Hu Ch'êng had done the deed. "No!" cried the magistrate ; "it was not he. It was you and this man here. [Here both began loudly to protest their innocence.] I have long known this ; but, fearing to leave the smallest loophole for escape, I have tarried thus long in elucidating the circumstances. How [to the woman], before the corpse was removed from the well, were you so certain that it was your husband's body ? *Because you already knew he was dead.* And does a trader who has several hundred ounces of silver about him dress as shabbily as your husband was dressed ? And you [to the man], how did you manage to find the head so readily ? *Because you were in a hurry to marry the woman.*" The two culprits stood there as pale as death, unable to utter a word in their defence ; and on the application of torture both confessed the crime. For this man, the woman's paramour, had killed her husband, curiously enough, about the time of Hu Ch'êng's braggart joke. He was accordingly released, but Fêng suffered the penalty of a false accuser ; he was severely bambooed, and banished for three years. The case was thus brought to a close without the wrongful punishment of a single person.

cases of rebellion, when the innocent and guilty are often indiscriminately massacred. In times of tranquillity, however, this is not the case ; and the execution of a criminal is surrounded by a number of formalities which go far to prevent the shedding of innocent blood. The *Hsi yüan lu* (see No. XIV., note 8) opens with the words, "There is nothing more important than human life."

[3] See No. LXVII., note 1.

CLVII. THE RUKH

Two herons built their nest under one of the ornaments on the roof of a temple at Tientsin. The accumulated dust of years in the shrine below concealed a huge serpent, having the diameter of a washing-basin ; and whenever the herons' young were ready to fly, the reptile proceeded to the nest and swallowed every one of them, to the great distress of the bereaved parents. This took place three years consecutively, and people thought the birds would build there no more. However, the following year they came again ; and when the time was drawing nigh for their young ones to take wing, away they flew, and remained absent for nearly three days. On their return, they went straight to the nest, and began amidst much noisy chattering to feed their young ones as usual. Just then the serpent crawled up to reach his prey ; and as he was nearing the nest the parent-birds flew out and screamed loudly in mid-air. Immediately, there was heard a mighty flapping of wings, and darkness came over the face of the earth, which the astonished spectators now perceived to be caused by a huge bird obscuring the light of the sun. Down it swooped with the speed of wind or falling rain, and, striking the serpent with its talons, tore its head off at a blow, bringing down at the same time several feet of the masonry of the temple. Then it flew away, the herons accompanying it as though escorting a guest. The nest too had come down, and of the two young birds one was killed by the fall ; the other was taken by the priests and put in the bell tower, whither the old birds returned to feed it until thoroughly fledged, when it spread its wings and was gone.[1]

[1] This story is inserted chiefly in illustration of the fact that all countries have a record of some enormous bird such as the *rukh* of *The Arabian Nights*.

CLVIII. THE FAITHFUL GANDER [1]

A sportsman of Tientsin, having snared a wild goose, was followed to his home by the gander, which flew round and round him in great distress, and only went away at night-fall. Next day, when the sportsman went out, there was the bird again ; and at length it alighted quite close to his feet. He was on the point of seizing it when suddenly it stretched out its neck and disgorged a piece of pure gold ; whereupon, the sportsman, understanding what the bird meant, cried out, " I see ! this is to ransom your mate, eh ? " Accordingly, he at once released the goose, and the two birds flew away with many expressions of their mutual joy, leaving to the sportsman nearly three ounces of pure gold. Can, then, mere birds have such feelings as these ? Of all sorrows there is no sorrow like separation from those we love ; and it seems that the same holds good even of dumb animals.

CLIX. THE ELEPHANTS AND THE LION

A huntsman of Kuang-si, who was out on the hills with his bow and arrows, lay down to rest awhile, and unwittingly fell fast asleep. As he was slumbering, an elephant came up, and, coiling his trunk around the man, carried him off. The latter gave himself up for dead ; but before long the elephant had deposited him at the foot of a tall tree, and had summoned up a whole herd of comrades, who crowded about the huntsman as though asking his assistance. The elephant who had brought him went and lay down under the tree, and first looked up into its branches and then looked down at the man, apparently requesting him to get up into the tree. So the latter jumped on the elephant's back and then clambered up to the topmost branch, not knowing what he was expected to do next. By-and-by a lion [1] arrived, and from among the frightened herd

[1] See No. XXXV., note 3.

[1] The term here used refers to a creature which partakes rather of the fabulous than of the real. The *Kuang yün* says it is " a kind of lion ; " but other authorities describe it as a horse. Its favourite food is tiger-flesh. Incense-burners are often made after the " lion " pattern and called by this name, the smoke of the incense issuing from the mouth of the animal, like our own gargoyles.

chose out a fat elephant, which he seemed as though about to devour. The others remained there trembling, not daring to run away, but looking wistfully up into the tree. Thereupon the huntsman drew an arrow from his quiver and shot the lion dead, at which all the elephants below made him a grateful obeisance. He then descended, when the elephant lay down again and invited him to mount by pulling at his clothes with its trunk. This he did, and was carried to a place where the animal scratched the ground with its foot, and revealed to him a vast number of old tusks. He jumped down and collected them in a bundle, after which the elephant conveyed him to a spot whence he easily found his way home.[2]

CLX. THE HIDDEN TREASURE

LI YÜEH-SHÊNG was a second son of a rich old man who used to bury his money, and who was known to his fellow-townsmen as " Old Crocks." One day the father fell sick, and summoned his sons to divide the property between them.[1] He gave four-fifths to the elder and only one-fifth to the younger, saying to the latter, " It is not that I love your brother more than I love you : I have other money stored away, and when you are alone I will hand that over to you." A few days afterwards the old man grew worse, and Yüeh-shêng, afraid that his father might die at any moment, seized an opportunity of seeing him alone to ask about the money that he himself was to receive. " Ah," replied the dying man, " the sum of our joys and of our sorrows is determined by fate. You are now happy in the possession of a virtuous wife, and have no right to an increase of wealth." For, as a matter of fact, this second son was married to a lady from the Ch'ê family whose virtue equalled that of any of the heroines of history : hence his father's remark. Yüeh-shêng, however, was not satisfied, and implored to be

[2] Compare the elephant story in the seventh voyage of Es-Sindibàd of the Sea (Lane's *Arabian Nights*, vol. iii., p. 77).
[1] All sons, whether by wife or concubine, share equally, and in preference to daughters, even though there should be a written will in favour of the latter, the power of bequeathing by will, except as regards trifling matters of detail, being practically non-existent.

allowed to have the money; and at length the old man got angry and said, " You are only just turned twenty; you have known none of the trials of life, and were I to give a thousand ounces of gold, it would soon be all spent. Go ! and, until you have drunk the cup of bitterness to its dregs, expect no money from me." Now Yüeh-shêng was a filial son, and when his father spoke thus he did not venture to say any more, and hoped for his speedy recovery, that he might have a chance of coaxing him to comply with his request. But the old man got worse and worse, and at length died ; whereupon the elder brother took no trouble about the funeral ceremonies, leaving it all to the younger, who, being an open-handed fellow, made no difficulties about the expense. The latter was also fond of seeing a great deal of company at his house, and his wife often had to get three or four meals a day ready for guests ; and, as her husband did very little towards looking after his affairs, and was further sponged upon by all the needy ones of the neighbourhood, they were soon reduced to a state of poverty. The elder brother helped them to keep body and soul together, but he died shortly afterwards, and this resource was cut off from them. Then, by dint of borrowing in the spring and repaying in the autumn,[2] they still managed to exist, until at last it came to parting with their land, and they were left actually destitute. At that juncture their eldest son died, followed soon after by his mother ; and Yüeh-shêng was left almost by himself in the world. He now married the widow of a sheep-dealer, who had a little capital ; and she was very strict with him, and wouldn't let him waste time and money with his friends. One night his father appeared to him and said, " My son, you have drained your cup of bitterness to the dregs. You shall now have the money. I will bring it to you." When Yüeh-shêng woke up, he thought it was merely a poor man's dream ; but the next day, while laying the foundations of a wall, he did come upon a quantity of gold. And then he knew what his father had meant by " when you are alone ; " for of those about him at that time, more than half were gone.

---

[2] This has reference to the " seed-time and harvest."

CLXI. THE BOATMEN OF LAO-LUNG

WHEN His Excellency Chu was Viceroy of Kuang-tung, there were constant complaints from the traders of mysterious disappearances ; sometimes as many as three or four of them disappearing at once and never being seen or heard of again. At length the number of such cases, filed of course against some person or persons unknown, multiplied to such an extent that they were simply put on record, and but little notice was further taken of them by the local officials. Thus, when His Excellency entered upon his duties, he found more than a hundred plaints of the kind, besides innumerable cases in which the missing man's relatives lived at a distance and had not instituted proceedings. The mystery so preyed upon the new Viceroy's mind that he lost all appetite for food ; and when, finally, all the inquiries he had set on foot resulted in no clue to an elucidation of these strange disappearances, then His Excellency proceeded to wash and purify himself, and, having notified the Municipal God,[1] he took to fasting and sleeping in his study alone. While he was in ecstasy, lo ! an official entered, holding a tablet in his hand, and said that he had come from the Municipal temple with the following instructions to the Viceroy :—

> Snow on the whiskers descending :
> Live clouds falling from heaven :
> Wood in water buoyed up :
> In the wall an opening effected.

The official then retired, and the Viceroy waked up ; but it was only after a night of tossing and turning that he hit upon what seemed to him the solution of the enigma. " The first line," argued he, " must signify old [*lao* in Chinese] ; the second refers to the *dragon* [2] [*lung* in Chinese]; the third is clearly a *boat* ; and the fourth a *door* [here taken in its secondary sense—*man*]." Now, to the east of the province, not far from the pass by which traders from the north connect their line of trade with the southern

---

[1] See No. I., note 1.

[2] Clouds being naturally connected in every Chinaman's mind with these fabulous creatures, the origin of which has been traced by some to waterspouts. See No. LXXXI., note 2.

seas, there was actually a ferry known as the Old Dragon (Lao-lung) ; and thither the Viceroy immediately despatched a force to arrest those employed in carrying people backwards and forwards. More than fifty men were caught, and they all confessed at once without the application of torture. In fact, they were bandits under the guise of boatmen ; [3] and after beguiling passengers on board, they would either drug them or burn stupefying incense until they were senseless, finally cutting them open and putting a large stone inside to make the body sink. Such was the horrible story, the discovery of which brought throngs to the Viceroy's door to serenade him in terms of gratitude and praise.[4]

CLXII. THE PIOUS SURGEON

A CERTAIN veterinary surgeon, named Hou, was carrying food to his field labourers, when suddenly a whirlwind arose in his path. Hou seized a spoon and poured out a libation of gruel, whereupon the wind immediately dropped. On another occasion, he was wandering about the municipal temple when he noticed an image of Liu Ch'üan presenting the melon,[1] in whose eye was a great splotch of dirt. "Dear me, Sir Liu!" cried Hou, "who has been ill-using you like this?" He then scraped away the dirt with his finger-nail, and passed on. Some years afterwards, as he was lying down very ill, two lictors walked in and carried him off to a yamên, where they insisted on his bribing them heavily. Hou was at his wit's end what to do ; but just

---

[3] " Boat-men " is the solution of the last two lines of the enigma.

[4] The author actually supplies a list of the persons who signed a congratulatory petition to the Viceroy on the arrest and punishment of the criminals.

[1] When the soul of the Emperor T'ai Tsung of the T'ang dynasty was in the infernal regions, it promised to send Yen-lo (the Chinese Yama or Pluto) a melon ; and when His Majesty recovered from the trance into which he had been plunged, he gave orders that his promise was to be fulfilled. Just then a man, named Liu Ch'üan, observed a priest with a hairpin belonging to his wife, and misconstruing the manner in which possession of it had been obtained, abused his wife so severely that she committed suicide. Liu Ch'üan himself then determined to follow her example, and convey the melon to Yen-lo ; for which act he was subsequently deified. See the Hsi yu chi, Section XI.

at that moment a personage dressed in green robes came
forth, who was greatly astonished at seeing him there, and
asked what it all meant. Our hero at once explained ;
whereupon the man in green turned upon the lictors and
abused them for not showing proper respect to Mr. Hou.
Meanwhile a drum sounded like the roll of thunder, and the
man in green told Hou that it was for the morning session,
and that he would have to attend. Leading Hou within,
he put him in his proper place, and, promising to inquire
into the charge against him, went forward and whispered
a few words to one of the clerks. " Oh," said the latter,
advancing and making a bow to the veterinary surgeon,
" yours is a trifling matter. We shall merely have to
confront you with a horse, and then you can go home
again." Shortly afterwards, Hou's case was called ; upon
which he went forward and knelt down, as did also a horse
which was prosecuting him. The judge now informed Hou
that he was accused by the horse of having caused its death
by medicines, and asked him if he pleaded guilty or not
guilty. " My lord," replied Hou, " the prosecutor was
attacked by the cattle-plague, for which I treated him
accordingly ; and he actually recovered from the disease,
though he died on the following day. Am I to be held
responsible for that ? " The horse now proceeded to tell
his story ; and after the usual cross-examination and cries
for justice, the judge gave orders to look up the horse's
term of life in the Book of Fate. Therein it appeared that
the animal's destiny had doomed it to death on the very
day on which it had died ; whereupon the judge cried out,
" Your term of years had already expired ; why bring this
false charge ? Away with you ! " and turning to Hou, the
judge added, " You are a worthy man, and may be permitted to live." The lictors were accordingly instructed
to escort him back, and with them went out both the clerk
and the man in green clothes, who bade the lictors take
every possible care of Hou by the way. " You gentlemen
are very kind," said Hou, " but I haven't the honour of
your acquaintance, and should be glad to know to whom
I am so much indebted." " Three years ago," replied the
man in green, " I was travelling in your neighbourhood,
and was suffering very much from thirst, which you relieved
for me by a few spoonfuls of gruel. I have not forgotten

that act." " And my name," observed the other, " is Liu
Ch'üan. You once took a splotch of dirt out of my eye that
was troubling me very much. I am only sorry that the
wine and food we have down here is unsuitable to offer you.
Farewell." Hou now understood all that had happened,
and went off home with the two lictors, where he would
have regaled them with some refreshment, but they refused
to take even a cup of tea. He then waked up and found
that he had been dead for two days. From this time forth
he led a more virtuous life than ever, always pouring out
libations to Liu Ch'üan at all the festivals of the year.
Thus he reached the age of eighty, a hale and hearty man,
still able to sit in the saddle ; until one day he met Liu
Ch'üan riding on horseback, as if about to make a long
journey. After a little friendly conversation, the latter
said to him, " Your time is up, and the warrant for your
arrest is already issued ; but I have ordered the constables
to delay awhile, and you can now spend three days in
preparing for death, at the expiration of which I will come
and fetch you. I have purchased a small appointment for
you in the realms below,[2] by which you will be more
comfortable." So Hou went home and told his wife and
children ; and after collecting his friends and relatives, and
making all necessary preparations, on the evening of the
fourth day he cried out, " Liu Ch'üan has come ! " and,
getting into his coffin,[3] lay down and died.

CLXIII.   ANOTHER SOLOMON

At T'ai-yüan there lived a middle-aged woman with her
widowed daughter-in-law. The former was on terms of
too great intimacy with a notably bad character of the

[2] As the Chinese believe that their disembodied spirits proceed
to a world organised on much the same model as the one they know,
so do they think that there will be social distinctions of rank and
emolument proportioned to the merits of each.

[3] A dying man is almost always moved into his coffin to die ;
and aged persons frequently take to sleeping regularly in the coffins
provided against the inevitable hour by the pious thoughtfulness of
a loving son. Even in middle life Chinese like to see their coffins
ready for them, and store them sometimes on their own premises,
sometimes in the outhouses of a neighbouring temple.

neighbourhood; and the latter, who objected very strongly to this, did her best to keep the man from the house. The elder woman accordingly tried to send the other back to her family, but she would not go; and at length things came to such a pass that the mother-in-law actually went to the mandarin of the place and charged her daughter-in-law with the offence she herself was committing. When the mandarin inquired the name of the man concerned, she said she had only seen him in the dark and didn't know who he was, referring him for information to the accused. The latter, on being summoned, gave the man's name, but retorted the charge on her mother-in-law; and when the man was confronted with them, he promptly declared both their stories to be false. The mandarin, however, said there was a *primâ facie* case against him, and ordered him to be severely beaten, whereupon he confessed that it was the daughter-in-law whom he went to visit. This the woman herself flatly denied, even under torture; and on being released, appealed to a higher court, with a very similar result. Thus the case dragged on, until a Mr. Sun, who was well known for his judicial acumen, was appointed district magistrate at that place. Calling the parties before him, he bade his lictors prepare stones and knives, at which they were much exercised in their minds, the severest tortures allowed by law being merely gyves and fetters.[1] However, everything was got ready, and the next day Mr. Sun proceeded with his investigation. After hearing all that each one of the three had to say, he delivered the following judgment:—"The case is a simple one; for although I cannot say which of you two women is the guilty one, there is no doubt about the man, who has evidently been the means of bringing discredit on a virtuous family. Take those stones and knives there and put him to death. I will be responsible." Thereupon the two women began to stone the man, especially the younger one, who seized the biggest stones she could see and threw them at him with all the might of her pent-up anger; while the mother-in-law chose small stones and struck him on non-vital parts.[2] So with the knives: the

---

[1] See No. LXXIII., note 2.

[2] The Chinese distinguish sixteen vital spots on the front of the body and six on the back, with thirty-six and twenty non-vital

daughter-in-law would have killed him at the first blow, had not the mandarin stopped her, and said, "Hold! I now know who is the guilty woman." The mother-in-law was then tortured until she confessed, and the case was thus terminated.

CLXIV. THE INCORRUPT OFFICIAL

MR. WU, Sub-prefect of Chi-nan, was an upright man, and would have no share in the bribery and corruption which was extensively carried on, and at which the higher authorities connived, and in the proceeds of which they actually shared. The Prefect tried to bully him into adopting a similar plan, and went so far as to abuse him in violent language ; upon which Mr. Wu fired up and exclaimed, "Though I am but a subordinate official, you should impeach me for anything you have against me in the regular way ; you have not the right to abuse me thus. Die I may, but I will never consent to degrade my office and turn aside the course of justice for the sake of filthy lucre." At this outbreak the Prefect changed his tone, and tried to soothe him. . . . [How dare people accuse the age of being corrupt, when it is themselves who will not walk in the straight path.] One day after this a certain fox-medium [1] came to the Prefect's yamên just as a feast was in full swing, and was thus addressed by a guest : —"You who pretend to know everything, say how many officials there are in this Prefecture " " *One*," replied the medium ; at which the company laughed heartily, until the medium continued, "There are really seventy-two holders of office, but Mr. Sub-prefect Wu is the only one who can justly be called an official."

---

spots in similar positions, respectively. They allow, however, that a severe blow on a non-vital spot might cause death, and *vice versâ*.

[1] Certain classes of soothsayers are believed by the Chinese to be possessed by foxes, which animals have the power of looking into the future, &c., &c.

APPENDIX I.

THE YÜ LI CH'AO CHUAN

VISITORS to Chinese temples of the Taoist persuasion usually make at once for what is popularly known amongst foreigners as the "Chamber of Horrors." These belong specially to Taoism, or the ethics of Right in the abstract, as opposed to abstract Wrong, and are not found in temples consecrated to the religion of Buddha. Modern Taoism, however, once a purely metaphysical system, is now so leavened with the superstitions of Buddhism, and has borrowed so much material from its younger rival, that an ordinary Chinaman can hardly tell one from the other, and generally regards them as to all intents and purposes the same. These rightly-named Chambers of Horrors—for Madame Tussaud has nothing more ghastly to show in the whole of her wonderful collection—represent the Ten Courts of Purgatory, through some or all of which erring souls must pass before they are suffered to be born again into the world under another form, or transferred to the eternal bliss reserved for the righteous alone. As a description of these Ten Courts may not be uninteresting to some of my readers, and as the subject has a direct bearing upon many of the stories in the previous collection, I hereto append my translation of a well-known Taoist work [1] which is circulated gratuitously all over the Chinese Empire by people who are anxious to lay up a store of good works against the day of reckoning to come. Those who are acquainted with Dante's *Divine Comedy* will recollect that the poet's idea of a Christian Purgatory was a series of nine lessening circles arranged one above the other, so as to form a cone. The Taoist believes that his Purgatory consists of Ten Courts of Justice situated in different positions at the bottom of a great ocean which lies down in the depths of the earth. These are subdivided into special wards, different forms of torture being inflicted in each. A perusal of this work will show what punishments the wicked Chinaman has to expect in the unseen world, and by what means he may hope to obtain a partial or complete remission of his sins.

> *The Divine Panorama, published by the Mercy of Yü Ti,*[2]
> *that Men and Women may repent them of their faults*
> *and make Atonement for their Crimes.*

On the birthday of the Saviour P'u-sa,[3] as the spirits of Purgatory were thronging round to offer their congratulations, the ruler of the Infernal Regions spake as follows:—" My wish is to release all souls, and every moon as this day comes round I would wholly

---

[1] The *Yü Li Ch'ao Chuan,* or *Divine Panorama.*
[2] The Divine Ruler, immediately below God Himself.   [3] See No. XXVI. note 5.

or partially remit the punishment of erring shades, and give them
life once more in one of the Six Paths.[4]   But alas ! the wicked are
many and the virtuous few.   Nevertheless, the punishments in the
dark region are too severe, and require some modification.   Any
wicked soul that repents and induces one or two others to do likewise
shall be allowed to set this off against the punishments which should
be inflicted." The Judges of the Ten Courts of Purgatory· then
agreed that all who led virtuous lives from their youth upwards
shall be escorted at their death to the land of the Immortals ;
that all whose balance of good and evil is exact shall escape the
bitterness of the Three States,[5] and be born again among men ;
that those who have repaid their debts of gratitude and friendship,
and fulfilled their destiny, yet have a balance of evil against them,
shall pass through the various Courts of Purgatory and then be born
again amongst men, rich, poor, old, young, diseased or crippled, to
be put a second time upon trial.   Then, if they behave well they
may enter into some happy state ; but if badly, they will be dragged
by horrid devils through all the Courts, suffering bitterly as they go,
and will again be born, to endure in life the uttermost of poverty
and wretchedness, in death the everlasting tortures of hell.   Those
who are disloyal, unfilial, who commit suicide, take life, or disbelieve
the doctrine of Cause and Effect,[6] saying to themselves that when a
man dies there is an end of him, that when he has lost his skin [7] he
has already suffered the worst that can befall him, that living men
can be tortured, but no one ever saw a man's ghost in the pillory,
that after death all is unknown, &c., &c.,—truly these men do not
know that the body alone perishes but the soul lives for ever and
ever ; and that whatsoever evil they do in this life, the same will
be done unto them in the life to come.   All who commit such crimes
are handed over to the everlasting tortures of hell ; for alas ! in
spite of the teachings of the Three Systems [8] some will persist in
regarding these warnings as vain and empty talk.   Lightly they
speak of Divine mercy, and knowingly commit many crimes, not
more than one in a hundred ever coming to repentance.   Therefore
the punishments of Purgatory were strictly carried out and the
tortures dreadfully severe.   But now it has been mercifully ordained
that any man or woman, young, old, weak or strong, who may have
sinned in any way, shall be permitted to obtain remission of the
same by keeping his or her thoughts constantly fixed on P'u-sa and
on the birthdays of the Judges of the Ten Courts, by fasting and
prayer, and by vows never to sin again.   Or for every good work
done in life they shall be allowed to escape one ward in the Courts
below.   From this rule to be excepted disloyal ministers, unfilial
sons, suicides, those who plot in secret against good people, those
who are struck by lightning (*lit.* thunder), those who perish by flood
or fire, by wild animals or poisonous reptiles [9]—these to pass through
all the Courts and be punished according to their deserts.   All other
sinners to be allowed to claim their good works as a set-off against

---

[4] See *Author's Own Record* (in *Introduction*), note 28.
[5] The three worst of the Six Paths.
[6] That the state of one life is the result of behaviour in a previous existence.
[7] *Lit.*—the skin purse (of his bones).   [8] Buddhism, Taoism, and Confucianism.
[9] Violent deaths are regarded with horror by the Chinese. They hold that a truly
virtuous man always dies either of illness or old age.

evil, thus partly escaping the agonies of hell and receiving some reward for their virtuous deeds.

This account of man's wickedness on the earth and the punishments in store for him was written in language intelligible to every man and woman, and was submitted for the approval of P'u-sa, the intention being to wait the return [10] of some virtuous soul among the sons of men, and by these means publish it all over the earth. When P'u-sa saw what had been done, he said it was good ; and on the 3rd of the 8th moon proceeded with the ten Judges of Purgatory to lay this book before God.[11]

Then God said, " Good indeed ! Good indeed ! Henceforth let all spirits take note of any mortal who vows to lead a virtuous life and, repenting, promises to sin no more. Two punishments shall be remitted him. And if, in addition to this, he succeeds in doing five virtuous acts, then he shall escape all punishment and be born again in some happy state—if a woman she shall be born as a man. But more than five virtuous acts shall enable such a soul to obtain the salvation of others, and redeem wife and family from the tortures of hell. Let these regulations be published in the *Divine Panorama* and circulated on earth by the spirits of the City Guardians.[12] In fear and trembling obey this decree and carry it reverently into effect."

THE FIRST COURT

His Infernal Majesty Ch'in Kuang is specially in charge of the register of life and death both for old and young, and presides at the judgment-seat in the lower regions. His court is situated in the great Ocean, away beyond the Wu-chiao rock,[13] far to the west near the murky road which leads to the Yellow Springs.[14] Every man and woman dying in old age whose fate it is to be born again into the world, if their tale of good and evil works is equally balanced, are sent to the First Court, and thence transferred back to Life, male becoming female, female male, rich poor, and poor rich, according to their several deserts. But those whose good deeds are outnumbered by their bad are sent to a terrace on the right of the Court, called the Terrace of the Mirror of Sin, ten feet in height. The mirror is about fifty feet [15] in circumference and hangs towards the east. Above are seven characters written horizontally :—
" Sin Mirror Terrace upon no good men." There the wicked souls are able to see the naughtiness of their own hearts while they were among the living, and the danger of death and hell. Then do they realise the proverb,—

> Ten thousand taels of yellow gold cannot be brought away :
> But every crime will tell its tale upon the judgment day.

When the souls have been to the Terrace and seen their wickednesses, they are forwarded into the Second Court, where they are tortured and dismissed to the proper hell.

Should there be any one enjoying life without reflecting that Heaven and Earth produce mortals, that father and mother bring

---

[10] Good people go to Purgatory in the flesh, and are at once passed up to Heaven without suffering any torture, or are sent back to earth again.
[11] The Supreme Ruler. [12] See No. I., note 1.
[13] Supposed to be the gate of the Infernal Regions.
[14] Hades. [15] Literally "ten armfuls."

the child to maturity—truly no easy matter ; and, ignoring the four obligations,[16] before receiving the summons, lightly sever the thread of their own existence by cutting their throats, hanging, poisoning, or drowning themselves :—then such suicides, if the deed was not done out of loyalty, filial piety, chastity, or friendship, for which they would go to Heaven, but in a trivial burst of rage, or fearing the consequences of a crime which would not amount to death, or in the hope of falsely injuring a fellow-creature—then such suicides, when the last breath has left their bodies, shall be escorted to this Court by the Spirits of the Threshold and of the Hearth. They shall be placed in the Hunger and Thirst Section, and every day from seven till eleven o'clock they will resume their mortal coil, and suffer again the pain and bitterness of death. After seventy days, or one or two years, as the case may be, they will be conducted back to the scene of their suicide, but will not be permitted to taste the funeral meats, or avail themselves of the usual offerings to the dead. Bitterly will they repent, unable as they will be to render themselves visible and frighten people,[17] vainly striving to procure a substitute.[18] For when the substitute shall have been harmlessly entrapped, the Spirits of the Threshold and Hearth will reconduct the erring soul back to this Court, whence it will be sent on to the Second Court, where its balance of good and evil will be struck, and dreadful tortures applied, being finally passed on through the Various Courts to the utter misery of hell. Should any one have such intention of suicide and thus threaten a fellow creature, even though he does not commit the act but continues to live not without virtue, yet shall it not be permitted in any way to remit his punishment. Any soul which after suicide shall not remain invisible, but shall frighten people to death, will be seized by black-faced, long-tusked devils and tortured in the various hells, to be finally thrust into the great Gehenna, for ever to remain hung up in chains, and not permitted to be born again.

Every Buddhist or Taoist priest who receives money for prayers and liturgies, but skips over words and misses out sentences, on arriving at this, the First Court, will be sent to the section for the completion of Prayer, and there in a small dark room he shall pick out such passages as he has omitted, and make good the deficiency as best he can, by the uncertain light of an infinitesimal wick burning in a gallon of oil. Even good and virtuous priests must also repair any omissions they may have (accidentally) made, and so must every man or woman who in private devotion may have omitted or wrongly repeated any part of the sacred writings from over-earnestness, their attention not being properly fixed on the actual words they repeat. The same applies to female priests. A dispensation from Buddha to remit such punishment is put in force on the first day of each month when the names are entered in the register of the virtuous.

O ye dwellers upon earth, on the 1st day of the 2nd moon, fasting

---

[16] To Heaven, Earth, sovereign, and relatives.

[17] Held to be a great relief to the spirits of the dead.

[18] It is commonly believed that if the spirit of a murdered man can secure the violent death of some other person he returns to earth again as if nothing had happened, the spirit of his victim passing into the world below and suffering all the misery of a disembodied soul in his stead. See No. XLV., note 8.

turn to the north and make oath to abstain from evil and fix your thoughts on good, that ye may escape hell ! The precepts of Buddha are circulated over the whole world to warn mankind to believe and repent, that when the last hour comes their spirits may be escorted by dark-robed boys to realms of bliss and happiness in the west.

THE SECOND COURT

His Infernal Majesty Ch'u Chiang reigns at the bottom of the great Ocean. Away to the south, below the Wu-chiao rocks, he has a vast hell, many leagues in extent, and subdivided into sixteen wards, as follows :—

In the first, nothing but black clouds and constant sand-storms. In the second, mud and filth. In the third, *chevaux de frise*. In the fourth, gnawing hunger. In the fifth, burning thirst. In the sixth, blood and pus. In the seventh, the shades are plunged into a brazen cauldron (of boiling water). In the eighth, the same punishment is repeated many times. In the ninth, they are put into iron clothes. In the tenth, they are stretched on a rack to regulation length. In the eleventh, they are pecked by fowls. In the twelfth, they have only rivers of lime to drink. In the thirteenth they are hacked to pieces. In the fourteenth, the leaves of the trees are as sharp as sword-points. In the fifteenth they are pursued by foxes and wolves. In the sixteenth, all is ice and snow.

Those who lead astray young boys and girls, and then escape punishment by cutting off their hair and entering the priesthood ; [19] those who filch letters, pictures, books, &c., entrusted to their care, and then pretend to have lost them ; those who injure a fellow-creature's ear, eye, hand, foot, fingers, or toes ; those who practise as doctors without any knowledge of the medical art ; those who will not ransom grown-up slave-girls ; [20] those who, contracting marriage for the sake of gain, falsely state their ages ; or those who in cases of betrothal, before actual marriage, find out that one of the contracting parties is a bad character, and yet do not come forward to say so, but inflict an irreparable wrong on the innocent one ;— such offenders, when their quota of crime has been cast up, their youth or age and the consequences of their acts taken into consideration, will be seized by horrid red-faced devils and thrust into the great Hell, and thence despatched to the particular ward in which they are to be tormented. When their time of suffering there has expired, they will be moved into the Third Court, there to be tortured and passed on to Gehenna.

O ye men and women of the world, take this book and warn all sinners, or copy it out and circulate it for general information ! If

[19] A very common trick in China. The drunken bully Lu Ta in the celebrated novel *Shui-hu* saved himself by these means, and I have heard that the Mandarin who in the war of 1842 spent a large sum in constructing a paddle-wheel steamer to be worked by men, hoping thereby to match the wheel-ships of the Outer Barbarians, is now expiating his failure at a monastery in Fukien. *A propos* of which, it may not be generally known at this moment (1880) there are small paddle-wheel boats for Chinese passengers, plying up and down the Canton River, the wheels of which are turned by gangs of coolies, who perform a movement precisely similar to that required on the treadmill.

[20] In order that their marriage destiny may not be interfered with. It is considered disgraceful not to accept the ransom of a slave girl of fifteen or sixteen years of age. See No. XXVI., note 8.

you see people sick and ill, give medicine to heal them. If you see people poor and hungry, feed them. If you see people in difficulties, give money to save them. Repent your past errors, and you will be allowed to cancel that evil by future good, so that when the hour arrives you will pass at once into the Tenth Court, and thence return again to existence on earth.

Let such as love all creatures endowed with life, and do not recklessly cut and slay, but teach their children not to harm small animals and insects—let these, on the 1st of the 3rd moon, register an oath not to take life, but to aid in preserving it. Thus they will avoid passing through Purgatory, and will also enter at once the Tenth Hall, to be born again in some happy state.

THE THIRD COURT

His Infernal Majesty Sung Ti reigns at the bottom of the great Ocean, away to the south-east, below the Wu-chiao rock, in the Gehenna of Black Ropes. This Hall is many leagues wide, and is subdivided into sixteen wards, as follows :—

In the first everything is Salt ; above, below, and all round, the eye rests upon Salt alone. The shades feed upon it, and suffer horrid torments in consequence. When the fit has passed away they return to it once again, and suffer agonies more unutterable than before. In the second, the erring shades are bound with cords and carry heavily-weighted *cangues*. In the third, they are perpetually pierced through the ribs. In the fourth, their faces are scraped with iron and copper knives. In the fifth, their fat is scraped away from their bodies. In the sixth, their hearts and livers are squeezed with pincers. In the seventh, their eyes are gouged. In the eighth, they are flayed. In the ninth, their feet are cut off. In the tenth, their finger-nails and toe-nails are pulled out. In the eleventh, their blood is sucked. In the twelfth, they are hung up head downwards. In the thirteenth, their shoulder-bones are split. In the fourteenth, they are tormented by insects and reptiles. In the fifteenth, they are beaten on the thighs. In the sixteenth, their hearts are scratched.

Those who enjoy the light of day without reflecting on the Imperial bounty ; [21] officers of State who revel in large emoluments without reciprocating their sovereign's goodness ; private individuals who do not repay the debt of water and earth ; [22] wives and concubines who slight their marital lords ; those who fail in their duties as acting sons, [23] or such as reap what advantages there are and then go off to their own homes ; slaves who disregard their masters ; official underlings who are ungrateful to their superiors ; working partners who behave badly to the moneyed partner ; culprits who escape from prison or abscond from their place of banishment ; those who break their bail and get others into trouble ;

[21] The soil of China belongs, every inch of it, to the Emperor. Consequently, the people owe him a debt of gratitude for permitting them to live upon it.
[22] Do their duty as men and women.
[23] A Chinaman may have three kinds of fathers : (1) his real father, (2) an adopted father, such as an uncle without children to whom he has been given as heir, and (3) the man his widowed mother may marry. The first two are to all intents and purposes equal ; the third is entitled only to one year's mourning instead of the usual three.

and those infatuated ones who have long omitted to pray and repent —all these, even though they have a set-off of good deeds, must pass through the misery of every ward.   Those who interfere with another man's Fêng-Shui ; those who obstruct funeral obsequies or the completion of graves ; those who in digging come on a coffin and do not immediately cover it up, but injure the bones ; those who steal or avoid paying up their quota of grain ; [24] those who lose all record of the site of their family burying-place ; those who incite others to commit crimes ; those who promote litigation ; those who write anonymous placards ; those who repudiate a betrothal ; those who forge deeds and other documents ; those who receive payment of a debt without signing a receipt or giving up the IOU ; those who counterfeit signatures and seals ; those who alter bills ; those who injure posterity in any way—all these, and similar offenders, shall be punished according to the gravity of each offence.   Devils with big knives will seize the erring ones and thrust them into the great Gehenna ; besides which they shall expiate their sins in the proper number of wards, and shall then be forwarded to the Fourth Court, where they shall be tortured and dismissed to the general Gehenna.

O ye sons of men, on the 8th day of the 2nd moon, register an oath that ye will do no evil.   Thus you may escape the bitterness of these hells.

THE FOURTH COURT

The Lord of the Five Senses reigns at the bottom of the great Ocean, away to the east below the Wu-chiao rock.   His Court is many leagues wide, and is subdivided into sixteen wards, as follows :—

In the first, the wicked shades are hung up and water is continually poured over them.   In the second, they are made to kneel on chains and pieces of split bamboo.   In the third, their hands are scalded with boiling water.   In the fourth, their hands swell and stream with perspiration.   In the fifth, their muscles are cut and their bones pulled out.   In the sixth their shoulders are pricked with a trident and the skin rubbed with a hard brush.   In the seventh, holes are bored into their flesh.   In the eighth, they are made to sit on spikes.   In the ninth, they wear iron clothes.   In the tenth they are placed under heavy pieces of wood, stone, earth, or tiles.   In the eleventh, their eyes are put out.   In the twelfth, their mouths are choked with dust.   In the thirteenth, they are perpetually dosed with nasty medicines.   In the fourteenth, it is so slippery, they are always falling down.   In the fifteenth, their mouths are painfully pricked.   In the sixteenth, their bodies are buried under broken stones, &c., the head alone being left out.

Those who cheat the customs and evade taxes ; those who repudiate their rent, use weighted scales, sell sham medicines, water their rice, [25] utter base coin, get deeply in debt, sell doctored [26] silks and satins, scrape [27] or add size to linen cloth ; those who do not

[24] As taxes.
[25] Visitors to Peking may often see the junkmen at T'ung-chou pouring water by t e bucketful on to newly arrived cargoes of Imperial rice in order to make up the right weight and conceal the amount they have filched on the way.
[26] That is, with a false gloss on them.
[27] In order to raise the nap and give an appearance of strength and goodness.

make way for the cripples, old and young; those who encroach upon petty trade rights [28] of old or young; those who delay in delivering letters entrusted to them; steal bricks from walls as they pass by, or oil and candles from lamps; [29] poor people who do not behave properly and rich people who are not compassionate to the poor; those who promise a loan and go back on their word; those who see people suffering from illness yet cannot bring themselves to part with certain useful drugs they may have in their possession; those who know good prescriptions but keep them secret; those who throw vessels which have contained medicine or broken cups and bottles into the street; those who allow their mules and ponies to be a nuisance to other people; those who destroy their neighbour's crops or his walls and fences; those who try to bewitch their enemies,[30] and those who try to frighten people in any way,—all these shall be punished according to the gravity of their offences, and shall be thrust by the devils into the great Gehenna until their time arrives for passing into the Fifth Court.

O ye children of this world, if on the 18th day of the 2nd moon you register an oath to sin no more, then you may escape the various wards of this Hall; and if to this book you add examples of rewards and punishments following upon virtues and crimes, and hand them down to posterity for the good of the human race, so that all who read may repent them of their wickedness—then they will be without sin, and you not without merit!

THE FIFTH COURT

His Infernal Majesty Yen Lo [31] said,—" Our proper place is in the First Court; but, pitying those who die by foul means, and should be sent back to earth to have their wrongs redressed, we have moved our judgment-seat to the great hell at the bottom of the Ocean, away to the north-east below the Wu-chiao rock, and have subdivided this hell into sixteen wards for the torment of souls. All those shades who come before us have already suffered long tortures in the previous four Courts, whence, if they are hardened sinners, they are passed on after seven days to this Court, where, if again found to be utterly hardened, corruption will overtake them by the fifth or seventh day. All shades cry out either that they have left some vow unfulfilled, or that they wish to build a temple or a bridge, make a road, clean out a river or well, publish some book teaching people to be virtuous, that they have not released their due number of lives, that they have filial duties or funeral obsequies to perform, some act of kindness to repay, &c.,

---

[28] Costermongers and others acquire certain rights to doorsteps or snug corners in Chinese cities which are not usually infringed by competitors in the same line of business. Chair-coolies, carrying-coolies, ferrymen, &c., alsc claim whole districts as their particular field of operations, and are very jealous of any interference. I know of a case in which the right of "scavengering" a town had been in the same family for generations, and no one dreamt of trying to take it out of their hands.

[29] Chiefly alluding to small temples where some pious spirit may have lighted a lamp or candle to the glory of his favourite P'u-sa.

[30] This is done either by making a figure of the person to be injured and burning it in a slow fire, like the old practice of the wax figure in English history; or by obtaining his nativity characters, writing them out on a piece of paper and burning them in a candle, muttering all the time whatsoever mischief it is hoped will befall him.

[31] Popularly known as the Chinese Pluto. The Indian *Yama*.

&c. For these reasons they pray to be allowed to return once more
to the light of day, and are always ready to make oath that henceforth they will lead most exemplary lives. We, hearing this, reply,
—In days gone by ye openly worked evil, but now that your boat
has reached the midstream, ye bethink yourselves of caulking the
leak. For although P'u-sa in his great mercy decreed that there
should be a modification of torture, and that good works might be
set off against evil, the same being submitted to God and ratified
by Divine Decree, to be further published in the realms below and
in the Infernal City—yet we Judges of the Ten Courts have not
yet received one single virtuous man amongst us, who, coming in
the flesh, might carry this *Divine Panorama* back with him to the
light of day. Truly those who suffer in hell and on earth cannot
complain, and virtuous men are rare ! But now ye have come to
my Court, having beheld your own wickedness in the mirror of sin.
No more—bull-headed, horse-faced devils, away with them to the
Terrace [32] that they may once more gaze upon their lost homes ! "
    This Terrace is curved in front like a bow ; it looks east, west,
and south. It is eighty-one *li* from one extreme to the other. The
back part is like the string of the bow ; it is enclosed by a wall of
sharp swords. It is 490 feet high ; its sides are knife-blades ; and
the whole is in sixty-three storeys. No good shade comes to this
Terrace ; neither do those whose balance of good and evil is exact.
Wicked souls alone behold their homes close by and can see and
hear what is going on. They hear old and young talking together ;
they see their last wishes disregarded and their instructions disobeyed. Everything seems to have undergone a change. The
property they scraped together with so much trouble is dissipated
and gone. The husband thinks of taking another wife ; the widow
meditates second nuptials.[33] Strangers are in possession of the
old estate ; there is nothing to divide amongst the children. Debts
long since paid are brought again for settlement, and the survivors
are called upon to acknowledge claims upon the departed. Debts
owed are lost for want of evidence, with endless recriminations,
abuse, and general confusion, all of which falls upon the three
families [34] of the deceased. They in their anger speak ill of him
that is gone. He sees his children become corrupt, and his friends
fall away. Some, perhaps, for the sake of bygone times, may stroke
the coffin and let fall a tear, departing quickly with a cold smile.
Worse than that, the wife sees her husband tortured in the yamên ;
the husband sees his wife victim to some horrible disease, lands gone,
houses destroyed by flood or fire, and everything in an unutterable
confusion—the reward of former sins.[35] All souls, after the misery
of the Terrace, will be thrust into the great Gehenna, and, when
the amount of wickedness of each has been ascertained, they will
be passed through the sixteen wards for the punishment of evil

[32] The celebrated " See-one's-home Terrace."
[33] Regarded by the Chinese with intense disgust.
[34] Father's, mother's, and wife's families.
[35] I know of few more pathetic passages throughout all the exquisite imagery of the
" Divine Comedy " than this in which the guilty soul is supposed to look back to the
home he has but lately left and gaze in bitter anguish on his desolate hearth and broken
household gods. For once the gross tortures of Chinese Purgatory give place to as
refined and as dreadful a punishment as human ingenuity could well devise.

hearts.   In the Gehenna they will be buried under wooden pillars,
bound with copper snakes, crushed by iron dogs, tied tightly hand and
foot, be ripped open and have their hearts torn out, minced up and
given to snakes, their entrails being thrown to dogs.   Then, when
their time is up, the pain will cease and their bodies become whole
once more, preparatory to being passed through the sixteen wards.
In the first are non-worshippers and sceptics.   In the second,
those who have destroyed or hurt living creatures.   In the third,
those who do not fulfil their vows.   In the fourth, believers in false
doctrines, magicians, and sorcerers.   In the fifth, those who tyran-
nise over the weak but cringe to the strong ;   also those who openly
wish for another's death.   In the sixth, those who try to put their
misfortunes on to other people's shoulders.   In the seventh, those
who lead immoral lives.   In the eighth, those who injure others
to benefit themselves.   In the ninth, those who are parsimonious
and will not help people in trouble.   In the tenth, those who steal
and involve the innocent.   In the eleventh, those who forget
kindness or seek revenge.   In the twelfth, those who by pernicious
drugs stir up others to quarrel, keeping themselves out of harm's
way.   In the thirteenth, those who deceive or spread false reports.
In the fourteenth, those who love brawling and implicate others.
In the fifteenth, those who envy the virtuous and wise.   In the
sixteenth, those who are lost in vice, evil speakers, slanderers, and
suchlike.

All who disbelieve the doctrine of Cause and Effect, who obstruct
good works, make a pretence of piety, talk of other people's sins,
burn or injure religious books, omit to fast when praying for the
sick, interfere with the adoration of Buddha, slander the priesthood, or, if scholars, abstain from instructing women and children ;
those who dig up graves and obliterate all traces thereof, set light to
woods and forests, allow their servants to be careless in handling
fire and thus endanger their neighbours' property ;   those who
wantonly discharge arrows and bolts, who try their strength against
the sick or weak, throw potsherds over a wall, poison fish, let off
guns, catch birds either with net, sticky pole,[36] or trap ;   those who
throw down salt to kill plants, who do not bury dead cats and
venomous snakes deep in the ground, who dig out corpses, who break
the soil or alter their walls and stoves at wrong seasons,[37] who
encroach on the public road or take possession of other people's
land, who fill up wells and drains &c., &c.,—all these, when they
return from the Terrace, shall first be tortured in the great Gehenna,
and then such as are to have their hearts minced shall be passed
into the sixteen wards, thence to be sent on to the Sixth Court for
the punishment of other crimes.   Those who in life have not been
guilty of the above sins, or, having sinned, did on the 8th day of the
1st moon, fasting, register a vow to sin no more, shall not only escape
the punishments of this Court, but shall also gain some further
remission of torture in the Sixth Court.   Those, however, who are
guilty of taking life, of gross immorality, of stealing and implicating

[36] A long pole tipped with a kind of birdlime is cautiously inserted between the branches
of a tree, and then suddenly dabbed on to some unsuspecting sparrow.
[37] If this is done in winter or spring the Spirits of the Hearth and Threshold are liable
to catch cold.

the innocent, of ingratitude and revenge, of infatuated vice which no warnings can turn from its course,—these shall not escape one jot of their punishments.

THE SIXTH COURT

This Court is situated at the bottom of the great Ocean, due north of the Wu-chiao rock. It is a vast, noisy Gehenna, many leagues in extent, and around it are sixteen wards. In the first, the souls are made to kneel for long periods on iron shot. In the second, they are placed up to their necks in filth. In the third, they are pounded till the blood runs out. In the fourth their mouths are opened with iron pincers and filled full of needles. In the fifth, they are bitten by rats. In the sixth, they are enclosed in a net of thorns and nipped by locusts. In the seventh, they are crushed to a jelly. In the eighth, their skin is lacerated and they are beaten on the raw. In the ninth, their mouths are filled with fire. In the tenth, they are licked by flames. In the eleventh, they are subjected to noisome smells. In the twelfth, they are butted by oxen and trampled on by horses. In the thirteenth, their hearts are scratched. In the fourteenth, their heads are rubbed till their skulls come off. In the fifteenth, they are chopped in two at the waist. In the sixteenth, their skin is taken off and rolled up into spills.

Those discontented ones who rail against Heaven and revile Earth, who are always finding fault either with the wind, thunder, heat, cold, fine weather or rain ; those who let their tears fall towards the north,[38] who steal the gold from the inside [39] or scrape the gilding from the outside of images ; those who take holy names in vain, who show no respect for written paper, who throw down dirt and rubbish near pagodas or temples, who use dirty cook-houses and stoves for preparing the sacrificial meats, who do not abstain from eating beef and dog flesh ; [40] those who have in their possession blasphemous or obscene books and do not destroy them, who obliterate or tear books which teach man to be good, who carve on common articles of household use the symbol of the origin of all things,[41] the Sun and Moon and Seven Stars, the Royal Mother and the God of Longevity on the same article,[42] or representations of any of the Immortals ; those who embroider the Svastika [43] on fancy work, or mark characters on silk, satin, or cloth, on banners, beds, chairs, tables, or any kind of utensil ; those who secretly wear clothes adorned with the dragon and the phœnix [44] only to be trampled under foot, who buy up grain and hold until the price is exorbitantly high—all these shall be thrust into the great and noisy

[38] I presume because God sits with his face to the south.

[39] Pious and wealthy people often give orders for an image of a certain P'u-sa to be made with an ounce or so of gold inside.

[40] Primarily, because no living thing should be killed for food. The ox and the dog are specified because of their kindly services to man in tilling the earth and guarding his home. [41] The symbol of the Yin and the Yang.

[42] One being male and the other female. This calls to mind the extreme modesty of a celebrated French lady, who would not put books by male and female authors on the same shelf.

[43] The symbol on Buddha's heart ; more commonly known to the Western world as Thor's Hammer. [44] Emblems of Imperial dignity.

Gehenna, there to be examined as to their misdeeds and passed accordingly into one of the sixteen wards, whence, at the expiration of their time, they will be sent for further questioning on to the Seventh Court.

All dwellers upon earth who on the 8th day of the 3rd moon, fasting, register a vow from that date to sin no more, and, on the 14th and 15th of the 5th moon, the 3rd of the 8th moon, and the 10th of the 10th moon, to practise abstinence, vowing, moreover, to exert themselves to convert others,—these shall escape the bitterness of all the above-mentioned wards.

THE SEVENTH COURT

His Infernal Majesty T'ai Shan reigns at the bottom of the great Ocean, away to the north-west, below the Wu-chiao rock. His is a vast, noisy Court, measuring many leagues in circumference and subdivided into sixteen wards, as follows :—

In the first, the wicked souls are made to swallow their own blood. In the second, their legs are pierced and thrust into a fiery pit. In the third, their chests are cut open. In the fourth, their hair is torn out with iron combs. In the fifth, they are gnawed by dogs. In the sixth, great stones are placed on their heads. In the seventh, their skulls are pierced. In the eighth, they wear fiery clothes. In the ninth, their skin is torn and pulled by pigs. In the tenth, they are pecked by huge birds. In the eleventh, they are hung up and beaten on the feet. In the twelfth, their tongues are pulled out and their jaws bored. In the thirteenth, they are disembowelled. In the fourteenth, they are trampled on by mules and bitten by badgers. In the fifteenth, their fingers are ironed with hot irons. In the sixteenth, they are boiled in oil.

All mortals who practise eating red lead [45] and certain other nauseous articles,[46] who spend more than they should upon wine, who kidnap human beings for sale, who steal clothes and ornaments from coffins, who break up dead men's bones for medicine, who separate people from their relatives, who sell the girl brought up in the house to be their son's wife, who allow their wives [47] to drown female children, who stifle their illegitimate offspring, who unite to cheat another in gambling, who act as tutors without being properly strict, and thus wrong their pupils, who beat and injure their slaves without estimating the punishment by the fault, who regard districts entrusted to their charge in the light of so much spoil, who disobey their elders, who talk at random and go back on their word, who stir up others to quarrel and fight—all these shall, upon verification of their sins, be taken from the great Gehenna and passed through the proper wards, to be forwarded when their time has expired to the Eighth Court, again to be tortured according to their deserts.

All things may not be used as drugs. It is bad enough to slay birds, beasts, reptiles, and fishes, in order to prepare medicine for the sick ; but to use red lead and many of the filthy messes in vogue is beyond all bounds of decency, and those who foul their mouths

---

[45] Supposed to confer immortality.   [46] Unfit for translation.

[47] This is ingeniously expressed, as if *mothers* were the prime movers in such unnatural acts.

with these nasty mixtures, no matter how virtuous they may otherwise be, will not only derive no benefit from saying their prayers, but will be punished for so doing without mercy.

Ye who hear these words, make haste to repent! From to-day forbear to take life, buy many birds and animals in order to set them free,[48] and every morning when you wash your teeth mutter a prayer to Buddha. Thus, when your last hour comes, a good angel will stand by your side and purify you of your former sins.

Some steal the bones of people who have been burnt to death or the bodies of illegitimate children, for the purpose of compounding medicines; others steal skulls and bones (from graves) with the same object. Worst of all are those who carry off bones by the basketful, using the hard ones for making various articles and grinding down the soft ones for the manufacture of pottery.[49] These, no matter what may have been their good works on earth, will not obtain thereby any remission of punishment; but when they are brought down below, the Ruler of the Infernal Regions will first pass them from the great Gehenna into the proper wards, and will send instructions to the Tenth Court that when they are born again on earth it shall be either without ears, or eyes, hand, foot, mouth, lips, or nose, or maimed in some way or other. Yet such as have thus sinned may still avoid this punishment, if only they are willing to pray and repent, vowing never to sin again. Or if they buy coffins for the poor and persuade others to do likewise, by these means giving a decent burial to many corpses—then, when the death-summons comes, the Spirits of the Home and Hearth will make a black mark upon the warrant, and punishment will be remitted.

Sometimes, when there is a famine, people have nothing to eat and die of hunger, and wicked men, almost before the breath is out of their bodies, cut them up and sell their flesh to others for food—a horrid crime indeed. Those who are guilty of such practices will, on arrival in the lower regions, be tortured in the various Courts for the space of forty-nine [50] days, and then the judge of the Tenth Court will be instructed to notify the judge of the First Court to put them down in his register for a new birth,—if among men, as hungry, famished outcasts, and if among animals as loathing the food that falls to their lot, and by-and-by perishing of hunger. Such is their reward. Besides the above, those who have eaten what is unfit for food and willingly continue to do so, will be punished either among men or animals according to their deserts. Their throats will swell, and though devoured by hunger they will be unable to swallow, and thus die. Those who do not err a second time may be forgiven as they deserve; but those who in times of distress subscribe money for the sufferers, prepare gruel, give away rice to the needy, or distribute ginger tea [51] and soup in the open street, and thus sustain life a little longer and do real good to their

---

[48] On fête days at temples it is not uncommon to see cages full of birds hawked about among the holiday-makers, that those who feel twinges of conscience may purchase a sparrow or two and relieve themselves from anxiety by the simple means of setting them at liberty.

[49] Bones are used in glazing porcelain, to give a higher finish.

[50] The seven periods of seven days each which occur immediately after a death and at which the departed shade is appeased with food and offerings of various kinds.

[51] To warm them.

fellow creatures—all these shall not only obtain remission of their sins, but carry on a balance of good to their account which shall ensure them a happy old age in the life to come.[52]

Of the above three clauses, two were proposed by the officials attached to this Seventh Court, the third by the Chief Justice of the great Gehenna, and the whole submitted together for the approval of God, the following Rescript being obtained :—" Let it be as proposed ; let the three clauses be copied into the *Divine Panorama*, and let the officials concerned be promoted or rewarded. Also, in case of crimes other than those already provided for, let such be punished according to the statutes of the Rulers of the Four Continents on earth, and let any evasion of punishment and implication of innocent people be at once reported by the proper officials for our consideration. This from the Throne ! Obey ! "

O ye sons and daughters of men, if on the 27th of the 3rd moon, fasting and turned towards the north, ye register a vow to pray and repent, and to publish the whole of the *Divine Panorama* for the enlightenment of mankind, then ye may escape the bitterness of this Seventh Court.

THE EIGHTH COURT

His Infernal Majesty Tu Shih reigns at the bottom of the great Ocean, due east below the Wu-chiao rock, in a vast noisy Court many leagues in extent, subdivided into sixteen wards as follows :— .In the first, the wicked souls are rolled down mountains in carts. In the second, they are shut up in huge saucepans. In the third, they are minced. In the fourth, their noses, eyes, mouths, &c., are stopped up. In the fifth, their uvulas are cut off. In the sixth they are exposed to all kinds of filth. In the seventh, their extremities are cut off. In the eighth, their viscera [53] are fried. In the ninth, their marrow is cauterised. In the tenth, their bowels are scratched. In the eleventh, they are inwardly burned with fire. In the twelfth, they are disembowelled. In the thirteenth, their chests are torn open. In the fourteenth, their skulls are split and their teeth dragged out. In the fifteenth, they are hacked and gashed. In the sixteenth, they are pricked with steel prongs.

Those who are unfilial, who do not nourish their relatives while alive or bury them when dead, who subject their parents to fright, sorrow, or anxiety—if they do not quickly repent them of their former sins, the Spirit of the Hearth will report their misdoings and gradually deprive them of what prosperity they may be enjoying. Those who indulge in magic and sorcery will, after death, when they have been tortured in the other Courts, be brought here to this Court, and dragged backwards by bull-headed, horse-faced devils to be thrust into the great Gehenna. Then when they have been tortured in the various wards they will be passed on to the Tenth Court, whence at the expiration of a *kalpa* [54] they will be sent back to earth with changed heads and faces for ever to find their place amongst the brute creation. But those who believe in the

---

[52] When they are born again on earth.
[53] Heart, lungs, spleen, liver, and kidneys.
[54] Many millions of years.

Divine Panorama, and on the 1st of the 4th moon make a vow of repentance, repeating the same every night and morning to the Spirit of the Hearth, shall, by virtue of one of three characters, *obedient, acquiescent,* or *repentant,* to be traced on their foreheads at death by the Spirit of the Hearth, escape half the punishments from the First to the Seventh Court, inclusive, and escape this Eighth Court altogether, being passed on to the Ninth Court, where cases of arson and poisoning are investigated, and finally born again from the Tenth Court among mankind as before.

To this God added, " Whosoever may circulate the *Divine Panorama* for the information of the world at large shall escape all punishment from the First to the Eighth Court, inclusive. Passing through the Ninth and Tenth Courts, they shall be born again amongst men in some happy state."

THE NINTH COURT

His Infernal Majesty P'ing Têng reigns at the bottom of the great Ocean, away to the south-west, below the Wu-chiao rock. His is the vast, circular hell of A-pi, many leagues in breadth, jealously enclosed by an iron net, and subdivided into sixteen wards, as follows :—

In the first, the wicked souls have their bones beaten and their bodies scorched. In the second, their muscles are drawn out and their bones rapped. In the third, ducks eat their heart and liver. In the fourth, dogs eat their intestines and lungs. In the fifth, they are splashed with hot oil. In the sixth, their heads are crushed in a frame, and their tongues and teeth are drawn out. In the seventh, their brains are taken out and their skulls filled with hedgehogs. In the eighth, their heads are steamed and their brains scraped. In the ninth, they are dragged about by sheep till they drop to pieces. In the tenth, they are squeezed in a wooden press and pricked on the head. In the eleventh, their hearts are ground in a mill. In the twelfth, boiling water drips on to their bodies. In the thirteenth, they are stung by wasps. In the fourteenth, they are tortured by ants and maggots ; they are then stewed, and finally wrung out (like clothes). In the fifteenth, they are stung by scorpions. In the sixteenth, they are tortured by venomous snakes, crimson and scarlet.

All who on earth have committed one of the ten great crimes, and have deserved either the lingering death, decapitation, strangulation, or other punishment, shall, after passing through the tortures of the previous Courts, be brought to this Court, together with those guilty of arson, of making *ku* poison,[55] bad books, stupefying drugs, and many other disgraceful acts. Then, if it be found that, hearkening to the words of the *Divine Panorama,* they subsequently destroyed the blocks of these books, burnt their prescriptions, and ceased practising the magical art, they shall escape the punishments of

---

[55] The following recipe for this deadly poison is given in the well-known Chinese work *Instructions to Coroners* :—" Take a quantity of insects of all kinds and throw them into a vessel of any kind ; cover them up, and let a year pass away before you look at them again. The insects will have killed and eaten each other, until there is only one survivor, and this one is *Ku*."

this Court and be passed on to the Tenth Court, thence to be born again amongst the sons of men. But if, having heard the warnings of the *Divine Panorama*, they still continue to sin, from the Second to the Eighth Court their tortures shall be increased. They shall be bound on to a hollow copper pillar, clasping it round with their hands and feet. Then the pillar shall be filled with fierce fire, so as to burn into their heart and liver ; and afterwards their feet shall be plunged into the great Gehenna of A-pi, knives shall be thrust into their lungs, they shall bite their own hearts, and gradually sink to the uttermost depths of hell, there to endure excruciating torments until the victims of their wickedness have either recovered the property out of which they were cheated, or the life that was taken away from them, and until every trace of book, prescription, picture, &c., formerly used by these wicked souls has disappeared from the face of the earth. Then, and only then, may they pass into the Tenth Court to be born again in one of the Six States of existence.

O ye who have committed such crimes as these, on the 8th of the 4th moon, or the 1st or 15th (of any moon), fasting swear that you will buy up all bad books and magical pamphlets and utterly destroy them with fire ; or that you will circulate copies of the *Divine Panorama* to be a warning to others ! Then, when your last moment is at hand, the Spirit of the Hearth will write on your forehead the two words *He obeyed*, and from the Second up to the Ninth Court your good deeds will be rewarded by a diminution of such punishments as you have incurred. People in the higher ranks of life who secure incendiaries or murderers, who destroy the blocks of bad books, or publish notices warning others, and offer rewards for the production of such books, will be rewarded by the success of their sons and grandsons at the public examinations. Poor people who, by a great effort, manage to have the *Divine Panorama* circulated for the benefit of mankind, will be forwarded at once to the Tenth Court, and thence be born again in some happy state on earth.

THE TENTH COURT

His Infernal Majesty Chuan Lun [56] reigns in the Dark Land, due east, away below the Wu-chiao rock, just opposite the Wu-cho of this world. There he has six bridges, of gold, silver, jade, stone, wood, and planks, over which all souls must pass. He examines the shades that are sent from the other courts, and, according to their deserts, sends them back to earth as men, women, old, young, high, low, rich, or poor, forwarding monthly a list of their names to the judge of the First Court for transmission to Fêng-tu. [57]

The regulations provide that all beasts, birds, fishes, and insects, whether biped, quadruped, or otherwise, shall after death become *chien*,[58] to be born again for long and short lives alternately. But such as may possibly have taken life, and such as must necessarily have taken life, will pass through a revolution of the Wheel, and

[56] He who " turns the wheel ; " a *chakravartti raja*.
[57] The capital city of the Infernal Regions.
[58] The ghosts of dead people are believed to be liable to death. The ghost of a ghost is called *chien*.

then, when their sins have been examined, they will be sent up on earth to receive the proper retribution. At the end of every year a report will be forwarded to Fêng-tu.

Those scholars who study the Book of Changes, or priests who chant their liturgies, cannot be tortured in the Ten Courts for the sins they have committed. When they come to this Court their names and features are taken down in a book kept for the purpose, and they are forwarded to Mother Mêng, who drives them on to the Terrace of Oblivion and doses them with the draught of forgetfulness. Then they are born again in the world for a day, a week, or it may be a year, when they die once more ; and now, having forgotten the holy words of the Three Religions,[59] they are carried off by devils to the various Courts, and are properly punished for their former crimes.

All souls whose balance of good and evil is exact, whose period of punishment is completed, or whose crimes are many and good deeds few, as soon as their future state has been decided,—man, woman, beautiful, ugly, comfort, toil, wealth, or poverty, as the case may be,—must pass through the Terrace of Oblivion.

Amongst those shades, on their way to be born again in the world of human beings, there are often to be found women who cry out that they have some old and bitter wrong to avenge,[60] and that rather than be born again amongst men they would prefer to enter the ranks of hungry devils.[61] On examining them more closely it generally comes out that they are the virtuous victims of some wicked student, who may perhaps have an eye to their money, and accordingly dresses himself out to entrap them, or promises marriage when sometimes he has a wife already, or offers to take care of an aged mother or a late husband's children. Thus the foolish women are beguiled, and put their property in the wicked man's hands. By-and-by he turns round upon and reviles them, and, losing face in the eyes of their relatives and friends, with no one to redress their wrong, they are driven to commit suicide. Then, hearing[62] that their seducer is likely to succeed at the examination, they beg and implore to be allowed to go back and compass his death. Now, although what they urge is true enough, yet that man's destiny may not be worked out, or the transmitted effects of his ancestors' virtue may not have passed away ;[63] therefore, as a compromise, these injured shades are allowed to send a spirit to the Examination Hall to hinder and confuse him in the preparation of his paper, or to change the names on the published list of successful candidates ; and finally, when his hour arrives, to proceed with the spirit who carries the death-summons, seize him, and bring him to the First Court for judgment.

Ye'who on the 17th of the 4th moon swear to carry out the precepts of the *Divine Panorama*, and frequently make these words the subject of your conversation, may in the life to come be born again

[59] Confucianism, Buddhism, and Taoism.
[60] Women are considered in China to be far more revengeful than men. *Cf.* " Sweet is revenge, especially to women."
[61] See *Author's Own Record* (in *Introduction*), note 28.
[62] While in Purgatory.
[63] It was mentioned above that the rewards for virtue would be continued to a man's sons and grandsons.

amongst men and escape official punishments, fire, flood, and all accidents to the body. The place where the Wheel of Fate goes round is many leagues in extent, enclosed on all sides by an iron palisade. Within are eighty-one subdivisions, each of which has its proper officers and magisterial appointments. Beyond the palisade there is a labyrinth of 108,000 paths leading by direct and circuitous routes back to earth. Inside it is as dark as pitch, and through it pass the spirits of priest and layman alike. But to one who looks from the outside everything is seen as clear as crystal, and the attendants who guard the place all have the faces and features they had at their birth. These attendants are chosen from virtuous people who in life were noted for filial piety, friendship, or respect for life, and are sent here to look after the working of the Wheel and such duties. If for a space of five years they make no mistakes they are promoted to a higher office ; but if found to be lazy or careless they are reported to the Throne for punishment.

Those who in life have been unfilial or have destroyed much life, when they have been tortured in the various Courts are brought here and beaten to death with peach twigs. They then become *chien*, and with changed heads and altered faces are turned out into the labyrinth to proceed by the path which ends in the brute creation.

Birds, beasts, fishes, and insects may after many myriads of *kalpas* again resume their original shapes ; and if there are any that during three existences do not destroy life, they may be born amongst human beings as a reward, a record being made and their names forwarded to the First Court for approval. But all shades of men and women must proceed to the Terrace of Oblivion.

Mother Mêng was born in the Earlier Han Dynasty. In her childhood she studied books of the Confucian school ; when she grew up she chanted the liturgies of Buddha. Of the past and the future she had no care, but occupied herself in exhorting mankind to desist from taking life and become vegetarians. At eighty-one years of age her hair was white and her complexion like a child's She lived and died a virgin, calling herself simply Mêng ; but men called her Mother Mêng. She retired to the hills and lived as a *religieuse* until the Later Han. Then because certain evil-doers, relying on their knowledge of the past, used to beguile women by pretending to have been their husbands in a former life, God commissioned Mother Mêng to build the Terrace of Oblivion, and appointed her as guardian, with devils to wait upon her and execute her commands. It was arranged that all shades who had been sentenced in the Ten Courts to return in various conditions to earth should first be dosed by her with a decoction of herbs, sweet, bitter, acrid, sour, or salt. Thus they forget everything that has previously happened to them, and carry away with them to earth some slight weaknesses, such as the mouth watering at the thought (of something nice), laughter inducing perspiration, fear inducing tears, anger inducing sobs, or spitting from nervousness. Good spirits who go back into the world will have their senses of sight, hearing, smell, and taste very much increased in power, and their physical strength and constitution generally will be much bettered. But evil spirits will experience the exact contrary of this, as a reward for previous sins and as a warning to others to pray and repent.

The Terrace is situated in front of the Ten Courts, outside the six bridges. It is square, measuring ten (Chinese) feet every way, and surrounded by 108 small rooms. To the east there is a raised path, one foot four inches in breadth, and in the rooms abovementioned are prepared cups of forgetfulness ready for the arrival of the shades. Whether they swallow much or little it matters not ; but sometimes there are perverse devils who altogether refuse to drink. Then beneath their feet sharp blades start up, and a copper tube is forced down their throats, by which means they are compelled to swallow some. When they have drunk, they are raised by the attendants and escorted back by the same path. They are next pushed on to the Bitter Bamboo floating bridge, with torrents of rushing red water on either side. Half-way across they perceive written in large characters on a red cliff on the opposite side the following lines :—

> To be a man is easy, but to act up to one's responsibilities as such is hard.
> Yet to be a man once again is perhaps harder still.

> For those who would be born again in some happy state there is no great difficulty ;
> It is only necessary to keep mouth and heart in harmony.

When the shades have read these words they try to jump on shore, but are beaten back into the water by two huge devils. One has on a black official hat and embroidered clothes ; in his hand he holds a paper pencil, and over his shoulder he carries a sharp sword. Instruments of torture hang at his waist, fiercely he glares out of his large round eyes and laughs a horrid laugh. His name is *Short Life*. The other has a dirty face smeared with blood ; he has on a white coat, an abacus in his hand and a rice sack over his shoulder. Round his neck hangs a string of paper money ; his brow contracts hideously, and he utters long sighs. His name is *They have their reward*, and his duty is to push the shades into the red water. The wicked and foolish rejoice at the prospect of being born once more as human beings ; but the better shades weep and mourn that in life they did not lay up a store of virtuous acts, and thus pass away from the state of mortals for ever.[64] Yet they all rush on to birth like an infatuated or drunken crowd ; and again, in their early childhood, hanker after the forbidden flavours.[65] Then, regardless of consequences, they begin to destroy life, and thus forfeit all claims to the mercy and compassion of God. They take no thought as to the end that must overtake them ; and finally, they bring themselves once more to the same horrid plight.

[64] That is, go to heaven.   [65] Of meat, wine, &c.

APPENDIX II.

ANCESTRAL WORSHIP

" The rudimentary form of all religion is the propitiation of dead ancestors, who are supposed to be still existing, and to be capable of working good or evil to their descendants."—SPENCER'S ESSAYS. Vol. iii., p. 102.—*The Origin of Animal Worship*.

BILOCATION

" As a general rule, people are apt to consider it impossible for a man to be in two places at once, and indeed a saying to that effect has become a popular saw. But the rule is so far from being universally accepted, that the word ' bilocation ' has been invented to express the miraculous faculty possessed by certain saints of the Roman Church, of being in two places at once ; like St. Alfonso di Liguori, who had the useful power of preaching his sermon in church, while he was confessing penitents at home."—TYLOR'S *Primitive Culture*. Vol. i., p. 447.

BURIAL RITES

" Hence the various burial rites—the placing of weapons and valuables along with the body, the daily bringing of food to it, &c. I hope hereafter to show that with such knowledge of facts as he has, this interpretation is the most reasonable the savage can arrive at."—SPENCER'S ESSAYS. Vol. iii., p. 104.—*The Origin of Animal Worship*.

DREAMS

" The distinction so easily made by us between our life in dreams and our real life is one which the savage recognises in but a vague way ; and he cannot express even that distinction which he perceives. When he awakes, and to those who have seen him lying quietly asleep, describes where he has been, and what he has done, his rude language fails to state the difference between seeing and dreaming that he saw, doing and dreaming that he did. From this inadequacy of his language it not only results that he cannot truly represent this difference to others, but also that he cannot truly represent it to himself."—SPENCER'S ESSAYS. Vol. iii., pp. 103, 104.

SHADE OR SHADOW

" The ghost or phantasm seen by the dreamer or the visionary is an unsubstantial form, like a shadow, and thus the familiar term of the *shade* comes in to express the soul. Thus the Tasmanian word for the shadow is also that for the spirit ; the Algonquin Indians describe a man's soul as *otahchuk*, ' his shadow ; ' the Quiché language uses *natub* for ' shadow, soul ; ' the Arawac *ueja* means ' shadow, soul, image ; ' the Abipones made the one word *loákal* serve for ' shadow, soul, echo, image.' "—TYLOR's *Primitive Culture*. Vol. i., p. 430.

SHADOW

" Thus the dead in Purgatory knew that Dante was alive when they saw that, unlike theirs, his figure cast a shadow on the ground." —TYLOR's *Primitive Culture*. Vol. i., p. 431.

THE SOUL

" The savage, conceiving a corpse to be deserted by the active personality who dwelt in it, conceives this active personality to be still existing, and his feelings and ideas concerning it form the basis of his superstitions."—SPENCER's ESSAYS. Vol. iii., p. 103.—*The Origin of Animal Worship.*

TRANSMIGRATION

" Whether the Buddhists receive the full Hindu doctrine of the migration of the individual soul from birth to birth, or whether they refine away into metaphysical subtleties the notion of continued personality, they do consistently and systematically hold that a man's life in former existences is the cause of his now being what he is, while at this moment he is accumulating merit or demerit whose result will determine his fate in future lives."—TYLOR's *Primitive Culture*. Vol. ii., p. 12.

TRANSMIGRATION

" Memory, it is true, fails generally to recall these past births, but memory, as we know, stops short of the beginning even of this present life."—TYLOR's *Primitive Culture*. Vol. ii., p. 12.

TRANSMIGRATION

" As for believers, savage or civilised, in the great doctrine of metempsychosis, these not only consider that an animal may have a soul, but that this soul may have inhabited a human being, and thus the creature may be in fact their own ancestor or once familiar friend."—TYLOR's *Primitive Culture*. Vol. i., p. 469.

TREE-SOULS

" Orthodox Buddhism decided against the tree-souls, and consequently against the scruple to harm them, declaring trees to have no mind nor sentient principle, though admitting that certain dewas or spirits do reside in the body of trees, and speak from within them."—TYLOR's *Primitive Culture.*—Vol. i., p. 475.